More praise for *The Little R*

"More than the shock of recognition, there is a jolt of pleasure, indistinguishable from wonder, in encountering *Ulysses* as its first intrigued readers would have in the proudly modern pages of the *Little Review*."—Maria DiBattista, Princeton University

"This canny edition of *Ulysses* episodes from the *Little Review* throws revealing light on transatlantic modernism by tracing the intertwined histories of a seminal journal and Joyce's masterpiece. It reconstructs serial reading by embedding the early versions in their periodical and period contexts while sending us to the 1922 *Ulysses* with refreshed vision for those who already know it, or with sharpened vision for first-time readers."—John Paul Riquelme, Boston University

"At last, the very first published version of *Ulysses* seen by readers, as it appeared in that courageous journal the *Little Review,* beautifully presented, its context clearly explained. This is a fascinating vision of the greatest twentieth-century novel in its first public appearance. The excitement radiates off every page. Here is a wondrous artwork's first outing, skillfully returned to the world."—Enda Duffy, University of California Santa Barbara

"A beautifully edited volume that allows contemporary readers to experience *Ulysses* as it was first published in serialization, warts and all. The scholarship is meticulous, helpful, and unobtrusive."
—Sam Slote, Trinity College Dublin

"A treasure—the *Ulysses* that readers first saw and that a court banned, beautifully presented to help us encounter this work in progress as it unfolded in the *Little Review*."—Michael Groden, author of *"Ulysses" in Progress* and *"Ulysses" in Focus*

THE LITTLE REVIEW "ULYSSES"

THE LITTLE REVIEW

Vol. V. MARCH, 1918 No. 11

ULYSSES

JAMES JOYCE

Episode 1

STATELY, plump Buck Mulligan came from the stairhead, bearing a bowl of lather on which a mirror and a razor lay crossed. A yellow dressing gown, ungirdled, was sustained gently behind him on the mild morning air. He held the bowl aloft and intoned:

—Introibo ad altare Dei.

Halted, he peered down the dark winding stairs and called up coarsely:

—Come up, Kinch. Come up, you fearful jesuit.

Solemnly he came forward and mounted the round gunrest. He faced about and blessed gravely thrice the tower, the surrounding country and the awaking mountains. Then, catching sight of Stephen Dedalus, he bent towards him and made rapid crosses in the air, gurgling in his throat and shaking his head. Stephen Dedalus, displeased and sleepy, leaned his arms on the top of the staircase and looked coldly at the shaking gurgling face that blessed him, equine in its length, and at the light untonsured hair, grained and hued like pale oak.

Buck Mulligan peeped an instant under the mirror and then covered the bowl smartly.

—Back to barracks, he said sternly.

He added in a preacher's tone:

—For this, O dearly beloved, is the genuine christine: body and soul and blood and ouns. Slow music, please. Shut your eyes, gents. One moment. A little trouble about those white corpuscles. Silence, all.

THE LITTLE REVIEW "ULYSSES"

JAMES JOYCE

EDITED BY MARK GAIPA,
SEAN LATHAM, AND
ROBERT SCHOLES

Yale UNIVERSITY PRESS
NEW HAVEN AND LONDON

Frontispiece: The opening page of *Ulysses* in the March 1918 issue of the *Little Review* (mistakenly identified as issue 5.11 instead of 4.11)

Published with assistance from the Andrew W. Mellon Foundation.
Published with assistance from the foundation established in memory of Calvin Chapin of the Class of 1788, Yale College.

Printed in the United States of America.

Library of Congress Cataloging-in-Publication Data
Joyce, James, 1882–1941.
The Little Review "Ulysses" / James Joyce ; edited by Mark Gaipa, Sean Latham, and Robert Scholes.
pages cm
Includes bibliographical references.
ISBN 978-0-300-18177-7 (paperback)
1. City and town life—Fiction. 2. Dublin (Ireland)—Fiction. 3. Joyce, James, 1882–1941. Ulysses. I. Gaipa, Mark, 1963–, editor. II. Latham, Sean, 1971–, editor. III. Scholes, Robert, 1929–, editor. IV. Title.
PR6019.O9U4 2015 823′.912—dc23 2014042988

A catalogue record for this book is available from the British Library.

This paper meets the requirements of ANSI/NISO Z39.48-1992 (Permanence of Paper).

10 9 8 7 6 5 4 3 2 1

CONTENTS

ILLUSTRATIONS

ACKNOWLEDGMENTS

The text from the *Little Review* used to create this edition of *Ulysses* is derived from the digital edition of the magazine produced by the Modernist Journals Project. The magazine images and underlying text were all produced with support from the National Endowment for the Humanities as well as from Brown University and the University of Tulsa. We are grateful for their ongoing support of the MJP.

We also want to thank several people who assisted us in assembling and proofing this text. Patrick Belk, David Chandler, Kent Emerson, Stewart Habig, Omer Kazmi, Susan Solomon, and Amelia Williamson provided invaluable editorial help, carefully confirming quotations and helping check the accuracy of the text—no small feat when dealing with the many strange spelling and printing errors that appeared in the *Little Review.* We are grateful for this help. This book is stronger and more useful thanks to them. Any remaining errors, of course, are entirely our own.

Finally, we would like to acknowledge the many sources of funding that helped support our work on this project. At the University of Tulsa, these include the Pauline McFarlin Walter Chair, the *James Joyce Quarterly,* and the Graduate School. At Brown University, we want to thank the Department of Modern Culture and Media. Finally, a grant to Robert Scholes from the Mellon Foundation made it possible for us to provide the color images in this book. In an age of diminished funding for the humanities, this support has proved particularly important for making possible a project like this one.

GENERAL INTRODUCTION

The first readers of James Joyce's *Ulysses* did not hold in their hands a massive volume with a blue cover, printed in Burgundy and published in Paris. They instead read installments of the novel, serialized in a magazine of many colors called the *Little Review,* edited just off Union Square in New York City (and later in Greenwich Village), with its episodes—or sections of episodes—sandwiched in among the diverse work of other experimental writers, some famous now and others not. These readers never saw the last four episodes of the book, for two reasons: first, the editors of the *Little Review,* Margaret Anderson and Jane Heap, were prosecuted and fined in early 1921 for publishing the thirteenth episode, and then the novel's book publication by Shakespeare and Company, initially slated for autumn 1921, squeezed out their efforts at serialization. As Heap notes in the Autumn 1921 issue: "Before we could revive from our trial for Joyce's 'Ulysses' it was announced for publication in book form. We limp from the field. — *jh*" (*LR* 8.1: 112). As it happened, the book did not appear until 1922, but the fifteenth episode, set in Dublin's red light district, would never have passed the American censors if the editors had been bold enough to publish it. They were probably wise to "limp from the field" when they did.

The aim of this edition of Joyce's novel is to offer interested people of our own time something like the experience of those first readers, who encountered not a book but a serialized novel that emerged slowly in a little magazine across the two and a half years between March 1918 and December 1920. The text here is not a facsimile of the *Little Review "Ulysses,"* but we have sought to preserve as many of the quirks of the original as possible, including botched text, misspelled words, and printing errors. We have also included, as the frontispiece to this volume, an image of the first page of the serialization, so readers can get some sense of just what the text looked like in the *Little Review.* (Those interested in seeing what the other pages of the novel originally looked like in the magazine should visit the Modernist Journals Project, www.modjourn.org, where full copies of each issue are available.) Joyce's novel got more complicated as it went along, and even more complicated when he revised it after this first publication—which he did at every stage in the process of printing the Paris edition. What readers will encounter in this book is a simpler version of *Ulysses,* one less than half the length of the 1922 book version. In no way can it rival the power and complexity of the complete text, but it can serve as an introduction to this masterpiece of modernism, afford readers insight into Joyce's early composition process, and focus attention on the original publication context of the novel.

For over a decade, Joyce's last novel, *Finnegans Wake,* was known as "Work In Progress," but *Ulysses* likewise was a work in progress for many years. Genetic critics have persuasively argued that a literary work is not to be confined to some supposedly finished text, but consists instead of an entire process of composition that includes early versions and afterthoughts as well. Joyce's sense of what he was doing in *Ulysses* changed as he went along; the novel moved from a relatively realistic narrative, in which interior monologues were a major feature, to other modes of narration in which an external schema and a variety of voices and methods dominate the book's events and characters—until it returns to a radically different kind of interior monologue in the final episode. Though *The Little Review "Ulysses"* stops well short of that end, it enables us to study closely the onset of these dramatic shifts in Joyce's methodology.

To allow readers to come as close as possible to the original experience of those who encountered Joyce's work in the *Little Review,* we have not intervened in the text of the novel by adding footnotes or marginal comments, nor have we corrected typographical errors in the original, which were a feature that many correspondents complained about to the editors. We have, however, tried to provide useful information in editorial commentary that follows the text of the novel. In "The Composition History of *Ulysses,*" we foreground some of the key differences between the text that appeared in the *Little Review* and the 1922 book edition, noting important changes that Joyce made as he continued to work on each episode after serialization. Then in "The Magazine Context for *The Little Review 'Ulysses,'*" we discuss the issues of the *Little Review* in which Joyce's episodes appeared, emphasizing the ways in which *Ulysses* operated in a constant—though perhaps not always intentional—dialogue with the magazine as whole. A final section reprints various documents from the *Little Review* that have some bearing on Joyce's novel. In this introduction, we are mainly concerned with the magazine itself and the story of how *Ulysses* came to appear in it.

ULYSSES AND THE *LITTLE REVIEW*

The *Little Review* was founded in 1914 in Chicago by a young woman named Margaret Anderson. It was, in many respects, the brash younger sibling of another Chicago magazine, *Poetry: A Magazine of Verse,* founded in 1912 by Harriet Monroe. As its title and subtitle indicate, *Poetry* published only poetical works and critical writing about such works. Anderson, however, wanted a journal that considered all the arts. She had a special interest in music and played the piano. Politically, she was well to the left of Monroe. The anarchist Emma Goldman's name was mentioned in twenty-five issues of the *Little Review,* but only once after 1917, in this sad comment by Anderson's fellow editor, Jane Heap: "I feel that the Government was right in deporting Emma Goldman and Alexander Berkman. They had become a tradition. Kind, loving, intelligent, intense, they had made anarchism a harmless, respected, even fashionable word in every kind of American home. For years they had kept young fire-brands from action simply out of courtesy to the Goldman-Berkman tradition" (*LR* 6.9: 36). After the war, anarchism was apparently no longer modernist. Jane Heap was an ironist, of course, suggesting that these political activists were deported not because they were radical but because they had become fashionable and were preventing young people from engaging in more active gestures of rebellion. This comment appeared, we may note, in the January 1920 issue, just a few months before the editors were hauled into court and fined for publishing *Ulysses.*

Throughout the magazine's existence, Anderson championed youth and modernism, as Mark Morrisson has shown so well in *The Public Face of Modernism.* She took the magazine to California for a few months in 1916, bringing with her Jane Heap, who had become coeditor. There, they made the supremely anarchistic gesture of leaving a dozen pages of the magazine blank, claiming that they did not have enough good material to fill an issue (plate 1). Back in Chicago at the end of the year, Anderson put this notice in her pages:

> We couldn't have an October issue, owing to our usual embarrassment about funds; so this will have to serve as a sort of October–November,

> though I can't put that on the cover because they tell me it would violate some new law.
>
> We are back in Chicago where we shall stay for a month before moving to New York. Word comes from every part of the country that young magazines are dying, and that even *The Masses* may have to succumb before the increasing cost of paper, etc. That *must* not be! *The Masses* is too valuable to lose and everybody must do something about it. As for *The Little Review,* we may have to come out on tissue paper pretty soon, but we shall *keep on coming out!* Nothing can stop us now.
>
> I feel as though we have an entirely new lease on life and were just starting with what we have to say. (*LR* 3.7: 21)

What was really new in the magazine's life was the addition of Heap, who helped inspire Anderson to continue the struggle to publish her magazine and whose work began to appear regularly over the signature "*jh,*" giving special meaning to the editorial "we" used by Anderson.

The magazine's move to New York in 1917 was energizing, no doubt, and another, greater change was in the wings. Ezra Pound, who had been connected with *Poetry* magazine since 1914 and was aware of its younger Chicago counterpart, had earlier written a letter to Anderson, which she published in the April 1916 issue:

> *Ezra Pound, London:*
>
> Thanks for the January–February issue. Your magazine seems to be looking up. A touch of light in Dawson and Seiffert—though THE LITTLE REVIEW seems to me rather scrappy and unselective. I thought you started out to prove Ficke's belief that the sonnet is "Gawd's own city." However, he seems to have abandoned that church. I still don't know whether you send me the magazine in order to encourage me in believing that my camp stool by Helicon is to be left free from tacks, or whether the paper is sent to convert me from error.
>
> I am glad to see in it some mention of Eliot, who is really of interest. (*LR* 3.2: 36)

Pound was associated by then with both *Poetry* and the London-based *Egoist.* He had sent Dora Marsden a copy of Joyce's first novel, which she and her coeditor Harriet Shaw Weaver serialized in the *Egoist* and then published in book form when no other English publisher would touch it. In addition, Pound was writing regularly for the *New Age,* also published in London.

Pound was constantly on the lookout for two things: a financial backer who would provide funds to pay authors, and a magazine that would allow him to select the authors that would be paid from those funds. He finally found the right financial backer in John Quinn, a New York lawyer, and the right magazine in the *Little Review.* As Forrest Read explains in *Pound/Joyce,* "Quinn and three of his friends staked the magazine to $1600 a year for two years, and Pound to $750 a year ($300 for his editorial duties, $450 for contributors)" (112). Pound described the arrangement succinctly in the course of a long letter to Margaret Anderson in January 1917:

> IN A NUT SHELL.
> The suggestion is this.
> You provide a certain number of pages.
> I fill, and pay for contributions to, said pages. (*Pound/The Little Review* 11)

The suggestion was accepted, and in the April 1917 issue Anderson announced the result (echoing Pound's own words from a letter to her):

> "Surprise"!
>
> THE "surprise" I promised in the last issue is this: Ezra Pound is to become Foreign Editor of "The Little Review."
>
> This means that he and T. S. Eliot will have an American organ (horrible phrase) in which they can appear regularly once a month, where James Joyce can appear when he likes, and where Wyndham Lewis can appear if he comes back from the war Also it means two or three other names of the "young blood" who will contribute from time to time, and altogether the most stunning plan that any magazine has had the good fortune to announce for a long, long time. (*LR* 3.10: 25)

In the issues that followed, work by those Pound approved of began to appear; Yeats, Eliot, Lewis, Ford Madox Ford (then still called Hueffer), and Pound himself took the lead. Almost a year after Pound joined the magazine, *Ulysses* began to run in the March 1918 issue.

Pound is well known for his important role in promoting the work of talented writers around him. He went to London from America in 1908 at the age of twenty-three, a young poet trying to get away from the stifling atmosphere of his own country and looking for people who took poetry seriously. He quickly got to know the Irish poet William Butler Yeats, working for him as a sort of secretary. It was Yeats who told Pound about a struggling young Irish author named James Joyce, which prompted him to write in December 1913: "From what W. B. Y. says I imagine we have a hate or two in common" (*Pound/Joyce* 18). He goes on to tell Joyce about his connections with magazines such as *Poetry* and the *Egoist* and offers to help him get published. Joyce, who had spent fourteen years trying to publish *Dubliners,* his collection of short stories, welcomed the assistance. He was then living in Europe, where he completed the second version of his autobiographical novel—the first had been called *Stephen Hero* and the second was *A Portrait of the Artist as a Young Man.* Joyce sent Pound a poem, which Pound got published in *Poetry,* and then began sending him *Portrait,* which Pound sent on to Dora Marsden for publication in the *Egoist. The Egoist* did not pay, but Pound felt that publication there might lead to better things—as indeed it did. One of those better things was Harriet Shaw Weaver, who became Joyce's patron and helped support his work for many years.

By the time Joyce started work on his next novel, Pound had established his connection with the *Little Review* and could use John Quinn's money to pay for things that interested him. In March 1917 he wrote to Joyce:

> I want SOMETHING from you, even if it is only 500 words.
>
> The "Little Review" has something like 3000 subscribers of the sort who read and buy books. They have a puff of you in the last number, promising long review in April. I think from purely practical point of view it will do you no harm to "keep in touch with" their readers. Remind them of your existence, at least six times a year. (*Pound/Joyce* 103)

At the time, Joyce had very little to offer, and wrote Pound that all he could send were a few excerpts from what would become the "Scylla and Charybdis" episode. When more pieces of *Ulysses* were ready for serialization later that year, he and Pound planned to bring them out in the *Egoist.* They would appear simultaneously in the *Little Review,* in large part, Pound emphasized, to "hold down the American copyright" (*Pound/Joyce* 126). He was aware, however, that the book would likely encounter legal trouble. "I think the chances of James getting £100 altogether for serial rights to 'Ulysses' (or as much of it as printers will print) are fairly good," he wrote to Joyce's companion, Nora (*Pound/Joyce* 126). Pound was right to be cautious: the *Egoist* could not find a printer willing to set *Ulysses* in type, and eventually only parts of four episodes appeared in its pages.

It is difficult for readers today to realize just how oppressive the censorship of that period was. In the United Kingdom, printers were legally liable for any work they set in type, meaning that their businesses could collapse if they ran afoul of the law. As a result, their rigorous self-censorship foiled the plan to place *Ulysses* in the *Egoist*—all without any direct intervention from the government. In the United States, federal postal authorities were empowered to seize materials deemed objectionable, and they worked with antivice societies to police anything considered obscene. At the time, mailing material that referred even vaguely to sexuality, prostitution, or birth control was a crime. Even before *Ulysses* appeared, an issue of the *Little Review* had been seized because it contained a story by Wyndham Lewis titled "Cantelman's Spring-Mate," which describes a sexual encounter in what now strikes us as vague and allusive language: "The nightingale sang ceaselessly in the small wood at the top of the field where they lay. He grinned up towards it, and once more turned to the devouring of his mate. He felt that he was raiding the bowels of Nature: not fecundating the Aspasias of our flimsy flesh, or assuaging, or competing with, the nightingale" (*LR* 4.6: 13). When Joyce's work began to appear, first Pound and then Anderson introduced several cuts designed to foil the censors. Despite these efforts, four issues of the magazine containing Joyce's novel were seized. Then, in 1920, the government prosecuted the editors themselves; they were fined $50 each and prevented from continuing their serialization of *Ulysses.*

When it appeared in the *Little Review,* Joyce's second novel was thought of and discussed as a continuation of *Portrait,* which it was, but it was also much, much more. While working on *Ulysses,* Joyce decided to go beyond his earlier books by connecting the world of his own time to that of Homer's ancient epic poem the *Odyssey.* But Joyce's knowledge of that poem was filtered through a version for young people written by Charles Lamb, called *The Adventures of Ulysses,* which had made a strong impression on him when he first read it. Lamb's version uses the Latin names for the characters, rather than the original Greek, which is one reason why Joyce's novel is not called *Odysseus.* Joyce took the adventures of that hero as models for events in a single day in the Dublin he had known as a young man, rearranging them to suit his own purposes: a single episode from the ancient epic echoes, sometimes ironically, in each section of his novel.

At some point in the writing of the novel, Joyce developed an elaborate schema in which most episodes were assigned repeating motifs. He sent different versions of his outline to friends such as Carlo Linati and Stuart Gilbert, who then used this information when writing about *Ulysses*. The schema gives the title, location, and hour of the day for each episode, and assigns to each a bodily organ, an art, a color, a symbol, and what Joyce called a "technic." In addition, he included a list of correspondences linking characters in his novel to their mythic counterparts in the *Odyssey*. It is still not clear exactly when Joyce codified this schema in his own mind, but he seems to have developed it during the composition and serial publication of the novel and did not have it in mind when he began writing. As a result, the schematized materials are much more visible in the later versions than in the serialized episodes reprinted here. The first readers of *Ulysses* in the *Little Review* knew little or nothing of Joyce's elaborate plan. They knew only the novel's title, but were left to decipher its meaning with few clues. We now have titles for every chapter because Joyce revealed them in his schemas, but in the magazine and the book publications the episodes appear without them. The notes that follow Joyce's text in our book provide some insight into Joyce's methods of composition, but the text that appears in the following pages is deliberately free of annotation so that readers can encounter the work as it first appeared: without aids or guides, spread across a sometimes choppy series of breaks and divisions.

Ulysses was anything but an isolated masterpiece. It was part of an ongoing dialogue about the modern world and the sort of art needed in that world. Thus, our notes include detailed information about the articles, poems, and images that surrounded Joyce's work as it appeared in the *Little Review*. Although this novel largely defined modernism (and indeed still defines it), when it first appeared its form and certainly its reputation were much more unstable. This indeterminacy is evident in the essays, comments, letters, and advertisements reprinted here. Drawn from the pages of the magazine, they debate the value of Joyce's experiments with form, his often shocking attention to naturalistic detail, and his relation to other artists working with and sometimes against him. We hope that the supplementary material will help contemporary readers understand the place of Joyce's novel in that world of almost a century ago, when modernism in literature and the other arts was being defined and contested in the pages of struggling magazines like the *Little Review*.

A NOTE ON THE TEXT

Although this is not a facsimile edition, we have done our best to reproduce the original look and feel of *Ulysses* as it appeared in the pages of the *Little*

Review. We have preserved the original typographical and printing errors as well as the sometimes odd spacing and inconsistent layout. We did, however, remove all the end-line hyphens in compound words that were introduced during typesetting to justify the margins of the printed pages. Joyce himself did not use this punctuation, and since the line endings in this edition do not match those of the original magazine pages, those marks would clearly be out of place here. References in our editorial essays to Joyce's text as reprinted in *The Little Review "Ulysses"* are cited as *LRU* followed by the appropriate page number.

ULYSSES

JAMES JOYCE

From the *Little Review,* 1918–1920

Episode 1

THE LITTLE REVIEW

THE MAGAZINE THAT IS READ BY THOSE WHO WRITE THE OTHERS

MARCH, 1918

MARGARET ANDERSON, Editor
EZRA POUND, Foreign Editor

24 *West Sixteenth Street, New York*
Foreign office:
5 *Holland Place Chambers, London W. 8.*

25 cents a copy $2.50 a year

Entered as second-class matter at P. O., New York, N. Y.
Published monthly by Margaret Anderson

STATELY, plump Buck Mulligan came from the stairhead, bearing a bowl of lather on which a mirror and a razor lay crossed. A yellow dressing gown, ungirdled, was sustained gently behind him on the mild morning air. He held the bowl aloft and intoned:

—*Introibo ad altare Dei.*

Halted, he peered down the dark winding stairs and called up coarsely:

—Come up, Kinch. Come up, you fearful jesuit.

Solemnly he came forward and mounted the round gunrest. He faced about and blessed gravely thrice the tower, the surrounding country and the awaking mountains. Then, catching sight of Stephen Dedalus, he bent towards him and made rapid crosses in the air, gurgling in his throat and shaking his head. Stephen Dedalus, displeased and sleepy, leaned his arms on the top of the staircase and looked coldly at the shaking gurgling face that blessed him, equine in its length, and at the light untonsured hair, grained and hued like pale oak.

Buck Mulligan peeped an instant under the mirror and then covered the bowl smartly.

—Back to barracks, he said sternly.

He added in a preacher's tone:

—For this, O dearly beloved, is the genuine christine: body and soul and blood and ouns. Slow music, please. Shut your eyes, gents. One moment. A little trouble about those white corpuscles. Silence, all.

He peered sideways up and gave a long low whistle of call, then paused awhile in rapt attention, his even white teeth glistening here and there with gold points. Chrysostomos.

—Thanks, old chap, he cried briskly. That will do nicely. Switch off the current, will you?

He skipped off the gunrest and looked gravely at his watcher, gathering about his legs the loose folds of his gown. The plump shadowed face and sullen oval jowl recalled a prelate, patron of arts in the middle ages. A pleasant smile broke quietly over his lips.

—The mockery of it! he said gaily .Your absurd name, an ancient Greek!

He pointed his finger in friendly jest and went over to the parapet, laughing to himself. Stephen Dedalus stepped up, followed him wearily halfway and sat down on the edge of the gunrest, watching him still as he propped his mirror on the parapet, dipped the brush in the bowl and lathered cheeks and neck.

Overleaf: table of contents, *Little Review,* March 1918

Buck Mulligan's gay voice went on :

—My name is absurd too. Malachi, Mulligan, two dactyls. But it has a Hellenic ring, hasn't it? Tripping and sunny like the buck himself. We must go to Athens. Will you come if I can get the aunt to fork out twenty quid?

He laid the brush aside and, laughing with delight, cried:

—Will he come? The jejune jesuit.

Ceasing, he began to shave with care.

—Tell me, Mulligan, Stephen said quietly.

—Yes, my love?

—How long is Haines going to stay in this tower?

Buck Mulligan showed a shaven cheek over his right shoulder.

—God, isn't he dreadful? he said frankly. A ponderous Saxon. He thinks you're not a gentleman. God, these bloody English! Bursting with money and indigestion. Because he comes from Oxford. You know, Dedalus, you have the real Oxford manner. He can't make you out. O, my name for you is the best: Kinch, the knifeblade.

He shaved warily over his chin.

—He was raving all night about a black panther, Stephen said. Where is his guncase?

—A woeful lunatic, Mulligan said. Were you in a funk?

—I was, Stephen said with energy and growing fear. Out here in the dark with a man I don't know raving and moaning to himself about shooting a black panther. You saved men from drowning . I'm not a hero, however. If he stays on here I am off.

Buck Mulligan frowned at the lather on his razor blade. He hopped down from his perch and began to search his trouser pockets hastily.

—Scutter, he cried thickly.

He came over to the gunrest and, thrusting a hand into Stephen's upper pocket, said:

—Give us a loan of your noserag to wipe my razor.

Stephen suffered him to pull out and hold up on show by its corner a dirty crumpled handkerchief. Buck Mulligan wiped the razor blade neatly. Then, gazing over the handkerchief, he said:

—The bard's noserag. A new art colour for our Irish poets: snotgreen. You can almost taste it, can't you?

He mounted to the parapet again and gazed out over Dublin bay, his fair oakpale hair stirring slightly.

—God! he said quietly. Isn't the sea what Algy calls it: a great sweet mother. The snotgreen sea. The scrotumtightening sea. *Epi oinopa ponton*. Ah, Dedalus, the Greeks! She is our great sweet mother. Come and look.

Stephen stood up and went over to the parapet. Leaning on it, he looked down on the water.

—Our mighty mother! Buck Mulligan said.

He turned abruptly his quick searching eyes from the sea to Stephen's face.

—The aunt thinks you killed your mother, he said. That's why she won't let me have anything to do with you.

—Someone killed her, Stephen said gloomily.

—You could have knelt down, damn it, Kinch, when your dying mother asked you, Buck Mulligan said. I'm hyperborean as much as you. But to think of your mother begging you with her last breath to kneel down and pray for her. And you refused. There is something sinister in you ....

He broke off and lathered again lightly his farther cheek. A tolerant smile curled his lips.

—But a lovely mummer! he murmured to himself. Kinch, the loveliest mummer of them all!

He shaved evenly and with care, in silence, seriously.

Stephen, an elbow rested on the jagged granite, leaned his palm against his brow and gazed at the fraying edge of his shiny black coatsleeve. Pain, that was not yet the pain of love, fretted his heart. Silently, in a dream she had come to him after her death, her wasted body within its loose brown graveclothes giving off an odour of wax and rosewood, her breath, that had bent upon him, mute, reproachful, a faint odour of wetted ashes. Across the threadbare cuffedge he saw the sea, hailed as a great sweet mother by the wellfed voice beside him. The ring of bay and skyline held a dull green mass of liquid. A bowl of white china had stood beside her deathbed, holding the green sluggish bile which she had torn up from her rotting liver by fits of loud groaning vomiting.

Buck Mulligan wiped again his razorblade.

—Ah, poor dogsbody! he said in a kind voice. I must give you a shirt and a few noserags. How are the secondhand breeks?

—They fit well enough, Stephen answered.

Buck Mulligan attacked the hollow beneath his underlip.

—The mockery of it, he said contentedly. Secondleg they should be. God knows what poxy bowsy left them off. I have a lovely pair with a hair stripe, grey. You'll look spiffing in them. I'm not joking, Kinch. You look damn well when you're dressed.

—Thanks , Stephen said. I can't wear them if they are grey.

—He can't wear them, Buck Mulligan told his face in the mirror. Etiquette is etiquette. He kills his mother but he can't wear grey trousers.

He folded his razor neatly and with stroking palps of fingers felt the smooth skin.

Stephen turned his gaze from the sea and to the plump face with its smoke-blue mobile eyes.

—That fellow I was with in the Ship with last night, said Buck Mulligan, says you have g. p. i. He's up in Dottyville with Conolly Norman. General paralysis of the insane!

He swept the mirror a half circle in the air to flash the tidings abroad in sunlight now radiant on the sea. His curling shaven lips laughed and the edges of his white glittering teeth. Laughter seized all his strong wellknit trunk.

—Look at yourself, he said, you dreadful bard!

Stephen bent forward and peered at the mirror held out to him, cleft by a crooked crack. Hair on end. As he and others see me. Who chose this face for me? It asks me too. I pinched it out of the skivvy's room, Buck Mulligan said. It does her all right. The aunt always keeps plain looking servants for Malachi. Lead him not into temptation. And her name is Ursula.

Laughing again, he brought the mirror away from Stephen's peering eyes.

—The rage of Caliban at not seeing his face in a mirror, he said. If Wilde were only alive to see you!

Drawing back and pointing, Stephen said with bitterness:

—It is a symbol of Irish art. The cracked looking-glass of a servant.

Buck Mulligan suddenly linked his arm in Stephen's and walked with him round the tower, his razor and mirror clacking in the pocket where he had thrust them.

—It's not fair to tease you like that, Kinch, is it? he said kindly. God knows you have more spirit than any of them.

Parried again. He fears the lancet of my art as I fear that of his.

—The cracked lookingglass of a servant! Tell that to the oxy chap down-stairs and touch him for a guinea. He's stinking with money and thinks you're not a gentleman. His old fellow made his tin by selling jalap to Zulus or some bloody swindle or other. God, Kinch, if you and I could only work together we might do something for the island. Hellenise it.

Cranly's arm. His arm.

—And to think of your having to beg from these swine. I'm the only one that knows what you are. Why don't you trust me more? What have you up your nose against me? Is it Haines? If he makes any noise here I'll bring down Seymour and we'll give him a ragging worse than they gave Clive Kempthorpe.

Young shouts of moneyed voices in Clive Kempthorpe's rooms. Palefaces: they hold their ribs with laughter, one clasping another, O, I shall expire! Break the news to her gently, Aubrey! I shall die! With slit ribbons of his shirt whipping the air he hops and hobbles round the table, with trousers down at heels, chased by Ades of Magdalen with the tailor's shears. A scared calf's face gilded with marmalade. I d.on't want to be debagged! Don't you play the giddy ox with me!

Shouts from the open window startling evening in the quadrangle. A deaf gardener, aproned, masked with Matthew Arnold's face, pushes his mower on the sombre lawn, watching narrowly the dancing motes of grasshalms.

To ourselves . . . . new paganism . . . . omphalos.

—Let him stay, Stephen said. There's nothing wrong with him except at night.

—Then what is it? Buck Mulligan asked impatiently. Cough it up. I'm quite frank with you. What have you against me now?

They halted, looking towards the blunt cape of Bray Head that lay on the water like the snout of a sleeping whale. Stephen freed his arm quickly.

—Do you wish me to tell you? he asked.

—Yes, what is it? Buck Mulligan answered. I don't remember anything.

He looked in Stephen's face as he spoke A light wind passed his brow, fanning softly his fair uncombed hair and stirring silver points of anxiety in his eyes.

Stephen, depressed by his own voice, said:

—Do you remember the first day I went to your house after my mother's death?

Buck Mulligan frowned quickly and said:

—What? Where? I can't remember anything. I remember only ideas and sensations. Why? What happened in the name of God?

—You were making tea, Stephen said, and I went across the landing to get more hot water. Your mother and some visitor came out of the drawingroom. She asked you who was in your room.

—Yes? Buck Mulligan said. What did I say? I forget.

—You said, Stephen answered, *O, it's only Dedalus whose mother is beastly dead.*

A flush which made him seem younger and more engaging rose to Buck Mulligan's cheek.

—Did I say that? he asked. Well? What harm is that?

He shook his constraint from him nervously.

—And what is death, he asked, your mother's or yours or my own? You saw only your mother die. I see them pop off every day in the Mater and Richmond and cut up into tripes in the dissecting room. It's a beastly thing and nothing else. It simply doesn't matter. You wouldn't kneel down to pray for your mother on her deathbed when she asked you. Why? Because you have the cursed jesuit strain in you only it's injected the wrong way. To me it's all a mockery and beastly. Her cerebral lobes are not functioning. She calls the doctor Sir Peter Teazle and picks buttercups off the quilt. Humour her till it's over. You crossed her last wish in death and yet you sulk with me because I don't whinge like some hired mute from Lalouette's. Absurd! I suppose I did say it. I didn't mean to offend the memory of your mother.

He had spoken himself into boldness. Stephen, shielding the gaping wounds which the words had left in his heart, said very coldly:

—I am not thinking of the offence to my mother.

—Of what, then? Buck Mulligan asked.

—Of the offence to me, Stephen answered.

Buck Mulligan swung round on his heel.

—O, an impossible person! he exclaimed.

He walked off quickly round the parapet. Stephen stood at his post, gazing over the calm sea towards the headland. Sea and headland now grew dim. Pulses were beating in his eyes, veiling their sight, and he felt the fever of his cheeks

A voice within the tower called loudly:

—Are you up there, Mulligan?

—I'm coming, Buck Mulligan answered.

He turned towards Stephen and said:

—Look at the sea. What does it care about offences? Chuck Loyola, Kinch, and come on down. The Sassenach wants his morning rashers.

His head halted again for a moment at the top of the staircase, level with the roof:

—Don't mope over it all day, he said. I'm inconsequent. Give up the moody brooding.

His head vanished but the drone of his descending voice boomed out of the stairhead.

—And no more turn aside and brood
Upon love's bitter mystery
For Fergus rules the brazen cars.

Woodshadows floated silently by through the morning peace from the stairhead seaward where he gazed. Inshore and farther out the mirror of water whitened, spurned by light-shod hurrying feet. White breast of the dim sea. The twining stresses, two by two. A hand plucking the harpstrings, merging their twining chords. Wavewhite wedded words shimmering on the dim tide.

A clod began to cover the sun slowly, wholly, shadowing the bay in deeper green. It lay beneath him, a bowl of bitter waters. Fergus' song. I sang it alone in the house, holding down the long dark chords. Her door was open: she wanted to hear my music. Silent with awe and pity I went to her bedside. She was crying in her wretched bed. For those words, Stephen: love's bitter mystery.

Where now?

Her secrets: old feather fans, tassled dancecards, powdered with musk, a gaud of amber beads in her locked drawer. A birdcage hung in the sunny window of her house when she was a girl. She heard old Royce sing in the pantomime of Turko the Terrible and laughed with others when he sang:

I am the boy
That can enjoy
Invisibility.

Phantasmal mirth, folded away: musk perfumed.

And no more turn aside and brood.

Folded away in the memory of nature with her toys. Memories beset his brooding brain. Her glass of water from the kitchen tap when she had approached the sacrament. A cored apple, filled with brown sugar, roasting for her at the hob on a dark autumn evening. Her shapely fingernails reddened by the blood of squashed lice from the children's shirts.

In a dream, silently, she had come to him, her wasted body within its loose graveclothes giving off an odour of wax and rosewood, her breath bent over him with mute secret words, a faint odour of wetted ashes.

Her glazing eyes, staring out of death, to shake and bend my soul. On me alone. The ghostcandle to light her agony. Ghostly light on the tortured face. Her hoarse loud breath rattling in horror, while all prayed on their knees. Her eyes on me to strike me down. *Liliata rutilantium te confessorum turma circumdet: iubilantium te virginum chorus excipiat.*

Ghoul! Chewer of corpses!

No, mother! Let me be and let me live

—Kinch ahoy!

Buck Mulligan's voice sang from within the tower. It came nearer up the staircase, calling again. Stephen, still trembling at his soul's cry, heard warm running sunlight and in the air behind him, friendly words.

—Dedalus, come down, like a good mosey. Breakfast is ready. Haines is apologising for waking us last night. It's all right.

—I'm coming, Stephen said, turning.

—Do, for Jesus' sake, Buck Mulligan said. For my sake and for all our sakes.

His head disappeared and reappeared.

—I told him your symbol of Irish art. He says it's very clever. Touch him for a quid, will you? A guinea, I mean.

—I get paid this morning, Stephen said.

—The school kip? Buck Mulligan said. How much? Four quid? Lend us one.

—If you want it, Stephen said.

—Four shining sovereigns, Buck Mulligan cried with delight. We'll have a glorious drunk to astonish the druidy druids. Four omnipotent sovereigns.

He flung up his hands and tramped down the stone stairs, singing out of tune with a Cockney accent.

—O, won't we have a merry time,
Drinking whiskey, beer and wine!
On coronation
Coronation day!
O won't we have a merry time
On coronation day !

Warm sunshine merry over the sea. The nickel shaving bowl shone, forgotten, on the parapet. Why should I bring it down? Or leave it there all day, forgotten friendship?

He went over to it, held it in his hands awhile, feeling its coolness, smelling the clammy slaver of the lather in which the brush was stuck. So I carried the boat of incense then at Clongowes. I am another now and yet the same. A servant too. A server of a servant.

In the gloomy domed livingroom of the tower Buck Mulligan's gowned form moved briskly about the hearth to and fro, hiding and revealing its yellow glow. Two shafts of soft daylight fell across the flagged floor from the high barbacans: and at the meeting of their rays a cloud of coalsmoke and fumes of fried grease floated, turning.

—We'll be choked, Buck Mulligan said. Haines, open that door, will you?

Stephen laid the shavingbowl on the locker. A tall figure rose from the hammock where it had been sitting, went to the doorway and pulled open the inner doors.

—Have you the key? a voice asked.

—Dedalus has it, Buck Mulligan said. Janey Mack, I'm choked!

He howled without looking up from the fire:

—Kinch!

—It's in the lock, Stephen said, coming forward.

The key scraped round harshly twice and, when the heavy door had been set ajar, welcome light and bright air entered. Haines stood at the doorway, looking out. Stephen hauled his up-ended valise to the table and sat down to wait. Buck Mulligan tossed the fry on to the dish beside him. Then he carried the dish and a large teapot over to the table, set them down heavily and sighed with relief.

—I'm melting, he said, as the candle remarked when ...... But hush! Not a word more on that subject . Kinch, wake up! Bread, butter, honey. Haines, come in. The grub is ready. Bless us, O Lord, and these they gifts. Where's the sugar? O, jay, there's no milk.

Stephen fetched the loaf and the pot of honey and the buttercooler from the locker. Buck Mulligan sat down in a sudden pet.

—What sort of a kip is this? he said. I told her to come before nine.

—We can drink it black, Stephen said. There's a lemon in the locker.

—O, damn you and your Paris fads! Buck Mulligan said. I want Sandycove milk.

Haines came in from the doorway and said quietly:

—That woman is coming up with the milk.

—The blessings of God on you! Buck Mulligan said, jumping up from his chair. Sit down. Pour out the tea there. The sugar is in the bag. Here, I can't go fumbling at the damned eggs.

He hacked through the fry on the dish and slapped it out on three plates, saying:

—*In nomine Patris et Filii et Spiritus Sancti.*

Haines sat down to pour out the tea.

—I'm giving you two lumps each, he said. But, I say, Mulligan, you do make strong tea, don't you?

Buck Mulligan, hewing thick slices from the loaf, said in an old woman's wheedling voice:

—When I makes tea I makes tea, as old mother Grogan said. And when I makes water I makes water.

—By Jove, it is tea, Haines said.

Buck Mulligan went on hewing and wheedling:

— So I do, Mrs. Cahill, says she. Begob, ma'am, says Mrs. Cahill, God send you don't make them in the one pot.

He lunged towards his messmates in turn a thick slice of bread, impaled on his knife.

—That's folk, he said very earnestly, for your book, Haines. Five lines of text and ten pages of notes about the folk and the fishgods of Dundrum.

He turned to Stephen and asked in a fine puzzled voice, lifting his brows:

—Can you recall, brother, is mother Grogan's tea and water pot spoken of in the Mabinogion or is it in the Upanishade?

—I doubt it, said Stephen gravely.

—Do you now? Buck Mulligan said in the same tone. Your reasons, pray?

—I fancy, Stephen said as he ate, it did not exist in or out of the Mabinogion. Mother Grogan was, one imagines, a kinswoman of Mary Ann.

Buck Mulligan's face smiled with delight.

—Charming! he said in a finical sweet voice, showing his white teeth and blinking his eyes pleasantly. Do you think she was? Quite charming!

Then, suddenly overclouding all his features, he growled in a hoarsened rasping voice as he hewed again vigorously at the loaf.

—For old Mary Ann
She doesn't care a damn
But, hising up her petticoats ......

He crammed his mouth with fry and munched and droned.

The doorway was darkened by an entering form.

—The milk, sir.

—Come in, ma'am, Mulligan said. Kinch, get the jug.

An old woman came forward and stood by Stephen's elbow.

—That's a lovely morning, sir, she said. Glory be to God.

—To whom? Mulligan said, glancing at her. Ah, to be sure!

Stephen reached back and took the milkjug from the locker.

—The islanders, Mulligan said to Haines casually, speak frequently of the collector of prepuces.

—How much, sir? asked the old woman.

—A quart, Stephen said.

He watched her pour into the measure and thence into the jug rich white milk, not hers. Old shrunken paps. She poured again a measurful and a tilly. Old and secret she had entered from a morning world, maybe a messenger. She praised the goodness of her milk, pouring it out. Crouching by a patient cow at daybreak in the lush field, a witch on her toadstool, her wrinkled fingers quick at the squirting dugs. They lowed about her whom they knew, dewsilky cattle. Silk of the kine and poor old woman, names given her in old times. A wandering queen, lowly form of an immortal serving her conqueror and her betrayer, a messenger from the secret morning. To serve or to upbraid, whether he could not tell: but scorned to beg her favour.

—It is indeed, ma'am, Buck Mulligan said, pouring milk into their cups.

—Taste it, sir, she said.

He drank at her bidding.

—If we could only live on good food like that, he said to her somewhat loudly, we wouldn't have the country full of rotten teeth and rotten guts. Living in a bogswamp, eating cheap food and the streets paved with dust, horsedung and consumptives' spits.

—Are you a medical student, sir? the old woman asked.

—I am, ma'am, Buck Mulligan answered.

Stephen listened in scornful silence She bows her old head to a voice that speaks to her loudly, her bonesetter, her medicineman: me she slights. To the voice that will shrive and oil for the grave all there is of her but her woman's unclean loins. And to the loud voice that now bids her be silent with wondering unsteady eyes.

—Do you understand what he says? Stephen asked her.

—Is it French you are talking, sir? the old woman said to Haines.

Haines spoke to her again a longer speech, confidently.

—Irish, Buck Mulligan said.

—I thought it was Irish, she said, by the sound of it. Are you from the west, sir?

—I am an Englishman, Haines answered.

—He's English, Buck Mulligan said, and he thinks we ought to speak Irish in Ireland.

—Sure we ought too, the old woman said, and I'm ashamed I don't speak the language myself . I'm told it's a grand language by them that knows.

—Grand is no name for it, said Buck Mulligan. Fill us out some more tea, Kinch. Would you like a cup, ma'am?

—No, thank you, sir, the old woman said, slipping the ring of the milkcan on her forearm and about to go.

Haines said to her:

—Have you your bill? We had better pay her, Mulligan, hadn't we?

Stephen filled again the three cups .

—Bill, sir? she said, halting. Well, it's seven mornings a pint at twopence is seven twos is a shilling and twopence over and these three mornings a quart at fourpence is three quarts is a shilling and one and two is two and two, sir.

Buck Mulligan sighed and, having filled his mouth with a crust thickly buttered on both sides, stretched forth his legs and began to search his trouser pockets.

—Pay up and look pleasant, Haines said to him smiling.

Stephen filled a third cup, a spoonful of tea colouring faintly the thick rich milk. Buck Mulligan brought up a florin, twisted it round in his fingers and cried:

—A miracle!

He passed it along the table towards the old woman, saying:

—Ask nothing more of me, sweet,
All I can give you I give.

Stephen laid the coin in her uneager hand.

—We'll owe twopence, he said.

—Time enough, sir, she said, taking the coin. Time enough. Good morning sir.

She curtseyed and went out, followed by Buck Mulligan's tender chant:

—Heart of my heart, were it more
More would be laid at your feet.

He turned to Stephen and said:

—Seriously, Dedalus, I'm stony . Hurry out to your school kip and bring us back some money. Today the bards must drink and junket. Ireland expects that every man this day will do his duty.

—That reminds me, Haines said, rising, that I have to visit your national library today.

—Our swim first, Buck Mulligan said.

He turned to Stephen and asked blandly:

—Is this the day for your monthly wash, Kinch?

Then he said to Haines:

—The bard makes a point of washing once a month.

—All Ireland is washed by the gulfstream, Stephen said as he let honey trickle over a slice of the loaf.

Haines from the corner where he was knotting easily a scarf about the loose collar of his tennis shirt spoke:

—I intend to make a collection of your sayings if you will let me.

Speaking to me.

—That one about the cracked lookingglass of a servant being the symbol of Irish art is deuced good.

Buck Mulligan kicked Stephen's foot under the table and said with warmth of tone:

—Wait till you hear him on Hamlet, Haines.

—Well, I mean it, Haines said, still speaking to Stephen. I was just thinking of it when that poor old creature came in.

—Would I make money by it? Stephen asked.

Haines laughed and as he took his soft grey hat from the holdfast of the hammock, said:

—I don't know, I'm sure.

He strolled out to the doorway. Buck Mulligan bent across to Stephen and said with coarse vigour:

— You put your hoof in it now. What did you say that for?

—Well? Stephen said. The problem is to get money. From whom? From the milkwoman or from him. It's a toss up, I think.

—I blow him out about you, Buck Mulligan said, and then you come along with your lousy leer and your gloomy jesuit jibes.

—I see little hope, Stephen said, from her or from him.

Buck Mulligan sighed tragically and laid his hand on Stephen's arm.

—From me, Kinch, he said.

In a suddenly changed tone he added:

—To tell you the God's truth I think you're right. Damn all else they are good for. Why don't you play them as I do? To hell with them all. Let us get out of the kip.

He stood up, gravely ungirdled and disrobed himself of his gown, saying resignedly:

—Mulligan is stripped of his garments.

He emptied his pockets on to the table.

—There's your snotrag, he said.

And putting on his stiff collar and rebellious tie, he spoke to them, chiding them, and to his dangling watchchain. His hands plunged and rummaged in his trunk while he called for a clean handkerchief. God, we'll simply have to dress the character. I want puce gloves and green boots. Contradiction. Do I contradict myself? Very well then. I contradict myself. Mercurial Malachi. A limp black missile flew out of his talking hands.

—And there's your Latin quarter hat, he said.

Stephen picked it up and put it on. Haines called to them from the doorway:

—Are you coming, you fellows?

—I'm ready, Buck Mulligan answered, going towards the door. Come out, Kinch. You have eaten all we left, I suppose .

Stepphen, taking his ashplant from its leaningplace, followed them out and, as they went down the ladder pulled to the slow iron door and locked it. He put the huge key in his inner pocket.

At the foot of the ladder Buck Mulligan asked:

—Did you bring the key?

—I have it, Stephen said, preceding them.

He walked on. Behind him he heard Buck Mulligan club with his heavy bathtowel upreared ferns or grasses.

—Down, sir! How dare you, sir!

Haines asked:

—Do you pay rent for this tower?

—Twelve quid, Buck Mulligan said.

—To the secretary of state for war, Stephen added over his shoulder.

They halted while Haines surveyed the tower and said at last:

—Rather bleak in wintertime, I should say. Martello you call it?

—Billy Pitt had them built, Buck Mulligan said, when the French were on the sea. But ours is the omphalos.

—What is your idea of Hamlet? Haines asked Stephen.

—No, no, Buck Mulligan shouted in pain. I'm not equal to Thomas Aquinas and the fifty-five reasons he has made to prop it up. Wait till I have a few pints in me first.

He turned to Stephen, saying as he pulled down neatly the peaks of his primrose waistcoat:

—You couldn't manage it under three pints, Kinch, could you?

—It has waited so long, Stephen said listlessly, it can wait longer.

—You pique my curiosity, Haines said amiably Is it some paradox?

—Pooh! Buck Mulligan said. We have grown out of Wilde and paradoxes.

It's quite simple. He proves by algebra that Hamlet's grandson is Shakespeare's grandfather and that he himself is the ghost of his own father.

—What? Haines said, beginning to point at Stephen. He himself?

Buck Mulligan slung his towel stolewise roun his neck and, bending in loose laughter, said to Stephen's ear:

—O, shade of Kinch the elder.

—I'm always tired in the morning, Stephen said to Haines. And it is rather long to tell.

Buck Mulligan, walking forward again, raised his hands.

—The sacred pint alone can unbind the tongue of Dedalus, he said.

—I mean to say, Haines explained to Stephen as they followed, this tower and these cliffs here remind me somehow of Elsinore.

—That beetles O'er his Base into the sea, isn't it?

Buck Mulligan turned suddenly for an instant towards Stephen but did not speak. In the bright silent instant Stephen saw his own image in cheap dusty mourning between their gay attires.

—It's a wonderful tale, Haines said bringing them to halt again.

He gazed southward over the bay. Eyes, pale as the sea the wind had freshened, paler, firm and prudent. The seas' ruler, he gazed over the bay, empty save for a sail tacking by the Muglins.

—I read a theological interpretation of it somewhere, he said bemused. The Father and the Son idea. The Son striving to be atoned with the Father.

Buck Mulligan at once put on a blithe broadly smiling face. He looked at them, his wellshaped mouth open happily, his eyes, from which he had suddenly withdrawn all shrewd sense, blinking with mad gaiety. He moved a doll's head to and fro, the brims of his Panama hat quivering, and began to chant in a quiet happy foolish voice:

—I'm the queerest young fellow that ever you heard.
My mother's a jew, my father's a bird.
With Joseph the joiner I cannot agree,
So here's to disciples and Calvary.

He held up a forefinger of warning

If anyone thinks that I amn't divine
He'll get no free drinks when I'm making the wine

But have to drink water and wish it were plain
That I make when the wine becomes water again.

He tugged swiftly at Stephen's ashplant in farewell and, running forward to a brow of the cliff, fluttered his hands at his sides like fins or wings of one about to rise in the air: and chanted

Goodbye, now, goodbye! Write down all I said
And tell Tom, Dick and Harry I rose from the dead.
What's bred in the bone cannot fail me to fly
And Olivet's breezy — Goodbye, now, goodbye!

He capered before them down towards the forty-foot hole, fluttering his winglike hands, leaping nimbly, Mercury's hat quivering in the fresh wind that bore back to them his brief birdlike cries.

Haines, who had been laughing guardedly, walked on beside Stephen, and said:

—We oughtn't to laugh, I suppose. He's rather blasphemous. I'm not a believer myself, that is to say. Still his gaiety takes the harm out of it somehow, doesn't it? What did he call it? Joseph the Joiner?

—The ballad of joking Jesus, Stephen answered.

—O, Haines said, you have heard it before?

—Three times a day, after meals, Stephen said drily.

—You're not a believer, are you? Haines asked. I mean, a believer in the narrow sense of the word. Creation from nothing and miracles and a personal God.

—There's only one sense of the word, it seems to me, Stephen said.

Haines stopped to take out a smooth silver case in which twinkled a green stone. He sprang it open with his thumb and offered it.

—Thank you, Stephen said, taking a cigarette.

Haines helped himself and snapped the case to. He put it back in his sidepocket and took from his waistcoatpocket a nickel tinderbox, sprang it open too, and having lit his cigarette, held the flaming spunk towards Stephen in the shell of his hands.

—Yes, of course, he said, as they went on again. Either you believe or you don't, isn't it? Personally I couldn't stomach that idea of a personal God. You don't stand for that, I suppose.

—You behold in me, Stephen said with grim displeasure, a horrible example of free thought.

He walked on, waiting to be spoken to, trailing his ashplant by his side. Its ferrule followed lightly on the path, squealing at his heels. My familiar, after me, calling Steeeeeeephen! A wavering line along the path. They will walk on it tonight, coming here in the dark. He wants that key. It is mine. I paid the rent. Now I eat his food. Give him the key too. All. He will ask for it. That was in his eyes.

—After all, Haines began—

Stephen turned and saw that the cold gaze which had measured him was not at all unkind.

—After all, I should think you are able to free yourself. You are your own master, it seems to me.

—I am the servant of two masters, Stephen said, an English and an Italian.

—Italian? Haines said.

—A crazy queen, old and jealous. Kneel down before me. And a third, Stephen said, there is who wants me for odd jobs.

—Italian? Haines said again. What do you mean?

—The imperial British state, Stephen answered, his colour rising, and the holy Roman catholic and apostolic church.

Haines detached from his underlip some fibres of tobacco before he spoke.

—I can quite understand that, he said calmly. An Irishman must think like that, I daresay. We feel in England that we have treated you rather unfairly. It seems history is to blame.

The proud potent titles clanged over Stephen's memory the triumph of their brazen bells: *et in unam sanctam catholican et apostolican ecclesiam.* Symbol of the apostles in the mass for pope Marcellus, the voices blended, singing alone, loud in affirmation: and behind their chant the vigilant angel of the church militant disarmed and menaced her heresiarchs. A horde of heresies fleeing with mitres awry: Photius and the brood of mockers of whom Mulligan was one, and Arius, waring his life long upon the consubstantiality of the Son with the Father and Valentine, spurning Christ's terrene body, and the subtle African heresiarch Sabellius who held that the Father was Himself His own Son. Words Mulligan had spoken a moment since in mockery to the stranger. Idle mockery. The void awaits surely all them that weave the wind: a menace, a disarming and a worsting from those embattled angels of the church, Michael's host, who defend her ever in the hour of conflict with their lances and their shields.

Hear, hear! Prolonged applause. *Zut! Nom de Dieu!*

—Of course I'm a Britisher, Haines's voice said, and I feel as one. I don't want to see my country fall into the hands of German jews either. That's our national problem, I'm afraid, just now.

Two men stood at the verge of the cliff, watching: businessman, boatman.

—She's making for Bullock harbour.

The boatman nodded towards the north of the bay with some disdain.

—There's five fathoms out there, he said. It'll be swept up that way when the tide comes in about one. It's nine days today.

The man that was drowned. A sail veering about the blank bay waiting for a swollen bundle to bob up, roll over to the sun a puffy face, saltwhite. Here I am.

They followed the winding path down to the creek. Buck Mulligan stood on a stone, in shirtsleeves, his unclipped tie rippling over his shoulder. A young man clinging to a spur of rock near him, moved slowly frogwise his green legs in the deep jelly of the water.

—Is the brother with you, Malachi?

—Down in Westmeath. With the Bannons.

—Still there? I got a card form Bannon. Says he found a sweet young thing down there. Photo girl he calls her.

—Snapshot, eh? Brief exposure.

Buck Mulligan sat down to unlace his boots. An elderly man shot up near the spur of rock a blowing red face. He scrambled up by the stones, water glistening on his pate and on its garland of grey hair, water rilling over his chest and paunch and spilling jets out of his black sagging loincloth.

Buck Mulligan made way for him to scramble past and, glancing at Haines and Stephen, crossed himself piously with his thumbnail at brow and lips and breastbone.

—Seymour's back in town, the young man said, grasping again his spur of rocks. Chucked medicine and going in for the army.

—Ah, go to God! Buck Mulligan said.

—Going over next week to stew. You know that red Carlisle girl? Lily.

—Yes.

—Spooning with him last night on the pier. The father is rotton with money.

—Is she up the pole?

—Better ask Seymour that.

—Seymour a bleeding officer! Buck Mulligan said.

He nodded to himself as he drew off his trousers and stood up, saying tritely:

—Redheaded women buck like goats.

He broke off in alarm, feeling his side under his flapping shirt.

—My twelth rib is gone, he cried. I'm the *Uebermensch*. Toothless Kinch and I, the supermen.

He struggled out of his shirt and flung it behind him to where his clothes lay.

—Are you going in here, Malachi?

—Yes. Make room in the bed.

The young man shoved himself backward through the water and reached the middle of the creek in two long clean strokes. Haines sat down on a stone, smoking.

—Are you not coming in, Buck Mulligan asked.

—Later on, Haines said. Not on my breakfast.

Stephen turned away.

—I'm going, Mulligan, he said.

—Give us that key, Kinch, Buck Mulligan said, to keep my chemise flat.

Stephen handed him the key. Buck Mulligan laid it across his heaped clothes.

—And twopence, he said, for a pint. Throw it there.

Stephen threw two pennies on the soft heap. Buck Mulligan erect, with joined hands before him, said solemnly:

—He who stealeth from the poor lendeth to the Lord. Thus spake Zarathustra.

His plump body plunged.

—We'll see you again, Haines said, turning as Stephen walked up the path.

—The Ship, Buck Mulligan cried. Half twelve.

—Good, Stephen said.

He walked along the upwardcurving path.

—*Liliata rutilantium. Turma circumdet.* The priest's grey nimbus in a niche where he dressed discreetly. *Jubilantium te virginum.* I will not sleep here tonight. Home also I cannot go.

A voice, sweettoned and sustained, called to him from the sea. Turning the curve he waved his hand. It called again. A sleek brown head far out on the water, round.

Usurper.

(*to be continued*)

Episode II

THE LITTLE REVIEW

THE MAGAZINE THAT IS READ BY THOSE
WHO WRITE THE OTHERS

APRIL, 1918

MARGARET ANDERSON, Editor
EZRA POUND, Foreign Editor

24 *West Sixteenth Street, New York*
Foreign office:
5 *Holland Place Chambers, London W. 8.*

25 cents a copy — $2.50 a year

Entered as second-class matter at P. O., New York, N. Y.
Published monthly by Margaret Anderson

— YOU, Cochrane, what city sent for him?

— Tarentum, sir.

— Very good . Well ?

— There was a battle, sir.

— Very good. Where?

The boy's blank face asked the blank window.

Fabled by the daughters of memory. And yet it was in some way if not as memory fabled it. A phrase, then, of impatience, thud of Blake's wings of excess. I hear the ruin of all space, shattered glass and toppling masonry, and time one livid final flame. What's left us then?

— I forget the place, sir. 279 B. C.

— Asculum, Stephen said, glancing at the name and year in the gorescarred book.

— Yes, sir. And he said: *Another victory like that and we are done for.*

That phrase the world had remembered. A dull ease of the mind. From a hill above a corpsestrewn plain a general, speaking to his officers, leaned upon his spear. Any general to any officers. They lend ear.

— You, Armstrong, Stephen said. What was the end of Pyrrhus?

— End of Pyrrhus, sir?

— I know, sir. Ask me, sir, Comyn said.

— Wait. You, Armstrong. Do you know anything about Pyrrhus?

A bag of figrolls lay snugly in Armstrong's satchel. He curled them between his palms at whiles and swallowed them softly. Crumbs adhered to the tissues of his lips. A sweetened boy's breath. Well off people, proud that their eldest son was in the navy. Vico Road, Dalkey.

— Pyrrhus, sir? Pyrrhus, a pier.

All laughed. Mirthless high malicious laughter. Armstrong looked round at his classmates, silly glee in profile. In a moment they will laugh more loudly, aware of my lack of rule and of the fees their papas pay.

— Tell me now, Stephen said, poking the boy's shoulder with the book, what is a pier.

— A pier, sir, Armstrong said. A thing out in the water. A kind of bridge. Kingstown pier, sir.

Some laughed again: mirthless but with meaning. Two in the back bench whispered. Yes. They knew: had never learned nor ever been innocent. All.

Overleaf: table of contents, *Little Review,* April 1918

With envy he watched their faces: Edith, Ethel, Gertie, Lily. Their likes: their breats, too, sweetened with tea and jam, their bracelets tittering in the struggle.

— Kingstown pier, Stephen said. Yes, a disappointed bridge.

The words troubled their gaze.

— How, sir? Comyn asked. A bridge is across a river.

For Haines's chapbook. No one here to hear. Tonight deftly amid wild drink and talk, to pierce the polished mail of his mind. What then? A jester at the court of his master, indulged and disesteemed, winning a clement master's praise. Why had they chosen all that part? Not wholly for the smooth caress. For them too history was a tale like any other too often heard, their land a pawnshop.

Had Pyrrhus not fallen by a beldam's hand in Argos or Julius Caesar not been knifed to death. They are not to be thought away. Time has branded them and fettered they are lodged in the room of the infinite possibilities they have ousted. But can those have been possible seeing that they never were? Or was that only possible which came to pass? Weave, weaver of the wind.

— Tell us a story, sir.

— Oh, do, sir. A ghoststory.

— Where do you begin in this? Stephen asked, opening another book.

— *Weep no more*, Comyn said.

— Go on then, Talbot.

—And the story, sir?

— After, Stephen said. Go on, Talbot.

A swarthy boy opened a book and propped it nimbly under the breastwork of his satchel. He recited jerks of verse with odd glances at the text.

Weep no more, woful shepherd, weep no more
For Lycidas, your sorrow, is not dead.
Sunk though he be beneath the watery floor.

It must be a movement then, an actuality of the possible as possible. Aristotle's phrase formed itself within the gabbled verses and floated out into the studious silence of the library of Saint Genevieve where he had read, sheltered from the sin of Paris, night by night. By his elbow a delicate Siamese conned a handbook of strategy. Fed and feeding brains about me: and in my mind's darkness a sloth of the underworld, reluctant, shy of brightness, shifting her dragon scaly folds. Thought is the thought of thought. Tranquil brightness.

The soul is in a manner all that is: the soul is the form of forms. Tranquility sudden, vast, candescent: form of forms.

Talbot repeated:

Through the dear might of Him that walked the waves
Through the dear might.

— Turn over, Stephen said quietly. I don't see anything.

— What, sir? Talbot asked simply, bending forward.

His hand turned the page over. He leaned back and went on again, having just remembered of Him that walked the waves. Here also over these craven hearts his shadow lies, and on the scoffer's heart and lips and on mine. It lies upon their eager faces who offered him a coin of the tribute. To Caesar what is Caesar's, to God what is God's. A long look from dark eyes, a riddling sentence to be woven and woven on the church's looms. Ay.

— Riddle me, riddle me, randy ro.
My father gave me seeds to sow.

Talbot slid his closed book into his satchel.

— Have I heard all? Stephen asked.

—Yes, sir. Hockey at ten, sir.

— Half day, sir. Thursday.

— Who can answer a riddle? Stephen asked.

They bundled their books away, pencils clacking, pages rustling. Crowding together they strapped and buckled their satchels, all gabbling gaily:

— A riddle. Ask me, sir.

— O, ask me, sir.

— A hard one, sir.

— This is the riddle, Stephen said:

The cock crew,
The sky was blue:
The bells in heaven
Were striking eleven.
'Tis time for this poor soul
To go to heaven.

— What is that?

— What, sir

— Again, sir. We didn't hear.

Their eyes grew bigger as the lines were repeated.

After a silence Cochrane said:

— What is it, sir? We give it up.

Stephen, his throat itching, answered:

— The fox burying his grandmother under a hollybush.

He stood up and gave a shout of nervous laughter to which their cries echoed dismay.

A stick struck the door and a voice in the corridor called:

— Hockey.

They broke asunder, sidling out of their benches, leaping them. Quickly they were gone and from the lumber room came the rattle of sticks and clamour of their boots and tongues.

Sargent who alone had lingered came forward slowly, showing an open sopybook. His thick hair and scraggy neck gave witness of unreadiness and through his misty glasses weak eyes looked up pleading. On his cheek, dull and bloodless, a soft stain of ink lay, dateshaped, recent and damp as a snail's bed.

He held out his copybook. The word *Sums* was written on the headline. Beneath were sloping figures and at the foot a crooked signature with blind loops and a blot. Cyril Sargent: his name and seal.

— Mr. Deasy told me to write them out all again, he said, and show them to you, sir.

Stephen touched the edges of the book. Futility.

— Do you understand how to do them now? he asked.

— Numbers eleven to fifteen, Sargent answered. Mr. Deasy said I was to copy them off the board, sir.

— Can you do them yourself? Stephen asked.

— No, sir.

Ugly and futile: lean neck and thick hair and a stain of ink, a snail's bed. Yet someone had loved him, borne him in her arms and in her heart. But for her the race of the world would have trampled him under foot, a squashed boneless snail. She had loved his weak watery blood drained from her own. Was that then real? The only true thing in life? She was no more: the trembling skeleton of a twig burnt in the fire, an odour of rosewood and wetted ashes. She had saved him from being trampled under foot and had gone, scarcely having been. A poor soul gone to heaven: and on a heath beneath winking stars a fox, red reek of rapine in his fur, with merciless bright eyes scraped in the earth, listened, scraped up the earth, listened, scraped and scraped.

Sitting at his side Stephen solved out the problem. He proves by algebra that Shakespeare's ghost is Hamlet's grandfather. Sargent peered askance, through his slanted glasses. Hockeysticks rattled in the lumberroom: the hollow knock of a ball and calls from the field.

Across the page the symbols moved in grave morrice, in the mummery of their letters, wearing quaint caps of squares and cubes. Give hands, traverse, bow to partner: so: imps of fancy of the Moors. Gone too from the world, Averroes and Moses Maimonides, dark men in mien and movement, flashing in their mocking mirrors the obscure soul of the world, a darkness shining in brightness which brightness could not comprehend.

— Do you understand now? Can you work the second for yourself?

— Yes sir .

In long shaky strokes Sargent copied the data. Waiting always for a word of help his hand moved faithfully the unsteady symbols, a faint hue of shame flickering behind his dull skin. *Amor matris*: subjective and objective genitive. With her weak blood and wheysour milk she fed him and hid from sight of others his swaddlingbands.

Like him was I, these sloping shoulders, this gracelessness. My childhood bends beside me. Too far for me to lay a hand of comfort there, one or lightly. Mine is far and his secret as our eyes. Secrets, silent, stony, sit in the dark palaces of both our hearts; secrets weary of their tyranny: tyrants willing to be dethroned.

The sum was done.

— It is very simple, Stephen said as he stood up.

— Yes, sir. Thanks, Sargent answered.

He dried the page with a sheet of thin blotting paper and carried his copybook back to his desk

— You had better get your stick and go out to the others, Stephen said as he followed towards the door the boy's graceless form.

— Yes, sir.

In the corridor his name was heard, called from the playfield.

— Sargent .

— Run on, Stephen said. Mr. Deasy is calling you.

He stood in the porch, and watched the laggard hurry towards the scrappy field where sharp voices were in strife. They were sorted in teams and Mr. Deasy came stepping over wisps of grass with gaitered feet. When he had reached the schoolhouse voices again contending called to him. He turned his angry white moustache.

— What is it now? he cried continually without listening.

— Cochrane and Halliday are on the same side, sir, Stephen cried.

— Will you wait in my study for a moment, Mr. Deasy said, till I restore order here.

And as he stepped fussily back across the field his old man's voice cried sternly.

— What is the matter? What is it now?

Their sharp voices cried about him on all sides: their many forms closed round him, garish sunshine bleaching the honey of his illdyed head.

Stale smoky air hung in the study with the smell of drab abraded leather of its chairs. As on the first day he bargained with me here. As it was in the beginning, is now. On the sideboard the tray of Stuart coins, base treasure of a bog: and ever shall be. And snug in tehir spooncase of purple plush, faded, the twelve apostles having preached to all the gentiles: world without end.

A hasty step over the stone porch and in the corridor. Blowing out his rare moustache Mr. Deasy halted at the table.

— First, our little financial settlement, he said.

He brought out of his coat a pocketbook bound by a rubber thong. It slapped open and he took from it two notes, one of joined halves, and laid them carefully on the table .

— Two, he said, strapping and stowing his pocketbook away.

And now his strongroom for the gold. Stephen's embarassed hand moved over the shells heaped in the cold stone mortar: whelks and money cowries and leopard shells: and this, whorled as an emir's turban, and this, the scallop of Saint James. An old pilgrim's hoard, dead treasure, hollow shells.

A sovereign fell, bright and new, on the soft pile of the tablecloth.

— Three, Mr. Deasy said, turning his little savings box about in his hand. These are handy things to have. See. This is for sovereigns. This is for shillings, sixpences, halfcrowns. And here crowns. See.

He shot from it two crowns and two shillings.

— Three twelve, he said. I think you'll find that's right.

— Thank you, sir, Stephen said, gathering the money together with shy haste and putting it all in a pocket of his trousers.

His hand, free again, went back to the hollow shells.

Symbols too of beauty and of power. A lump in my pocket. Symbols soiled by greed and misery.

— Don't carry it like that, Mr. Deasy said. You'll pull it out somewhere and lose it. You just buy one of these machines. You'll find them very handy.

Answer something.

— Mine would be often empty, Stephen said.

That same room and hour, the same wisdom: and I the same. Three times now. Three nooses round me here. Well, I can break them in this instant if I will.

— Because you don't save, Mr. Deasy said, pointing his finger. You don't know yet what money is. Money is power, when you have lived as long as I have. I know, I know. If youth but knew. But what does Shakespeare say: *Put money in thy purse.*

— Iago, Stephen murmured.

He lifted his gaze from the idle shells to the old man's stare.

— He knew what money was, Mr. Deasy said. He made money. A poet, yes, but an Englishman too. Do you know what is the pride of the English Do you know what is the proudest word you will ever hear from an Englishman's mouth?

The seas' ruler. His seacold eyes looked on the empty bay; it seems history is to blame: on me and on my words, unhating.

— That on his empire, Stephen said, the sun never sets.

— Ba! Mr. Deasy cried. That's not English. A French Celt said that.

He tapped his savingsbox against his thumbnail.

— I will tell you, he said solemnly, what is his proudest boast. *I paid my way.*

Good man, good man.

— *I paid my way. I never borrowed a shilling in my life.* Can you feel that *I owe nothing.* Can you?

Mulligan, nine pounds, three pairs of socks, ties. Curran, ten guineas. McCann, one guinea. Fred Ryan, two shillings. Temple, two lunches, Russell, one guinea, Cousins, ten shillings, Bob Reynolds, half a guinea, Köhler, three guineas, Mrs. McKernan, five week's board. The lump I have is useless.

— For the moment, no, Stephen answered.

Mr. Deasy stared sternly for some moments over the mantelbox.

— I knew you couldn't, he said joyously. But one day you must feel it. We are a generous people but we must also be just.

— I fear those big words, Stephen said, which make us so unhappy.

Mr. Deasy stared sternly for some moments over the mantelpiece at the shapely bulk of a man in tartan fillibegs: Albert Edward, Prince of Wales.

— You think me an old fogey and an old tory, his thoughtful voice said. I saw three generations since O'Connell's time. I remember the famine in '46. Do you know that the orange lodges agitated for repeal of the union twenty years before O'Connell did or before the prelates of your communion denounced him as a demagogue? You fenians forget some things.

Stephen sketched a brief gesture.

— I have rebel blood in me too, Mr. Deasy said. On the spindle side. I am descended from Sir John Blackwood who voted against the union. We are all Irish, all kings' sons.

— Alas, Stephen said.

— *Per vias rectas*, Mr. Deasy said firmly, was his motto. He voted against it: and put on his topboots to ride to Dublin from the Ards of Down to do so.

Lal-the-ral-the-ra: the rocky road to Dublin. A gruff squire on horseback with shiny topboots. Soft day, sir John. Soft day, your honour .... Day .... Day .... Two topboots jog jangling on to Dublin. Lal-the-ral-the-ra, lal-the-ral-the raddy.

— That reminds me, Mr. Deasy said. You can do me a favour, Mr. Dedalus, with some of your literary friends. I have a letter here for the press. Sit down a moment. I have just to copy the end.

He went to the desk near the window, pulled in his chair twice and read off some words from the sheet on the drum of his typewriter.

—Sit down. Excuse me, he said over the shoulder, *the dictates of common sense.* Just a moment.

He peered from under his shaggy brows at the manuscript by his elbow and, muttering, began to prod the stiff buttons of the keyboard slowly, sometimes blowing as he screwed up the drum to erase an error.

Stephen seated himself noiselessly before the princely presence. Framed around the walls images of vanished horses stood in homage, their meek heads poised in air: lord Hastings' *Repulse*, the duke of Westminster's *Shotover*, the duke of Beaufort's *Ceylon*, *prix de Paris*, 1866. Elfin riders sat them, watchful of a sign. He saw their speeds and shouted with the shouts of vanished crowds.

— Full stop, Mr. Deasy bade his keys. *But prompt ventilation of this all important question .....*

Where Cranly led me to get rich quick, hunting his winners among the mudsplashed brakes, amid the bawls of bookies and reek of the canteen, over the motley slush. Even money *Fair Rebel.* Ten to one the field. Dicers and thimbleriggers we hurried by, after the hoofs, the vying caps and jackets and past the meatfaced woman, a butcher's dame, nuzzling thirstily her clove of orange.

Shouts rang shrill from the boys' playfield and a whirring whistle. Again: a goal. I am among them, among their battling bodies in a medley, the joust of life. You mean that knock-kneed mother's darling who seems to be slightly crawsick? Jousts. Time shocked rebounds, shock by shock. Jousts, slush and uproar of battles, the frozen deathspew of the slain, a shout of spearspikes baited with men's bloodied guts.

— Now then, Mr. Deasy said rising.

He came to the table, pinning together his sheets. Stephen stood up.

— I have put the matter into a nutshell, Mr. Deasy said. It's about the foot and mouth disease. Just look through it. There can be no two opinions on the matter.

May I trespass on your valuable space . That doctrine of *laissez faire* which so often in our history. Our cattle trade. The way of all our old industries. Liverpool ring which jockeyed the Galway harbour scheme. European conflagration. Grain supplies through the narrow waters of the channel. The pluterperfect imperturbability of the department of agriculture. Pardoned a classical allusion. Cassandra. By a woman who was no better than she should be. To come to the point at issue.

— I don't mince words, do I? Mr. Deasy asked as Stephen read on.

Foot and mouth disease. Known as Koch's preparation. Serum and virus. Percentage of salted horses. Rinderpest. Emperor's horses at Mürzsteg, lower Austria. Veterinary surgeons. Mr. Henry Blackwood Price. Courteous offer a fair trial. Dictates of common sense. All important question. In every sense of the word take the bull by the horns. Thanking you for the hospitality of your columns.

— I want that to be printed and read, Mr. Deasy said. You will see at the next outbreak they will put an embargo on Irish cattle. And it can be cured. It is cured. My cousin, Blackwood Price, writes to me it is regularly treated and cured in Austria by cattle doctors there. They offer to come over here. I am trying to work up influence with the department. Now I'm going to try publicity. I am surrounded by difficulties, by . . . intrigues by . . . .

He raised his forefinger and beat the air oldly before his voice spoke.

— Mark my words, Mr. Dedalus, he said. England is in the hands of the jews. In all the highest places: her finance, her press. And they are the signs of a nation's decay. Wherever they gather they eat up the nation's vital strength.

I have seen it coming these years. As sure as we are standing here the jew merchants are already at their work of destruction. Old England is dying.

He stepped swiftly off, his eyes coming to blue life as they passed a broadsunbeam. He faced about and back again.

— Dying, he said, if not dead by now.

The harlot's cry from street to street
Shall weave old England's windingsheet.

His eyes open wide in vision stared sternly across the sunbeam in which he halted.

— A merchant, Stephen said, is one who buys cheap and sells dear, jew or gentile, is he not?

— They sinned against the light, Mr. Deasy said gravely. And you can see the darkness in their eyes. And that is why they are wanderers on the earth to this day.

On the steps of the Paris stock exchange the goldskinned men quoting prices on their gemmed fingers. Gabble of geese. They swarmed loud, uncouth, about the temple, their heads thick plotting under maladroit silk hats. Not theirs: these clothes, this speech, these gestures. Their full slow eyes belied the words, the gestures eager and unoffending, but knew the rancours massed about them and knew their zeal was vain. Vain patience to heap and hoard. Time surely would scatter all. A hoard heaped by the roadside: plundered and passing on. Their eyes knew their years of wandering and, patient, knew the dishonours of their flesh.

— Who has not? Stephen said.

— What do you mean? Mr. Deasy asked.

He came forward a pace and stood by the table. His underjaw fell sideways open uncertainly. Is this old wisdom? He waits to hear from me.

— History, Stephen said, is a nightmare from which I am trying to awake.

From the playfield the boys raised a shout. A whirring whistle: goal.

— The ways of the Creator are not our ways, Mr. Deasy said. All history moves towards one great goal, the manifestation of God.

Stephen jerked his thumb towards the window, saying:

— That is God.

Hooray! Ay! Whrrwhee!

What? Mr. Deasy asked.

— A shout in the street, Stephen answered, shrugging his shoulders.

Mr. Deasy looked down and held for a while the wings of his nose tweaked between his fingers. Looking up again he set them free.

—I am happier than you are, he said. We have committed many errors and many sins. A woman brought sin into the world. For a woman who was no better than she should be, Helen, the runaway wife of Menelaus, ten years the Greeks made war on Troy. A faithless wife first brought the strangers to our shore here, O'Rourke's wife, Prince of Breffni. A woman too brought Parnell low. Many errors, many failures but not the one sin. I am a struggler now at the end of my days. But I will fight for the right till the end.

For Ulster will fight
And Ulster will be right.

Stephen raised the sheets in his hand.

— Well, sir, he began.

— I foresee, Mr. Deasy said, that you will not remain here very long at this work. You were not born to be a teacher, I think. Perhaps I am wrong.

— A learner rather, Stephen said.

And here what will you learn more?

Mr. Deasy shook his head.

— Who knows? he said. To learn one must be humble. But life is the great teacher.

Stephen rustled the sheets again.

— As regards these, he began.

— Yes, Mr. Deasy said. You have two copies there. If you can have them published at once.

Telegraph. Irish Homestead.

— I will try, Stephen said, and let you know tomorrow. I know two editors slightly.

— That will do. Mr. Deasy said. There is no time to lose. to the Mr. Field, M. P. There is a meeting of the cattle trade association today at the City Arms Hotel. I asked him to lay my letter before the meeting. You see if you can get it into your two papers. What are they

— The *Evening Telegraph* .....

— That will do, Mr. Deasy said. There is no time to lose. Now I have to answer that letter from my cousin.

— Good morning, sir, Stephen said putting the sheets in his pocket. Thank you.

— Not at all, Mr. Deasy said as he searched the papers on his desk. I like to break a lance with you, old as I am.

— Good morning, sir, Stephen said again, bowing again to his bent back.

He went out by the open porch and down the gravel path under the trees, hearing the cries of voices and crack of sticks from the playfield. The lions couchant on the pillars as he passed out through the gate; toothless terrors. Still I will help him in his fight. Mulligan will dub me a new name: the bullock-befriending bard.

— Mr. Dedalus!

Running after me. No more letters, I hope.

— Just one moment.

— Yes, sir, Stephen said, turning hard and swallowing his breath.

— I just wanted to say, he said. Ireland, they say, has the honour of being the only country which never persecuted the jews. Do you know that? No. And do you know why?

He frowned sternly on the bright air.

— Why, sir? Stephen asked, beginning to smile.

— Because she never let them in, Mr. Deasy said solemnly,

A coughball of laughter leaped from his throat dragging after it a rattling chain of phlegm. He turned back quickly, coughing, laughing, his lifted arms waving to the air.

— She never let them in, he cried again through his laughter as he stamped on gaitered feet over the gravel of the path. That's why.

On his wise shoulders through the checkerwork of leaves the sun flung spangles, dancing coins.

(*to be continued*)

Episode III

THE LITTLE REVIEW

THE MAGAZINE THAT IS READ BY THOSE
WHO WRITE THE OTHERS

MAY, 1918

MARGARET ANDERSON, Editor
EZRA POUND, Foreign Editor

24 *West Sixteenth Street, New York*
Foreign office:
5 *Holland Place Chambers, London W. 8.*

25 cents a copy $2.50 a year

Entered as second-class matter at P. O., New York, N. Y.
Published monthly by Margaret Anderson

INELUCTABLE modality of the visible: at least that if no more, thought through my eyes. Signatures of all things I am here to read, seaspawn and seawrack, the nearing tide, that rusty boot. Snotgreen, bluesilver, rust: coloured signs. Limits of the diaphane. But he adds: in bodies. Then he was aware of them, bodies, before of them coloured. How? By knocking his sconce against them, sure. Go easy. Bald he was and a millionaire, *maestro di color ceh sanno*. Limit of the diaphane in. Why in? Diaphane, adiaphane. If you can put your five fingers through it it is a gate, if not a door. Shut your eyes and see.

Stephen closed his eyes to hear his boots crush crackling wrack and shells. You are walking through it howsomeever. I am, a stride at a time. A very short space of time through very short times of space. Five, six: the *Nacheinander*. Exactly: and that is the ineluctable modality of the audible. Open your eyes. No. Jesus ! If I fell over a cliff that beetles o'er his base, fell through the *Nebeneinander* ineluctably I am getting on nicely in the dark. My ash sword hangs at my side. Tap with it: they do. My two feet in his boots are at the end of my two legs, *nebeneinander*. Sounds solid: made by the mallet of Los demiurgos. Am I walking into eternity along Sandymount strand? Crush, crack, crick, crick. Wild sea money. Dominie Deasy kens them a'.

Won't you come to Sandymount,
Madeline the mare?

Rhythm begins, you see. I hear. Catalectic tetrameter of iambs marching. No, agallop: deline the mare.

Open your eyes now. I will. One moment. Has all vanished since? If I open and am for ever in the black adiaphana! *Basta*. I will see if I can see.

See now. There all the time without you: and ever shall be,. world without end.

They came down the steps from Leahy's terrace prudently, *Frauenzimmer*: and down the shelving shore flabbily, their splayed feet sinking in the silted sand. Like me, like Algy, coming down to our mighty mother. Number one swung lourdily her midwife's bag, the other a gamp poking in the beach. From the liberties, out for the day. Mrs. Florence MacCabe, relict of the late Patk MacCabe, deeply lamented, of Bride Street. One of her sisterhood lugged me squealing into life. Creation from nothing. What has she in the bag? A misbirth with a trailing navelcord, hushed in ruddy wool. The cords of all link

Facing page: table of contents, *Little Review,* May 1918

back, strandentwining cable of all flesh. That is why mystic monks. Will you be as gods? Gaze in your *omphalos*. Hello. Kinch here. Put me on to Edenville. Aleph, alpha: nought, nought, one.

Spouse and helpmate of Adam Kadmon: Heva, naked Eve. She had no navel. Gaze. Belly without belmish, bulging big, a buckler of taut vellum, no, whiteheaped corn, orient and immortal, standing from everlasting to everlasting. Womb of sin.

Wombed in sin darkness I was too, made not begotten. By them, the man with my voice and my eyes and a ghostwoman with ashes on her breath. They clasped and sundered, did the couple's will. From before the ages He willed me and now may not will me away or ever. A *lex eterna* stays about him. Is that then the divine substance wherein Father and Son are consubstantial? When is Arius to answer? Warring his life long on the contrnasmagnificandjewbangtantiality? Illstarred heresiarch! In a Greek watercloset he breathed his last: *euthanasia*. With beaded mitre and with crozier, stalled upon his throne, widower of a widowed see, with upstiffed *omophorion*, with clotted hinderparts.

Airs romped around him, nipping and eager airs. They are coming, waves. The whitemaned seahorses, champing, brightwindbridled.

I mustn't forget his letter for the press. And after? The Ship, half twelve. By the way go easy with that money like a good young imbecile. Yes, I must.

His pace slackened. Here. Am I going to Aunt Sara's or not? My consubstantial father's voice. Did you see anything of your artist brother Stephen lately? No? Sure re's not down in Strasburg terrace with his aunt Sally? Couldn't he strike a bit higher than that, eh? And and and tell us Stephen, how is uncle Si? O, weeping God, the things I married into! De boys up in de hayloft. The drunken little costdrawer and his brother, the cornet player. Highly respectable gondoliers! And skeweyed Walter sirring his father, no less! Sir. Yes, sir. No, sir. Jesus wept: and no wonder by Christ!

I pull the wheezy bell of their shuttered cottage: and wait. They take me for a dun, peer out from a coign of vantage.

—It's Stephen, sir.

—Let him in. Let Stephen in.

A bolt drawn back and Walter welcomes me.

—We thought you were someone else.

In his broad bed uncle Richie, pillowed and blanketed, extends over the hillock of his knees a sturdy forearm. Cleanchested. He has washed the upper moiety.

—Morrow, nephew.

He lays aside the lapboard whereon he drafts his bills of costs for the eyes of Master Goff and Master Tandy, filing consents and common searches and a writ of *Duces Tecum*. A bogoak frame over his bald head: Wilde's *lequiescat*. The drone of his misleading whistle brings Walter back.

—Yes, sir?

—Malt for Richie and Stephen, tell mother. Where is she?

—Bathing Crissie, sir.

Papa's little lump of love.

—No, uncle Richie . . . .

—Call me Richie. Whusky!

—Uncle Richie, really . . . .

—Sit down or by the law Harry I'll knock you down.

Walter squints vainly for a chair.

—He has nothing to sit down on, sir.

—He has nowhere to put it, you mug. Bring in our Chippendale chair. Would you like a bite of something? None of your damned lawdeedaw airs here; a rasher fried with a herring? Sure? So much the better. We have nothing in the house but backache pills.

All'erta!

He drones bars of Ferrando's *aria di sortita*. The grandest number Stephen, in the whole opera. Listen.

His tuneful whistle sounds again, finely shaded, with rushes of air, his fists bigdrumming on his padded knees.

This wind is sweeter.

Houses of decay, mine, his and all. You told the Clongowes gentry you had an uncle a judge and an uncle a general in the army. Come out of them, Stephen. Beauty is not there. Nor in the stagnant bay of Marsh's library where you read the fading prophecies of Joachim Abbas. For whom? The hundredheaded rabble of the cathedral close. A hater of his kind ran from them to the wood of madness, his mane foaming in the moon, his eyeballs stars. Houyhnhnm, horsenostrilled. The oval equine faces, Temple, Buck Mulligan, Foxy Campbell, Lanternjaws. Abbas father, furious dean what offence laid fire to their brains. Paff! *Descende, calve, ut ne amplius decalveris*. A garland of grey hair on his comminated head see him now clambering down to the footpace, (*descende*), clutching a monstrance, basliskeyed. Get down, baldpoll! A choir gives back menace and echo, assisting about the altar's horns, the snorted Latin of jackpriests moving burly in their albs, tonsured and oiled and gelded, fat with the fat of the kidneys of wheat. And at the same instant perhaps a priest round the corner is elevating it. Dringdring! And two streets off another locking it into a pyx. Dringadring! And in a ladychapel another taking housel all to his own cheek. Dringdring! Down, up, forward back. Occam thought of that, invincible doctor. A misty English morning the imp tickled his brain. Brining his host down and kneeling he heard twine with his second bell the first bell in the transept (he is lifting his) and, rising, heard (now I am lifting) their two bells (he is kneeling) twang in diphthong.

Cousin Stephen, you will never be a saint. Isle of saints. You were awfully holy, weren't you? You prayed to the Blessed Virgin that you might not have a red nose. You prayed to the devil in Serpentine avenue that the buxom widow in front might lift her clothes still more from the wet street. *O si, certo!* Sell your soul for that, do, dyed rags pinned round a squaw. More tell me, more still! On the top of the Hewth tram alone crying to the rain: *naked women! naked women!* What about that, eh?

What about what? what else were they invented for?

Reading two pages apiece of seven books every night eh? I was young. You bowed to yourself in the mirror, stepping forward to applause earnestly, striking face. Hurray for the Goddamned idiot! Hray! No-one saw: tell no-one. Books you were going to write with letters for titles. Have you read his F? O yes, but I prefer Q. Yes, but W is wonderful. O yes, W. Remember your epiphanies on green oval leaves, deeply deep, copies to be sent if you died to all the great libraries of the world, including Alexandria? Someone was to read them there after a few thousand years, a mahamanyantara. Pico della Mirandola like. Ay, very like a whale. When one reads these strange pages of one long gone one feels that one is at one with one who once . . . .

The grainy sand had gone from under his feet. His boots trod again a damp crackling mast, razorshells, squeaking pebbles, that on the unnumbered pebbles beats, wood sieved by the shipworm, lost armada. Unwholesome sandflats waited to suck his treading soles, breathing upward sewage breath. He coasted them, walking warily. A porterbottle stood up, pitted to its waist, in the cakey sand dough. A sentinel: isle of dreadful thirst. Broken hoops on the shore; at the land a maze of dark cunning nets; farther away chalkscrawled backdoors and on the higher beach a dryingline with two crucified shirts. Ringsend: wigwams of brown steersmen and master mariners. Human shells.

He halted. I have passed the way to aunt Sara's. Am I not going there? Seems not. No-one about. He turned northeast and crossed the firmer sand towards the Pigeonhouse.

—Qui vous a mis dans cette fichue position?

—C'est le pigeon, Joseph.

Patrice, home on furlough, lapped warm milk with me in the bar MacMahon. Son of the wild goose, Kevin Egan of Paris. My father's a bird, he lapped the sweet *lait chaud* with pink young tongue, plump bunny's face. Lap, *lapin*. He hopes to win in the groslets. About the nature of women he read in Michelet. But he must send me *La Vie de Jésus* by Mr. Léo Taxil. Lent it to his friend.

—C'est tordant, *vous savez. Moi, je suis socialiste. Je ne crois pas à l'existence de Dieu. Paut pas le dire à mon père.*

—Il croit?

—Mon père, oui.

Schluss. He laps.

My latin quarter hat. God, we simply must dress the character. I want puce gloves. You were a student, weren't you? Of what in the other devil's name? Paysayenn. P. C. N., you know: *physiques, chimiques et naturelles*. Aha. Eating your groatsworth of *mou en civet*, fleshpots of Egypt, elbowed by belching cabmen. Just say in the most natural tone: when I was in Paris I used to. Yes, used to carry punched tickets to prove an alibi if they arrested you for murder somewhere. Justice. On the night of the seventeenth of February 1904 the prisoner was seen by two witnesses. Other fellow did it: other me. Hat, tie, overcoat, nose. *Lui, c'est moi*. You seem to have enjoyed yourself.

Proudly walking. Whom were you trying to walk like? Forget: a dispossessed. With mother's money order, eight shillings, the barrier of the post office shut in your face by the usher. Hunger toothache. *Encore deux minutes*. Look clock. Must get. *Fermé*. Hired dog! Shoot him to bloody bits with a bang shotgun, bits man spattered walls all brass buttons. Bits all khrrrklak in place clack back. Not hurt? O, that's all right. Shake hands. See what I meant, see? O, that's all right. Shake a shake. O, that's all only all right.—

You were going to do wonders, what? Missionary to Europe after fiery Columbanus. Pretending to speak broken English as you dragged your valise, porter threepence, across the slimy pier at Newhaven. *Comment?* Rich booty you brought back; five tattered numbers of *Pantalon Blanc et Culotte Rouge;* a blue French telegram, curiosity to show:

—Mother dying come home father.

The aunt thinks you killed your mother. That's why she won't.

—Then here's a health to Mulligan's aunt
And I'll tell you the reason why.

She always kept things decent in
The Hannigan familеye.

His feet marched in sudden proud rhythm over the sand furrows, along by the boulders of the south wall. He stared at them proudly, piled stone mammoth skulls. Gold light on sea, on sand, on boulders. The sun is there, the slender trees, the lemon houses.

Paris rawly waking, crude sunlight on her lemon streets. Moist pith of farls of bread, the froggreen wormwood, her matin incense, court the air. Belluomo rises from the bed of his wife's lover's wife, the kerchiefed housewife is astir, a saucer of acetic acid in her hand. In Rodot's Yvonne and Madeleine newmake there tumbled beauties, shattering with gold teeth *chaussons* of pastry, their mouths yellowed with the *pus* of *flan brêton*. Faces of Paris men go by, their well pleased pelasers, curled *conquistadores*.

Noon slumbers. Kevin Egan rolls gunpowder cigarettes through fingers smeared with printer's ink, sipping his green fairy as Patrice his white. About us gobblers fork spiced beans down their gullets. *Un demi setier!* A jet of coffee steam from the burnished caldron. She serves me at his beck. Your postprandial, do you know that word? Postprandial. There was a fellow I knew once in Barcelona, queer fellow, used to call it his postprandial. Well: *sláinte!* Around the slabbed tables the tangle of wined breaths and grumbling gorges. His breath hangs over our saucestained plates, the green fairy's fang thrusting between his lips. Of Ireland, the Dalcassians, of hopes, conspiracies, of Arthur Griffith now. To yoke me as his yokefellow, our crimes our common cause. His fustian shirt sanguineflowered, trembles its Spanish tassels at his secrets. Mr. Drumont, famous journalist, Drumont, know what he called queen Victoria? Old hag with the yellow teeth. *Vieille ogresse* with the *dents jaunes*. Maud Gonne, *la Patrie*, Mr. Millevoye, Felix Faure, know how he died? Licentious men. The *froeken* who rubbed his nakedness in the bath at Upsala. *Moi faire*, she said. *Tous les messieurs*. Most licentious custom. Bath a most private thing. I wouldn't let my brother, not even my own brother, most lascivious thing. Green eyes, I see you. Fang, I feel. Lascivious people.

The blue fuse burns deadly between hands and burns clear. Loose tobaccoshreds catch fire: a flame and acrid smoke lights our corner. Raw facebones under his peep of day boy's hat. How the head centre got away, true version. Got up as a young bride, man, veil, orangeblossoms, drove out the road to Malahide. Did, faith. Of lost leaders, the betrayed, wild escapes. Disguises, clutched at, gone, not here.

Spurned lover. I was a strapping young gossoon at that time, I tell you. I'll show you my likeness one day. I was faith. Lover, for her love he prowled with colonel Richard Burke, tanist o his sept, under the walls of Clerkenwell and, crouching, saw a flame of vengeance hurl them upward in the fog. Shattered glass and toppling masonry. In gay Paree he hides, Egan of Paris, unsought by any save by me. Making his day's stations, the dingy printingcase, his three taverns, the lair in Butte Montmartre he sleeps short night in *rue de la Goutte d'Or*, damascened with flyblown faces of the gone. Loveless, landless, wifeless. She is quite nicey comfy without her outcast man, madame, in *rue Git-le-Coeur*, canary and two buck lodgers. Peachy cheeks, a zebra skirt, frisky as a young thing! Spurned and undespairing. *Mon fils,* soldier of France. I taught him to sing T*he boys of Kilkenny are stout roaring blades*. Know that old lay? I taught Patrice that. Old Kilkenny: saint Canice, Strongbow's castle on the Nore. Goes like this . O, O. He takes me, Napper Tandy, by the hand.

—O, O the boysof

Kilkenny . . . .

Weak wasting hand on mine. They have forgotten Kevin. Egan, not he them. Remembering thee, O Sion.

He had come nearer the edge of the sea and wet sand slapped his boots. The new air greeted him, harping in wild nerves, wind of wild air of seeds of brightnes.s Here, I am not walking out to the Kish lightship, am I? He stood suddenly, his feet beginning to sink slowly in the quaking soil. Turn back.

Turning, he scanned the shore south, his feet sinking again slowly in new sockets. The cold domed room of the tower waits. Through the barbacans the shafts of light are moving ever, slowly ever as my feet are sinking, creeping duskward over the dial floor. Blue dusk, nightfall, deep blue night. In the darkness of the dome they wait, their pushedback chairs, my obelisk valise, around a board of abandoned platters. Who to clear it? He has the key. I will not sleep there when this night comes. A shut door of a silent tower entombing their blind bodies, the panthersahib and his pointer, Call: no answer. He lifted his feet up from the suck and turned back by the mole of boulders. Take all. My soul walks with me, form of forms. So in the moon's midwatches I pace the path above the rocks, in sable silvered, hearing Elsinore's tempting flood.

The flood is following me. I can watch it flow past from here. Get back then by the Poolbeg road to the strand there. He climbed over the sedge and eely oarweeds and sat on a stool of rock, resting his ashplant by him.

A bloated carcase of a dog lay lolled on bladderwrack. Before him the gunwale of a boat, sunk in sand. *Un coche ensablé* Louis Veuillot called Gautier's prose. These heavy sands are language tide and wind have silted here. And these, the stoneheaps of dead builders, a warren of weasel rats. Hide gold there. Try it. You have some. Sands and stones. Heavy of the past. Sir lout's toys. Mind you don't get one bang on the ear. I'm the bloody well gigant rolls all them bloody well boulders, bones for my steppingstones. Feefawfum. I zmellz de bloodz odz an Iridzman.

A point, live dog, grew into sight running across the sweep of sand. Lord, is he going to attack me? Respect his liberty. You will not be master of others or their slave. I have my stick. Sit tight. From farther away, walking shoreward across from the crested tide, figures, two. The two maries. They have tucked it safe mong the bulrushes. Peekaboo. I see you. No, the dog. He is running back to them. Who?

Galleys of the Lochlanns ran here to beach, in quest of prey, their bloodbeaked prows riding low on a molten pewter surf. Dane vikings, tores of tomahawks aglitter on their breasts when Malachi wore the collar of gold. A school of turlehide whales stranded in hot noon, spouting, hobbling in the shallows. Then from the starving cagework city a horde of jerkined dwarfs, my people, with flayers' knives, running, scaling, hacking in green blubbery whalemeat. Famine, plague and slaughters. Their blood is in me, their lusts my waves. I moved among them on the frozen Liffey, that I, a changeling, among the spluttering resin fires. I spoke to no-one: none to me.

The dog's bark ran toward him, stopped, ran back. Dog of my enemy. I just simply stood pale, silent, bayed about. *Terribilia meditans.* A primrose doublet, fortune's knave, smiled on my fear. For that are you pining, the bark of their applause? Pretenders: live their lives. The Bruce's brother, Thomas Fitzgerald, silken knight, Perkin Warbeck, York's false scion, in breechers of silk of whiterose ivory, wonder of a day, and Lambert Simnel, a scullion crowned. All kings' sons. Paradise of pretenders then and now. He saved men from drowning and you shake at a cur's yelping. But the courtiers who mocked Guido in or san Michele were in their own house. House of . . . . We don't want any of your medieval abstrusiosities. Would you do what he did? A boat would be near, a lifebuoy. *Natürlich*, put there for you. Would you or would you not? The man that was drowned nine days ago off Maiden's rock. They were waiting for him now. The truth, spit it out. I would want to. I would try. I am not a strong swimmer. Water cold soft. When I put my face into it in the basin at Clongowes. Out quickly, quickly! Do you see the tide flowing quickly in an all sides, sheeting the beds of sand quickly, shellcocoacoloured? If I had land under my feet. I want his life still to be his, mine to be mine. A drowning man. His human eyes scream to me out of horror of his death. I . . . With him together down . . . . I could not save her. Waters: bitter death: lost.

A woman and a man. I see her skirties. Pinned up, I bet.

Their dog ambled about a bank of dwindling sand, trotting, sniffing on all sides. Looking for something lost in a past life. Suddenly he made off like a bounding hare, ears flung back, chasing the shadow of a lowskimming gull. The man's shrieked whistle struck his limp ears. He turned, hounded back, came nearer, trotted on twinkling shanks. On a field tenney a buck trippant, proper, unattired. At the lacefringe of the tide he halted with stiff forehoofs, seawardpointed ears. His snout lifted barked at the wavenoise. They serpented towards his feet, curling, unfurling many crests, every ninth, breaking, plashing, from far, from farther out, waves and waves.

Cocklepickers. They wade a little way in the water and, stooping, soused their bags, and, lifting them again, waded out. The dog yelped running to them, reared up and pawed them, dropping on all fours, again reared up at them with mute bearish fawning. Unheeded he kept by them as they came towards the drier sand, a rag of wolf's tongue redpanting from his jaws. His speckled body ambled ahead of them and then set off at a calf's gallop. The carcase lay on his path. He stopped, sniffed, stalked round it, brother, nosing closer, went round it, sniffling rapidly, dogsniff, eyes on the ground, moves to one great goal. Ah poor dogsbody! Here lies dogsbody's body.

—Tatters! Out of that you mongrel!

The cry brought him skulking back to his master and a blunt bootless kick sent him unscathed across a spit of sand, crouched in flight. He slunk back in a curve. Doesn't see me. Along by the edge of the mole he dawdled, smelt a rock and, from under a edge of the mole he dawdled, smelt a rock. Something he buried there, his grandmother. He rooted in the sand, dabbling and delving and stopped to listen to the air; scraped up the sand again with a fury of his claws, soon ceasing, a pard, a panther, got in spousebreach, vulturing the dead.

After he woke me up last night same dream or was it? Wait. Open hallway. Street of harlots. Remember. I am almosting it. That man led me, spoke. I was not afraid. The melon he had he held against my face. Smiled: creamfruit smell. That was the rule said. In. Come. Red carpet spread. You will see who.

Shouldering their bags they passed. His blued feet out of turnedup trousers slapped the clammy sand, a dull red muffler strangling his unshaven neck.

With woman steps she followed: the ruffian and his strolling mort, spoils slung at her back. Loose sand and shellgrit crusted her bare feet. About her windraw face her hair trailed. Behind her lord his helpmate, trudging to Romeville. When night hides her body's flaws calling under her brown shawl from an archway where dogs have mired. Her fancyman is treating two Royal Dublins in O'Loughlin's of Blackpitts. Buss her, wap in rogues' rum lingo, for, O, my dimber wapping dell A shefiend's whitenes under her rancid rage. Fumbally's lane that night: the tanyard smells.

White thy fambles, red thy gan
And thy quarrons dainty is.
Couch a hogshead with me then:
In the darkmans clip and kiss.

Morose delectation Aquinas tunbelly calls this, *frate porcospino*. Call away let him: thy quarrons dainty is. Language no whit worse than his. Monkwords, marybeads jabber on their girdles: roguewords, tough nuggets patter in their pockets.

Passing now.

A side-eye at my Hamlet hat. If I were suddenly naked here as I sit? I am not. Across the sands of all the world, followed by the sun's flaming sword, to the west, to evening lands. She trudges, schlepps, trains, drags, trascines her load. A tide westering, moondrawn, in her wake, Ides, myriadislanded, within her, blood not mine, *oinopa ponton,* a winedark sea. Behold the handmaid of the moon. In sleep the wet sign calls her hour, bids her rise. Bridebed, childbed, bed of death, ghostcandled. *Omnis caro ad te veniet.* He comes, pale vampire, through storm his eyes, his bat sails bloodying the sea, mouth to her mouth's kiss.

Here. Put a pin in that chap, will you? My tablet. Mouth to her kiss. No. Must be two of em. Glue em well. Mouth to her mouth's kiss.

His lips lipped and mouthed fleshless lips of air: mouth to her moomb. Oomb, allwombing tomb. His mouth moulded issuing breath, unspeeched: ooeeehah: roar of oataractic planets, globed, blazing, roaring wayawayawayawayawayaway. Paper. The banknotes, blast them. Old Deasy's letter. Here. Thanking you for the hospitality tear the blank end off. Turning his back to the sun he bent over far to a table of rock and scribbled words. That's twice I forgot to take slips from the library counter.

His shadow lay over the rocks as he bent, ending. Why not endless till the farthest star? Darkly they are there behind this light, darkness shining in the brightness, delta of Cassiopeia, worlds. Me sits there with his augur's rod of ash, in borrowed sandals, by day beside a livid sea, unbeheld, in violet night walking beneath a reign of uncouth stars. I throw this ended shadow from me, call it back. Endless, would it be mine, form of my form? Who watches me here? Who ever anywhere will read these written words? Signs on a white field. Somewhere to someone in your flutiest voice. The good bishop of Cloyne took the veil of the temple out of his shovel hat: veil of space with coloured emblems hatched on its field. Hold hard. Coloured on a flat: yes, that's right. Flat I see, then think distance, near, far, flat I see, east, back . Ah, see now! Falls back suddenly frozen in stereoscope. Click does the trick. You find my words dark. Darkness is in our souls do you not think? Flutier. Our souls, shamewounded by our sins, cling to us yet more, a woman to her lover clinging, the more the more.

She trusts me, her hand gentle, the longlashed eyes. Now where the blue hell am I bringing her beyond the veil? Into the ineluctable modality of the ineluctable visuality. She, she, she. What she? The virgin at Hodges Riggis' window on Monday looking in for one of the alphabet books you were going to write. Keen glance you gave her. Wrist through the braided jesse of her sunshade. She lives in Leesonp ark, a lady of letters. Talk that to someone else, Stevie: a pickmeup. Bet she wears those curse of God stays suspenders and yellow stockings, darned with lumpy wool. Talk about apple dumpling, *piuttosto*. Where are your wits?

Touch me. Soft eyes. Soft soft soft hand. I am lonely here. O, touch me soon, now. What is that word known to all men? I am quiet here alone. Sad too. Touch, touch me.

He lay back at full stretch over the sharp rocks, cramming the scribbled note and pencil into a pocket, his hat tilted down on his eyes. That is Kevin Egan's movement I made, nodding for his nap. *Hlo! Bonjour*. Under its leaf he watched through peacocktwittering lashes the southing sun. I am caught in this burning scene. Pan's hour, the faunal noon. Among gumheavy serpentplants, milkoozing fruits, where on the tawny waters leaves lie wide. Pain is far.

And no more turn aside and brood.

His gaze brooded on his broadtoed boots, a buck's castoffs, *nebeneinander*. He counted the creases of rucked leather wherein another's foot had nested warm. The foot that beat the ground in tripudium, foot I dislove. But you were delighted when Esther Osvalt's shoe went on you: girl I knew in Paris. *Tiens, quel petit pied!* Staunch friend, a brother soul: Wilde's love that dare not speak its name. He now will leave me. And the blame? As I am. All or not at all.

In long lassos from the Cock lake the water flowed full, covering grenngoldenly lagoons of sand, rising, flowing. My ashplant will float away. I shall wait. No, they will pass on, passing chafing agains the low rocks, swirling, passing. Better get this job over quick. Listen: a fourworded wavespeech: seesoo, hrss, rsseeiss ooos. Vchement breath of waters amid seasnakes, rearing horses, rocks. In cups of rocks it slops: flop, slop, slap: bounded in barrels. And, spent, its speech ceases. It flows purling, widely flowing, floating foampool, flower unfurling.

Under the upswelling tide he saw the writhing weeds lift languidly and sway reluctant arms, hising up their petticoats, in whispering water swaying and upturning coy silver fronds. Day by day: night by night: lifted, flooded and let fall: Lord, they are weary: and, whispered to, they sigh. Saint Ambrose heard it, sigh of leaves and waves, waiting, awaiting the fulness of their times, *diebus ac noctibus iniurias patiens ingemiscit.* To no end gathered: vainly then released, forthflowing, wending back: loom of the moon. Weary too in sight of lovers, lascivious men, a naked woman shining in her court, she draws a toil of waters.

Five fathoms out there. Full fathom five thy father lies. At one he said. High water at Dublin bar. Driving before it a loose drift of rubble, fanshoals of fishes, silly shells. A corpse rising saltwhite from the undertow, bobbing landward. There he is. Hook it quick. Pull. We have him. Easy now.

Bag of corpsegas sopping in foul brine. A quiver of minnows, fat of a spongy titbit, flash through the slits of his buttoned trouserfly. God becomes man becomes fish becomes barnacle goose becomes featherbed mountain. Dead breaths I living breathe, tread dead dust, devour a urinous offal from all dead. Hauled stark over the gunwale he breathes upward the stench of his green grave, his leprous nosehole snoring to the sun.

A seachange this. Seadeath, mildest of all death's known to man. *Prix de Paris*: beware of imitations. Just you give it a fair trial. We enjoyed ourselves immensely.

Come. Clouding over. No black clouds anywhere, are there? Thunderstorm. No. My cockle hat and staff and hismy sandal shoon. Where? To evening lands. Evening will find itself.

He took the hilt of his ashplant, lunging with it softly, dallying still. Yes, evening will find itself in me, without me. All days make their end. By the way next when is it Tuesday will be the longest day. Of all the glad new year, mother, the rum tum tiddledy tum. Lawn Tennyson, gentleman poet. *Gia.* For the old hag with the yellow teeth. And Monsieur Drumont, gentleman journalis *Gia.* My teeth are very bad. Why, I wonder? Feel. That one is going to. Shells. Ought I go to a dentist, I wonder, with that money? That one. This. Toothless Kinch, the superman. Why is that, I wonder, or does it mean something perhaps?

My handkerchief. He threw it. I remember. Did I not take it up?

His hand groped vainly in his pockets. No. I didn't. Better buy one. He laid the dry snot picked from his nostril on a ledge of rock, carefully. For the rest let look who will.

Behind. Perhaps there is someone.

He turned his face over a shoulder, rere regardant. Moving through the air high spars of a threemaster, her sails brailed up on the crosstrees, homing, silently moving, a silent ship.—

(*to be continued*)

Episode IV

THE LITTLE REVIEW

THE MAGAZINE THAT IS READ BY THOSE WHO WRITE THE OTHERS

JUNE, 1918

MARGARET ANDERSON, **Editor**
EZRA POUND, ***Foreign Editor***

24 *West Sixteenth Street, New York*
Foreign office:
5 *Holland Place Chambers, London W. 8.*

25 cents a copy $2.50 a year

Entered as second-class matter at P. O., New York. N. Y., under the act March 3, 1879.

***Published monthly** by Margaret Anderson*

MR. LEOPOLD BLOOM ate with relish the inner organs of beasts and fowls. He liked thick giblet soup, nutty gizzards, a stuffed roast heart, liver-slices fried with crust-crumbs, fried cods' roes. Most of all he liked grilled mutton kidneys which gave to his palate a fine tang of faintly scented urine.

Kidneys were in his mind as he moved about the kitchen softly, righting her breakfast things on the humpy tray. Gelid light and air were in the kitchen but out of doors gentle summer morning everywhere. Made him feel a bit peckish.

The coals were reddening.

Another slice of bread and butter: three, four: right. She didn't like her plate full. Right . He turned from the tray, lifted the kettle off the hob and set it sideways on the fire. It sat there, dull and squat, its spout stuck out .

The cat walked stiffly round a leg of the table with tail on high.

Mkgnao!

—O, there you are, Mr. Bloom said, turning from the fire.

The cat mewed in answer and stalked again stiffly round a leg of the table, mewing.

Mr. Bloom watched curiously, kindly the lithe black form. Clean to see: the gloss of her sleek hide, the white button under the butt of her tail, the green flashing eyes. He bent down to her, his hands on his knees.

—Milk for the pussens , he said.

—Mrkgnao! the cat cried.

They call them stupid. They understand what we say better than we understand them. She understands all she wants to.

—Afraid of the chickens she is, he said mockingly. Afraid of the chookchooks. I never saw such a stupid pussens as the pussens.

—Mrkgnao! The cat said loudly.

She blinked up out of her avid eyes, mewing plaintively and long, showing him her milkwhite teeth. He watched the dark eyeslits narrowing with greed till her eyes were green stones. Then he went to the dresser, poured milk on a saucer and set it for her slowly on the floor.

—Gurrhr! she cried, running to lap.

He watched the bristles shining wirily in the weak light. Wonder is it true if you clip them they can't mouse after. Why? They shine in the dark perhaps, the tips. Or kind of feelers in the dark, perhaps.

Facing page: table of contents, *Little Review,* June 1918

He listened to her licking lap. Thursday: good day for a mutton kidney at Buckley's. Fried with butter, a shake of pepper. Or better a pork kidney at Dlugacz's. While the kettle is boiling. She lapped slower, then licking the saucer clean. Why are their tongues so rough? To lap better , all porous holes. Nothing she can eat? He glanced round him. No.

He went up the staircase to the hall, paused by the bedroom door. She might like something tasty. Thin bread and butter she likes in the morning. Still perhaps: once in a way.

He said softly in the bare hall :

—I am going round the corner. Be back in a minute.

And when he had heard his voice say it he added:

—You don't want anything for breakfast?

A sleepy soft grunt answered:

—Mn.

No. She did not want anything. He heard then a warm heavy sigh, softer, as she turned over and the loose brass quoits of the bedstead jingled. Must get those settled really. Pity. All the way from Gibraltr. Wonder what her father gave for it. Old style. Ah yes, of course. Bought it at the governor's auction. Got a short knock. Hard as nails at a bargain, old Tweedy. Yes , sir. At Plevna that was. I rose from the ranks, sir, and I'm proud of it. Still he had brains enough to make that corner in stamps. Now that was farseeing .

His hand took his hat from the peg. Stamps: stickyback pictures. Daresay lots of officers are in the swim too. Course they do. The sweated legend in the crown of his hat told him mutely: Plasto's high grade ha. He peered quickly inside the leather headband. White slip of paper. Quite safe.

On the doorstep he felt in his hip pocket for the latchkey. Not there. In the trousers I left off. Creaky wardrobe. No use disturbing her. She turned over sleepily that time. He pulled the halldoor to after him very quietly, more, till the footleaf dropped gently over the threshold, a limp lid. Looked shut. All right till I come back anyhow.

He crossed to the brgiht side . The sun was nearing the steeple of George's church. Be a warm day I fancy. Specially in these black clothes feel it more. Black conducts, reflects, (refracts is it?) the heat. His eyelids sank quietly often as he walked in happy warmth. Makes you feel young. Somewhere in the east: early morning: set off at dawn. Walk along a strand, strange land, come to a city gate, sentry there, old ranker too, old Tweedy's big moustaches, leaning on a long kind of spear. Wander through awned streets . Turbaned faces going by. Dark caves of carpet shops, big man, Turk, seated crosslegged smoking a coiled pipe. Cries of sellers in the streets. Drink water scented with fennel, sherbet. Wander along all day. Getting on to sundown. The shadows of the mosques among the pillars: priest with a scroll rolled up. A shiver of the trees, signal, the evening wind. I pass on. Fading gold sky. A mother watches me from her doorway. She calls her children home in their dark language. High wall: beyond strings twanged. Night sky, moon, violet, colour of Molly's new garters. Strings. Listen. A girl playing one of those instruments what do you call them: dulcimers. I pass.

Probably not a bit like it really. Kind of stuff you read: in the track of the sun. Sunburst on the titlepage. He smiled, pleasing himself. What Arthur Griffith said about the headpiece over the *Freeman* leader: a homerule sun rising up in the northwest from the laneway behind the bank of Ireland. He prolonged his pleased smile. Ikey touch that: homerule sun rising up in the northwest.

He approached Larry O'Rourke's. From the cellar grating floated up the flabby gush of porter. Through the open doorway the bar squirted out whiffs of ginger, teadust, biscuitmush. Good house however: just the end of the city traffic. For instance M'Auley's down there.: n. g. as position . Of course if they ran a tramline along the North Circular from the cattle market to the quays value would go up like a shot.

Baldhead over the blind. Cute old dodger. No use canvassing him for an order ad. Still he knew his own business best. There he is, sure enough, my bold arry, leaning against the sugarbin in his shirtsleeves watching the aproned curate swab up with mop and bucket. Simon Dedalus takes him off to a tea, with his eyes screwed up. Do you know what I'm going to tell you? What's that, Mr. O'Rourke? Do you know what: the Russians, they are only an eight o'clock breakfast for the Japanese.

Stop and say a word: about the funeral perhaps. Sad thing about poor Dignam, Mr. O'Rourke.

Turning into Dorset street he said freshly in greeting through the doorway:

—Good day, Mr. O'Rourke.

—Good day to you.

—Lovely weather, sir.

—'Tis all that.

Where do they get the money? Coming up redheaded curates from the country eitrim, rinsing empties in the cellar. Then, lo and behold, they blossom out as publicans. Save it they can't. Off the drunks perhaps. What is that A bob here and there, dribs and drabs. On the wholesale orders perhaps. Doing a double shuffle with the town travellers. Square it with the boss and we'll split the job, see?

How much would that tot to off the porter in the month? Say ten barrels of stuff. Say he got ten per cent off. Or more. Fifteen.

He halted before Dlugacz's window, staring at the hanks of sausages, polonies, black and white. Fifteen multiplied by. The figures whitened in his mind unsolved: displeased, he let them fade. The shiny link packed with forcemeat, fed his gaze and he breathed in tranquilly the lukewarm breath of cooked spicy pig's blood .

A kidney oozed bloodgouts on the willow-patterned dish: the last. He stood near the nextdoor girl at the counter. Would she buy it too, calling the items from a slip in her hand? Chapped: washing soda. And a pound and a half of sausages. His eyes rested on her vigorous hips. Strong pair of arms. Whacking a carpet on the clothesline. She does whack it, by George. The way her crooked skirt swings at each whack.

The ferreteyed porkbutcher folded the sausage he had snipped off with blotchy fingers, sausagepink.

Sound meat there: like a stallfed heifer. He took a page up from the pile of cut sheets: the model farm at Kinnereth on the lakeshore of Tiberias. I thought he was. Farmhouse, wall round it, blurred cattle cropping. He held the page from him: interesting: read it nearer, the title, the blurred cropping cattle, the page rustling. A young white heifer. Those mornings in the cattle market, the beasts lowing in their pens, flop and fall of dung, the bdeeders in hobnailed boots trudging through the litter, slapping a palm on a meaty hindquarter, there's a prime one, unpeeled switches in their hands. He held the page aslant patiently, bending his senses and his will, his soft subject gaze at rest. The crooked skirt swinging whack by whack by whack.

The porkbutcher snapped two sheets from the pile, wrapped up her sausages and made a red grimace.

—Now, my miss, he said.

She tendered a coin, smiling boldly, holding her thick wrist out.

—Thank you my miss. And one shilling threepence change. For you, please?

Mr. Bloom pointed quickly. To catch up and walk behind her if she went slowly, behind her moving hams. Hurry up, damn it. She stood outside the shop in sunlight and turned lazily to the right. He sighed down his nose: they never understand. Soda chapped hands. Crusted toenails too. Brown scapulars in tatters, defending her both ways. The sting of disregard glowed to weak pleasure within his breast. For another: a constable off duty cuddled her in Eccles' Lane.

—Threepence, please.

His hand accepted the moist tender gland and slid it into a sidepocket. Then it fetched up three coins from his trousers' pocket and laid them on the rubber prickles. They lay, were read quickly and quickly slid, disc by disc, into the till.

—Thank you, sir. Another time.

A speck of eager fire from foxeyes thanked him. He withdrew his gaze after an instant. No: better not: another time.

—Good morning, he said, moving away.

—Good morning, sir.

No sign. Gone. What matter?

He walked back along Dorset street, reading gravely. Agendath Netaim: planters' company. You pay eighty marks, and they plant a dunam of land for you with olives, oranges, almonds or citrons. Olives cheaper: oranges need artificial irrigation. Every year you get a sending of the crop. Your name entered for life as owned in the book of the union. Can pay ten down and the balance in yearly instalments. Bleibtreustrasse 34 Berlin, W. 15.

Nothing doing. Still an idea behind it.

He looked at the cattle, blurred in silver heat. Silvered powdered olivetrees. Quiet long days: pruning, ripening. Olives are packed in jars, eh? I have a few left from Andrews. Molly spitting them out. Knows the taste of them now. Oranges in tissue paper packed in crates. Citrons too. Wonder is poor Citrin still alive in saint Kevin's parade. And Mastiansky with the old cither. pleasant evenings we had then. Molly in Citrin's basketchair. Nice to hold, cool waxen fruit, hold in the hand, lift it to the nostrils and smell the perfume. Like that heavy sweet, wild perfume. Always the same , year after year. They fetched high prices too, Moisel told me. Arbutus place: Pleasants street: pleasant old times. Must be without a flaw, he said. Coming all that way: Spain, Gibralter, Mediterranean, the Levant. Crates lined up on the quayside at Jaffa, chap ticking them off in a book, navvies handling them in soiled dungarees.

A cloud began to cover the sun slowly, wholly. Grey. Far.

No, not like that. A barren land, bare waste. Vulcanic lake, the dead sea: no fish, weedless, sunk deep in the earth. No wind could lift those waves, grey metal, poisonous foggy waters. Brimstone they called it raining down: the cities of the plain: Sodom, Gommorah, Edom. All dead names. A dead sea in a dead land, grey and old. Old now. It bore the oldest, the first race. A bent hag crossed from Cassidy's, clutching a naggin bottle by the neck. The oldest people. Wandered far away over all the earth, multiplying, dying, being born everything. It lay there now. Now it could bear no more. Dead: an old woman's: the grey sunken belly of the world.

Desolation.

Grey horror seared his fiesh. Folding the page into his pocket he turned into Eccles' Street, hurrying homeward. Cold oils slid along his veins, chilling his blood: age crusting him with a salt cloak. Well, I am here now. Blotchy brown brick houses. Number seven still unlet. Why is that? Valuation is only twenty-eight. Towers, Battersby , North, MacArthur: parlour windows plastered with bills. Plasters on a sore eye . To smell the gentle smoke of tea, fume of the pan, sizzling butter. Be near her ample bedwarmed flesh. Yet, yes.

Quick warm sunlight came running from Berkeley Road, swiftly, in slim sandals, along the brightening footpath. Runs, she runs to meet me, a girl with gold hair on the wind.

Two letters and a card lay on the hall floor. He stooped and gathered them. Mrs. Marion Bloom. His quickened heart slowed at once. Bold hand, Mrs. Marion . . .

—Poldy!

Entering the bedroom he halfclosed his eyes and walked through warm yellow twilight towards her tousled head.

—Who are the letters for?

He looked at them. Mullinger, Milly.

—A letter for me from Milly , he said carefully, and a crad to you. And a letter for you.

He laid her card and letter on the twill bedspread near the curve of her knees.

—Do you want the blind up?

Letting the blind up by gentle tugs halfway his backward eye saw her glance at the letter and tuck it under her pillow.

—That do? he asked, turning.

She was reading the card, propped on her elbow.

—She got the things, she said.

He waited till she had laid the card aside and curled herself back slowly with a snug sigh.

—Hurry up with that tea, she said. I'm parched.

—The kettle is boiling, he said.

But he delayed to clear the chair: her striped petticoat, tossed soiled linen: and lifted all in an armful on to the foot of the bed.

As he went down the kitchen stairs she called:

—Poldy!

—What?

—Scald the teapot.

Boiling sure enough: a plume of steam from the spout. He scalded and rinsed out the teapot and put in four full spoons of tea, tilting the kettle then to let water flow in. Having set it to draw he took off the kettle, crushed the pan flat on the live coals and watched the lump of butter slide and melt. While he unwrapped the kidney the cat mewed hungrily against him. He let the blood-smeared paper fall to her and dropped the kidney amid the sizzling butter sauce. Pepper. He sprinkled it through his fingers, ringwise, from the chipped eggcup.

Then he slit open his letter, glancing down the page and over. Thanks: new tam: Mr. Coghlan: lough Owel picnic: young student: Blazes Boylan's seaside girls.

The tea was drawn. He filled his own moustache cup, sham crown Derby, smiling. Silly Milly's birthday gift. Only nine she was then. No, wait: eight. I gave her the necklace she broke. He smiled, pouring.

O, Milly Bloom, you are my darling.
You are my looking glass from night to morning.
I'd rather have you without a farthing
Than Katey Keogh with her ass and garden.

Poor old professor Goodwin. Dreadful old case. Still he was a courteous old chap. Oldfashioned way he used to bow Molly off the platform. And the little mirror in his silk hat. The night Milly brought it into the parlour. O, look what I found in professor Goodwin's hat! All we laughed. Pert little piece she was.

He prodded a fork into the kidney and slapped it over: then fitted the teapot on the tray . Its hump bumped as he took it up. Everything on it? Bread and butter; four, sugar, spoon, her cream. Yes. He carried it upstairs, his thumb hooked in the teapot handle.

Nudging the door open with his knee he carried the tray in and set it on the chair by the bedhead.

—What a time you were? she said.

She set the brasses jingling as she raised herself briskly, an elbow on the pillow. He looked calmly down on her bulk and between her large soft bubs, sloping within her nightdress like a shegoat's udder. The warmth of her couched body rose on the air, mingling with the fragrance of the tea she poured.

A strip of torn envelope peeped from under the dimpled pillow. In the act of going he stayed to straighten the bedspread.

—Who was the letter from? he asked.

Bold hand. Marion.

—O, Boylan, she said. He's bringing the programme.

—What are you singing?

—*Là ci darem* with J. C. Doyle, she said, and *Love's Old Sweet Song*.

Her full lips, drinking, smiled. Rather stale smell that incense leaves next day.

—Would you like the window open a little?

She doubled a slice of bread into her mouth, asking:

—What time is the funeral?

—Eleven, I think, he answered. I didn't see the paper.

Following the pointing of her finger he took up a leg of her soiled drawers from the bed. No. Then, a twisted grey garter looped round a stocking: rumpled, shiny sole.

—No: that book.

Other stocking. Her petticoat.

—It must have fell down, she said.

He felt here and there. *Voglio e non vorrei*. Wonder if she pronounces that right: *voglio*. Not in bed. Must have slid down. He stooped and lifted the valance. The book, fallen, sprawled against the bulge of the orangekeyed chamberpot.

—Show here, she said. I put a mark in it. There's a word I wanted to ask you.

She swallowed a draught of tea and, having wiped her fingertips smartly on the blanket, began to search the text with the hairpin till she reached the word.

—Met him what? he asked.

—Here, she said. What does that mean?

He leaned downward and read near her polished thumbnail.

—Metempsychosis?

—Yes. What's that?

—Metempsychosis, he said, frowning. It's Greek: from the Greek. That means the transmigration of souls.

—O, rocks! she said. Tell us in plain words.

He smiled, glancing askance at her mocking eyes. The same young eyes. The first night after the charade at Dolphin's Barn. He turned over the smudged pages. *Ruby*: a tale of circus life. That we live after death. Our souls. That a man's soul after he dies, Dignam's soul . . .

—Did you finish it? he asked.

—Yes, she said. There's nothing smutty in it. Is she in love with the first fellow all the time?

—Never read it. Do you want another?

—Yes. Get another of Paul de Kock's. Nice name he has.

She poured more tea into her cup, watching it flow sideways.

Reincarnation: that's the word.

—Some people believe, he said, that we go on living in another body after death, that we lived before. They call it reincarnation. That we all lived before on the earth thousands of years ago or some other planet. They say we have forgotten it. Some say they remember their past lives.

The sluggish cream wound curdling spirals through her tea. Better remind her of the word: metempsychosis. An example would be better. An example?

The Bath of the Nymph over the bed. Given away with the easter number of *Photo Bits*: splendid masterpiece in art colours. Tea before you put milk in. Not unlike her with her hair down: slimmer. Three and six I gave for the frame. She said it would look nice over the bed. Naked nymphs: Greece: and for instance all the people that lived then.

He turned the pages back.

—Metempsychosis, he said, is what the ancient Greeks called it. They used to believe you could be changed into an animal or a tree, for instance. What they called nymphs for example.

Her spoon ceased to stir up the sugar. She gazed straight before her, inhaling through her arched nostrils.

—There's a smell of burn, she said. Did you leave anything on the fire?

—The kidney? he cried suddenly.

He fitted the book roughly into his inner pocket and hurried out towards the smell, stepping hastily down the stairs with a flurried stork's legs. Pungent smoke shot up in an angry jet from a side of the pan. By prodding a prong of the fork under the kidney he detached it and turned it over on its back. Only a little burned . He tossed it off the pan on to a plate and let the scanty brown gravy trickle over it.

Cup of tea now. He sat down, cut and buttered a slice of the loaf. He shore away the burnt flesh and flung it to the cat. Then he put a forkful into his mouth, chewing with discernment the toothsome pliant meat. Done to a turn. A mouthful of tea. Then he cut many dies of bread, sopped one in the gravy and put it in his mouth. What was that about some young student and a picnic? He creased out the letter at his side, reading it slowly as he chewed, sopping another die of bread in the gravy and raising it to his mouth.

Dearest Papli :

Thanks ever so much for the lovely birthday present. It suits me splendid. Everyone says I'm quite the belle in my new tam. I got mummy's lovely box of cerams and am writing . They are lovely. I am getting on swimming in the photo business now. Mr. Coghlan took one of me and Mrs. will send when developed. We did great biz yesterday. Fair day and all the beef to the heels were in. We are going to lough Owel on Monday with a few friends to make a scrap picnic. Give my love to mummy and to yourself a big kiss and thanks. I hear them at the piano downstairs. There is to be concert in the Greville Armson Saturady. There is a young student comes here some evenings named Bannon his cousins or something are swells; he sings Boylan's (I was on the pop of writing Blazes Boylan's) song about those seaside girls . Tell him silly Milly sends my best respects. Byby again and lots of love.

Your fond daughter

Milly

P. S. Excuse bad writing, am in hurry.

Fifteen yesterday. Curious, fifteenth of the month too. Her first birthday away from home. Separation . Remember the morning she was born, running to knock up Mrs. Thornton in Denzille street. Jolly old woman. Lots of babies she must have helped into the world. She knew from the first poor little Rudy wouldn't live. Well, God is good, sir. She knew at once. He would be eleven now if he had lived.

His vacant face stared pitying at the postscript. Excuse bad writing. Hurry. Piano downstairs. He sopped other dies of bread in the gravy and ate piece after piece of kidney. Twelve and six a week. Not much. Still, she might do worse. Musichall stage. Young student. He drank a draught of cold tea to wash down his meal. Then he read the letter again: twice.

O well: she knows how to mind herself. But if not? No, nothing had happened. Of course it might . Wait in any case till it did. A wild piece of goods. Her slim legs running up the staircase. Destiny. Ripening now. Vain: very.

He smiled with troubled affection at the kitchen window. Day I caught her in the street pinching her cheeks to make them red. On the *Erin's King* that day round the Kish. Damned old tub pitching about. Not a bit funky. Her pale blue scarf loose in the wind with her hair.

All dimpled cheeks and curls,
Your head it simply swirls.

Seaside girls. Torn envelope. Hands stuck in his trousers' pockets, singing. Swurls, he says. Pier with lamps, summer evening, band.

Those girls, those girls,
Those lovely seaside girls.

Milly too. Young kisses: the first. Far away now past. Mrs. Marion. Reading lying back now, counting the strands of her hair.

A soft qualm, regret, flowed down his backbone, increasing . Will happen, yes. Prevent. Useless: can't move. Girl's sweet light lips. Will happen too. He felt the flowing qualm spread over him. Useless to move now. Lips kissed, kissing, kissed. Full gluey woman's lips.

Better where she is down there: away. Might take a trip down there. August bank holiday, only five and six return. Six weeks off however. Might work a press pass. Or through M'Coy.

The cat, having cleaned all her fur, returned to the meatstained paper, nosed at it and stalked to the door. She looked back at him, mewing. Wants to go out. Let her wait.

He felt heavy, full: then a gentle loosening. He stood up. The cat mewed to him.

—Miaow! he said in answer. Wait till I'm ready.

Heaviness: hot day coming. Too much trouble to fag up the stairs to the landing.

In the table drawer he found an old number of *Titbits*. He folded it under his armpit, went to the door and opened it. The cat went up in soft bounds. Ah, wanted to go upstairs, curl up in a ball on the bed.

Listening, he heard her voice:

—Come, come, pussy. Come.

He went out into the garden: stood to listen towards the next garden. No sound. Perhaps hanging clothes out to dry. Fine morning.

He bent down to regard a lean file of spearmint growing by the wall. Want to manure the whole place over, scabby soil. A coat of liver of sulphur. All soil like that without dung. Loam, what is this that is? The hens in the next garden; their droppings are very good I heard. Best of all though are the cattle, specially when they are fed on those oilcakes. Mulch of dung. Reclaim the whole place. Grow peas in that corner there. Lettuce. Always have fresh greens then.

He walked on. Where is my hat, by the way? Must have put it back on the peg. Funny I don't remember that . Picking up the letters. Drago's shopbell ringing. Queer I was just thinking that moment. Black brillantined hair over his collar. Just had a wash and brush up. Wonder have I time for a bath this morning.

Deep voice that fellow Dlugacz has . Agendath what is it? Now, my miss. Enthusiast.

Something new and easy. Our prize titbit. *Matcham's Masterstroke*. Written by Mr. Philip Beaufoy, Playergoers' Club, London. Payment at the rate of one guinea a column has been made to the writer. Three and a half. Three pounds three. Three pounds, thirteen and six.

Life might be so. It did not move or touch him but it was something quick and neat. He read on. Neat certainly. Matcham often thinks of the masterstroke by which he won the laughing witch who now. Hand in hand. Smart. He glanced back through what he had read and envied kindly Mr. Beaufoy who had written it and received payment of three pounds, thirteen and six.

Might manage a sketch . . Time I used to try jotting down on my cuff what she said dressing. Biting her nether lip hooking the placket of her skirt. Timing her. 9.15. Did Roberts pay you yet? 9.20. What had Gretta Conroy on? 9.23. What possessed me to buy this comb? 9.24. I'm swelled after that cabbage. A speck of dust on the patent leather of her boot.

Rubbing smartly in turn each welt against her stockinged calf. Morning after the bazaar dance when May's band played Ponchielli's dance of the hours. Explain that: morning hours, noon, then evening coming on, then night hours. Washing her teeth. That was the first night: Is that Boylan well off? He has money. Why? I noticed he had a good rich smell off his breath dancing. No use humming then. Allude to it. Strange kind of music that last night. The mirror was in shadow. She rubbed her handglass briskly on her woolen vest against her full wagging bub. Peering into. Lines in her eyes. It wouldn't pan out somehow.

Evening hours, girls in grey gauze. Night hours then, black with daggers and eyemasks. Poetical idea; pink, then golden, then grey, then black. Still, true to life also. Day: then the night.

In the bright light he eyed carefully his black trousers : the ends, the knees, the houghs of the knees. What time is the funeral? Better find out in the paper.

A creak and a dark whirr in the air high up. The bells of George's church. They tolled the hour: loud dark iron.

Heigho! Heigho!
Heigho! Heigho!
Heigho! Heigho!

Quarter to. There again: the overtone following through the air. A third. Poor Dignam!

(*to be continued*)

Episode v

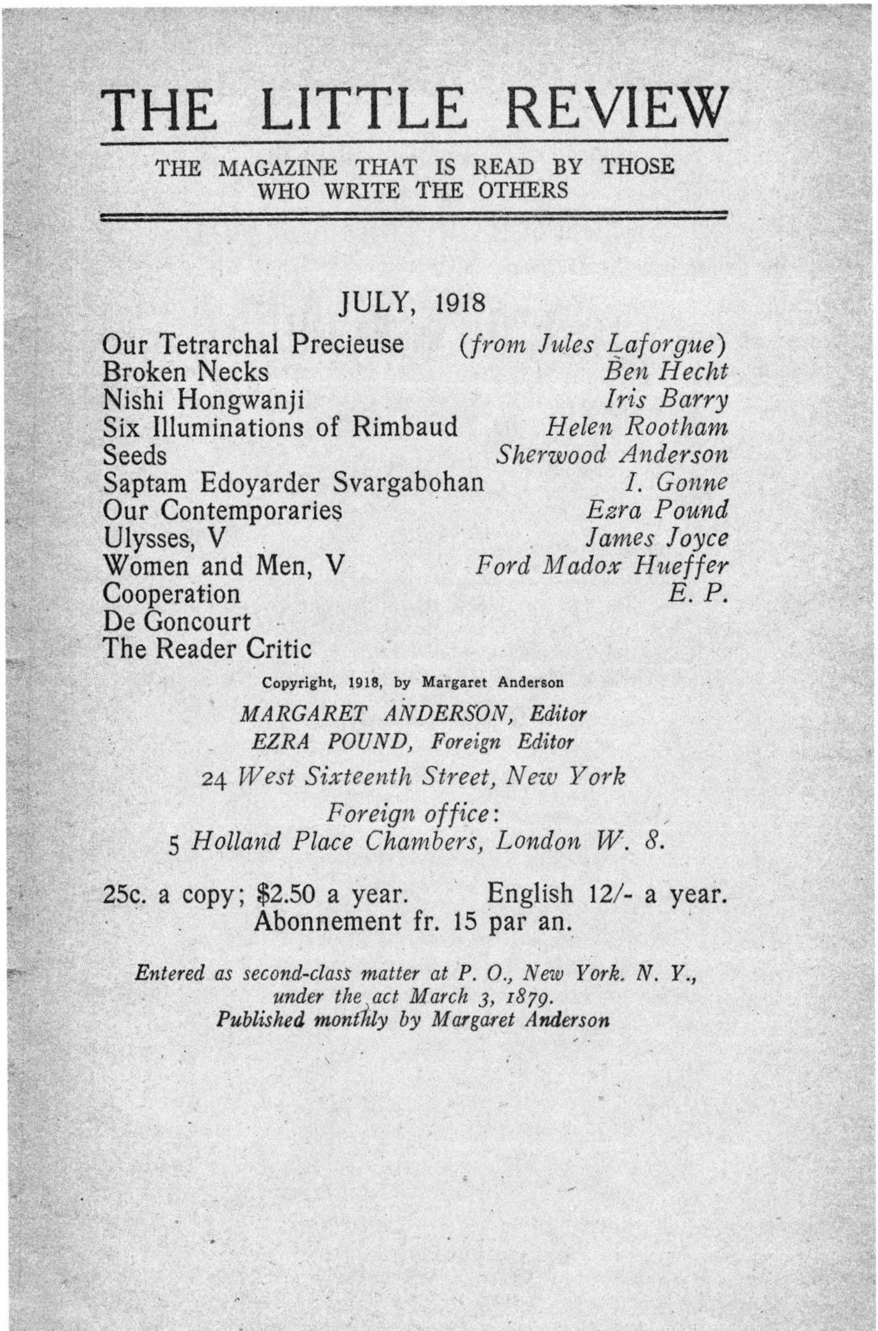
THE LITTLE REVIEW

THE MAGAZINE THAT IS READ BY THOSE WHO WRITE THE OTHERS

JULY, 1918

MARGARET ANDERSON, Editor
EZRA POUND, Foreign Editor

24 *West Sixteenth Street, New York*

Foreign office:
5 *Holland Place Chambers, London W. 8.*

25c. a copy; $2.50 a year. English 12/- a year.
Abonnement fr. 15 par an.

Entered as second-class matter at P. O., New York. N. Y., under the act March 3, 1879.
Published monthly by Margaret Anderson

BY lorries along Sir John Rogerson's quay Mr. Bloom walked soberly, past Windmill lane, Leask's the linseed crusher's, the postal telegraph office. Could have given that address too. And past the sailors' home. He turned from the morning noises of the quayside and walked through Lime street. Slack hour : won't be many there. He crossed Townsend street, passed the frowning face of Bethel. El, yes: house of: Aleph, Beth. And past Nichols' the undertaker's At eleven it is. Time enough. Daresay Corny Kelleher bagged that job for O'Neill's.

In Westland row he halted before the window of the Belfast and Oriental Tea Company and read the legends of lead-papered packets: choice blend, finest quality, family tea. Rather warm. Tea . Must get some from Tom Kernan. Couldn't ask him at a funeral, though. While his eyes still read blandly he took off his hat quietly and sent his right hand with slow grace over his brow and hair. Very warm morning. Under their dropped lids his eyes found the tiny bow of the leather headband inside his high grade hat. Just there. His right hand came down into the bowl of his hat. His fingers found quickly a card behind the headband and transferred it to his waistcoat pocket.

So warm . His right hand once more more slowly went over his brow and hair. Then he put on his hat again, relieved: and read again: choice blend, made of the finest Ceylon brands. Lovely spot it must be: the garden of the world, big lazy leaves, shaky lianas they call them. Wonder is it like that. Those Cinghalese lobbing around in the sun, not doing a damn tap all day. Influence of the climate. Where was the chap I saw in that picture somewhere? Ah, in the dead sea, floating on his back, reading a book with a parasol open. Couldn't sink if you tried: so thick with salt. Because the weight of the water, no, the weight of the body in the water is equal to the weight of the what. Or is it the volume is equal to the weight? It's a law something like that. What is weight really when you say the weight? Thirtytwo feet per second per second. Law of falling bodies: per second per second. They all fall to the ground. The earth. It's the force of gravity of the earth is the weight.

He turned away and sauntered across the road. As he walked he took the folded *Freeman* from his sidepocket, unfolded it, rolled it lengthwise in a baton and tapped it at each sauntering step against his trouserleg. Careless air: just drop in to see. Per second per second. Per second for every second it means. From the curbstone he darted a keen glance through the door of the postoffice . No-one. In.

Facing page: table of contents, *Little Review*, July 1918

He handed the card through the brass grill.

—Are there any letters for me? he asked.

While the postmistress searched a pigeonhole he gazed at the recruiting poster with soldiers of all arms on parade: and held the tip of his baton against his nostrils, smelling freshprinted rag paper. No answer probably. Went too far last time.

The postmistress handed him back through the grill his card with a letter. He thanked her and glanced rapidly at the typed envelope.

Henry Flower Esq,
℅ P. O. Westland Row,
City.

Answered anyhow. He slipped card and letter into his sidepocket, reviewing again the soldiers on parade. Where's old Tweedy's regiment ? There: bearskin cap and hackle plume. No, he's a grenadier. Pointed cuffs. There he is: royal Dublin fusiliers. Redcoats. Too showy. That must be why the women go after them. Take them off O'Connell street at night: disgrace to our Irish capital. Griffith's paper is on the same tack now: an army rotten with disease: overseas or halfseasover. Half baked they look: hypnotised like. Eyes front!

He strolled out of the postoffice and turned to the right. Talk: as if that would mend matters. His hand went into his pocket and a forefinger felt its way under the flap of the envelope, ripping it open in jerks. Women will pay a lot of heed, I don't think. His fingers drew forth the letter and crumpled the envelope in his pocket. Something pinned on: photo perhaps. Hair? No .

M'Coy. Get rid of him quickly.

—Hello, Bloom. Where are you off to?

—Hello, M'Coy. Nowhere in particular.

—How's the body?

—Well. How are you?

—Just keeping alive, M'Coy said.

His eyes on the black tie and clothes, he asked with low respect.

—Is there any . . . . no trouble I hope? I see you're . . . .

—O no, Mr. Bloom said. Poor Dignam, you know . The funeral is today.

—To be sure, poor fellow. So it is. What time?

A photo it isn't. A badge maybe.

—E . . eleven, Mr. Bloom answered.

—I must try to get out there, M'Coy said. Eleven, is it? I only heard it last night. Who was telling me? Holohan. You know Hoppy?

—I know.

Mr. Bloom gazed across the road at the outsider drawn up before the door of the Grosvenor. The porter hoisted the valise up on the well. She stood still, waiting, while the man, husband, brother, like her, searched his pockets for change. Stylish kind of coat with that roll collar, warm for a day like this, looks like blanketcloth. Careless stand of her with her hands in those patch pockets.

—I was with Bob Doran, he's on one of his periodical bends, and what do you call him Bantam Lyons. Just down there in Conway's we were.

Doran, Lyons in Conway's. She raised a gloved hand to her hair. In came Hoppy. Having a wet. Drawing back his head and gazing far from beneath his veiled eyelids he saw the bright fawn skin shine in the glare, the braided drums. Talking of one thing or another. Lady's hand. Which side will she get up?

—And he said: *Sad thing about our poor friend Paddy! What Paddy?* I said. *Poor little Paddy Dignam*, he said .

Off to the country: Broadstone probably. High brown boots with laces dangling. Wellturned foot. What is he foostering over that change for?

—*Why?* I said. *What's wrong with him?* I said.

Proud: rich: silk stockings.

—Yes, Mr. Bloom said.

He moved a little to the side of M'Coy's talking head. Getting up in a minute.

—*What's wrong with him?* he said. *He's dead*, he said. And, faith he filled up. *Is it Paddy Dignam?* I said. I couldn't believe it when I heard it. I was with him no later than Friday last or Thursday was it in the Arch. *Yes,* he said. *He's gone. He died on Monday, poor fellow.*

Watch! Watch! Silk flash rich stockings white. Watch!

A heavy tramcar honking its gong slewed between.

Lost it. Curse your noisy pugnose. Always happening like that. The very moment.

—Yes, yes, Mr. Bloom said after a dull sigh. Another gone.

—One of the best, M'Coy said.

The tram passed. They drove off towards the Loop Line bridge, her rich gloved hand on the steel grip. Flicker, flicker: the laceflare of her hat in the sun: flicker, flick.

—Wife well I suppose? M'Coy's changed voice said.

—O yes, Mr. Bloom said. Tiptop, thanks.

He unrolled the newspaper baton idly and read idly:

What is home without
Plumtree's Potted Meat?
Incomplete.
With it an abode of bliss.

—My missus has just got an engagement. At least it's not settled yet.

Valise tack again. I'm off that, thanks.

Mr. Bloom turned his largelidded eyes with unhasty friendliness:

—My wife too, he said. She's going to sing at a swagger affair in the Ulster hall, Belfast, on the twentyfifth.

—That so? M'Coy said. Glad to hear that, old man. Who's getting it up?

Mrs. Marion Bloom. Not up yet. No book. Blackened court cards laid along her thigh by sevens. Dark lady and fair man. Cat furry black ball. Torn strip of envelope.

Love's
Old
Sweet
Song
Comes love's old . . . .

—It's a kind of a tour, don't you see? Mr. Bloom said thoughtfully . *Sweeeet song*. There's a committee formed. Part shares and part profits.

M'Coy nodded, picking at his moustache stubble.

—O well, he said. That's good news.

He moved to go.

—Well, glad to see you looking fit, he said. Meet you knocking around.

—Yes, Mr. Bloom said.

—Tell you what, M'Coy said. You might put down my name at the funeral, will you? I'd like to go but I mightn't be able, you see. You just shove in my name if I'm not there, will you?

—I'll do that, Mr. Bloom said, moving. That'll be all right.

—Right, M'Coy said brightly. Thanks, old man. I'd go if I possibly could. Well, tolloll. Just C. P. M'Coy will do.

—That will be done, Mr. Bloom answered firmly.

Didn't come off that wheeze.

Mr. Bloom, strolling towards Brunswick street, smiled. My missus has just got an. Reedy freckled soprano. Nice enough in its way: for a little ballad. No guts in it. You and me, don't you know? In the same boat. Give you the needle that would. Can't he hear the difference? Thought that Belfast would fetch him. Your wife and my wife.

Wonder is he pimping after me?

Mr. Bloom stood at the corner, his eyes wandering over the multicoloured hoardings. Cantrell and Cochrane's Ginger Ale (Aromatic). Clery's summer sale. No, he's going on straight. Hello. *Leah* tonight: Mrs. Bandmann Palmer. Like to see her in that again. Poor papa! How he used to talk about Kate Bateman in that! Outside the Adelphi in London waited all the afternoon to get in. Year before I was born that was: sixtyfive. And Ristori in Vienna. What is this the right name is? By Mosenthal it is. *Rachel*, is it? No. The scene he was always talking about where the old blind Abraham recognises the voice and puts his fingers on his face.

Nathan's voice! His son's voice! I hear the voice of Nathan who left his father to die of grief and misery in my arms, who left the house of his father and left the God of his father.

Every word is so deep, Leopold.

Poor papa! Poor man! I'm glad I didn't go into the room to look at his face. That day! O dear! O dear! Ffoo! Well, perhaps it was the best for him.

Mr. Bloom went round the corner and passed the drooping horses of the hazard. No use thinking of it any more. Nosebag time. Wish I hadn't met that M'Coy fellow. He came nearer and heard a crunching of the oats, the gently champing teeth. Their full buck eyes regarded him as he went by. Poor jugginses! Damn all they know or care about anything with their long noses stuck in nosebags. Still they get their feed all right and their doss. Gelded too: Might be happy all the same that way. Good poor brutes they look.

He drew the letter from his pocket and folded it into the newspaper he carried. Might just walk into her here. The lane is safer.

He hummed, passing the cabman's shelter:

Là ci darem la mano

La la lala la la.

He turned into Cumberland street and, going on some paces, halted in the lee of the station wall. No-one. Meade's timberyard . Ruins and tenements. He opened the letter within the newspaper.

A flower. A yellow flower with flattened petals. Not annoyed then? What does she say?

Dear Henry

I got your last letter to me and thank you very much for it. I am sorry you did not like my last letter. Why did you enclose the stamps? I am awfully angry with you. I do wish I could punish you for that. I called you naughty boy because I do not like that other word. Please tell me what is the real meaning of that word. Are you not happy in your home, you poor little naughty boy? I do wish I could do something for you. Please tell me what you think of poor me. I often think of the beautiful name you have. Dear Henry, when will we meet? I think of you so often you have no idea. I have never felt myself so much drawn to a man as you. I feel so bad about. Please write me a long letter and tell me more. Remember if you do not I will punish you. So now you know what I will do to you, you naughty boy, if you do not write. O how I long to meet you. Henry dear, do not deny my request before my patience are exhausted. Then I will tell you all. Goodbye now, naughty darling. I have such a bad headache today and write soon to your longing

Martha

P. S. Do tell me what kind of perfume does your wife use. I want to know.

He tore the flower gravely from its pinhold and placed it in his heart pocket. Then, walking slowly forward, he read the letter again, murmuring here and there a word. Having read it all he took it from the newspaper and put it back in his sidepocket.

Weak joy opened his lips. Changed since the first letter. Doing the indignant: a girl of good family like me, respectable character. Could meet one Sunday after mass. Thank you: not having any. Go further next time. Naughty boy: punish: afraid of words of course. Brutal, why not? Try it anyhow. A bit at a time.

Fingering still the letter in his pocket he drew the pin out of it. Common pin, eh? He threw it on the road. Out of her clothes somewhere: pinned together. Queer the number of pins they always have.

Flat Dublin voices bawled in his head. Those two sluts that night in the Coombe, linked together in the rain:

Mairy lost the pin of her drawers
She didn't know what to do
To keep it up
To keep it up

It? Them. Such a bad headache. What perfume does your wife use? Now could you make out a thing like that?

To keep it up.

Martha, Mary. I saw that picture somewhere I forget now. He is sitting in their house, talking. Mysterious. Also the two sluts in the Coombe would listen.

To keep it up.

Nice kind of evening feeling. No more wandering about. Just loll there: quiet dusk: let everything rip. Tell about places you have been, strange customs. The other one was getting the supper: fruit, olives, lovely cool water out of the well, things like that. She listens with big dark soft eyes. Tell her: more and more: all. Then a sigh: silence. Long long long rest.

Going under the railway arch he took out the envelope, tore it swiftly in shreds and scattered them towards the road. The shreds fluttered away, sank in the dank air: a white flutter then all sank.

Henry Flower. You could tear up a cheque for a hundred pounds in the same way. Simple bit of paper. Lord Iveagh once cashed a cheque for a million in the bank of Ireland. Shows you the money to be made out of porter. A million pounds, wait a moment. Twopence a pint, fourpence a quart, eightpence a gallon of porter, no, one and fourpence a gallon of porter. One and four into twenty: fifteen about. Yes, exactly. Fifteen millions of barrels of porter.

What am I saying, barrels? Gallons. About a million barrels all the same.

An incoming train clanked heavily above his head, coach after coach. Barrels bumped in his head: dull porter slopped and churned inside. The bungholes sprang open and a huge dull flood leaked out, flowing together, winding through mudflats all over the level land, a lazy pooling swirl of liquor bearing along wideleaved flowers of its froth.

He had reached the open backdoor of All Hallows. Stepping into the porch he doffed his hat, took the card from his pocket and tucked it again behind the leather headband. Damn it. I might have tried to work M'Coy for a pass to Mullingar.

Same notice on the door. Sermon by the Very Reverend John Conmee S.J. on saint Peter Claver S. G. and the African mission. Conmee: Martin Cunningham knows him: distinguished looking. He's not going out to baptise blacks, is he? Like to see them sitting round in a circle, listening. Lap it up like milk, I suppose.,

The cold smell of sacred stone called him. He pushed the swingdoor and entered softly by the rear.

Something going on: some sodality. Women knelt in the benches with crimson halters round their necks, heads bowed. A batch knelt at the altar rails. The priest went along by them, murmuring, holding the thing in his hands. He stopped at each, took out a communion, shook a drop or two (are they in water?) off it and put it neatly into her mouth. Her hat and head sank. Then the next one: a small old woman. The priest bent down to put it into her mouth, murmuring all the time. Latin. The next one. What? *Corpus*. Body. Corpse. They don't seem to chew it: only swallow it down. Rum idea: eating bits of a corpse.

He stood aside watching their blind masks pass down the aisle, one by one, and seek their places. He approached a bench and seated himself in its corner, nursing his hat and newspaper. They were about him here and there, with heads still bowed in their crimson halters, waiting for it to melt in their stomachs. Something like those mazzoth: it's that sort of bread: unleavened bread. Look at them. Now I bet it makes them feel happy. It does. Yes, bread of angels it's called. There's a big idea behind it, kind of heavenly feel inside. Then feel all like one family, all in the same swim. They do. I'm sure of that. Not so lonely. Thing is if you really believe in it.

He saw the priest stow the communion cup away, well in, and kneel an instant before it, showing a large grey bootsole from under the lace affair he had on. Letters on his back: I. H. S. Molly told me one time I askd her. I have sinnd: or no: I have suffered it is.

Meet one Sunday after mass. Do not deny my request. She might be here with a ribbon round her neck and do the other thing all the same on the sly. Their character. That fellow that turned queen's evidence on the invincibles he used to receive the—, Carey was his name—the communion every morning. This very church. Peter Carey. No, Peter Claver I am thinking of. Denis Carey. And just imagine that. And plotting that murder all the time. Those crawthumpers, now that's a good name for them, there's always something shiftylooking about them. They're not straight men of business either. O no she's not here: the flower: no, no. By the way did I tear up that envelope? Yes: under the bridge.

The priest was rinsing out the chalice: then he tossed off the dregs smartly. Doesn't give them any of the wine: only the other. Quite right: otherwise they'd have one old booser worse than another coming along, cadging for a drink. Spoil the whole atmosphere of the. Quite right. Perfectly right that is.

Mr. Bloom looked back towards the choir. Not going to be any music. Pity. Who has the organ here I wonder? Old Glynn, he knew how to make that instrument talk, the *vibrato*: fifty pounds a year they say he had in Gardiner street. Molly was in fine voice that day, the *Stabat Mater* of Rossini. I told her to pitch her voice against that corner. I could feel the thrill in the air, the people looking up:

Quis est homo

Some of that old sacred music splendid. Mercadante: seven last words. Mozart's twelfth mass: *Gloria* in that. Those old popes keen on music, on art and statues and pictures of all kinds. Palestrina for example too. They had a gay old time while it lasted. Still, having eunuchs in their choir that was coming it a bit thick. What kind of voice is it? Must be curious to hear. Connoisseurs. Suppose they wouldn't feel anything after. Kind of a placid. No worry. Fall into flesh don't they? Who knows? Eunuch. One way out of it.

He saw the priest bend down and kiss the altar and then face about and bless all the people. All crossed themselves and stood up. Mr. Bloom glanced about him and then stood up, looking over the risen hats. Stand up at the gospel of course. Then all settled down on their knees again and he sat back quietly in his bench. The priest came down from the altar, holding the thing out from him, and he and the massboy answered each other in Latin. Then the priest knelt down and began to read off a card:

O God, our refuge and our strength,

Mr. Bloom put his face forward to catch the words. Glorious and immaculate virgin. Joseph her spouse. Peter and Paul. More interesting if you understood what it was all about. Wonderful organization certainly, goes like clockwork. Squareheaded chaps those must be in Rome: they work the whole show. And don't they rake in the money too? Bequests also: to say so many masses. The priest in the Fermanagh will case in the witnessbox. No browbeating him . He had his answer pat for everything. Liberty and exaltation of our holy mother the church. The doctors of the church: they mapped out the whole theology of it.

The priest prayed:

—*Blessed Michael, archangel, defend us in the hour of conflict. Be our safeguard against the wickedness and snares of the devil (may God restrain him we humbly pray) : and do thou, O prince of the heavenly host by the power of God thrust Satan down to hell and with him those other wicked spirits who wander through the world for the ruin of souls.*

The priest and the massboy stood up and walked off. All over. The women remained behind: thanksgiving.

Better be shoving along.

He stood up. Hello. Were those two buttons of my waistcoat open all the time? He passed, discreetly buttoning, down the aisle and out through the main door into the light. Trams: a car of Prescott's dyeworks: a widow in her weeds. He covered himself. How goes the time? Quarter past. Time enough yet. Better get that lotion made up. Where is this? Ah yes, the last time, Sweny's in Lincoln place.

He walked southward along Westland row. But the recipe is in the other trousers. O, and I forgot that latchkey too. Bore this funeral affair. O well, poor fellow, it's not his fault. When was it I got it made up last? Wait. I changed a sovereign I remember. First of the month it must have been or the second. O he can look it up in the prescriptions book.

The chemist turned back page after page. Sandy shrivelled smell he seems to have. Living all the day among herbs and ointments. The first fellow that picked an herb to cure himself had a bit of pluck. Want to be careful. Enough stuff here to send you off.

—About a fortnight ago, sir?

—Yes, Mr. Bloom said.

He waited by the counter, inhaling the keen reek of drugs, the dusty dry smell of sponges.

—Sweet almond oil and tincture of benzoin, Mr. Bloom said, and then orangeflower water . . .

It certainly did make her skin so delicate white like wax.

—And whitewax also, he said.

Brings out the darkness of her eyes. Looking at me, the sheet up to her eyes, when I was fixing the links in my cuffs. Those homely recipes are often the best: oatmeal they say steeped in buttermilk. But you want a perfume too. That orangeflower water is so fresh. Nice smell these soaps have. Time to get a bath round the corner. Feel fresh then all day. Funeral be rather glum.

—Yes, sir, the chemist said. That was two and nine. Have you brought a bottle?

—No, Mr. Bloom said. Make it up, please. I'll call later in the day and I'll take one of those soaps. How much are they?

—Fourpence, sir.

Mr. Bloom raised a cake to his nostrils. Sweet lemony wax.

—I'll take this one, he said. That makes three and a penny.

—Yes, sir, the chemist said. You can pay all together, sir, when you come back.

—Good, Mr. Bloom said.

He strolled out of the shop, the newspaper baton under his armpit, the cool wrappered soap in his left hand.

At his armpit Bantam Lyons' voice and hand said:

—Hello, Bloom. Is that today's? Show us a minute.

Shaved off his moustache again, by Jove! Long cold upper lip. To look younger. He does look balmy.

Bantam Lyons' yellow blacknailed fingers unrolled the baton. Wants a wash too.

I want to see about that French horse that's running today, Bantam Lyons' said.

He rustled the pleated pages, jerking his chin on his high collar. Better leave him the paper and get shut of him.

—You can keep it, Mr. Bloom said.

—Ascot. Gold cup. Wait, Bantam Lyons muttered. Maximum the second.

—I was just going to throw it away, Mr. Bloom said.

Bantam Lyons raised his eyes suddenly and leered weakly.

—What's that? his sharp voice said.

—I say you can keep it, Mr. Bloom answered. I was going to throw it away that moment.

Bantam Lyons doubted an instant, leering: then thrust the outspread sheets back on Mr. Bloom's arms.

—I'll risk it, he said. Here, thanks.

He sped off towards Conway's corner.

Mr. Bloom folded the sheets again to a neat square and lodged the soap on it, smiling. Silly lips of that chap. He walked cheerfully towards the mosque of the baths. Remind you of a mosque, redbaked bricks, the minarets. College sports today I see. He eyed the horseshoe poster over the gate of the college park: cyclist doubled up like a cod in a pot. Damn bad ad. Now if they had made it round like a wheel. Then the spokes: sports, sports, sports: and the hub big: college. Something to catch the eye.

There's Hornblower standing at the porter's lodge. Keep him on hands: might take a turn in there on the nod. How do you do, Mr. Hornblower? How do you do, sir?

Heavenly weather really. If life was always like that. Won't last. Always passing, the stream of life, which in the stream of life we trace is dearer thaaan them all.

Enjoy a bath now: clean trough of water, cool enamel, the gentle tepid stream. He foresaw his pale body reclined in it at full, naked, oiled by scented melting soap, softly laved. He saw his trunk and limbs riprippled over and sustained, buoyed lightly upward, lemonyellow.

(*to be continued*)

Episode VI

THE LITTLE REVIEW

THE MAGAZINE THAT IS READ BY THOSE WHO WRITE THE OTHERS

SEPTEMBER, 1918

MARGARET ANDERSON, Editor

EZRA POUND, London Editor

JULES ROMAINS, French Editor

Foreign office:
5 *Holland Place Chambers, London W. 8.*

25c. a copy; $2.50 a year. English 12/- a year.
Abonnement fr. 15 par an.

Entered as second-class matter at P. O., New York. N. Y.,
under the act March 3, 1879.
Published monthly by Margaret Anderson

MARTIN CUNNINGHAM, first, poked his silk hatted head into the creaking carriage and, entering deftly, seated himself. Mr. Power stepped in after him, curving his height with care.

—Come on, Simon.

—After you, Mr. Bloom said.

Mr. Dedalus covered himself quickly and got in, saying:

—Yes, yes.

— Are we all here now? Martin Cunningham asked. Come along, Bloom.

Mr. Bloom entered and sat in the vacant place. He pulled the door to after him and slammed it tight till it shut tight. He passed an arm through the armstrap and looked seriously from the open carriage window at the lowered blinds of the avenue. One dragged aside: an old woman peeping. Thanking her stars she was passed over. Extraordinary the interest they take in a corpse. Job seems to suit them. Huggermugger in corners. Then getting it ready. Wash and shampoo. I believe they clip the nails and the hair. Grow all the same after.

All waited. Nothing was said. Stowing in the wreaths probably. I am sitting on something hard. Ah, that soap in my hip pocket. Better shift it out of th-at. Wait for an opportunity.

All waited. Then wheels were heard from in front, turning then nearer: then horses' hoofs. A jolt. Their carriage began to move, creaking and swaying. Other hoofs and creaking wheels started behind. The blinds of the avenue passed and number ten with its craped knocker, door ajar. At walking pace.

They waited still, their knees jogging, till they had turned and were passing along the tramtracks. Tritonville road. Quicker. The wheels rattled rolling over the cobbled causeway and the crazy glasses shook rattling in the doorframes.

—What way is he taking us? Mr. Power asked of both windows.

—Through Irishtown, Martin Cunningham said. Ringsend. Brunswick street.

Mr. Dedalus nodded, looking out.

—That's a fine old custom, he said. I am glad to see it has not died out.

All watched awhile through their windows caps and hats lifted by passers. Respect. The carriage swerved from the tramtrack to the smoother road. Mr. Bloom at gaze saw a lithe young man, clad in mourning, a wide hat.

—There's a friend of yours gone by, Dedalus, he said.

—Who is that?

Overleaf: table of contents, *Little Review,* September 1918

—Your son and heir.

—Where is he? Mr. Dedalus said, stretching over, across.

The carriage lurched round the corner and, swerving back to the tramtrack, rolled on noisily with chettering wheels. Mr. Dedalus fell back, saying:

—Was that Mulligan cad with him?

—No, Mr. Bloom said. He was alone.

—Down with his aunt Sally, I suppose, Mr. Dedalus said, and the drunken little costdrawer and Crissie, papa's little lump of dung, the wise child that knows her own father.

Mr. Bloom smiled joylessly on Ringsend road. Wallace Bros. the bottleworks. Dodder bridge.

Ritchie Goulding and the legal bag Goulding, Colles and Ward he calls the firm. His jokes are getting a bit damp. Great card he was. Waltzing in Stamer street with Ignatius Gallaher on a Sunday morning, the landlady's two hats pinned on his head. Out on the rampage all night. Beginning to tell on him now: that backache of his, I fear. Thinks he'll cure it with pills. All breadcrumbs they are. About six hundred per cent profit.

—He's in with a lowdown crowd, Mr. Dedalus snarled. That Mulligan is a contaminated bloody ruffian. His name stinks all over Dublin. But with the help of God and his blessed mother I am going to write a letter one of those days to his mother or his aunt or whatever she is that will open her eye as wide as a gate. I'll tickle his catastrophe, believe you me.

He cried above the clatter of the wheels.

—I won't have her bastard of a nephew ruin my son. A counter jumper's son. Selling tapes in my cousin, Peter Paul M'Swiney's. Not likely.

He ceased. Mr. Bloom glanced from his angry moustache to Mr. Power's mild face and Martin Cunningham's eyes and beard, gravely shaking. Noisy selfwilled man. Full of his son. He is right. Something to hand on. If little Rudy had lived. See him grow up, hear his voice in the house. Walking beside Molly. My son. Me in his eyes. Strange feeling it would be. From me. Just a chance. Must have been that morning she was at the window, watching the two dogs at it by the wall of the cease to do evil. And the warder grinning up. She had that cream gown on with the rip she never stitched. Give us a touch, Poldy. God, I'm dying for it. How life begins.

Got big then. Had to refuse the Greystones concert. My son inside her. I could have helped him on in life. I could. Make him independent. Learn German too.

—Are we late? Mr. Power asked.

—Ten minutes, Martin Cunningham said, looking at his watch.

Molly. Milly. Same thing watered down. Her tomboy oath. O jumping Jupiter! Still, she's a dear girl. Soon be a woman. Mulligan. Dearest Papli. Young student. Yes yes: a woman too. Life, life.

The carriage heeled over and back, their four trunks swaying.

—Corny might have given us a more commodious yoke, Mr. Power said .

—He might, Mr. Dedalus said, if he hadn't that squint troubling him. Do you follow me?

He closed his left eye. Martin Cunningham began to brush away crust-crumbs from under his thighs.

—What is this? he said, in the name of God? Crumbs?

—Someone seems to have been making a picnic party here lately, Mr. Power said.

All raised their thighs, eyed with disfavour the mildewed buttonless leather of the seats. Mr. Dedalus, twisting his nose, frowned downward and said:

—Unless I'm greatly mistaken. What do you think, Martin?

—It struck me too, Martin Cunningham said.

Mr. Bloom set his thigh down. Glad I took that bath. Feel my feet quite clean.

Mr. Dedalus sighed resignedly.

—After all, he said, it's the most natural thing in the world.

—Did Tom Kernan turn up? Martin Cunningham asked, twirling the peak of his beard gently.

—Yes, Mr. Bloom answered. He's behind with Ned Lambert and Hynes.

—And Corny Kelleher himself? Mr. Power asked.

—At the cemetery, Martin Cunningham said.

—I met M'Coy this morning, Mr. Bloom said. He said he'd try to come.

The carriage halted short.

—What's wrong?

—We're stopped.

—Where are we?

Mr. Bloom put his head out of the window.

—The grand canal, he said.

Gasworks. Whooping cough they say it cures. Good job Milly never got it. Poor children. Doubles them up black and blue. Shame really. Dogs' home over there. Poor old Athos! Be good to Athos, Leopold, is my last wish. He took it to heart, pined away. Quiet brute. Old men's dogs usually are.

A raindrop spat on his hat. He drew back and saw an instant of shower spray dots over the grey flags . Apart. Curious. Like through a colander. I thought it would. My boots were creaking, I remember now.

—The weather is changing, he said quietly.

—A pity it did not keep up fine, Martin Cunningham said.

—Wanted for the country, Mr. Powers said. There's the sun again coming out.

Mr. Dedalus, peering through his glasses towards the veiled sun, hurled a mute curse at the sky.

—It's as uncertain as a child's bottom, he said.

—We're off again.

The carriage turned again its stiff wheels and their trunks swayed gently. Martin Cunningham twirled more quickly the peak of his beard.

—Tom Kernan was immense last night, he said.

—O draw him out, Martin, Mr. Power said eagerly. Wait till you hear him, Simon, on Ben Dollard's singing of The Croppy Boy.

—Immense, Martin Cunningham said pompously. His singing of that simple ballad, Martin, is the most trenchant rendering I ever heard in the whole course of my experience.

—Trenchant, Mr. Power said laughing. He's dead nuts on that. And the retrospective arrangement.

—Did you read Dan Dawson's speech? Martin Cunningham asked.

—I did not then, Mr. Dedalus said. Where is it?

—In the paper this morning.

Mr. Bloom took the paper from his inside pocket. That book I must change for her.

—No, no, Mr. Dedalus said quickly. Later on, please.

Mr. Bloom's glance travelled down the edge paper scanning the deaths. Callan, Coleman, Dignam, Fawcett, Lowry, Naumann, Peake, what Peake is that, is it the chap was in Crosbie and Alleyne's? no, Sexton, Urbright. Inked characters fast fading on the frayed breaking paper. Thanks to the little flowers of Mary. Month's mind Quinlan .

It is now a month since dear Henry fled
To his home up above in the sky
While his family weeps and mourns his loss
Hoping some day to meet him on high.

I tore up the envelope? Yes. Where did I put her letter after I read it in the bath? He patted his waistcoat pocket. There all right. Dear Henry fled. Before my patience are exhausted.

National school. Meade's yard. The hazard. Only two there now. Nodding. Full as a tick. Too much bone in their skulls. The other trotting round with a fare. An hour ago I was passing there. The jarvies raised their hats.

A pointsman's back straightened itself upright suddenly by Mr. Bloom's window. Couldn't they invent something automatic so that the wheel itself: much handier? Well but that fellow would lose his job then? Well but then another fellow would get a job making the new invention?

Antient concert rooms. Nothing on there. A man in a buff suit with a crape armlet. Not much grief there. People in law, perhaps.

They went past the bleak pulpit of saint Mark's' under the railway bridge, past the Queen's theatre: in silence. Hoardings. Eugene Stratton. Mrs. Bandmann Palmer. Could I go to see Leah tonight, I wonder. Or the Lily of Killarney? Wet bright bills for next week. Fun on the Bristol. Martin Cunningham could work a pass for the Gaiety. Have to stand a drink or two. As broad as it's long.

He's coming in the afternoon. Her songs.

Plasto's.

—How do you do? Martin Cunningham said, raising his palm to his brow in salute.

—He doesn't see us, Mr. Power said. Yes he does. How do you do?

—Who? Mr. Dedalus asked.

—Blazes Boylan, Mr. Power said. There he is airing his quiff.

Just that moment I was thinking.

Mr. Dedalus bent across to salute. From the door of the Red Bank the white disc of a straw hat flashed reply: passed.

Mr. Bloom reviewed the nails of his left hand, then those of his right hand. The nails, yes. Is there anything more in him than that she sees? That keeps him alive. They sometimes feel what a person is. Instinct. But a type like that. My nails. I am just looking at them : well pared. And after: thinking alone. Body getting a bit softy. I would notice that from remembering. What causes that? I suppose the skin can't contract quickly enough when the flesh falls off. But the shape is there. The shape is there still.

He clasped his hands between his knees and, satisfied, sent his vacant glance over their faces.

Mr. Power asked:

—How is the concert tour getting on, Bloom?

—O very well, Mr. Bloom said. I hear great accounts of it. It's a good idea, you see. . . .

—Are you going yourself?

—Well no, Mr. Bloom said. I am not sure, that is. You see the idea is to tour the chief towns. What you lose on one you can make up the other.

—Quite so, Martin Cunninghm said. Mary Anderson is up there now. Have you good artists?

—Louis Werner is touring her, Mr. Bloom said. O yes, we have all top nobbers. J. C. Doyle and John McCormack and. The best, in fact.

—And madame, Mr. Power said, smiling. Last but not least.

Mr. Bloom unclasped his hands in a gesture of soft politeness and clasped them. The carriage wheeling by Smith O'Brien stature united noiselesly their unresisting knees.

Oot: a dullgarbed old man from the curbstone tendered his wares, his mouth opening: oot.

—Four bootlaces for a penny.

Wonder why he was struck off the rolls. Has that silk hat ever since. Mourning too. Terrible comedown, poor wretch! Relics of old decency.

And madame. Twenty past eleven. Up. Mrs. Fleming is in to clean. Doing her hair, humming: voglio e non vorrei. No: vorrei e non. Looking at the tips of her hairs to see if they are split. Mi trema un poco il. Beautiful on that tre her voice is: weeping tone. A thrush. A throstle. There is a word throstle that expresses that .

His eyes passed lightly over Mr. Power's goodlooking face. Greyish over the ears. Madame: smiling. I smiled back. Only politeness perhaps. Nice fellow. Who knows is that true about the woman he keeps? Not pleasant for the wife. Yet they say, who was it told me, there is no carnal. You would imagine that would get played out pretty quick. Yes, it was Crofton met him one evening bringing her a pound of rumpsteak. What is this she was? Barmaid in Jury's. Or the Moira, was it?

Martin Cunningham nudged Mr. Power.

—Of the tribe of Reuben, he said.

A tall blackbearded figure, bent on a stick, stumping round the corner of Elvery's elephant house showed them a curved hand open on his spine.

—In all his pristine beauty, Mr. Power said.

Mr. Dedalus looked after the stumping figure and said mildly:

—The devil break the hasp of your back !

Mr. Power, collapsing in laughter, shaded his face from the carriage window.

—We have all been there, Martin Cuningham said broadly.

His eyes met Mr. Bloom's eyes. He caressed his beard, adding

—Well, nearly all of us.

Mr. Bloom began to speak with sudden eagerness to his companions' faces.

— That's an awfully good one that's going the rounds about Reuben J and the son.

—About the boatman? Mr. Power asked.

—Yes. Isn't it awfully good?

—What is that? Mr. Dedalus asked. I didn't hear it.

—There was a girl in the case, Mr. Bloom began, and he determined to send him to the isle of Man out of harm's way but when they were both . . . . .

—What? Mr. Dedalus asked. That hobbledehoy is it?

—Yes, Mr. Bloom said. They were both on the way to the boat and he tried to drown . . . . .

—Drown Barabbas! Mr. Dedalus cried. I wish to Christ he did!

Mr. Power sent a long laugh down his shaded nostrils.

—No, Mr. Bloom said, the son himself . . . . .

Martin Cunningham thwarted his speech rudely.

—Reuben J and the son were piking it down the quay next the river on their way to the isle of Man boat and the young chisell suddenly got loose and over the wall with him into the Liffey.

—For God' sake! Mr. Dedalus exclaimed in fright. Is he dead?

—Dead! Martin Cunningham cried. Not he! A boatman got a pole and fished him out by the slack of the breeches and he was landed up to the father on the quay. Half the town was there.

—Yes, Mr. Bloom said. But the funny part is . . .

—And Reuben J, Martin Cunningham said, gave the boatman a florin for saving his son's life.

A stifled sigh came from under Mr. Power's hand.

—O, he did, Martin Cunningham affirmed. Like a hero. A silver florin.

—Isn't it awfully good? Mr. Bloom said eagerly.

—One and eightpence too much, Mr. Dedalus said drily.

Mr. Power's choked laugh burst quietly in the carriage.

Nelson's pillar.

—Eight plums a penny. Eight for a penny.

—We had better look a little serious, Martin Cunningham said.

Mr. Dedalus sighed.

—Ah the indeed, he said, poor little Paddy wouldn't grudge us a laugh. Many a good one he told himself.

—The Lord forgive me! Mr. Power said, wiping his wet eyes with his fingers. Poor Paddy! I little thought a week ago when I saw him last that I'd be driving after him like this.

—As decent a little man as ever wore a hat, Mr. Dedalus said. He went very suddenly.

—Breakdown, Martin Cunningham said. Heart.

He tapped his chest sadly.

Blazing face: redhot.

Mr. Power gazed at the passing houses with rueful apprehension.

—He had a sudden death, poor fellow, he said.

—The best death, Mr. Bloom said.

Their wideopen eyes looked at him.

—No suffering, he said. A moment and all is over.

—No-one spoke.

Horses with white frontlet plumes came round the Rotunda corner, galloping. A tiny coffin flashed by. A mourning coach.

—Sad, Martin Cunningham said. A child.

A dwarf's face mauve and wrinkled like little Rudy's was. Dwarf's body, weak as puty, in a whitelined box. Meant nothing. Mistake of nature.

—Poor little thing, Mr. Dedalus said. It's well out of it.

The carriage climbed more slowly the hill of Rutland square.

—In the midst of life, Martin Cunningham said.

—But the worst of all, Mr. Power said, is the suicide.

Martin Cunningham drew out his watch briskly, coughed and put it back.

—The greatest disgrace to have in the family, Mr. Power added.

—Temporary insanity, of course, Martin Cunningham said decisively, We must take a charitable view of it.

—They say a man who does it, is a coward, Mr. Dedalus said.

—It is not for us to judge, Martin Cunningham said.

Mr. Bloom, about to speak, closed his lips again. Martin Cunningham's large eyes. Looking away now. Sympathetic human man he is. Intelligent. Like Shakespeare's face. Always a good word to say. And that awful drunkard of a wife of his. Setting up house for her time after time and then pawning the furniture on him. Wear out a man's heart. Lord, she must have looked a sight that night Dedalus told me he was in there. Drunk about the place and capering with Martin's umbrella.

—And they call me the jewel of Asia,
Of Asia
The geisha.

He looked away from me. He knows.

That afternoon of the inquest. The redlabelled bottle on the table. The room in the hotel with hunting pictures. Stuffy it was. Sunlight through the slats of the Venetian blinds. The coroner's ears, big and hairy. Boots giving evidence. Thought he was asleep first. Then saw like yellow streaks on his face. Verdict: overdose. The letter. For my son Leopold.

No more pain. Wake no more.

The carriage rattled swiftly along Berkeley road.

—We are going the pace, I think, Martin Cunningham said.

—God grant he doesn't upset us on the road, Mr. Power said.

—I hope not, Martin Cunningham said. That will be a great race tomorrow in Germany, The Gordon Bennett.

—Yes, by Jove, Mr. Dedalus said. That will be worth seeing, faith.

The carriage galloped round a corner: stopped.

—What's wrong now?

A divided drove of cattle passed the windows, lowing, slouching by on padded hoofs, whisking their tails slowly on their clotted bony croups.

—Emigrants, Mr. Power said.

—Huuu! the drover's voice cried, his switch sounding on their flanks. Huuu out of that!

Thursday of course. Springers. Cuffe sold them about twenty-seven quid each. For Liverpool probably. Roast beef for old England. They buy up all the juicy ones. And then the fifth quarter lost: all that raw stuff, hide, hair, horns. Comes to a big thing in a year. Wonder if that dodge works now getting dicky meat off the train at Clonsilla.

The carriage moved on through the drove.

—I can't make out why the corporation doesn't run a tramline from the parkgate to the quays, Mr. Bloom said. All those animals could be taken in trucks down to the boats.

—Instead of blocking up the throughfare, Martin Cunningham said. Quite right. They ought to.

—Yes, Mr. Bloom said, and another thing I often thought is to have funeral trams like they have in Milan. You know. Run the line out to the cemetery gates and have special trams, hearse and carriage and all. Don't you see what I mean?

—O that be damned for a story, Mr. Dedalus said.

—A poor lookout for Corny, Mr. Power added.

—Why? Mr. Bloom asked, turning to Mr. Dedalus. Wouldn't it be more decent than galloping two abreast?

—Well, there's something in that, Mr. Dedalus granted.

—And, Martin Cunningham said, we wouldn't have scenes like that when the hearse capsized round Dunphy's and upset the coffin on to the road.

—That was terrible, Mr. Power's shocked face said, and the corpse fell about the road. Terrible!

—First round Dunphy's, Mr. Dedalus said, nodding.

—Praises be to God! Martin Cunningham said piously.

Bom! Upset. A coffin bumped out on to the road. Burst open. Paddy Dignam shot out and rolling over stiff in the dust in a brown habit too large for him. Red face: grey now. Mouth fallen open. Asking what's up now. Quite right to close it. Looks horrid open. Then the insides decompose quickly. Much better to close up all the orifices. Yes, also. With wax. Seal up all.

—Dunphy's, Mr. Power announced as the carriage turned right.

Dunphy's corner. Mourning coaches drawn up, drowning their grief. Tiptop position for a pub. Expect we'll pull up here on the way back to drink his health.

But suppose now it did happen. Would he bleed if a nail say cut him in the knocking about? He would and he wouldn't, I suppose. Depends on where. The circulation stops. Still some might ooze out of an artery. It would be better to bury them in red: a dark red.

In silence they drove along Phibsborough road. An empty hearse trotted by, coming from the cemetery: looks relieved.

Crossguns bridge: the royal canal.

Water rushed roaring through the sluices. A man stood on his dropping barge between clamps of turf. On the towpath by the lock a slacktethered horse. Aboard of the Bugabu.

Their eyes watched him. On the slow weedy waterway he had floated on his raft coastward over Ireland. Athlone, Mullingar Moyvalley, I could make a walking tour to see Milly by the canal, come as a surprise, Leixlip, Clonsilla. Dropping down, lock by lock to Dublin. With turf from the midland bogs. Salute. He lifted his brown straw hat, saluting Paddy Dignam.

They drove on. Near it now.

—I wonder how is our friend Fogarty getting on, Mr. Power said.

—Better ask Tom Kernan, Mr. Dedalus said.

—How is that? Martin Cunningham said. Left him weeping I suppose.

The carriage steered left for Finglas road.

The stonecutter's yard on the right. Last lap. Crowded on the spit of land silent shapes appeared, white, sorrowful, holding out calm hands, knelt in grief, pointing. Fragments of shapes, hewn. In white silence: appealing. Thos H. Dennany, monumental builder and sculptor.

Passed.

Gloomy gardens then went by, one by one: gloomy houses.

Mr. Power pointed.

—That is where Childs was murdered, he said. The last house.

—So it is, Mr. Dedalus said. A queer case. Seymour Bushe got him off. Murdered his brother. Or so they said.

—The crown had no evidence, Mr. Power said.

—Only circumstantial, Martin Cunningham said. That's the maxim of the law. Better for ninetynine guilty to escape than for one innocent person to be wrongfully condemned.

They looked . Murderer's ground. It passed darkly. Wrongfully condemned.

Cramped in this carriage. She mightn't like me to come that way without letting her know. Must be careful about women. Fifteen.

The high railings of Prospect rippled past their gaze. Dark poplars, rare white forms. Forms more frequent, white shapes thronged amid the trees, white forms and fragments streaming by mutely, sustaining vain gestures on the air.

They fell harshly against the curbstone: stopped. Martin Cunningham put out his arm and, wrenching back the handle, shoved the door open with his knee. He stepped out. Mr. Power and Mr. Dedalus followed.

Change that soap now. Mr. Bloom's hand unbuttoned his hip pocket swiftly and transferred the paperstuck soap to his inner handkerchief pocket. He stepped out of the carriage, replacing the newspaper his other hand still held.

Paltry funeral: coach and three carriages. Beyond the hind carriage a hawker stood by his barrow of cakes and fruit. Simnel cakes those are, stuck together: cakes for the dead. Who ate them? Mourners coming out.

He followed his companions. Mr. Kernan and Ned Lambert followed,

Hynes walking after them. Corny Kelleher stood by the opened hearse and took out the two wreaths. He handed one to the boy.

Where is that child's funeral disappeared to?

Coffin now. Got here before us, dead as he is. Horse looking round at it with his plume skeowways. Dull eye: collar tight on his neck, pressing on a blood-vessel or something. Do they know what they cart out here every day. Must be twenty or thirty funerals every day. Then Mount Jerome for the prostestants. Funerals all over the world every where every minute. Shovelling them under by the thousand doublequick. Too many in the world.

Mourners came out through the gates: woman and girl. Leanjawed harpy, hard woman at a bargain, her bonnet awry. Girl's face stained with dirt and tears, holding the woman's arm looking up at her for a sign to cry. Fish's face, bloodless and livid.

The mutes shouldered the coffin and bore it in through the gates. First the stiff: then the friends of the stiff. Corny Kelleher and the boy followed with their wreaths. Who is that beside them? Ah, the brother-in-law.

All walked after.

Martin Cunningham whispered:

—You made it damned awkward talking of suicide before Bloom.

—Did I? Mr. Power whispered. How so?

—His father poisoned himself, Martin Cunningham said. Had the Queen's hotel in Ennis.

—O God! Mr. Power said. First I heard of it. Poisoned himself!

He glanced behind him to where a face with dark thinking eyes followed. Speaking.

—Was he insured? Mr. Bloom asked.

—I believe so, Mr. Kernan answered, but the policy was heavily mortgaged. Martin is trying to get the boy into Artane.

—How many children did he leave?

—Five. Ned Lambert says he'll try to get one of the girls into Todd's.

—A sad case, Mr. Bloom said gently. Five young children.

—A great blow to the poor wife, Mr. Kernan added.

—Indeed yes, Mr. Bloom agreed.

Has the laugh at him now.

He looked down at the boots he had blacked and polished. She had outlived him. One must outlive the other. She would marry another. Him? No. Yet who knows after? One must go first: alone, under the ground: and lie no more in her warm bed.

—How are you, Simon? Ned Lambert said, shaking hands. Haven't seen you for a month of Sundays.

—Can't complain. How are all in Cork's own town?

—I was there for the races, Ned Lambert said. Same old six and eightpence. Stopped with Dick Tivy.

—And how is Dick, the solid man?

—Nothing between himself and heaven, Ned Lambert answered.

—For God' sake—! Mr. Dedalus said. Dick Tivy bald?

—Martin is going to get up a whip for the youngsters, Ned Lambert said, pointing ahead. A few bob a skull. Just to keep them going till the insurance is cleared up.

—Yes, yes, Mr. Dedalus said dubiously. Is that the eldest boy in front?

—Yes, Ned Lambert said, with the wife's brother. John Henry Menton is behind. He put down his name for a quid.

—I'll engage he did, Mr. Dedalus said. I often told poor Paddy he ought to mind that job. John Henry is not the worst in the world.

—How did he lose it? Ned Lambert asked. Liquor, what?

—Many a good man's fault, Mr. Dedalus said with a sigh.

They halted about the door of the mortuary chapel. Mr. Bloom stood behind the boy with the wreath, looking down at his sleekcombed hair and at the slender furrowed neck inside his brandnew collar. Poor boy! Was he there when the father? Would he understand? The mutes bore the coffin into the chapel. Which end is his head?

After a moment he followed the others in, blinking in the screened light. The coffin lay on its bier before the chancel, four tall yellow candles at its corners. Always in front of us. Corny Kelleher, laying a wreath at each fore corner, beckoned to the boy to kneel. The mourners knelt here and there in prayingdesks. Mr. Bloom stood behind near the font and, when all had knelt, dropped carefully his unfolded newspaper from his pocket and knelt his right knee upon it. He fitted his black hat gently on his left knee and, holding its brim, bent over piously.

A server, bearing a brass bucket with something in it, came out through a door. The whitesmocked priest came after him tidying his stole with one hand, balancing with the other a little book against his toad's belly.

They halted by the bier and the priest began to read out of his book with a fluent croak.

Father Coffey. I knew his name was like a coffin. Dominenamine. Bully about the muzzle he looks. Bosses the show. Woe betide anyone that looks crooked at him: priest. Burst sideways like a sheep in clover, Dedalus says he will. Most amusing expressions that man finds. Hhhn: burst sideways.

—*Non intres in judicium cum servo tuo, Domine.*

Makes them feel more important to be prayed over in Latin. Chilly place this. Want to feed well, sitting in there all the morning in the gloom kicking his heels waiting for the next one. Eyes of a toad too. What swells him up that way? Molly gets swelled after cabbage. Air of the place maybe. Looks full up of bad gas. Must be a lot of bad gas round the place. Butchers for instance: they get like raw beefsteaks. Who was telling me? Mervyn Brown. Down in the vaults of saint Werburgh's lovely old organ hundred and fifty they have to bore a hole in the coffins sometimes to let out the bad gas and burn it. Out it rushes: blue. One whiff of that and you're a doner.

My kneecap is hurting me. Ow. That's better.

The priest took a stick with a knob at the end of it out of the boy's bucket and shook it over the coffin. Then he walked to the other end and shook it again. Then he came back and put it back in the bucket. As you were before you rested. It's all written down: he has to do it.

—*Et ne nos inducas in tentationem.*

The server piped the answers in the treble. I often thought it would be better to have boy servants. Up to fifteen or so. After that of course. . . .

Holy water that was, I expect. Shaking sleep out of it. He must be fed up with that job, shaking that thing over all the corpses they trot up. What harm if he could see what he shaking it over. Every mortal day a fresh batch: middle-aged men, old women, children, women dead in childbirth, men with beards, baldheaded business men, consumptive girls' with little sparrows' breasts. All the year round he prayed the same thing over them all and shook water on top of them: sleep. On Dignam now.

—*In paradisum.*

Said he was going to paradise or is in paradise. Says that over everybody. Tiresome kind of a job. But he has to say something.

The priest closed his book and went off, followed by the server. Corny Kelleher opened the sidedoors and the gravediggers came in, hoisted the coffin again, carried it out and shoved it on their cart. Corny Kelleher gave one wreath to the boy and to the brother-in-law. All followed them out of the side-door into the mild grey air. Mr. Bloom came last, folding his paper again into his pocket. He gazed gravely at the ground till the coffincart wheeled off to the left. The metal wheels ground the gravel with a sharp grating cry and the pack of blunt boots followed the barrow along a lane of sepulchres.

The ree the ra the ree the ra the roo. Lord, I musn't lilt here.

—The O'Connell circle, Mr. Dedalus said about him.

Mr. Power's soft eyes went up to the apex of the lofty cone.

—He's at rest, he said, ,in the middle of his people, old Dan O'. But his heart is buried in Rome. How many broken hearts are buried here, Simon!

—Her grave is over there, Jack, Mr. Dedalus said. I'll soon be stretched beside her. Let him take me whenever He likes.

He began to weep to himself quietly, stumbling a little in his walk. Mr. Power took his arm.

—She's better where she is, he said kindly

—I suppose so, Mr. Dedalus said with a weak gasp. I suppose she is in heaven if there is a heaven.

Corny Kelleher stepped aside from his rank and allowed the mourners to plod by.

—Sad occasions, Mr. Kernan began politely.

—They are, indeed, Mr. Bloom said.

—The others are putting on their hats, Mr. Kernan said. I suppose we can do so too. We are the last. This cemetery is a treacherous place.

They covered their heads.

—The reverend gentleman read the service too quickly, don't you think? Mr. Kernan said with reproof.

Mr. Bloom nodded gravely, looking in the quick bloodshot eyes. Secret eyes, secret searching eyes. Mason, I think: not sure. Beside him again. We are the last. In the same boat.

Hope he'll say something else.

Mr. Kernan added:

—The service of the Irish church, used in Mount Jerome, is simpler, more impressive, I must say.

Mr. Bloom gave prudent assent. The language of couse was different.

Mr. Kernan said with solemnity:

—I am the resurrecton and the life. That touches a man's inmost heart.

—It does, Mr. Bloom said.

Your heart perhaps but what price the fellow in the six feet by two? No touching that. A pump after all, pumping thousands of gallons of blood every day. One fine day it gets bunged up and there you are. Lots of them lying around here: lungs, hearts, livers. Old rusty pumps: damn the thing else. The resurrection and the life. Once you are dead you are dead. That last day idea. Knocking them all up out of their graves. Get up! Last day! Then every fellow mousing around for his liver and his lights and the rest of his traps. Find damn all of himself that morning. Pennyweight of powder in a skull. Twelve grammes one pennyweight.

Corny Kelleher fell into step at their side.

—Everything went off A 1, he said. What?

He looked on them from his drawling eye. Policeman's shoulders.

—As it should be, Mr. Kernan said.

—What? Eh? Corny Kelleher said.

Mr. Kernan assured him.

—Who is that chap behind with Tom Kernan? John Henry Menton asked, I know his face.

Ned Lambert glanced back.

—Bloom, he said. Madam Marion Tweedy that was, the soprano. She's his wife.

—O, to be sure, John Henry Menton said. I haven't seen her for some time. She was a fine looking woman. I danced with her—wait—fifteen seventeen golden years ago at Mat Dillon's in Roundtown. And a good armful she was.

He looked behind through the others.

—What is he? he asked. What does he do? Wasn't he in the stationery line? I fell foul of him one evening, I remember, at bowls.

Ned Lambert smiled.

—Yes, he was, he said, in Wisdom Hely's. A traveller for blotting paper.

—In God's name, John Henry Menton said, what did she marry a coon like that for? She had plenty of game in her then.

—Has still, Ned Lambert said. He does some canvassing for ads.

John Henry Menton's large eyes stared ahead.

The barrow turned into a side lane. A portly man ambushed among the grasses, raised his hat in homage. The gravediggers touched their caps.

—John O'Connell, Mr. Power said, pleased. He never forgets a friend. Mr. O'Connell shook all their hands in silence. Mr. Dedalus said:

—I am come to pay you another visit.

—My dear Simon, the caretaker answered in a low voice. I don't want your custom at all.

Saluting Ned Lambert and John Henry Menton he walked on at Martin Cunningham's side, puzzling two long keys at his back.

—Did you hear that one, he asked them, about Mulcahy from the Coombe?

—I did not, Martin Cunningham said.

They bent their silk hats in concert and Hynes inclined his ear. The caretaker hung his thumbs in the loops of his gold watchchain and spoke in a discreet tone to one to their vacant smiles.

—They tell the story, he said, that two drunks came out here one foggy evening to look for the grave of a friend of theirs. They asked for Mulcahy from the Coombe and were told where he was buried. After traipsing about in the fog they found the grave sure enough. One of the drunks spelt out the name: Terence Mulcahy. The other drunk was blinking up at a statue of our Saviour the widow had got put up.

The caretaker blinked up at one of the sepulchres they passed. He resumed:

—And after blinking up at it. *Not a bloody bit like the man,* says he. *That's not Mulcahy*, says he*, whoever done it.*

Rewarded by smiles he fell back and spoke with Corny Kelleher, accepting the dockets given him, turning them over and scanning them as he walked.

— That's all done with a purpose, Martin Cunningham explained to Hynes.

—I know, Hynes said, I know that.

—To cheer a fellow up, Martin Cunningham said. It's pure goodheartedness: nothing else.

Mr. Bloom admired the caretaker's properous bulk. Keys: like Keyes's ad: no fear of anyone getting out. I must see about that ad after the funeral. Be the better of a shave. Grey sprouting beard. That's the first sign when the hairs come out grey. Fancy being his wife. Wonder how he had the gumption to propose to any girl. Come out and live in the graveyard. Night here with all the dead stretched about. The shadows of the tombs and Daniel O'Connell must be a descendant I suppose who is this used to say he was a queer breedy man great catholic all the same like a big giant in the dark. Want to keep her mind off it to conceive at all. Women especially are so touchy.

He has seen a fair share go under in his time, lying around him field after field. Holy fields. All honeycombed the ground must be: oblong cells. And very neat he keeps it too, trim grass and edgings. His garden Major Gamble calls Mount Jerome. Well so it is. Ought to be flowers of sleep. Chinese cemeteries with giant poppies growing produce the best opium, Mastiansky told me.

I daresay the soil would be quite fat with corpsemanure, bones, flesh, nails. Dreadful. Turning green and pink, decomposing. Then a kind of a tallowy kind of a cheesy. Then begin to get black treacle oozing out of them. Then dried up. Of course the cells or whatever they are go on living. Changing about. Live for ever practically.

But they must breed a devil of a lot of maggots. Soil must be simply swirling with them. *Your head it simply swurls. Your head it simply swurls.* He looks cheerful enough over it. Gives him a sense of power seeing all the others go under first. Wonder how he looks at life. Cracking his jokes too: warms the cockles of his heart. Keep out the damp. Hard to imagine his funeral. Seems a sort of a joke.

—How many have you for tomorrow? the caretaker asked.

—Two, Corny Kelleher said. Half ten and eleven.

The caretaker put the papers in his pocket. The barrow had ceased to trundle. The mourners split and moved to each side of the hole, stepping with care round the graves. The gravediggers bore the coffin and set its nose on the brink, looping the bands round it.

Burying him. We come to bury Caesar. He doesn't know who is here.

Now who is that lanky looking galoot, over there in the mackintosh? Now who is he I'd like to know? Now, I'd give a trifle to know who he is. Always someone turns up you never dreamt of. A fellow could live on his lonesome all his life. Yes, he could. Still he'd have to get someone to sod him after he died . Say Robinson Crusoe was true to life. Well then Friday buried him.

How could you possibly do so?
O poor Robinson Crusoe

Poor Dignam! His last lie on the earth in his box. When you think of them all it does seem a waste of wood. All gnawed through. They could invent a handsome bier with a kind of panel sliding, let it down that way. Ay but they might object to be buried out of another fellow's. I see what it means. I see. To protect him as long as possible even in the earth.

Mr. Bloom stood far back, his hat in his hand, counting the bared heads. Twelve. I'm thirteen. No. The chap in the mackintosh is thirteen. Where the deuce did he pop out of? He wasn't in the chapel, that I'll swear. Silly superstition that about thirteen.

Nice soft tweed Ned Lambert has in that suit. Tinge of purple. I had one like that when we lived in Lombard street west. Dressy fellow he was once. Used to change three suits in the day. Hello. It's dyed. His wife, I forgot he's not married, or his landlady ought to have picked out those threads for him.

The coffin dived out of sight, easied down by the men straddled on the grave trestles. They struggled up and out: and all uncovered. Twenty.

Pause.

If we were all suddenly somebody else.

Gentle sweet air blew round the bared heads in a whisper. Whisper. The boy by the gravehead held his wreath with both hands staring quietly in the black open space. Mr. Bloom moved behind the portly kindly caretaker. Well-cut frockcoat. Weighing them up perhaps to see which will go next. Well it is a long rest. Feel no more. It's the moment you feel. Must be damned unpleasant. Can't believe it at first. Mistake must be: someone else. People talk about you a bit: forget you. Then they follow: dropping into a hole one after the other.

We are praying now for the repose of his soul.

Does he ever think of the hole waiting for himself? They say you do when you shiver in the sun. Someone walking over it. Mine over there towards Findglas, the plot I bought. Mamma, poor mamma, and little Rudy.

The gravediggers took up their spades and flung heavyclods of clay in on the coffin. Mr. Bloom turned his face. And if he was alive all the time? Whew! By Jingo, that would be awful! No, no: he is dead, of course. Of course he is dead. Monday he died. Three days. Rather long to keep them in the summer. Just as well to get shut of them as soon as you are sure there's no.

The clay fell softer. Begin to be forgotten. Out of sight.

The caretaker moved away a few paces and put on his hat. The mourners took heart of grace, one by one, covering themselves without show. Mr. Bloom put on his hat and saw the portly figure make its way deftly through the maze of graves. Quietly, sure of his ground, he traversed the dismal fields.

Hynes jotting down something in his notebook. Ah, the names. But he knows them all. No: coming to me.

—I am just taking the names, Hynes said below his breath. What is your christian name? I'm not sure.

—L, Mr. Bloom said. Leopold. And you might put down M'Coy's name too. He asked me to.

—Charley, Hynes said writing. I know. He was on the Freeman once.

So he was. Got the run. Levanted with the cash of a few ads. That was why he asked me to. O well, does no harm. I saw to that, M'Coy. Thanks, old chap: much obliged. Leave him under an obligation: costs nothing.

—And tell us, Hynes said, do you know that fellow in the, fellow was over there in the. . . .

He looked around.

—Mackintosh. Yes I saw him, Mr. Bloom said. Where is he now?

—Mackintosh, Hynes said, scribbling. I don't know who he is. Is that his name?

He moved away, looking about him.

—No, Mr. Bloom began, turning and stopping. I say, Hynes! Didn't hear. What? Where has he disappeared to? Not a sign. Well of all the. Good Lord, what became of him?

A seventh gravedigger came beside Mr. Bloom to take up an idle spade.

O, excuse me.

He stepped aside nimbly.

Clay, brown, damp, began to be seen in the hole. It rose. Nearly over. A mound of damp clods rose more, rose, and the gravediggers rested their spades. All uncovered again for a few instants. The boy propped his wreath against a corner: the brother-in-law his on a lump. The gravediggers put on their caps and carried their earthy spades towards the barrow. Then knocked the blades lightly on the turf: clean. One bent to pluck from the heft a long tuft of grass. Silently at the gravehead another coiled the coffin band. The brother-in-law, turning away, placed something in his free hand. Thanks in silence. Sorry, sir: trouble. Headshake. I know that. For yourselves just.

The mourners moved away slowly without aim, by devious paths, staying awhile to read a name on a tomb.

—Let us go round by the chief's grave, Hynes said. We have time.

—Let us, Mr. Power said.

They turned to the right following their slow thoughts. With awe Mr. Power's blank voice spoke:

—Some say he is not in that grave at all. That the coffin was filled with stones. That one day he will come again.

Hynes shook his head.

—Parnell will never come again, he said.

Mr. Bloom walked unheeded along his grove. Who passed away. Who departed this life. As if they did it of their own accord . Got the shove, all of them. Rusty wreaths hungs on knobs, garlands of bronzefoil. Better value that for the money. Still, the flowes are more poetical. The other gets rather tiresome, never withering. Expresses nothing.

A bird sat tamely perched on a poplar branch. Like stuffed. Like the wedding present alderman Hooper gave us. Hu! Not a budge out of him. Knows there are no catapults to let fly at him.

The sacred Heart that is: showing it. Red it should be painted like a real heart. Would birds come then and peck like the boy with the basket of fruit but he said no because they ought to have been afraid of the boy. Apollo that was.

How many . All these here once walked round Dublin.

Besides how could you remember everybody? Eyes, walk, voice. Well, the voice, yes: gramopohne. Have a gramophone in every grave or keep it in the house. Remind you of the voice like the photograph reminds you of the face. Otherwise you couldn't remember the face after fifteen years, say. For instance who? For instance some fellow that died when I was in Wisdom Hely's.

Ssld! A rattle of pebbles. Wait. Stop.

He looked down intently into a stone crypt. Some animal. Wait. There he goes.

An obese grey rat toddled along the side of the crypt, moving the pebbles. An old stager: grandfather: he knows the ropes. The grey alive crushed itself in under the plinth, wriggled itself in under it.

Who lives there? Are laid the remains of Robert Elliot. Robert Emmet was buried here by torchlight, wasn't he? Making his rounds.

Tail gone now.

One of those chaps would make short work of a fellow. Pick the bones clean no matter who it was. Ordinary meat for them. A corpse is meat gone bad. I read in that voyags in China that the Chinese say a white man smells like a corpse. Wonder does the news go about whenever a fresh one is let down. Wouldn't be surprised. Regular square feed for them. Got wind of Dignam. They wouldn't care about the smell of it. Saltwhite crumbling mush of corpse: smell, taste like raw white turnips.

The gates glimmered in front: still open. Back to the world again. Enough of this place. A little goes a long way. Brings you a bit nearer every time. Last time I was here was Mrs. Sinico's funeral. Give you the creeps after a bit. Plenty to see and hear and feel yet. Feel live warm beings near you. Let them sleep in their maggoty beds. They are not going to get me this innings. Warmbeds: warm fullblooded life.

Martin Cunninghm emerged from a sidepth, talking gravely.

Solicitor, I think. I know his face. Menton. Dignam used to be in his office. Mat Dillon's long ago. Got his rag out that evening on the bowlinggreen because I sailed inside him. Pure fluke of mine: the bias. Molly and Floey Dillon linked under the lilactree, laughing. Fellow always like that if women are by.

Got a dinge in the side of his hat. Carriage probably.

—Excuse me, sir, Mr. Bloom said beside them.

They stopped.

—Your hat is a little crushed, Mr. Bloom said, pointing.

John Henry Menton stared at him for an instant without moving.

—There, Martin Cunningham helped, pointing also.

John Henry Menton took off his hat, bulged out the dinge and smoothed the nap with care on his coatsleeve. He clapped the hat on his head again.

—It's all right now, Martin Cunningham said.

John Henry Martin jerked his head down in aknowledgement.

—Thank you, he said shortly.

They walked on towards the gates. Browbeaten Mr. Bloom fell behind a few paces so as not to overhear. Martin laying down the law. Martin could wind a fathead like that round his little finger without his seeing it. . .

Oyster eyes. Never mind. Be sorry after perhaps when it dawns on him. Get the pull over him that way.

Thank you. How grand we are this morning!

Episode VII

THE LITTLE REVIEW

THE MAGAZINE THAT IS READ BY THOSE WHO WRITE THE OTHERS

OCTOBER, 1918

MARGARET ANDERSON, Editor

EZRA POUND, London Editor

JULES ROMAINS, French Editor

Foreign office:

5 *Holland Place Chambers, London W. 8.*

25c. a copy; $2.50 a year. English 12/- a year.

Abonnement fr. 15 par an.

Entered as second-class matter at P. O., New York, N. Y., under the act March 3, 1879.

Published monthly by Margaret Anderson

GROSSBOOTED draymen rolled barrels dullhudding out of Prince's stores and bumped them up on the brewery float.

Grossbooted draymen rolled barrels dullthudding out of Prince's stores and bumped them up on the brewery float.

— There it is, John Murray said. Alexander Keyes.

— Just cut it out, will you? Mr. Bloom said, and I'll take it round to the *Telegraph* office.

— The door of Ruttledge's office creaked again.

John Murray's long shears sliced out the advertisement from the newspaper in four clean strokes.

— I'll go through the printing works, Mr. Bloom said, taking the cut square.

— Of course, if he wants a par, John Murray said earnestly, we can do him one.

— Right, Mr. Bloom said with a nod. I'll rub that in.

We.

John Murray touched Mr. Bloom's arm with the shears and whispered:

— Brayden.

Mr. Bloom turned and saw the liveried porter raise his lettered cap as a stately figure entered from Prince's street. Dullthudding Guinness's barrels. It passed statelily up the stair case, steered by an umbrella, a solemn beardframed face. The broadcloth back ascended each step: back. All his brains are in the nape of his neck, Simon Dedalus says. Fat folds of neck, fat, neck, fat, neck.

— Don't you think his face is like Our Saviour? John Murray whispered.

The door of Ruttledge's office whispered: ee: cree.

Our Saviour: beardframed oval face: talking in the dusk. Mary, Martha. Steered by an umbrella sword to the footlights: Mario the tenor.

— Or like Mario, Mr. Bloom said.

— Yes, John Murray agreed. But Mario was said to be the picture of Our Saviour.

Jesusmario with rougy cheeks, doublet and spindle legs. Hand on his heart. In Martha.

Co-ome thou lost one,
Co-ome thou dear one!

— His grace phoned down twice this morning, John Murray said gravely.

They watched the knees, legs, boots vanish Neck.

Facing page: table of contents, *Little Review,* October 1918

Mr. Bloom said slowly:

— Well, he is one of our saviours also.

A meek smile accompanied him as he lifted the counter-flap, as he passed in through the sidedoor and along the warm dark stairs and passage, along the now reverberating boards. Thumping, thumping.

He pushed in the glass swingdoor and entered, stepping over strewn packing paper. Through a lane of clanking drums he made his way towards Nannetti's reading closet.

Hynes here too: account of the funeral probably. Thumping thump. This morning the remains of the late Mr. Patrick Dignam. Machines. His machineries are pegging away too. Like these, got out of hand: fermenting. Working away, tearing away. And that old grey rat tearing to get in.

Mr. Bloom halted behind the foreman's spare body, admiring the glossy crown.

Strange he never saw his real country. Ireland my country . Member for College green. He ran that workaday worker tack for all it was worth.

The machines clanked in threefour time. Thump, thump, thump. Now if he got paralysed there and no-one knew how to stop them they'd clank on and on the same, print it over and over and up and back. Monkeydoodle the whole thing. Want a cool head.

— Well, get it into the evening edition, councillor, Hynes said.

Soon be calling him my lord mayor. Long John is backing him they say.

The foreman, without answering, scribbled press on a corner of the sheet and made a sign to a typesetter. He handed the sheet silently over the dirty glass screen.

— Right: thanks, Hynes said moving off.

Mr. Bloom stood in his way.

— If you want to draw, the cashier is just going to lunch, he said, pointing backward with his thumb.

— Did you? Hynes asked.

— Mm, Mr. Bloom said. Look sharp and you'll catch him.

— Thanks, old man, Hynes said. I'll tap him too.

He hurried on eagerly towards the *Freeman's Journal.*

Three bob I lent him in Meagher's.

Mr. Bloom laid his cutting on Mr. Nannetti's desk.

— Excuse me, councillor, he said. This ad, you see. Keyes, you remember.

Mr. Nannetti considered the cutting awhile and nodded.

— He wants it in for July, Mr. Bloom said.

The foreman moved his pencil towards it.

— But wait, Mr. Bloom said. He wants it changed. Keyes, you see. He wants two keys at the top.

Hell of a row they make. Maybe he understands what I.

The foreman turned round to hear patiently and, lifting an elbow, began to scratch slowly in the armpit of his alpaca jacket.

— Like that, Mr. Bloom said, crossing his forefingers at the top.

Let him take that in first . . .

Mr. Bloom, glancing sideways up from the cross he had made, saw the foreman's sallow face, think he has a touch of jaundice, and beyond the obedient reels feeding in the huge webs of paper. Clank it. Clank it. Miles of it unreeled. What becomes of it after? O, wrap up meat, parcels: various uses, one thing or anothe.r.

Slipping his words deftly into the pauses of the clanking he drew swiftly on the scarred woodwork.

— Like that, see. Two crossed keys here. A circle. Then here the name Alexander Keyes, tea, wine and spirit merchant. So on.

Better not teach him his own business.

— You know yourself, councillor, just what he wants. Then round the top in leaded: the house of keys. You see? Do you think that's a good idea?

The foreman moved his scratching hand to his lower ribs and scratched there quietly.

— The idea, Mr. Bloom said, is the house of keys. You know, councillor, the Manx parliment. Tourists, you know, from the isle of Man. Catches the eye, you see. Can you do that?

I could ask him perhaps about how to pronounce that *voglio*. But then if he didn't know only make it awkard for him. Better not.

— We can do that, the foreman said. Have you the design?

— I can get it, Mr. Bloom said. It was in a Kilkenny paper. He has a house there too. I'll just run out and ask him. Well, you can do that and just a little par calling attention. You know the usual Highclass licensed premises. Longfelt want. So on.

The foreman thought for an instant.

— We can do that, he said. Let him give us a three month's renewal .

A typesetter brought him a limp galleypage. He began to check it silently. Mr. Bloom stood by, hearing the loud throbs of cranks, watching the silent typesetters at their cases.

Want to be sure of his spelling. Martin Cunningham forgot to give us his spellingbee conundrum this morning. It is amusing to view the unpar one ar alleled embarra two ars is it? double ess ment of a harassed pedlar while gauging au the symmetry of a peeled pear under a cemetery wall. Silly isn't it? Cemetery put in of course on account of the symmetry.

I could have said when he clapped on his topper. Thank you. I ought to have said something about an old hat or something . No, I could have said. Looks as good as new now. See his phiz then.

Sllt. The nethermost deck of the first machine jogged forward its flyboard with sllt the first batch of quirefolded papers. Sllt. Almost human the way it sllt to call attention. Doing its level best to speak. That door too sllt creaking, asking to be shut. Everything speaks in its own way. Sllt.

The foreman handed back the galleypage suddenly, saying:

— Wait. Where's the archbishop's letter? It's to be repeated in the *Telegraph*. Where's what's his name

He looked about him round his loud unanswering machines.

— Monks, sir?

— Ay. Where's Monks?

— Monks!

Mr. Bloom took up his cutting. Time to get out.

—Then I'll get the design, Mr. Nannetti, he said, and you'll give it a good place I know.

— Monks!

— Yes, sir.

Three month's renewal. Want to get some wind off my chest first. Try it anyhow. Rub in August: good idea: horseshow month. Ballsbridge. Tourists over for the show.

He walked on throught the caseroom, passing an old man, bowed, spectacled, aproned. Old Monks, the dayfather. Queer lot of stuff he must have put through his hands in his time: obituary notices, pubs' ads, speeches, divorce suits, found drowned. Nearing the end of his tether now. Sober serious man with a bit in the savings bank I'd say. Wife a good cook and washer. Daughter working the machine in the parlour. Plain Jane, no damn nonsense.

He stayed in his walk to watch a typesetter neatly distributing type. Reads it backwards first. Quickly he does it. Must require some practice that. mangiD kcirtaP. Poor papa with his haggadah book, reading backwards with his finger to me. Pessach. Next year in Jerusalem. Dear, O dear! All that long business about that brought us out of Egypt *alleluia*. *Shema Israel Adonai Elohenu* .

No, that's the other. Then the twelve brothers, Jacob's sons. And then the lamb and the cat and the dog and the stick and the water and the butcher and then then the angel of death kills the butcher and he kills the ox and and the dog kills the cat. Sounds a bit silly till you come to look into it well. Justice it means but it's everybody eating everyone else. That's what life is after all. How quickly he does that job. Seems to see with his fingers.

Mr. Bloom passed on out of the clanking noises through the gallery on to the landing. Now am I going to tram it out all the way and then catch him out perhaps. Better phone him up first . Number? Same as Citron's house. Twentyeight. Twentyeight double four.

He went down the house staircase. Who the deuce scrawled all over these walls with matches? Looks as if they did it for a bet. Heavy greasy smell there always is in those works.

He took out his handerchief to dab his nose. Citronlemon? Ah, the soap I put there. Lose it out of that pocket. Putting back his handerkerchief he took out the soap and stowed it away, buttoned, into the hip pocket of his trousers .

What perfume does your wife use? I could go home still: tram: something I forgot. Just to see: before: dressing. No. Here. No.

A sudden screech of laughter came from the *Evening Telegraph* office. Know who that is. What's up? Pop in a minute to phone. Ned Lambert it is.

He entered softly.

— The ghost walks, professor MacHugh murmured softly, biscuitfully to the dusty windowpane.

Mr. Dedalus, staring from the empty fireplace at Ned Lambert's quizzing face, asked of it sourly:

— Agonizing Christ, would'nt it give you a heartburn on your arse?

Ned Lambert, seated on the table, read on:

— *Or follow the meanderings of some purling rill as it babbles on its way to Neptune's blue domain, mid mossy banks, played on by the glorious sunlight or among the shadows cast upon its pensive bosom by the overarching leafage of the giants of the forest.* What about that, Simon? he asked over the fringe of his newspaper.

— Changing his drink, Mr. Dedalus said.

Ned Lambert, laughing, struck the newspaper on his knees repeating:

— *The pensive bosom and the overarching leafage.* O boys! O boys!

— That will do, professor MacHugh cried from the window. I don't want to hear any more of the stuff.

He ate off the crescent of water biscuit he had been nibbling and made ready to nibble the biscuit in his other hand.

High falutin stuff. Ned Lambert is taking a day off I see. Rather upsets a man's day a funeral does. He has influence, they say. Old Chatterton, the vicechancellor is his granduncle or his greatgranduncle. Ninetyfive they say. The right honourable Hedges Eyre Chatterton. Daresay he writes him an odd shaky cheque or two.

— Just another spasm, Ned Lambert said .

— What is it? Mr. Bloom asked .

— A recently discovered fragment of Cicero's, professor MacHugh answered with pomp of tone. *Our lovely land.*

— Whose land? Mr. Bloom said simply.

— Most pertinent question, the professor said between his chews, with an accent on the whose.

— Dan Dawson's land, Mr. Dedalus said.

— Is it his speech last night? Mr. Bloom asked.

Ned Lambert nodded.

— But listen to this, he said.

The doorknob hit Mr. Bloom in the small of the back as the door was pushed in.

— Excuse me, J . J. O'Molloy said, entering.

Mr. Bloom moved nimbly aside.

— I beg yours, he said.

— Good day, Jack.

— Come in. Come in.

— Good day.

— How are you, Dedalus?

— Well. And yourself?

J. J. O'Molloy shook his head.

Cleverest fellow at the junior bar he used to be. Decline, poor chap. Touch and go with him.

— *Or again if we but climb the towering mountain peaks.*

— You're looking as fit as a fiddle.

— Is the editor to be seen? J. J. O'Molloy asked, looking towards the inner door.

— Very much so, professor MacHugh said. To be seen and heard. He's in his sanctum with Lenehan.

J. J. O'Molloy strolled to the sloping desk and began to turn back the pink pages of the file.

Practice dwindling. Losing heart. Used to get good retainers from D. and T. Fitzgerald. Believe he does some literary work for the *Express* with Gabriel Conroy. Well-read fellow. Myles Crawford began on the *Independent*. Funny the way they veer about. Go for one another baldheaded in the papers and then hail fellow well met the next moment.

— Ah, listen to this for God's sake, Ned Lambert pleaded. *Or again if we but climb the towering mountain peaks ....*

— Bombast! the professor broke in testily. Enough of the windbag!

—*Peaks*, Ned Lambert went on, *to bathe our souls, as it were ....*

— Bathe his lips, Mr. Dedalus said. Yes?

— *As it were, in the peerless panorama of bosky grove and undulating plain and luscious pastureland, steeped in the transcendent translucent glow of our mild mysterious Irish twilight....*

— The moon, professor MacHugh said. He forgot Hamlet.

—*That mantles the vista far and wide and wait till the glowing orb of the moon shines forth to irradiate her silver effulgence...*

— O! Mr. Dedalus groaned helplessly. Onions! That'll do, Ned . Life is too short.

He took off his silk hat and, blowing out impatiently his bushy moustache, began to rake through his hair with his fingers.

Ned Lambert tossed the newspaper aside, chuckling with delight. An instant after a hoarse bark of laughter burst over professor MacHugh's unshaven blackspectaled face.

— Doughy Daw! he cried.

All very fine to jeer at it now in cold print but it goes down like hot cake that stuff. He was in the bakery line too wasn't he? Why they call him doughy Daw. Feathered his nest well anyhow. Daughter engaged to that chap in the inland revenue office with the motor. Hooked that nicely. Entertainments. Big blowout. Wetherup always said that. Get a grip of them by the stomach.

The inner door was opened violently and a scarlet beaked face, crested by a comb of feathery hair, thrust itself in. The bold blue eyes stared about them and the harsh voice asked:

— What is it?

And here comes the sham squire himself, professor MacHugh said grandly.

— Getououthat, you bloody old pedagogue! the editor said in recognition.

— Come, Ned, Mr. Dedalus said, putting on his hat. I must get a drink after that.

—Drrink! the editor cried. No drink served before mass.

— Quite right too, Mr. Dedalus said, going out. Come on, Ned.

Ned Lambert sidled down from the table. The editor's blue eyes roved towards Mr. Bloom's face, shadowed by a smile.

— Will you join us, Myles? Ned Lambert asked.

— North Cork militia! the editor cried, striding to the mantelpiece. We won every time! North Cork and Spanish officers!

— Where was that, Myles? Ned Lambert asked with a reflective glance at his toecaps.

— In Ohio! the editor shouted.

— So it was, begad, Ned Lambert agreed.

Passing out, he whispered to J. J. O'Molloy:

— Incipient jigs. Sad case.

— Ohio! the editor crowed in high treble from his uplifted scarlet face. My Ohio!

— A perfect cretic! the professor said. Long, short and long.

He took a reel of dental floss from his waistcoat pocket and, breaking off a piece, twanged it smartly between two and two of his resonant unwashed teeth.

— Bingbang, bangbang.

Mr. Bloom seeing the coast clear, made for the inner door .

— Just a moment, Mr. Crawford, he said. I just want to phone about an ad. He went in.

— What about that leader this evening? professor MacHugh asked, coming to the editor and laying a firm hand on his shoulder.

— That'll be all right, Myles Crawford said more calmly. Never you fret. Hello, Jack.

— Good day, Myles, J. J. O'Molloy said, letting the pages he held slip limply back on the file. Is that Canada swindle case on today?

The telephone whirred inside.

— Twenty eight. . . No, twenty. . . Doublefour. . Yes.

Lenehan came out of the inner office with tissues.

— Who wants a dead cert for the Gold cup? he asked. Sceptre with O. Madden up.

He tossed the tissues on to the table.

Screams of newsboys barefoot in the hall rushed near and the door was flung open. Professor MacHugh strode across the room and seized the cringing urchin by the collar as the others scampered out of the hall and down the steps. The tissues rustled up in the draught, floated softtly in the air blue scrawls and under the table came to earth.

— It wasn't me, sir. It was the big fellow shoved me, sir.

— Throw him out, the editor said. What does he want?

Lenehan began to paw the tissues up from the floor, grunting as he stooped twice.

—Waiting for the racing special, sir, the newsboy said. It was Pat Mullins shoved me in, sir.

He pointed to two faces peering in round the doorframe.

—Him, sir.

— Out of this with you, professor MacHugh said gruffly.

He thrust the boy out and banged the door to.

— Yes . . . *Evening Telegraph* here, Mr. Bloom phoned from the inner office. Is the boss . . . ? Yes, *Telegraph* . . . To where? . . . Aha! Which auction rooms? . . Aha! I see. . . Right. I'll catch him.

The bell whirred again as he rang off. He came in quickly and bumped against Lenehan who was struggling up with the second tissue.

— *Pardon, monsieur*, Lenehan said, clutching him for an instant and making a grimace.

— My fault, Mr. Bloom said, suffering his grip. Are you hurt? I'm in a hurry.

—Knee, Lenehan said.

He made a comic face and whined, rubbing his knee:

— The accumulation of the *anno Domini.*

— Sorry , Mr. Bloom said.

He went to the door and, holding it ajar, paused. The noise of two shrill voices, a mouthorgan, echoed in the bare hallway from the newsboys squatted on the doorsteps:

— *We are the boys of Wexford*

Who fought with heart and hand.

—I'm just running round to Bachelor's walk, Mr. Bloom said, about this ad of Keyes's. Want to fix it up. They tell me he's round there in Dillon's.

He looked indecisively for a moment at their faces. The editor who, leaning against the mantelshelf, had propped his head on his hand, suddenly stretched forth an arm amply.

— Go, he said. The world is before you.

—Back in no time, Mr. Bloom said, hurrying out.

J. J. O'Molloy took the tissues from Lenehan's hand and read them without comment.

— He'll get that advertisement, the professor said, staring through his black-rimmed spectacles over the crossblind. Look at the young scamps after him.

— Show. Where? Lenehan cried, running to the window.

Both smiled over the crossblind at the file of capering newsboys in Mr. Bloom's wake, the last zigzagging white on the breeze a mocking kite, a tail of white bowknots.

— Look at the young guttersnipes behind him, Lenehan said, and you'll kick. Taking off his flat spaugs and the walk. Steal upon larks.

He began to mazurka swiftly across the floor on sliding feet past the fireplace to J. J. O'Molloy who placed the tissues in his receiving hands. .

—What's that? Myles Crawford said with a start. Where are the other two gone?

— Who? the professor said turning. They're gone round to the Oval for a drink.

—Come on then, Myles Crawford said. Wher's my hat?

He walked jerkily into the office behind, jingling his keys in his pocket. They jingled then in the air and against the wood as he locked his desk drawer.

— He's pretty well on professor, MacHugh said in a low voice.

— Seems to be, J. J. O'Molloy said, taking out a cigarette case. Who has the most matches?

He offered a cigarette to the professor and took one himself. Lenehan promptly struck a match for them and lit their cigarettes in turn. J. J. O'Molloy opened his case again and offered it.

— Thanky vous, Lenehan said, helping himself.

The editor came from the inner office, a straw hat awry on his brow. He declaimed in song, pointing sternly at professor MacHugh:

—'Twas rank and fame that tempted thee,

'Twas empire charmed thy heart.

The professor grinned, locking his long lips.

—Eh? You bloody old Roman empire? Myles Crawford said.

He took a cigarette from the open case. Lenehan, lighting it for him with quick grace, said:

— Silence for my brandnew riddle!

— *Imperium romanum,* J. J. O'Molloy said gently. It sounds nobler than British or Brixton. The word reminds one somehow of fat in the fire.

Myles Crawford blew his first puff violently towards the ceiling.

— That's it, he said. We are the fat. You and I are the fat in the fire. We haven't got the chance of a snowball in hell.

— Wait a moment, professor MacHugh said, raising two quiet claws. We musn't be led away by words, by sounds of words. We think of Rome imperial, imperious, imperative.

He extended his arms, pausing:

— What was their civilization? Vast, I allow: but vile. *Cloacae*: sewer. The jews in the wilderness and on the mountaintop said: It is meet to be here. Let us build an altar to Jehovah. The Roman, like the Englishman who follows in his footsteps, brought to every new shore on which he set his foot (on our shore he never set it) only his cloacal obsession. He gazed about h˙m in his toga and he said: It is meet to be here. Let us construct a watercloset.

— Our old ancient ancestors, Lenehan said, were partial to the running stream.

— They were nature's gentlemen, J. J O'Molloy murmured. But we have also Roman law.

— And Pontius Pilate is its prophet, professor MacHugh responded.

— Do you know that story about chief baron Palles? J. J. O'Molly asked .

— First my riddle, Lenehan said. Are you ready?

Mr. O'Madden Burke, tall in copious grey, came in from the hallway. Stephen Dedalus, behind him, uncovered as he entered.

— *Entrez, mes enfants!* Lenehan cried.

— I escort a suppliant, Mr. O'Madden Burke said melodiously.

— How do you do? the editor said, holding out a hand. Come in . Your governor is just gone.

Lenehan said to all:

— Silence! What opera resembles a railwayline? reflect, ponder, excogitate, reply.

Stephen handed over the typed sheets., pointing to the title and signature.

— Who? the editor asked.

Bit torn off.

— Mr. Garrett Deasy, Stephen said.

—That old pelters, the editor said. Who tore it? Was he short taken?

On swift sail flaming
From storm and south
He comes, pale phantom,
Mouth to my mouth.

— Good day, Stephen, the professor said, coming to peer over their shoulders. Foot and mouth. ? Are you turned. . . ?

Bullockbefriending bard.

— Good day, sir, Stephen answered, blushing. The letter is not mine. Mr. Garret Deasy asked me to . . . . . .

— O, I know him, Myles Crawford said, and knew his wife too. The bloodiest old tartar God ever made. By Jesus, she had the foot and mouth disease and no mistake! The night she threw the soup in the waiter's face in the Star and Garter. Oho!

A woman brought sin into the world. For Helen, the runaway wife of Menelaus, ten years the Greek's. O'Rourke's wife, prince of Breffni.

— Is he a widower? Stephen asked.

—Ay, a grass one, Myles Crawford said. Emperor's horses. Habsburg. An Irishman saved his life on the ramparts of Vienna. Don't you forget! Maximilian Karl O'Donnell, graf von Tirconnel in Ireland. Wild geese. O, yes, every time. Don't you forget that!

—The point is did he forget it. J. J. O'Molloy said quietly. Saving princes is a thankyou job.

Professor MacHugh turned on him.

— And if not? he said.

— I'll tell you how it was, Myles Crawford began. A Hungarian it was one day. . .

— We were always loyal to lost causes, the professor said. Success for us is the death of the intellect and of the imagination. We were never loyal to the successful. We serve them. I teach the blatant Latin language. I speak the tongue of a race the acme of whose mentality is the maxim: time is money. Material domination. *Dominus!* Lord! Where is the spirituality? Lord Jesus! Lord Salisbury . A sofa in a westend club. But the Greek!

A smile of light brightened his darkrimmed eyes, his long lips.

— The Greek! he said again. *Kyrios!* Shining word! *Kyrie!* The radiance of the intellect. I ought to profess Greek, the language of the mind. *Kyrie eleison!* The closetmaker and the cloacamaker will never be lords of our spirit. We are liege subjects of the catholic chivalry of Europe that foundered at Trafalgar and of the empire of the spirit, not an *imperium,* that went under with the Athenian fleets at Aegospotami. Yes, yes. They went under. Pyrrhus, misled by an oracle, made a last attempt to retrieve the fortunes of Greece. Loyal to a lost cause.

He strode away from them towards the window.

— They went forth to battle, Mr. O'Madden Burke said greyly, but they always fell.

— *There's a ponderous pundit MacHugh*
Who wears goggles of ebony hue:
As he mostly sees double,
To wear them why trouble?
I can't see the Joe Miller. Can you?

In my mourning for Sallust, Mulligan says. Whose mother is beasty dead..

Myles Crawford crammed the sheets into a sidepocket.

— That'll be all right, he said. I'll read the rest after. That'll be all right.

Lenehan extended his hands in protest.

— But my riddle! he said. What opera is like a railwayline?

— Opera? Mr. O'Madden Burke's vague face repeated.

Lenehan announced gladly:

— *The Rose of Castile.* See the wheeze? Rows of cast steel. Gee!

He poked Mr. O'Madden Burke mildly in the spleen. Mr. O'Madden Burke fell back with grace on his umbrella, feigning a gasp.

— Help! he sighed.

Lenehan, rising to tiptoe, fanned his face rapidly with the rustling tissues.

The professor, returning by way of the files, swept his hand across Stephen's and Mr. O'Madden Burke's loose ties.

— Paris, past and present, he said. You look like communards.

— Like fellows who had blown up the Bastile, J. J. O'Molloy said in quiet mockery. Or was it you shot the lord lieutenant of Finland between you. You look as though you had done the deed. General Bobrikoff.

— We were only thinking about it, Stephen said.

— All the talents, Myles Crawford said. Law, the classics...

— The turf, Lenehan put in.

— Literature, the press.

— If Bloom were here, the professor said. The gentle art of advertisement.

— And Madam Bloom, Mr. O'Madden Burke added. The vocal muse. Dublin's prime favorite.

Lenehan gave a loud cough.

— Ahem! he said very softly. I caught a cold in the park. The gate was open.

The editor laid a nervous hand on Stephen's shoulder.

— I want you to write something for me, he said. Something with a bite in it. You can do it. I see it in your face.

See it in your face. See it in your eye. Lazy idle little schemer.

— Foot and mouth disease! the editor cried scornfully. Great nationalist meeting in Borris-in-Ossory. All balls! Bulldozing the public . Give them something with a bite in it. Put us all into it, damn its soul. Father, Son and Holy Ghost.

— We can all supply mental pabulum, Mr. O'Madden Burke said.

Stephen raised his eyes to the bold unheeding stare.

— He wants you for the pressgang, J. J. O'Malloy said.

— You can do it, Myles Crawford repeated, clenching his hand in emphasis. Wait a minute. We'll paralyse Europe as Ignatius Gallaher used to say when he was on the shaughranun. That was pressman for you. You know how he made his mark? I'll tell you. That was the smartest piece of journalism ever known. That was in eightytwo, time of the invincibles, murder in Phoenix park, before the you were born. I'll show you.

He pushed past them to the files.

— Look at here, he said, turning. The *New York World* cabled for a special. Remember that time?

Professor MacHugh nodded.

— The *New York World*, the editor said, excitedly pushing back his straw hat. Where it took place. Where Skin-the goat-drove the car. Whole route, see?

— Skin-the-goat, Mr. O'Madden Burke said. Fitzharris. He has that cabman's shelter they say, down there at Butt bridge. Holohan told me. You know Holohan?

— Hop and carry one, is it? Myles Crawford said.

— And poor Gumly is down there too, he told me minding stones for the corporation. A nightwatchman.

Stephen turned in surprise.

— Gumly? he said. A friend of my father's, is he?

— Never mind Gumly, Myles Crawford cried angrily. Let Gumly mind the stones, see they don't run away. Look at here. What did Ignatius Gallaher do? I'll tell you. Inspiration of genius Cabled right away. Have you *Weekly Freeman* of 17 March? Right. Have you got that?

He flung back pages of the files and stuck his finger on a point.

— Take page four, advertisement for Bransom's coffee, let us say. Have you got that? Right.

The telephone whirred,

— I'll answer it, the professor said, going.

— B is parkgate. Good.

His finger leaped and struck point after point, vibrating.

— T is viceregal lodge. C is where the murder took place. K. is Knockmaroon gate.

The loose flesh of his neck shook like a cock's wattles. An illstarched dicky jutted up and with a rude gesture he thrust it back into his waiscoat.

— Hello? *Evening Telegraph* here... Hello? ... Who's there? ... Yes... Yes... Yes.

— F to P is the route Skin-the-goat drove the car. F. A. B. P. Got that? X is Burke's publichouse 'n Baggot street.

The professor came to the inner door.

— Bloom is at the telephone, he said.

— Tell him to go to hell, the editor said promptly. X is Burke's publichouse, see?

— Clever, Lenehan said.

— Gave it to them on a hot plate, Myles Crowford said, the whole bloody history.

Nightmare from which you will never awake.

— I saw it, the editor said proudly. I was present, Dick Adams and myself. Out of an advertisement. That gave him the leg up. Then Tay Pay took him on to the Star. Now he's got in with Blumenfeld. That's press. That's talent.

— Hello? ... Are you there? .... Yes, he's here still. Come across your self.

— Where do you find a pressman like that now, eh? the editor cried.

He flung the pages down.

— Clever idea, Lenehan said to Mr. O'Madden Burke.

— Very smart, Mr. O'Madden Burke said.

Professor MacHugh came from the inner office.

— Talking about the invincibles, he said, did you see that some hawkers were up before the recorder .....

— O yes, J. J. O'Molloy said eagerly. Lady Dudley was walking home through the park and thought she'd buy a view of Dublin. And it turned out to be a commemoration postcard of Joe Brady or Skin-the-goat. Right outside the viceregal lodge, imagine!

— They're only in the hook and eye department, Myles Crawford said . Psha! Press and the bar! Where have you a man now at the bar like those fellows, like Whiteside, like Isaac Butt, like silvertongued O'Hagan? Eh? Ah, bloody nonsense! Only in the halfpenny place!

His mouth continued to twitch unspeaking in nervous curls of disdain.

Would anyone wish that mouth for her kiss? How do you know? Why did you write it then?

Mouth, south. Is the mouth south someway?- Or the south a mouth? Must be some. South, pout, out, shout, drouth. Rymes: two men dressed the same, looking the same, two by two.

.... *la tua pace*

.... *che parlar ti piace*

.... *Mentreche il vento, come fa, si tace*

He saw them three by three, approaching girls, in green, in rose, in russet, entwining, *per l'aer perso,* in mauve, in purple, *quella pacifica oriafiamma,* in gold of oriflamme, *di rimirar fe piu ardenti.* But I old men, penitent, leadenfooted: mouth, south: tomb womb.

— Speak up for yourself, Mr. O'Madden Burke said.

J. J. O'Molloy, smiling palely, took up the gage.

— My dear Myles, he said, flinging his cigarette aside, your Cork legs are running away with you. Why not bring in Henry Grattan and Flood and Demosthenes and Edmund Burke? Ignatius Gallaher we all know and his Chapelized boss, Harmsworth of the farthing press, and his American cousin of the Bowery guttersheet. Why bring in a master of forensic eloquence like Whiteside? Sufficient for the day is the newspaper thereof.

— Grattan and Flood wrote for this very paper, the editor cried in his face. Irish volunteers. Where are you now? Dr. Lucas. Who have you now like John Philpot Curran? Psha!

— Well, J. J. O'Molloy said, Seymour Bushe, for example.

— Bushe? the editor said. Well, yes. : Bushe, yes . He has a strain of it in his blood. Kendal Bushe or I mean Seymour Bushe.

— He would have been on the bench long ago, the professor said. . . .

J. J. O'Molloy turned to Stephen and said quietly and slowly:

— One of the most polished periods I think I ever listened to in my life fell from the lips of Seymour Bushe. It was in that case of fratricide, the Childs murder case. Bushe defended him.

And in the porches of mine ear did pour

By the way how did he find that out? He died in his sleep . Or the other story, beast with two backs?

— What was that? the professor asked.

— He spoke on the law of evidence, J. J. O'Molloy said, of Roman justice as contrasted with the earlier Mosaic code, the *lex talionis*. And he spoke of the Moses of Michelangelo in the vatican.

— Ha.

Pause. J. J. O'Molloy took out his cigarettcase.

False lull. Something quite ordinary.

Messenger took out his matchbox thoughtfully and lit his cigar.

I have often thought since on looking back over that strange time that it was that small act, trivial in itself, the striking of a match, that determined the whole aftercourse of both our lives.

J. J. O'Molloy resumed, moulding his words:

— He said of it: *that stony effigy, horned and terrible, that eternal symbol of wisdom and of prophecy which, if aught that the imagination or the hand of sculptor has wrought in marble of soultransfigured and of soultransfiguring deserves to live, deserves to live.*

His slim hand with a wave graced echo and fall.

— Fine! Myles Crawford said at once.

— You like it? J. J. O'Molloy asked Stephen.

Stephen, his blood wooed by grace of language and gesture, blushed. He took a cigarette from the case. J. J. O'Molloy offered his case to Myles Crawford. Lenehan lit their cigarettes as before and helped himself.

— Professor Magennis was speaking to me about you, J. J. O'Molloy said to Stephen. What do you think really of that hermetic crowd the opal hush poets: A. E. the mastermystic? That Blavatsky woman started it. She was a nice old bag of tricks. A. E. has been telling some interviewer that you came to him in the small hours of the morning to ask him about planes of consciousness. Magennis thinks you must have been pulling A. E. 's leg. He is a man of the very highest morale, Magennis.

Speaking about me. What did he say? What did he say? What did he say about me? Don't ask.

— No, thanks, professor MacHugh said, waving the cigarettecase aside . Wait a moment. Let me say one thing. The finest display of oratory I ever heard was a speech made by John F. Taylor at the college historical society. Mr. Justice Fitzgibbon, the present lord justice of appeal, had spoken and the paper under debate was an essay (new for those days) advocating the revival of the Irish tongue.

He turned towards Myles Crawford and said:

— You know Gerald Fitzgibbon. Then you can imagine the style of his discourse.

— He is sitting with Tim Healy, J. J. O'Molly said on the Trinity college estates commission.

— He is sitting with a sweet thing in a child's frock, Myles Crawford said. Go on. Well?

— It was the speech, mark you, the professor said, of a finished orator, full of courteous haughtiness and pouring I will not say the vials of his wrath but pouring the proud man's contumely upon the new movement. It was then a new movement.

He closed his long thin lips an instant but, eager to be on, raised an outspanned hand to his spectacles and, with trembling thumb and ringfinger touching lightly the black rims, steadied them to a new focus.

In ferial tone he addressed J. J. O'Molloy:

— Taylor had come there, you must know, from a sick bed. That he had prepared his speech I do not believe. His dark lean face had a growth of shaggy beard round it. He wore a loose neckcloth and altogether he looked (though he was not) a dying man.

His gaze turned at once towards Stephen's face and then bent at once to the ground, seeking. His unglazed linen collar appeared behind his bent head, soiled by his withering hair. Still seeking, he said:

— When Fitzgibbon's speech had ended John F. Taylor rose to reply. As well as I can bring them to mind his words were these.

He raised his head firmly. His eyes bethought themselves once more. Witless shellfish swam in the gross lenses to and fro, seeking outlet.

He began:

— *Mr. chairman, ladies and gentlemen: in listening to the remarks addressed to the youth of Ireland a moment since by my learned friend it seemed to me that I had been transported into a country far away from this country, into an age remote from this age, that I stood in ancient Egypt and that I was listening to the speech of some highpriest of that land addressed to the youthful Moses.*

His listeners held their cigarettes poised to hear, smokes ascending in frail stalks that flowered with his speech. *And let our crooked smokes.* Noble words coming. Look out. Could you try your hand at it yourself?

— *And it seemed to me that I heard the voice of that Egyptian highpriest raised in a tone of like haughtiness and like pride. I heard his words and their meaning was revealed to me.*

It was revealed to me that those things are good which yet are corrupted which neither if they were supremely goond nor unless they were good, could be corrupted. Ah, curse you! That's saint Augustine.

— *Why will you jews not accept our culture, our religion and our language? You are a tribe of nomad herdsmens we are a mighty people. You have no cities nor no wealth: our cities are hives of humanity and our galleys, trireme and quadrireme, laden with all manner of merchandise furrow the waters of the known globe. You have but emerged from primitive condition: we have a literature, a priesthood, an agelong history and a polity.*

Nile.

Child, man, effigy,

By the Nilebank the babemaries kneel, cradle of bulrushes: a man supple in combat: stonehorned, stonebearded, heart of stone.

— *You pray to a local and obscure idol: our temples, majestic and mysterious, are the abodes of Isis and Osiris, of Horus and Ammon Ra. Vagrants and daylabourers are you called: the world trembles at our name.*

A dumb belch of hunger cleft his speech. He lifted his voice above it boldly:

—*But, ladies and gentlemen, had the youthful Moses listened to and accepted that view of life, had he bowed his head and bowed his will and bowed his spirit before that arrogant admonition he would never have brought the chosen people out of their house of bondage nor followed the pillar of the cloud by day. .He would never have spoken with the Eternal amid lightnings on Sinai's mountaintop nor ever have come down with the light of inspiration shining in his countenance and bearing in his arms the tables of the law, graven in the language of the outlaw.*

He ceased and looked at them, enjoying silence.

J.J. O'Molloy said not without regret:

— And yet he died without having entered the land of promise.

—A-sudden-at-the-moment-though-from-lingering_illness-often-previousy-expectorated-demise, Lenehan said. And with a great future behind him.

The troop of bare feet was heard rushing along the hallway and pattering up the staircase.

— That is oratory, the professor said, uncontradicted.

Gone with the wind. Hosts at Mullaghmast and Tara of the kings. Miles of ears of porches. The tribune's words howled and scattered. Dead noise. Akasic records of all that ever anywhere wherever was.

I have money.

— Gentlemen, Stephen said. May I suggest that the house do now adjourn?

— It is not a French compliment? Mr. O'Madden Burke asked.

— All who are in favour say ay, Lenehan announced. The contrary no. I declare it carried. To which particular boosingshed . .? Mooney's?

He led the way.

Mr. O'Madden Burke, following close, said with an ally's lunge of his umbrella:

— *Lay on, Macduff!*

— Chip of the old block! the editor cried, slapping Stephen on the shoulder. Let us go. Where are those bloody keys?

He fumbled in his pocket, pulling out the crushed typesheets.

— Foot and mouth. I know. That'll be all right. That'll go in. Where are they?

He thrust the sheets back and went into the inner office .

J. J. O'Molloy, about to follow him in, said quietly to Stephen:

— I hope you will live to see it published. Myles, one moment.

He went into the inner office, closing the door behind him.

— Come along, Stephen, the professor said. That is fine, isn't it? It has the prophetic vision.

The first newsboy came pattering down the stairs at their heels and rushed out into the street, yelling:

— Racing special!

Dublin.

They turned to the left along Abbey street.

— I have a vision too, Stephen said.

— Yes? the professor said, skipping to get into step. Crawford will follow.

Another newsboy shot past them, yelling as he ran:

— Racing special!

Dubliners.

— Two Dublin vestals, Stephen said, elderly and pious, have lived fifty and fiftythree years in Fumbally's lane.

— Where is that? the professor asked.

— Off Blackpitts, Stephen said.

Damp night reeking of hungry dough. Against the wall. Face glistening. tallow under her fustian shawl. Frantic hearts. Akasic records. Quicker, darlint!

On now. Let there be life.

— They want to see the views of Dublin from the top of Nelson's pillar. They save up three and tenpence in a red tin letterbox moneybox. They shake out threepenny bits and a sixpence and coax out the pennies with the blade of a knife. Two and three in silver and one and seven in coppers. They put on their bonnets and best clothes and take their umbrellas for fear it may come on to rain.

— Wise virgins, professor MacHugh said.

— They buy oneandfourpenceworth of brawn and four slices of panloaf at the north city diningrooms in Marlborough street from Miss Kate Collins, proprietress . . They purchase four and twenty ripe plums from a girl at the foot of Nelson's pillar to take off the thirst of the brawn. They give two threepenny bits to the gentleman at the turnstile and begin to waddle slowly up the winding staircase, grunting, encouraging each other, afraid of the dark, panting, one asking the other have you the brawn, praising God and the Blessed Virgin, threatening to come down, peeping at the airslits. Glory be to God. They had no idea it was that high.

Their names are Anne Kearns and Florence MacCabe. Anne Kearns has the lumbago for which she rubs on Lourdes water given her by a lady who got a bottleful from a passionist father. Florence MacCabe takes a crubeen and a bottle of double X for supper every Saturday.

— Antithesis, the professor said, nodding twice. I can see them. What's keeping our friend?

He turned.

A bevy of scampering newsboys rushed down the steps, scampering in all directions, yelling, their white papers fluttering. Hard after them Myles Crawford appeared on the steps, his hat aureoling his scarlet face, talking with J. J. O'Molloy.

— Come along, the professor cried waving his arm.

He set off again to walk by Stephen's side.

— Yes, he said, I see them.

Mr. Bloom, caught in a whirl of wild newsboys near the steps, called:

— Mr. Crawford! A moment!

— *Telegraph!* Racing special!

— What is it? Myles Crawford said, falling back a pace.

A newsboy cried in Mr. Bloom's face:

— Terrible tragedy in Rathmines! A child bit by a bellows!

— Just this ad, Mr. Bloom said, pushing through and taking the cutting from his pocket. I spoke with Mr. Keyes just now. He'll give a renewal for two months, he says. After he'll see. But he wants a par to call attention in the *Telegraph* too, the Saturday pink. And he wants it if it's not too late. I told councillor Nannetti from the *Kilkenny People*. I can get it in the National library. House of keys, don't you see? His name is Keyes. It's a play on the name. But he says he'll give the renewal. But he wants the par. What will I tell him, Mr. Crawford?

— Will you tell him he can kiss my arse? Myles Crawford said, throwing out his arm for emphasis. Tell him that straight from the stable.

A bit nervy. All off for a drink. Lenehan's yachting cap on the cadge beyond. Wonder is that young Dedalus standing. Has a good pair of boots on him today. Last time I saw him he had his heels on view. Been walking in muck somewhere. Careless chap. What was he doing in Irishtown?

— Well, Mr. Bloom said, his eyes returning, if I can get the design I suppose it's worth a short par. He'd give the ad. I think. I'll tell him . . . .

— He can kiss my royal Irish arse, Myles Crawford cried loudly over his shoulder. Any time he likes, tell him.

While Mr. Bloom stood weighing the point and about to smile he strode on jerkily.

— *Nulla bona*, Jack, he said, raising his hand to his chin. I'm up to here. I've been through the hoop myself. I was looking for a fellow to back a bill for me no later than last week. Sorry, Jack. With a heart and a half if I could.

J. J. O'Molloy pulled a long face and walked on silently They caught up on the others and walked abreast.

— When they have eaten the brawn and the bread and wiped their twenty fingers in the paper the bread was wrapped in they go nearer the railings.

— Something for you. the professor explained to Myles Crawford. Two old Dublin women on the top of Nelson's pillar.

— That's new, Myles Crawford said. Out for the waxies' Dargle. Two old trickies, what?

— But they are afraid the pillar will fall, Stephen went on. They see the roofs and argue about where the different churches are: Rathmines' blue dome, Adam and Eve's, saint Laurence O'Toole's. But it makes them giddy to look so they pull up their skirts . . . .

— Easy all, Myles Crawford said. We're in the archdiocese here.

— And settle down on their striped petticoats, peering up at the statue of the onehandled adulterer.

— Onehandled adulterer! the professor cried. I like that. I see the idea. I see what you mean.

— It gives them a crick in their necks, Stephen said, and they are too tired to look up or down or to speak. They put the bag of plums betwen them and eat the plums out of it, one after another wiping off with their handkerchiefs the plumjuice that dribbles out of their mouths and spitting the plumstones slowly out between the railways.

He gave a sudden loud young laugh as a close. Lenehan and Mr. O'Madden Burke, hearing, turned, beckoned and led on across towards Mooney's.

— Finished? Myles Crawford said. So long as they do no worse.

— You remind me of Antisthenes, the professor said, a disciple of Gorgias the sophist. It is said of him that none could tell if he were bitterer against others or against himself. He was the son of a noble and a bondwoman. And he wrote a book in which he took away the palm of beauty from Argive Helen and handed it to poor Penelope.

Poor Penelope. Penelope Rich.

They made ready to cross O'Connell street.

— But what do you call it? Myles Crawford asked. Where did they get the plums?

— Call it, wait, the professor said, opening his long lips wide to reflect. Call it, let me see. Call it: *deus nobis haec otia fecit.*

— No, Stephen said, I call it *A Pisgah Sight of Palestine.*

— I see, the professor said.

He laughed richly.

— I see, he said again with new pleasure. Moses and the promised land. We gave him that idea, he added to J. J. O'Molloy.

J .J .O'Molloy sent a weary sidelong glance towards the statue and held his peace.

— I see, the professor said.

He halted on Sir John Gray's pavement island and peered aloft at Nelson through the meshes of his wry smile.

— Onehandled adulterer, he said grimly. That tickles me I must say.

— Tickled the old ones too, Myles Crawford said, if the truth was known.

(*To be continued*)

Episode VIII

THE LITTLE REVIEW

THE MAGAZINE THAT IS READ BY THOSE WHO WRITE THE OTHERS

JANUARY, 1919

MARGARET ANDERSON, **Editor**
EZRA POUND, **London Editor**
JULES ROMAINS, **French Editor**

24 *West Sixteenth Street, New York*

Foreign office:
5 *Holland Place Chambers, London W. 8.*

25c. a copy; $2.50 a year. **English 12/- a year.**
Abonnement fr. 15 par an.

Entered as second-class matter at P. O., New York, N. Y., under the act March 3, 1879.

Published monthly by Margaret Anderson

PINEAPPLE rock, lemon platt, butter-scotch. A sugarsticky girl shovelling scoopfuls of creams for a christian brother. Some school treat. Bad for their tummies. Lozenge and comfit manufacturer to His Majesty the King. God. Save. Our. Sitting on his throne, sucking jujubes.

A sombre young man, watchful among the warm sweet fumes of Graham Lemon's, placed a throwaway in a hand of Mr. Bloom.

Heart to heart talks.

Bloo . . . . Me? No.

Blood of the Lamb.

His slow feet walked him riverward, reading. All are washed in the blood of the lamb. Elijah is coming. Dr. John Alexander Dowie restorer of the church in Zion is coming.

Is coming! Is coming!! Is coming!!!

All heartily welcome.

Paying game. Where was that ad some Birmingham firm the luminous crucifix? Our saviour. Wake up in the dead of night and see him on the wall, hanging. Pepper's ghost idea. Iron nails ran in.

Phosphorous it must be done with. If you leave a bit of codfish for instance. I could see the bluey silver over it. Night I went down to the pantry in the kitchen. What was it she wanted? The Malaga raisins. Before Rudy was born. The phosphorescence, that bluey greeny. Very good for the brain.

From Butler's monument house corner he glanced along Bachelor's walk. Dedalus' daughter there still outside Dillon's auction rooms. Must be selling off some old furniture. Knew her eyes at once from the father. Lobbing about waiting for him. Home always breaks up when the mother goes. Fifteen children he had. Birth every year almost. That's in their theology or the priest won't give the poor woman the confession, the absolution. Increase and multiply. Did you ever hear such an idea? No families themselves to feed. Living on the fat of the land. A housekeeper of one of those fellows if you could pick it out of her. Never pick it out of her: his reverence: mum's the word.

Good Lord that poor child's dress is in flitters. Under fed she looks too. It's after they feel it. Undermines the constitution.

As he set foot on O'Connell bridge a puffball of smoke plumed up from the parapet. Brewery barge with export stout. England. Sea air sours it, I heard. Be interesting some day get a pass through Hancock to see the brewery. Regu-

Facing page: table of contents, *Little Review,* January 1919

lar town in itself. Vats of porter wonderful. Rats get in too. Drink themselves bloated as big as a collie floating. Dead drunk on the porter. Drink till they puke again like christians. Imagine drinking that! Rats: vats. Well of course if we knew all the things.

Looking down he saw flapping strongly, wheeling between the gaunt quaywalls, gulls. Rough weather outside. If I threw myself down? Reuben J's son must have swallowed a good bellyful of that sewage. One and eightpence too much. Hhhm. It's the droll way he comes out with the things.

They wheeled lower. Looking for grub. Wait.

He threw down among them a crumpled paper ball. Elijah thirtytwo feet per sec is come. Not a bit. The ball bobbed unheeded on the wake of swells, floated under by the bridgepiers. Not such damn fools . They wheeled, flapping.

The hungry famished gull
Flaps o'er the waters dull.

That is how poets write, the similar sounds. But then Shakespeare has no rhymes: blank verse. The flow of the language it is. The thoughts. Solemn.

Hamlet, I am thy father's spirit
Doomed for a certain time to walk the earth.

— Two apples a penny! Two for a penny!

His gaze passed over the glazed apples serried on her stand. Australians they must be this time of year. Shiny peels: polishes them up with a rag or a handkerchief.

Wait. Those poor birds.

He halted again and bought from the old applewoman two Banbury cakes for a penny and broke the brittle paste and threw its fragments down into the Liffey. See that? The gulls swooped silently, two, then all, from their heights, pouncing on prey. Gone. Every morsel.

Aware of their greed and cunning he shook the powdery crumb from his hands. They never expected that. Manna. Live on fish, fishy flesh they have, all seabirds, gulls, seagoose. Robinson Crusoe had to live on them.

They wheeled, flapping weakly. I'm not going to throw any more. Penny quite enough. Lot of thanks I get. Not even a caw. If you fatten a turkey say on chesnut meal it tastes like that. But then why is it that saltwater fish are not salty? How is that?

His eyes sought answer from the river and saw a rowboat rock at anchor on the treacly swells lazily its plastered board.

Hyam's

11/

Trousers.

Good idea that. Wonder if he pays rent to the corporation. How can you own water really? It's always flowing in a stream, never the same, which in the stream of life we trace. Because life is a stream. All kinds of places are good for ads. That quackdoctor for the clap used to be stuck up in all the greenhouses. Never see it now. Strictly confidential. Dr. Hy Franks. Didn't cost him a red. Got fellows to stick them up or stick them up himself for that matter on the q. t., running in to loosen a button. Just the place too.

If he . . . . ?

O!

Eh?

No . . . . No

No, no. I don't believe it. He wouldn't surely?

No, no.

Mr. Bloom moved forward, raising his troubled eyes. Think no more about that. After one. Timeball on the ballast-office is down. Dunsink time. Fascinating little book that is of sir Robert Ball's . Parallax. I never exactly understood. Par it's Greek: parallel, parallax. Met him pikehoses she called it till I told her about the transmigration. O rocks!

Mr. Bloom smiled O rocks at two windows of the ballast-office. She's right after all. Only big words for ordinary things on account of the sound. She's not exactly witty. Still I don't know. She used to say Ben Dollard had a base barreltone voice. He has legs like barrels and you'd think he was singing into a barrel. Now, isn't that wit? They used to call him big Ben. Not half as witty as calling him base barreltone. Powerful man he was at stowing away number one Bass. Barrel of Bass. See? It all works out.

A procession of whitesmocked sandwich men marched slowly towards him along the gutter, scarlet sashes across their boards. Bargains. Like that priest they are this morning: we have sinned: we have suffered. He read the scarlet letters on their five tall white hats: H. E. L. Y. S. Wisdom Hely's. Y lagging behind drew a chunk of bread from under his foreboard, crammed it into his mouth and munched as he walked. Three bob a day, walking along the gutters, street after street. Just keep skin and bone together, bread and skilly. They are not Boyl: no: M'Glade's men. Doesn't bring in any business either. I suggested to him about a transparent showcart with two smart girls sitting inside writing letters, copybooks, envelopes, blottingpaper. I bet that would have caught on. Smart girls writing something catch the eye at once. Everyone dying to know what she's writing. Wouldn't have it of course because he didn't think of it himself first. Well out of that ruck I am. Devil of a job it was collecting accounts of those convents. Tranquilla convent. That was a nice nun there, really sweet face. Sister? Sister? I am sure she was crossed in love by her eyes. Very hard to bargain with that sort of woman. I disturbed her at her devotions that morning. Our great day, she said. Feast of Our Lady of Mount Carmel. Sweet name too: caramel. She knew I, I think she knew by the way she. If she had married she would have changed. I suppose they really were short of money. Fried everything in the best butter all the same. Sister? It was a nun they say invented barbed wire.

He crossed Westmoreland street when apostrophe S had plodded by. Rover cycleshop. Those races are on today. How long ago is that? Year Phil Gilligan died. We were in Lombard street west. Wait: was in Thom's . Got the job in Wisdom Hely's year we married. Six years. Ten years ago: ninetyfour he died, yes that's right the big fire at Arnott's. Val Dillon was lord mayor. Milly was a kiddy then. Molly had that elephant grey dress with the braided frogs. She didn't like it because I sprained my ankle first day she wore it, choir picnic at the Sugarloaf. As if that. Never put a dress on her back like it. Fitted her like a glove, shoulder and hips. Just beginning to plump it out well. Rabbitpie we had that day. People looking after her.

Happy. Happier then. Snug little room that was with the red wallpaper. Milly's tubbing night. American soap I bought: elder flower. Cosy smell of her bathwater. Funny she looked soaped all over. Shapely too.

He walked along the curbstone.

Stream of life. What was the name of that priesty-looking chap was always squinting in when he passed? Stopped in Citron's saint Kevin's parade. Pen something. Pendennis? My memory is getting. Pen . . . ?

Bartell d'Arcy was the tenor, just coming out then. Seeing her home after practice. Conceited fellow with his waxedup moustache. Gave her that song *Winds that blow from the south.*

Windy night that was I went to fetch her, there was that lodge meeting on about those lottery tickets after Goodwin's concert in the supperroom of the mansion house. He and I behind. Sheet of her music blew out of my hand against the high school railings . Lucky it didn't. Thing like that spoils the effect of a night for her. Professor Goodwin linking her in front. Shaky on his pins, poor old sot. Remember her laughing at the wind, her blizzard collar up.

Corner of Harcourt road remember that gust? Brrfoo! Blew up all her skirts and her boa nearly smothered old Goodwin. She did get flushed in the wind. Remember when we got home raking up the fire and frying up those pieces of lap of mutton for her with the Chutney sauce she liked. And the mulled rum. Could see her in the bedroom from the hearth unclasping her stays. White.

Swish and soft flop her stays made on the bed. Always warm from her. Always liked to let herself out. Sitting there after till near two, taking out her hairpins. Milly tucked up in beddyhouse. Happy. Happy. That was the night ....

— O Mr. Bloom, how do you do?

— O how do you do, Mrs. Breen?

— No use complaining. How is Molly those times? Haven't seen her for ages.

— In the pink, Mr. Bloom said gaily. Milly's down in Mullingar, you know.

— Is that so?

— Yes, in a photographer's there. Getting on like a house on fire. How are all your charges?

— All on the baker's list, Mrs. Breen said

How many has she? No other in sight.

— You're in black I see. You have no ....

— No Mr. Bloom said. I have just come from a funeral.

Going to crop up all day, I foresee.

— O dear me, Mrs. Breen said, I hope it wasn't any near relation.

May as well get her sympathy.

— Dignam, Mr Bloom said. An old friend of mine. He died quite suddenly poor fellow. Heart trouble, I believe. Funeral was this morning.

Your funeral's tomorrow

While you're coming through the rye.

Diddlediddle dumdum

Diddlediddle ....

— Sad to lose the old friends, Mrs Breen's womaneyes said melancholily.

Now that's quite enough about that. Just: quietly: husband.

— And your lord and master?

Mrs Breen turned up her two large eyes. Hasn't lost them anyhow.

—O, don't be talking, she said. He's a caution to rattlesnakes. He's in there now with his lawbooks finding out the law of libel. He has me heartscalded. Wait till I show you.

Hot mockturtle vapour and steam of newbaked jampuffs poured out from Harrison's. The heavy noonreek tickled the top of Mr. Bloom's gullet. A barefoot arab stood over the grating breathing in the fumes. Deaden the gnaw of hunger that way,

Opening her handbag, chipped leather. Hatpin: ought to have a guard on those things. Stick it in a chap's eye in the tram. Rummaging. Soiled handkerchief: medicine bottle. What is she? . . . . .

— There must be a new moon out, she said. He's always bad then. Do you know what he did last night?

Her hand ceased to rummage. Her eyes fixed themselves on him, wide in alarm, yet smiling.

— What? Mr Bloom asked.

Let her speak. Look straight in her eyes. I believe you. Trust me.

— Woke me up in the night, she said. Dream he had, a nightmare.

Indiges.

— Said the ace of spades was walking up the stairs.

— The ace of spades! Mr Bloom said .

She took a folded postcard from her handbag.

— Read that, she said. He got it this morning.

— What is it? Mr Bloom asked, taking the card. U. P.?

— U. P: up, she said. Someone taking a rise out of him. It's a great shame for them whoever he is.

— Indeed it is, Mr Bloom said.

She took back the card sighing.

— And now he's going round to Mr Menton's office. He's going to take an action for ten thousand pounds, he says.

She folded the card into her untidy bag and snapped the catch.

Same blue serge dress she had two years ago, the nap bleaching. Seen its best days. Wispish hair over her ears. And that dowdy toque, three old grapes to take the harm out of it. She used to be a smart dresser. Lines round her mouth. Only a year or so older than Molly.

See the eye that woman gave her, passing. Cruel.

He looked still at her, holding back behind his look his discontent. Pungent mockturtle oxtail mulligatawny. I'm hungry too. Flakes of pastry on the gusset of her dress: daub of sugary. flour stuck to her cheek. Josie Powell that was. U. P: up.

Change the subject.

— Do you ever see anything of Mrs. Beaufoy, Mr. Bloom asked.

— Mina Purefoy? she said.

Philip Beaufoy I was thinking. Playgoers' club. Matcham often thinks of the masterstroke. Did I pull the chain?

— Yes.

— I just called to ask on the way in is she over it. She's in the lyingin hospital in Holles street. Dr Horne got her in. She's three days bad now.

— O, Mr Bloom said. I'm sorry to hear that.

— Yes, Mrs Breen said. And a houseful of kids at home. It's a very stiff birth, the nurse told me.

— O, Mr. Bloom said.

His heavy pitying gaze absorbed her news. His tongue clacked in compassion. Dth! Dth!

— I'm sorry to hear that, he said. Poor thing! Three days! That's terrible for her.

Mrs Breen nodded.

— She was taken bad on the Tuesday .....

Mr Bloom touched her funnybone gently, warning her.

— Mind! Let this man pass.

A bony form strode along the curbstone from the river, staring with a rapt gaze into the sunlight through a heavy-stringed glass. Tight as a skullpiece a tiny hat gripped his head.

From his arm a folded dustcoat, a stick and an umbrella dangled to his stride.

— Watch him, Mr. Bloom said. He always walks outside the lampposts. Watch!

— Who is he when he's at home? Mrs Breen asked. Is he dotty?

— His name is Cashel Boyle O'Connor Fitzmaurice Tisdall Farrell, Mr .Bloom said, smiling. Watch!

— He has enough of them, she said. Denis will be like that one of these days.

She broke off suddenly.

— There he is, she said. I must go after him. Goodbye. Remember me to Molly, won't you?

— I will, Mr Bloom said.

He watched her dodge through passers towards the shop-fronts. Denis Breen in skimpy frockcoat and blue canvas shoes shuffled out of Harrison's, hugging two heavy tomes to his ribs. Like old times. He suffered her to overtake him without surprise and thrust his dull grey beard towards her, his loose jaw wagging as he spoke earnestly.

Off his chump.

Mr Bloom walked on again easily, seeing ahead of him in sunlight the tight skullpiece, the dangling stickumbrelladustcoat. Going the two days. Watch him! Out he goes again. And that other old mosey lunatic. Hard time she must have with him.

U. P: up. I'll take my oath that's Alf Bergan or Richie Goulding. Wrote it for a lark in the Scotch house I bet anything. Round to Menton's office. His oyster eyes staring at the postcard. Be a feast for the gods.

He passed the *Irish Times*. There might be other answers lying there. At their lunch now. Clerk with the glasses there doesn't know me. O, let them stay there. Enough bother wading through fortyfour of them. Wanted smart lady typist to aid gentleman in literary work. I called you naughty darling because I do not like that other world. Please tell me what is the meaning. Please tell me what perfume your wife. Tell me who made the world. The way they spring those questions on you. And the other one Lizzie Twigg. My literary efforts have had the good fortune to meet with the approval of the eminent poet A. E. (Mr Geo. Russell). No time to do her hair drinking sloppy tea with a book of poetry.

Best paper by long chalks for a small ad. James Carlisle made that. Six and a half per cent dividend. Cunning old Scotch fox. All the toady news. Our gracious and popular vicereine. Bought the *Irish Field* now. Lady Mountcashel has quite recovered after her confinement and rode out with the Meath hounds. Strong as a brood mare some of those horsey women. Toss off a glass of brandy neat while you'd say knife. That one at the Grosvenor this morning. Up with her on the car: wishswish. Think that pugnosed driver did it out of spite.

Poor Mrs. Purefoy!

He stood at Fleet street crossing. A sixpenny at Rowe's? Must look up that ad in the national library. An eightpenny in the Burton. Better. On my way.

He walked on past Bolton's Westmoreland house. Tea. Tea. Tea. I forgot to tap Tom Kernan.

Sss. Dth, dth, dth! Three days imagine groaning on a bed with a vinegarded handkerchief round her forehead, her belly swollen out. Phew! Dreadful simply! Child's head too big: forceps. Doubled up inside her trying to butt its way out blindly, groping for the way out. Kill me that would. Lucky Molly got over hers lightly. They ought to invent something to stop that. Twilight sleep idea: queen Victoria was given that. Time someone thought about it instead of gassing about the what was it the pensive bosom of the silver effulgence. They could easily have big establishments whole thing quite painless out of all the taxes, give every child born five quid at compound interest up to twentyone five per cent is a hundred shillings and five tiresome pounds multiply by twenty decimal system encourage people to put by money save hundred and ten and a bit twentyone years want to work it out on paper come to a tidy sum more than you think.

Not stillborn of course. They are not even registered. Trouble for nothing.

How flat they look after all of a sudden! Peaceful eyes. Weight off their minds. Old Mrs Thornton was a jolly old soul. Snuffy Dr Brady. People knocking them up at all hours. For God' sake, doctor. Wife in her throes. Then keep them waiting months for their fee. No gratitude in people.

A squad of constables debouched from College street, marching in Indian file. Foodheated faces, sweating helmets, patting their truncheons. After their feed with a good load of fat soup under their belts. They split up into groups and scattered, saluting towards their beats. Let out to graze. A squad of others, marching irregularly, rounded Trinity railings, making for the station. Bound for their troughs. Prepare to receive cavalry. Prepare to receive soup.

He crossed under Tommy Moore's roguish finger. They did right to put him up over a urinal: meeting of the waters. *There is not in this wide world a vallee.* Great song of Julia Morkan's. Kept her voice up to the very last. Pupil of Michael Balfe's, wasn't she?

He gazed after the last broad tunic. Nasty customers to tackle. Jack Power could tell a few tales; father a G man. If a fellow gives them trouble being lagged they let him have it hot and heavy in the bridewell. Can't blame them after all with the job they have. That horsepoliceman the day Joe Chamberlain was given his degree in Trinity he got a run for his money. My word he did! His horses' hoofs clattering after us down Abbey street. Lucky I had the presence of mind to dive into Manning's. He did come a wallop, by George. Must have cracked his skull on the cobblestones. I oughtn't to have got myself swept along with those medicals. All skedaddled. Why he fixed on me. Right here it began.

— Up the Boers!

— Three cheers for De Wet!

— *We'll hang Joe Chamberlain on a sourapple tree.*

Silly billies: mob of young cubc yelling their guts out. Few years time half of them magistrates and civil servants. War comes on: into the army helterskelter: same fellows used to: *whether on the scaffold high.*

Never know who you're talking to. Corny Kelleher he has Harvey Duff in his eye. Like that Peter or Denis or James Carey that blew the gaff on the invincibles. Member of the corporation too. Egging raw youths on to get in the know all the time drawing secret service pay from the castle. Why those plainclothes men are always courting slaveys. Squarepushing up against a backdoor. Maul her a bit. And who is the gentleman does be visiting there? Was the young master saying anything? Peeping Tom through the key hole. Decoy duck. Hotblooded young student fooling round her fat arms ironing.

— Are those yours, Mary?

— I don't wear such things ..... Stop or I'll tell the missus on you. Out half the night.

—There are great times coming, Mary. Wait till you see.

— Ah, golong with your great times coming.

Barmaids too. Tobaccoshopgirls.

James Stephens' idea was the best. He knew them. Circles of ten so that a fellow couldn't inform on more than his own ring. Turnkey's daughter got him out of Richmond, off from Lusk. Putting up in the Buckingham Palace hotel under their very noses. Garibaldi.

You must have a certain fascination: Parnell. Arthur Griffith is a squareheaded fellow but he has no go in him for the mob. Want to gas about our lovely land. Have your daughters inveigling them to your house. Stuff them up with meat and drink. The not far distant day. Homerule sun rising up in the northwest.

His smile faded as he walked, a heavy cloud hiding the sun slowly, shadowing Trinity's surly front. Trams passed one another, ingoing, outgoing, clanging. Useless words. Things go on: same: day after day: squads of police marching out, back: trams in, out. Those two loonies mooching about. Dignam carted off. Mina Purefoy swollen belly on a bed groaning to have a child tugged out of her. One born every second somewhere. Other dying every second. Since I fed the birds five minutes. Three hundred kicked the bucket. Other three hundred born, washing the blood off, all are washed in the blood of the lamb, bawling maaaaaa.

Cityful passing away, other cityful coming, passing away too: other coming on, pasing on. Houses, lines of houses, streets, miles of pavements, piled up bricks, stones. Changing hands. This owner, that. Landlord never dies they say. Other steps into his shoes when he gets his notice to quit. They buy the place up with gold and still they have all the gold. Swindle in it somewhere. Piled up in cities, worn away age after age. Pyramids in sand. Babylon. Big stones left. Rest rubble, sprawling suburbs, jerrybuilt. Kerwan's houses, built of breeze. Shelter for the night.

No-one is anything.

„ This is the very worst hour of the day. Vitality. Dull, gloomy: hate this hour. Feel as if I had been eaten and spewed .

Provost's house. The reverend Dr. Salmon: tinned salmon. Well tinned in there. Wouldn't live in it if they paid me. Hope they have liver and bacon today.

The sun freed itself slowly and lit glints of light among the silverware in Walter Sexton's window opposite by which John Howard Parnell passed, unseeing.

There he is: the brother. Image of him. Haunting face. Now that's a coincidence. Course hundreds of times you think of a person and don't meet him. Like a man walking in his sleep. No-one knows him. Must be a corporation meeting today. They say he never put on the city marshal's uniform since he got the job. Charley Kavanagh used to come out on his high horse, cocked hat, puffed, powdered and shaved. Look at the woebegone walk of him. Great man's brother: his brother's brother. Drop into the D. B. C. probably for his coffee, play chess there. Let them all go to pot. Afraid to pass a remark on him. Freeze them up with that eye of his. That's the fascination: the name. Still David Sheehy beat him for south Meath. Simon Dedalus said when they put him in parliament that Parnell would come back from the grave and lead him out of the house of commons by the arm.

Of the twoheaded octopus, one of whose heads is the head upon which the ends of the world have forgotten to come while the other speaks with a Scotch accent. The tentacles . . . .

They passed from behind Mr. Bloom along the curbstone. Beard and bicycle. Young woman.

And there he is too. Now that's really a coincidence: second time. With the approval of the eminent poet Mr. Geo. Russell. That might be Lizzie Twigg with him. A. E.: What does that mean? Initials perhaps. Albert Edward, Arthur Edmund, Alphonsus Eb Ed El Esquire. What was he saying? The end of the world with a Scotch accent. Tentacles: octopus. Something occult:

symbolism. Holding forth. She's taking it all in. Not saying a word. To aid gentleman in literary work.

His eyes followed the high figure in homespun, beard and bicycle, a listening woman at his side. Coming from the vegetarian. Only wegebobbles and fruit. They say its healthier. Wind and watery though. Tried it. Why do they call that thing they gave me nutsteak? To give you the idea you are eating rumpsteak. Absurd.

Her stockings are loose over her ankles. I detest that: so tasteless. Those literary etereal people they are all. Dreamy, cloudy, symbolistic. Esthetes they are. I wouldn't be surprised if it was that kind of food you see produces the like waves of the brain the poetical. For example one of those policemen sweating Irish stew into their shirts you couldn't squeeze a line of poetry out of him. Don't know what poetry is even. Must be in a certain mood.

The dreamy cloudy gull
Waves o'er the waters dull

He crossed at Nassau street corner and stood before the window of Yeates and Son, pricing the fieldglasses. Or will I drop into old Harris's and have a chat with young Sinclair? Well mannered fellow. Probably at his lunch. Must get those old glasses of mine set right. Goerz lenses seven guineas. Germans making their way everywhere. Sell on easy terms to capture trade. Might chance on a pair in the railway lost property office. Astonishing the things people leave behind them in trains and cloakrooms. What do they be thinking about? Women too. Incredible. There's a little watch up there on the roof of the bank to test those glasses by.

His lids came down on the lower rims of his irises. Can't see it. If you imagine it's there you can almost see it. Can't see it.

He faced about and, standing between the awnings, held out his right hand at arm's length towards the sun. Wanted to try that often. Yes: completely. The tip of his little finger blotted out the sun's disk. Must be the focus where the rays cross. If I had black glasses. Interesting. There was a lot of talk about those sunspots when we were in Lombard street west. Terrific explosions they are. There will be a total eclipse this year: autumn some time.

Now that I come to think of it that ball falls at Greenwich time. It's the clock is worked by an electric wire from Dunsink. Must go out there some first Saturday of the month. If I could get an introduction to professor Joly or learn up something about his family. That would do to: man always feels complimented.

Ah.

His hand fell again to his side.

Never know anything about it. Waste of time. Gasballs spinning about crossing each other, passing. Same old dingdomg always. Gas: then solid: then world: then cold: then dead shell drifting around, frozen rock like that pineapple rock. The moon. Must be a new moon out, she said. I believe there is.

He went on by la maison Claire.

Wait. The full moon was the night we were Sunday fortnight exactly there is a new moon. Walking down by the Tolka. She was humming: *The young May moon she's beaming, love.* He other side of her. Elbow, arm. He. *Glow-worm's lamp is gleaming, love.* Touch. Fingers. Asking . Answer. Yes.

Stop. Stop. If it was it was. Must.

Mr. Bloom, quickbreathing, slowlier walking, passed Adam court.

With a deep quiet relief his eyes took note this is the street here middle of the day Bob Doran's bottle shoulders. On his annual bend, M'Coy said. Up in the Coombe with chummies and streetwalkers and then the rest of the year as sober as a judge,

Yes. Thought so. Sloping into the Empire. Gone. Where Pat Kinsella had his Harp theatre. Broth of a boy Dion Boucicault business with his harvestmoon face in a poky bonnet. *Three Purty Maids from School.* How time flies, eh? Showing long red pantaloons under his skirts. Drinkers, drinking, laughed. More power, Pat. Coarse red: fun for drunkards: guffaw and smoke. His parboiled eyes. Where is he now? Beggar somewhere. The harp that once did starve us all.

I was happier then. Or was that I? Or am I now I? Twenty eight I was. She twentythree. Can't bring back time. Like holding water in your hand. Would you go back to then? Just beginning then. Would you? Are you not happy in your home, you poor little naughty boy? Wants to sew on buttons for me. I must answer. Write it in the library.

Grafton street gay with housed awnings lured his senses. Muslin prints, silkdames and dowagers, jingle of harnesses, hoof-thuds lowringing on the baking causeway. Thick feet that woman had in the white stockings. Countrybred. All the beef to the heels were in . Always gives a woman clumsy feet. Molly looks out of plumb.

He passed, dallying, the windows of Brown Thomas, silk mercers. A tilted urn poured from its mouth a flood of bloodhued poplin: lustrous blood. The huguenots brought that here. *Lacaus esant tara tara.* Great chorus that. *Taree tara.* Must be washed in rainwater. Meyerbeer. *Tara: bom bom bom.*

Pincushions. I'm a long time threatening to buy one. Sticks them all over the place.

He bared slightly his left forearm. Scrape: nearly gone. Not today anyhow. Must go back for that lotion. For her birthday perhaps. Junejulyaugseptember eighth. Nearly three months off. Then she mightn't ilke it. Women won't pick up pins. Say it cuts lo.

Gleaming silks, petticoats on slim brass rails, rays of flat silk stockings.

Useless to go back. Had to be. Tell me all.

High voices. Sunwarm silk. Jingling harnesses. All for a woman, home and houses, silkwebs, silver, rich fruits spicy from Jaffa. Agendath Netaim. Wealth of the world.

A warm human plumpness settled down on his brain. His brain yielded. Perfume of embraces all him assailed. With hungered flesh obscurely he mutely craved to adore.

Duke street. Here we are. Must eat. The Burton. Feel better then.

He turned Combridge's corner, still pursued. Jingling hoofthuds. Perfumed bodies, warm, full. All kissed, yielded: in deep summer fields, tangled pressed grass, in trickling hallways of tenements, along sofas, creaking beds.

— Jack, love!

— Darling!

— Kiss me, Reggie!

— My boy!

— Love!

His heart astir he pushed in the door of the Burton restaurant. Stink gripped his trembling breath: pungent meatjuice, slush of greens.

Men, men, men.

Perched on high stools by the bar, hats shoved back, at the tables calling for more bread no charge, swilling wolfing gobfuls of sloppy food, their eyes bulging, wiping wetted moustaches. A man with an infant's napkin tucked round him spooned gurgling soup down his gullet. A man spitting back on his plate: gristle gums: no teeth to chew it. Chump chop he has. Sad booser's eyes.

— Roast beef and cabbage.

— One stew.

Smells of men. Spaton sawdust, sweetish warmish cigarette smoke, reek of plug, spilt beer, the stale of ferment.

His gorge rose.

Couldn't eat a morsel here. Get out of it.

He gazed round the stooled and tabled eaters, tightening the wings of his nose.

— Two stouts here.

— One corned and cabbage.

That fellow ramming a knifeful of cabbage down. Give me the fidgets to look. Second nature to him. Born with a silver knife in his mouth. That's witty, I think. Or no. Silver means born rich. Born with a knife. But then the allusion is lost.

An illgirt server gathered sticky clattering plates. Rock, the bailiff, standing at the bar blew the foamy crown from his tankard. Well up: it splashed yellow near his boot.

Mr. Bloom raised two fingers doubtfully to his lips. His eyes said:

— Not here. Don't see him.

Out.

He backed towards the door. Get something light in Davy Byrnes'. Keep me going. Had a good breakfast.

— Roast and mashed here.

— Pint of stout.

Every fellow for his own, tooth and nail. Gulp. Grub. Gulp.

He came out into clearer air and turned back towards Grafton street. Eat or be eaten.

Suppose that communal kitchen years to come perhaps. All trotting down with a porringer to be filled John Howard Parnell example the provost of Trinity every mother's son *don't talk of your provosts and provost of Trinity* women and children cabmen priest parsons fieldmarshals archbishops *Father O'Flynn would make hares of them all.* Want a souppot as big as the Phoenix park. Then who'd wash up all the plates and forks? Might be all feeding on tabloids that time. Teeth getting worse and worse.

After all there's a lot in that vebetarian fine flavour of things from the earth garlic of course it stinks Italian organgrinders crisp of onions mushrooms truffles. Pain to the animal too. Wretched brutes there at the cattlemarket waiting for the poleaxe to split their skulls open. Moo. Poor trembling calves. Meh. Staggering bob. Bubble and squeak. Butchers' buckets wobble lights. Give us that brisket off the hook. Plup. Flayed glasseyed sheephung from their haunches, sheepsnouts bloodypapered snivelling nosejam on sawdust. Top and lashers going out. Don't maul them pieces, young one.

Hot fresh blood they prescribe for decline. Insidious. Lick it up smoking-hot. Famished ghosts.

Ah, I'm hungry.

He entered Davy Byrne's.

What will I take now? He drew his watch. Let me see now.

— Hello, Bloom, Nosey Flynn said from his nook.

— Hello, Flynn.

— How's things?

— Tiptop ..... Let me see. I'll take a glass of burgundy and . . . let me see.

Sardines on the shelves. Potted meats. *What is home without Plumtree's potted meat?* Incomplete. What a stupid ad! Under the obituary notices they stuck it. Dignam's potted meat Cannibals would with lemon and rice. White men too salty. Like pickled pork. *With it an abode of bliss.* Lord knows what concoction. Cauls mouldy tripes windpipes faked up. Kosher. Hygiene that was what they call now.

— Have you a cheese sandwich?

— Yes sir.

Like a few olives too if they had them. Good glass of burgundy take away that. A cool salad. Tom Kernan can dress . . .

— Wife well?

— Quite well, thanks . . . . . . A cheese sandwich, then. Gorgonzola, have you?

— Yes, sir.

Nosey Flynn sipped his grog.

— Doing any singing those times? ,

Look at his mouth. Could whistle in his own ear. Flap ears to match. Music. Knows as much about it as my coachman. Still better tell him. Does no harm.

— She's engaged for a big tour end of this month. You may have heard perhaps.

—No. O, that's the style. Who's getting it up?

The curate served.

— How much is that?

— Seven d., sir . . . . . Thank you, sir.

Mr. Bloom cut his sandwich into slender strips.

— Mustard, sir?

— Thank you.

He studded under each lifted strip yellow blobs.

— Getting it up? he said. Well, it's like a company idea, you see. Part shares and part profits.

— Ay, now I remember, Nosey Flynn said, putting his hand in his pocket to scratch his groin. Who is this was telling me? Isn't Blazes Boylan mixed up in it?

A warm shock of air heat of mustard hauched on Mr. Bloom's heart. He raised his eyes and met the stare of a bilious clock. Two. Pub clock five minutes fast. Time going on. Hands moving. Two. Not yet.

His midriff yearned then upward, sank within him, yearned more longly, longingly.

Wine.

He smellsipped the cordial juice and, bidding his throat strongly to speed it, set his wineglass delicately down.

— Yes, he said. He's the organiser in point of fact.

No fear. No brains.

Nosey Flynn snuffled and scratched. Flea having a good square meal.

— He made a tidy bit, Jack Mooney was telling me over that boxing match Myler Keogh won against that soldier in the Portobello barracks. By God he had Myler down in the country Carlow he was telling me . . . .

Hope that dewdrop doesn't come down into his glass. No, snuffled it up.

— For near a month, man, before it came off. Sucking duck eggs by God till further orders. Keep him off the booze, see? O, by God, Blazes is a hairy chap.

Davy Byrne came forward from the hindbar in shirtsleeves, cleaning his lips with two wipes of his napkin. Herring's blush.

— And here's himself and pepper on him, Nosey Flynn said. Can you give us a good one for the Gold cup?

— I'm off that, Mr. Flynn, Davy Byrne answered. I never put anything on a horse.

— You're right there, Nosey Flynn said.

Mr. Bloom ate his strips of sandwich, fresh clean bread, with relish of disgust, pungent mustard the feety savour of green cheese. Sips of his wine soothed his palate.

Nice quiet bar. Nice piece of wood in that counter. Nicely planed. Like the way it curves there.

— I wouldn't do anything at all in that line, Davy Byrne said. It ruined many a man the same horses.

Vintners' sweepstake. Licensed for the sale of beer, wine and spirits for consumption on the premises. Heads I win tails you lose.

— True for you, Nosey Flynn said. Unelss you're in the know. There's no straight sport going now. Lenehan gets some good ones. He's giving *Sceptre* today. *Zinfandel's* the favourite, lord Howard de Walden's, won at Epsom. Morny Cannon is riding him. I could have got seven to one against *Saint Amant* a fortnight before.

— That so? Davy Byrne said . .

He went towards the window and, taking up the pettycash book, scanned its pages.

— I could, faith, Nosey Fylnn said, snuffling. That was a rare bit of horseflesh. She won in a thunderstorm, Rothschild's filly, with wadding in her ears. Bad luck to big Ben Dollard and his *John o' Gaunt*. He put me off it. Ay.

He drank resignedly from his tumbler, running his fingers down the flutes.

— Ay, he said, sighing.

Mr. Bloom, champing standing, looking upon his sigh. Nosey numbskull. Will I tell him that horse Lenehan? He knows already. Better let him forget. Go and lose more. Fool and his money. Dewdrop coming down again. Cold nose he'd have kissing a woman. Still they might like. Prickly beards they like. Dogs' cold noses. Old Mrs. Riordan with the rumbling stomach's Skye terrier in the City Arms hotel. Molly fondling him in her lap. O the big doggybowwowsywowsy!

Wine soaked and softened rolled pith of bread mustard a moment mawkish cheese. Nice wine it is. Taste it better because I'm not thirsty. Bath of course does that. Just a light snack. Then about six o'clock I can. Six, six. Time will be gone then. She . . .

Mild fire of wine kindled his veins. I wanted that badly. Felt so off colour. His eyes unhungrily saw shelves of tins, sardines, gaudy lobsters' claws. All the odd things people pick up for food. Out of shells, periwinkles with a pin, off trees, snails out of the ground the French eat, out of the sea with bait on a hook. Silly fish learn nothing in a thousand years. If you didn't know risky thing putting anything into your mouth. Poisonous berries. One fellow told another and so on. Try it on the dog first. Led on by the smell or the look. Instinct. Orangegroves for instance. Need artificial irrigation. Bleibtreustrasse. Yes but what about oysters. Unsightly like a clot of phlegm. Filthy shells. Devil to open them too. Who found them out? Garbage, sewage they feed on. Fizz and Red bank oysters. Effect on the sexual. Aphrodis. He was in the

Red bank this morning. Was he oysters old fish at table perhaps he young flesh in bed no June has no "r" no oysters. But there are people like tainted game that archduke Leopold was it, no, yes, or was it Otto one of those Habsbourgs, of course aristocrats, then the others copy to be in the fashion. Half the catch of oysters they throw back in the sea to keep up the price. Cheap no-one would buy. Caviare. Do the grand. Hock in green glasses. Swell blow out. Lady this. Powdered bosom pearls. May I tempt you to a little more filleted sole, miss Dubedat? Yes, do bedad. And she did bedad. Huguenot name I expect that. A miss Dubedat lived in Killiney I remember. Du de la French. Still it's the same fish perhaps old Mickey Hanlon of Moore street ripped the guts out of making money hand over fist finger in fishes' gills can't write his name on a cheque think he was painting the landscape with his mouth twisted Moooikill Aitcha Ha ignorant as a kish of brogues worth fifty thousand pounds.

Stuck on the pane two flies buzzed, stuck.

Glowing wine on his palate lingered swallowed. Crushing in the winespress grapes of Burgundy. Sun's heat it is. Seems to a secret touch telling me memory. Touched his sense moistened remembered. Hidden under wild ferns on Howth below us bay sleeping: sky. No sound. The sky. The bay purple by the Lion's head. Pillowed on my coat she had her hair earwigs in the heather scrub my hand under her nape you'll toss me all. O wonder! Coolsoft with ointments her hand touched me, caressed: her eyes upon me did not turn away. Ravished over her I lay full lips full open kissed her mouth. Yum. Softly she gave me in my mouth the seedcake warm and chewed. Mawkish pulp her mouth had mumbled sweet and sour with spittle. Joy: I ate it: joy. Young life, her lips that gave me pouting. Soft warm sticky gumjelly lips. Flowers her eyes were take me willing eyes. Pebbles fell. She lay still. A goat. No-one. High on Ben Howth rhododendrons a nannygoat walking surefooted, dropping currants. Screened under ferns she laughed warm folded. Wildly I lay on her, kissed her: eyes, her lips, her stretched neck beating, woman's breasts full in her blouse of nun's veiling, fat nipples upright. Hot I tongued her. She kissed me. I was kissed. All yielding she tossed my hair. Kissed, she kissed me.

Me. And me now.

Stuck, the flies buzzed.

His downcast eyes followed the silent veining of the oaken slab. Beauty: it curves: curves are beauty. Shapely goddesses, Venus, Juno: curves the world admires. Can see them museum library standing in the round hall, naked goddesses. They don't care what man looks. All to see. Never speaking. I mean to say to fellows like Flynn. Quaffing nectar at mess with gods golden dishes all ambrosial. Not like a tanner lunch we have, boiled mutton carrots and turnips bottle of Allsop. Nectar imagine it drinking electricity: god's food. Lovely forms of woman Junonian. Immortal lovely. And we stuffing food in one hole and out behind. They have no. Never looked. I'll look today. Keeper won't see. Bend down let some thing fall see if she.

Dribbling a quiet message from his bladder came. A man and ready he drained his glass to the lees and walked to men too they gave themselves manly conscious lay with men lovers a youth enjoyed her to the yard.

When the sound of his boots had ceased Davy Byrne said from his book:

— What is this he is? Isn't he in the insurance line?

— He's out of that long ago, Nosey Flynn said. He does canvassing for the *Freeman*.

— I know him well to see, Davy Byrne said. Is he in trouble?

— Trouble? Nosey Flynn said. Not that I heard of. Why?

— I noticed he was in mourning.

— Was he? Nosey Flynn said. So he was, faith. I asked him how was all at home. You're right, by God. So he was.

— I never broach the subject, Davy Byrne said humanely, if I see a gentleman is in trouble that way. It only brings it up fresh in their minds.

— It's not the wife anyhow, Nosey Flynn said. I met him the day before yesterday and he coming out of that Irish farm dairy John Wyse Nolan's wife has in Henry street with a jar of cream in his hand taking it home to his better half. She's well nourished, I tell you. Plovers on toast.

— And is he doing for the *Freeman?* Davy Byrne said.

Nosey Flynn pursed his lips.

— He doesn't buy cream on the ads he picks up. You may take that from me.

— How so? Davy Byrne asked, coming from his book.

Nosey Flynn made swift passes in the air with juggling fingers. He winked.

— He's in the craft, he said.

— Do you tell me so? Davy Byrne said.

— Very much so, Nosey Flynn said. Ancient free and accepted order. Light, life and love, by God. They give him a leg up. I was told that by a — well, I won't say who.

— Is that a fact?

— O, it's a fine order, Nosey Flynn said. They stick to you when you're down. I know a fellow was trying to get into it but they're as close as damn it. By God they did right to keep the women out of it.

Davy Byrne smiledyawnednodded all in one:

— Iiiiichaaaaaaach!

— There was one woman, Nosey Flynn said, hid herself in a clock to find out what they do be doing. But be damned but they smelt her out and swore her in on the spot a master mason. That was one of the Saint Legers of Doneraile.

Davy Byrne, sated after his yawn, said with tearwashed eyes.

— And is that a fact? Decent quiet man he is. I often saw him in here and I never once saw him — you know, over the line.

—God Almighty couldn't make him drunk, Nosey Flynn said firmly. Slips off when the fun gets too hot. Didn't you see him look at his watch? Ah, you weren't there. If you ask him to have a drink first thing he does he outs with the watch to see what he ought to imbibe. Declare to God he does.

— There are some like that, Davy Byrne said. He's a safe man, I'd say.

— He's not too bad, Nosey Flynn said, snuffling it up. He has been known to put his hand down too to help a fellow. Give the devil his due. O, Bloom has his good points. But there's one thing he'll never do.

His hand scrawled a dry pen signature beside his grog.

— I know, Davy Byrne said

— Nothing in black and white, Nosey Flynn said .

Paddy Leonard and Bantam Lyons came in. Tom Rochford followed, a plaining hand on his claret waistcoat.

— Day, Mr. Byrne.

— Day, gentlemen.

They paused at the counter.

— Who's standing? Paddy Leonard asked.

— I'm sitting anyhow, Nosey Flynn answered.

— Well, what'll it be? Paddy Leonard asked.

— I'll take a stone ginger, Bantam Lyons said.

— How much? Paddy Leonard cried. Since when, for God' sake? What's yours, Tom?

— How is the main drainage? Nosey Flynn asked, sipping.

For answer Tom Rochford pressed his hand to his breastbone and hiccoughed.

— Would I trouble you for a glass of fresh water, Mr. Byrne? he said.

— Certainly, sir.

Paddy Leonard eyed his alemates.

— Lord love a duck, he said, look at what I'm standing drinks to! Cold water and gingerpop! Two fellows that would suck whisky off a sore leg. He has some bloody horse up his sleeve for the Gold cup. A dead snip.

— Zinfandel is it? Nosey Flynn asked.

Tom Rochford spilt powder from a twisted paper into the water set before him.

— That cursed dyspepsia, he said before drinking.

— Breadsoda is very good, Davy Byrne said.

Tom Rochford nodded and drank.

— Is it *Zinfandel?*

— Say nothing, Bantam Lyons winked. I'm going to plunge five bob on my own.

— Tell us and be damned to you, Paddy Leonard said. Who gave it to you?

Mr Bloom on his way out raised three fingers in greeting.

— So long, Nosey Flynn said.

The others turned.

— That's the man now that gave it to me, Bantam Lyons whispered.

— Prrwht! Paddy Leonard said with scorn. Mr. Byrne, sir, we'll take two of your small Jamesons after that and a . . . . .

— Stone ginger, Davy Byrne added civilly.

— Ay, Paddy Leonard said. A suckingbottle for the baby.

(*to be continued*)

Episode VIII (continued)

THE LITTLE REVIEW

THE MAGAZINE THAT IS READ BY THOSE WHO WRITE THE OTHERS

FEBRUARY-MARCH, 1919

MARGARET ANDERSON, Editor
EZRA POUND, London Editor
JULES ROMAINS, French Editor

24 *West Sixteenth Street, New York*

Foreign office:
5 *Holland Place Chambers, London W. 8.*

25c. a copy; $2.50 a year. English 12/- a year.
Abonnement fr. 15 par an.

Entered as second-class matter March 16, 1917, at P. O., New York, N. Y., under the act March 3, 1879.

Published monthly by Margaret Anderson

Mr. Bloom walked towards Dawson street, his tongue brushing his teeth smooth. Something green it would have to be: spinach say. Then with those Röntgen rays searchlight you could.

At Duke lane a terrier choked up a sick knuckly cud on the cobblestones and lapped it with new zest. Mr. Bloom coasted warily. Ruminants. Wonder if Tom Rochford will do anything with that invention of his. Wasting time explaining it to Flynn's mouth. Lean people long mouths. Ought to be a hall or a place where inventors could go in and invent free. Course then you'd have all the cranks pestering.

He hummed, prolonging in solemn echo, the closes of the bars:

— *Don Giovanni, a cenar teco*

M' invitasti.

Feel better. Burgundy. Good pick me up. Who distilled first? Some chap in the blues. Dutch courage. That *Kilkenny People* in the national library now I must.

Bare clean closestools, waiting, in the window of William Miller, plumber, turned back his thoughts. They could: and watch it all the way down changing biliary duct spleen squirting liver gastric juice coils of intestines like pipes. But the poor buffer would have to stand all the time with his insides entrails on show. Science.

— *A cenar teco.*

What does that *teco* mean? Tonight perhaps.

— *Don Giovanni, thou hast me invited*

To come to supper tonight

The rum the rumdum,

Doesn't go properly.

Keyes: two months if I get Nannetti to. That'll be two pounds ten about two pounds eight. Three Hynes owes me. Two eleven. Presscott's dyeworks van over there. If I get Billy Presscott's ad. Two fifteen. Five guineas about. On the pig's back.

Could buy one of those silk petticoats for Molly, colour of her new garters.

Today. Today. Not think.

Tour the south then. What about English wateringplaces? Brighton, Margate. Piers by moonlight. Her voice floating out. *Those lovely seaside girls.*

He turned at Gray's confectioner's window of unbought tarts and passed

Overleaf: table of contents, *Little Review,* February–March 1919

the reverend Thomas Connellan's bookstore. *Why I left the church of Rome.* Bird's nest women run him. They say they used to give pauper children soup to change to protestants. *Why we left the church of Rome.*

A blind stripling stood tapping the curbstone with his slender cane. No tram in sight. Wants to cross .

— Do you want to cross? Mr. Bloom asked.

The blind stripling did not answer. His wallface frowned weakly. He moved his head uncertainly.

— You're in Dawson street, Mr Bloom said. Molesworth street is opposite. Do you want to cross? There's nothing in the way.

The cane moved out trembling to the left. Mr. Bloom's eye followed its line and saw again the dye works' van drawn up before Drago's. Where I saw his brillantined hair just when I was. Horse drooping. Driver in John Long's. Slaking his draught.

— There's a van there, Mr. Bloom said, but it's not moving. I'll see you across. Do you want to go to Molesworth street?

— Yes, the stripling answered. South Frederick street.

— Come, Mr. Bloom said.

He touched the thin elbow gently: then took the limp seeing hand to guide it forward.

Say something to him. Better not do the condescending. Pass a remark.

— The rain kept off.

No answer.

Stains on his coat. Slobbers his food I suppose. Like a child's hand his hand. Like Milly's was. Sensitive. Sizing me up I daresay from my hand. Van. Keep his cane clear of the horse's legs: tired drudge get his doze. That's right. Clear. Behind a bull: in front of a horse.

— Thanks, sir.

Knows I'm a man. Voice.

— Right now? First turn to the left.

The blind stripling tapped the curbstone and went on his way, drawing his cane back, feeling again.

Mr. Bloom walked behind him. Poor young fellow! How on earth did he know that van was there? Must have felt it. See things in their foreheads perhaps. Kind of sense of volume. Weight or size of it, something blacker than the dark. Wonder would he feel it if something was removed. Feel a gap. Queer idea of Dublin he must have, tapping his way round by the stones. Could he walk in a beeline if he hadn't that cane? Bloodless pious face like a fellow going in to be a priest.

Penrose! That was that chap's name.

Look at all the things they can learn to do. Read with their fingers. Tune pianos. Of course the other senses are more. Embroider. Plait baskets. People ought to help. Work basket I could buy Molly's birthday. Hates sewing. Might take an objection. Dark men they call them.

Sense of smell must be stronger too. Smells on all sides bunched together. Each street different smell. Each person too. Then the spring, the summer: smells. Tastes. They say you can't taste wines with your eyes shut. Also smoke in the dark they say get no pleasure.

And with a woman, for instance. Must be strange not to see her. Kind of a form in his mind's eye. The voice temperature when he touches her with his fingers must almost see the lines, the curves. His hands on her hair, for instance. Say it was black for instance. Good. We call it black. Then passing over her white skin. Different feel perhaps. Feeling of white.

Postoffice. Must answer. Fag today. Send her a postal order two shillings half a crown. Accept my little present. Stationer's just here too. Wait. Think over it.

With a gentle finger he felt ever so slowly the hair combed back above his ears. Again. Fibres of fine fine straw. Then gently his finger felt the skin of his right cheek. Dawny hair there too. Not smooth enough. The belly is the smoothest. No-one about. There he goes into Frederick street. Perhaps to Levenston's dancing academy: piano. Might be settling my braces.

Walking by Doran's publichouse he slid his hand between waistcoat and trousers and, pulling aside his shirt gently, felt a slack fold of his belly. But I know it's whitey yellow. Want to try in the dark to see.

He withdrew his hand and pulled his dress to.

Poor fellow! Quite a boy. Terrible. Really terrible. Where is the justice being born that way. All those women and children excursion beanfeast burned and drowned in New York, Holocaust. Karma they call that transmigration for sins you did in a past life the reincarnation met him pikehoses. Dear, dear, dear. Pity of course: but somehow you can't cotton on to them someway.

Sir Frederick Falkiner going into the freemason's hall. Solemn as Troy. After his good lunch in Earlsfort terrace. I suppose he'd turn up his nose at that wine I drank. Has his own ideas of justice in the recorder's court. Wellmeaning old man. Police chargesheets crammed with cases get their percentage manufacturing crime. Sends them to the rightabout. The devil on moneylenders. Gave Reuben J. a great strawcalling. Now he's really what they call a dirty jew. Power those judges have. Grumpy old topers in wigs. And may the Lord have mercy on your soul.

Hello placard. Mirus bazaar. His excellency the lord lieutenant. Sixteenth. Today it is. In aid of funds for Mercer's hospital. The *Messiah* was first given for that. Yes. Handel. What about going out there. Ballsbridge. Drop in on Keyes. No use sticking to him like a leech. Sure to know someone on the gate.

Mr Bloom came to Kildare street. First I must. Library.

Straw hat in sunlight. Tan shoes. Turnedup trousers. It is. It is.

His heart quopped softly. To the right. Museum. Goddesses. He swerved to the right.

Is it? Almost certain. Won't look. Wine in my face. Why did I? Yes, it is. The walk. Not see. Not see. Get on.

Making for the museum gate with long windy strides he lifted his eyes. Handsome building. Sir Thomas Deane designed. Not following me?

Didn't see me perhaps. Light in his eyes.

The flutter of his breath came forth in short sighs. Quick. Cold statues: quiet there. Safe in a minute.

No didn't see me. After two. Just at the gate.

My heart!

His eyes beating looked steadfastly at cream curves of stone. Sir homas Deane was the Greek architecture.

Look for something I.

His hasty hand went quick into a pocket, took out, read unfolded Agendath Netaim. Where did I?

Busy looking for.

He thrust back quickly Agendath.

Afternoon she said.

I am looking for that. Yes, that. Try all pockets. Handker. *Freeman*. Where did I? Ah, yes. Trousers. Potato. Purse. Where?

Hurry. Walk quietly. Moment more. My heart.

His hand looking for the where did I put found in his hip pocket soap lotion have to call tepid paper stuck. Ah soap there I yes. Gate.

Safe!

(to be continued)

Episode IX

THE LITTLE REVIEW

THE MAGAZINE THAT IS READ BY THOSE WHO WRITE THE OTHERS

Vol. V. APRIL 1919 No. 11.

MARGARET ANDERSON, **Editor**
EZRA POUND, **London Editor**
JULES ROMAINS, **French Editor**
24 *West Sixteenth Street, New York*
Foreign office:
5 *Holland Place Chambers, London W. 8.*

25c. a copy; $2.50 a year. English 12/- a year.
Abonnement fr. 15 par an.

Entered as second-class matter March 16, 1917, at P. O., New York, N. Y., under the act March 3, 1879.
Published monthly by Margaret Anderson

URBANE, to comfort them, the quaker librarian purred:

— And we have, have we not, those priceless pages of "Wilhelm Meister"? A great poet on a great brother poet. A hesitating soul taking arms against a sea of troubles, torn by conflicting doubts, as one sees in real life.

He came a step, a sinkapace, forward on neatsleather creaking and a step backward a sinkapace on the solemn floor.

A noiseless attendant, setting open the door but slightly made him a noiseless beck.

Directly, said he, creaking to go, albeit lingering. The beautiful ineffectual dreamer who comes to grief against hard facts. One always feels that Goethe's judgments are so true. True in the larger analysis.

Twicreakingly analysis he corantoed off. Bald, most zealous by the door he gave his large ear all to the attendant's words: heard them: and was gone.

Two left.

— Monsieur de la Palice, Stephen sneered, was alive fifteen minutes before his death.

— Have you found those six brave medicals, John Eglinton asked with elder's gall, to write Paradise Lost at your dictation?

Smile. Smile Cranly's smile.

First he tickled her
Then he patted her
Then he passed the female catheter
For he was a medical
Jolly old medi. . . . .

I feel you would need one more for Hamlet. Seven is dear to the mystic mind. The shining seven W. B. calls them.

Glittereyed, his rufous skull close to his greencapped desklamp sought the face, bearded amid darkgreener shadow, an ollav, holyeyed. He laughed low: a sizar's laugh of Trinty: unanswered.

Orchestral Satan, weeping many a rood
Tears such as angels weep.
Ed egli avea del cul fatto trombetta.
He holds my follies hostage.

Cranly's eleven true Wicklowmen to free their sireland. Gaptoothed Kath-

Facing page: table of contents, *Little Review,* April 1919 (mistakenly identified as issue 5.11 instead of 5.12)

leen, her four beautiful green fields, the stranger in her house. And one more to hail him: *ave, rabbi*. The Tinahely twelve. In the shadow of the glen he cooes for them. My soul's youth I gave him, night by night. Godspeed. Good hunting.

Mulligan has my telegram.

Folly. Persist.

— Our young Irish bards, John Eglinton censured, have yet to create a figure which the world will set beside Saxon Shakespeare's Hamlet though I admire him, as old Ben did, on this side idolatry

— All these questions are purely academic, Russell oracled out of his shadow. I mean, whether Hamlet is Shakespeare or James I or Essex. Clergyman's discussions of the historicity of Jesus. Art has to reveal to us ideas, formless spiritual essences. The supreme question about a work of art is out of how deep a life does it spring. The painting of Gustave Moreau is the painting of ideas. The deepest poetry of Shelley, the words of Hamlet bring our mind into contact with the eternal wisdom, Plato's world of ideas. All the rest is the speculation of schoolboys for schoolboys.

A. E. has been telling some interviewer. Wall, tarnation strike me!

— The schoolmen were schoolboys first, Stephen said superpolitely. Aristotle was once Plato's schoolboy.

— And has remained so, one should hope, John Eglinton sedately said. One can see him, a model schoolboy with his diploma under his arm.

He laughed again at the now smiling bearded face.

Formless spiritual. Father, Son and Holy Breath. This verily is that. I am the fire upon the altar. I am the sacrificial butter.

Dunlop, Judge, the noblest Roman of them all, A. E., Arval in heaven hight, K. H, their master. Adepts of the great white lodge always watching to see if they can help. The Christ with the bridesister, moisture of light, born of a virgin, repentant sophia, departed to the plane of buddhi. Mrs. Cooper Oakley once glimpsed our very illustrious sister H. P. B's elemental.

O, fie! Out on't! *Pfuiteufel!* You naughtn't to look, missus, so you naugh't when a lady's ashowing of her elemental.

Mr. Best entered, tall, young, mild, light. He bore in his hand with grace a notebook, new, large, clean, bright.

— That model schoolboy, Stephen said, would find Hamlet's musings about the afterlife of his princely soul, the improbable, insignificant and undramatic monologue, as shallow as Plato's.

John Eglinton, frowning, said, waxing wroth:

— Upon my word it makes my blood boil to hear anyone compare Aristotle with Plato.

— Which of the two, Stephen asked, would have banished me from his commonwealth?

Unsheathe your dagger definitions. Streams of tendency and eons they worship. God: noise in the street: very peripatetic. Space: what you damn well have to see. Through spaces smaller than red globules of man's blood they creepycrawl after Blake's buttocks into eternity of which this vegetable world is but a shadow. Hold to the now, the here, through which all future plunges to the past.

Mr. Best came forward, amiable, towards his colleague.

— Haines is gone, he said.

— Is he?

— I was showing him Jubainville's book. He's quite enthusiastic, don't you know, about Hyde's "Lovesongs of Connacht." I couldn't bring him in to hear the discussion. He's gone to Gill's to buy it.

Bound thee forth, my booklet, quick
To greet the callous public
Writ, I ween, 'twas not my wish
In lean unlovely English.

— The peatsmoke is going to his head, John Eglinton opined.

We feel in England. Penitent thief. Gone. I smoked his baccy. Green twinkling stone. An emerald set in the ring of the sea.

— People do not know how dangerous lovesongs can be, the auric egg of Russell warned occultly. The movements which work revolutions in the world are born out of the dreams and visions in a peasant's heart on the hillside. For them the earth is not an exploitable ground but the living mother. The rarefied air of the academy and the arena produce the sixshilling novel, the musichall song. France produces the finest flower of corruption in Mallarmé but the desirable life is revealed only to the poor of heart, the life of Homer's Phaeacians.

From these words Mr. Best turned an unoffending face to Stephen.

— Mallarmé, don't you know, he said, has written those wonderful prose poems Stephen MacKenna used to read to me in Paris. The one about "Hamlet". He says: *il se promène, lisaut au livre de luimême*, don't you know, reading the book of himself. He describes "Hamlet" given in a French town, don't you know, a provincial town. They advertised it.

His free hand graciously wrote tiny signs in air.

Hamlet
ou
Le Distrait
pièce de Shakespeare

He repeated to John Eglinton's newgathered frown:

— *Pièce de Shakespeare.* don't you know. It's so French, the French point of view. *Hamlet ou.....*

— The absentminded beggar, Stephen ended.

John Eglinton laughed.

— Yes, I suppose it would be, he said. Excellent people, no doubt, but distressingly shortsighted in some matters.

Sumptuous and stagnant exaggeration of murder.

— A deathsman of the soul Robert Greene called him, Stephen said. Not for nothing was he a butcher's son, wielding the sledded pole-axe and spitting in his palm. Nine lives are taken off for his father's one, Our Father who art in purgatory. Khaki Hamlets don't hesitate to shoot. The shambles in act five is a forecast of the concentration camp sung by Mr. Swinburne.

Cranly, I his mute orderly, following battles from afar.

Whelps and dams of murderous foes whom none
But we had spared....

— He will have it that "Hamlet" is a ghost story, John Eglinton said for Mr. Best's behoof. Like the fat boy in Pickwick he wants to make our flesh creep.

List! List! O list!
My flesh hears him creeping, hears.
If thou didst ever........

— What is a ghost? Stephen said with tingling energy. One who has faded into impalpability through death, through absence, through change of manners. Elizabethan London lay as far from Stratford as corrupt Paris lies from virgin Dublin. Who is the ghost, returning to the world that has forgotten him? Who is king Hamlet?

John Eglinton shifted his spare body, leaning back to judge.

Lifted.

— It is this hour of a June day, Stephen said, begging with a swift glance their hearing. The flag is up on the playhouse by the bankside. The bear Sackerson growls in the pit near it, Paris garden. Canvasclimbers who sailed with Drake chew their sausages among the groundlings.

Local colour. Work in all you know. Make them accomplices.

— Shakespeare has left the huguenot's house in Silver street and walks by the swanmews along the riverbank. But he does not stay to feed the pen chivying her game of cygnets towards the rushes. The swan of Avon has other thoughts.

Composition of place. Ignatius Loyola, make haste to help me!

— The play begins. A player comes on under the shadow, clad in the cast-off mail of a court buck, a wellset man with a bass voice. He is the ghost king Hamlet, and the player Shakespeare. He speaks the words to Burbage, the young player who stands before him, calling him by a name:

Hamlet, I am thy father's spirit

bidding him list. To a son he speaks, the son of his soul, the prince, young Hamlet and to the son of his body, Hamlet Shakespeare who has died in Stratford that his namesake may live for ever.

Is it possible that that player Shakespeare, a ghost by absence, and in the vesture of buried Denmark, a ghost by death, speaking his own words to his own son's name (had Hamlet Shakespeare lived he would have been prince Hamlet's twin) is it possible, I want to know, or probable that he did not draw or foresee the logical conclusion of those premises: you are this dispossessed son. I am the murdered father: your mother is the guilty queen, Ann Shakespeare, born Hathaway?

— But this prying into the family life of a great man, Russell began impatiently.

Art thou there, truepenny?

—Interesting only to the parish clerk. I mean, we have the plays. I mean when we read the poetry of "King Lear" what is it to us how the poet lived? As for living our servants can do that for us, Villiers de l'Isle said. Peeping and prying into greenroom gossip of the day, the poet's drinking, the poet's debts. We have "King Lear": and it is immortal.

Mr. Best's face appealed to, agreed.

Flow over them with your waves and with your waters, Mananaan, Mananaan MacLir. . . . .

By the way, that pound he lent you when you were hungry?

I wanted it.

Take thou this noble.

You spent most of it in . . . .

Do you intend to pay it back?

O, yes.

When? Now?

Well. . . no.

When, then?

I paid my way. I paid my way.

Steady on. He's from north of Boyne water. You owe it.

Wait. Five months. Molecules all change. I am other I now. Other I got pound.

Buzz. Buzz.

But I, entelechy, form of forms, am I by memory under ever changing forms.

I that sinned and prayed and fasted.

A child Conmee saved from pandies.

I, I and I. I.

A. E. I. O. U.

— Do you mean to fly in the face of the tradition of three centuries? John Eglinton's carping voice asked. Her ghost at least has been laid for ever. She died, for literature at least, before she was born.

— She died, Stephen retorted, sixtyseven years after she was born. She saw him into and out of the world. She took his first embraces. She bore his children and she laid pennies on his eyes to keep his eyelids closed when he lay on his deathbed.

Mother's deathbed. Candle. The sheeted mirror. Who brought me into this world lies there, bronzelidded, under few cheap flowers. *Liliata rutilantium.*

I wept alone.

John Eglinton looked in the tangled glowworm of his lamp.

— The world believes that Shakespeare made a mistake, he said, and got out of it as quickly and as best he could.

— Bosh! Stephen said rudely. A man of genius makes no mistakes. His errors are volitional and are the portals of discovery.

Portal of discovery opened to let in the quaker librarian, softcreakedfooted, bald, eared and assiduous.

— A shrew, John Eglinton said shrewdly, is not a useful portal of discovery, one should imagine. What useful discovery did Socrates learn from Xanthippe?

— Dialectic, Stephen answered: and from his mother how to bring thought into the world. But neither the midwife's lore nor the caudlelectures saved him from the archons of Sinn Fein and their naggin of hemlock.

— But Ann Hathaway? Mr. Best's quiet voice said forgetfully. Yes, we seem to be forgetting her as Shakespeare himself forgot her.

His look went from brooder's beard to carper's skull, to remind, to chide them not unkindly, then to the baldpink lollard costard, guiltless though maligned.

— He had a good groatsworth of wit, Stephen said, and no truant memory. He carried a memory in his wallet as he trudged to Romeville whistling *The girl I left behind me*. If the earthquake did not time it we should know where to place poor Wat, sitting in his form, the studded bridle and her blue windows. That memory, *Venus and Adonis,* lay in the bedchamber of every light-of-love in London. Is Katherine the shrew ill favored? Hortensio calls her young and beautiful. Do you think the writer of "Anthony and Cleopatra," a passionate pilgrim, had his eyes in the back of his head that he chose the ugliest doxy in all Warwickshire to lie withal? Good: he left her and gained the world of men. But his boywomen are the women of a boy. Their life, thought, speech are lent them by males. He chose badly? He was chosen, it seems to me. If others have their will Ann hath a way. By cock, she was to blame. She put the comether on him, sweet and twentysix. The goddess who bends over the boy Adonis is a boldfaced Stratford wench who tumbles in a cornfield a lover younger than herself.

And my turn? When?

Come!

— Ryefield, Mr. Best said brightly, gladly, raising his new book, gladly, brightly.

He murmured then with blond delight for all:

Between the acres of the rye
These pretty countryfolk would lie.

Paris: the wellpleased pleaser.

A tall figure in bearded homespun rose from shadow and unveiled its cooperative watch.

— I am afraid I am due at the Homestead.

Whither away? Exploitable ground.

— Are you going, John Eglinton's eyebrows asked. Shall we see you at Moore's tonight? Piper is coming.

— Piper! Mr. Best piped. Is Piper back?

Peter Piper pecked a peck of pick of peck of pickled pepper.

— I don't know if I can. Thursday. We have our meeting. If I can get away in time.

Yogibogeybox in Dawson chambers. "Isis Unveiled." Their Palibook we tried to pawn. Crosslegged under an umbrel umbershoot he thrones an Aztec logos, functioning on astral levels, mahamahatma. The faithful hermetists await the light, ringroundabout him. Louis H. Victory. T. Caulfield Irwin. Lotus ladies tend them i' the eyes, their pineal glands aglow. Filled with his god he thrones, Buddha under plantain. Gulfer of souls, engulfer. Hesouls, shesouls, shoals of souls. Engulfed with wailing creecries, whirled, whirling, they bewail.

In quintessential triviality
For years in this fleshcase a shesoul dwelt.

— They say we are to have a literary surprise, the quaker librarian said, friendly and earnest. Mr. Russell, rumour has it, is gathering together a sheaf of our younger poets' verses. We are all looking forward anxiously.

Anxiously he glanced in the cone of lamplight where three faces, lighted, shone.

See this. Remember.

Stephen looked down on a wide headless caubeen, hung on his ashplant-handle over his knee. My casque and sword.

Listen.

Young Colum and Starkey. George Roberts is doing the commercial part. Longworth will give it a good puff in the *Express*.. O, will he? I like Colum's drover. Yes, I think he has that queer thing, genius. Do you think he has genius really? Yeats admired h's line. *As in wild earth a Grecian vase*. Did he? I hope you'll be able to come tonight. Malachi Mulligan is coming too. Moore asked him to bring Haines. Did you hear Miss Mitchell's joke about Moore and Martyn? That Moore is Martyn's wild oats? Awfully clever, isn't it? They remind one of don Quixote and Sancho Panza. Our national epic has yet to be written. Moore is the man for it. A knight of the rueful countenance here in Dublin. With a saffron kilt? O'Neill Russell? O, yes, he must speak the grand old tongue. And his Dulcinea? James Stephens is doing some clever sketches. We are becoming important, it seems.

Cordelia. *Cordoglio*. Lir's loniest daughter.

Now your best French polish.

— Thank you very much, Mr. Russell, Stephen said, rising. If you will be so kind as to give the letter to Mr. Norman.....

—O, yes. If he considers it important it will go in. We have so much correspondence.

— I understand, Stephen said. Thank you.

The pigs' paper. Bullockbefriending.

Synge has promised me an article for Dana too. Are we going to be read? I feel we are. The Gaelic league wants something in Irish. I hope you will come round tonight. Bring Starkey.

Stephen sat down.

The quaker librarian came from the leavetakers. Blushing his mask said:

— Mr. Dedalus, your views are most illuminating.

He creaked to and fro, tiptoing up nearer heaven by the altitude of a chopine, and, covered by the noise of outgoing, said low:

— Is it your view, then, that she was not faithful to the poet?

Alarmed face asks me. Why did he come? Courtesy or an inward light?

— Where there is a reconciliation, Stephen said, there must have been first a sundering.

— Yes.

Christfox in leather trews, hiding, a runaway in blighted treeforks from hue and cry. Knowing no vixen, walking lonely in the chase. Women he won to him, tender people, a whore of Babylon, ladies of justices, bully tapsters' wives. Fox and geese. And in New place a slack dishonoured body that once was comely, once as sweet, as fresh as cinnamon, now her leaves falling, all bare, frighted of the narrow grave and unforgiven.

— Yes. So you think.....

The door closed behind the outgoer.

Rest, suddenly possessed the discreet vaulted cell, rest of warm and brooding air.

A vestal's lamp.

Here he ponders things that were not: what Caesar would have lived to do had he believed the soothsayer: what might have been: possibilities of the possible as possible: things not known: what name Achilles bore when he lived among women.

Coffined thoughts around me, in mummycases, embalmed in spice of words. Thoth, god of libraries, a birdgod, moonycrowned. And I heard the voice of that Egyptian highpriest. *In painted chambers loaded with tilebooks.*

They are still. Once quick in the brains of men. Still: but an itch of death is in them, to tell me in my ear a maudlin tale, urge me to wreaktheirwill

— Certanly, John Eglinton mused, of all great men he is the most enigmatic. We know nothing but that he lived and suffered. Not even so much. Others abide our question. A shadow hangs over all the rest.

— But "Hamlet" is so personal, isn't it — Mr. Best pleaded. I mean a kind of private paper, don't you know, of his private life. I mean I don't care a button, don't you know, who is killed or who is guilty.....

He rested an innocent book on the edge of the desk, smiling his defiance. His private papers. *Ta an bad ar an tir. .Taim imo shagart.* Put *beurla* on it, littlejohn.

Quoth littlejohn Eglinton:

— I was prepared for paradoxes from what Malachi Mulligan told us but I may as well warn you that if you want to shake my belief that Shakespeare is Hamlet you have a stern task before you.

Bear with me.

Stephen withstood the bane of miscreant eyes, glinting stern under wrinkling brows. A basilisk. *E quando vede l'uomo l'attosca.* Messer Brunetto, I thank thee for the word.

—As we, or mother Dana, weave and unweave our bodies, Stephen said, from day to day, their molecules shuttled to and fro, so does the artist weave and unweave his image. And as the mole on my right breast is where it was when I was born though all my body has been woven of new stuff time after time so through the ghost of the unquiet father the image of the unliving son looks forth. In the intense instant of imagination, when the mind, Shelley says, is a fading coal, that which I was is that which I am and that which in possibility I may come to be. So in the future, the sister of the past, I may see myself as I sit here now but by reflection from that which then I shall be.

Drummond of Hawthornden helped you at that stile.

—Yes, Mr. Best said youngly. I feel Hamlet quite young. The bitterness might be from the father but the passages with Ophelia are surely from the son.

Has the wrong sow by the lug.

—That mole is the last to go, Stephen said, laughing.

John Eglinton made a nothing pleasing mow.

— If that were the birthmark of genius, he said, genius would be a drug in the market. The plays of Shakespeare's later years which Renan admired so much breathe another spirit.

— The spirit of reconciliation, the quaker librarian breathed.

— There can be no reconciliation, Stephen said, if there has not been a sundering.

Said that.

— If you want to know what are the events which cast their shadow over the hell of time of "King Lear," "Othello," "Hamlet," "Troilus and Cressida," look to see when and how the shadow lifts. What softens the heart of a man, shipwrecked in life's storms, tried, like another Ulysses, Pericles, prince of Tyre?

Head, redconecapped, buffeted, brineblinded.

— A child, a girl placed in his arms Marina.

— The leaning of sophists towards the bypaths of apocrypha is a constant quantity, John Eglinton detected. The highroads are dreary but they lead to the town.

Good Bacon: gone musty. Shakespeare Bacon's wild oats. Cypherjugglers going the highroads. What town, good masters? Mummed in names: A. E, eon: Magee, John Eglinton. East of the sun, west of the moon: *Tir nan og*. Booted the twain and staved.

How many miles to Dublin?
Three score and ten, sir.
Will we be there by candlelight?

— Mr. Brandes accepts it, Stephen said, as the first play of the closing period.

— Does he? What does Mr. Sidney Lee, or Mr. Simon Lazarus, as some aver his name is, say of it?

— Marina, Stephen said, a child of storm, Miranda, a wonder, Perdita, that which was lost. What was lost is given back to him. his daughter's child. *My dearest wife,* Pericles says, *was like this maid.* Will any man love the daughter if he has not loved the mother?

— The art of being a grandfather, Mr. Best gan murmur. *L'art d'être grand-p.....*

— His own image to a man with that queer thing genius is the standard of all experience, material and moral. Such an appeal will touch him. The images of other males of his blood will repel him. He will see in them grotesque attempts of nature to foretell or repeat himself.

The benign forehead of the quaker librarian enkindled rosily with hope.

— I hope Mr. Dedalus will work out his theory for the enlightenment of the public. And we ought to mention another Irish commentator, Mr. Frank Harris. His articles on Shakespeare in the *Saturday Review* were surely brilliant. Oddly enough he too draws for us an unhapply relation with the dark lady of the sonnets. The favored rival is William Herbert, earl of Pembroke. I own that if the poet must be rejected such a rejection would seem more in harmony with — what shall I say? — our notions of what ought not to have been.

Felicitously he ceased and held out a meek head among them, auk's egg, prize of their fray.

He thous and thees her with grave husbandwords. Dost love, Miriam? Dost love thy man?

— That may be too, Stephen said. There is a saying of Goethe's which Mr. Magee likes to quote. Beware of what you wish for in youth because you will get it in middle life. Why does he send to one who is a *buonaroba*, a bay where all men ride, a maid of houour with a scandalous girlhood, a lordling to woo for him? He was himself a lord of language and had made himself a coistrel gentleman and had written "Romeo and Juliet." Why? Belief in himself has been untimely killed. He was overborne in a cornfield first (a rye field, I should say) and he will never be a victor in his own eyes after nor play victoriously the game of laugh and lie down. Assumed dongiovannism will not save him. No later undoing will undo the first undoing. If the shrew is worsted there remains to her woman's invisble weapon. There is, I feel in the words, some goad of the flesh driving him into a new passion, a darker shadow of the first, darkening even his own understanding of himself. A like fate awaits him and the two rages commingle in a whirlpool.

They list. And in the porches of their ears I pour.

— The soul has been before stricken mortally, a poison poured in the porch of a sleeping ear. But those who are done to death in sleep cannot know the manner of their quell unless their Creator endow their souls with that knowledge in the life to come. The poisoning and the beast with two backs that urged it king Hamlet's ghost could not know of were he not endowed with knowledge by his creator. That is why the speech is always turned elsewhere, backward. Ravisher and ravished go with him from Lucrece's bluecircled ivory globes to Imogen's breast, bare, with its mole cinquespotted. He goes back, weary of the creation he has piled up to hide him from himself, an old dog licking an old score. But, because loss is his gain, he passes on towards eternity in undiminished personality, untaught by the wisdom he has written or by the laws he has revealed. His beaver is up. He is a ghost, a shadow now, the wind by Elsinore's rocks or what you will, the sea's voice, a voice heard only in the heart of him who is the substance of his shadow, the son consubstantial with the father.

— Amen! responded from the doorway.

Hast thou found me, O mine enemy?

A ribald face, sullen as a dean's, Buck Mulligan came forward, then blithe in motley, towards the greeting of their smiles. My telegram.

(*to be continued*)

Episode IX (continued)

THE LITTLE REVIEW

Vol. VI. MAY, 1919 No. 1

CONTENTS

Subscription price, payable in advance, in the United States and Territories, $2.50 per year; Canada, $2.75; Foreign, $3.00. Published monthly, and copyrighted, 1919, by Margaret C. Anderson.

Manuscripts must be submitted at author's risk, with return postage.

Entered as second class matter March 16, 1917, at the Post Office at New York, N. Y., under the act of March 3, 1879.

MARGARET C. ANDERSON, Publisher
24 West Sixteenth Street, New York, N. Y.
Foreign Office: 43 Belsize Park, Gardens, London N. W. 3.

— You were speaking of the gaseous vertebrate, if I mistake not? he asked of Stephen.

Primrosevested he greeted gaily with his doffed Panama as with a bauble.

They make him welcome.

Brood of mockers: Photius, pseudomalachi, Johann Most.

He Who Himself begot, middler the Holy Ghost, and Himself sent Himself, agenbuyer, between Himself and others, Who, put upon by His fiends, strippd and whipped, was nailed like a bat to a barndoor, starved on crosstree, Who let Him bury, stood up, harrowed hell, fared into heaven and there these nineteen years sitteth on the right hand of His Own Self but yet shall come in the latter day to doom the quick and dead when all the quick shall be dead already.

Glo-ria in ex-cel-sis De-o.

He lifts his hands. Veils fall. O, flowers! Bells with bells, with bells aquiring.

— Yes, indeed, the quaker librarian said. A most instructive discussion. Mr. Mulligan, I'll be bound, has his theory too of the play and of Shakespeare. All sides of life should be represented.

He smiled on all sides equally.

Buck Mulligan thought, puzzled:

— Shakespeare? he said. I seem to know the name.

A flying sunny smile rayed in his loose features.

— To be sure, he said, remembering brightly. The chap that writes like Synge.

Mr. Best turned to him:

—Haines missed you, he said. Did you meet him? He'll see you after at the D. B. C. He's gone to Gill's to buy Hyde's *Lovesongs of Connacht*.

— I came through the museum, Buck Mulligan, said. Was he here?

— The bard's fellowcountrymen, John Eglinton answered, are rather tired. perhaps of our brilliancies of theorising. I hear that an actress is playing Hamlet in Dublin. Vining held that the prince was a woman. Has no-one made him out to be an Irishman? He swears by saint Patrick.

— The most brilliant of all is that story of Wilde's, Mr. Best said lifting his

Overleaf: table of contents, *Little Review,* May 1919

brilliant notebook. That *Portrait of Mr. W. H.* where he proves that the sonnets were written by a Willie Hughes, a man all hues.

— For Willie Hughes, is it not? the quaker librarian asked.

Or Hughie Wills.

— I mean, for Willie Hughes, Mr. Best said, amending his gloss easily. Of course it's all paradox, don't you know, Hughes and hews and hues the colour, but it's so typical the way he works it out . It's the very essence of Wilde, don't you know. The light touch.

His glance touched their faces lightly as he smiled, a blond ephebe. Tame essence of Wilde.

You're darned witty. Three drams of usquebaugh you drank with Dan Deasy's ducats.

How much did I spend? O, a few shillings.

For a plump of pressmen. Humour wet and dry.

Wit. You would give your five wits for youth's proud livery he pranks in. Lineaments of gratified desire.

There be many mo. Take her for me. In pairing time. Jove, a cool ruttime send them. Yea, turtledove her.

Eve. Naked wheatbellied sin. A snake coils her, fang in's kiss.

— Do you think it is only a paradox, the quaker librarian was asking. The mocker is never taken seriously when he is most serious.

They talked seriously of mocker's seriousness.

Buck Mulligan's again heavy face eyed Stephen awhile. Then, his head wagging, he came near, drew a folded telegram from his pocket. His mobile lips read, smiling with new delight.

— Telegram! he said. Wonderful inspiration! Telegram! A papal bull!

He sat on a corner of the unlit desk, reading aloud joyfully:

— *The sentimentalist is he who would enjoy without incurring the immense debtorship for a thing done.* Signed: Dedalus. Where did you launch it from? The kips? No. College Green. Have you drunk the four quid? Telegram! Malachi Mulligan, The Ship, lower Abbey street. O, you peerless mummer! O, you priestified kinchite!

Joyfully he thrust message and envelope into a pocket but keened in querulous brogue:

— It's what I'm telling you, mister honey, it's queer and sick we were, Haines and myself, the time himself brought it in. And we one hour and two hours and three hours in Connery's sitting civil waiting for pints apiece.

He wailed:

—And we to be there, mavrone, and you to be unbeknownst sending your conglomerations the way we to have our tongues out a yard long like the drouthy clerics do be fainting for a pussful.

Stephen laughed.

Quickly, warningfully Buck Mulligan bent down:

— The tramper Synge is looking for you, he said, to murder you. He heard you . . . . . . on his halldoor in Glasthule. He's out in pampoe ties to murder you.

— Me! Stephen exclaimed. That was your contribution to literature.

Buck Mulligan gleefully bent back, laughing to the dark eavesdropping ceiling.

— Murder you! he laughed.

Harsh gargoyle a face that warred against me over our mess of hash of lights in *rue saint André des arts*. In words of words for words, palabras. Oisin with Patrick. Faunman he met in Clamart woods, brandishing a wine bottle. *C'est vendredi saint!* His image, wandering he met. I mine. I met a fool i' the forest.

— Mr. Lyster, an attendant said from the door ajar.

— . . . . . in which everyone can find his own. So Mr. Justice Madden in his "Diary of Master William Silence" has found the hunting terms. . . . . Yes What is it?

— Ther's a gentleman here, sir, the attendant said, coming forward and offering a card. From the *Freeman*. He wants to see the files of the *Kilkenny People for last year*.

— Certainly, certainly, certainly. Is the gentleman. . . . . . . ?

He took the eager card, glanced, not saw, laid down, unglanced, looked, asked, creaked, asked:

— Is he. . . . . ? O. there!

Brisk in a galliard he was off and out. In the daylit corridor he talked with voluble pains of zeal, in duty bound, most fair, most kind, most honest broadbrim.

— This gentleman? *Freeman's Journal? Kilkenny People?* To be sure. Good day, sir. *Kilkenny*. . . . We have certainly. . .

A patient silhouette waited, listening.

— All the leading provincial . . . . *Northern Whig. Cork Examiner. Enniscorthy Guardian*. 1903. . . . . . Will you please...? Evans, conduct this gentleman. . . . If you just follow the atten. . . . Or please allow me. . . . . This way. . .Please, sir. . . . .

Voluble, dutiful, he led the way to all the provincial papers, a bowing dark figure following his hasty heels.

The door closed.

— The sheeny! Buck Mulligan cried.

He jumped up and snatched the card.

— What's his name? Ikey Moses? Bloom.

He rattled on.

— Jehovah, collecto,r of prepuces, is no more, I found him over in the museum where I went to hail the foamborn Aphrodite. The Greek mouth that has never been twisted in prayer. Every day we must do homage to her. *Life of life, thy lips enkindle.*

Suddenly he turned to Stephen:

— He knows you. He knows your old fellow. O, I fear me, he is Greeker than the Greeks. His pale Galilean eyes were upon her mesial groove. Venus Kalipyge. O, the thunder of those loins! *The god pursuing the maiden hid.*

— We want to hear more, John Eginton decided with Mr. Best's approval. We begin to be interested in Mrs. S. Till now we had thought of her, if at all, as a patient Griselda, a Penelope stay-at-home.

— Antisthenes, pupil of Gorgias, Stephen, took the palm of beauty from Kyrios Menelaus' broodmare, Argive Helen, and handed it to poor Penelope. Twenty years he lived in London and, during part of that time, he drew a salary equal to that of the lord chancellor of Ireland. His life was rich. His art, more than the art of feudalism, as Walt Whitman called it, is the art of surfeit. Hot herring pies, green mugs of sack, honeysauces, gooseberried pigeons, ringocandies. Sir Walter Raleigh, when they arrested him, had half a million francs on his back. The gombeenwoman Eliza Tudor had underlinen enough to vie with her of Sheba. Twenty years he dallied there. You know Manningham's story of the burgher's wife who bade Dick Burbage to her bed after she had seen him in "Richard III" and how Shakespeare, overhearing, took the cow by the horns and, when Burbage came knocking, answered from the blankets: *William the conqueror came before Richard III.* And mistress Fitton, mount and cry O, and his dainty birdsnies, lady Penelope Rich, and the punks of the bankside, a penny a time.

Cours la reine. Encore vingt sous. Nous ferons des petites cochonnerise. . Mnette? Tu veux?

— The height of fine society. And Sir William Davenant of Oxford's mother with her cup of canary for every cockcanary.

Buck Mulligan, his pious eyes upturned, prayed:

— Blessed Margaret Mary Anycock!

— And Harry of six wives' daughter and other lady friends from neighbour seats, as Lawn Tennyson, gentleman, poet sings. But all those twenty years what do you suppose poor Penelope in Stratford was doing behind the diamond panes?

Do and do. Thing done. In a rosery of Fetter lane of Gerard, herbalist, he walks, greyedauburn. An azured harebell like her veins. Lids of Juno's eyes, violets. He walks. One life is all. One body. Do. But do. Afar, in a reek of lust and squalor, hands are laid on whiteness.

Buck Mulligan rapped John Eglinton's desk sharply.

— Whom do you suspect? he challenged.

— Say that he is the spurned lover in the sonnets. Once spurned twice spurned. But the court wanton spurned him for a lord, his dreamy love.

Love that dare not speak its name.

— As an Englishman, you mean, John sturdy Eglinton put in, he loved a lord.

Old wall where sudden lizards flash. At Charenton I watched them.

—It seems so, Stephen said, ... * Maybe, like Socrates, he had a midwife to mother as he had a shrew to wife. But she, the wanton, did not break a bed vow. Two deeds are rank in that ghost's mind: a broken vow and the dullbrained yokel on whom her favour has declined. Sweet Ann I take it, was hot in the blood. Once a wooer twice a wooer.

Stephen turned boldly in his chair.

— The burden of proof is with you not with me, he said, frowning. If you deny that in the fifth scene of "Hamlet" he has branded her with infamy tell me why there is no mention of her during the thirtyfour years between the day she married him and the day she buried him. All those women saw their men down and under: Mary, her goodman John, Ann, her William, Joan, her four brothers, Judith, her husband and all her sons, Susan, her husband too, while Susan's daughter, Elizabeth, to use granddaddy's words, wed her second, having killed her first.

---

*The Post Office authorities objected to certain passages in the January installment of "Ulysses," which prevents our mailing any more copies of that issue. To avoid a similiar interference this month I have ruined Mr. Joyce's story by cutting certain passages in which he mentions natural facts known to everyone. —M. C. A.)

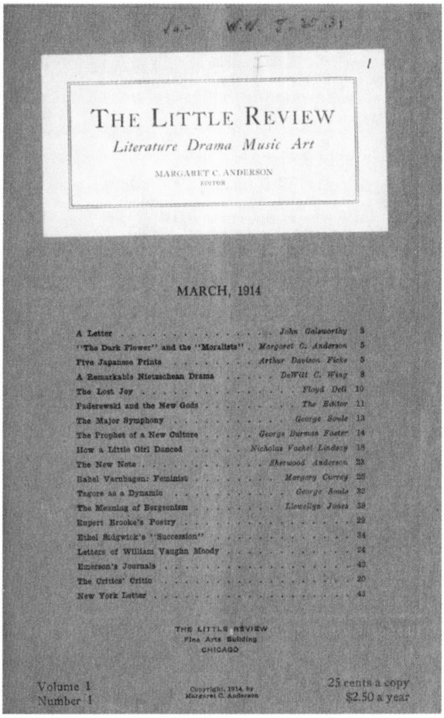

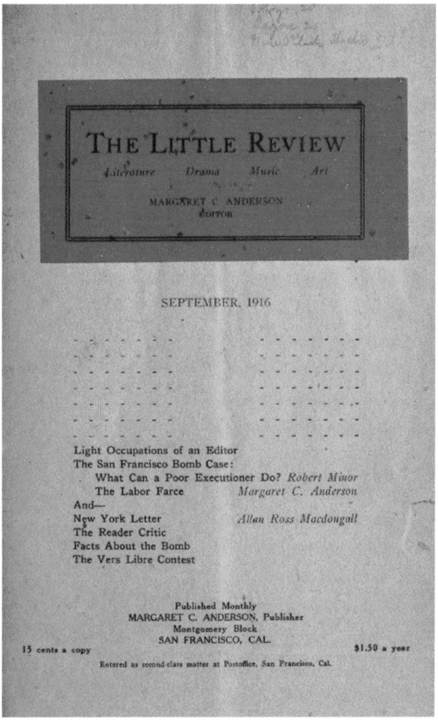

The covers of the first issue of the *Little Review* (March 1914) and the famous September 1916 issue, in which the editors protested the lack of acceptable submissions by leaving the first thirteen pages blank

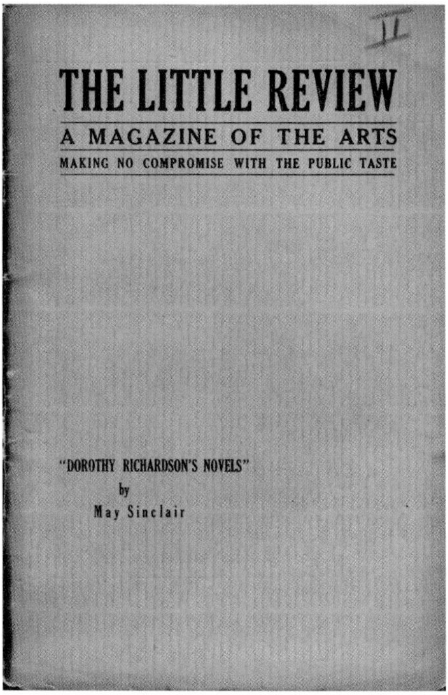

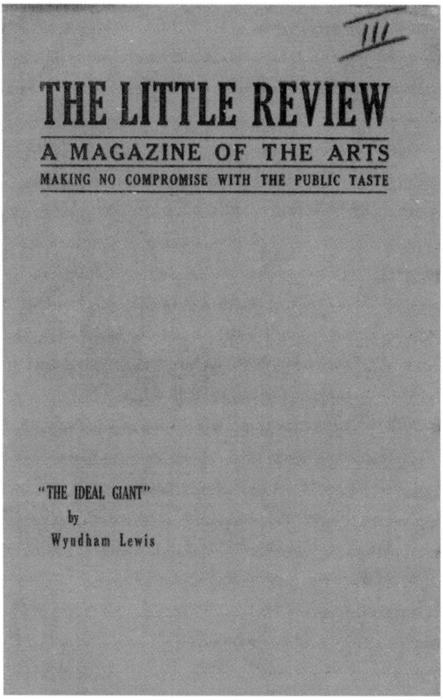

The covers of the first four issues with installments of *Ulysses:* March 1918, Episode I, top left; April 1918, Episode II, top right; May 1918, Episode III, bottom left; June 1918 Episode IV, bottom right

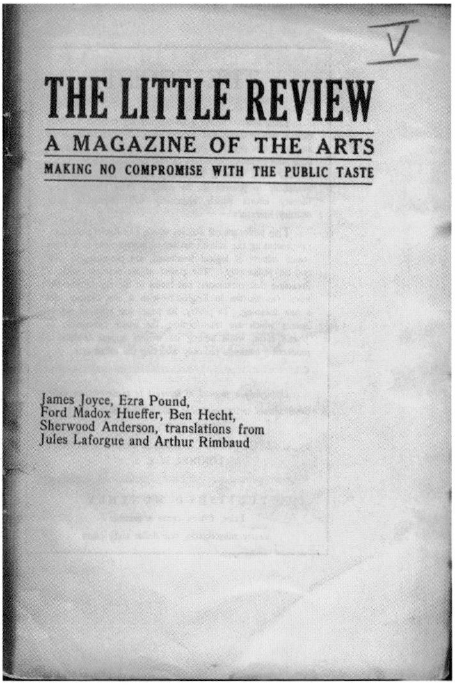

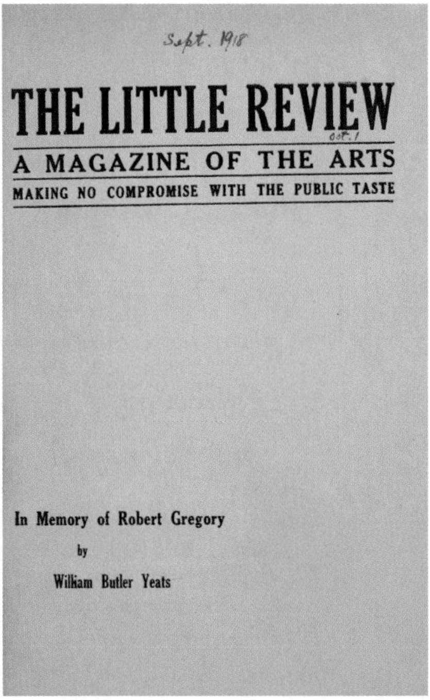

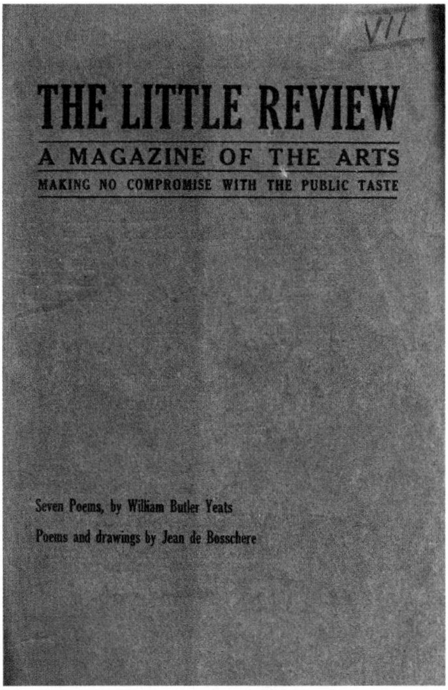

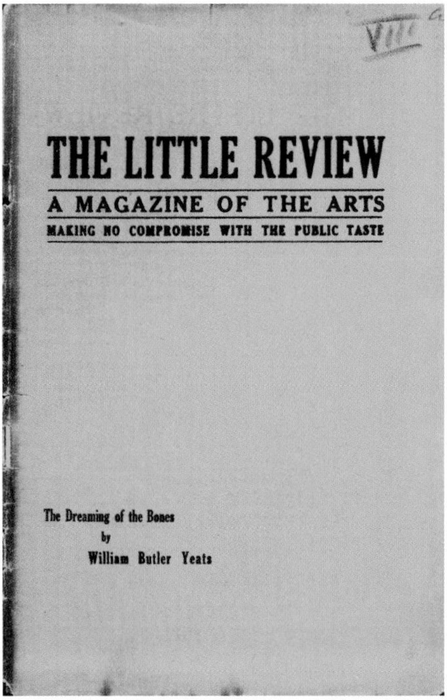

The covers of the next four issues with installments of *Ulysses:* July 1918, Episode V, top left; September 1918, Episode VI, top right; October 1918, Episode VII, bottom left; January 1919, Episode VIII, bottom right

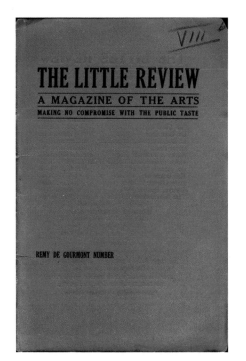

The covers of the next four issues with installments of *Ulysses:* February–March 1919, Episode VIII (cont.), top left; April 1919, Episode IX, top right; May 1919, Episode IX (cont.), bottom left; June 1919, Episode X, bottom right

The covers of the next four issues with installments of *Ulysses:* July 1919, Episode X (cont.), top left; August 1919, Episode XI, top right; September 1919, Episode XI (cont.), bottom left; November 1919, Episode XII, bottom right

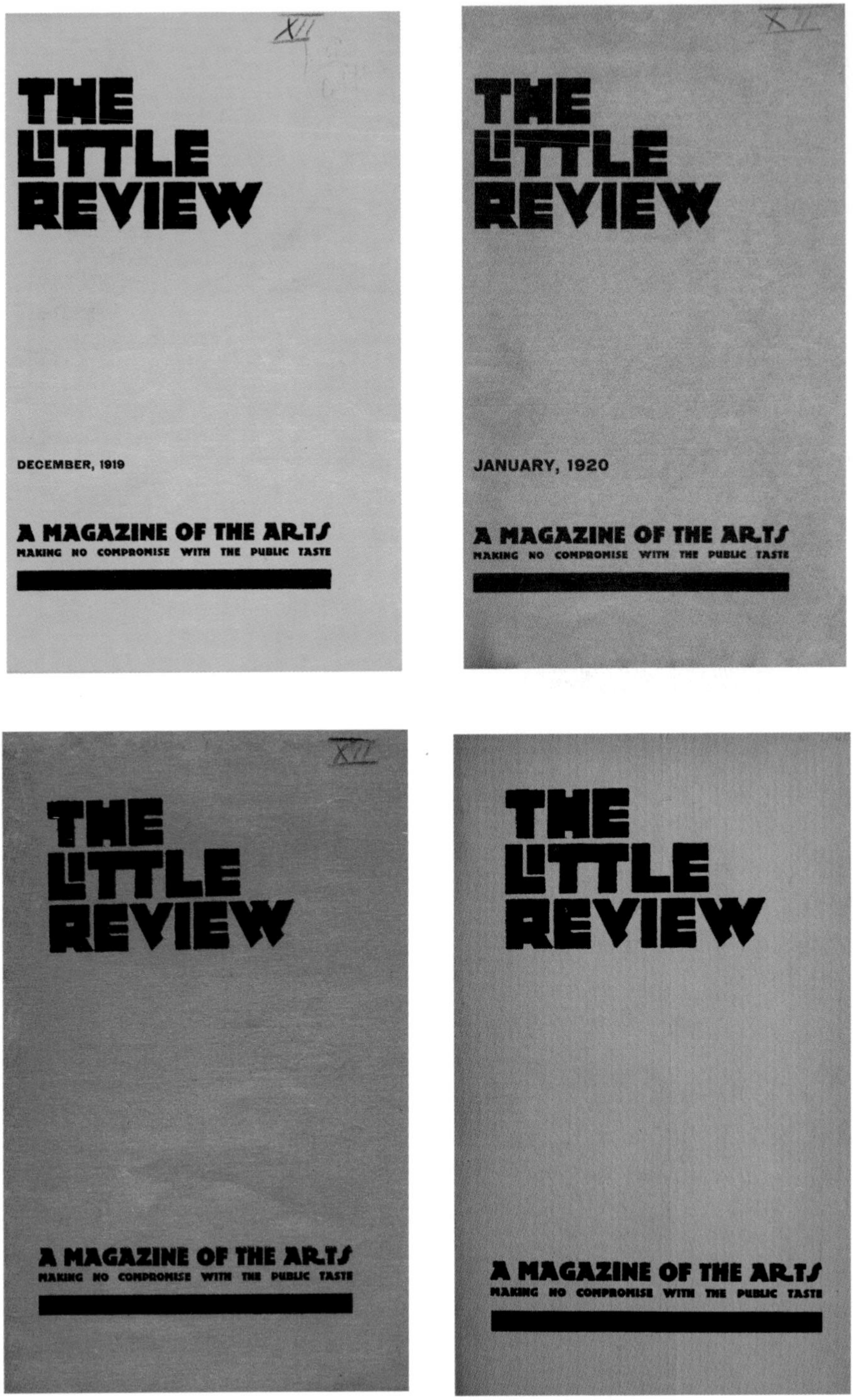

The covers of the next four issues with installments of *Ulysses:* December 1919, Episode XII (cont.), top left; January 1920, Episode XII (cont.), top right; March 1920, Episode XII (cont.), bottom left; April 1920, Episode XIII, bottom right

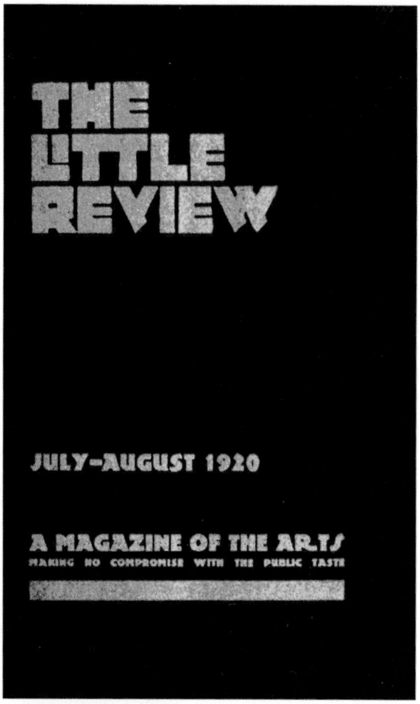

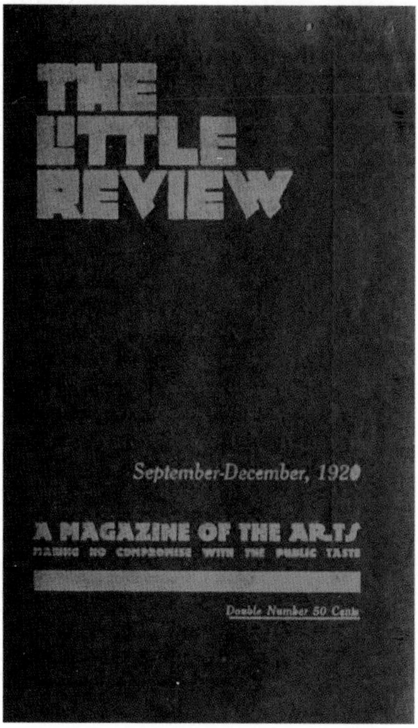

The covers of the last three issues with installments of *Ulysses:* May–June 1920, Episode XIII (cont.), top left; July–August 1920, Episode XIII (cont.), top right; September–December 1920, Episode XIV, bottom

ULYSSES

by

JAMES JOYCE

will be published in
the Autumn of 1921
by

"SHAKESPEARE AND COMPANY"

— SYLVIA BEACH —

8, RUE DUPUYTREN, PARIS — VIe

Advance Press Notices.

— Mr. EZRA POUND in — *Instigations* — His profoundest work . . . an impassioned meditation on life . . . He has done what Flaubert set out to do in Bouvard et Pécuchet, done it better, more succinct.

— Mr. RICHARD ALDINGTON in — *The English Review* — A most remarkable book . . . Bloom is a rags and tatters Hamlet, a proletarian Lear . . .

— THE TIMES — . . . . of the utmost sincerity . . . complete courage.

— Mrs. EVELYN SCOTT in — *The Dial* — A contemporary of the future . . . His technique has developed unique aspects that indicate a revolution of style for the future . . . This Irish artist is recreating a portion of the English language . . . He uses the stuff of the whole world to prove one man.

— THE NEW AGE — . . . "One of the most interesting literary symptoms in the whole literary world, and its publication is very nearly a public obligation".

— Mr. VALERY LARBAUD in — *La Nouvelle Revue Française* — Avec *ULYSSES,* l'Irlande fait une rentrée sensationnelle et triomphante dans la haute littérature européenne.

ULYSSES suppressed four times during serial publication in "The Little Review" will be published by "SHAKESPEARE AND COMPANY" complete as written.

This edition is private and will be limited to 1,000 copies:

100 copies signed on Dutch hand made paper . . . . **350** fr.
150 copies on vergé d'Arches . . . . **250** fr.
750 copies on hand made paper . . . . **150** fr.

The work will be a volume in-8° crown of 600 pages.

Subscribers will be notified when the volume appears, which will be sent to them by registered post immediately on receipt of payment.

All correspondence, cheques, money-orders should be addressed to:

Miss SYLVIA BEACH
"SHAKESPEARE AND COMPANY"
8, RUE DUPUYTREN, PARIS — VIe

ORDER FORM

Please send me ULYSSES by JAMES JOYCE

NUMBER OF COPIES *	
....	Edition on Dutch hand made paper with signature of the Author **350** fr.
....	Edition on vergé d'Arches . . . . **250** fr.
....	Edition on hand made paper . . . . **150** fr.

I will pay on receipt of notice announcing that the volume has appeared.

Name.. *Signature:*

Address..

* Please cancel editions not required.

107

A full-page advertisement for the book version of *Ulysses* from the Autumn 1921 issue

O, yes, mention there is. In the years when he was living richly in royal London to pay a debt she had to borrow forty shillings from her father's shepherd. Explain you then. Explain the swansong too wherein he has commended her to posterity.

He faced their silence.

To whom thus Eglinton:

You mean the will.
That has been xplained, I believe, by Jurists.
She was entitled to her widow's dower
At common law. His legal knowledge was great
Our judges tell us.

Him Satan fleers,
Mocker:

And therefore he left out her name
From the first draft but he did not leave out
The presents for his granddaughter, for his daughters,
For his sister, for his old cronies in Stratford
And in London. And therefore he was urged,
As I believe, to name her
He left her his
Second best
Bed.

Punkt.

Leftherhis
Secondbest
Leftherhis
Bestabed
Secabest
Leftabed.

Woa!

— Pretty countryfolk had a few chattels then, John Eglinton observed, as they have still if our peasant plays are true to type.

— He was a rich countrygentleman, Stephen said, with a coat of arms and landed estate at Stratford and a house in Ireland yard, capitalist shareholder, a bill promoter, a tithefarmer. Why did he not leave her his best bed if he wished her to snore away the rest of her nights in peace?

— It is clear that there were two beds, a best and a secondbest, Mr. Secondbest Best said finely.

— *Separatio a mensa et a thalamo*, said Buck Mulligan and was smiled on.

— Antiquity mentions famous beds, John Eglinton puckered, bedsmilng. Let me think.

— Do you mean he died so? Mr. Best asked with concern. I mean.....

— He died dead drunk, Buck Mulligan stated. A quart of ale is a dish for a king. O, I must tell you what Dowden said!

— What? asked Besteglinton.

William Shakespeare and company, limited. The people's Willam. For terms apply: E. Dowden, Highfield house......

— Lovely! Buck Mulligan suspired amorously. I asked him what he thought of the charge of pederasty brought against the bard. He lifted his hands and said: *All we can say is that life ran very high in those days*. Lovely!

Catamite.

— The sense of beauty leads us astray, Mr. Best with some sadness said.

Will they wrest from us, from me the palm of beauty?

— And the sense of property, Stephen said. He drew Shylock out of his own long pockset. The son of a maltjobber and moneylender he was himself a cornjobber and moneylender with ten tods of corn hoarded in famine years. His borrowers are no doubt those divers of worship mentioned by Chettle Falstaff who reported his uprightness of dealing. He sued a fellowplayer for the price of a few bags of malt and exacted his pound of flesh in interest for every money lent. How else could Aubrey's ostler and callboy get rich quick? All events brought grist to his mill. Shylock chimes with the jewbaiting that followed the hanging and quartering of the queen's leech Lopez, his Jew's heart being plucked forth while the sheeny was yet alive: "Hamlet" and "Macbeth" with the coming to the throne of a Scotch philosphaster with a turn for witchroasting. The lost armada is his jeer in "Love's Labour Lost." His pageants, the histories, sail fullbellied on a tide of Mafeking enthusiasm. Warwickshire jesuits are tried and we have a porter's theory of equivocation. The *Sea Venture* comes home from Bermudas and the play Renan admired is written with Patsy Caliban, our American cousin. The sugared sonnets follow Sidney's. As for fay Elizabeth, the gross virgin who inspired "The Merry Wives of Windsor" let some meinherr from Almany grope his life long for deephid meanings in the depths of the buckbasket.

I think you're getting on very nicely. Just mix up a mixture of theolologicophilolological. *Mingo, minxi, mictum, mingere.*

— Prove that he was a jew, John Eglinton dared, expectantly. Your dean of studies holds he was a holy Roman.

Sufflaminandus sum.

— He was made in Germany, Stephen replied, as the champion French polisher of Italian scandals.

— A myriadminded man, Mr. Best reminded. Coleridge called him myriadminded.

Amplius. In societate humana hoc est maxime necessarium ut sit amicitia inter multos.

— Saint Thomas, Stephen began.........

— *Ora pro nobis*, Monk Mulligan groaned, sinking to a chair.

There he keened a wailing rune.

— It's destroyed we are from this day! It is destroyed we are surely!

All smiled their smiles.

— Saint Thomas, Stephen, smiling, said, writing of incest from a stand point different from that of the Viennese school Mr. Magee spoke of, likens it in his wise and curious way to an avarice of the emotions. He means that the love so given to one near in blood is covetously withheld from some stranger who, it may be, hungers for it. Jews, whom christians tax with avarice, are of all races the most given to intermarriage. Accusations are made in anger. The christians laws which built up the hoards of the jews (for whom, as for the lollards, storm was shelter) bound their affections too with hoops of steel. Whether these be sins or virtues old Nobodaddy will tell us at doomsday leet. But a man who holds so tightly to what h calls his rights over what he calls his debts will hold tightly also to what he calls his rights over her whom he calls his wife. No sir smile neighbour shall covet his ox or his wife or his manservant or his maidservant or his jackass.

— Or his jennyass, Buck Mulligan antiphoned.

— Gentle Will is being roughly handled, gentle Mr. Best said gently.

— Which will? asked sweetly Buck Mulligan. We are getting mixed.

— The will to live, John Eglinton philosophised, for poor Ann, Will's widow, is the will to die.

— *Requiescat!* Stephen prayed.

What of all the will to do?
It has vanished long ago...

— She lies laid out in stark stiffness in that secondbest bed even though you prove that a bed in those days was as rare as a motorcar is now and that its carvings were the wonder of seven parishes. In old age she takes up with gospellers (one stayed at New Place and drank a quart of sack the town paid for but in which bed he slept it skills not to ask) and heard she had a soul. Venus has twisted her lips in prayer. Agenbite of inwit: remorse of conscience. It is an age of exhausted whoredom groping for its god.

— History shows that to be true, *inquit Eglinton Chronolologos*. The ages succeed one another. But we have it on high authority that a man's worst enemies shall be those of his own house and family. I feel that Russell is right. What do we care for his wife and father. I should say that only family poets have family lives. Falstaff was not a family man. I feel that the fat knight is his supreme creation.

Lean, he lay back. Shy, deny thy kindred, the unco guid. Shy supping with the godless, he sneaks the cup. A sire in Ultonian Antrim bade it him. Visits him here on quarter days. Mr. Magee, sir, there's a gentleman to see you. Me? Says he's your father, sir. Give me my Wordsworth. Enter Magee Mor Matthew, a rugged, rough, rugheaded kern, his nether stocks bemired with clauber of ten forests, a wilding in his hand.

Your own? He knows your old fellow.

Hurrying to her squalid deathlair from gay Paris on the quayside I touched his hand . The voice, new warmth, speaking. Dr. Bob Kenny is attending her. The eyes that wish me well. But do not know me.

— A father, Stephen said, battling against hopelessness, is a necessary evil. He wrote the play in the months that followed his father's death. If you hold that he, a greying man with two marriageable daughters, with thirtyfive years of life, *nel mezzo del cammin di nostra vita*, with fifty of experience is the beardless undergraduate from Wittenberg then you must hold that his seventyyear old mother is the lustful queen. No. The corpse of John Shakespeare does not walk the night. From hour to hour it rots and rots. He rests, disarmed of fatherhood, having devised that mystical estate upon his son. Boccaccio's Calandrino was the first and last man who felt himself with child. Fatherhood, in the sense of conscious begetting, is unknown to man. It is a mystical estate, an apostolic succession, from only begetter to only begotton. On that mystery and not on the madonna which the cunning Italian intellect flung to the mob of Europe the church is founded and founded irremovably because founded, like the world, macro-and microcosm, upon the void. Upon incertitude, upon unlikelihood. *Amor matris* subjective and objective genitive, may be the only true thing in life. Paternity may be a legal fiction. Who is the father of any son that any son should love him or he any son?

What the h--l are you driving at?

I know. Shut up. Blast you! I have reasons.

Amplius. Adhuc. Iterum. Postea.

Are you condemned to do this?

— They are sundered by bodily shame so steadfast that the criminal annals of the world, stained with all other incests and bestialities, do not record its breach: . . . . * The son unborn mars beauty: born, he brings pain, divides affection, increases care. He is a male: his growth is his fathers decline, his youth his father's envy, his friend his father's enemy.

In *rue Monsieur le Prince* I thought it.

— What links them in nature? An instant of blind rut.

Am I a father? If I were?

Shrunken uncertain hand.

— Sabellius, the African, subtlest heresiarch of all the beasts of the field, held that the Father was Himself His Own Son. The bulldog of Aquin, with whom no word shall be impossible, refutes him. Well: if the father who has not a son be not a father can the son who has not a father be a son? When Rutlandbaconsouthamptonshakespeare wrote "Hamlet" he was not the father of his own son merely but, being no more a son, he was and felt himself the father of all his race, the father of his own grandfather, the father of his unborn grandson who, by the same token, never was born for nature, as Mr. Magee understands her, abhors perfection.

Eglintoneyes, quick with pleasure, looked up shybrightly.

Flatter. Rarely. But flatter.

— Himself his own father, Sonmulligan told himself. Wait. I am big with child. I have an unborn child in my brain. Pallas Athena! A play! The play's the thing! Let me parturiate!

He clasped his paunchbrow with both birthaiding hands.

— As for his family, Stephen said, his mother's name lives in the forest of Arden. Her death brought from him the scene with Volumnia in "Coriolanus". His boyson's death is the deathscene of Arthur in "King John." Hamlet, the black prince, is Hamlet Shakespeare. Who the girls in "The Tempest," in "Pericles," in "Winter's Tale" are Cleopatra fleshpot of Egypt and Cressid and Venus are we may guess. But there is another member of his family who is recorded.

— The plot thickens, John Eglinton said.

The quaker librarian, quaking, tiptoed in quake, his mask, quake, with haste, quake, quack.

Door closed. Cell. Day.
They list. Three. They.
I you he they.

Stephen

He had three brothers, Gilbert, Edmund, Richard. Gilbert in his old age told some cavaliers he seen his brud on time in a play wud a man on his back. The playhouse sausage filled Gilbert's soul. He is nowhere: but an Edmund and a Richard are recorded in the works of Sweet William.

Johneglinton

Names! What's in a name?

Best

That is my name, Richard, don't you know. I hope you are going to say a good word for Richard, don't you know, for my sake.

(*laughter*)

Buckmulligan

(*piano, diminuendo*)
(*Then outspoke medical Dick*
To his comrade medical Davy. . .

Stephen

In his trinity of black Wills, the villian shakebags, Iago, Richard Crookback, Edmund in *King Lear*, two bear his brother's names. Nay, that last play was written or being written while his brother Edmund lay dying in Southwark.

Johneglinton

I give thanks to providence there was no brother of my name.

(*laughter*)

Best

I hope Edmund is going to catch it. I don't want Richard, my name. . . . .

Quakerlyster

(*a tempo*) But he that filches from me my good name. . . .

Stephen

(*stringendo*)

He has hidden his own name, a fair name, William, in the plays, a super here a clown there, as a painter of old Italy set his face in a dark corner of his canvas. He has revealed it in the sonnets where there is Will in overplus. Like John o' Gaunt his name is dear to him, as dear as the coat of arms he toadied for, on a bend sable a spear or steeled argent, *honorificabilitudinitatibus*, dearer than his glory of greatest shakescene in the country. What's in a name? That is what we ask ourselves in childhood when we write the name that we are told is ours. A star, a daystar, a firedrake rose at his birth. It shone by day in the heavens alone, brighter than Venus in the night, and by night it shone over delta in Cassiopeia, the recumbent constellation which is the signature of his initial among the stars. His eyes watched it, lowlying on the horizon, eastward of the bear, as he walked by the slumberous summer fields at midnight, returning from Shottery and from her arms.

Both satisfied. I too.

Don't tell them he was nine years old when it was quenched.

And from her arms.

Wait to be wooed and won. Ay, imbecile. Who will woo you?

Read the skies. *Autontimerumenos. Bous Stephanoumenos.* Where's your configurations S. D: *sua donna. Gia*: *di lui. Gelindo risolve di non amar S. D.*

—What is that, Mr. Dedalus? the quaker librarian asked. Was it a celestial phenomenon.

— A star by night, Stephen said, a pillar of the cloud by day.

What more's to speak?

Stephen looked on his hat, his stick, his boots.

Stephanos, my crown. My sword. His boots are spoiling the shape of my feet. Buy a pair. Holes in my socks. Handkerchief too.

—You make good use of the name, John Eglinton allowed. Your own name is strange enough. I suppose it explains your fantastical humour.

Me, Magee and Mulligan.

Fabulous artificer, the hawklike man. You flew. Whereto? Newhaven-Dieppe, steerage passenger. Paris and back. Lapwing. Icarus *Pater, ait.* Seabedabbled, fallen weltering. Lapw˙ng you are. Lapwing be.

Mr. Best eagerquietly lifted his book to say:

—That's very interesting because that brother motive, don't you know, we find also in the old Irish myths. Just what you say. The three brothers Shakespeare. In Grimm too, don't you know, the fairy-tales. The third brother that always marries the sleep˙ng beauty and wins the best prize.

Best of Best brothers. Good, better, best.

The quaker librarian springhalted near.

—I should like to know, he said, which brother you ..... I understand you suggest there was misconduct with one of the brothers...... But perhaps I am anticipating?

He caught himself in the act: looked at all: refrained.

An attendant from the doorway called:

— Mr. Lyster! Father Dineen wants . . .

—O! Father Dineen! Directly.

Swiftly rectly creaking rectly rectly he was rectly gone.

John Eglinton touched the foil.

—Come, he said. Let us hear what you have to say of Richard and Edmund. You kept them for the last, didn't you?

—In asking you to remember those two noble kinsmen, nuncle Richie and nuncle Edmund, Stephen answered, I feel I am asking too much perhaps. A brother is as easily forgotten as an umbrella.

Lapwing.

Where is your brother? Apothecaries' hall. My whetstone. Him, then Cranley, Mulligan: now these. Speech, speech. But act. Act speech. They mock to try you. Act. Be acted on.

Lapwing.

I am tired of my voice.

On.

—You will say those names were already in the chronicles from which he took the stuff of his plays. Why did he take them rather than others? Richard, a crookback, misbegotten, makes love to a widowed Ann (what's in a name?), woos an wins her. Richard the conqueror, third brother, came after William the conquered. The other four acts of that play hang limply from that first. Of all his kings Richard is the only king unshielded by Shakepeare's reverence, the angel of the world. Why is the underplot of "King Lear" in which Edmund figures lifted out of Sidney's "Arcadia" and spatchcocked on to a Celtic legend older than history?

—That was Will's way, John Eglinton defended. We should not now combine a Norse saga with an excerpt from a novel by George Meredith. *Que voulez-vous*, Moore would say. He puts Bohemia on the seacost and makes Ulysses quote Aristotle.

—Why? Stephen answered himself. Because the theme of the false or the usurping or the adulterous brother or all three in one is to Shakespeare what the poor it not, always with him. The note of banishment, banishment from the heart, banishment from home, sounds uninterruptedly from the "The Two Gentlemen of Verona" onward till Prospero breaks his staff, buries it certain fathoms in the earth and drowns his book. It doubles itself in the middle of his life, reflects itself in another, repeats itself. It repeats itself again when he is near the grave, when his married daughter Susan, chip of the old block, is accused of adultery. But it was the original sin that darkened his understanding, weakened h's will and left in him a strong inclination to evil. The words are those of my lords bishops of Maynooth—an original sin and, like original sin, committed by another in whose sin he too has sinned. It is between the lines of his last written words, it is petrified on his tombstone under which her four bones are not to be laid. Age has not withered it. Beauty and peace have not done it away. It is in infinite variety everywhere in the world he has created, in "Much Ado about Nothing", twice in "As you Like It", in "The Tempest", in "Hamlet", in "Measure for Measure"—and in the other plays which I have not read.

He laughed to free his mind from his mind's bondage.

Judge Eglinton summed up.

—The truth is midway, he affirmed. He is the ghost and the prince. He is all in all.

—He is, Stephen said. The boy of act one is the mature man of act five. All in all. In "Cymbeline", in "Othello" he is bawd and cuckold. He acts and is acted on. His unremitting intellect is the Iago ceaselessly that the moor in him shall suffer.

—Cuckoo! Cuckoo! Buck Mulligan clucked lewdly. O word of fear!

Dark dome received, reverbed.

—And what a character is Iago! undaunted John Eglinton exclaimed. When all is said Dumas fils (or is it Dumas père) is right. After God Shakespeare has created most.

—Man delights him not nor woman neither, Stephen said. He returns after a life of absence—to that spot of earth where he was born, where he has always been a silent witness and there, his journey of life ended, he plants his mulberrytree in the earth. Then dies, Gravediggers bury Hamlet *père* and Hamlet *fils*. If you like the last scene look long on it: prosperous Prospero, the good man rewarded, Lizzie, grandpa's lump of love, and nuncle Richie, the bad man taken off by poetic justice to the place where the bad niggers go. He found in the world without as actual what was in his world within as possible. Maeterlinck says: If Socrates leave his house today he will find the sage seated on his doorstep, if Judas go forth tonight it is to Judas his steps will tend. Every life is many days, day after day. We walk through ourselves, meeting robbers, ghosts, giants, old men, young men, wives, but always meeting ourselves. The playwright who wrote this world and wrote it badly (He gave us light first and the sun two days later), the lord of things as they are whom the most Roman of catholics call *dio boia*, hangman god, is doubtless all in all in all of us, ostler and butcher, and would be bawd and cuckold too but that in the economy of heaven, foretold by Hamelt, there are no more marriages, glorified man being a wife unto himself.

— Eureka!, Buck Mulligan cried. *Eureka!*

Suddenly happied he jumped up and reached in a stride John Eglinton's desk.

— May I? he said. The Lord has spoken to Malachi.

He began to scribble on a slip of paper.

Take some slips from the counter going out.

— Those who are married, Mr. Best douce herald, said, all save one, shall live. The rest shall keep as they are.

He laughed, unmarried, at Eglinton Johannes, of arts a bachelor.

Unwed, unfancied, ware of wiles, they fingerponder nightly each his variorum edition of "The Taming of the Shrew."

— You are a delusion, said roundly John Eglinton to Stephen. You have brought us all this way to show us a French triangle. Do you believe your own theory?

— No, Stephen said promptly.

— Are you going to write it? Mr. Best asked. You ought to make it a dialogue, don't you know, like the Platonic dialogues Wilde wrote.

John Eglinton smiled doubly.

— Well, in that case, he said, I don't see why you should expect payment for it since you don't believe it yourself. Dowden believes there is some mystery in "Hamlet" but will say no more. Herr Bleibtreu, the man Piper met in Berlin who is working up that Rutland theory, believes that the secret is hidden in the Stratford monument. He is going to visit the present duke, Piper says, and prove to him that his ancestor wrote the plays. It will come as a surprise to his grace. But he believes his theory.

I believe, O Lord, help my unbelief. That is, help me to believe or help me to unbelieve? Who helps to believe? *Egomen*. Who to unbelieve? Other chap.

— You are the only contributor to *Dana* who asks for pieces of silver. Then I don't know about the next number. Fred Ryan wants a space for an article on economics.

Fraidrine. Two pieces of silver he lent me. Tide you over. Economics.

— For a guinea, Stephen said, you can publish this interview.

Buck Mulligan stood up from his laughing scribbling, laughing: and then gravely said, honeying malice:

— I called upon the bard Kinch at his summer residence in upper Mecklenburgh street and found him deep in the study of the *Summa contra Gentiles* in the company of two gonorrheal ladies, Fresh Nelly and Rosalie, the coalquay whore.

He broke away.

— Come, Kinch. Come, wandering Aengus of the birds.

Come, Kinch, you have eaten all we left. Ay. I will serve you your orts and offals.

Stephen rose.

Life is many days. This will end.

— We shall see you tonight, John Eglinton said. *Notre ami* Moore says Malachi Mulligan must be there.

Buck Mullgani flaunted his slip and panama.

— Monsieur Moore, he said, lecturer on French letters to the youth of Ireland. I'll be there. Come Kinch. the bards must drink. Can you walk straight?

Laughing he. . . . .

Swill till eleven. Irish nights entertainment.

Lubber. . . . .

Stephen followed a lubber. . .

One day in the national library we had a discussion Shakes. After his lub back I followed.

Stephen, greeting, then all amort, followed a lubber jester, a wellkempt head, newbarbered, out of the vaulted cell into a shattering daylight of no thoughts.

What have I learned? Of them? Of me?

Walk like Haines now.

The constant readers' room. In the readers' book Cashel Boyle O'Connor Fitzmaurice Tisdall Farrell parafes his polysyllables. Item: was Hamlet mad? The quaker's pate godlily with a priesteen in booktalk.

The turnstile.

Is that? . . .? Blueribboned hat. . . . . Idly writing . . . . . What? Looked. . . ?

The curving balustrade, smoothsliding Mincius.

Puck Mulligan, panamahelmeted, went step by step, iambing, trolling:

— *John Eglinton, my jo, John,*
Why won't you wed a wife?

He spluttered to the air:

— O, the chinless Chinaman! We went over to their playbox, Haines and I, the plumbers' hall. Abbey theatre! I smell the pubic sweat of monks.

He spat blank.

Forgot: any more than he forgot the whipping lousy Lucy gave him. And left the *femme de trente ans*. And why no other children born?

Afterwit. Go back.

The dour recluse still there and the douce youngling, minion of pleasure, Phedo's toyable fair hair.

Eh... I just eh... wanted... I forgot... eh...

— Longworth and M'Curdy Atkinson were there...

Puck Mulligan footed featly, trilling:

—I hardly hear a purlieu cry
Or a Tommy talk as you pass one by
Before my thoughts begin to run
On F. M'Curdy Atkinson,
The same that had the wooden leg
And that filibustering filibeg
Who never dared to slake his drought,
—Magee that had the chinless mouth...

Jest on. Know thyself.

Halted below me, a quizzer looks at me. I halt.

— Mournful mummer, Buck Mulligan moaned. Synge has left off wearing black to be like nature. Only crows, priests and English coal are black.

A laugh tripped over his lips.

— Longworth is awfully sick, he said, after what you wrote about that old hake Gregory. O you inquisitional drunken jewjesuit! She gets you a job on the paper and then you go and slate her book to Jaysus. Couldn't you do the Yeats' touch?

He went on and down, chanting with waving graceful arms:

— The most beautiful book that has come out of Ireland in my time.

He stopped at the stairfoot

— I have conceived a play for the mummers, he said solemnly.

The pillared Moorish hall, shadows entwined. Gone the nine men's morrice with caps of indices.

In sweetly varying voices Buck Mulligan read his tablet:

Everyman His Own Wife
(a national immorality in three orgasms)
by
Ballocky Mulligan

He turned a happy patch's smirk to Stephen, saying:

— The disguise, I fear, is thin. But listen.

He read, marcato:

— Characters:

Toby Tostoff (a ruined Pole)
Crab (a bushranger)
Medical Dick
and (two birds with one stone)
Medical Davy
Mother Grogan (a watercarrier)
Fresh Nelly
and
Rosalie (the coalquay whore)

He laughed, lolling a to and fro head, walking on, followed by Stephen: and mirthfully he told the shadows, souls of men:

— O, the night in the Camden hall when the daughters of Erin had to lift their skirts to step over you as you lay in your mulberry coloured, multicoloured, multitudinous vomit!

— The most innocent son of Erin, Stephen said, for whom they ever lifted them.

About to pass through the doorway, feeling one behind, he stood aside.

Part. The moment is now. Where then? If Socrates leave his house today, if Judas go forth tonight. Why? That lies in space which I in time must come to, ineluctably.

My will: his will that fronts me. Seas between.

A man passed out between them, bowing, greeting:

— Good day again, Buck Mulligan said.

The portico.

Here I watched the birds for augury. Aengus of the birds. They go, they come. Last night I flew. Easily flew. Men wondered.—Street of harlots after. A creamfruit melon he held to me. In. You will see.

— The wandering jew, Buck Mulligan whispered with clown's awe. Did you see his eye? He looked upon you to lust after you. I fear thee, ancient mariner. O, Kinch, thou art in peril. Get thee a breechpad.

Manner of Oxenford.

Day. Wheelbarrow sun over arch of bridge.

A dark back went before them, step of a pard, down, out by the gateway, under portcullis barbs.

They followed.

Offend me still. Speak on.

Kind air defined the coigns of houses in Kildare street. No birds. Frail from the housetops two plumes of smoke ascended, pluming, and in a flaw of softness, softly were blown.

Cease to strive. Peace of the druids priests of "Cymbeline" hierophantic: from wide earth an altar.

Laud we the gods
And let our crooked smokes climb to their nostrils
From our bless'd altars.

(*to be continued*)

Episode x

THE LITTLE REVIEW

VOL. VI. JUNE, 1919 NO. 2

CONTENTS

Subscription price, payable in advance, in the United States and Territories, $2.50 per year; Canada, $2.75; Foreign, $3.00. Published monthly, and copyrighted, 1919, by Margaret C. Anderson.

Manuscripts must be submitted at author's risk, with return postage.

Entered as second class matter March 16, 1917, at the Post Office at New York, N. Y., under the act of March 3, 1879.

MARGARET C. ANDERSON, Publisher
24 *West Sixteenth Street, New York, N. Y.*
Foreign Office: 43 *Belsize Park, Gardens, London N. W.* 3.

THE superior, the very reverend John Conmee S. J. reset his smooth watch in his interior pocket as he came down the presbytery steps. Five to three. Just nice time to walk to Artane. What was that boy's name again? Dignam, yes. *Vere dignum et istum est.* Brother Swan was the person to see. Mr. Cunningham's letter. Yes. Oblige him, if possible. Good practical catholic: useful at mission time.

A one legged sailor, swinging himself onward by lazy jerks of his crutches, growled some notes. He jerked short before the convent of the sister of charity and held out a peaked cap for alms towards the very reverend John Conmee S. J. Father Conmee blessed him in the sun for his purse held, he knew, one silver crown.

Father Conmee crossed to Mountjoy Square. He thought, but not for long, of soldiers and sailors whose legs were shot off by cannonballs, of cardinal Wolsey's words: *If I had served my God as I have served my King He would not have abandoned me in my old days.* He walked by the treeshade of sunnywinking leaves: and towards him came the wife of Mr. David Sheehy M. P.

—Very well, indeed, father. And you, father?

Father Conmee was wonderfully well indeed. He would go to Buxton probably for the waters. And her boys, were they getting on well at Belvedere? Was that so? Father Conmee was very glad indeed to hear that. And Mr. Sheehy himself? Still in London. The house was still sitting, to be sure it was. Beautiful weather it was, delightful indeed. Yes, it was very probable that Father Bernard Vaughan would come again to preach. O, yes: a very great success. A wonderful man really.

Father Conmee was very glad to see the wife of Mr. David Sheehy M. P. looking so well and he begged to be remembered to Mr. David Sheehy M. P. Yes, he would certainly call.

—Good afternoon, Mrs. Sheehy.

Father Conmee doffed his silk hat, as he took leave, at the jet beads of her mantilla inkshining in the sun. And smiled yet again in going. He had cleaned his teeth, he knew, with arecanut paste.

Father Conmee walked and, walking, smiled for he thought on Father Bernard Vaughan's droll eyes and cockney voice.

—Pilate! Wy don't you oldback that owlin mob?

A zealous man, however. Really he was. And really did great good in his way. Beyond a doubt. Of good family too would one think it? Welsh, were they not?

Overleaf: table of contents, *Little Review,* June 1919

O, lest he forget. That letter to Father provincial.

Father Conmee stopped three little schoolboys at the corner of Mountjoy square. Yes: they were from Belvedere. The little house: Aha. And were they good boys at school? O. That was good now. And what was his name? Jack Sohan. And his name? Ger. Gallaher. And the other little man? His name was Brunny Lynam. O, that was a very nice name to have.

Father Conmee gave a letter from his breast to master Brunny Lynam and pointed to the red pillarbox at the corner of Fitzgibbon Street.

—But mind you don't post yourself into the box, little man, he said.

The boys sixeyed Father Conmee and laughed.

—O, Sir.

—Well, let me see if you can post a letter, Father Conmee said.

Master Brunny Lynam ran across the road and put Father Conmee's letter to Father provincial into the mouth of the bright red letterbox, Father Conmee smiled and nodded and smiled and walked along Mountjoy square east.

Was that not Mrs. McGuinness?

Mrs. McGuinness stately, silverhaired, bowed to Father Conmee Conmee from the further footpath along which she sailed. And Father Conmee smiled and saluted. How did she do?

A fine carriage she had . Like Mary, queen of Scots, something. And to think that she was a pawnbroker. Well, now! Such a. . . . what should he say? . . . . . such a queenly mien.

Father Conmee walked down Great Charles Street and glanced at the shut up free church on his left. The reverend T. R. Greene B. A. . . . The incumbent they called him. He felt it incumbent on him to say a few words. But one should be charitable. Invincible ignorance. They acted according to their lights.

Father Conmee turned the corner and walked along the North Circular road. It was a wonder that there was not a tramline in such an important thoroughfare. Surely, there ought to be.

A band of satchelled schoolboys crossed from Richmond Street. All raised untidy caps. Father Conmee greeted them more than once begnignly. Christian brother boys.

Father Conmee smelled incense on his right hand as he walked. St. Joseph's church, Portland row. For aged and virtuous females. Father Conmee raised his hat to the Blessed Sacrament. Virtuous: but occasionally they were also bad tempered.

Near Aldborough house Father Conmee thought of that spendthrift nobleman. And now it was an office or something.

Father Conmee, began to walk along the North Strand road and was saluted by Mr. William Gallagher who stood in the doorway of his shop. Father Conmee saluted Mr. William Gallagher and perceived the odours that came from baconflitches and ample cools of butter. He passed Grogan's the tobacconist against which newsboards leaned, and told of a dreadful catastrophe in New York. In America these things were continually happening. Unfortunate people to die like that, unprepared. Still, an act of perfect contrition.

Father Conmee went by Daniel Bergin's publichouse against the window of which two unlabouring men lounged. They saluted him and were saluted.

Father Conmee passed H. J. O'Neill's funeral establishment where Corny Kelleher toted figures on the daybook while he chewed a blade of hay. A constable on his beat saluted Father Conmee and Father Conmee saluted the constable. In Yonkstett the porkbutcher's Father Conmee observed pigs' puddings white, and black and red lying neatly curled in tubes.

Moored under the trees of Charleville Mall Father Conmee saw a turfbarge, a towhorse with pendent head, a bargeman with a hat of dirty straw seated amidships, smoking and staring at a branch of elm above him. It was idyllic: and Father Conmee reflected on the providence of the Creator who had made turf to be in bogs where men might dig it out and bring it to make fires in the houses of poor people.

On Newcomen bridge the very reverend John Conmee S. J. of St. Francis Xavier's church, upper Gardiner street, stepped on to an outward bound tram.

Off an inward bound tram stepped the reverend Nicholas Dudley C. C. of Saint Agatha's church, North William street, on to Newcomen bridge.

At Newcomen bridge Father Conmee stepped into an outward bound tram for he disliked to traverse on foot the dingy way past mud island.

Father Conmee sat in a corner of the tramcar, a blue ticket tucked with care in the eye of one plump kid glove, while four shillings, a sixpnce and five pennies chuted from his other plump glovepalm into his purse.

It was a peaceful day. The gentleman with the glasses opposite Father Conmee had finished explaining and looked down. His wife, Father Conmee supposed. A tiny yawn opened the mouth of the wife of the gentleman with the glasses. She raised her small gloved fist, yawned ever so gently, tiptapping her small gloved fist on her opening mouth.

Father Conmee perceived her perfume in the car. He perceived also that the awkward man at the other side of her was sitting on the edge of the seat.

Father Conmee at the altarrails placed the host with difficulty in the mouth of the awkward old man who had the shaky head.

At Annesley bridge the tram halted and, when it was about to go, an old woman rose suddenly from her place to alight. The conductor pulled the bell-strap to stay the car for her. She passed out with her basket and a marketnet: and Father Conmee saw the conductor help her and net and basket down: and Father Conmee thought that she was one of those good souls who had always to be told twice bless you, my child, that they have been absolved, pray for me. But they had so many worries in life, so many cares, poor creatures.

From the hoardings Mr. Eugene Stratton grinned with thick niggerlips at Father Conmee.

Father Conmee thought of the souls of black and brown and yellow men and of his sermon on saint Peter Claver S. J. and the African mission and of the propagation of the faith and of the millions of black and brown and yellow souls that had not received the baptism of water. That book by the Belgian jesuit, "Le Nombre des Elus", seemed to Father Conmee a reasonable plea. Those were millions of human souls created by God in His Own likeness to whom the faith had not been brought. But they were God's souls created by God. It seemed to Father Conmee a pity that they should all be lost, a waste, if one might say.

At the Howth road stop Father Conmee alighted, was saluted by the conductor and saluted in his turn.

The Malahide road was quiet. It pleased Father Conmee, road and name. The joybells were ringing in gay Malahide. Those were old worldish days, loyal times, in joyous townlands, old times in the barony.

Father Conmee, walking, thought of his little book "Old Times in the Barony" and of the book that might be written about Jesuit houses and of Ellen, first countess of Belvedere.

A listless lady, no more young, walked alone the shore of lough Owel, Ellen, first countess of Belvedere, listlessly walking in the evening, not startled when an otter plunged. Who could know the truth? Not the jealous lord Belvedere, and not her confessor if she had not committed adultery fully, *eiaculatio seminis intra vas mulieris*, with her husband's brother? She would half confess if she had not all sinned as women did. Only God knew and she and he, her husband's brother.

Father Conmee thought of that tyrannous incontinence, needed however for men's race on earth, and of the ways of God which were not our ways.

Don John Conmee walked and moved in times of yore. He was humane and honoured there. He bore in mind secrets confessed and he smiled at smiling noble faces in a beeswaxed drawingroom, ceiled with full fruit clusters. And the hands of a bride and of a bridegroom, noble to noble, were impalmed by by Don John Conmee.

It was a charming day.

The lychgate of a field showed Father Conmee breadths of cabbages, curtseying to him with ample underleaves. The sky showed him a flock of small white clouds going slowly down the wind. *Moutonnés*, the French said. A homely and just word.

Father Conmee, reading his office, watched a flock of muttoning clouds over Rathcoffee. His thinsocked ankles were tickled by the stubble of Clongowes field. He walked there, reading in the evening and heard the cries of the boys' lines at their play, young cries in the quiet evening. He was their rector: his reign was mild.

Father Conmee, reading his office, watched a flock of mutbreviary out. An ivory bookmark told him the page.

Nones. He should have read that before lunch. But lady Maxwell had come.

Father Conmee read in secret *Pater* and *Ave* and crossed his breast. *Deus in adiutorium.*

He walked calmly and read mutely the nones, walking and reading till he came to, *Res* in *Beati immaculati*: *Principium verborum tuorum veritas*: *in eternum omnia indicia justitiae tuae.*

A flushed young man came from the gap of a hedge and after him came a young woman with wild nodding daisies in her hand. The young man raised his hat abruptly: the young woman abruptly bent and with slow care detached from her light skirt a clinging twig.

Father Conmee blessed both gravely and turned a thin page of his breviary. *Sin*: *Principes persecuti sunt me gratis*: *et a verbis tuis formidavit cor meum.*

+

+ +

Corny Kelleher closed his long daybook and glanced with his drooping eye at a pine coffinlid sentried in a corner.

He pulled himself erect, went to it and spinning it on its axle, viewed its shape.

Chewing his blade of hay he laid the coffinlid by and came to the doorway. There he tilted his hatbrim to give shade to his eys and leaned against the doorcase, looking idly out. Father John Conmee stepped in to the Dollymount tram on Newcomen bridge.

Corny Kelleher locked his largefooted boots and gazed, his hat downtilted, chewing his blade of hay.

Constable 57 C, on his beat, stood to pass the time of day.

—That's a fine day, Mr. Kelleher.

—Ay, Corny Kelleher said.

—It's very close, the constable said.

Corny Kelleher sped a silent jet of hayjuice arching from his mouth, while a generous white arm from a window in Eccles street flung forth a coin.

—What's the best news, he asked.

— I seen that particular party last evening, the constable said with bated breath.

+

\+ +

A onelegged sailor crutched himself round MacConnell's corner, skirting Rabaiotti's icecream car, and jerked himself up Eccles street. Towards Larry O'Rourke, in shirtsleeves in his doorway, he growled unamiably.

—For England,

He swung himself violently forward past Katey and Boody Dedalus, halted and growled:

—home and beauty.

J. J. O'Molloy's white careworn face was told that Mr. Lambert was in the warehouse with a visitor.

A stout lady stopped, took a copper coin from her purse and dropped it into the cap held out to her. He grumbled thanks and glanced sourly at the unheeding windows, sank his head and swung himself forward four strides.

He halted and growled angrily:

—For England,

Two barefoot urchins, sucking long liquorice laces, halted near him, gaping at his stump with their yellow slobbered mouths.

He swung himself forward in vigorous jerks, lifted his head towards a window and bayed deeply.

—home and beauty.

The gay sweet whistling within went a bar or two, ceased. The blind of the window was drawn aside. A plump bare generous arm shone, was seen, held forth from a white petticoatbodice and taut shiftstraps. A woman's hand flung forth a coin over the area railings. It fell on the path.

One of the urchins ran to it, picked it up and dropped it into the minstrel's cap, saying:

—there, sir.

\+

\+ \+

Katey and Boody Dedalus shoved in the door of the close steaming kitchen.

—Did you put in the books? Boody asked.

Maggie at the range rammed down a greyish mass beneath bubbling suds twice with her potstick and wiped her brow.

—They wouldn't give anything on them, she said.

Father Conmee walked through Clongowes fields, his thinsocked ankles tickled by stubble.

—Where did you try? Boody asked.

—McGuinness's.

Boody stamped her foot, and threw her satchel on the table.

—Bad cess to her ibg face, she cried.

Katey went to the range and peered with squinting eyes.

—What's in the pot? she asked.

—Shirts, Maggie said.

Boody cried angrily:

—Crickey, is there nothing for us to eat?

Katey, lifting the kettlelid in a pad of her stained skirt, asked:

—and what's in this?

A heavy fume gushed in answer.

—Peasoup, Maggie said.

—Where did you get it? Katey asked.

—Sister Mary Patrick, Maggie said.

The Lacquey rang his bell.

—Barang!

Boody sat down at the table and said hungrily:

—Give us it here!

Maggie, poured yellow thick soup from the kettle into a bowl. Katey, sitting opposite Boody, said quietly:

— A good job we have that much. Where's Dilly?

—Gone to meet father, Maggie said.

Boody, breaking big chunks of bread into the yellow soup, added:

—Our father, who art not in heaven.

Maggie, pouring yellow soup in Katey's bowl, exclaimed:

—Boody! For shame!

A skiff, a crumpled throwaway, Elijah is coming, rode lightly down the Liffey, under loopline bridge, sailing eastward past hulls and anchorchains, between the Customhouse old dock and Georges quay.

+

+ +

The blond girl in Thornton's bedded the wicker basket with rustling fibre. Blazes Boylan handed her the bottle swathed in pink tissue paper and a small jar.

—Put these in first, will you? he said.

—Yes, sir, the blond girl said, and the fruit on top.

—That'll do, game ball, Blazes Boylan said.

She bestowed fat pears neatly, head by tail, and among them ripe shamefaced peaches.

Blazes Boylan walked here and there in new tan shoes about the fruitsmelling shop, lifting fruits, sniffing smells.

H. E. L. Y. S. filed before him, tall whitehatted, past Tangier lane, plodding towards their goal.

He turned suddenly from a chip of strawberries, drew a gold watch from his fob and held it at its chain length.

—Can you send them by tram? Now?

A darkbacked figure under Merchant's arch scanned books on the hawker's car.

—Certainly, sir. Is it in the city?

—O, yes, Blazes Boylan said. Ten minutes.

The blond girl handed him a docket and pencil.

—Will you write the address, sir?

Blazes Boylan at the counter wrote and pushed the docket to her.

—Send it at once, will you? he said. It's for an invalid.

—Yes, sir. I will, sir.

Blazes Boylan rattled merry money in his trousers' pocket.

—What's the damage? he asked.

The blond girl's slim fingers reckoned the fruits.

Blazes Boylan looked into the cut of her blouse. A young pullet. He took a red carnation from the tall stemglass. —This for me? he asked gallantly.

The blond girl glanced sideways up, blushing. — Yes, sir, she said.

Bending archly she reckoned again fat pears and blushing peaches.

Blazes Boylan looked in her blouse with more favour, the stalk of the red flower between his smiling teeth. May I say a word to your telephone missy? he asked roguishly.

+

+ +

—*Ma!* Almidano Artifoni said.

He gazed over Stephen's shoulder at Goldsmith's knobby poll.

Two carsfull of tourists passed slowly, their women sitting fore, gripping frankly the handrests. Palefaces. Men's arms frankly round their stunted forms. They looked from Trinity to the blind columned porch of the bank of Ireland, where pigeons roocoocooed.

—*Anch'io ho avuto di queste idee,* Almidano Artifoni said, *quand' ero giovine come Lei. Eppoi mi sono convinto che il mondo è ma bestia. E pecatto. Perche la sua voce . . . sarebbe un cespite di rendita, via. Invece, Lei si sacrifica.*

— *Sacrifizio incruento*, Stephan said smiling.

— *Speriamo*, the round mustachioed face said pleasantly. *Ma, diaretta a me. Ci refletta.*

By the stern stone hand of Grattan, bidding halt, an Inchicore tram unloaded straggling Highland soldiers of a band.

—*Ci riflettero*, Stephen said, glancing down the solid trouserleg.

—*Ma, sul serio, eh*? Almidano Artifoni said.

His heavy hand took Stephen's firmly. Human eyes. They gazed curiously an instant and turned quickly towards a Dalkey tram.

—Eccolo, Almidano Artifoni said in friendly haste. Venga a trovarmi e ci pensi. Addio, caro.

—*Arrivederlo, maestro*, Stephen said, raising his hat when his hand was freed. *Egrazie.*

—*Di che?* Almidano Artifoni said. *Scusi, eh?*

Almidano Artifoni, holding up a baton of rolled music as a signal, trotted on stout trousers after the Dalkey tram. In vain he trotted, signaling in vain among the rout of barekneed gillies smuggling implements of music through Trinity gates.

+

+ +

Miss Dunne hid the Capel street library copy of "The Woman in White" far back in her drawer and rolled a sheet of gaudy notepaper into her typewriter.

Too much mystery business in it? Is he in love with that one, Marion? Change it and get another by Mary Cecil Haye.

The disk shot down the groove, wobbled a while, ceased and ogled them: six.

Miss Dunne clicked on the keyboard: —

—16 June 1904.

Five tallwhitehatted sandwichmen between Moneypeny's corner and the slab where Wolfe Tone's statue was not, eeled themselves turning H. E. L. Y. S. and plodded back as they had come.

Then she stared at the large poster of Marie Kendall, charming soubrette. Mustard hair and dauby cheeks. She's not nice looking, is she? The way she is holding up her bit of a skirt. Wonder will that fellow be at the band tonight. If I could, get that dressmaker to make a concertina skirt like Susy Nagle's. They kick out grand. Shannon and all the boatclub swells never took his eyes off her. Hope to goodness he won't keep me here till seven.

The telephone rang rudely by her ear.

—Hello. Yes, sir. No, sir. Yes, sir. I'll ring them up after five. Only those two, sir, for Belfast and Liverpool. All right, sir. Then I can go after six if you're not back. A quarter after. Yes, sir. Twenty-seven and six. I'll tell him. Ye: one, seven, six. No, sir. Yes, sir. I'll ring them up after five.

—Mr. Boylan! Hello! That gentleman from *Sport* was in looking for you. Mr. Lenehan, yes. He said he'll be in the Ormond. No, sir. Yes, sir. I'll ring them up after five.

+

\+ +

Two pink faces turned in the flare of the tiny torch.

—Who's that? Ned Lambert asked. Is that Crotty?

—Ringabella and Crosshaven, a voice replied, groping for foothold.

—Hello, Jack, is that yourself? Ned Lambert said, raising in salute his pliant lath among the flickering arches. Come on. Mind your steps there.

The vesta in the clergyman's uplifted hand consumed itself in a long soft flame and was let fall. At their feet its red speck died: and mouldy air closed round them.

—How interesting! a refined accent said in the gloom.

—Yes, sir, Ned Lambert said heartily. We are standing in the historic council chamber of St. Mary's abbey: where silken Thomas proclaimed himself a rebel. You were never down here before, Jack, were you?

—No, Ned.

—He rode down through Dame walk, the refined accent said, if my memory serves me. The mansion of the Kildares was in Thomas court.

—That's right, Ned Lambert said. That's quite right.

—If you will be so kind then, the clergyman said, the next time to allow me perhaps . . . .

—Certainly, Ned Lambert said. Bring the camera whenever you like. I'll get those bags cleared away from the windows. You can take it from here or from here.

In the still faint light he moved about, tapping with his lath the piled seedbags and points of vantage on the floor.

From a long face a beard and gaze hung on a chessboard.

—I'm deeply obliged, Mr. Lambert . . . the clergyman said. I won't trespass on your valuable time . . . . .

—You're welcome, sir, Ned Lambert said Drop in whenever you like. Next week, say. Can you see?

—Yes, yes. Good afternoon, Mr. Lambert. Very pleased to have met you.

—Pleasure is mine, sir, Ned Lambert answered.

He followed his guest to the outlet and then whirled his lath away, among the pillars. With J. J. O'Molloy he came forth slowly into Mary's abbey where draymen were loading floats

He stood to read the card in his hand.

—The reverend Hugh C. Love, the vicarage, Rathcoffey. Nice young chap he is. He's writing a book about the Fitzgeralds he told me. He's well up in history, faith.

The young woman with slow care detached from her light skirt a clinging twig.

—I thought you were at a new gunpowder plot, J. J. O'Molloy asid.

Ned Lambert cracked his fingers in the air.

—God! he cried. I forgot to tell him that one about the earl of Kildare after he set fire to Cashel cathedral. You know that one? *I'm bloody sorry I did it*, says he, *but I declare to God I thought the archbishop was inside*. He mightn't like it, though. What? God, I'll tell him anyhow. That was the great earl, the Fitzegerald Mor. Hot members they were all of them, the Geraldines.

The horses he passed started nervously under their slack harness. He slapped a piebald haunch quivering near him and cried:

—Woa, sonny!

He turned to J. J. O'Molloy and asked:

—Well, Jack. What is it? What's the trouble? Wait a while. Hold hard.

With gaping mouth and head far back he stood still and, after an instant, sneezed loudly.

—Chow! he said. Blast you!

—The dust from those sacks, J. J. O'Molloy said politely.

—No, Ned Lambert gasped, I caught a . . . . . . cold night before . . . . . . blast your soul . . . . night before last . . . and there was a hell of a lot of draught . . . . .

He held his handekrchief ready for the coming . . . . .

— I was . . . .   this morning . . . . poor little . . . . . what do you call him . . . . . . Chow! . . . . . Holy Moses!

(*To be continued.*)

Episode x (continued)

THE LITTLE REVIEW

VOL. VI. JULY, 1919 No. 3

CONTENTS

Subscription price, payable in advance, in the United States and Territories, $2.50 per year; Canada, $2.75; Foreign, $3.00. Published monthly, and copyrighted, 1919, by Margaret C. Anderson.

Manuscripts must be submitted at author's risk, with return postage.

Entered as second class matter March 16, 1917, at the Post Office at New York, N. Y., under the act of March 3, 1879.

MARGARET C. ANDERSON, Publisher
24 *West Sixteenth Street, New York, N. Y.*
Foreign Office: 43 *Belsize Park, Gardens, London N. W.* 3.

TOM ROCHFORD took the top disk from the pile he clasped against his claret waistcoat.

—See? he said. Say it's turn six. In here, see. Turn Now On.

He slid into the left slot for them. It shot down the groove, wobbled a while, ceased, ogling them: six.

Lawyers of the past, haughty, pleading, beheld pass to Nisi Prius court Richie Goulding carrying the costbag of Goulding, Colles and Ward.

—See? he said. See now the last one I put in is over here: Turns Over... The impact. Leverage, see?

He showed them the rising column of disks on the right.

—Smart idea, Nosey Flynn said, snuffling . So a fellow coming in late can see what turn is on and what turns are over.

—See? Tom Rochford said.

He slid in a disk for himself: and watched it shoot, wobble, ogle, stop: four. Turn Now On.

—I'll see him now in the Ormond, Lenehan said, and sound him. One good turn deserves another.

—Do, Tom Rochford said. Tell him I'm Boylan with impatience.

—Goodnight, McCoy said abruptly, when you two begin ....

Nosey Flynn stooped towards the lever, snuffling at it.

—But how does it work here, Tommy? he asked.

—Tooraloo, Lenehan said, see you later.

He followed McCoy out across the tiny square of Crampton court.

—He's a hero, he said simply.

—I know, McCoy said. The drain, you mean.

—Drain? Lenehan said. It was down a manhole.

They passed Dan Lowry's musichall where Marie Kendall, charming soubrette, smiled on them from a poster a dauby smile.

Going down the path of Sycamore street Lenehan showed McCoy how the whole thing was. One of those manholes like a bloody gaspipe and there was the poor devil stuck down in it, half choked with sewer gas. Down went Tom Rochford anyhow, booky's vest and all, with the rope round him. And be damned but he got the rope round the poor devil and they two were hauled up.

—The act of a hero, he said.

At the Dolphin he halted.

Facing page: table of contents, *Little Review*, July 1919

—This way, he said, walking to the right. I want to pop into Lyaan's to see Sceptre's starting price. What's the time by your gold watch and chain?

M'Coy peered into Marcus Tertius Moses sombre office, then at O'Neill's clock.

—After three, he said. Who's riding her?

—O Madden, Lenehan said. And a game filly she is.

While he waited in Temple bar M'Coy dodged a banana peel with gentle pushes of his toe from the path to the gutter. Fellow might damn easy get a nasty fall there coming along tight in the dark.

The gates of the drive opened wide to give egress to the viceregal cavalcade.

—Even money, Lenehan said returning. Bantom Lyons was in there going to back a bloody horse someone gave him that hasn't an earthly. Through here.

They went up the steps and under Merchants' arch. A darkbacked figure scanned books on the hawker's cart.

—There he is, Lenehan said.

—Wonder what he is buying, M'Coy said, glancing behind.

—*Leopoldoor the Bloom is on the Rye*, Lenehan said.

—He's dead nuts on sales, M'Coy said. I was with him one day and he bought a book from an old one in Liffey street for two bob. There were fine plates in it worth double the money, the stars and the moon and comets with long tails. Astronomy it was about.

Lenehan laughed.

—I'll tell you a damn good one about comet's tails, he said. Come over in the sun.

They crossed to the metal bridge and went along Wellington quay by the river wall.

Master Patrick Aloysius Dignam came out of Mangan's, late Fehrenbach's carrying a pound and a half of porksteaks.

—There was a big spread out at Glencree reformatory, Lenehan said eagerly. The annual dinner you know. The Lord mayor was there, Val Dillon it was, and Sir Charles Cameron and Dan Dawson spoke and there was music. Bartell D'Arcy sang and Benjamin Dollard . . . .

—I know, M'Coy broke in. My missus sang there once.

—Did she? Lenehan said.

He checked his tale a moment but broke out in a wheezy laugh.

—But wait till I tell you, he said, Delahunt of Camden street had the catering and yours truly was chief bottlewasher. Bloom and the wife were there. Lashings of stuff we put up: port wine and sherry and curacoa. Cold joints galore and mince pies .....

—I know, M'Coy said. The year the missus was there ....

Lenehan linked his arm warmly.

—But wait till I tell you, he said. We had a midnight lunch after it too and when we sallied forth it was blue o'clock in the morning , Coming home it was a gorgeous winter's night on the featherbed mountain. Bloom and Chris Callanan were on one side of the car and I was with the wife on the other. We started singing glees and duets: *Lo, the early beam of morning*. She was well primed with a good load of Delahunt's port under her belly band. Every jolt the bloody car gave I had her bumping up against me. Hell's delight! She has a fine pair, God bless her. Like that.

He held his caved hands a cubit from him, frowning:

—I was tucking the rug under her and settling her boa all the time. Know what I mean?

His hands moulded ample curves of the air. He shut his eyes tight in delight, his body shrinking, and blew a sweet chirp from his lips.

—The lad stood to attention anyhow, he said with a sigh. She's a gamey mare and no mistake . Bloom was pointing out all the stars and the comets in the heavens to Chris Callanan and the jarvey: the Great bear and Hercules and the dragon and the whole jingbang lot. But, by God, I was lost, so to speak, in the milky way. He knew them all, faith. At last she spotted a weeny one miles away. *And what star is that, Poldy?* says she. By God, she had Bloom cornered. *That one, is it?* says Chris Callanan, *sure that's only what you might call a pinprick.* By God, he wasn't far wide of the mark.

Lenehan stopped and leaned on the riverwall, panting with soft laughter.

—I'm weak, he gasped.

Mc'Coy's white face smiled about it at instants and grew grave Lenehan walked on again. He lifted his yachting cap and scratched his hindhead rapidly. He glanced sideways in the sunlight at Mc'Coy.

—He's a cultured chap, Bloom is, he said seriously. He's not one of your common or garden ..... you know ..... There's a touch of the artist about Bloom.

+

+ +

Mr Bloom turned over idly pages of *Maria Monk*, then of Aristotle's *Masterpiece*. Crooked botched print. Plates: infants cuddled in a ball in bloodred wombs like livers of slaughtered cows. Lots of them like that at this moment all over the world. All butting with their skulls to get out of it. Child born every minute somewhere. Mrs. Purefoy.

He laid both books aside and glanced at the third. *Tales of the Ghetto* by Sacher Masoch.

— That I had, he said, pushing it by.

The shopman let two volumes fall on the counter.

—Them are two good ones, he said.

Onions of his breath came across the counter out of his ruined mouth. He bent to make a bundle of the other books, hugged them against his unbuttoned waistcoat and bore them off behind the dingy curtain.

Mr. Bloom, lone, looked at the titles. *Fair Tyrants* by James Lovebirch. Know the kind that is.

He opened it. Thought so.

A woman's voice behind the dingy curtain. Listen: The man.

No: she wouldn't like that much. Got her one once.

He read the other title: *Sweets of Sin*. More in her line. Let us see.

He read where his finger opened.

—All the dollarbills her husband gave her were spent in the stores on wondrous gowns and costliest frillies. For him! For Raoul!

Yes. This. Here. Try.

—Her mouth glued on his in a luscious voluptuous kiss while his hands felt for the opulent curves inside her deshabille.

Yes. Take this. The end.

—You are late, he spoke hoarsely, eyeing her with a suspicious glare.

The beautiful woman threw off her sabletrimmed wrap, displaying her queenly shoulders and heaving embonpoint. An inperceptible smile played round her perfect lips as she turned to him calmly.

Mr. Bloom read again: *The beautiful woman* . . . .

Warmth showered gently over him, cowing his flesh. Flesh yielded amply amid rumpled clothes: Whites of eyes swooning up His nostrils arched themselves for prey. Melting breast ointments (*for him! For Raoul!*) Armpits' oniony sweat. Fishgluey slime. (*her heaving embonpoint!*) Feel! Press! Chrished! Sulphur dung of lions!

Young! Young!

Phlegmy coughs shook the air of the bookshop, bulging out the dingy curtains. The shopman's uncombed grey head came out and his unshaven reddened face, coughing. He raked his throat rudely, spat phlegm on the floor.

He put his boot on what he had spat, wiping his sole along it and bent, showing a raw-skinned crown, scantily haired.

Mr. Bloom beheld it.

Mastering his troubled breath, he said:

—I'll take this one.

The shopman lifted eyes bleared with old rheum.

—*Sweets of Sin*, he said, tapping on it. That's a good one.

+

\+ +

The lacquey by the door of Dillon's auctionrooms shook his handbell twice again and viewed himself in the chalked mirror of the cabinet.

Dilly Dedalus, listening by the curbstone, heard the beats of the bell, the cries of the auctioneer within. Four and nine. Those lovely curtains. Five shillings? Cosy curtains. Selling new at two guineas. Any advance of five shillings? Going for five shillings.

The lacquey lifted his handbell and shook it:

—Barang!

Bang of the lastlap bell spurred the halfmile wheelmen to their spirit. J. A. Jackson, W. E. Wylie, A. Munro and H. T. Gahan, their stretched necks wagging, negotiated the curve by the College library.

Mr. Dedalus, tugging a long moustache, came round from William's row. He halted near his daughter.

—It's time for you, she said.

—Stand up straight for the love of the Lord Jesus, Mr. Dedalus said. Are you trying to imitate your uncle John the cornetplayer, head upon shoulders?

Dilly shrugged her shoulders. Mr. Dedalus placed his hands on them and held them back.

—Stand up straight, girl, he said. You'll get curvature of the spine. Do you know what you look like?

He let his head sink suddenly down and forward, hunching his shoulders and dropping his underjaw.

—Give it up, father, Dilly said. All the people are looking at you.

Mr. Dedalus drew himself upright and tugged again at his moustache.

—Did you get any money? Dilly asked.

—Where would I get money? Mr. Dedalus said. There is no one in Dublin would lend me four pence.

—You got some, Dilly said, looking in his eyes.

—How do you know that? Mr. Dedalus asked, his tongue in his cheek.

Mr. Kernan, pleased with the order he had booked, walked boldly along James's street.

—I know you did, Dilly answered. Were you in the Scotch house now?

—I was not there, Mr. Dedalus said, smiling. Was it the little nuns taught you to be so saucy? Here.

He handed her a shilling.

—See if you can do anything with that, he said.

—I suppose you got five, Dilly said. Give me more than that.

—Wait awhile, Mr Dedalus said threateningly. You're like the rest of them, are you? An insolent pack of little bitches since your poor mother died. But wait awhile. You'll get a short shrift and a long day from me.

He left her and walked on. Dilly followed quickly and pulled his coat.

—Well, what is it? he said, stopping.

The lacquey rang his bell behind their backs.

—Barang!

—Curse your bloody blatant soul, Mr. Dedalus cried, turning on him.

The lacquey, aware of comment, shook the lolling clapper of his bell: but feebly:

—Bang!

—You got more than that, father, Dilly said.

—I'm going to show you a little trick, Mr. Dedalus said. I'll leave you all where Jesus left the Jews. Look, that's all I have. I got two shillings from Jack Power and I spent two pence for a shave for the funeral.

He drew forth a handful of copper coins nervously.

—Can't you look for some money somewhere? Dilly said.

Mr. Dedalus thought and nodded.

—I will, he said gravely, I looked all along the gutter in O'Connell street. I'll try this one now.

—You're very funny Dilly said, grinning.

—Here, Mr. Dedalus said, handing her two pennies. Get a glass of milk for yourself and a bun or a something. I'll be home shortly.

He put the other coins in his pocket and started to walk on.

The viceregal cavalcade passed, greeted by obsequious policemen, out of Park gate.

—I'm sure you have another shilling, Dilly said.

The lacquey banged loudly.

Mr. Dedalus amid the din walked off, murmuring to himself with a pursing mincing mouth.

—The little nuns! Nice little things! O, sure they wouldn't do anything! O, sure they wouldn't really! Is it little sister Monica!

From the sundial towards James' Gate walked Mr. Kernan, pleased with the order he had booked for Pullbrook Robertson boldly along James's street. Got round him all right. How do you do, Mr. Crimmin? First rate, Sir. How are things going? Just keeping alive. Lovely weather we are having. Yes, indeed. Good for the country. I'll just take a thimble full of your best gin, Mr. Crimmins. A small gin, sir. Yes, sir. Terrible affair that General Slocum explosion. Terrible, terrible. A thousand casualties. And heartrending scenes. Men trampling down women and children. Most brutal thing. What do they say was the cause? Spontaneous combustion: most scandalous revelation. Not a single lifeboat would float and the firehose all burst. What I cann't understand is how the inspectors ever allowed a boat like that ...... Now you're talking straight, Mr. Crimmins. You know why? Palm oil. Is that a fact? Without a doubt. Well, now, look at that. And America they say is the land of the free. I thought we were bad here.

I smiled at him. America, I said, quietly, just like that. What is it? The sweepings of every country including our own. Isn't that true? That's a fact.

Graft, my dear sir. Well, of course, where there's money going there's always someone to pick it up.

Saw him looking at my frock coat. Dress does it. Nothing like a dressy appearance. Bowls them over.

—Hello, Simon, Father Cowley said.

—Hello, Bob, old man, Mr. Dedalus answered.

Mr. Kernan halted and preened himself before the sloping mirror of Peter Kennedy, hairdresser. Stylish coat, you know. Scott of Dawson street. Well worth the half sovereign I gave Nearly for it. Never built under three guinas. Fits me down to the ground. Some Kildare street club toff had it probably.

Aham! Must dress the character for those fellows. Gentlemen. And now, Mr. Crimmins may we have the honour of your custom again, sir. The cup that cheers but not inebriates, as the old saying has it.

North wall and Sir John Rogerson's quay, with hulls and anchor chains, sailing westward, sailed by a skiff, a crumpled throwaway, rocked on the ferrywash, Elijah is coming.

Mr. Kernan glanced in farewell at his image. High colour, of course. Grizzled moustache. Returned Indian officer. Bravely he bore his stumpy body forward on spatted feet, squaring his shoulders.

Aham! Hot spirit of juniper juice warmed his vitals and his breath. Good drop of gin, that was. His frock's tails winked in bright sunshine to his fat strut.

Down there Emmet was hanged, drawn and quartered. Greasy black rope. Dogs licking the blood off the street when the Lord lieutenant's wife drove by in her noddy .

Let me see. Is he buried in Saint Michan's? or no there was a midnight burial in Glasnevin. Corpse brought in through a secret door in the wall. Dignam is there now. Went out in a puff. Well, well. Better turn down here.

Mr. Kernan turned and walked down the slope of Watling street. Denis Breen with his tomes, weary of having waited an hour in John Henry Menton's office, led his wife over O'Connell bridge, bound for the office of Messrs. Collis and Ward.

Times of the troubles. Must ask New Lambert to lend me those reminiscences of Sir Jonah Barrington. When you look back on it all now in a kind of retrospective arrangement. Gaming at Daly's. No cardsharping then. One of those fellows got his hand nailed to the table by a dagger.

Somewhere here Lord Edward Fitzgerald escaped from major Sirr. Island street. Stables behind Moira house.

Damn good gin that was.

Fine dashing young nobleman. Good stock, of course. That ruffian, that sham squire, with his violet gloves, gave him away. Course they were on the wrong side. They rose in dark and evil days. Fine poem that is: Ingram. They were gentlemen. Ben Dollard does sing that ballad touchingly. Masterly rendition.

At the siege of Ross did my father fall.

A cavalcade in easy trot along Penbroke quay, passed, outriders leaping gracefully in their saddles. Frockcoats. Cream sunsheds.

Mr. Kernan hurried forward, blowing pursily.

His Excellency! Too bad! Just missed that by a hair. Damn it! What a pity!

\+

\+ +

Stephen Dedalus watched through the webbed window the lapidary's fingers prove a timedulled chain. Dust webbed the window dust darkened the toiling fingers with their vulture nails. Dust slept on dull coils of bronze and silver, lozenges of cinnabar, on rubies, leprous and winedark stones.

Born all in the dark wormy earth, cold specks of fire, evil lights shining in the darkness. Muddy swinesnouts, hands, root and root, gripe and wrest them.

She dances in a foul gloom where gum burns with garlic. A sailorman, rustbearded sips from a beaker rum and eyes her. A long and seafed silent rut. She dances, capers, wagging her sowish haunches and her hips, on her gross belly flapping a ruby egg.

Old Russell with a smeared shammy rag, burnished again his gem, turned it and held it at the point of his Moses' beard. Grandfather ape gloating on a stolen hoard.

And you who wrest old images from the burial earth! The brainsick words of sophists: Antisthenes. A lore of drugs. Orient and immortal wheat standing from everlasting to everlasting.

Two old women from their whiff of the briny drudged through Irishtown along London bridge road, one with a sanded unbrella, one with a midwife's bag in which eleven cockles rolled.

The whirr of flapping leathern bands and hum of dynamos from the powerhouse urged Stephen to be on. Beingless beings. Stop! Throb always without you and the throb always within. Your heart you sing of. I between them. Where? Between two roaring worlds where they swirl, I. Shatter them, one and both. But stun myself too in the blow. Shatter me you who can. Bawd and butcher, were the words. I say! Not yet awhile. A look around.

Yes, quite true. Very large and wonderful and keeps famous time. You say, right Sir, a Monday morning. Twas so, indeed.

Stephen went down Bedford row. In Clohisey's window a faded print of Heenan boxing Sayers held his eye. Staring backers with square hats stood round the ropering. The heavy weights in light loincloths proposed gently each to other his bulbous fists. And they are throbbing: heros' hearts.

He turned and halted by the slanted bookcart.

—Twopence each, the huckster said. Four for sixpence.

Tattered pages. *The Irish Beekeeper. Life and Miracles of the Curé of Ars. Pocket Guide to Killarney.*

I might find here one of my pawned schoolprizes. *Stephano Dedalo, alumno optimo, palmam ferenti.*

Father Conmee, having read his little hours, walked through the hamlet of Donnycarney, murmuring vespers.

Binding too good probably. What is this? Eighth and ninth book of Moses secret of all secrets. Seal of King David. Thumbed pages: read and read. Who has passed here before me? How to soften chapped hands. Recipe for white wine vinegar. How to win a woman's love. For me this. Say the following talisman three times with hands folded:

—*Se el yilo nebrakada femininum! Amor me solo! Sanktus! Amen.*

Who wrote this? Charms and invocations of the most blessed abbot Peter Salanka to all true believers divulged. As good as any other abbot's charms, as mumbling Joachim's. Down, baldynoddle, or we'll wool your wool.

—What are you doing here, Stephen?

Dilly's high shoulders and shabby dress.

Shut the book quick. Don't let see.

—What are you doing? Stephen said.

A Stuart face of nonesuch Charles, lank locks falling at its sides. It glowed as she crouched feeding the fire with broken boots. I told her of Paris. Late lieabed under a quilt of old overcoats fingering a pinchbeck bracelet, Dan Kelly's token. *Nebrakada femininum*. .

—What have you there? Stephen asked.

—I bought it from the other cart for a penny, Dilly said, laughing nervously. Is it any good?

My eyes they say she has. Do others see me so? Quick, far and daring. Shadow of my mind.

He took the coverless book from her hand. Bué's French primer.

—What did you buy that for? He asked. To learn French?

She nodded, reddening and closing tight her lips.

Show no surprise. Quite natural.

—Here, Stephen said. It's all right. Mind Maggie doesn't pawn it on you. I suppose all my books are gone.

—Some, Dilly said. We had to.

She is drowning. Save her. All against us. She will drown me with her, eyes and hair. Lank coils of seaweed hair around me, my heart, my soul. Salt green death.

We.

Misery! Misery!

+

\+ +

—Hello, Simon, Father Cowley said.

—Hello, Bob, old man, Mr. Dedalus answered, stopping.

They clasped hands loudly outside Keddy and Daughter's. Father Cowley brushed his moustache often downward with a scooping hand.

—What's the best news? Mr. Dedalus said.

—Why then not much Father Cowley said. I'm barricaded up, Simon, with two men prowling around the house trying to effect an entrance.

—Jolly, Mr. Dedalus said. Who is it?

—O, Father Cowley said. A certain gombeen man of our acquaintance.

—With a broken back, is it? Mr. Dedalus asked.

—The same, Simon, Father Cowley answered.

—Reuben of that ilk. I'm just waiting for Ben Dollard. He's going to say a word to Long John to get him to take those two men off. All I want is a little time.

He looked with vague hope up and down the quay, a big apple bulging in his neck.

—I know, Mr. Dedalus said, nodding. Poor old bockedy Ben! He's always doing a good turn for someone. Hold hard!

He put on his glasses and gazed towards the metal bridge an instant.

—There he is, by God, he said, arse and pockets.

Ben Dollard's loose blue cutaway and square hat above large slops crossed the quay in full gait from the metal bridge. He came towards them at an amble, scratching actively behind his coattails.

As he came near Mr. Dedalus greeted:

—Hold that fellow with the bad trousers.

—Hold him now, Ben Dollard said.

He stood beside them beaming on them first and on his roomy clothes from points of which Mr. Dedalus flicked fluff, saying:

—They were made for a man in his health.

—Bad luck to the jewman that made them, Ben Dollard said. Thanks be to God he is not paid yet.

—And how is that *basso profondo*, Benjamin, Father Cowley asked.

Cashel Boyle O'Connor Fitzmaurice Tisdall Farrell, murmuring, glassy eyed strode past the Kildare street club.

Ben Dollard frowned and, making suddenly a chanter's mouth, gave forth a deep note.

—Aw! he said.

—That's the style, Mr. Dedalus said, nodding to its drone.

—What about that? Ben Dollard said. Not too dusty? What?

He turned to both.

—That'll do, Father Cowley said, nodding also.

The reverend Hugh C. Love walked from the old Chapterhouse of saint Mary's abbey past James and Charles Kennedy, rectifiers, attended by Geraldines tall and personable, towards the Tholsel beyond the Ford of Hurdles.

Ben Dollard with a heavy list towards the shopfronts led them forward, his joyful fingers in the air.

—Come along, with me to the subsheriff's office, he said. I saw John Henry Menton in the Bodega. We're on the right lay, Bob, believe you me.

—For a few days tell him, Father Cowley said anxiously.

Ben Dollard halted and stared, his loud orifice open.

—What few days? be boomed. Hasn't your landlord distrained for rent.

—He has, Father Cowley said.

—Then our friend's writ is not worth the paper it's printed on, Ben Dollard said. The landlord has the prior claim.

—Are you sure of that?

—You can tell Barabbas from me, Ben Dollard said, that he can put that writ where Jacko put the nuts.

He led Father Cowley boldly forward linked to his bulk.

—Filbert's I believe they were, Mr. Dedalus said, as he dropped his glasses on his coatfront, following them.

+

+ +

—The youngster will be all right Martin Cunningham said, as they passed out of the Castle yard gate.

The policeman touched his forehead.

—God bless you, Martin Cunningham said, cheerily.

He signed to the waiting jarvey who chucked at the reins and set on towards Lord Edward street.

Bronze by gold, Miss Kennedy's head with Miss Douce's head, appeared above the crossblind of the Ormond hotel.

—Yes, Martin Cunningham said. I wrote to Father Conmee and laid the whole case before him.

—You could try our friend, Mr. Power suggested backward.

—Boyd? Martin Cunningham said shortly. Touch me not.

John Wyse Nolan, lagging behind, reading the list, came after them quickly down Cork hill.

On the steps of the City hall Councillor Nannetti descending, hailed Alderman Cowley and Councillor Abraham Lyon ascending.

The castle car wheeled empty into upper Exchange street.

—Look here Martin, John Wyse Nolan said, overtaking them at the *Mail* office. I see Bloom put his name down for five shillings.

—Quite right, Martin Cunningham said, taking the list. And put down the five shillings too.

—Without a second word either, Mr. Power said.

—Strange but true, Martin Cunningham added.

John Wyse Nolan opened wide eyes.

—I'll say there is much kindness in the Jew, he quoted elegantly.

They went down Parliament street.

—There's Jimmy Henry, Mr. Power said, just heading for Kavanagh's.

—Righto, Martin Cunningham said. Here goes.

Outside la Maison Claire Blazes Boylan waylaid Jack Mooney's brother-in-law, humpy, tight, making for the liberties.

John Wyse Nolan fell back with Mr. Power, while Martin Cunningham took the elbow of a little man in a shower of hail suit who walked uncertainly with hasty steps, past Nicky Anderson's watches.

—The assistant town clerk's corns are giving him some trouble, John Wyse Nolan told Mr. Power.

They followed round the corner towards James Kavanagh's winerooms. The empty castle car fronted them at rest in Essex gate. Martin Cunningham, speaking always, showed often the list at which Jimmy Henry did not glance.

—And long John Fanning is here too, John Wyse Bolan said, as large as life.

The tall form of long John Fanning filled the doorway where he stood.

—Good day, Mr. Sheriff, Martin Cunningham said, as all halted and greeted.

Long John Fanning made no way for them. He removed his large Henry Clay decisively, and his large fierce eyes scowled intelligently over all their faces.

—Are the conscript fathers pursuing their peaceful deliberations? he said, with rich acrid utterance to the assistant town clerk.

—Hell open to Christians they were having, Jimmny Henry said pettishly, about their damned Irish language. Where was the marshal, he wanted to know to keep order in the council chamber. And old Barlow the macebearer laid up with asthma and Harrington in Llandudno and little Lorcan Sherlock doing *locum tenens* for him. Damned Irish language, language of our forefathers.

Long John Fanning blew a plume of smoke from his lips.

Martin Cunningham spoke by turns to the assistant town clerk and the sub-sheriff, while John Wyse Nolan held his peace.

—That Dignam was that? Long John Faninng asked.

Jimmy Henry made a grimace and lifted his left foot.

—O, my corns! he said plaintively. Come upstairs for goodness' sake till I sit down somewhere. Uff! Ooo! Mind!

Testily he made room for himself beside Long John Fanning's flank and passed in and up the stirs.

—Come on up, Martin Cunningham said to the subsheriff! I don't think you knew him, or perhaps you did though.

With John Wyse Nolan, Mr. Power followed them in.

—Decent little soul he was, Mr. Power said to the stalwart back of Long John Fanning, ascending towards Long John Fanning in the mirror.

—Rather lowsized, Dignam of Menton's office that was, Martin Cunningham said.

Long John Fanning could not remember him.

Clatter of horsehoofs sounded from the air.

—What's that? Martin Cunningham said.

All turned where they stood; John Wyse Nolan came down again. From the cool shadow of the doorway he saw the horses pass Parliament street, harness and glossy pasterns in sunlight shimmering. Gaily they went past before his cool unfriendly eyes, not quickly.

—What was it? Martin Cunningham asked, as they went on up the staircase.

—The lord lieutenant general and general governor of Ireland, John Wyse Nolan answered from the stairfoot.

+

+ +

As they trod across the thick carpet Buck Mulligan whispered behind his hat to Haines.

—Parnell's brother. There in the corner.

They choose a small table near the window opposite a longfaced man whose beard and gaze hung intently down on a chessboard.

—Is that he? Haines asked, twisting round in his seat.

—Yes, Mulligan said. That's John Howard, his brother, our city marshal.

John Howard Parnell translated a white bishop quietly, and his grey claw went up again to his forehead whereat it rested.

An instant after, under its screen, his eyes looked quickly, ghostbright, at his foe and fell once more upon a working corner. I'll take a *mélange*, Haines said to the waitress.

—Two *mélanges,* Buck Mulligan said. And bring us some scones and butter, and some cakes as well.

When she had gone he said, laughing:

—We call it D. B. C. because they have damn bad cakes. O, but you missed Dedalus on *Hamlet.*

Haines opened his newbought book.

—I'm sorry, he said. Shakespeare is the happy hunting ground of all minds that have lost their balance.

The onelegged sailor growled at the area of 17 Helson street:

—England expects.

Buck Mulligan's primrose waistcoat shook gaily to his laughter.

—You should see him, he said, when his body loses its balance. Wandering Aengus I call him.

—I am sure he has an *idée fixe,* Haines said, pinching his chin thoughtfully with thumb and forefinger. How I am speculating what it would be likely to be. Such persons always have.

Buck Mulligan bent across the table gravely.

—They drove his wits astray, he said, by visions of hell. He will never capture the attic note. The note of Swinburne, of all poets, the white death and the ruddy birth. That is his tragedy. He can never be a poet. The joy of creation . . . . .

—Eternal punishment, Haines said, nodding curtly. I see. I tackled him this morning on belief. There was something on his mind, I saw. It's rather interesting because Professor Pokorny of Vienna makes an interesting point of that.

Buck Mulligan's watchful eyes saw the waitress come. He helped her to unload her tray.

—He can find no trace of hell in ancient Irish myth, Haines said, amid the cheerful cups. The moral idea seems lacking, the sense of destiny, of retribution. Rather strang he should have just that fixed idea. Does he write anything for your movement?

He sank two lumps of sugar deftly longwise through the whipped cream. Buck Mulligan slit a steaming scone in two and plastered butter over its smoking pith. He bit off a soft piece hungrily.

—Ten years he said, chewing and laughing. He is going to write something in ten years.

—Seems a long way off, Haines said, thoughtfully lifting his spoon. Still, I shouldn't wonder if he did, after all.

He tasted a spoonful from the creamy cone of his cup.

—This is real Irish cream I take it, he said with forbearance. I don't want to be imposed on.

Elijah, skiff, light crumpled throwaway, sailed eastward by flanks of ships and trawlers, beyond new Wapping street past Benson's ferry, and by the threemasted schooner *Rosevean* from Bridgwater with bricks.

+

+ +

Almidano Artifoni walked past Holles street, past Sewell's yard. Behind him Cashel Boyle O'Connor Fitzmaurice Tisdall Farrell with stickumbrelladustcoat dangling, shunned the lamp before Wilde's house and walked along Merrion square. Distantly behind him a blind stripling tapped his way by the wall of College Park.

Cashel Boyle O'Connor Fitzmaurice Tisdall Farrell walked as far as Mr. Lewis Werner's cheerful windows, then turned and strode back along Merrion square, his stickumbrelladustcoat dangling.

At the corner of Wilde's house he halted, frowned at Elijah's name announced on the Metropolitan Hall, frowned at the distant pleasance of duke's lawn. His eyeglass flashed frowning in the sun. With ratsteeth bared he muttered:

Coatus volui.

He strode on for Clare street, grinding his fierce word.

As he strode past Mr. Bloom's dental windows the sway of his dustcoat brushed rudely from its angle a slender tapping cane and swept onwards, having buffeted a thewless body. The blind stripling turned his sickly face after the striding form.

—God's curse on you, he said sourly, whoever you are! You're blinder nor I am, you bitch's bastard!

+

+ +

Opposite Ruggy O'Donohoe's Maszer Patrick Aloysius Dignam, pawing the pound and a half of Mangan's, late Fehrenbach's, portporksteaks he had been sent for, went along warm Wicklow dawdling. It was too blooming dull, sitting in the parlour with Mrs. Stoer and Mrs. Quigly and ma and the blind down and they all at their sniffles and sipping sups of the superior old sherry uncle Barney brought from Tunney's. And they eating crumbs of the cottage fruit cake, jawing the whole blooming time and sighing. After Wicklow lane the window of Madame Doyle court dress milliner stopped him. He stood looking in at the two puckers stripped to their pelts and putting up their props. From the sidemirrors two mourning Masters Dignam gaped silently. Myler Keogh, Dublin's pet lamb, will meet Sergeant major Bennett, the Portobello bruiser, for a purse of twelve sovereigns. Gob, that'd be a good pucking match to see. Myler Keogh, that's the chap sparring out to him with the green sash. Two bar entrance, soldiers half price. I could easy do a bunk on ma. Master Dignam on his left turned as he turned. That's me in mourning. When is it? May the twentysecond. Sure, the blooming thing is all over. He turned to the right and on his right Master Dignam turned, his cap awry, his collar sticking up. Buttoning it down, his chin lifted, he saw the image of Marie Kendall, charming soubrette, beside the two puckers. One of them mots that do be in the packets of fags Stoer smokes that his old fellow welted hell out of him for one time he found out.

Master Dignam got his collar down and dawdled on. The best pucker going for strength was Fitzsimons. One puck in the wind from that fellow would knock you into the middle of next week, man. But the best pucker for science was Jem Corbet before Fitzsimons knocked the stuffings out of him, dodging and all.

In Grafton street Master Dignam saw a red flower in a toff's mouth and a swell pair of kicks on him and he listening to what the drunk was telling him and grinning all the time.

+

\+ +

No Sandymount tram.

Master Dignam walked along Nassau Strret, shifted the porksteaks to his other hand. His collar sprang up again and he tugged it down. The blooming stud was too small for the buttonhole of the shirt, blooming end to it. He met schoolboys with satchels. I'am not going tomorrow either, stay away till Mondy. He met other schoolboys. Do they notice I'm in mourning? Uncle Barney said he'd get it into the paper tonight. Then they'll all see it in the paper and read my name printed, and pa's name.

His face got all grey instead of being red like it was and there was a fly walking over it up to his eye. The scrunch that was when they were screwing the screws into the coffin: and the bumps when they were bringing it downstairs.

Pa was inside it and ma crying in the parlour and uncle Barney telling the men how to get it round the bend. A big coffin it was and high and heavy-looking. How was that? The last night pa was boosed he was standing on the landing there bawling out for his boots to go out to Tunney's for to boose more and he looked butty and short in his shirt. Never see him again. Death that is. Pa is dead. My father is dead. He told me to be a good son to ma. I couldn't hear the other things he said but I saw his tongue and his teeth trying to say it better. Poor pa. That was Mr. Dignam, my father. I hope he is in purgatory now because he went to confession to father Conroy on Saturday night.

+

+ +

William Humble, earl of Dudley, and Lady Dudley, accompanied by lieutenant-colonel Hesseltime, drove out after luncheon from the viceregal lodge. In the following carriage were the honourable Mrs. Paget, Miss de Courcy and the honourabl Gerald Ward A. D. C. in attendance.

The cavalcade passed out by the lower gate of Phoneix Park saluted by obsequious policemen and proceeded along the northern quays. The viceroy was most cordially greeted on his way through the metropolis. At bloody bridge Mr. Thomas Kernan beyond the river greeted him vainly from afar. In the porch of four courts Richie Goulding with the costsbag of Goulding Colles and Ward saw him with surprise. From its sluice in Wood quay wall under Tom Devon's office Poodle river hung out in fealty a tongue of liquid sewage. Above the crossblind of the Ormond Hotel, bronze by gold, Miss Kennedy's head by Miss Douce's head watched and admired. On Ormond quay Mr. Simon Dedalus, on his way from the greenhouse to the subsheriff's office, stood still in midstreet and brought his hat low. His Excellency graciously returned Mr. Dedalus' greeting. From Cahill's corner the reverend Hugh C. Love made obeisance unperceived mindful of lords deputies whose hands benignant had held of yore rich advowsons. On Grattan bridge Lenehan and McCoy, taking leave of each other, watched the carriage go by. From the shaded door of Kavanagh's winerooms John Wyse Nolan smiled with unseen coldness towards the lord liutenant general and general governor of Ireland. Over against Dame gate Tom Rochford and Nosey Flynn watched the approach of the cavalcade. Tom Rochford, seeing the eyes of lady Dudley fixed on him, took his thumbs quickly out of the pockets of his claret waistcoat and duffed his cap to her. A charming soubrette, great Marie Kendall, with dauby cheeks and lifted skirt smiled daubily from her poster upon William Humble ,earl of Dudley, and upon lieutenant colonel H. G. Hesseltime, and also upon the honourable Gerald Ward A. D. C. From the window of the

D. B. C. Buck Mulligan gaily, and Haines gravely, gazed down on the viceregal carriages over the shoulders of eager guests, whose mass of forms darkened the chessboard whereon John Howard Parnell looked intently. In Fownes's street, Dilly Dedalus, straining her sight upward from Bue's first French primer, saw sunshades spanned and wheelspokes spinning in the glare. John Henry Menton, filling the doorway of Commercial Buildings, stared from winebig oyster eyes. Where the foreleg of King Billy's horse pawed the air Mrs. Breen plucked her hastening husband back from under the hoofs of the outriders. She shouted in his ear the tidings. Understanding, he shifted his tomes to his left breast and saluted the second carriage. The honourable Gerald Ward A. D. C., agreeably surprised, made haste to reply. At Ponsonby's Corner a jaded white flagon H. halted and four tallhatted white flagons halted behind him, E. L. Y. S, while outriders pranced past and carriages. By the provost's wall came jauntily Blazes Boylan, stepping in tanned shoes and socks with skyblue clocks to the refrain of *My girl's a Yorkshire girl.*

Blazes Boylan presented to the leaders' skyblue frontlets and high action a skyblue tie, a widebrimmed straw hat at a rakish angle and a suit of indigo serge. His hands in his jacket pockets forgot to salute but he offered to the three ladies the bold admiration of his eyes and the red flower between his lips. As they drove along Nassau street his excellency drew the attention of his bowing consort to the programme of music which was being discoursed in College park. Unseen brazen highland laddies blared and drumthumped after the cortège:

But though she's a factory lass
And weares no fancy clothes
Baraabum
Yet I've a sort of a
Yorkshire relish for
My little Yorkshire rose
Baraabum.

Thither of the wall the quartermile flat handicappers, M. C. Green, H. Thrift, T. M. Patey, S. Scaife, J. B. Joffs, G. N. Morphy, F. Stevenson, C. Adderly, and W. C. Huggard started in pursuit. Striding past Finn's hotel, Cashel Boyle O'Connor Fitzmaurice isdall Farrell stared through a fierce eyeglass across the carriages at the head of Mr. M. E. Solomons in the window of the Austro-Hungarian vice-consulate. Deep in Leintser street, by Trinity's postern, a loyal King's man, Hornblower, touched his tallyho cap. As the glossy horses pranced by Merrion square Master Patrick Aloysius Dignam, waiting, saw salutes being given to the gent with the topper and raised also his new black cap with fingers greased by porksteak paper. His collar too sprang up . The Viceroy, on his way to inaugurate the Mirus bazaar in aid of funds for Mercer's Hospital, drove with his following towards Lower Mount street. He passed a blind stripling opposite Broadbent's. In Lower Mount street a pedestrian in a brown mackintosh, eating dry bread, passed swiftly and unscathed across the viceroy's path. At the Royal Canal bridge, from his hoarding, Mr. Eugene Stratton, his blub lips agrin, bade all comers welcome to Pembroke township. At Haddington road corner two sandled women halted themselves, an umbrella and a bag in which eleven cockles rolled to view with wonder the lord mayor and lady mayoress without his golden chain. On Northumberland road his excellency acknowledged punctually salutes from rare male walkers the salute of two small schoolboys at a garden gate and the salute of Almidano Artifoni's sturdy trousers swallowed by a closing door.

(*To be continued.*)

Episode XI

THE LITTLE REVIEW

VOL. VI. AUGUST, 1919 No. 4

CONTENTS

Subscription price, payable in advance, in the United States and Territories, $2.50 per year; Canada, $2.75; Foreign, $3.00. Published monthly, and copyrighted, 1919, by Margaret C. Anderson.
Manuscripts must be submitted at author's risk, with return postage.
Entered as second class matter March 16, 1917, at the Post Office at New York, N. Y., under the act of March 3, 1879.

MARGARET C. ANDERSON, Publisher

24 *West Sixteenth Street, New York, N. Y.*

Foreign Office: 43 *Belsize Park, Gardens, London N. W.* 3.

Bronze by gold heard the hoofirons, steelyringing.
Imperthnthn thnthnthn.
Chips, picking chips off rocky thumbnail, chips.
Horrid! And gold flushed more.
A husky fifenote blew.
Blew. Blue bloom is on the
Gold pinnacled hair.
A jumping rose on satiny breasts of satin, rose of Castile.
Trilling, trilling: Idolores.
Peep! Who's in the . . . . . . peepofgold?
Tink cried to bronze in pity.
And a call, pure, long and throbbing. Longindying call.
Decoy. Soft word. But look! The bright stars fade. O rose!
Notes chirruping answer. Castile. The morn is breaking.
Jingle jingle jaunted jingling.
Coin rang. Clock clacked.
Avowal. Sonnez. I could. Rebound of garter. Not leave thee.
Smack. La cloche! Thigh smack. Avowal. Warm. Sweetheart, goodbye!
Jingle. Bloo
Boomed crashing chords. When love absorbs. War! War! The tympanum.
A sail! A veil awave upon the waves.
Lost. Throstle fluted. All is lost now.
Horn. Hawhorn.
When first he saw. Alas!
Full tup. Full throb.
Warbling. Ah, lure! Alluring.
Martha! Come!
Clapclop. Clipclap. Clappyclap.
Goodgod henev erheard inall
Deaf bald Pat brought pad knife took up.
A moonlit hightcall: far: far.
I feel so sad. P. S.. So lonely blooming.
Listen!
The spiked and winding cold seahorn. Have you the? Each and for other plash and silent roar.

Overleaf: table of contents, *Little Review,* August 1919

Pearls: when she. Liszt's rhapsodies. Hissss.
You don't?
Did not: no, no: believe: Lidlyd. With a cock with a carra.
Black.
Deepsounding. Do, Ben, do.
Wait while you wait. Hee hee. Wait while you hee.
But wait!
Low in dark middle earth. Embedded ore.
Naminedamine. All gone. All fallen.
Tiny, her tremulous fernfoils of maidenhair.
Amen! He gnashed in fury.
Fro. To, fro. A baton cool protruding.
Bronzelydia by Minagold.
By bronze, by gold, in oceangreen of shadow. Bloom. Old Bloom.
One rapped, one tapped with a carra, with a cock.
Pray for him! Pray, good people!
His gouty fingers nakkering.
Big Benaben. Big Benben.
Last rose Castile of summer left bloom I feel so sad alone.
Pwee Little wind piped wee.
True men. Lid Ker Cow De and Doll. Ay, ay, like you men.
Will lift your tschink with tschunk.
Fff! Oo!
Where bronze from anear? Where gold from afar? Where hoofs?
Rrrpr. Kraa. Kraandl.
Then, not till then. My eppripfftaph. Be pfwritt.
Done.
Begin!

Bronze by gold, Miss Douce's head by Miss Kennedy's head, over the crossblind of the Ormond bar heard the viceregal hoofs go by, ringing steel.
—Is that her? asked Miss Kennedy's head.

Miss Douce said yes, sitting with his ex, pearl grey and eau de Nil.
—Exquisite contrast, Miss Kennedy said.

When all agog Miss Douce said eagerly:
—Look at the fellow in the tall silk.
—Who? Where? gold asked more eagerly.

—In the second carriage, Miss Douce's wet lips said, laughing in the sun. He's looking. Mind till I see.

She darted, bronze, to the backmost corner, flattening her face against the pane in a halo of hurried breath.

Her wet lips tittered:

—He's killed looking back.

She laughed:

—O wept! Aren't men frightful idiots

With sadness.

Miss Kennedy sauntered sadly from bright light, twining a loose hair behind an ear. Sauntering sadly, gold no more, she twisted twined a hair. Sadly she twined in sauntering gold hair behind a curving ear.

—It's them has the fine times, sadly then she said.

A man.

Bloom went by Moulang's pipes, bearing in his breast the sweets of sin, by Wine's antiques in memory bearing sweet sinful words, by Carroll's dusky battered plate, for Raoul.

The boots to them, them in the bar, them barmaids came. For them unheeding him he banged on the counter his tray of chattering china. And

—There's your teas, he said.

Miss Kennedy with manners transposed the teatray down to an upturned lithia crate, safe from eyes, low

—What is it? loud boots unmannerly asked.

—Find out, Miss Douce retorted, leaving her spyingpoint.

—Your beau, is it?

A haughty bronze replied:

—I'll complain to Mrs. de Massey on you if I hear any more of your impertinent insolence.

—Imperthnthn thnthnthn, bootsnout sniffed rudely, as he retreated as she threatened as he had come.

Bloom.

On her flower frowning Miss Douce said:

—Most aggravating that young brat is. If he doesn't conduct himself I'll wring his ear for him a yard long.

Ladylike in exquisite contrast.

—Take no notice, Miss Kennedy rejoined.

She poured in a teacup tea, then back in the teapot tea. They cowered under their reef of counter, waiting on footstools, crates upturned, waiting for their teas to draw. They pawed their blouses, both of black satin, two and nine a yard, waiting for their teas to draw, and two and seven.

Yes, bronze from anear, by gold, from afar, heard steel, from anear, hoofs ring, from afar, and heard steel hoofs ringhoof ringsteel.

—Am I awfully sunburnt?

Miss bronze unbloused her neck.

—No, said Miss Kennedy. It gets brown after. Did you try the borax with the cherry laurel water?

Miss Douce halfstood to see her skin askance in the barmirror where hock and claret glasses shimmered and in their midst a shell.

—And leave it to my hands, she said.

—Try it with the glycerine, Miss Kennedy advised.

Bidding her neck and hands adieu Miss Douce

—Those things only bring out a rash, replied, reseated. I asked that old fogey in Boyd's for something for my skin.

Miss Kennedy, pouring now fulldrawn tea, grimaced and prayed:

—O, don't remind me of him for mercy' sake!

—But wait till I tell you, Miss Douce entreated.

Sweet tea Miss Kennedy having poured with milk plugged both two ears with little fingers.

—No, don't, she cried.

—I won't listen, she cried.

But Bloom?

Miss Douce grunted in snuffy fogey's tone:

—For your what? says he.

Miss Kennedy unplugged her ears to hear, to speak: but said, but prayed again:

—Don't let me think of him or I'll expire. The hideous old wretch! That night in the Antient Concert Rooms.

She sipped distastefully her brew, hot tea, a sip, sipped sweet tea.

—Here he was, Miss Douce said, cocking her bronze head three quarters, ruffling her nosewings. Hufa! Hufa!

Shrill shriek of laughter sprang from Miss Kennedy's throat. Miss Douce huffed and snorted down her nostrils that quivered imperthnthn like a snout in quest.

—O! shrieking, Miss Kennedy cried. Will you ever forget his goggle eye?

Miss Douce chimed in in deep bronze laughter, shouting:

—And your other eye!

Bloom's dark eye read Aaron Figatner's name. Why do I always think Figather? Gathering figs I think. And Prosper Loré's huguenot name. By Bassi's blessed virgins Bloom's dark eyes went by. Bluerobed, white under, come to me. God they believe she is: or goddess. Those today. I could not see. That fellow spoke. A student. After with Dedalus' son. He might be Mulligan. All comely virgins. That brings those rakes of fellows in: her white.

By went his eyes. The sweet of sin, Sweet are the sweets.

Of sin.

In a giggling peal young goldbronze voices blended, Douce with Kennedy, your other eye. They threw young heads back, bronze by gold, to let freefly their laughter, screaming, your other, signals to each other, high piercing notes.

Ah, panting, sighing, sighing, ah, fordone their mirth died down.

Miss Kennedy lipped her cup again, raised drank a sip. Miss Douce, bending again over the teatray, ruffled again her nose and rolled droll fattened eyes. Again Miss Kennedy, stooping her fair pinnacles of hair, stooping, her tortoise napecomb showed, spluttered out of her mouth her tea, choking in tea and laughter, coughing with choking, crying:

—O greasy eyes! Imagine being married to a man like that, she cried. With his bit of beard!

Douce gave full vent to a splendid yell, a full yell of full woman, delight, joy, indignation.

—Married to the greasy nose! she yelled.

Shrill, with deep laughter, after bronze in gold, they urged each each to peal after peal, ringing in changes, bronzegold goldbronze, shrilldeep, to laughter after laughter. And then laughed more. Greasy I knows. Exhausted, breathless their shaken heads they laid, braided and pinnacled by glossycombed against the counterledge. All flushed (O!), panting, sweating (O!), all breathless.

Married to Bloom, to greaseaseabloom.

—O saints above! Miss Douce said, sighed above her jumping rose.
I wished I hadn't laughed so much. I feel all wet.

—O, Miss Douce! Miss Kennedy protested. You horrid thing!

And flushed yet more, (you horrid!), more goldenly.

By Cantwell's offices roved Greaseabloom, by Ceppi's virgins, bright of their oils. Nannetti's father hawked those things about, wheedling at doors. Religion pays. Must see him about Keyes's par. Eat first. I want. Not yet. At four, she said. Time ever passing. Clockhands turning. On. Where eat? The Clarence, Dolphin. On. For Raoul. Eat. If I net five guineas with those ads. The violet silk petticoats. Not yet. The sweets of sin.

Flushed less, still less, goldenly paled.

Into their bar strolled Mr. Dedalus. Chips, picking chips off one of his rocky thumbnails. Chips. He strolled.

—O welcome back, Miss Douce.

He held her hand. Enjoyed her holidays?

—Tiptop.

He hoped she had nice weather in Rostrevor.

—Gorgeous, she said. Look at the holy show I am. Lying out on the strand all day.

Bronze whiteness.

—That was exceedingly naughty of you, Mr. Dedalus told her and pressed her hand indulgently. Tempting poor simple males.

Miss Douce of satin douced her arm away.

—O go away, she said. I'm sure you're very simple.

He was.

—Well now, I am, he mused. I looked so simple in the cradle they christened me simple Simon.

—Yes I don't think, Miss Douce made answer. And what did the doctor order today?

—Well now, he mused, whatever you say yourself. I think I'll trouble you for some fresh water and a half glass of whisky.

Jingle.

—With the greatest alacrity, Mlss Douce agreed.

With grace of alacrity towards the mirror she turned herself. With grace she tapped a measure of gold whisky from her crystal keg. Forth from the skirt of his coat Mr. Dedalus brought pouch and pipe. Alacrity she served. He blew through the flue two husky fifenotes.

—By Jove, he mused. I often wanted to see the Mourne mountains. Must be a great tonic in the air down there. But a long threatening comes at last, they say. Yes, yes.

Yes. He fingered shreds into the bowl. Chips. Shreds. Musing. Mute.

None not said nothing. Yes.

Gaily Miss Douce polished a tumbler, trilling:

—O, Idolares, queen of the eastern seas!

—Was Mr. Lidwell in today?

In came Lenehan. Round him peered Lenehan. Mr. Bloom reached Essex bridge. Yes, Mr. Bloom crossed bridge of Yessex. To Martha I must write. Buy paper. Daly's Girl there civil. Bloom. Old Bloom. Blue bloom is on the rye.

—He was in at lunchtime, Miss Douce said.

Lenehan came forward.

—Was Mr. Boylan looking for me?

He asked. She answered:

—Miss Kennedy, was Mr. Boylan in while I was upstairs?

She asked. Miss voice of Kennedy answered, a second teacup poised. her gaze upon a page.

—No. He was not.

Miss gaze of Kennedy, heard not seen, read on. Lenehan round the sandwichbell wound his round body round.

—Peep! Who's in the corner?

No glance of Kennedy rewarding him he yet made overtures. To mind her stops. To read only the black ones: round o and crooked ess.

Jingle jaunty jingle.

Girlgold she read and did not glance. Take no notice. She took no notice while he read by rote a solfa fable for her, plappering flatly:

—Ah fox met ah stork. Said thee fox too thee stork: Will you put your bill down inn my troath and pull upp ah bone?

He droned in vain. Miss Douce turned to her tea aside.

He sighed a sigh:

—Ah me! O my!

He greeted Mr. Dedalus and got a nod.

—Greetings from the famous son of a famous father.

—Who may he be? Mr. Dedalus asked.

Lenehan opened most genial arms. Who?

—Can you ask? he asked. Stephen, the youthful bard.

Dry.

Mr. Dedalus famous father laid by his dry filled pipe.

—I see, he said. I didn't recognise him for the moment. I hear he is keeping very select rompany. Have you seen him lately?

He had.

—I quaffed the nectarbowl with him this very day, said Lenehan. In Mooney's *en ville and* in Mooney's *sur mer*. He had received the rhino for the labour of his muse.

He smiled at bronze's teabathed lips, as listening lips and eyes.

—The *élite* of Erin hung on his lips. The ponderous pundit, Hugh MacHugh, Dublin's most brilliant scribe and editor and that *minstrel* boy of the wild wet west who is known by the euphonious appellation of the O'Madden Burke.

After an interval Mr. Dedalus raised his grog and

—That must have been highly diverting, said he. I see.

He see. He drank. Set down his glass.

He looked towards the saloon door.

—I see you have moved the piano.

—The tuner was in today, Miss Douce replied, tuning it for the smoking concert and I never heard such an exquisite player.

—Is that a fact?

—Didn't he, Miss Kennedy? The real classical, you know. And blind too, poor fellow. Not twenty I'm sure he was.

—Is that a fact? Mr. Dedalus said.

He drank and strayed away.

—So sad to look at his face, Miss Douce condoled.

God's curse on bitch's bastard.

Tink to her pity cried a diner's bell. To the door of the diningroom came bald Pat, came bothered Pat, came Pat, waiter of Ormond. Lager for diner. Lager without alacrity she served.

With patience Lenehan waited for Boylan with impatience, for jingle jaunty blazes boy.

Upholding the lid he (who?) gazed in the coffin (coffin?) at the oblique triple (piano!) wires. He pressed (the same who pressed indulgently her hand), soft pedalling a triple of keyes to see the thicknesses of felt advancing, to hear the muffled hammertall in action.

Two sheets cream vellum paper one reserve two envelopes when I was in Wisdom Hely's wise Bloom in Daly's Henry Flower bought. Are you not happy in your home? Flower to console me and a pin cuts lo. Means something, language of flow. Was it a daisy? Innocence that is. Respectable girl meet after mass. Thanks awfully muchly. Wise Bloom eyed on the door a poster, a swaying mermaid smoking mid nice waves. Smoke mermaids, coolest whiff of all. Hair streaming: lovelorn. For some man. For Raoul. He eyed and saw afar on Essex bridge a gay hat riding on a jauntingcar. It is. Third time. Coincidence.

Jingling on supple rubbers it jaunted from the bridge to Ormond quay. Follow. Risk it. Go quick. At four. Near now. Out.

—Twopence, sir, the shopgirl dared to say.

—Aha . . . . I was forgetting . . . Excuse . . .

—And four.

At four she. Winsomely she smiled on Bloom. Bloo smi qui go. Ternoon. Think you're the only pebble on the beach? Does that to all. For men.

In drowsy silence gold bent on her page.

From the saloon a call came, long in dying. That was a tuning fork the tuner had that he forgot that he now struck. A call again. That he now poised that it now throbbed. You hear? It throbbed, pure, purer, softly and softlier, its buzzing prongs. Longer in dying call

Pat paid for diner's popcorked bottle: and over tumbler tray and popcorked bottle ere he went he whispered, bald and bothered, with Miss Douce.

—*The bright stars fade . . .*

—. . . . . A voiceless song sang from within, singing:

—. . . . . the morn is breaking.

A duodene of birdnotes chirruped bright treble answer under sensitive hands. Brightly the keyes, all twinkling, linked, all harpsichording, called to a voice to sing the strain of dewy morn, of youth, of love's leavetaking, life's, love's morn.

—*The dewdrops pearl . . . . . .*

Lenehan's lips over the counter lisped a low whistle of decoy.

—But look this way, he said, rose of Castile.

Jingle jaunted by the curb and stopped.

She rose and closed her reading, rose of Castile. Fretted forlorn, dreamily rose.

—Did she fall or was she pushed? he asked her.

She answered, slighting:

—Ask no questions and you'll hear no lies.

Like lady, ladylike.

Blazes Boylan's smart tan shoes creaked on the barfloor where he strode. Yes, gold from anear by bronze from afar. Lenehan heard and knew and hailed him:

—See the conquering hero comes.

Between the car and window, warily walking, went Bloom, unconquered hero. See me he might. The seat he sat on: warm. Black wary hecat walked towards Richie Goulding's legal bag, lifted aloft, saluting.

—*And I from thee* . . . .

—I heard you were round, said Blazes Boylan.

He touched to fair Miss Kennedy a rim of his slanted straw. She smiled on him. But sister bronze outsmiled her, preening for him her richer hair, a bosom and a rose.

Boylan bespoke potions.

—What's your cry? Glass of bitter? Glass of bitter, please, and a sloegin for me. Wire in yet?

Not yet. At four he. All said four.

Cowley's red lugs and Adam's apple in the door of the sheriff's office. Avoid. Goulding a chance. What is he doing in the Ormond? Car waiting. Wait.

Hello. Where off to? Something to eat? I too was just. In here. What, Ormond Best value in Dublin. Is that so? Diningroom. Sit tight there. See, not be seen. I think I'll join you. Come on. Richie led on. Bloom followed bag. Dinner fit for a prince.

Miss Douce reached high to take a flagon, stretching her satin arm, her bust.

—O! O! jerked Lenehan, gasping at each stretch. O!

But easily she seized her prey and led it low in triumph.

—Why don't you grow? asked Blazes Boylan.

She bronze, dealing from her jar thick syrupy liquor for his lips, looked as it flowed (flower in his coat: who gave him?), and syrupped with her voice:

—Fine goods in small parcels.

That is to say she. Neatly she poured slowsyrupy sloe.

—Here's fortune, Blazes said.

He pitched a broad coin down. Coin rang.

—Hold on, said Lenehan, till I . . . .

—Fortune, he wished, lifting his bubbled ale.

—Sceptre will win in a canter, he said.

—I plunged a bit, said Boylan. Not on my own, you know. Fancy of a friend of mine.

Lenehan still drank and grinned at his tilted ale and at Miss Douce's lips that all but hummed, not shut, the oceansong her lips had trilled. Idolores. The eastern seas.

Clock whirred. Miss Kennedy passed their way(flower, wonder who gave), bearing away teatray. Clock clacked.

Miss Douce took Boylan's coin, struck boldly the cashregister. It clanged. Clock clacked. Fair one of Egypt teased and sorted in the till and hummed and handed coins in change. Look to the west. A clack. For me.

—What time is that? asked Blazes Boylan. Four?

O'clock.

Lenehan, small eyes ahunger on her humming, bust ahumming, tugged Blazes Boylan's elbowsleeve.

—Let's hear the time, he said.

The bag of Goulding, Colles, Ward led Bloom by ryebloom flowered tables. Aimless he chose with agitated aim, bald Pat at ending, a table near the door. Be near. At four. Has he forgotten? Perhaps a trick. Not come: whet appetite. I couldn't do. Wait, wait. Pat, waiter, waited.

Sparkling bronze azure eyed Blazes' skyblue bow and eyes.

—Go on, pressed Lenehan. There's no-one. He never heard.

— . . . . *to Flora's lips did hie*

High, a high note, pealed in the treble, clear.

Bronzedouce, communing with her rose that sank and rose sought Blazes Boylan's flower and eyes.

—Please, please.

He pleaded over returning phrases of avowal.

—I could not leave thee . . . .

—Afterwits, Miss Douce promised coyly.

—No, now, urged Lenehan *Sonnez la cloche!* O do! There's no-one.

She looked. Quick. Miss Kenn out of earshot. Sudden bent. Two kindling faces watched her bend.

Quavering the chords strayed from the air, found it again, lost chord, and lost and found it faltering.

—Go on! Do! *Sonnez!*

Bending, she nipped a peak of skirt above her knee. Delayed. Taunted them still, bending, suspending, with wilful eyes.

—Sonnez!

Smack. She let free sudden in rebound her nipped elastic garter smackwarm against her smackable a woman's warmhosed thigh.

—*La cloche!* cried gleeful Lenehan. Trained by owner. No sawdust there.

She smilesmirked supercilious, (wept! aren't men?), but, lightward gliding, mild she smiled on Boylan.

—You're the essence of vulgarity, she said in gliding.

Boylan eyed, eyed. Tossed to fat lips his chalice, drank off his tiny, chalice, sucking the last fat violet syrupy drops. His spellbound eyes went after her gliding head as it went down the bar by mirrors, hock and claret glasses shimmering, a spiky shell, where it concerted, mirrored, bronze with sunnier bronze.

Yes, bronze from anearby.

— . . . . *sweetheart, goodbye!*

—I'm off, said Boylan with impatience.

He slid his chalice brisk away, grasped his change.

—Wait a shake, begged Lenehan, drinking quickly. I wanted to tell you. Tom Rochford . . .

—Come on to blazes, said Blazes Boylan, going.

Lenehan gulped to go.

—Got the horn or what? he said. Half a mo. I'm coming.

He followed the hasty creaking shoes but stood by nimbly by the threshold, saluting forms, a bulky with a slender.

—How do you do, Mr. Dollard?

—Eh? How do? How do? Ben Dollard's vague bass answered, turning an instant from Father Cowley's woe. He won't give you any trouble, Bob. Alf Bergan will speak to the long fellow. We'll put a barleystraw in that Judas Iscariot's ear this time.

Sighing, Mr. Dedalus came through the saloon, a finger soothing an eyelid.

—Hoho, we will, Ben Dollard yodled jollily. Come on, Simon, give us a ditty. We heard the piano.

Bald Pat, bothered waiter, waited for drink orders. Power for Richie. And Bloom? Let me see. Four now. How warm this black is. Course nerves a bit. Refracts (is it?) heat. Let me see. Cider. Yes, bottle of cider.

—What's that? Mr. Dedalus said. I was only vamping, man.

—Come on, come on, Ben Dollard called. Begone, dull care. Come, Bob.

He ambled Dollard, bulky slops, before them (hold that fellow with the: hold him now) into the saloon. He plumped him Dollard on the stool. His gouty paws plumped chords. Plumped, stopped abrupt.

Bald Pat in the doorway met tealess gold returning. Bothered he wanted Power and cider. Bronze by the window watched, bronze from afar.

Jingle a tinkle jaunted.

Bloom heard a jing, a little sound. He's off. Light sob of breath Bloom sighed on the silent flowers. Jingling. He's gone. Jingle. Hear.

—Love and war, Ben, Mr. Dedalus said. God be with old times.

Miss Douce's brave eyes, unregarded, turned from the crossblind, smitten by sunlight. Gone. Pensive (who knows?), smitten (the smiting light), she lowered the dropblind with a sliding cord. She drew down pensive (why did he go so quick when I?) about her bronze, over the bar where bald stood by sister gold, in exquisite contract, contrast inexquisite nonexquisite, slow cool dim seagreen sliding depth of shadow, eau de Nil.

—Poor old Goodwin was the pianist that night, Father Cowley reminded them. There was a slight difference of opinion between himself and the Collard grand.

There was.

—A symposium all his own, Mr. Dedalus said. The devil wouldn't stop him. He was a crotchety old fellow in the primary stage of drink.

—God, do you remember? Ben bulky Dollard said, turning from the punished keyboard. And by Japers I had no wedding garment.

They laughed all three. He had no wed. They all three laughed. No wedding garment.

—Our friend Bloom turned in handy that night, Mr. Dedalus said. Where's my pipe by the way?

He wandered back to the bar to the lost chord pipe. Bald Pat carried two diners' drinks, Richie and Poldy. And Father Cowley laughed again.

—I saved the situation, Ben, I think.

—You did, averred Ben Dollard. I remember those tight trousers too. That was a brilliant idea, Bob.

Father Cowley blushed to his brilliant purply lobes. He saved the situa. Tight trou. Brilliant ide.

—I knew he was on the rocks, he said. The wife was playing the piano in the coffee palace on Saturdays for a very trifling consideration and who was it gave me the wheeze she was doing the other business? Do you remember? We had to search all Holles street to find them till the chap in Keogh's gave us the number. Remember?

Ben remembered, his broad visage wondering.

—By God she had some luxurious operacloaks and things there.

Mr. Dedalus wandered back, pipe in hand.

—Merrionsquare style. Balldresses by God, nd court dresses. He wouldn't take any money either. What? Any God's quantity of cocket hats and boleros and trunkhose. What?

—Ay, ay, Mr. Dedalus nodded. Mrs. Marion Bloom has left off clothes of all descriptions.

Jingle jaunted down the quays. Blazes sprawled on bounding tyres.

Liver and bacon. Steak and kidney pie. Right, sir. Right, Pat.

Mrs. Marrion met him pike hoses. Smell of burn of Paul de Kock. Nice name he.

—What's this her name was? A buxom lassy. Marion . . .

—Tweedy.

—Yes. Is she alive?

—And kicking.

—She was a daughter of . . . . .

—Daughter of the regiment.

—Yes, begad. I remember the old drummajor.

Mr. Dedalus struck, whizzed, lit, puffed savoury puffafter.

—Irish? I don't know, faith. Is she, Simon?

Puff after stiff, a puff, strong, savoury, crackling.

—Buccinator muscle is . . . What? . . . Bit rusty . . . O, she is . . . My Irish Molly, O.

He puffed a pungent plumy blast.

—From the rock of Gibraltar . . . all the way.

They pined in depth of ocean shadow, gold by the beerpull, bronze by maraschino, thoughtful all two, Mina Kennedy, 4 Lismore terrace, Drumcondra with Idolores, a queen, silent.

Pat served uncovered dishes. Leopold cut liverslices. As said before he ate with relish the inner organs, nutty gizzards, fried cods' roes while Richie Goulding, Colles, Ward ate steak and kidney, steak then kidney, bite by bite of pie he ate Bloom ate they ate.

Bloom with Goulding, married in silence, ate. Dinners fit for princes.

By Bachelor's walk jogjaunty jingled Blazes Boylan, bachelor, in sun in heat, mare's glossy rump atrot, with flick of whip, on bounding tyres: sprawled, warmseated, Boylan impatience, ardentbold. Horn. Have you the? Horn. Have you the? Haw haw horn.

Over their voices Dollard bassooned attack booming over bombarding chords:

—When love absorbs my ardent soul . . .

—War! War! cried Father Cowley. You're the warrior.

—So I am, Ben Dollard laughed.

He stopped. He wagged huge beard, huge face over his blunder huge.

—Sure, you'd burst the tympanum of her ear, man, Mr. Dedalus said through smoke aroma, with an organ like yours.

In bearded abundant laughter Dollard shook upon the keyboard. He would.

—Not to mention another membrane, Father Cowley added. Half time, Ben. Amoroso ma non troppo. Let me there.

Miss Kennedy served two gentlemen with tankards of cool stout. She passed a remark. It was indeed, first gentleman said, beautiful weather. They drank cool stout, did she know where the lord lieutenant was going? And heard steel hoofs ring hoof ring. No, she couldn't say. But it would be in the paper. O, she needn't trouble. No trouble. She waved about her outspread Independent searching the lord lieutenant her pinnacles of hair slowmoving lord lieuten. Too much trouble, first gentleman said. O, not in the least. Way he looked that. Lord lieutenant. Gold by bronze heard iron steel

—. *my ardent soul*

I care not foror the morrow.

In liver gravy Bloom mashed mashed potatoes. Love and war someone is. Ben Dollard's famous. Night he ran round to us to borrow a dress suit for that concert. Trousers tight as a drum on him. Molly did laugh when he went out. Threw herself back across the bed, screaming, kicking. With all his belongings on show. O, saints above, I'm drenched! O, the women in the front row! O, I never laughed so much! Well, of course, that's what gives him the base barreltone. For instance eunuchs. Wonder who's playing. Nice touch. Must be Cowley. Musical. Knows whatever note you play. Bad breath he has, poor chap. Stopped.

Stopped.

George Lidwell, gentleman, entering. Good afternoon. She gave her moist, a lady's, hand to his firm clasp. Afternoon.

—Your friends are inside, Mr. Lidwell.

George Lidwell, suave, solicited, held a Lydia's hand.

Bloom ate liv as said before. Clean here at least. That chap in the Burton, gummy with gristle. No-one here: Goulding and I. Clean tables, flowers, mitres of napkins. Pat to and fro, bald Pat. Nothing to do. Best value in Dub.

Piano again. Cowley it is. Way he sits in to it, like one together, mutual understanding. Tiresome shapers scraping fiddles, sawing the cello, remind you of toothache. Night we were in the box. Trombone under blowing like a grampus, other brass chap unscrewing, emtying spittle. Conductor's legs too, bagstrousers, jiggedy jiggedy. Do right to hide them.

Jiggedy jingle jaunty jaunty.

Only the harp. LovelyGold glowering light. Girl touched it. Poop of a lovely. Gravy's rather good fit for a. Golden ship. Erin. The harp that once or twice. Cool hands. Ben Howth, the rhododendrons. We are their harps. I. He. Old. Young.

—Ah, I couldn't, man, Mr. Dedalus said, shy, listless.

Strongly.

—Go on blast you, Ben Dollard growled. Get it out in bits.

—*M'appari*, Simon, Father Cowley said.

Down stage he strode some paces, grave, tall in affliction, his long arms outheld. Hoarsely the apple of his throat hoarsed softly. Softly he sang to a dusty seascape there: *A Last Farewell.* A headland, a ship, a sail upon the billows. Farewell. A lovely girl, her veil awave upon the wind upon the headland, wind around her.

Cowley sang:

—*M'appari tutt'amor*:

Il mio sguardo . . . . .

She waved, unhearing Cowley, her veil to one departing, dear one, to wind, love, speeding sail, return.

—Go on, Simon.

—Ah, sure my dancing days are done, Ben . . . Well . . .

Mr Dedalus laid his pipe to rest beside the tuningfork and, sitting, touched the obedient keys,

—No, Simon, Father Cowley turned Play it in the original. One flat.

The keys, obedient, rose higher, told, faltered, confessed, confused.

Up stage strode Father Cowley.

—Here, Simon. I'll accompany you, he said. Get up.

By Graham Lemon's pineapple rock, by Elvery's elephant jingle jogged.

Steak, kidney, liver, mashed at meat fit for princes sat princes Bloom and Goulding. Princes at meat they raised and drank Power and cider.

Most beautiful tenor air ever written, Richie said: *Sonam bula.* He heard Joe Maas sing that one night. Ah, what M'Guckin! Yes. In his way. Choirboy style. Maas was the boy. Massboy. A lyrical tenor if you like. Never forget it. Never.

Tenderly Bloom over liverless bacon saw the tightened featuresstrain. Backache he. Bright's bright eye. Net item on the programme. Pills, pounded bread, worth a guinea a box. Stave it off awhile. Sings too: *Down among the dead men.* Appropriate. Kidney pie. Sweets to the. Not making much hand of it. Best value in. Characteristic of him. Power. Particular about his drink. Fecking matches from counters to save. Then squander a sovereign in dribs and drabs. And when he's wanted not a farthing. Curious types.

Never would Richie forget that night. As long as he lived, never. In the gods of the old royal with little Peake. And when the first note.

Speech paused on Richie's lips.

Coming out with a whopper now . Rhapsodies about damn all. Believes his own lies. Does really. Wonderful liar.

—Which air is that? asked Leopold Bloom.

—*All is lost now.*

Richie cocked his lips apout. A low incipient note sweet murmured: alla thrush. Athrostle. His breath, birdsweet, good teeth he's proud of, fluted with plaintive woe. Is lost. Rich sound. Two notes in one there. Blackbird I heard in the hawthorn valley. How is that done? All lost now. Mournful he whistled. Fall, surrender, lost.

Bloom bent leopold ear, turning a fringe of doyley down under the vase. Order. Yes, I remember. Lovely air. In sleep she went to him. Innocence in the moon. Still hold her back. Brave, don't know their danger. Call name. Touch water. Jingle jaunty. Too late. She longed to go. That's why. Woman. As easy stop the sea. Yes: all is lost.

—A beautiful air, said Bloom lost Leopold. I know it well.

Never in all his life had Richie Goulding.

He knows it well too. Or he feels. Wise child that knows her father, Dedalus said. Me?

Bloom askance over liverless saw. Face of the all is lost. Rollicking Richie once. Jokes old stale now. Wagging his ear. Napkinring in his eye.

Piano again. Sounds better than last time I heard. Tuned probably. Stopped again.

Dollard and Cowley still urged the lingering singer out with it.

—With it, Simon.
—It, Simon.
—Ladies and gentlemen, I am most deeply obliged by your kind solicitations.
—It, Simon.
—I have no money but if you will lend me your attention I shall endeavour to sing to you of a heart bowed down.

By the sandwichbell in screening shadow, Lydia her bronze and rose, a lady's grace, gave and withehld: as in cool glaucous eau de Nil Mina to tankards two her pinnacles of gold.

The harping chords of prelude closed. A chord longdrawn, expectant drew a voice away.

—*When first I saw that form endearing,*

Richie turned.

—Si Dedalus' voice, he said.

Bloom signed to Pat, bald Pat is a waiter hard of hearing to set ajar the door of the bar. The door of the bar. So. That will do. Pat, waiter, waited to hear for he was hard of hear by the door.

—*Sorrow from me seemed to depart.*

Through the hush of air a voice sang to them, low, not rain, not leaves in murmur, like no voice of strings or reeds or what do you call them dulcimers, touching their still ears with words, still hearts of their each his remembered lives. Good, good to hear: sorrow from them each seemed to from both depart when first they heard. When first they saw, lost Richie, Poldy, mercy of beauty, heard from a person wouldn't expect it in the least her first merciful lovesoft word.

Love that is singing: love's old sweet song. Bloom unwound slowly the elastic band of his packet. Love's old sweet *sonnez la* gold. Bloom wound a skein round four forkfingers, stretched it, relaxed, and wound it round his troubled double, fourfold, in octave: gyved them fast.

—*Full of hope and all delighted . . .*

Tenors get women by the score. Jingle all delighted. He can't sing for tall hats. Your head it simply swurls. Perfumed for him. What perfume does your wife? I want to know. Jing. Stop. Knock. Last look at mirror always before she answers the door. The hall. There? How do you? I do well. There? What? Or? Phial of cachous, kissing comfits, in her satchel. Yes? Hands felt for the opulent.

Alas! The voice rose, sighing, changed: loud, full, shining, proud.

—*But alas 'twas idle dreaming . . .*

Glorious tone he has still. Silly man! Could have made oceans of money. Wore out his wife: now sings. But hard to tell. Only the two themselves. If he doesn't break down. Drink. Nerves overstrung. Must be abstemious to sing.

Tenderness it welled: slow swelling. Full it throbbed. That's the chat. Ha, give! Take! Throb, a throb, a pulsing proud erect.

Words? Music? No: it's what's behind.

Bloom looped, unlooped, noded, disnoded.

Bloom. Flood of warm jimjam lickitup secretness flowed to flow in music out, in desire, dark to lick flow, invading. Tup. Pores to dilate dilating. Tup. The joy the feel the warm the. Tup. To pour o'er sluices pouring gushes. Flood, gush, flow joygush, tupthrob. Now! Language of love.

— . . . . *ray of hope* . . . .

Beaming. Lydia for Lidwell squeak scarcely hear so ladylike the muse unsqueaked a cork.

Martha it is. Coincidence. Just going to write. Lionel's song. Lovely name you have. Can't write. Accept my little pres. She's a. I called you naughty boy. Still the name: Martha. How strange! Today.

The voice of Lionel returned, weaker but unwearied. It sang again to Richie Poldy Lydia Lidwell also sang to Pat open mouth ear waiting to wait. How first he saw that form endearing, how sorrow seemed to part, how look, form, word charmed him Gould Lidwell, won Pat Bloom's heart.

Wish I could see his face, though. Explain better. Why the barber in Drago's always looked my face when I spoke his face in the glass.

—*Each graceful look* . . . .

First night when first I saw her at Mat Dillon's in Terenure. Yellow, black lace she wore. Musical chairs. We two the last. Fate. After her. Fate. Round and round slow. Quick round. We two. All looked. Halt. Down she sat. Lips laughing. Yellow knees.

—*Charmed my eye* . . . .

Singing. *Waiting* she sang. I turned her music. Full voice of perfume of what perfume does your lilactrees. Bosom I saw, both full, throat warbling. First I saw. She thanked me. Why did she me? Fate. Spanishy eyes. At me. Luring. Ah, alluring.

—*Martha! Ah, Martha!*

Quitting all langour Lionel cried in grief, in cry of passion to love to return with deepening yet with rising chords, chords of harmony. In cry of lionel loneliness that she should know, must martha feel. For only her he waited. Where? Somewhere.

—*Co-ome, thou lost one!*
Co-ome thou dear one!

Alone. One love. One hope. One comfort me. Martha, chestnote return.

—*Come!*

It soared, a bird, it held its flight, a swift pure cry, soar silver orb it leaped serene, speeding, sustained, to come, don't spin it out too long long breath he breath long life, soaring high, high resplendent, aflame, crowned high in the effulgence symbolistic, high of the etherial bosom, high, of the high vast irradiation everywere all soaring all around about the all, the endlessnessness-ness . . . .

—*To me!*

Consumed.

Come. Well sung. All clapped. She ought to. Come. To me, to him, to her, you too, me, us.

—Bravo! Clapclap. Goodman, Simon. Clappyclapclap. Encore! Clapclipclap. Sound as a bell. Bravo, Simon! Clapclopclap. Encore, enclap, said, cried, clapped all, Ben Dollard, Lydia Douce. George Lidwell, Pat, Mina two gentlemen with two tankards, Cowley, first gent with tank and bronze Miss Douce and gold Miss Mina.

Blazes Boylan's smart tan shoes creaked on the bar-floor, said before. Jingle by monuments of sir John Gray, Horatio onehandled Nelson, reverend father Theobald Matthew, jaunted as said before just now. Atrot, in heat, heatseated. *Cloche. Sonnez la. Cloche. Sonnez la.* Slower the mare went up the hill by the Rotunda, Rutland square. Too slow for Boylan, blazes Boylan, impatience Boylan, joggled the mare.

An afterclang of Cowley's chords closed, died on the air made richer.

And Richie Goulding drank his Power and Leopold Bloom his cider drank, Lidwell his Guinness, second gentleman said they would partake of two more tankards if she did not mind. Miss Kennedy smirked, disserving, coral lips, at first, at second. She did not mind.

—Seven days in gaol, Ben Dollard said, on bread and water. Then you'd sing, Simon, like a garden thrush.

Lionel Simon, singer, laughed. Father Bob Cowley played. Mina Kennedy served. Second gentleman paid. Tom Kernan strutted in . Lydia, admired, admired.

Admiring.

Richie, admiring, descanted on that man's glorious voice. He remembered one night long ago. Never forget that night. Si sang *'Twas rank and fame*: in Ned Lambert's 'twas. Good God he never heard in all his life a note like that he never did *then false one we had better part* so clear so God he never heard *since love lives not* a clinking voice ask Lambert he can tell you too.

Goulding, a flush struggling in his pale, told Mr. Bloom, face of the night, Si in Ned Lambert's, Dedalus house sang *'Twas rank and fame.*

He Mr. Bloom, listened while he, Richie Goulding, told him, Mr. Bloom, of the night he Richie heard him, Si Dedalus, sing *'Twas rank and fame* in his, Ned Lambert's house.

Brothers-in-law: relations. Rift in the lute I think. Treats him with scorn. See. He admires him all the more. The night Si sang. The human voice, two tiny silky cords. Wonderful, more than all the others.

That voice was a lamentation. Calmer now. It's in the silence you feel you hear. Vibrations. Now silent air.

Bloom ungyved his crisscrossed hands and, with slack fingers plucked the slender catgut thong. He drew and plucked. It buzz, it twanged. While Goulding talked of Barraclough's voice production, while Tom Kernan, harking back in a retrospective sort of arrangement, talked to listening Father Cowley who played a voluntary, who nodded as he played. While big Ben Dollard talked with Simon Dedalus lighting, who nodded as he smoked, who smoked.

Thou lost one. All songs on that theme. Yet more Bloom stretched his string. Cruel it seems. Let people get fond of each other: lure them on. Then tear asunder. Death. Explos. Knock on the head. Outtohelloutofthat. Human life. Dignam. Ugh, that rat's tail wriggling! Five bob I gave. *Corpus paradisum.* Corncrake croker: belly like a poisoned pup. Gone. They sing. Forgotten. I too. And one day she with. Leave her: get tired. Suffer then. Snivel. Big Spanishy eyes goggling at nothing. Hair uncombed.

Yet too much happy bores. He stretched more, more. Are you not happy in your? Twang. It snapped.

Jingle into Dorset street.

Miss Douce withdrew her satiny arm, reproachful, pleased.

—Don't make half so free, said she, till we're better acquainted.

George Lidwell told her really and truly: but she did not believe.

First gentleman told Mina that was so. She asked him was that so. And second tankard told her so. That that was so.

Miss Douce, Miss Lydia, did not believe: Miss Kennedy, Mina, did not believe: George Lidwell, no: Miss Dou did not: the first, the first: gent with the tank: believe, no, no: did not, Miss Kenn: Lidlydiawell: the tank.

Better write it here. Quills in the postoffice chewed and twisted.

Bald Pat at a sign drew night. A pen and ink. He went, A pad. He went. A pad to blot. He heard, deaf Pat.

—Yes, Mr. Bloom said, teasing the curling satgut line. It certainly is. Few lines will do. My present. All that Italian florid music is. Who is this wrote? Know the name you know better. Take out sheet notepaper, envelope: unconcerned. It's so characteristic.

—Grandest number in the whole opera, Goulding said.

—It is, Bloom said.

Numbers it is. All music when you come to think. Two multiplied by two divided by half is twice one. Vibrations: chords those are One plus two plus six is seven. Do anything you like with figures juggling. Always find out this equal to that, symmetry under a cemetery wall. He doesn't see my mourning. Callous: all for his own gut. Musemathematics. And you think you're listening to the etherial. But suppose you said it like: Martha, seven times nine minus x is thirtyfive thousand. Fall quite flat. It's on account of the sounds it is.

Instance he's playing now. Might be what you like till you hear the words. Want to listen sharp. Hard. Begin all right: then hear chards a bit off: feel lost a bit. Time makes the tune. Question of mood you're in. Still always nice to hear. Except scales up and down, girls learning. Milly no taste. Queer because we both I mean. Ought to invent dummy pianos for that.

Bald deaf Pat brought quite flat pad ink. Pat set with ink pen quite flat pad. Pat took plate dish knife fork. Pat went.

It was the only language Mr. Dedalus said to Ben. He heard them as a boy in Ringabella, Crosshaven, Ringabella, singing their barcaroles. Queenstown harbour full of Italian ships. Walking, you know, Ben, in the moonlight with those earthquake hats. Blending their voices. God, such music, Ben. Heard as a boy.

Sour pipe removed he held a shield of hand beside his lips that cooed a moonlight nightcall, clear from anear, a call from afar, replying.

Down the edge of his *Freeman* baton ranged Bloom's your other eye, scanning for where did I see that. Callan, Coleman, Dignam Patrick. Heigho! Heigho! Fawcett. Aha! Just I was looking . . .

Hope he's not looking, cute as a cat. He held unfurled his *Freeman*. Can't see now. Remember write Greek ees. Bloom dipped, Bloom mur: dear sir. Dear Henry wrote: dear Mady. Got your lett and flower. Hell did I put? Some pock or oth. It is utterly imposs. Underline imposs. To write today.

Bore this. Bored Bloom tambourined gently with I am just reflecting fingers on flat pad Pat brought.

On. Know what I mean. No, change that ee. Accept my poor little pres enclos. Hold on. Five Dig. Two about here. Penny the gulls. Elijah is com. Seven Davy Byrne's. Is eight about, Say half a crown. My poor little pres: p. o. two and six. Write me a long. Do you despise? Jingle, have you the? So excited. Why do you call me naught? You naughty too? O, Mairy lost the pin of her. Bye for today. Yes, yes, will tell you. Want to. To keep it up. Call me that other. Other world she wrote. My patience are exhaust. To keep it up. You must believe. Believe. The tank. It. Is. True.

Folly am I writing? Husbands don't. That's marriage does, their wives. Because I'm away from. Suppose. But how? She must. Keep young. If she found out. Card in my high grade ha. No, not tell all. Useless pain. If they don't see. Woman. Sauce for the gander.

A hackney car, number three hundred and twentyfour, driver Barton James of number one Harmony avenue, Donnybrook, on which sat a fare, a young gentleman, stylishly dressed in an indigoblue serge suit made by George Robert Mesias, tailor and cutter, of number five Eden quay, and wearing a straw hat very dressy, bought of John Plasto of number one Great Brunswick street, hatter. Eh? This is the jingle that joggled and jingled. By Dlugacz' porkshop bright tubes of Agendath trotted a gallantbuttocked mare.

—Answering an ad? Keen Richie's eyes asked Bloom.

—Yes, Mr. Bloom said. Town traveller. Nothing doing, I expect.

Bloom mur: best references. But Henry wrote: it will excite me. You know how. In haste. Henry. Greekee. Better add postscript. What is he playing now? Improvising intermezzo. P. S. The rum tum tum. How will you pun? You punish me? Crooked skirt swinging, whack by. Tell me I want to. Know. O. Course if I didn't I wouldn't ask. La la la ree. Trails off there sad in minor. Why minor sad? Sign H. They like sad tail at end. P. P. S. La la la ree. I feel so sad today La ree. So lonley. Dee.

He blotted quick on pad of Pat. Envel. Address. Just copy out of paper. Murmured: Messrs Callan, Coleman and Co., limited. Henry wrote:

Miss Martha Clifford
c|o P. O.
Dolphin's barn lane
Dublin

Blot over the other so he can't read. Right. Idea prize titbit. Something detective read off blottingpad. Payment at the rate of guinea per col. Matcham often thinks the laughing witch. Poor Mrs. Purefoy. U. p: up.

Too poetical that about the sad. Music did that. Music hath charms. Shakespeare said. Quotations every day in the year. To be or not to be. Wisdom while you wait.

In Gerard's rosery of Fetter lane he walks, greyedauburn. One life is all. One body. Do. But do.

Done anyhow. Postal order stamp. Post office lower down. Walk now. Enough. Barney Kiernan's I promised to meet them. Dislike that job. House of mourning. Walk. Pat! Doesn't hear.

Car near there now. Talk. Talk. Pat! Doesn't. Settling those napkins. Lot of ground he must cover in the day . . Wish they'd sing more. Keep my mind off.

Bald Pat who is bothered settled the napkins. Pat is a waiter hard of his hearing. Pat is a waiter who waits while you wait. Hee hee hee hee. He waits while you wait. Hee hee. A waiter is he. Hee hee hee hee. He waits while you wait. While you wait if you wait he will wait while you wait. Hee hee hee hee. Wait while you wait.

(*to be continued*)

Episode XI (continued)

THE LITTLE REVIEW

VOL. VI. SEPTEMBER, 1919 No. 5

CONTENTS

Subscription price, payable in advance, in the United States and Territories, $2.50 per year; Single copy 25 c., Canada, $2.75; Foreign, $3.00. Published monthly, and copyrighted, 1919 by Margaret C. Anderson.

Manuscripts must be submitted at author's risk, with return postage.

Entered as second class matter March 16, 1917, at the Post Office at New York, N. Y., under the act of March 3, 1879.

MARGARET C. ANDERSON, Publisher
24 *West Sixteenth Street, New York, N. Y*
Foreign Office: 43 *Belsize Park, Gardens, London N. W.* 3.

Douce now. Douce Lydia. Bronze and rose.

She had a gorgeous, simply gorgeous, time. And look at the lovely shell she brought.

To the end of the bar to him she bore lightly the spiked and winding seahorn that he, George Lidwell, solicitor, might hear.

—Listen! she bade him.

Under Tom Kernan's ginhot words the accompanist wove music slow. Authentic fact. How Walter Bapty lost his voice. The husband took him by the throat. *Scoundrel,* said he. *You'll sing no more lovesongs.* He did, sir Tom. Bob Cowley wove. Tenors get wom. Cowley lay back.

Ah, now he heard, she holding it to his ear. Hear! He heard. Wonderful. She held it to her own and through the sifted light pale gold in contrast glided. To hear.

Tap.

Bloom through the bardoor saw a shell held at their ears. He heard more faintly that that they heard, each for herself alone, then each for other, hearing the plash of waves, loudly, a silent roar.

Bronze by a weary gold, anear, afar, they listened.

Her ear too is a shell, the peeping lobe there. Been to the seaside. Lovely seaside girls. Skin tanned raw. Should have put on cold cream first make it brown. Buttered toast. O and that lotion mustn't forget. Fever near her mouth. Your head it simply. Hair braided over: shell with seaweed. Why do they hide their ears with seaweed hair? And Turks their mouth, why? Her eyes over the sheet, a yashmak. Find the way in. A cave. No admittance except on business.

The sea they think they hear. Singing. A roar. The blood it is. Souse in the ear sometimes. Well, it's a sea. Corpuscle islands.

Wonderful really. So distinct. Again. George Lidwell held its murmur, hearing: then laid it by, gently.

—What are the wild waves saying? he asked her, smiled.

Charming, seasmiling and unanswering Lydia on Lidwell smiled.

Tap.

By Larry O'Rourke's, by Larry, bold Larry O',Boylan swayed and Boylan turned.

From the forsaken shell Miss Mina glided to her tankard waiting. No, she was not so lonely archly Miss Douce's head let Mr. Lidwell know. Walks in the

Facing page: table of contents, *Little Review,* September 1919

moonlight by the sea. No, not alone. With whom? She nobly answered: with a gentleman friend.

Bob Cowley's twinkling fingers in the treble played again. The landlord has the prior. A little time. Long John. Big Ben. Lightly he played a light bright tinkling measure for tripping ladies, arch and smiling, and for their gallants, gentleman friends. One: one, one, one: two, one, three, four.

Sea, wind, leaves, thunder, waters, cows lowing, the cattle market, cocks, hens don't crow, snakes hissss. There's music everywhere. Ruttledge's door: ee creaking. No, that's noise. Minuet of *Don Giovanni* he's playing now. Court dresses of all descriptions in castle chambers dancing. Misery. Peasants outside. Green starving faces eating dockleaves. Nice that is. Look: look, look, look, look, look: you look at us.

That's joyful I can feel. Never have written it. Why? My joy is other joy. But both are joys. Yes, joy it must be. Mere fact of music shows you are. Often thought she was in the dumps till she began to lilt. Then know.

M'Coy valise. My wife and your wife. Squealing cat. Molly in *quis est homo*: Mercadante. My ear against the wall to hear. Want a woman who can deliver the goods.

Jog jig jogged stopped. Dandy tan shoe of dandy Boylan came to earth.

O, look we are so! Chamber music. Could make a kind of pun on that. 'Tis kind of music I often thought when she. Acoustics that is Tinkling. Because the acoustics, the resonance changes according as the weight of the water is equal to the law of falling water. Like those rhapsodies of Liszt's, Hungarian, gipsyeyed. Pearls. Drops Rain. Diddle some iddle addle addle oodle oodle. Hiss. Now. Maybe now. Before.

One rapped on a door, one tapped with a knock, did he knock Paul de Kock, with a loud proud knocker, with a cock carracarracarra cock. Cockcock.

Tap.

—*Qui sdegno*, Ben, said Father Cowley.

—No, Ben, Tom Kernan interferred. *The Croppy Boy*. Our native Doric.

—Ay do, Ben, Mr. Dedalus said. Good men and true.

—Do, do, they begged in one.

I'll go. Here, Pat. How much?

—What key? Six sharps?

—F sharp major, Ben Dollard said.

Bob Cowley's outstretched talons griped the black deep-sounding chords.

Must go prince Bloom told Richie prince. No, Richie said. Yes, must. Got money somewhere. He's on for a razzle backache spree. Much? One and nine. Penny for yourself. Here. Give him twopence tip. Deaf, bothered. But perhaps he has wife and family waiting, waiting Patty come home. Hee hee hee hee. Deaf wait while they wait.

But wait. But hear. Chords dark. Lugugugubrious. Low. In a cave of the dark middle earth. Embedded ore. Lumpmusic.

The voice of dark age, of unlove, earth's fatigue made grave approach, called on good men and true. The priest he sought. With him would he speak a word.

Tap.

Ben Dollard's voice base barreltone. Doing his level best to say it. Other comedown. Big ships' chandler's business he did once. Remember: rosiny ropes, ships' lanterns. Failed to the tune of ten thousand pounds. Now in the Iveagh home. Cubicle number so and so. Number one Bass did that for him.

The priest's at home. A false priest's servant bade him welcome. Step in. The holy father. Curlycues of chords.

Ruin them. Wreck their lives. Then build them cubicles to end their days in. Hushaby. Lullaby. Die, dog. Little dog, die.

The voice of warning, solemn warning, told them the youth had entered a lonely hall, told them how solemn fell his footsteps there, told them the gloomy chamber, the vested priest sitting to shrive.

Decent soul. Bit addled now. Thinks he'll win in *Answers* poets' picture puzzle. Bird sitting hatching in a nest. Lay of the last minstrel he thought it was. Good voice he has still. No eunuch yet with all his belongings.

Listen. Bloom listened. Richie Goulding listened. And by the door deaf Pat, bald Pat, tipped Pat, listened.

The chords harped slower.

The voice of penance and of grief came slow, embellished tremulous. Ben's contrite beard confessed: *in nomine Domini,* in God's name. He knelt. He beat his hand upon his breast, confessing: *mea culpa.*

Latin again. That holds them like birdlime. Priest with the communion corpus for those women. Chap in the mortuary, coffin or coffey, *corpusnomine.* Wonder where that rat is by now. Scrape.

Tap.

They listened: tankards and Miss Kennedy, George Lidwell eyelid well expressive, fullbusted satin, Kernan, Si.

The sighing voice of sorrow sang. His sins. Since easter he had cursed three times. You bitch's bast. And once at masstime he had gone to play. Once by the churchyard he had passed and for his mother's rest he had not prayed. A boy. A croppy boy.

Bronze, listening by the beerpull, gazed far away. Soulfully. Doesn't half know I'm. Molly great dab at seeing anyone looking.

Bronze gazed far sideways. Mirror there. Is that best side of her face? They always know. Knock at the door. Last tip to titivate.

Cockcarracarra.

What do they think when they hear music. Way to catch rattlesnakes. Night Michael Gunn gave us the box. Tuning up. Shah of Persia liked that best. Wiped his nose in curtain too. Custom his country perhaps. That's music too. Tootling. Brasses braying asses. Doublebasses helpless, gashes in their sides. Woodwinds mooing cows. Woodwind like Goodwin's name.

She looked fine. Her crocus dress she wore, lowcut, belongings on show. Clove her breath was always in theatre when she bent to ask a questnion. Told her what Spinoza says in that book of poor papa's. Hypnotised, listening. Eyes like that. She bent. Chap in dresscircle, staring down into her with his operaglass for all he was worth. Met him pike hoses. Philosophy. O rocks!

All gone. All fallen. At the siege of Ross his father, at Gorey all his brothers fell. To Wexford, we are the boys of Wexford, he would. Last of his name and race.

I too, last of my race. Milly young student. Well, my fault perhaps. No son. Rudy. Too late now. Or if not? If not? If still?

He bore no hate.

Hate. Love. Those are names. Rudy. Soon I am old.

Big Ben his voice unfolded. Great voice Richie Goulding said, a flush struggling in his pale, to Bloom, soon old but when was young.

Ireland comes now. My country above the king. She listens. Time to be shoving. Looked enough.

—*Bless me, father,* Dollard the croppy cried. Bless me *and let me go.*

Tap.

Bloom looked, unblessed to go. Got up to kill: on eighteen bob a week. Fellows shell out the dibs. Want to keep your weather eye open. Those girls, those lovely. Chorusgirl's romance. Letters read out for breach of promise. From Chickabiddy's own Mumpsypum. Laughter in court. Henry. The lovely name you.

Low sank the music, air and words. Then hastened. The false priest rustling soldier from his cassock. A yoeman captain. They know it all by heart. The thrill they itch for. Yeoman cap.

Tap. Tap.

Thrilled, she listened, bending in sympathy to hear.

Blank face. Virgin should say: or fingered only. Write something on it: page. If not what becomes of them? Decline, despair. Keeps them young. Even admire themselves. See. Play on her. Lip blow. Body of white woman, a flute alive. Blow gentle. Loud. Three holes all women. Goddess I didn't see. They want it: not too much polite. That's why he gets them. Gold in your pocket, brass in your face. With look to look: songs without words. Molly that hurdygurdy boy. She knew he meant the monkey was sick. Understand animals too that way. Gift of nature.

Ventriloquise. My lips closed. Think in my stom. What?

Will? You? I. Want. You. To.

With hoarse rude fury the yoeman cursed. Swelling in apoplectic bitch's bastard. A good thought, boy to come. One hour's your time to live, your last.

Tap. Tap.

Thrill now. Pity they feel. For all things dying, for all things born. Poor Mrs. Purefoy. Hope she's over. Because their wombs .

A liquid of womb of woman eyeball gazed under a fence of lashes, calmly, hearing. See real beauty of the eye when she not speaks. On yonder river. At each slow satiny heaving bosom's wave (her heaving embon) red rose rose slowly, sank red rose. Heartbeats her breath: breath that is life. And all the tiny tiny fernfoils trembled of maidenhair.

But look. The bright stars fade. O rose! Castile. The morn.

Ha. Lidwell that is. For him then, not for me she. His eyes infatuated. I like that? See her from here though. Popped corks, splashes of beerfroth, stacks of empties.

On the smooth jutting beerpull laid Lydia hand lightly, plumply, leave it to my hands. All lost in pity for croppy. Fro, to: to, fro: over the polished knob (she knows his eyes, my eyes, her eyes) her thumb and finger passed in pity: passed, repassed and, gently touching, then slid so smoothly, slowly down, a cool firm white enamel baton protruding through their sliding ring.

With a cock with a carra.

Tap. Tap. Tap.

I hold this house. Amen. He gnashed in fury. Traitors swing.

The chords consented. Very sad thing. It had to be.

Get out before the end. Pass by her. Can leave that *Freeman*. Letter I have. Suppose she were the? No. Walk, walk, walk.

Well, I must be. Are you off? Yes. Bloom stood up. Soap feeling rather sticky behind. Must have sweated behind: music. That lotion, remember. Well, so long. High grade. Card inside yes.

By deaf Pat in the doorway, straining ear, Bloom passed.

At Geneva barrack that young man died. At Passage was his body laid. The voice of the mournful chanter called to prayer .

By rose, by satiny bosom, by the fondling hand, by slops, by empties, by popped corks, greeting in going past eyes and maidenhair, bronze and faint gold in deepseashadow, went Bloom, soft Bloom, I feel so lonely Bloom.

Tap. Tap. Tap.

Pray for him, prayed the bass of Dollard. You who hear in peace. Breathe a prayer, drop a tear, good men, good people. He was the croppy boy.

Scaring eavesdropping boots croppy bootsboy Bloom in the Ormond hallway heard growls and roars of bravo, fat backslapping, their boots all treading, boots not the boots the boy. General chorus off for a swill to wash it down. Glad I avoided.

—Come on, Ben, Simon Dedalus said. By God, you're as good as ever you were.

—Better, said Tomgin Kernan. Most masterly rendition of that ballad, upon my soul and honour it is .

—Lablache, said Father Cowley.

Ben Dollard bulkily cachuchad towards the bar, mightily praisefed and all big roseate, on heavyfooted feet, his gouty fingers nakkering castagnettes in the air.

Big Benaben Dollard. Big Benben. Big Benben.

Rrr.

And deepmoved, all, Simon trumping compassion from his nose, all laughing, they brought him forth, Ben Dollard, in right good cheer.

—You're looking rubicund, George Lidwell said.

Miss Douce composed her rose to wait.

—He is, said Mr. Dedalus, clapping Ben's fat back shoulderblade. He has a lot of a adipose dispose tissue concealed about his person..

Rrrrrrsss.

—Fat of death, Simon, Ben Dollard growled.

Richie rift in the lute alone sat: Goulding, Colles, Ward. Uncertainly he waited. Unpaid Pat too.

Tap. Tap. Tap.

Miss Mina Kennedy brought near her lips to ear of tankard one.

—Mr. Dollard, they murmured low.

—Dollard, murmured tankard.

Tank one believed: Miss Kenn when she: that doll he was: she doll: the tank.

He murmured that he knew the name. The name was familiar to him, that is to say. That was to say he had heard the name of Dollard, was it? Dollard, yes.

Yes, her lips said more loudly, Mr. Dollard. He sang that song lovely, murmured Mina. And *The last rose of summer* was a lovely song. Mina loved that song. Tankard loved the song that Mina.

'Tis the last rose of summer dollard left bloom felt wind wound round inside.

Gassy thing that cider: binding too. Wait. Postoffice near Reuben J's one and eightpence too. Get shut of it. Dodge round by Greek street. Wish I hadn't promised to meet. Freer in air. Music. Gets on your nerves. Beerpull. Her hand that rocks the cradle rules the. Ben Howth. That rules the world.

Far. Far. Far. Far.

Tap. Tap. Tap. Tap.

Leopold Bloom with letter for Mady, naughty Henry, with sweets of sin with frillies for Raoul with met himpike hoses went Poldy on.

Tap blind walked tapping by the tap the curbstone tapping, tap by tap.

Cowley, he stuns himself with it: kind of drunkenness. Instance enthusiasts. All ears. Not lose a semidemiquaver. Eyes shut. Head nodding in time. Dotty. You daren't budge. Thinking strictly prohibited. Always talking shop. Fiddle-faddle about notes.

All a kind of attempt to talk. Unpleasant when it stops because you never know exac. Organ in Gardiner street. Old Glynn fifty quid a year. Queer up there in the cockloft alone with stops and locks and keys. Maunder on for hours, talking to himself or the other fellow, blowing the bellows. Growl angry, then shriek cursing (want to have wadding or something in his no don't she cried), then all of a soft sudden wee little wee little pipey wind.

Pwee! A wee little wind piped eeee. In Bloom's little wee.

—Was he? Mr. Dedalus said, returning with fetched pipe. I was with him this morning at poor little Paddy Dignam's . . . . . .

—Ay, the Lord have mercy on him.

—By the bye there's a tuning fork in there on the . . . .

Tap. Tap. Tap. Tap.

—The wife has a fine voice. Or had. What? Lidwell asked.

—O, that must be the tuner, Lydia said to Simonlionel first I saw, forgot it when he was here.

Blind he was she told George Lidwell second I saw. And played so exquisitely, treat to hear. Exquisite contrast: bronzelid minagold.

—Shout! Ben Dollard shouted, pouring.

—'lldo! cried Father Cowley.

Rrrrrr.

I feel I want . . . .

Tap. Tap. Tap. Tap. Tap.

—Very, Mr. Dedalus said, staring hard at a headless sardine.

Under the sandwichbell lay on a bier of bread one last, one lonely, last sardine of summer. Bloom alone.

—Very, he stared. The lower register, for choice.

Tap. Tap. Tap. Tap. Tap. Tap. Tap. Tap.

Bloom went by Barry's. Wish I could. Wait. Twentyfour solicitors in that one house. Litigation. Love one another. Piles of parchment. Goulding, Colles, Ward.

But for example the chap that wallops the big drum. His vocation: Micky Rooney's band. Wonder how it first struck him. Sitting at home after pig's cheek and cabbage nursing it in the armchair Pom. Pompedy. Jolly for the wife. Asses' skins. Welt them through life, then wallop after death. Pom. Wallop. Seems to be what you call yashmak or I mean kismet. Fate.

Tap. Tap. A stripling, blind, with a tapping cane, came taptaptapping by Daly's window where a mermaid, hair all streaming, (but he couldn't see), blew whiffs of a mermaid (blind couldn't), mermaid, coolest whiff of all.

Instruments. Even comb and tissuepaper you can knock a tune out of. Molly in her shift in Lombard street west, hair down. I suppose each kind of trade made its own, don't you see? Hunter with a horn. Haw. Have you the? *Cloche. . Sonnez la!* Shepherd his pipe. Policeman a whistle. All is lost now. Drum? Pompedy. Wait, I know. Towncrier, bumbailiff. Long John. Waken the dead. Pom. Dignam. Poor little *nominedomine*. Pom. It is music. I mean of course it's all pom pom pom very much what they call *da capo*. Still you can hear.

I must really. Fff. Now if I did that at a banquet. Just a question of custom shah of Persia. Breathe a prayer, drop a tear. All the same he must have been a bit of an natural not to see it was a yeoman cap. Muffled up. Wonder who was that chap at the grave in the brown mackin. O, the whore of the lane!

A frowsy whore with black straw sailor hat askew came glazily in the day along the quay towards Mr. Bloom. When first he saw that form endearing. Yet, it is. I feel so lonely. Wet night in the lane. Off her beat here. What is she? Hope she. Psst! Any chance of your wash. Knew Molly. Had me decked. Stout lady does be with you in the brown costume. Put you off your stroke, that. Sees me, does she? Looks a fright in the day. Face like dip. Damn her! O, well, she has to live like the rest. Look in here.

In Lionel Mark's antique window Lionel Leopold dear Henry Flower earnestly Mr. Leopold Bloom envisaged candlesticks melodeon oozing maggoty blowbags. Bargain: six bob. Might learn to play. Cheap. Let her pass. Course everything is dear if you don't want it. That's what good salesman is. Make you buy what he wants to sell. She's passing now. Six bob.

Must be the cider or perhaps the burgund.

Near bronze from anear near gold from afar they chinked their clinking glasses all, brighteyed and gallant, before bronze Lydia's tempting last rose of summer, rose of Castile. First Lid, De, Cow, Ker, Doll, a fifth: Lidwell, Si Dedalus, Bob Cowley. Kernan and Big Ben Dollard.

Tap. A youth entered a lonely Ormond hall.

Bloom viewed a gallant pictured hero in Lionel Mark's window. Robert Emmet's last words. Seven last words. Of Meyerbeer that is.

—True men like you men.

—Ay ay, Ben.

—Will lift your glass with us.

They lifted.

Tschink. Tschunk.

Tip. An unseeing stripling stood in the door. He saw not bronze. He saw not gold. Nor Ben nor Bob nor Tom nor Si nor George nor tanks nor Richie nor Pat. Hee hee hee hee. He did not see.

Seabloom, greaseabloom viewed last words. Softly. *When my country takes her place among.*

Prrprr.

Must be the bur.

Fff. Oo. Rrpr.

The nations of the earth. No-one behind. She's passed. *Then and not till then.* Tram. Kran, kran, kran. Good oppor. Coming. Krandlkrankran. I'm sure it's the burgund. Yes. One, two. *Let my epitaph be.* Kraaaaaaaa. *Written. I have.*

Pprrpffrrppfff.

Done.

(*to be continued*)

Episode XII

THE LITTLE REVIEW

VOL. VI NOVEMBER, 1919 No. 7

CONTENTS

Subscription price, payable in advance, in the United States and Territories, $2.50 per year; Single copy 25 c., Canada, $2.75; Foreign, $3.00. Published monthly, and copyrighted, 1919 by Margaret C. Anderson.

Manuscripts must be submitted at author's risk, with return postage.

Entered as second class matter March 16, 1917, at the Post Office at New York, N. Y., under the act of March 3, 1879.

MARGARET C. ANDERSON, Publisher

24 *West Sixteenth Street, New York, N. Y.*

Foreign Office: 43 *Belsize Park, Gardens, London N. W.* 3.

I WAS just passing the time of day with old Troy of the D. M. P. at the corner of Arbour hill there and be damned but a bloody sweep came along and he near drove his gear into my eye. I turned around to let him have the weight of my tongue when who should I see dodging along Stony Batter. . . . . only Joe Hynes.

—Lo, Joe, says I. How are you blowing? Did you see that bloody chimnysweep near shove my eye out with his brush?

—Soot's luck, says Joe. Who is the old ballocks you were talking to?

—Old Troy, says I, was in the force. I'm on two minds not to give that fellow in charge for obstructing the thoroughfares with his brooms and ladders.

—What are you doing round those parts? says Joe.

—Devil a much, says I. There is a bloody gig foxy thief beyond by the garrison church at the corner of Chicken Lane—old Troy was just giving me a wrinkle about him—I lifted any God's quantity of tea and sugar to pay three bob a week said he had a farm in the country Down off a hop of my thumb by the name of Moses Herzog over there near Heylesbury Street.

—Circumcised? says Joe.

—Ay, says I. A bit of the top. An old Plumber named Geraghty.

I'm hanging on to his tow now for the past fortnight and I can't get a penny out of him.

—That the lay you're on now? says Joe.

—Ay, says I. How are the mighty fallen! Collector of bad and doubtful debts. But that's the most notorious bloody robber you'd meet in a day's walk and the face on him all pockmarks would hold a shower of rain. *Tell him,* says he, *I dare him,* says he and *I double dare him to send you round here again, or if he does,* says he, *I'll have him summonsed up before the court, so I will, for trading without a licence.* And he after stuffing himself till he's fit to burst! Jesus. I had to laugh at the little jewy getting his shirt out. *He drink me my teas. He eat me my sugars. Why he no pay me my moneys?*

For nonperishable goods bought of Moses Herzog, of 13 Saint Kevin's parade. Wood quay ward, merchant, hereinafter called the vendor, and sold and delivered to Michael E. Geraght, Esquire, of 29 Arbour Hill in the city of Dublin, Arran quay ward, gentleman, hereinafter called the purchaser, videlicet, five pounds avoirdupois of first choice tea at three shillings per pound avoirdupois and three stone avoirdupois of sugar, crushed crystal, at three pence per

Facing page: table of contents, *Little Review,* November 1919

pound avoirdupois, the said purchaser debtor to the said vendor of 1 pound 5 shilings and six pence sterling for value received which amount shall be paid by said purchaser to said vendor in weekly instalments every seven calendar days of three shillings and no pence sterling: and the said nonperishable goods shall not be pawned or pledged or sold or otherwise alienated by the said purchaser but shall be and remain and be held to the sole and exclusive property of the said vendor to be disposed of at his good will and pleasure until the said amount shall have been duly paid by the said purchaser to the said vendor in the manner herein set forth as this day hereby agreed between the said vendor, his heirs, successors, trustees and assigns, of the one part and the said purchaser, his heirs, successors, trutees and assigns of the other part.

—Are you a strict t. t? says Joe.

—Not taking anything between drinks, says I.

—What about paying our respects to our friend? says Joe.

—Who? says I. Sure he's in John of God's off his head, poor man.

—Drinking his own stuff? says Joe.

—Ay, says I. Whisky and water on the brain.

—Come around to Barney Kienan's, says Joe. I want to see the citizen.

—Barney mavourneen's be it, says I. Anything strange or wonderful, Joe?

—Not a word, says Joe. I was up at that meeting in the City Arms.

—What was that, Joe? says I.

—Cattle traders, says Joe, about the foot and mouth disease. I want to give the citizen the hard word about it.

So we went around by the Linenhall barracks and the back of the court house talking of one thing or another. Decent fellow Joe when he has it but sure like that he never has it. Jesus, I couldn't get over that bloody foxy Geraghty. For trading without a licence, says he.

In Inisfail the fair there lies a land the land of holy Michan. There rises a watchtower beheld of men afar. There sleep the mighty dead as in life they slept warriors and princes of high renown. A pleasant land it is in sooth of murmuring waters, fishful streams where sport the gunnard, the plaice, the halibut, the flounder and other denizons of the acqueous kingdom too numerous to be enumerated. In the mild breezes of the west and of the east the lofty trees wave in different directions their first class foliage, the sycamore, the Lebanonian cedar, the exalted planetree, the eucalyptus and other ornaments of the arboreal world with which that region is thoroughly well supplied. Lovely maidens sit in close proximity to the roots of the lovely trees singing the most lovely songs while they play with all kinds of lovely objects as for eaxmple golden ingots, silvery fishes, purple seagems and playful insects. And heroes voyage from afar to woo them, the sons of Kings.

And there rises a shining palace whose crystal glittering roof is seen by mariners who traverse the extensive sea in barks built for that purpose and thither come all herds and fatlings and first fruits . . . . . of that land for O'Connell Fitzsimon takes toll of them, a chieftain descended from chieftains. Thither the extremely large wains bring foison of the fields, spherical potatoes and irridescent kale and onions, pearls of the earth, and red, green, yellow, brown, russet, sweet, big, bitter ripe pomellated apples and strawberries fit for princes and rapsberries from their canes

I dare him says he, and I doubledare him.

And thither wend the herds innumerable of heavyhooved kine from pasturelands of Lush and Rush and Carrickmines and from the streamy vales of Thomond and from the gentle declivities of the place of the race of Kiar, their udders distended with superabundance of milk and butter and rennets of cheese and oblong eggs, various in size, the agate with the dun.

So we turned into Barney Kiernan's, and there sure enough was the citizen as large as life up in the corner having a great confab with himself and that bloody mangy mongrel. Garryowen, and he waiting for what the sky would drop in the way of drink.

—There he is, says I, in his glory hole, with his load of papers, working for the cause.

The bloody mongrel let a grouse out of him would give you the creeps. Be a corporal work of mercy if someone would take the life of that bloody dog. I'm told for a fact he ate a good part of the breeches off a constabulary man in Santry that came round one time with a blue paper about a licence.

—Stand and deliver, says he.

—That's all right, citizen, says Joe. Friends here.

—Pass, friends, says he.

Then he rubbed his hand in his eye and says he:

—What's your opinion of the times?

Doing the rapparee. But, begob, Joe was equal to the occasion.

—I think the markets are on a rise, says he, sliding his hand down his fork.

So begob the citizen claps his paw on his knee and he says:

—Foreign wars is the cause of it.

And says Joe, sticking his thumb in his pocket:

—It's the Russians wish to tyrannise.
—Arrah, give over your bloody coddling Joe, says I, I've a thirst on me I wouldn't sell for half a crown.
—Give it a name, citizen, says Joe.
—Wine of the country, says he.
—What's yours? says Joe.
—Ditto Mac Anaspey, says I.
—Three pints, Terry, says Joe. And how's the old heart, citizen? says he.
—Never better, *a chara,* says he. What Garry? Are we going to win? Eh?

And with that he took the bloody old towser by the scruff of the neck and, by Jesus, he near throttled him.

The figure seated on a large boulder was that of a broadshouldered, deep-chested, stronglimbed, frankeyed, redhaired, freely freckled, shaggybearded, widemouthed, largenosed, longheaded, deepvoiced, barekneed, brawnyhanded, hairylegged, ruddyfaced, sinewyarned hero. From shoulder to shoulder he measured several ells and his rocklike knees were covered, as was likewise the rest of his body wherever visible, with a strong growth of tawny prickly hair in hue and toughness similar to the mountain gorse (*Ulex Europeus*). The wide-winged nostrils from which bristles of the same tawny hue projected, were of such capaciousness that within their cavernous obscurity the fieldlark might easily have lodged her nest. The eyes in which a tear and a smile strove ever for the mastery were of the dimension of a goodsized cauliflower. A powerful current of warm beath issued at regular intervals from the profound cavity of his mouth while in rhythmic resonance the loud strong hale reverberations of his formidable heart thundered rumblingly causing the ground and the lofty walls of the cave to vibrate and tremble.

He wore a long unsleeved garment of recently flayed oxhide reaching to the knees in a loose kilt and this was bound about his middle by a girdle of plaited straw and rushes. Beneath this he wore trews of deerskin, roughly stitched with gut. His nether extremities were encased in high buskins dyed in lichen purple, the feet being shod with brogues of salted cowhide laced with the windpipe of the same beast. From his girdle hung a row of seastones which dangled at every movement of his portentous frame and on these were graven with rude yet striking art the tribal images of many heroes of antiquity, Cuchulin, Conn of hundred battles, Niall of nine hostages, Brian of Kincara, the Ardri Malachi, Art Mac Murragh, Shane O'Neill, Father John Murphy, Owen Roe, Patick Sarsfield, Red Hugh O'Donnell, Don Philip O'Sullivan Beare. A spear of acuminated granite rested by him while at his feet reposed a savage animal of the canine tribe whose stertorous gasps announced that he was sunk in uneasy slumber, a supposition confirmed by hoarse growls and spasmodic movements which his master repressed from time to time by tranquilizing blows of a mighty cudgel rudely fashioned out of paleolithic stone.

So anyhow Terry brought the three pints Joe was standing and begob the sight nearly left my eyes when I saw him hand out a quid. O, as true as I am telling you. A goodlooking sovereign.

—And there's more where that came from, says he.

—Were you robbing the poorbox, Joe? say I?

—Sweat of my brow, says Joe. 'Twas the prudent member gave me the wheeze.

—I say him before I met you, says I, sloping around by Pill lane with his cod's eye counting up all the guts of the fish.

Who comes through Michan's land, bedight in sable armour? O'Bloom, the son of Rory: it is he. Impervious to fear is Rory's son: he of the prudent soul.

'—For the old woman of Prince's Street, says the citizen, the subsidized organ. The pledgebound party on the floor of the house. And look at this blasted rag, says he.

—Look at this, says he. *The Irish Independent,* if you please, founded by Parnell to be the workingman's friend. Listen to the births and deaths in the *Irish all for Ireland Independent* and I'll thank you, and the marriages.

And he starts reading them out:

—Gordon, Barnfield Crescent, Exeter; Redmayne of Iffley, Saint Anne's on Sea, the wife of William T. Redmayne, of a son. How's that, eh? Wright and Flint, Vincent and Gillett to Rotha Marion Daughter of Rosa and the late George Alfred Gillett 179 Clapham Road, Stockwell, Playwood and Ridsdale at Saint Jude's Kensington by the very reverend Dr. Forrest, Dean of Worcester, eh? Deaths. Bristow, at whitehall lane, London: Carr, Stoke Newington of gastritis and heart disease: Cockburn, at the Moat house., Chepstow . . .

—I know that fellow, says Joe, from bitter experience.

—Cockburn. Dimsey, wife of David Dimsey, late of the admiralty: Miller, Tottenham, aged eightyfive: Welsh, June 12, at 35 Canning Street, Liverpool, Isabella Helen. How's that, for a national press, eh? How's that for Martin Murphy, the Bantry Jobber?

—Ah, well, says Joe, handing round the boose.

Thanks be to God they had the start of us. Drink that, citizen.

—I' wil, says he, honourable person.

—Health, Joe, says I.

Aw! Ow! Don't be talking! I was blue mouldy for the want of that pint. Declare to God I could hear it hit the pit of my stomach with a click.

And lo, as they quaffed their cup of joy, a godlike messenger came running in, radiant as the eye of heaven, a comely youth and behind him there passed an elder of noble gait and countenance, bearing the sacred scrolls of law and with him his lady wife, a dame of peerless lineage, fairest of her race.

'Little Alf Bergan popped in round the door and hid behind Barney's snug, squeezed up with the laughing, and who was sitting up there in the corner that I hadn't seen snoring drunk, blind to the world, only Bob Doran. I didn't know what was up and Alf' kept making signs out of the door. And begob what was it only that bloody old pantaloon Denis Breen in his bath slippers, with two bloody big books tucked under his oxter and the wife hotfoot after him, unfortunate wretched woman trotting like a poodle. I thought Alf would split.

—Look at him, says he. Breen. He's traipsing all round Dublin with a postcard someone sent him with u. p. : up on it to take a li . . . . .

And he doubled up.

—Take a what? says I.

—Libel action, says he, for ten thousand pounds.

—O hell! says I.

The bloody mongrel began to growl seeing something was up but the citizen gave him a kick in the ribs. Begob he wakened Bob Doran anyhow.

—*Bi i dho husht*, says he.

—Who? says Joe.

—Breen, says Alf. He was in John Henry Menton's and then he went round to Colles and Ward's and then Tom Rochford met him and sent him round to the subsheriff's for a lark. O God, I've a pain laughing. U. p: up. The long fellow gave him an eye as good as a process and now the bloody old lunatic is gone round to Green Street to look for a G. man.

—When is that long John going to hang that fellow in Mountjoy? says Joe.

—Bergan, says Bob Doran, waking up. Is that Alf Bergan.

—Yes, says Alf. Hanging? Wait till I show you. Here, Terry, give us a pony of stout. That bloody old fool! Ten thousand pounds. You should have seen long Johns eye. U. p . . . . .

And he started laughing.

—Who are you laughing at? says Bob Doran? Is that Bergan?

—Hurry up, Terry boy, says Alf, with the stout.

Terence O'Ryan heard him and straightway brought him a crystal cup full of the foaming ebon ale which the noble twin brothers Bungiveagh and Bungardilaun brew ever in their divine alevats, cunning as the sons of deathless Leda. For they garner the succulent berries of the hop and mass and sift and bruise and brew them and they mix therewith sour juices and bring the must to the sacred fire and cease not night or day from their toil, those cunning brothers, lords of the vat.

Then did you, Terence, hand forth, as to the manner born, that nectarous beverage and you offered the crystal cup to him that thirsted, in beauty akin to the immortals

But he, the young chief of the O'Bergan's, could ill brook to be outdone in generous deeds but gave therefore with gracious gesture a testoon of costliest bronze Thereon embossed in excellent smithwork was seen the image of a queen of regal port, Victoria her name, by grace of God, queen of Great Britain and Ireland, Empress of India, defender of the faith, even she, who bore rule, a victress over many peoples, the wellbeloved, for they knew and loved her from the rising of the sun to the going down thereof, the pale, the dark, the ruddy and the ethiop.

—What's that bloody freemason doing, says the citizen, prowling up and down outside?

—What's that? says Joe.

—Here you are, says Alf, chucking out the rhino. Talking about hanging, I'll show you something you never saw. Hangmens' letters, look at here.

So he took a bundle of wisps of letters and envelopes out of his pocket.

—Are you codding? say I.

—Honest injun, says Alf. Read them.

So Joe took up the letters.

—Who were you laughing at? says Bob Doran.

So I saw there was going to be a bit of adust Bob's a queer chap when the porter's up in him so says I just to make talk:

—How's Willie Murray those times, Alf?

—I don't know, says Alf. I saw him just now in Capel Street with Paddy Dignam. Only I was running after that.....

—You what? says Joe, throwing down the letters. With who?

—With Dignam, says Alf.

—Is it Paddy? says Joe.

—Yes, says Alf. Why?

—Don't you know he's dead? says Joe.

—Paddy Dignam dead? says Alf.

—Ay, says Joe.

—Sure I am after seeing him not five minutes ago, says Alf, as plain as a pikestaff.

—Who's dead? says Bob Doran.

—You saw his ghost then, says Joe, God between us and harm.

—What? says Alf. Good Christ, only five...... What?...... and Willie Murray with him, the two of them there near what do you call him's...... What? Dignam dead?

What about Dignam? says Bob Doran. Who's talking about......?

—Dead! says Alf. He is no more dead than you are.

—Maybe so, says Joe. They took the liberty of burying him this morning anyhow.

—Paddy? says Alf.

—Ay, says Joe. He paid the debt of nature, God be merciful to him.

—Good Christ! says Alf.

Begod he was what you might call flabbegasted.

In the darkness, spirit hands were felt to flutter, and when prayer by .... had been directed to the proper quarter a faint but increasing luminosity of dark ruby light became gradually visible, the apparition of the etheric double being particularly lifelike owing to the discharge of jivic rays from the crown of the head and face. Communication was effected through the pituitary body and also by means of the orangefiery and scarlet rays emanating from the sacral region and solar plexus. Questioned as to his whereabouts he stated that he was now on the path of pralaya or return but was still submitted to trial at the hands of certain bloodthirsty entities on the lower astral levels. In reply to a question as to his first sensations beyond he stated that previously he had seen as in a glass darkly but that those who had passed over had summit possibilities of atmic development opened up to them. Interrogated as to whether life there resembled our experience in the flesh he stated that he heard from more favoured beings that their abodes were equipped with every modern comfort and that the highest adepts were steeped in waves of volupcy of the very purest nature. Having requested a quart of buttermilk this was brought and evidently afforded relief. Asked if he had any message for the living he exhorted all who were still at the wrong side of Maya to acknowledge the true path for it was repoted in devanic circles that Mars and Jupiter were out for mischief on the eastern angle where the ram has power. It was then queried whether there were any special desires on the part of the defunct and the reply was: *Mind C. K. doesn't pile it on.* It was ascertained that the reference was to Mr. Cornelius Kelleher manager of Messrs. H. J. O'Neill's popular funeral establishment, a personal friend of the defunct who had been responsible for the carrying out of the internment arrangements. Before departing he requested that it should be told to his dear son Patsy that the other boot which he had been looking for was at present under the commode, in the return room and that the pair should be sent to Cullen's to be sold only as the heels were still good. He stated that this had greatly perturbed his peace of mind in the other region and earnestly requested that his desire should be made known. Assurances were given that the matter would be attended to and it was intimated that this had given satisfaction.

He is gone from mortal haunts: O'Dignam, sun of our morning. Fleet was his foot on the bracken: Patrick of the beamy brow. Wail, Banba, with your wind: and Wail, O ocean, with your whirlwind.

—There he is again, says the citizen, staring out.

—Who,? says I.

—Bloom, says he. He's on point duty up and down there for the last ten minutes.

And, begob, I saw him do a peep in and then slidder off again.

Little Alf was knocked bawways. Faith, he was.

—Good Christ! says he. I could have sworn it was him.

And says Bob Doran, with the hat on the back of his poll, he's the lowest blackguard in Dublin when he's under the influence.

—Who said Christ is good?

—I beg your parsnips, says Alf.

—Is that a good Christ, says Bob Doran, to take away poor little Willie Dignam?

—Ah, well, says Alf, trying to pass it off. He's over all his troubles.

But Bob Doarn shouts out of him.

—He's a bloody ruffian, I say, to take away poor little Willie Dignam.

Terry came down and tipped him the wink to keep quiet, that they didn't want that kind of talk in a respectable licensed premises. And Bob Doran starts doing the weeps about Paddy Dignam, true as you're there.

—The finest man, says he, snivelling, the finest, purest character.

Talking through his bloody hat. Fitter for him to go home to the little sleepingwalking bitch he married, Mooney, the bailiff's daughter, Mother kept a kip in Hardwick street that used to be stravaging about the landings Bantan Lyons told me that was stopping there at two in the morning without a stitch on her, exposing her person open to all comers, fair field and no favor.

—The noblest, the truest, says he. And he's gone, poor little Willie, poor little Paddy Dignam.

And mournful and with a heavy heart he bewept the extinction of that beam of heaven.

Old Garryowen started growling again at Bloom that was skeezing round the door.

—Come in, come on, he won't eat you, says the citizen.

So Bloom slopes in with his cod's eye on the dog and asks Terry was Martin Cunningham there.

—O, Christ Mackeon, says Joe, reading one of the letters. Listen to this, will you?

And he starts reading out one.

7, Hunter Street,
Liverpool.

To the High Sheriff of Dublin,

Dublin.

Honoured sir i beg to offer my services in the above mentioned painful case i hanged Joe Gann in Bootle jail on the 12 of Febuary 1900 and i hanged . . . . . .

—Show us, Joe says I.

. . . private Arthur Chace for fowl murder of Jessie Tilsit in Pentonville prison and i was assistant when . . . . .

—Jesus, says I.

. . . Billington executed the awful murderer Toad Smith. . . .

The citizen made a grab at the letter.

—Hold hard, says Joe,

i have a special nack of putting the noose once in he can't get out hoping to be favoured i remain, honoured sir, my terms is five ginnees.

H. Rumbold
Master Barber

—And a barbarous bloody barbarian he is too, says the citizen.

—And the dirty scrawl of the wretch, says Joe. Here, says he, take them to hell-out of my sight, Alf. Hello, Bloom, says he, what will you have?

They started arguing about the point, Bloom saying he wouldn't and he couldn't and excuse him no offence and all to that and then he said well he'd just take a cigar. Gob, he's a prudent member and no mistake.

—Give us one of your prime stinkers, Terry, says Joe.

Any Alf was telling us there was one chap sent in a mounring card with a black border round it.

—They're all barbers, says he, from the black country that would hang their own fathers for five quid down and travelling expenses.

And he was telling us they chop up the rope after and sell the bits for a few bob each.

In the dark land they hide, the vengeful knights of the razor. Their deadly coil they grasp: ya, and therein they lead to Erebus whatsoever wight hath done a deed of blood for I will on nowise suffer it even so saith the Lord.

So they started talking about capital punishment and of course Bloom comes out with the why and the wherefore and all the codology of the business and the old dog smelling him all the time I'm told those Jews have a sort of queer odour coming off them for dogs about I don't know what all deterrent effect and so forth and so on.

—There's one thing it hasn't a deterrent effect on, says Alf.*

. . . .

So of course the citizen was only waiting for the wink of the word and he starts gassing out of him about the invincibles and who fears to speak of ninety-eight and Joe with him about all the fellows that were hanged for the cause by

---

*A passage of some twenty lines has been omitted to avoid the censor's possible suppression.

drumhead court marshal and a new Ireland and new this that and the other. Talking about new Ireland he ought to go and get a new dog so he ought. Mangy ravenous brute sniffling and sneezing all round the place and scratching his scabs and round he goes to Bob Doran that was standing Alf a half one sucking up for what he could get So of course Bob Doran starts doing the bloody fool with him:

—Give us the paw! Give us the paw, doggy! Good old doggy. Give us the paw here! Give us the paw!

Arrah! bloody end to the paw he'd give and Alf trying to keep him from tumbling off the bloody stool atop of the bloody old dog and he talking all kinds of drivel about training by kindness and thoroughbred dog and intelligent dog: give you the bloody pip. Then he starts scraping a few bits of old biscuit out of the bottom of a Jacob's tin he told Terry to bring. Gob, he golloped it down like old boots and his tongue hanging out for more. Near ate the tin and all, hungry bloody mongrel.

And the citizen and Bloom having an argument about the point, Robert Emmet and die for your country, the Tommy Moore touch about Sarah Curran and she's far from the land. And Bloom of course, with his knock me down cigar putting on swank with his lardy face. Phenomenon! The fat heap he married is a nice old phenomenon. Time they were stopping up in the *City Arms* Pisser Burke told me there was an old one there with a cracked nephew and Bloom trying to get the soft side of her doing the molly coddle playing bézique to come in for a bit of the wampum in her will and not eating meat of a Friday because the old one was always thumping her craw and taking the lout out for a walk. And one time he brought him back as drunk as a boiled owl and he said he did it to teach him the evils of alcohol, and, by herrings the women bear roasted him, the old one, Bloom's wife and Mrs. O'Dowd that kept the hotel—Jesus, I had to laugh at Pisser Burke taking them off chewing the fat and Bloom with his *but don't you see?* and *but on the other hand*. Phenomenon!

—The memory of the dead, says the citizen taking up his pintglass and glaring at Bloom.

—Ay, ay, says Joe.

—You don't grasp my point, says Bloom. What I mean is. . . . .

—*Sinn Fein!* says the citizen. *Sinn fein amhain!* The friends we love are by our side and the foes we hate before us.

The last farewell was affecting in the extreme. From the belfries far and near the funereal deathbell tolled unceasingly, while all around the gloomy precincts rolled the ominous warning of a hundred muffled drums punctuated by the hollow booming of ordnance. The deafening claps of thunder and the dazzling flashes of lightning which lit up the ghastly scene testified that the artillery of heaven had lent its supernatural pomp to the already gruesome spectacle. A torrential rain poured down from the floodgates of the angry heavens upon the bared heads of the assembled multitude which numbered at the lowest computation five hundred thousand persons. The learned prelate who administred the last comforts of holy religion to the hero martyr knelt in a most christian spirit in a pool of rain water, his cassock above his hoary head, and offered up to the throne of grace fervent prayers of supplication. Hard by the block stood the grim figure of the executioner, his visage concealed in a ten gallon pot with two circular perforated apetures through which his eyes glowered furiously. As he waited the fatal signal he tested the edge of his horrible weapon by honing it upon his brawny forearm or decapitated in rapid succession a flock of sheep which had been provided by the admirers of his fell but necessary office. On a handsome mahogany table near him were neatly arranged the quartering knife, the various finely tempered disembowelling appliances, a terracotta saucepan for the reception of the duodenum, colon, blind intestine and appendix etc., when successfully extricated and two commodious milkjugs destined to receive the most precious blood of the most precious victim. The housesteward of the amalgamated cats' and dogs' home was in attendance to convey these vessels when replenished to that beneficent institution. Quite an excellent repast consisting of rashers and eggs, fried steak and onions, delicious hot breakfast rolls and invigorating tea had been considerately provided by the authorities for the consumption of the central figure of the tragedy but he expressed the dying wish (immediately acceded to) that the meal should be divided in aliquot parts among the members of the sick and indigent roomkeepers association as a token of his regard and esteem. The non plus ultra of emotion was reached when the blushing bride elect burst her way through the serried ranks of the bystanders and flung herself upon the muscular bosom of him who was about to die for her sake. The hero folded her willowy form in a loving embrace murmuring fondly *Sheila, my own*. Encouraged by this use of her christian name she kissed passionately all the various suitable areas of his person which the decencies of prison garb permitted her adour to reach. She swore to him as they mingled the salt streams of their tears that she would cherish his memory, that she would never forget her hero boy. She brought back to his recollection the happy days of blissful childhood together on the banks of Anna Liffey when they had indulged in the innocent pastimes of the young, and, oblivous of the dreadful present, they both laughed heartily, all the spectators, including the venerable pastor, joining in the general merriment. But anon they were overcome with grief and clasped their hands for the last time. A fresh torrent of tears burst from their lachrymal ducts and the vast concourse of people, touched to the inmost core, broke into heartrending sobs, not the least affected being the aged prebendary himself. A most romantic incident occured when a handsome young Oxford graduate noted for his chivalry towards the fair sex, stepped forward and, presenting his visiting card, bankbook and genealogical tree solicited the hand of the hapless young lady and was accepted on the spot. This timely and generous act evoked a fresh outburst of emotion: and when he placed on the finger of his blushing *fiancée* an expensive engagement ring with three emeralds set in the form of a shamrock excitment knew no bounds. Nay, even the stern provost marshal, lieutenant colonel Tomkin—Maxwell Frenchmullen Tomlinson, who presided on the sad occasion, he who had blown a considerable number of sepoys from the cannonmouth without flinching, could not now restrain his natural emotion. With his mailed gaunlet he brushed away a furtive tear and was overheard by those privileged burghers who happened to be in his immediate *entourage,* to murmur to himself in a faltering undertone:

—God blimey it makes me kind of cry, straight, it does, when I sees her cause I thinks of my old mashtub what's waiting for me down Limehouse way.

So then the citizen begins talking about the Irish language and the cooperation meeting and all to that and the shoneens that can't speak their own language and Joe chipping in his old goo with his twopenny stump that he cadged off Joe and talking about the Gaelic league and the antitreating league and drink, the curse of Ireland. Antitreating is about the size of it. Gob, he'd let you pour all manner of drink down his throat till the Lord would call him before you'd ever see the froth of his pint. And one night I went in with a fellow into one of their musical evenings, song and dance and there was a fellow with a badge spiffing out of him in Irish and a lot of colleen bawns going about with temperance beverages and selling medals. And then an old fellow starts blowing into his bagpipe and all shuffling their feet to the tune the old cow died of. And one or two sky pilots having an eye around that there was no goings on with the females, hitting below the belt.

So, as I was saying, the old dog seeing the tin was empty starts mousing around Joe and me. I'd train him by kindness, so I would, if he was my dog. Give him a rousing fine kick now and again where it wouldn't blind him.

—Afraid he'll bite you? says the citizen sneering.

—No, says I, but he might take my leg for a lamppost.

So he calls the old dog over.

—What's on you, Garryowen? says he.

Then he starts hauling and mauling and talking to him in Irish and the old towser growling, letting on to answer, like a duet in the opera. Such growling you never heard as they let off between them. Someone that has nothing better to do ought to write a letter *pro bono publico* to the papers about the muzzling order for a dog the like of that. Growling and grousing and his eye all bloodshot and the hydrophobia dropping out of his jaws.

All those who are interested in the spread of human culture among the lower animals (and their name is legion) should make a point of not missing the really marvellous exhibition of cynanthropy given by the famous animal Garryowen. The exhibition, which is the result of years of training by kindness and a carefully thought out dietary system, comprises, among other achievements, the recitation of verse. Our phonetic experts have left no stone unturned in their efforts to delucidate and compare the verse recited and have found it bears a striking resemblance to the rauns of ancient Celtic bards. We are not speaking so much of those delightful lovesongs with which the writer who conceals his identity under the title of the little sweet branch has familiarised the bookloving world but rather of the harsher and more personal note which is found in the satirical effusions of the famous Raftery and of Donal Mac Considine. We subjoin a specimen which has been rendered into English by an eminent scholar whose name for the moment we are not at liberty to disclose though we believe that our readers will find the topical allusion rather more than an indication. The metrical system of the canine original, which recalls the intricate alliterative and isosyllabic rules of the Welsh englyn, is infinitely more complicated but we believe our readers will agree that the spirit has been well caught. Perhaps it should be added that the effect is greatly increased if the verse be spoken somewhat slowly and indistinctly in a tone suggestive of suppressed rancour.

The curse of my curses
Seven days every day
And seven dry Thursdays
On you, Barney Kiernan,
Has no sup of water
To cool my courage,

And my guts red roaring
After Lowry's lights.

So he told Terry to bring some water for the dog and, gob, you could hear him lapping it up a mile off. And Joe asked him would he love another.

—I will, says he, to show there's no ill feeling.

Gob, he's not as green as he's cabbagelooking. Arsing around form one pub to another with a dog and getting fed up by the ratepayers. Entertainment for man and beast. And says Joe:

—Could you make a hole in another pint?

—Could a swim duck? says I.

—Same again Terry, says Joe. Are you sure you won't have anything in the way of liquid refreshment? says he.

—Thank you, no, says Bloom. As a matter of fact I just wanted to meet Martin Cunningham, don't you see, about this insurance of Dignam's. Martin asked me to go to the house. You see, he, Dignam, I mean, didn't serve any notice of the assignment on the company at the time and really under the act the mortgagee can't recover on the policy.

—That's a good one by God, says Joe laughing, if old Bridgeman is landed. So the wife comes out top dog, what?

—Well, that's a point, says Bloom, for the wife's admirers.

—Whose admirers? says Joe.

—The wife's advisers, I mean, says Bloom.

Then he starts all confused mucking it up about the mortgagor under the act and for the benefit of the wife and that a trust is created but on the other hand that Dignam owes the money and if now the wife or the widow contested the mortagee's right till he near gave me a pain in my head with his mortagagor under the act. He was bloody safe he wasn't run in himself under the act that time as a rogue and vagabond only he had a friend in court. Selling bazaar tickets or what do you call it royal Hungarian privileged lottery. O, commend me to an israelite! Royal and privileged Hungarian robbery.

(*To be continued*)

THE LITTLE REVIEW

VOL. VI   DECEMBER, 1919   No. 8

CONTENTS

Subscription price, payable in advance, in the United States and Territories, $2.50 per year; Single copy 25 c., Canada, $2.75; Foreign, $3.00. Published monthly, and copyrighted, 1919 by Margaret C. Anderson.

Manuscripts must be submitted at author's risk, with return postage.

Entered as second class matter March 16, 1917, at the Post Office at New York, N. Y., under the act of March 3, 1879.

MARGARET C. ANDERSON, Publisher

24 *West Sixteenth Street, New York, N. Y.*

Foreign Office: 43 *Belsize Park, Gardens, London N. W.* 3.

SO Bob Doran comes lurching around asking Bloom to tell Mrs. Dignam he was sorry for her trouble and he was very sorry about the funeral and to tell her that he said and everyone who knew him said that there was never a truer, a finer than poor little Willie that's dead to tell her. Choking with bloody foolery. And shaking Bloom's hand doing the tragic to tell her that. Shake hands brother. You're a rogue and I'm another.

—Let me, said he, so far presume upon our acquaintance which, however slight it may appear if judged by the standard of mere time, is founded, as I hope and believe, on a sentiment of mutual esteem as to request of you this favour. But, should I have overstepped the limits of reserve let the sincerity of my feelings be the excuse for my boldness.

—No, rejoined the other, I appreciate to the full the motives which actuate your conduct and I shall discharge the office you entrust to me consoled by the reflection that, though the errand be one of sorrow, this proof of your confidence sweetens in some measure the bitterness of the cup.

—Then suffer me to take your hand, said he. The goodness of your heart, I feel sure, will dictate to you better than my inadequate words the expressions which are most suitable to convey an emotion whose poignanc,y were I to give went to my feelings, would deprive me even of speech.

And off with him and out trying to walk straight. Boosed at five o'clock. Night he was near being lagged only Paddy Leonard knew the bobby. Boosed up in a shebeen in Bride street after closing time with two shawls and a bully on guard drinking porter out of teacups. And calling himself a Frenchy, for the shawls, Joseph Manuo, and talking against the catholic religion who wrote the new testament and the old testament and hugging and smuggling. And the two shawls killed with the laughing, picking his pockets the bloody fool and he spilling the porter all over the bed and the two shawls screeching laughing at one another. *How is your testament? Have you got an old testament?* Only Paddy was passing there, I tell you what. Then see him of a Sunday with his little wife, and she wagging her tail up the aisle of the chapel, with her patent boots on her no less, and her violets, nice as pie, doing the little lady. Jack Mooney's sister. And the old prostitute of a mother letting rooms to street couples. Bob, Jack made him toe the line. Told him if he didn't patch up the pot, Jesus, he'd kick the guts out of him.

So Terry brought the three pints

Overleaf: table of contents, *Little Review*, December 1919

—Here, says Joe, doing the honours. Here, citizen.

—*Slan leat,* says he.

—Fortune, Joe, says I. Good health, citizen.

Gob, he had his mouth half way down the tumbler already. Want a small fortune to keep him in drinks.

—Who is the long fellow running for the mayoralty, Alf? says Joe.

—Friend of yours, says Alf.

—Nan, Nan? says Joe.

—I won't mention names, says Alf.

—I thought so, says Joe, I saw him up at that meeting now with William Field, M. P., the cattle trader.

—Hairy Iopas, says the citizen, the darling of all countries and the idol of his own.

So Joe starts telling the citizen about the foot and mouth disease and the cattle traders and taking action in the matter and the citizen sending them all the rightabout and Bloom coming out with his guaranteed remedy for timber tongue in calves. Because he was up one time in a knacker's yard. Walking about with his book and pencil here's my head and my heels are coming till Joe Cuffe gave him the order of the boot for giving lip to a grazier. Mister Knowall. Teach your grandmother how to milk ducks. Pisser Burke was telling me in the hotel the wife used to be in rivers of tears some times with Mrs. O'Dowd. Couldn't loosen her . . . . strings but old codseye was walking around her showing her how to do it. Ay. Humane methods. Because the poor animals suffer and experts say and the best known remedy that doesn't cause pain to the animal and on the sore spot administer gently. Gob, he'd have a soft hand under a hen.

Ga Ga Gara. Klook Klook Klook. Black Liz is our hen. She lays eggs for us. When she lays her eggs she is so glad. Gara. Klook Klook Klook. Then comes good uncle Leo. He puts his hand under black Liz and takes her fresh egg, Ga ga Gara Klook Klook Klook.

—Anyhow, says Joe, Field and Nannetti are going over tonight to London to ask about it in the House of Commons.

—Are you sure, says Bloom, the councillor is going. I wanted to see him, as it happns.

—Well, he's going off by the mailboat, says Joe, tonight.

—That's too bad, says Bloom. I wanted particularly. Perhaps only Mr. Field is going. I coudn't phone. No. You're sure?

—Nan Nan's going too, says Joe. The league told him to ask a question tomorrow about the commissioner of police forbidding Irish games in the park. What do you think of that, citizen.
The Sluagh na h-Eireann.
Mr. Cowe Conacre (Multifarnham. Nat.): Arising out of the question of my honourable friend may I ask the right honourable gentleman whether the government has issued orders that these animals shall be slaughtered though no medical evidence is forthcoming as to their pathological condition?
Mr. Allfours (Tamoshant. Con.): Honourable members are already in possession of the evidence. The answer to the honourable member's question is in the affirmative.
Mr. Orelli O'Reilly (Montenotte. Nat.): Have similar orders been issued for the slaughter of human animals who dare to play Irish games in the phoenix park?
Mr. Allfours: The answer is in the negative.
Mr. Cowe Canocre: Has the right honourable gentleman's famous Mitchelstown telegram inspired the policy of gentlemen on the treasury bench? (O! O!)
Mr. Allfours: I must have notice of that question.
Mr. Staylewit: (Buncombe. Ind.): Don't hesitate to shoot.
(Ironical opposition cheers)
The speaker: Order! Order!
—There's the man, says Joe, that made the Gaelic sports revival. There he is sitting there. The man that got away James Stephens. The champion of all Ireland at putting the 56 pound shot. What was your best throw, citizen?
—*Na bacleis*, says the citizen, letting on to be modest. I was as good as the next fellow anyhow.
—You were, says Joe, and a bloody sight better.
—Is that really a fact? says Alf.
—Yes, says Bloom. That's well known. Do you not know that?

So off they started about Irish support and Shoneen games the like of the lawn tennis and about hurley and putting the stone and racy of the soil and building up a nation once again. And of course Bloom had to have his say too about if a fellow had a weak heart violent exercise was bad. I declare to God if you took up a straw from the floor and if you said to Bloom: *Look at Bloom, do you see that straw? that's a straw.* Declare to my aunt he'd talk about it for an hour so he would and talk steady.

A most interesting discussion took place in the ancient hall of the O'Kiernan's under the auspices of *Sluagh na h-Eireann*, on the revival of ancient

Gaelic sports and the importance of physical culture, as understood in ancient Greece and ancient Rome and ancient Ireland, for the development of the race. The venerable president of this noble order was in the chair, and the attendance was of large dimensions. After an instructive discourse by the chairman a most interesting and instructive discussion ensued as to the desirability of the revivability of the ancient games and sports of our ancient high forefathers. The wellknown and highly respected worker in the cause of our old tongue Mr. Joseph Carthy Hynes made an eloquent appeal for the resuscitation of the ancient Gaelic sports and pastimes as calculated to revive the best traditions of manly strength and powers handed down to us from ancient ages. L. Bloom having espoused the negative the chairman brought the discussion to a close, in response to repeated requests and hearty plaudits from all parts of the house, by a remarkably noteworthy rendering of Thomas Osborne Davis' immortal verses. *A nation once again* in the execution of which the veteran patriot champion may be said without fear of contradiction to have fairly excelled himself. His stentorian notes were heard to the greatest advantage in the timehonoured anthem and and his superb highclass vocalism was vociferously applauded by the large audience amongst which were to be noticed many prominent members of the clergy as well as representatives of the press and the bar and the other learned professions. The proceedings then terminated.

—Talking about violent exercise, says Alf, were you at that Keogh-Bennett match?

—No, says Joe.

—I heard Boylan made a cool hundred quid over it, says Alf.

—Who? Blazes? says Joe.

And says Bloom:

—What I meant about tennis, for example, is the agility and training of the eye.

—Ay, Blazes, says Alf. He let out that Myler was on the beer to run up the odds and he swatting all the time.

—We know him, says the citizen. The traitor's son. We know what put english gold in his pocket.

—True for you, says Joe.

And Bloom cuts in again about lawn tennis and the circulation of the blood, asking Alf:

—Now don't you think, Bergan?

—Myler dusted the floor with him, says Alf. Heenan & Sayers was only a bloody fool to it. See the little kipper not up to his navel and the big fellow swiping. God, he gave him one last puck in the wind, Queensberry rules and all, made him puke what he never ate.

It was a historic battle. Handicapped as he was by lack of poundage Dublin's pet lamb made up for it by superlative skill in ringcraft. The final bout of fireworks was a gruelling for both champions. Bennett had tapped some lively claret in the previous mixup and Myler came on looking groggy. The soldier got to business leading off with a powerful left jab to which Myler retaliated by shooting out a stiff one to Bennett's face. The latter ducked but the Dubliner lifted him with a left hook the punch being a fine one. The men came to handigrips and the bout ended with Bennett on the ropes Myler punishing him. The Englishman was liberally drenched with water and when the bell went came on gamey and full of pluck. It was a fight to a finish and the best man for it. The two fought like tigers and excitement ran fever high. After a brisk exchange of courtesies during which a smart upper cut of the military man brought blood freely from his opponent's mouth the lamb suddenly landed a terrific left to Bennett's stomach, flooring him flat. It was a knockout clean and clever. Amid tense expectation the Portobello bruiser was counted out and Myler declared victor to the frenzied cheers of the public who broke through the ringropes and fairly mobbed him with delight.

—He knows which side his bread is buttered, says Alf. I hear he's running a concert tour now up in the north.

—He is, says Joe. Isn't he?

—Who? says Bloom, ah, yes. That's quite true. Yes, a kind of summer tour, you see. Just a holdiay.

—Mrs. B. is th bright particular star, isn't she? says Joe.

—My wife? says Bloom. She's singing, yes. I think it will be a success too. He's an excellent man to organize. Excellent.

Hoho begob says I to myself says I. That explains the milk in the cocoanut and absence of hair on the animal's chest. Blazes doing the tootle on the flute. Concert tour. Dirty Dan the dodger's son that sold the same horses twice over to the government to fight the Boers. That's the bucko that'll organize her take my tip. Twixt me and you Caddereesh.

Pride of Calpe's rocky mount, the ravenhaired daughter of Tweedy. There grew she to peereless beauty where loquat and almond scent the air. The gardens of Alameda knew her step: the garths of olives knew and bowed. The chaste spouse of Leopold is she: Marion of the bountiful bosoms.

And lo, there entered one of the clan of the O'Molloy's a comely hero of white face yet withal somewhat ruddy, his majesty's counsel learned in the law and with him the prince and heir of the noble line of Lambert.

—Hello, Ned.

—Hello, Alf.

—Hello. Jack.

—Hello, Joe.

—God save you, says the citizen.

—Save you kindly, says J. J. What'll it be, Ned?

—Half one, says Ned.

So J. J. ordered the drinks.

—Were you round at the court? says Joe.

—Yes, says J. J. He'll square that, Ned, says he.

—Hope so, says Ned.

Now what were those two at? J. J. getting him off the jury list and the other give him a leg over the stile. With his name in Stubb's. Playing cards, hobnobbing with flash toffs, drinking fizz and he half smothered in writs and garnishee orders. Gob, he'll come home by weeping, cross one of these days I'm thinking.

—Did you see that bloody lunatic Breen round there, says Alf. U. p. up—

—Yes, says J. J. Looking for a private detective.

—Ay, says Ned, and he wanted right go wrong to address the court, only Corny Kelleher got round him telling him to get the handwriting examined first.

—Ten thousand pounds says Alf, laughing. God I'd give anything to hear him before a judge and jury.

—Was it you did it? Alf? says Joe. The truth the whole truth and nothing but the truth, so help you Jimmy Johnson.

—Me? says Alf. Don't cast your nasturtiums on my character.

—Whatever statement you make, says Joe, will be taken down in evidence against you.

—Of course an action would lie, says J. J. It implies that he is not *compos mentis*. U. p. up.

—Compos what? says Alf, laughing. Do you know that he's balmy?

Look at his head. Do you know that some mornings he has to get his hat on with a shoehorn.

—Yes, says J J., but the truth of a libel is no defence to an indictment for publishing it in the eye of the law.

—Ha, ha, Alf, says Joe.

—Still, says Bloom, on account of the poor woman, I mean his wife.

—Pity about her, says the citizen. Or any other woman marries a half and half.

—How half and half? says Bloom. Do you mean he.....

—Half and half I mean says the citizen. A fellow that's neither fish nor flesh.

—Nor good red herring, says Joe.

—That's what's I mean, says the citizen, a pishogue, if you know what that is.

Begob I saw there was trouble coming. And Bloom explained he meant on account of it being cruel for the wife having to go round after the old stuttering fool. Cruelty to animals so it is to let that bloody Breen out on grass with his beard out tripping him. And she with her nose cocked up after she married him because a cousin of his old fellow's was pew opener to the Pope. Picture of him on the wall with his Turk's moustaches, the signor from summer hill, two pair back and passages, and he covered with all kinds of breastplates bidding defiance to the world.

—And moreover, says J. J., a postcard is publication. It was held to be sufficient evidence of malice in the testcase Sadgrove V. Hole. In my opinion an action might lie.

Six and eightpence, please. Who wants your opinion? Let us drink our pints in peace. Gob, we want be let even do that much.

—Well good health, Jack, says Ned.

—Good health, Ned, says J. J.

—There he is again, says Joe.

—Where? says Alf.

And begob there he was passing the door with his books under his oxter and the wife beside him and Corny Kelleher with his wall eye looking in as they went past, talking to him like a father, trying to sell him a second hand coffin.

—How did that Canada swindle case go off? says Joe.

—Remanded, says J. J.

One of the bottlenosed tribe it was went by the name of James Wought alias Saphiro alias Spark and Spiro put an ad in the papers saying he'd give a passage to Canada for twenty bob. What? Course it was a bloody barney. What? Swindled them all, skivvies and badhacks from the country Meath, ay, and his own Kidney too. J. J. was telling us there was an ancient Hebrew Zaretsky or something weeping in th witness box with his hat on him swearing by the holy Moses he was stuck for two quid.

—Who tried the case? says Joe.

—Recorder, says Ned.
—Poor old Sir Frederick Falkiner, says Alf, you can cod him up to the two eyes.
—Heart as big as a lion, says Ned. Tell him a tale of woe about arrears of rent and a sick wife and a squad of kids and, faith, he'll dissolve in tears on the bench.
—Ay, says Alf. Reuben J. was bloody lucky he didn't clap him in the dock the other day for suing poor little Gumly that's minding stones for the corporation there near Butt bridge.

And he starts taking off the old recorder letting on to cry:
—A most scandalous thing! This poor hardworking man! How many children? Ten, did you say ?
—Yes, your worship. And my wife has the typhoid!
—And a wife with the typhoid fever! Scandalous! Leave the court immediately, Sir. No, sir, I'll make no order for payment. How dare you, sir, come up before me and ask me to make an an order! A poor hardworking industrious man! I dismiss the case.

And on the sixteenth day of the month of the oxeyed goddess the daughter of the skies, the virgin moon, being then in her first quarter those learned judges repaired them to the halls of law. There master Courtenay, sitting in his own chamber, gave his rede and master Justice Andrews, sitting without a jury in the probate court, weighed well and pondered the claims of the first chargeant upon the property in the matter of the will propounded and final testamentary disposition of the real and personal estate of the late lamented Jacob Halliday, vintner, deceased, versus Livingstone, of unsound mind, and another. And to the solemn court of Green street there came Sir Frederick the Falconer. And he sat him there to administer the law of the bretons at the commission to be holden in and for the county of the city of Dublin. And there sat with him the high sinhedrium of the twelve tribes of Iar, for every tribe one man, of the tribe of Patrick and of the tribe of Hugh and of the tirbe of Owen and of the tribe of Conn and of the tribe Oscar and of the tribe of Fergus and of the tribe of Finn and of the tribe of Dermot and of the tribe of Cormac and of the tribe of Kevin and of the tribe of Caolte and of the tribe of Ossian, there being in all twelve good men and true. And he conjured them by him who died on rood that they should well and truly try and true deliverance make in the issue joined between their sovereign lord the king and the prisoner at the bar and true verdict give according to the evidence so help them God and kiss the book. And they rose in their seats, those twelve of Iar, and they swore by the name of him who is everlasting that they'd do His rightwiseness. And straightway the minions of the law led forth from their Donjon keep one whom the sleuthhounds of justice had apprehended in consequence of information received. And they shackled him hand and foot and would take of him ne bail ne mainprise but perferred a charge against him for he was a malefactor. —Those are nice things, says the citizen, coming over here to Ireland filling the country with bugs.

So Bloom let on he heard nothing and he starts talking with Joe, telling him he needn't trouble about that little matter till the first but if he would just say a word to Mr. Crawford. And so Joe swore high and holy he'd do the devil and all.

—Because you see, says Bloom, for an advertisement you must have repetition. That's the whole secret.

—Rely on me, says Joe.

—Swindling the peasants, says the citizen, and the poor of Ireland. We want no more strangers in our house.

—O I'm sure that will be all right, Hynes, says Bloom. It's just that Keyes, you see.

—Consider that done, says Joe.

—Very kind of you, says Bloom.

—The strangers, says the citizen. Our own fault. We let them come in. We brought them in. The adulteress and her paramour brought the Saxon robbers here.

—Decree *nisi*, says J. J.

And Bloom letting on to be awfully deeply interested in nothing, a spider's web in the corner behind the barrel and the citizen scowling after him and the old dog at his feet looking up to know who to bite and when.

—A dishonoured wife, says the citizen, that what the cause of all our misfortunes.

—And here she is, says Alf, that was giggling over the *Police Gazette* with Terry on the counter, in all her warpaint.

—Give us a squint at her, says I.

—O, jakers, Jenny, says Joe, how short your shirt is!

—There's hair, Joe, says I. Get a queer old sirloin off that one, what?

So anyhow in came John Wyse Nolan and Lenehan with him with a face on him as long as a late breakfast.

—Well, says the citizen, what did these tinkers in the cityhall decide about the Irish language?

O'Nolan, clad in shining armour, low bending made obeisance to the puissant chief of Erin and did him to wit of that which had befallen, how that the grave elders of the most obedient city, second of the realm, had met them in the tholsel, and there, after due prayers to the gods who dwell in an ether supernal, had taken solemn counsel whereby they might, if so be it might be, bring once more into honour among mortal men the winged speech of the seadivided Gael.

—It's on the march, says the citizen. To hell with the bloody brutal Sassenachs and their language.

So J. J. puts in a word doing the toff, and Bloom trying to back him up. Moderation and botheration.

—To hell with them, says the citizen. The curse of a good for nothing God light sideways on the bloody thicklugged sons of whores gets! Any civilisation they have they stole from us. Tonguetied sons of bastards' ghosts.

—The European family, says J. J. . . .

—There're not European, says the citizen. I was in Europe with Kevin Egan of Paris. You woudn't see a trace of them or their language anywhere in Europe except in a *cabinet d'aisance.*

And says John Wyse:

—Full many a flower is born to blush unseen.

And says Lenehan, that knows a bit of the lingo:

—*Conspuez les Anglais! Perfide Albion!*

Then lifted he in his rude great brawny strengthy hands the medher of dark strong foamy ale and he drank to the undoing of his foes, a race of mighty valorous heroes, rulers of the waves, who sit on throwns of alabaster silent as the deathless gods.

—What's up with you, says I to Lenehan. You look like a fellow that had lost a bob and found a tanner.

—Gold cup, says he.

—Who won, Mr. Lenehan? says Terry.

—*Throwaway,* says he, at twenty to one. A rank outsider.

—And Bass's mare? says Terry.

—Still running, says he. We'er all in a cart. Boylan plunged two quid on my tip *Sceptre* for himself and a lady friend.

— I had half a crown myself, says Terry, on *Zinfandel* that Mr. Flynn gave me . Lord Howard de Walden's.

—Twenty to one, says Lenehan. Such is life in an outhouse. *Throwaway,* says he. Takes the biscuit and talking about bunions. Frailty, thy name is *Sceptre.*

So he went over to the biscuit tin Bob Doran left to see if there was anything he could lift on the nod the old cur after him backing his luck with his mangy snout up. Old mother Hubbard went to the cupboard.

—Not there, my child, says he.

—Keep your pecker up, says Joe. She'd have won the money only for the other dog.

And J. J. and the citizen arguing about law and history with Bloom sticking in an odd word.

—Some people, says Bloom, can see the mote in others' eyes but they can't see the beam in their own.

—*Raimeis,* says the citizen. Where are the twenty millions of Irish should be here today instead of four? And our potteries and textiles, the nest in the world! And the beds of the Barrow and Shannon they won't deepen with a million acres of marsh and bog to make us all die of consumptoin.

—As treeless as Portugal we'l be soon, says John Wyse, if something is not to reafforest the .and. Larches, firs, all the trees of the conifer family are going fast. I was reading a report. . . . . . .

—Save them, says the citizen, save the trees of Irland for the future men of Ireland on the fair hills of Eire, O.

—Europe has its eyes on you, says Lenehan.

(*to be continued*)

Episode XII (continued)

THE LITTLE REVIEW

VOL. VI   JANUARY, 1920   No. 9

CONTENTS

Subscription price, payable in advance, in the United States and Territories, $2.50 per year; Single copy 25 c., Canada, $2.75; Foreign, $3.00. Published monthly, and copyrighted, 1919 by Margaret C. Anderson.

Manuscripts must be submitted at author's risk, with return postage.

Entered as second class matter March 16, 1917, at the Post Office at New York, N. Y., under the act of March 3, 1879.

MARGARET C. ANDERSON, Publisher

24 *West Sixteenth Street, New York, N. Y.*

Foreign Office: 43 *Belsize Park, Gardens, London N. W.* 3.

THE fashionable international world attended en masse this afternoon at the wedding of the chevalier Jean Wyse de Nolan, grand high chief ranger of the Irish National Foresters, with Miss Fir Conifer of Pine Valley. The bride looked exquisitely charming in a creation of green mercerised silk, moulded on an underslip of gloaming grey, sashed with a yoke of broad emerald and finished with a triple flounce of darker hued fringe, the scheme being relieved by bretelles and hip insertions of acorn bronze. The maids of honour, Miss Larch Conifer and Miss Spruce Conifer, sisters of the bride, wore very becoming costumes in the same tone, a dainty *motif* of plume rose being worked into the pleats in a pinstripe and repeated capriciously in the jadegreen toques in the form of heron feathers of paletinted coral.

—And our eyes are on Europe, says the citizen. We had our trade with Spain and the French and with the Flemings before those mongrels were pupped, Spanish ale in Galway, the winebark on the winedark waterway.

—And will again, says Joe.

—And with the help of the holy mother of God we will again, says the citizen. Our harbours that are empty will be full again, Queenstown, Kinsale, Galway, Killybegs, the third largest harbour in the wide world. And will again, says he, when the first Irish battleship is seen breasting the waves with the green flag to the fore.

And he took the last swig out of the pint, Moya. Cows in Connacht have long horns. Ought to go down and address the multitude in Shanagolden where he daren't show his nose fear the Molly Maguires would let daylight through him for grabbing the holding of an evicted tenant.

—Hear, hear to that, says John Wyse What will you have?

—An imperial yeomanry, says Lenehan, to celebrate the occasion

—Half one, Terry, says John Wyse, and a hands up. Terry! Are you asleep?

—Yes, sir, says Terry. Small whisky and bottle of Allsop. Right, sir.

Hanging over the bloody paper with Alf looking for spicy bits instead of attending to the general public. Picture of a butting match, trying to crack their bloody skulls, one chap going for the other with his head down like a bull at a gate. And another one: *Black Beast Burned in Omaha. Ga.* A lot of Deadwood Dicks in slouch hats and they firing at a sambo strung up on a tree with his tongue out and a bonfire under him. Gob, they ought to drown him in the sea, after, and electrocute and crucify to make sure of the job.

Overleaf: table of contents, *Little Review,* January 1920

—But what about the fighting navy, says Ned, that keeps our foes at bay?
—I'll tell you what about it, says the citizen. Hell upon earth it is. Read the revelations that's going on in the papers about flogging on the training ships at Portsmouth. A fellow writes that calls himself *Disgusted One.*

So he starts telling us about corporal punishment and about the crew of tars and officers and rearadmirals drawn up in cocked hats and the parson with his protestant bible to witness punishment and a young lad brought out, howling for his ma, and they tie him down on the buttend of a gun.
—A rump and dozen, says the citizen, was what that old ruffian Sir John Beresford called it but the modern God's Englishman calls it caning on the breech.

And says John Wyse:
—'Tis a custom more honoured in the breech than in the observance.

Then he was telling us the master at arms comes along with a long cane and he draws out and he flogs the bloody backside off of the poor lad till he yells meila murder.
—That's your glorious British navy, says the citizen, that bosses the earth. The fellows that never will be slaves, with the only hereditary chamber in Europe and their land in the hands of a dozen gamehogs and cottonball barons. That's the great empire they boast about of drudges and whipped serfs.
—On which the sun never rises, says Joe.
—And the tragedy of it is, says the citizen, they believe it. The unfortunate Yahoos believe it.

They believe in rod, the scourger almighty, creator of hell upon earth and in Jacky Tar, the son of a gun, who was conceived of unholy boast, born of the fighting navy, suffered under rump and dozen, was scarified, flayed and curried, yelled like bloody hell, the third day he arose from the bed, steered into haven, sitteth on his beamend till further orders when he shall come to drudge for a living and be paid.
—But, says Bloom, isn't discipline the same everywhere. I mean wouldn't it be the same here if you put force against force?

Didn't I tell you? As true as I'm drinking this porter if he was at his last gasp he'd try to downface you that dying was living.
—We'll put force against force, says the citizen. We have our greater Ireland beyond the sea. They were driven out of house and home in the black 47. Their mudcabins by the roadsire were laid low by the batteringram and the *Times* rubbed its hands and told the whitelivered Saxons there would soon be as few Irish in Ireland as redskins in America. Even the Turks sent us help. But the

Sassenach tried to starve the nation at home while the land was full of crops that the British hyenas bought and sold in Rio de Janeiro. Ay, they drove out the peasants in hordes. Twenty thousand of them died in the coffin ships. But those that came to the land of the free remember the land of bondage. And they will come again and with a vengeance: the sons of Granuaile.

—Perfectly true, says Bloom. But my point was . . . . .

—We are a long time waiting for that day, citizen, says Ned. Since the French landed at Killala.

—Ay, says John Wyse. We gave our best blood to France and Spain, the wild geese. Fontenoy, eh? And Sarsfield and O'Donnell, duke of Tetuan in Spain and Ulysses Browne of Camus that was fieldmarshal to Maria Teresa. But what did we ever get for it?

—The French! says the citizen. Set of dancing masters! Do you know what it is? They were never worth a roasted fart to Ireland. Aren't they trying to make an Entente cordial now with perfidious Albion? Firebrands of Europe and they always were.

—*Conspuez les francais,* says Lenehan, nobbling his beer.

—And as for the Germans, says Joe, haven't we had enough of those sausage-eating bastards on the throne from George the elector down to the flatulent old bitch that's dead?

Jesus, I had to laugh at the way he came out with that about the old one with the winkers on her blind drunk in her royal palace every night with her jorum of mountain dew and her coachman carrying her up body and bones to roll into bed and she pulling him by the whiskers and singing him old bits of songs about *Ehren on the Rhine* and come where the boose is cheaper.

—Well! says J. J. We have Edward the peacemaker now.

—Tell that to a fool, says the citizen. There's a bloody sight more pox than pax about that boyo.

—And what do you think, says Joe, of the holy boys, the priests and bishops of Ireland doing up his room in Maynooth in his racing colours and sticking up pictures of all the horses his jockeys rode.

—They ought to have stuck up all the women he rode, says little Alf. And says J.J.:

—Considerations of space influenced their lordships' decision.

—Will you try another, citizen? says Joe.

—Yes, sir, says he, I will.

—You? says Joe.

—Thank you, Joe, says I.
—Repeat that dose, says Joe.

Bloom was talking and talking with John Wyse and he quite excited with his old plumeyes rolling about.
—Persecution, says he, all the history of the world is full of it. Perpetuating national hatred among nations.
—But do you know what a nation means? says John Wyse.
—Yes, says Bloom.
—What is it? says John Wyse.
—A nation? says Bloom. A nation is the same people living in the same place.
—By God, then says Ned, laughing, if that's so I'm a nation for I'm living in the same place for the past five years.

So of course everyone had a laugh at Bloom and says he, trying to muck out of it:
—Or also living in different places.
—That covers my case, says Joe.
—What is your nation if I may ask, says the citizen.
—Ireland, says Bloom. I was born here. Ireland.

The citizen said nothing only cleared the spit out of his gullet and, gob, he spat an oyster out of him right in the corner.
—After you with the push, Joe, says he.
—Here you are, citizen, says Joe. Take that in your right hand and repeat after me the following words.
—Which is which? says I.
—That's mine, says Joe, as the devil said to the dead policeman.
—And I belong to a race too, says Bloom, that is hated and persecuted. Also now. This very moment. This very instant.

Gob, he near burnt his fingers with the butt of his old cigar.
—Robbed, says he. Plundered. Insulted. Persecuted. Taking what belongs to us by right. At this very moment, says he, putting up his fist.
—Are you talking about the new Jerusalem? says the citizen.
—I'm talking about injustice, says Bloom.
—Right, says John Wyse. Stand up to it then with force like men.

That's an almanac picture for you. Old lardyface standing up to the business end of a gun. Gob, he'd adorn a sweeping brush, so he would, if he only had a nurse's apron on him. And then he collapses all off a sudden, twisting around all the opposite, as limp as a wet rag.

—But it's no use, says he. Force, hatred, history, all that. That's not life for men and women, insult and hatred. And everybody knows that it's the very opposite of that that is really life.
—What? says Alf.
—Love, says Bloom. I mean the opposite of hatred. I must go now, says he to John Wyse. Just round to the court a moment to see if Martin is there. If he comes just say I'll be back in a second. Just a moment.

And off he pops.
—A new apostle, to the gentiles, says the citizen. Universal love.
—Well, says John Wyse. Isn't that what we're told. Love your neighbours.
—That chap? says the citizen. Beggar my neighbour is his motto. Love, Moya He's a nice pattern of a Romeo and Juliet.

Love loves to love love. Nurse loves the new chemist. Constable 25 A loves Mary Kelly. Gertie Mac Dowell loves the boy that has the bicycle. M. B. loves a fair gentleman. Li chi Han lovey up kissy Cha Pu Chow. Jumbo, the elephant, loves Alice, the elephant. Old Mr. Verschoyle wtih the ear trumpet loves old Mrs. Verschoyle with the turned in eye. The man in the brown mackintosh loves a lady who is dead. His Majesty the King loves her majesty the Queen. Mrs. Norman W. Tupper loves officer Taylor. You love a certain person. And this person loves that other person because everybody loves somebody but God loves everybody.
—Well, Joe, says I, your very good health and song. More power, citizen.
—Hurrah, there, says Joe.
—The blessing of God and Mary and Patrick on you, says the citizen.

And he ups with his pint to wet his whistle.
—We know those canters, says he, preaching and piking your pocket. What about Cromwell that put the women and children of Drogheda to the sword with the bible texts *God is love* pasted round the mouth of his cannon. The bible! Did you read that skit in the *United Irishman* today about that Zulu chief that's visiting England?
—What's that? says Joe.

So the citizen takes up one of his papers and he starts reading out:
—A delegation of the chief cotton magnates of Manchester was presented yesterday to his Majesty the Alaki of Abeakuta by Gold Stick in Waiting, Lord Walkup of Walkup on Eggs, to tender to his majesty the heartfelt thanks of British traders for the facilities afforded them in his dominions. The dusky potentate, in the course of a gracious speech, freely translated by the British

chaplain the reverend Ananias Praisegod Barebones, tendered his best thanks to Massa Walkup and emphasized the cordial relations existing between Abeakuta and the British Empire, stating that he treasured as one of his dearest possessions an illuminated bible presented to him by the white chief woman, the great squaw Victoria. The Alaki then drank a loving cup to the toast *black and white* from the skull of his immediate predecessor in the dynasty Kakachakachak, surnamed Forty Warts.

—Widow woman, says Ned, I wouldn't doubt her. Wonder did he put that bible to the same use as I would.

—Same only more so, says Lenehan. And therafter in that fruitful the broad-leaved mango flourished exceedingly.

—Is that by Griffith? says John Wyse.

—No, says the citizen. It's not signed Shanganagh. It's only initialled: P.

—And a very good initial too, says Joe.

—That's how it's worked, says the citizen. Trade follows the flag.

—Well, says J. J., if they're any worse than those Belgians in the Congo Free State they must be bad. Did you read that report by a man what's this his name is?

—Casement, says the citizen. He's an Irishman.

—Yes, that's the man, says J. J. Raping the women and girls and flogging the natives on the belly to squeeze all the red rubber they can out of them.

—I know where he's gone, says Lenehan, cracking his fingers.

—Who? says I.

—Bloom, says he. The courthouse is a blind. He had a few bob on *Throwaway* and he's gone to gather in the shekels.

—Is it that Kaffir? says the citizen, that never backed a horse in anger in his life.

—That's where he's gone, says Lenhan. I met Bantam Lyons going to back that horse only I put him off it and he told me Bloom gave him the tip. Bet you what you like he has a hundred shillings to five on. He's the only man in Dublin has it. A dark horse.

—He's a bloody dark horse himself, says Joe.

—Mind, Joe says I, show us the entrance out.

—There you are, says Terry.

So I just went round to the back of the yard and begob (hundred shillings to five) while I was letting off my (*Throwaway* twenty to) letting off my load gob says I to myself I knew he was uneasy in his (two pints off Joe and one in Slattery's off) in his mind to get off the mark to (Hundred shillings is five quid) and when they were in the (dark horse) Burke told me card party and letting on the child was sick (gob, must have done about a gallon) flabbyarse of a wife speaking down the tube *she's better* or *she's* (ow!) all a plan, so he could vamoose with the pool if he won or (Jesus, full up I was) trading without a licence (ow!) never be up to those bloody(there's the last of it) Jerusalem (ah!) cuckoos.

So anyhow when I got back they were at it dingdong, John Wyse saying it was Bloom gave the idea for Sinn Fein to Griffith to put in his paper all kinds of jerrymandering, packed juries and the world to walk about selling Irish industries. Robbing Peter to pay Paul. Gob, that puts the bloody Kybosh on it if old sloppy eyes is mucking up the show. God save Ireland from the likes of that bloody mouseabout. Mr. Bloom with his argol bargol; Gob, he's like Lanty MacHale's goat that'd go a piece of the road with every one.

—Well, it's a fact, says John Wyse. And there's the man now that'll tell you all about it, Martin Cunningham.

Sure enough the castle car drove up with Martin on it and Jack Power with him and a fellow named Crofter or Crofton pensioner out of the collector general's an orangeman Blackburn has on the registration and he drawing his pay, or Crawford jaunting around the country at the King's expense.

Our travellers reached the rustic hostelry and alighted from their palfreys.

—Ho, Varlet! cried he, who by his mien seemed the leader of the party. Saucy Knave. To us!

So saying he knocked loudly with his swordhilt upon the open lattice.

Mine host came forth at the summons girding him with his tabard.

—Give you good den, my masters, said he with an obsequious bow.

—Bestir thyself, sirah! cried he who had knocked. Look to our steeds. And for ourselves give us of your best for faith we need it.

—Lackaday, good masters, said the host, my poor house has but a bare larder. I know not what to offer your lordships.

—How now, fellow? cried the second of the party, a man of pleasant countenance, so serve you the King's messengers, Master Taptun?

An instantaneous change overspread the landlord's visage.

—Cry you mercy, gentlemen, he said humbly. An you be the King's messengers (God shield his majesty!) You shall not want for aught. The kings friends (God bless his majesty!) Shall not go afasting in my house I warrant me.

—Then about! cried the traveller who had not spoken, a lusty trencherman, by his aspect. Hast aught to give us?

Mine host bowed again as he made answer:
—What say you, good masters, to a cold pigeon pasty, a boar's head with pistachios and a flagon of old Rhenish?
——Gadzooks! cried the last speaker. That likes me well. Pistachios!
—Aha! cried he of the pleasant countenance. A poor house, and a bare larder, quotha! 'Tis a merry rogue.

So in comes Martin asking where was Bloom.
—Where is he? says Lenehan. Defrauding widows and orphans.
—Isn't that a fact, says John Wyse, that I was telling the citizen about Bloom and the Sinn Fein.
—That's so, says Martin. Or so they allege.
—Who made those allegations says Alf.
—I, says Joe. I'm the alligator.
—And after all, says John Wyse, why can't a jew love his country like the next fellow?
—Why not? says J. J., when he's quite sure which country it is.
—Is he a jew or a gentile or what the hell is he? says Ned.
—He's a perverted jew, says Martin, from a place in Hungary and it was he drew up all the plans according to the Hungarian system. We know that in the castle.
—Isn't he a cousin of Bloom the dentist, says Jack Power.
—Not at all, says Martin. His name was Virag, the father's name that poisoned himself. He changed it by deedpoll, the father did.
—That's the new Messiah for Ireland! says the citizen. Island of saints and sages!
—Well, they're still waiting for their redeemer, says Martin. For that matter so are we.
—Yes, says J. J., and every male that's born they think it may be their Messiah And every jew is in a tall state of excitement, I believe, till he knows if he's a father or a mother.
—Expecting every moment will be his next, says Lenehan.
—O, by God, says Ned, you should have seen Bloom before that son of his that died was born. I met him one day in the south city markets buying a tin of Neave's food six weeks before the wife was delivered.
—En ventre sa mère, says J. J.
—Do you call that a man? says the citizen.
—I wonder did he ever put it out of sight, says Joe.

—Well, there were two children born anyhow, says Jack Power.
—And who does he suspect? says the citizen.

Gob, there's many a true word spoken in jest. One of those mixed middlings he is. Lying up in the hotel, Pisser Burke told me, once a month with headache like a totty with her courses. Why are things like that let live? Then sloping off with his five quid without putting up a pint like a man.

—Charity to the neighbour, says Martin. But where is he? We can't wait.
—A wolf in sheep's clothing, says the citizen. That's what he is. Virag from Hungary! Ahasuerus I call him. Cursed by God.
—Have you time for a brief libation, Martin? says Ned.
—Only one, says Martin. We must be quick. John Jameson.
—You Jack? Crofton? Three half ones, Terry.
—Saint Patrick would want to come and convert us again, says the citizen, after allowing things like that to contanminate our shores.
—Well, says Martin, taking his glass. God bless all here is my prayer.
—Amen, says the citizen.
And I'm sure he will, says Joe.

(*To be continued*)

Episode XII (continued)

THE LITTLE REVIEW

VOL. VI MARCH, 1920 No. 10

CONTENTS

* *From the H. Gandier-Brzeska Portfolio, published by the Ovid Press. Twenty drawings on Japanese vellum. (15 s.)*

Subscription price, payable in advance, in the United States and Territories, $2.50 per year; Single copy 25 c., Canada, $2.75; Foreign, $3.00. Published monthly and copyrighted, 1920 by Margaret C. Anderson.

Manuscripts must be submitted at author's risk, with return postage.

Entered as second class matter March 16, 1917, at the Post Office at New York, N. Y., under the act of March 3, 1879.

MARGARET C. ANDERSON, Publisher

24 *West Sixteenth Street, New York, N. Y.*

Foreign Office: 43 *Belsize Park, Gardens, London N. W.* 3.

AND at the sound of the sacring bell the blessed company drew nigh of monks and friars the monks of Benedict of Spoleto, Carthusians and Camaldolesi, Cistercians and Olivetans, Oratorians and Vallombrosans, and the friars of Augustine, Brigittines, Premonstratesians, Servi, Trinitarians, and the children of Peter Nolasco; and therewith from Carmel mount the children of Elijah prophet led by Albert bishop and by Teresa of Avila, calced and other: and friars brown and grey, sons of poor Francis, capuchins, cordeliers, minimes and observants and the daughters of Clara: and the sons of Dominic and of Vincent; and Ignatius his children: and the confraternity of the christian brothers led by reverend brother Rice. And after came all saints and martyrs, virgins and confessors: S. Isidore arator and S. James the Less and S. Phocas of Sinope and S. Julian Hospitator and S. Felix de Cantalice and S. Stephen Protomartyr and S. John Nepomuc and S. Thomas Aquinas and S. Ives of Brittany and S. Herman-Joseph and the saints Gevasius, Servasius and Bonifacius and S. Bride and the saints Rose of Lima and of Viterbo and S. Martha of Bethany and S. Mary of Egypt and S. Barbara and S. Scholastica and S. Ursula with eleven thousand virgins. And all came with nimbi and aureoles and gloriae, bearing palms and harps and swords and olive crowns in robes whereon were woven the blessed symbols of their efficacies, ink horns, arrows, loaves, cruses, fetters, axes, trees, bridges, babes in a bathtub, shells, wallets, shears, keys, dragons, lilies, buckshot, beards, hogs, lamps, bellows, beehives, soupladles, stars, snakes, anvils, boxes of vaseline, bells, crutches, forceps, stags' horns, watertight boots, hawks, millstones, eyes on a dish, wax candles, aspergills, unicorns. And as they wended their way by Nelson's Pillar, Henry Street, Mary Street, Capel Street, Little Britain Street, chanting the introit in *Epiphania Domini* which beginneth *Surge, illuminare* and thereafter most sweetly the gradual *Omnes* which saith *de Saba venient* they did divers wonders such as casting out devils, raising the dead to life, multiplying fishes, healing the halt and the blind, discovering various articles which had been mislaid, interpreting and fulfilling the scriptures, blessing and prophesying. And last, beneath a canopy of cloth of gold came the reverend Father O'Flynn attended by Malachi and Patrick. And when all had reached the appointed place the celebrant blessed the house and censed and sprinkled the lintels thereof with blessed water and prayed that God would bless that house as he had blessed the house of Abraham and Isaac and Jacob and make the angels

Overleaf: table of contents, *Little Review,* March 1920

of His light to inhabit therein. And entering he blessed the viands and the beverages and the company of all the blessed answered his prayers.

—*Adiutorium nostrum in nomine Domini.*
—*Qui fecit coelum et Terram.*
—*Dominus vobiscum.*
—*Et cum spiritu tuo.*

And he laid his hands upon that he blessed and gave thanks and he prayed and they all with him prayed:
—*Deus, cuius verbo sanctificantur omnia, benedictionem tuam effunde super creaturas istas: et praesta ut quisquis eis secundum legem et voluntatem tuam cum gratiarum actione usus fuerit per invocationem sanctissimi nominis tui corporis sanitatem et animae tutelam, te anctore percipiat per Christum, dominum nostrum.*
—And so say all of us, says Jack.
—Thousand a year, Lambert, says Crofton.
—Right, says Ned. And butter for fish.
I was just looking round to see who the happy thought would strike when, be damned but Bloom comes in again letting on to be in a hell of a hurry.
—I was just round at the court house, says he, looking for you. I hope I'm not ......
—No, says Martin, we're ready.
Courthouse my eye. And your pockets hanging down with gold and silver. Mean bloody scut. Stand us a drink itself. There's a jew for you! Hundred to five.
—Don't tell anyone, says the citizen.
—Beg your pardon, says Bloom.
—Come on boys, says Martin, seeing it was looking blue. Come along now.
—Don't tell anyone, says the citizen, letting a bawl out of him.
And the bloody dog woke up and let a growl.
—Bye bye all, says Martin.
And he got them out as quick as he could, Jack Power and Crofton or whatever you call him and old Bloom in the middle of them letting on to be all at sea and up with them on the bloody car.
—Off with you, says Martin to the jarvey.
The milkwhite dophine tossed his mane and rising in the golden poop, the

helmsman spread the bellying sail upon the wind. A many comely nymphs drew nigh to starboard and to larboard and, clinging to the sides of the noble bark, they linked their shining forms as doth the cunning wheelwright when he fashions about the heart of his wheel the equidistant rays whereof each one is sister to another and he binds them all with an outer ring and giveth speed to the feet of men when as they ride to a hosting or contend for the smile of ladies fair. Even so did they come and set them, those willing nymphs, the undying sisters. And they laughed, sporting in a circle of their foam: and the bark clave the waves.

But begob I was just lowering the last of the pint when I saw the citizen getting up to waddle to the door and he cursing bell book and candle in Irish and Joe and little Alf trying to hold him back.

—Let me alone, says he.

And begob he got as far as the door and they holding him and be bawls out of him:

—Three cheers for Israel!

Arrah, sit down on the parlimentary side of your arse and don't be making an exhibition of yourself. Jesus, there's always some bloody clown or other kicking up a bloody murder about bloody nothing. Gob, it'd turn the porter sour in your guts, so it would.

And all the ragamuffins and sluts of the place round the door and Martin telling the jarvey to drive ahead and the citizen bawling and Alf and Joe at him to whisht and Bloom on his high horse about the jews and the loafers calling for a speech and Jack Power trying to get him to sit down on the car and hold his bloody jaw and a young lad starts singing *The Boys of Wexford* and a slut shouts out of her:

—Eh, mister! Your fly is open, mister!

And says Bloom:

—Mendelssohn was a jew and Karl Marx and Mercadante and Spinoza. And your god was a jew and his father was a jew.

—He had no father, says Martin. That'll do now. Drive ahead.

—Whose god! says the citizen.

—Well, his uncle was a jew, says Bloom. Your god was a jew. Christ was a jew like me.

Gob, the citizen made a plunge into the shop.

—By Jesus, says he, I'll brain that bloody jewman for using the holy name. By Jesus, I'll crucify him so I will. Give us that biscuit box here.

—Stop! stop! says Joe.

A large and appreciative gathering of friends and acquaintances assembled to bid farewell to Mr. L. Virag on the occasion of his departure for a distant clime. The ceremony which went off with great *èclat* was characterized by the most affecting cordiality. An illuminated scroll, the work of Irish artists, was presented to the distinguished visitor on behalf of a large section of the community and was accompanied by the gift of a silver casket, tastefully executed in the style of ancient Celtic ornament, a work which reflects every credit on the makers Messrs. Jacob and Jacob. The departing guest was the recipient of a hearty ovation, many of those who were present being visibly moved when the select orchestra of Irish pipes struck up the wellknown strains of *Come Back to Erin*. Amid cheers that rent the welkin the vessel slowly moved away saluted by a final floral tribute from the representatives of the fair sex who were present in large numbers. Gone but not forgotten.

He got hold of the bloody tin anyhow and out with him, and little Alf hanging on to his elbow and he shouting like a stuck pig.

—Where is he till I murder him?

And Ned and J. J. paralysed with the laughing.

—Gob, says I, I'll be in for the last gospel.

But as luck would have it the jarvey got the nag's head round the other way and off with him.

—Hold on, citizen, says Joe. Stop!

Begob he made a swipe and let fly. Mercy of God the sun was in his eyes. Gob, he near sent it into the country Longford. The bloody nag took fright and the old mongrel after the car and all the populace shouting and laughing and the old tinbox clattering along the street.

The catastrophe was terrific and instantaneous in its effect. The observatory of Dunsink registered in all eleven shocks and there is no record extant of a similar seismic disturbance in our island since the earthquake of 1534, the year of the rebellion of Silken Thomas. The epicentre appears to have been that part of the metropolis which constitutes the Inn's Quay Ward and parish of Saint Michan. All the lordly residences in the vicinity of the palace of Justice were demolished and that noble edifice itself, in which at the time of the catastrophe, important legal debates were in progress, is literally a mass of ruins beneath which it is to be feared all the occupants have been buried alive. From the reports of eyewitnesses it transpires that the seismic waves were accompanied by a violent atmospheric perturbation of cyclonic character. An article of headgear since ascertained to belong to the much respected clerk of the crown and peace Mr. George Fottrell and a silk umbrella with gold handle with the engraved initials, coat of arms and house number of the erudite and worshipful chairman of quarter sessions Sir Frederick Falkiner, recorder of Dublin, have been discovered by search parties in remote parts of the island respectively the former on the third basaltic ridge of the giant's causeway, the latter embedded to the extent of one foot three inches in the sandy beach of Haleopen bay near the old head of Kinsale. Other eyewitnesses depose that they observed an incandescent object of enormous proportions hurling through the atmosphere at a terrifying velocity in a trajectory directed southwest by west. Messages of condolence and sympathy are being hourly received from all parts of the different continents and the sovereign pontiff has been graciously pleased to decree that a special missa *pro dejunctis* shall be celebrated simultaneously by the ordinaries of each and every parish church of all the episcopal dioceses subject to the spiritual authority of the holy see in suffrage of the souls of those faithful departed who have been so unexpectedly called away from our midst. The work of salvage, removal of *debris,* human remains, etc., has been entrusted to Messrs. Michael Meade and son, Great Brunswick Street, and Messrs. T. & C. Martin, North Wall, assisted by the men and officers of the Duke of Cornwall's light infantry under the general supervision of H. R. H., near admiral, the right horourable Sir Hercules Hannibal Habeas Corpus Anderson K. G., K. P., K . T., P. C., K. C. B., M. P., J. P., M. B., D. S. O., S. O. D., M. F. H., M. R. I. A., B. L., Mus. Doc. P. L. G., F. R. C. P. I., and F. R. C. S. I.

You never saw the like of it in all your born puff. Gob, if he got that on the side of his poll he'd remember the gold cup, so he would, but begob the citizen would have been lagged for assault and battery and Joe for aiding and abetting. The jarvey saved his life as sure as God made me. What? O, Jesus, he did. And he let a volley of oaths after him.

—Did I kill him, says he, or what?

And he shouting to the bloody dog:

—After him, Garry! After him, boy!

And the last we saw was the bloody car rounding the corner and old sheepsface on it gesticulating and the bloody mongrel after it with his lugs back for all he was bloody well worth. Hundred to five! Jesus, he took the value of it out of him, I promise you.

When, lo, there came about them all a great brightness and they beheld the chariot wherein he stood ascend to heaven. And they beheld him in the chariot, clothed upon in the glory of the brightness, having raiment as of the sun, fair as the moon and terrible that for awe they durst not look upon him. And there came a voice out of heaven, calling: *Elijah! Elijah!* And he answered with a main cry: *Abba! Adonai!* And they beheld him even him, ben Bloom Elijah, amid clouds of angels ascend to the glory of the brightness at an angle of forty-five degrees over Donohoe's in Little Green Street like a short off a shovel.

(*To be continued*)

Episode XIII

THE LITTLE REVIEW

VOL. VI APRIL 1920 No. 11

CONTENTS

Subscription price, payable in advance, in the United States and Territories, $2.50 per year; Single copy 25c.; Canada, $2.75; Foreign, $3.00. Published monthly and copyrighted, 1920, by Margaret C. Anderson.

Manuscripts must be submitted at author's risk, with return postage.

Entered as second class matter March 16, 1917, at the Post Office at New York, N. Y., under the act of March 3, 1879.

MARGARET C. ANDERSON, Publisher

27 *West Eighth Street, New York, N. Y.*

Foreign Office: 43 *Belsize Park, Gardens, London, N. W.* 3.

THE summer evening had begun to fold the world in its mysterious embrace. Far away in the west the sun was setting and the last glow of all too fleeting day lingered lovingly on sea and strand, on the proud promontory of dear old Howth guarding as ever the waters of the bay, on the weedgrown rocks along Sandymount shore and, last but not least, on the quiet church whence there streamed forth at times upon the stillness the voice of prayer to her who is in her pure radiance a beacon ever to the storm-tossed heart of man, Mary, star of the sea.

The three girl friends were seated on the rocks, enjoying the evening scene and the air which was fresh but not too chilly. Many a time and oft were they wont to come there to that favourite nook to have a cosy chat and discuss matters feminine, Cissy Caffrey and Edy Boardman with the baby in the pushcar and Tommy and Jacky Caffrey, two little curly headed boys, dressed in sailor suits with caps to match and the name H. M. S. Belle Isle printed on both. For Tommy and Jacky Caffrey were twins, scarce four years old and very noisy and spoiled twins sometimes but for all that darling little fellows with bright merry faces and endearing ways about them. They were dabbling in the sand with their spades and buckets, building castles as children do, or playing with their big coloured ball, happy as the day was long. And Edy Boardman was rocking the chubby baby to and fro in the pushcar while that young gentleman fairly chuckled with delight. He was but eleven months and nine days old and, though still a tiny toddler, was just beginning to lisp his first babish words. Cissy Caffrey bent over him to tease his fat little plucks and the dainty dimple in his chin.

— Now, baby, Cissy Caffrey said. Say out big, big. I want a drink of water.

And baby prattled after her:

—A jink a jing a jawbo.

Cissy Caffrey cuddled the wee chap for she was awfully fond of children, so patient with little sufferers and Tommy Caffrey could never be got to take his castor oil unless it was Cissy Caffrey that held his nose. But to be sure baby was as good as gold, a perfect little dote in his new fancy bib. None of your spoilt beauties was Cissy Caffrey. A truer-hearted girl never drew the breath of life, always with a laugh in her gipsylike eyes and a frolicsome word on her cherryripe red lips, a girl lovable in the extreme. And Edy Boardman laughed too at the quaint language of little brother.

Facing page: table of contents, *Little Review,* April 1920

But just then there was a slight altercation between Master Tommy and Master Jacky. Boys will be boys and our two twins were no exception to this rule. The apple of discord was a certain castle of sand which Master Jacky had built and Master Tommy would have it right or wrong that it was to be architecturally improved by a frontdoor like the Martello tower had. But if Master Tommy was headstrong Master Jacky was selfwilled too and, true to the maxim that every little Irishman's house is his castle, he fell upon his hated rival and to such purpose that the would-be assailant came to grief and (alas to relate!) the coveted castle too. Needless to say the cries of discomfited Master Tommy drew the attention of the girl friends.

—Come here, Tommy, his sister called imperatively, at once! And you, Jacky, for shame to throw poor Tommy in the dirty sand. Wait till I catch you for that.

His eyes misty with unshed tears Master Tommy came at her call for their big sister's word was law with the twins. And in a sad plight he was after his misadventure. His little man-o'-war top and unmentionables were full of sand but Cissy was a past mistress in the art of smoothing over life's tiny troubles and very quickly not one speck of sand was to be seen on his smart little suit. Still the blue eyes were glistening with hot tears that would well up so she shook her hand at Master Jacky the culprit, her eyes dancing in admonition.

—Nasty bold Jacky! she cried.

She put an arm around the little mariner and coaxed winningly:

—What's your name? Butter and cream?

—Tell us who is your sweetheart, spoke Edy Boardman. Is Cissy your sweetheart?

—Nao, tearful Tommy said.

—Is Edy Boardman your sweetheart? Cissy queried.

—Nao, Tommy said.

—I know, Edy Boardman said none too amiably with an arch glance from her shortsighted eyes. I know who is Tommy's sweetheart. Gerty is Tommy's sweetheart.

—Nao, Tommy said on the verge of tears.

Cissy's quick motherwit guessed what was amiss and she whispered to Edy Boardman to take him there behind the pushcar where the gentlemen couldn't see and to mind he didn't wet his new tan shoes.

But who was Gerty?

Gerty MacDowell who was seated near her companions, lost in thought, gazing far away in to the distance was in very truth as fair a specimen of winsome Irish girlhood as one could wish to see. She was pronounced beautiful by all who knew her though, as folks folks often said, she was more a Giltrap than a MacDowell. Her figure was slight and graceful inclining even to fragility but those iron jelloids she had been taking of late had done her a world of good and she was much better of those discharges she used to get. The waxen pallor of her face was almost spiritual in its ivorylike purity. Her hands were of finely veined alabaster with tapering fingers and as white as lemonjuice and queen of ointments could make them though it was not true that she used to wear kid gloves in bed. Bertha Supple told that once to Edy Boardman when she was black out with Gerty (the girl chums had of course their little tiffs from time to time like the rest of mortals) and she told her not to let on whatever she did that it was her that told her or she'd never speak to her again. No. Honour where honour is due. There was an innate refinement, a languid queenly hauteur about Gerty which was unmistakeably evidenced in her delicate hands and higharched instep. Had kind fate but willed her to be born a gentlewoman of high degree in her own right and had she only received the benefit of a good education Gerty MacDowell might easily have held her own beside any lady in the land and have seen herself exquisitely gowned with jewels on her brow and patrician suitors at her feet vying with one another to pay their devoirs to her. Mayhap it was this, the love that might have been, that lent to her softly featured face at whiles a look, tense with suppressed meaning, that impatted a strange yearning tendency to the beautiful eyes, a charm few could resist. Why have woman such eyes of witchery? Gerty's were of the bluest Irish blue, set off by lustrous lashes and dark expressive brows. Time was when those brows were not so silkily seductive. It was Madame Vera Verity, directress of the Woman Beautiful page of the Princess novelette, who had first advised her to try eyebrowleine which gave that haunting expression to the eyes, so becoming in leaders of fashion, and she had never regretted it. But Gerty's crowning glory was her wealth of hair. It was dark brown with a natural wave in it. She had cut it that very morning on account of the new moon and it nestled about her pretty head in a profusion of luxuriant clusters. And just now at Edy's words as a telltale flush, delicate as the faintest rosebloom, crept into her cheeks she looked so lovely in her sweet girlish shyness that of surety God's fair land of Ireland did not hold her equal.

For an instant she was silent with rather sad downcast eyes. She was about to retort but something checked the words on her tongue. Inclination prompted her to speak out: dignity told her to be silent. The pretty lips pouted a while but then she glanced up and broke out into a joyous little laugh which had in it all the freshness of a young May morning. She knew right well, no one better, what made squinty Edy say that. As per usual somebody's nose was out of joint about the boy that had the bicycle always riding up and down in front of her window. Only now his father kept him in the evenings studying hard to get an exhibition in the intermediate that was on and he was going to Trinity college to study for a doctor when he left the high school like his brother W. E. Wylie who was racing in the bicycle races in Trinity college university. Little recked he perhaps for what she felt, that dull ache in her heart sometimes, piercing to the core. Yet he was young and perchance he might learn to love her in time. They were protestants in his family and, of course, Gerty knew Who came first and after Him the blessed virgin and then saint Joseph. But he was undeniably handsome and he was what he looked, every inch a gentleman the shape of his head too at the back without his cap on something off the common and the way he turned the bicycle at the lamp with his hands off the bars and also the nice perfume of those good cigarettes and besides they were both of a size and that was why Edy Boardman thought she was so frightfully clever because he didn't go and ride up and down in front of her bit of a garden.

Gerty was dressed simply but with instinctive taste for she felt that there was just a might that he might be out. A neat blouse of electric blue, selftinted by dolly dyes, with a smart vee opening and kerchief pocket (in which she always kept a piece of cottonwool scented with her favourite perfume because the handkerchief spoiled the sit) and a navy threequarter skirt cut to the stride showed of her slim graceful figure to perfection. She wore a coquettish wideleaved hat of nigger straw with an underbrim of eggblue chenille and at the side a butterfly bow to tone. All Tuesday week afternoon she was hunting to match that chenille but at last she found what she wanted at Clery's summer sales, the very it slightly shopsoiled but you would never notice seven fingers two and a penny. She did it up all by herself and tried it on then smiling back at her lovely reflection in the mirror and when she put it on the waterjug to keep the shape she knew that that would take the shine out of some people she knew. Her shoes were the newest thing in footwear (Edy Boardman prided herself that she was very *petite* but she never had a foot like Gerty McDowell a five and never would ash oak or elm) with patent toecaps and just one smart buckle. Her wellturned ankle displayed its proportions beneath her skirt and just the proper amount and no more of her shapely leg encased in finespun hose with highspliced heels and wide garter tops. As for undies they were Gerty's chief care and who that knows the fluttering hopes and fears of sweet seventeen (though Gerty would never see seventeen again) can find it in his heart to blame her? She had four dinky sets, three articles and nighties extra, and each set slotted with different coloured ribbons, rosepink, pale blue, mauve and peagreen and she aired them herself and blued them when they came home from the wash and ironed them and she had a brickbat to keep the iron on because she wouldn't trust those washerwoman as far as she'd see them scorching the things. She was wearing the blue for luck, her own colour and the lucky colour too for a bride to have a bit of blue somewhere on her because the green she wore that day week brought grief because his father brought him in to study for the intermediate exhibition and because she thought perhaps she might be out because when she was dressing that morning she nearly slipped up the old pair on her inside out and that was for luck and lovers' meetings if you put those things on inside out so long as it wasn't of a Friday.

And yet—and yet! A gnawing sorrow is there all the time. Her very soul is in her eyes and she would give worlds to be in her own familiar chamber where she could have a good cry and relieve her pentup feelings. The paly light of evening falls upon a face infinitely sad and wistful. Gerty MacDowell yearns in vain. Yes, she had known from the first that it was not to be. He was too young to understand. He would not believe in love. The night of the party long ago in Stoers' (he was still in short trousers) when they were alone and he stole an arm round her waist she went white to the very lips. He called her little one and half kissed her (the first!) but it was only the end of her nose and then he hastened from the room with a remark about refreshments. Impetuous fellow! Strength of character had never been Reggy Wylie's strong point and he who would woo and win Gerty MacDowell must be a man among men. But waiting, always waiting to be asked and it was leap year too and would soon be over. No prince charming is her beau ideal to lay a rare and wondrous love at her feet but rather a manly man with a strong quiet face, perhaps his hair slightly flecked with grey, and who would understand, take her in his sheltering arms, strain her to him in all the strength of his deep passionate nature and comfort her with a long long kiss. For such a one she yearns this balmy summer eve. With all the heart of her she longs to be his only, his affianced bride for riches for poor in sickness in health till death us two part from this to this day forward.

And while Edy Boardman was with little Tommy behind the pushcar she was just thinking would the day ever come when she could call herself his little wife to be. Then they could talk about her, Bertha Supple too, and Edy, the spitfire, because she would be twentytwo in November. She would care for him with creature comforts too for Gerty was womanly wise and knew that a mere man liked that feeling of homeyness. Her griddlecakes and queen Ann's pudding had won golden opinions from all because she had a lucky hand also for lighting a fire, dredge in the fine flour and always stir in the same direction then cream the milk and sugar and whisk well the white of eggs and they would have a nice drawingroom with pictures and chintz covers for the chairs and that silver toastrack in Clery's summer sales like they have in rich houses. He would be tall (she had always admired tall men for a husband) with glistening white teeth under his carefully trimmed sweeping moustache and every morning they would both have brekky for their own two selves and before he went out to business he would give her a good hearty hug and gaze for a moment deep down into her eyes.

Edy Boardman asked Tommy Caffrey was he done and he said yes and so then she buttoned up his little knickerbockers for him and told him to run off and play with Jacky and to be good and not to fight. But Tommy said he wanted the ball and Edy told him no that baby was playing with the ball and if he took it there'd be wigs on the green but Tommy said it was his ball and he wanted his ball his ball and he pranced on the ground, if you please. The temper of him! O, he was a man already was little Tommy Caffrey. Edy told him no, no and to be off now with him and she told Cissy Caffrey not to give in to him.

—You're not my sister, naughty Tommy said. It's my ball.

But Cissy Caffrey told baby Boardman to look up, look up high at her finger and she snatched the ball quickly and threw it along the sand and Tommy after it in full career, having won the day.

—Anything for a quite life, laughed Ciss.

And she tickled baby's two cheeks to make him forget and played here's the lord mayor, here's his two horses, here's his gigger bread carriage and here he walks in, chinchopper, chinchopper, chinchopper chin. But Edy got as cross as two sticks about his getting his own way like that from everyone always petting him.

—I'd like to give him something, she said, so I would, where I won't say.

—On the beeoteetom, laughed Cissy merrily.

Gerty McDowell bent down her head at the idea of Cissy saying a thing like that out she'd be ashamed of her life to say flushing a deep rosy red and Edy

Boardman said she was sure the gentleman opposite heard what she said. But not a pin cared Ciss.

—Let him! she said with a pert toss of her head and a piquant tilt of her nose. Give it to him too on the same place as quick as I'd look at him.

Madcap Ciss. You had to laugh at her sometimes. For instance when she asked you would you have some more Chinese tea and jaspberry ram and when she drew the jugs too and the men's faces make you plit your sides or when she said she wanted to run and pay a visit to the miss white. That was just like Cissycums. O, and will you ever forget the evening she dressed up in her father's suit and hat and walked down Tritonville road, smoking a cigarette. But she was sincerity itself, one of the bravest and truest hearts heaven ever made, not one of your twofaced things, too sweet to be wholesome.

(*to be continued*)

Episode XIII (continued)

THE LITTLE REVIEW

VOL. VII MAY-JUNE No. 1

CONTENTS

Subscription price, payable in advance, in the United States and Territories, $2.50 per year; Single copy, 25c.; Canada, $2.75; Foreign, $3.00. Published monthly and copyrighted, 1920, by Margaret C. Anderson.

Manuscripts must be submitted at author's risk, with return postage.

Entered as second class matter March 16, 1917, at the Post Office at New York, N. Y., under the act of March 3, 1879.

MARGARET C. ANDERSON, Publisher

27 West Eighth Street, New York, N. Y.

Foreign Office: 43 Belsize Park Gardens, London, N. W. 3.

AND THEN there came out upon the air the sound of voices and the pealing anthem of the organ. It was the men's temperance retreat conducted by the missioner, the reverend John Hughes S. J. rosary, sermon and benediction of the most blessed sacrament. They were there gathered together without distinction of social class (and a most edifying spectacle it was to see) in that simple fane beside the waves after the storms of this weary world, kneeling before the feet of the immaculate, beseeching her to intercede for them, holy Mary, holy virgin of virgins. How sad to poor Gerty's ears! Had her father only avoided the clutches of the demon drink she might now be rolling in her carriage, second to none. Over and over had she told herself that as she mused by the dying embers in a brown study or gazing out of the window by the hour at the rain falling on the rusty bucket. But that vile decoction which has ruined so many hearts and homes had cast its shadow over her childhood days. Nay, she had even witnessed in the home circle deeds of violence caused by intemperance and had seen her own father, a prey to the fumes of intoxication, forget himself completely for if there was one thing of all things that Gerty knew it was that the man who lifts his hand to a woman save in the way of kindness deserves to be branded as the lowest of the low.

And still the voices sang in supplication to the virgin most powerful, virgin most merciful. And Gerty, wrapt in thought, scarce saw or heard her companions or the twins at their boyish gambols or the gentleman off Sandymount green that Cissy Caffrey called the man that was so like himself passing along the strand taking a short walk. You never saw him anyway screwed but still and for all that she would not like him for father because he was too old or something or on account of his face (it was a palpable case of doctor Fell) or his carbuncly nose with the pimples on it. Poor father! With all his faults she loved him still when he sang *Tell me, Mary, how to woo thee* and they had stewed cockles and lettuce with salad dressing for supper and when he sang *The moon hath raised* with Mr. Dignam that died suddenly and was buried, God have mercy on him, from a stroke. Her mother's birthday that was and Charley was home on his holidays and Tom and Mr. Dignam and Mrs. and Patsy and Freddy Dignam and they were to have had a group taken. No one would have thought the end was so near. Now he was laid to rest. And her mother said to him to let that be a warning to him for the rest of his days and he couldn't even go to the

Facing page: table of contents, *Little Review,* May–June 1920

funeral on account of the gout, and she had to go into town to bring him the letters and samples from his office about Catesby's cork line, artistic designs, fit for a palace, gives tiptop wear and always bright and cheery in the home.

A sterling good daughter was Gerty just like a second mother in the house, a ministering angel too. And when her mother had those splitting headaches who was it rubbed on the menthol cone on her forehead but Gerty though she didn't like her mother taking pinches of snuff and that was the only single thing they ever had words about, taking snuff. It was Gerty who turned off the gas at the main every night and it was Gerty who tacked up on the wall of that place Mr. Tunney the grocer's christmas almanac the picture of halcyon days where a young gentleman in the costume they used to wear then with a threecornered hat was offering a bunch of flowers to his ladylove with oldtime chivalry through her lattice window. The colours were done something lovely. She was in a soft clinging white and the gentleman was in chocolate and he looked a thorough aristocrat. She often looked at them dreamily when she went there for a certain purpose and thought about those times because she had found out in Walker's pronouncing dictionary about the halcyon days what they meant.

The twins were now playing in the most approved brotherly fashion, till at last Master Jacky who was really as bold as brass there was no getting behind that deliberately kicked the ball as hard as ever he could down towards the seaweedy rocks. Needless to say poor Tommy was not slow to voice his dismay but luckily the gentleman in black who was sitting there by himself came to the rescue and intercepted the ball. Our two champions claimed their plaything with lusty cries and to avoid trouble Cissy Caffrey called to the gentleman to throw it to her please. The gentleman aimed the ball once or twice and then threw it up the strand towards Cissy Caffrey but it rolled down the slope and stopped right under Gerty's skirt near the little pool by the rock. The twins clamoured again for it and Cissy told her to kick it way and let them fight for it, so Gerty drew back her foot but she wished their stupid ball hadn't come rolling down to her and she gave a kick but she missed and Edy and Cissy laughed.

—If you fail try again, Edy Boardman said.

Gerty smiled assent. A delicate pink crept into her pretty cheek but she was determined to let them see so she just lifted her skirt a little but just enough and took good aim and gave the ball a jolly good kick and it went ever so far and the two twins after it down towards the shingle. Pure jealousy of course it was nothing else to draw attention on account of the gentleman opposite looking.

She felt the warm flush, a danger signal always with Gerty MacDowell, surging and flaming into her cheeks. Till then they had only exchanged glances of the most casual but now under the brim of her new hat she ventured a look at him and the face that met her gaze there in the twilight, wan and strangely drawn, seemed to her the saddest she had ever seen.

Through the open window of the church the fragrant incense was wafted and with it the fragrant names of her who was conceived without stain of original sin, spiritual vessel, pray for us, honourable vessel, pray for us, vessel of singular devotion, pray for us, mystical rose. And careworn hearts were there and toilers for their daily bread and many who had erred and wandered, their eyes wet with contrition but for all that bright with hope for the reverend father Hughes had told them what the great saint Bernard said in his famous prayer of Mary, the most pious virgin's intercessory power that it was not recorded in any age that those who implored her powerful protection were ever abandoned by her.

The twins were now playing again right merrily for the troubles of childhood are but as passing summer showers. Cissy played with baby Boardman till he crowed with glee, clapping baby hands in air. Peep she cried behind the hood of the pushcar and Edy asked where was Cissy gone and then Cissy popped up her head and cried ah! and, my word, didn't the little chap enjoy that! And then she told him to say papa.

—Say papa, baby, say pa pa pa pa pa pa pa.

And baby did his level best to say it for he was very intelligent for eleven months everyone said and he would certainly turn out to be something great they said.

—Haja ja ja haja.

Gerty wiped his little mouth with the dribbling bib and wanted him to sit up properly and say pa pa pa but when she undid the strap she cried out, holy saint Denis, that he was possing wet and to double the half blanket the other way under him. Of course his infant majesty was most obstreperous at such toilet formalities and he let everyone know it:

—Habaa baaaahabaaa baaaa.

It was all no use soothering him with no, nono, baby and telling him all about the geegee and where was the puffpuff but Ciss, always readywitted, gave him in his mouth the teat of the suckingbottle and the young heathen was quickly appeased.

Gerty wished to goodness they would take their squalling baby home out of that, no hour to be out, and the little brats of twins. She gazed out towards the distant sea. It was like a picture the evening and the clouds coming out and the Bailey light on Howth and to hear the music like that and the perfume of those incense they burned in the church. And while she gazed her heart went pitapat. Yes, it was her he was looking at and there was meaning in his look. His eyes burned into her as though they would search her through and through, read her very soul. Wonderful eyes they were, superbly expressive, but could you trust them? She could see at once by his dark eyes that he was a foreigner but she could not see whether he had an aquiline nose from where he was sitting. He was in deep mourning, she could see that, and the story of a haunting sorrow was written on his face. She would have given worlds to know what it was. He was looking up so intensely, so still and he saw her kick the ball and perhaps he could see the bright steel buckles of her shoes if she swung them like that thoughtfully. She was glad that something told her to put on the transparent stockings thinking Reggy Wylie might be out but that was far away. Here was that of which she had so often dreamed. The heart of the girl-woman went out to him. If he had suffered, more sinned against than sinning, or even, even, if he had been himself a sinner, a wicked man, she cared not. There were wounds that wanted healing and she just yearned to know all, to forgive all if she could make him fall in love with her, make him forget the memory of the past. Then mayhap he would embrace her gently, crushing her soft body to him and love her for herself alone.

Refuge of sinners. Comfortess of the afflicted. *Ora pro nobis*. Well has it been said that whosoever prays to her with faith and constancy can never be lost or cast away: and fitly is she too a haven of refuge for the afflicted because of the seven dolours which transpierced her own heart. Gerty could picture the whole scene in the church, the stained glass windows lighted up, the candles, the flowers and the blue banner of the blessed virgin's sodality and Father Conroy was helping Canon O'Hanlon at the altar, carrying things in and out with his eyes cast down. He looked almost a saint and his confession-box was so quiet and clean and dark and his hands were just like white wax. He told her that time when she told him about that in confession crimsoning up to the roots of her hair for fear he could see, not to be troubled because that was only the voice of nature and we were all subject to nature's laws, he said in this life and that that was no sin because that came from the nature of woman instituted by God, he said, and that Our Blessed Lady herself said to the archangel Gabriel be it done unto me according to Thy Word. He was so kind and holy and often and often she thought could she work an embroidered teacosy for him as a present or a clock but they had a clock she noticed on the mantelpiece white and gold with a canary that came out of a little house to tell the time the day she went there about the flowers for the forty hours' adoration because it was hard to know what sort of a present to give or perhaps an album of illuminated views of Dublin or some place.

The little brats of twins began to quarrel again and Jacky threw the ball out towards the sea and they both ran after it. Little monkeys common as ditch-water. Someone ought to take them and give them a good hiding for themselves to keep them in their places the both of them. And Cissy and Edy shouted after them to come back because they were afraid the tide might come in on them and be drowned.

—Jacky! Tommy!

Not they! What a great notion they had! So Cissy said it was the very last time she'd ever bring them out. She jumped up and called and then she ran down the slope past him, tossing her hair behind her which had a good enough colour if there had been more of it but with all the thingamerry she was always rubbing in to it she couldn't get it to grow long because it wasn't natural so she could just go and throw her hat at it. She ran with long gandery strides it was a wonder she didn't rip up her skirt at the side that was too tight on her because there was a lot of the tomboy about Cissy Caffrey whenever she thought she had a good opportunity to show off and just because she was a good runner she ran like that so that he could see all the end of her petticoat running, and her skinny shanks up as far as possible. It would have served her just right if she had tripped up over something with her high French heels on her to make her look tall and got a fine tumble. That would have been a very charming expose for a gentleman like that to witness.

Queen of angels, queen of patriarchs, queen of prophets, of all saints, they prayed, queen of the most holy rosary and then Father Conroy handed the thurible to Canon O'Hanlon and he put in the incense and censed the blessed sacrament and Cissy Caffrey caught the two twins and she was itching to give them a good clip on the ear but she didn't because she thought he might be watching but she never made a bigger mistake in her life because Gerty could see without looking that he never took his eyes off of her and then Canon O'Hanlon handed the thurible back to Father Conroy and knelt down looking up at the blessed sacrament and the choir began to sing *Tantum ergo* and she just swung her foot in and out in time to the *Tantumer gosa cramen tum*. Three and eleven she paid for those stockings in Sparrow's of George's street on the Tuesday, no the Monday before easter and there wasn't a brack on them and that was what he was looking at, transparent, and not at hers that had neither shape nor form because he had eyes in his head to see the difference for himself.

Cissy came up along the strand with the two twins and their ball with her hat anyhow on her on one side after her run and she did look like a streel tugging the two kids along with the blouse she bought only a fortnight before like a rag on her back. Gerty just took off her hat for a moment to settle her hair and a prettier, a daintier head of nutbrown tresses was never seen on a girl's shoulder—a radiant little vision, in sooth, almost maddening in its sweetness. You would have to travel many a long mile before you found a head of hair the like of that. She could almost see the swift answering flush of admiration in his eyes that set her tingling in every nerve. She put on her hat so that she could see from underneath the brim and swung her buckled shoe faster for her breath caught as she caught the expression in his eyes. He was eyeing her as a snake eyes its prey. Her woman's instinct told her that she had raised the devil in him and at the thought a burning scarlet swept from throat to brow till the lovely colour of her face became a glorious rose.

Edy Boardman was noticing it too because she was squinting at Gerty, half smiling with her specs, like an old maid, pretending to nurse the baby. Irritable little gnat she was and always would be and that was why no one could get on with her, poking her nose into what was no concern of hers. And she said to Gerty:

—A penny for your thoughts.

—What, laughed Gerty. I was only wondering was it late.

Because she wished to goodness they'd take the snotty-nosed twins and their baby home to the mischief out of that so that was why she just gave a gentle hint about its being late. And when Cissy came up Edy asked her the time and Miss Cissy, as glib as you like, said it was half past kissing time, time to kiss again. But Edy wanted to know because they were told to be in early.

—Wait, said Cissy, I'll run ask my uncle Peter over there what's the time by his conundrum.

So over she went and when he saw her coming she could see him take his hand out of his pocket, getting nervous and beginning to play with his watchchain, looking at the church. Passionate nature though he was Gerty could see that he had enormous control over himself. One moment he had been there, fascinated by a loveliness that made him gaze and the next moment it was the quiet gravefaced gentlman, selfcontrol expressed in every line of his distinguished-looking figure.

Cissy said to excuse her would he mind telling her what was the right time and Gerty could see him taking out his watch listening to it and looking up and he said he was very sorry his watch was stopped but he thought it must be after eight because the sun was set. His voice had a cultured ring in it and there was a suspicion of a quiver in the mellow tones. Cissy said thanks and came back with her tongue out and said his waterworks were out of order.

Then they sang the second verse of the *Tantum ergo* and Canon O'Hanlon got up again and censed the blessed sacrament and knelt down and he told Father Conroy that one of the candles was just going to set fire to the flowers and Father Conroy got up and settled it all right and she could see the gentleman winding his watch and listening to the works and she swung her leg more in and out in time. It was getting darker but he could see and he was looking all the time that he was winding the watch or whatever he was doing to it and then he put it back and put his hands back into his pockets. She felt a kind of a sensation rushing all over her and she knew by the feel of her scalp and that irritation against her stays that that thing must be coming on because the last time too was when she clipped her hair on account of the moon. His dark eyes fixed themselves on her again, drinking in her every contour, literally worshipping at her shrine. If ever there was undisguised admiration in a man's passionate gaze it was there plain to be seen on that man's face. It is for you, Gertrude MacDowell, and you know it.

Edy began to get ready to go and she noticed that that little hint she gave had the desired effect because it was a long way along the strand to where there was the place to push up the pushcar and Cissy took off the twins' caps and tidied their hair to make herself attractive of course and Canon O'Hanlon stood up with his cope poking up at his neck and Father Conroy handed him the card to read off and he read out *Panem de coelo praestitisti eis* and Edy and Cissy were talking about the time all the time and asking her but Gerty could pay them back in their own coin and she just answered with scathing politeness when Edy asked her was she heartbroken about her best boy throwing her over. Gerty winced sharply. A brief cold blaze shot from her eyes that spoke of scorn immeasurable. It hurt—O yes, it cut deep because Edy had her own quiet way of saying things like that she knew would wound like the confounded little cat she was. Gerty's lips parted swiftly but she fought back the sob that rose to her throat, so slim, so flawless, so beautifully moulded it seemed one an artist might have dreamed of. She had loved him better than he knew. Lighthearted deceived and fickle like all his sex he would never understand what he had meant to her and for an instant there was in the blue eyes a quick stinging of tears. Their eyes were probing her mercilessly but with a brave effort she sparkled back in sympathy as she glanced at her new conquest for them to see.

—O, she laughed and the proud head flashed up. I can throw my cap at who I like because it's leap year.

Her words rang out crystal clear, more musical than the cooing of the ring-dove but they cut the silence icily. There was that in her young voice that told that she was not a one to be lightly trifled with. Miss Edy's countenance fell to no slight extent and Gerty could see by her looking as black as thunder that she was simply in a towering rage because that shaft had struck home and they both knew that she was something aloof, apart in another sphere, that she was not of them and never would be and there was somebody else too that knew it and saw it so they could put that in their pipe and smoke it.

Edy straightened up baby Boardman to get ready to go and Cissy tucked in the ball and the spades and buckets and it was high time too because the sand-man was on his way for Master Boardman junior and Cissy told him too that Billy Winks was coming and that baby was to go deedaw and baby looked just too ducky, laughing up out of his gleeful eyes, and Cissy poked him like that out of fun in hihs wee fat tummy and baby, without as much as by your leave, sent up his compliments to all and sundry on to his brand new dribbling bib.

—O my! Puddney pie! protested Ciss.

The slight contretemps claimed her attention but in two twos she set that little matter to rights.

Gerty stifled a smothered exclamation and Edy asked what and she was just going to tell her to catch it while it was flying but she ever ladylike in her deportment so she simply passed it off by saying that that was the benediction because just then the bell rang out from the steeple over the quiet seashore because Canon O'Hanlon was up on the altar with the veil that Father Conroy put round him round his shoulders giving the benediction with the blessed sacrament in his hands.

How moving the scene there in the gathering twilight, the last glimpse of Erin, the touching chime of those evening bells and at the same time a bat flew forth from the ivied belfry through the dusk, hither, thither, with a tiny lost cry. And she could see far away the lights of the lighthouses and soon the lamplighter would be going his rounds lighting the lamp near her win-dow where Reggy Wylie used to turn the bicycle like she read in that book *The Lamplighter* by Miss Cummins, author of *Mabel Vaughan* and other tales. For Gerty had her dreams that no one knew of. She loved to read poetry and she got a keepsake from Berha Supple of that lovely confession album with the coralpink cover to write her thoughts in she laid it in the drawer of toilet-table which though it did not err on the side of luxury, was scrupulously neat and clean. It was there she kept her girlish treasure trove the tortoiseshell combs, her child of Mary badge, the whiterose scent, the eyebrowleine, her alabaster pouncetbox and the ribbons to change when her things came home from the wash and there were some beautiful thoughts written in it in violet ink that she bought in Wisdom Hesly's for she felt that she too could write poetry if she could only express herself like that poem she had copied out of the newspaper she found one evening round the potherbs *Art thou real, my ideal?* it was called by Louis J. Walshe, Magherafelt, and after there was something about *twilight, wilt thou ever?* and often the beauty of poetry, so sad in its transient loveliness had misted her eyes with silent tears that the years were slipping by for her, one by one, and but for that one shortcoming she knew she need fear no competition and that was an accident coming down the hill and she always tried to conceal it. But it must end she felt. If she saw that magic lure in his eyes there would be no holding back for her. Love laughs at locksmiths. She would make the great sacrifice. Dearer than the whole world would she be to him and gild his days with happiness. There was the all important question and she was dying to know was he a married man or a widower who had lost his wife or some tragedy like the nobleman with the foreign name from the land of song had to have her put into a madhouse, cruel only to be kind. But even if—what then? Would it make a very great difference? From everything in the least indelicate her finebred nature instinctively recoiled. She loathed that sort of person, the fallen woman off the accommodation walk beside the Dodder that went with the soldiers and coarse men, degrading the sex and being taken up to the police station. No, no: not that. They would be just good friends in spite of the conventions of society with a big ess. Perhaps it was an old flame he was in mourning for from the days beyond recall. She thought she understood. She would try to understand him because men were so different. The old love was waiting, waiting with little white hands stretched out, with blue appealing eyes. She would follow the dictates of her heart for love was the master guide. Nothing else mattered. Come what might she would be wild, untrammelled, free.

(*To be continued*)

Episode XIII (continued)

THE LITTLE REVIEW

VOL. VII JULY-AUGUST No. 2

CONTENTS

Subscription price, payable in advance, in the United States and Territories, $2.50 per year; Single copy, 25c; Canada, $2.75; Foreign, $3.00. Published monthly and copyrighted, 1920, by Margaret C. Anderson.

Manuscripts must be submitted at author's risk, with return postage.

Entered as second class matter March 16, 1917, at the Post Office at New York, N. Y., under the act of March 3, 1879.

MARGARET C. ANDERSON, Publisher

27 West Eighth Street, New York, N. Y.

Foreign Ofice: 43 Belsize Park Gardens, London, N. W. 3

CANON O'HANLON put the blessed sacrament back into the tabernacle and the choir sang *Laudate Dominum omnes gentes* and then he locked the tabernacle door because the benediction was over and Father Conroy handed him his hat to put on and Edy asked was she coming but Jacky Caffrey called out:

—O, look, Cissy!

And they all looked was it sheet lightning but Tommy saw it too over the trees beside the church, blue and then green and purple.

—It's fireworks, Cissy Caffrey said.

And they all ran down the strand to see over the houses and the church, helterskelter, Edy with the pushcar with baby Boardman in it and Cissy holding Tommy and Jacky by the hand so they wouldn't fall running.

—Come on, Gerty, Cissy called. It's the bazaar fireworks.

But Gerty was adamant. She had no intention of being at their beck and call. If they could run like rossies she could sit so she said she could see from where she was. The eyes that were fastened upon her set her pulses tingling. She looked at him a moment, meeting his glance, and a light broke in upon her. Whitehot passion was in that face, passion silent as the grave, and it had made her his. At last they were left alone without the others to pry and pass remarks, and she knew he could be trusted to the death, steadfast, a man of honour to his fingertips. She leaned back far to look up where the fireworks were and she caught her knee in her hands so as not to fall back looking up and there was no one to see only him and her when she revealed all her graceful beautifully shaped legs like that, supply soft and delicately rounded, and she seemed to hear the panting of his heart his hoarse breathing, because she knew about the passion of men like that, hotblooded, because Bertha Supple told her once in secret about the gentleman lodger that was staying with them out of the record office that had pictures cut out of papers of those skirtdancers and she said he used to do something not very nice that you could imagine sometimes in the bed. But this was different from a thing like that because there was all the difference because she could almost feel him draw her face to his and the first quick hot touch of his handsome lips. Besides there was absolution so long as you didn't do the other thing before being married and there ought to be woman priests that would understand without telling out and Cissy Caffrey too sometimes had that dreamy kind of dreamy look in her eyes so that she too,

Facing page: table of contents, *Little Review,* July–August 1920

my dear, and besides it was on account of that other thing coming on the way it did.

And Jacky Caffrey shouted to look, there was another and she leaned back and the garters were blue to match on account of the transparent and they all saw it and shouted to look, look there it was and she leaned back ever so far to see the fireworks and something queer was flying about through the air, a soft thing to and fro, dark. And she saw a long Roman candle going up over the trees up, up, and they were all breathless with excitement as it went higher and higher and she had to lean back more and more to look up after it, high, high, almost out of sight, and her face was suffused with a divine, an entrancing blush from straining back and he could see her other things too, nainsook knickers, four and eleven, on account of being white and she let him and she saw that he saw and the it went so high it went out of sight a moment and she was trembling in every limb from being bent so far back that he could see high up above her knee where no-one ever and she wasn't ashamed and he wasn't either to look in that immodest way like that because he couldn't resist the sight like those skirtdancers behaving so immodest before gentlemen looking and he kept on looking, looking. She would fain have cried to him chokingly, held out her snowy slender arms to him to come, to feel his lips laid on her white brow. And then a rocket sprang and bang shot blind blank and O! then the Roman candle burst and it was like a sigh of O! and everyone cried O! O! and it gushed out of it a stream of rain gold hair threads and they shed and ah! they were all greeny dewy stars falling with golden, O so lovely! O so soft, sweet, soft!

Then all melted away dewily in the grey air: all was silent. Ah! She glanced at him as she bent forward quickly, a glance of piteous protest, of shy reproach under which he coloured like a girl. He was leaning back against the rock behind. Leopold Bloom (for it is he) stands silent, with bowed head before those young guileless eyes. What a brute he had been! At it again? A fair unsullied soul had called to him and, wretch that he was, how had he answered? An utter cad he had been! But there was an infinite store of mercy in those eyes, for him too a word of pardon even though he had erred and sinned and wandered. That was their secret, only theirs, alone in the hiding twilight and there was none to know or tell save the little bat that flew so softly through the evening to and fro and little bats don't tell.

Cissy Caffrey whistled, imitating the boys in the football field to show what a great person she was: and then she cried

—Gerty Gerty! We're going. Come on. We can see from farther up.

Gerty had an idea. She slipped a hand into her kerchief pocket and took out the wadding and waved in reply of course without letting him and then slipped it back. Wonder if he's too far to. She rose. She had to go but they would meet again, there, and she would dream of that till then, tomorrow. She drew herself up to her full height. Their souls met in a last lingering glance and the eyes that reached her heart, full of a strange shining, hung enraptured on her sweet flower-like face. She half smiled at him, a sweet forgiving smile—and then they parted.

Slowly without looking back she went down the uneven strand to Cissy, to Edy, to Jacky and Tommy Caffrey, to little baby Boardman. It was darker now and there were stones and bits of wood on the strand and slippy seaweed. She walked with a certain quiet dignity characteristic of her but with care and very slowly because—because Gerty MacDowell was . . .

Tight boots? No. She's lame! O!

Mr. Bloom watched her as she limped away. Poor girl! That's why she's left on the shelf and the others did a sprint. Thought something was wrong by the cut of her jib. Jilted beauty. Glad I didn't know it when she was on show. Hot little devil all the same. Near her monthlies, I expect, makes them feel ticklish. I have such a bad headache today. Where did I put the letter? Yes, all right. All kinds of crazy longings. Girl in Tranquilla convent told me liked to smell rock oil. Sister? That's the moon. But then why don't all women menstruate at the same time with same moon? I mean. Depends on the time they were born, I suppose. Anyhow I got the best of that. Made up for that tramdriver this morning. That gouger M'Coy stopping me to say nothing. And his wife's engagement in the country valise voice like a pickaxe. Thankful for small mercies. Cheap too. Yours for the asking. Because they want it themselves. Shoals of them every evening poured out of offices. Catch 'em alive. O. Pity they can't see themselves. A dream of wellfilled hose. Where was that? Ah, yes. Mutoscope pictures in Capel street: for men only. Peeping Tom. Willie's hat and what the girls did with it. Do they snapshot those girls or is it all a fake. *Lingerie* does it. Felt for the curves inside her *deshabille*. Excites them also when they're. Molly. Why I bought her the violet garters. Say a woman loses a charm with every pin she takes out. Pinned together. O Mairy lost the pin of her. Dressed up to the nines for some body. In no hurry either. Always off to a fellow when they are. Out on spec probably. They believe in chance because like themselves. And the others inclined to give her an odd dig. Mary and Martha. Girl friends at school, arms round each other's necks, kissing and whispering secrets about nothing in the convent garden. Nuns with whitewashed faces, cool coifs and their rosaries going up and down, vindictive too for what they can't get. Barbed wire. Be sure now and write to me. And I'll write to you. Now won't you? Molly and Josie Powell. Then meet once in a blue moon. *Tableau.* O, look who it is for the love of God! How are you at all? What have you been doing with yourself? Kiss and delighted to, kiss, to see you. Picking holes in each other's appearance. You're looking splendid. Wouldn't lend each other a pinch of salt.

Ah.

Devils they are when that's coming on them. Molly often told me feel things a ton weight. Scratch the sole of my foot. O that way! O, that's exquisite! Feel it myself too. Good to rest once in a way. Wonder if it's bad to go with them then. Safe in one way. Something about withering plants I read in a garden. Besides they say if the flower withers she wears she's a flirt. All are. Daresay she felt I. When you feel like that you often meet what you feel. Liked me or what? Dress they look at. Always know a fellow courting: collars and cuffs. Same time might prefer a tie undone or something. Trousers? Suppose I when I was? No. Gently does it. Dislike rough and tumble. Kiss in the dark and never tell. Saw something in me. Wonder what. Sooner have me as I am than some poet chap with bearsgrease plastery hair, lovelock over his dexter optic. To aid gentleman in literary. Ought to attend to my appearance my age. Didn't let her see me in profile. Still, you never know. Pretty girls and ugly men marrying. Beauty and the beast. Besides I can't be so if Molly. Took off her hat to show her hair. Wide brim bought to hide her face, meeting someone might know her, bend down or carry a bunch of flowers to smell. Hair strong in rut. Ten bob I got for Molly's combings when we were on the rocks in Holles street. Why not? Suppose he gave her money. Why not? All a prejudice. She's worth ten, fifteen, more a pound. What? I think so. All that for nothing. Bold hand. Mrs Marion. Did I forget to write address on that letter like the postcard I sent to Flynn. And the day I went to Drimmie's without a necktie. Wrangle with Molly it was put me off. No, I remember. Ritchie Goulding. He's another. Weighs on his mind. Funny my watch stopped at half past four. Was that just when he, she?

O, he did. Into her. She did. Done.

Ah.

Mr. Bloom with careful hand recomposed his shirt. O Lord, that little limping devil. Begins to feel cold and clammy. After effect not pleasant. They don't care. Complimented perhaps. Go home and say night prayers with the kiddies. Well, aren't they? Still I feel. The strength it gives a man. That's the secret of it.

Good job I let off there behind coming out of Dignam's. Cider that was. Otherwise I couldn't have. Makes you want to sing after. *Lacaus esant tatatara.* Suppose I spoke to her. What about? Bad plan however if you don't know how to end the conversation. Ask them a question they ask you another. Good idea if you're stuck. Gain time. But then you're in a cart. Wonderful of course if you say: Good evening, and you see she's on for it: good evening. Girl in Meath street that night. All the dirty things I made her say. Parrots. Wish she hadn't called me sir. O, her mouth in the dark! And you a married man with a single girl. That's what they enjoy. Taking a man from another woman. French letter still in my pocketbook. But might happen sometime. I don't think. Come in. All is prepared. I dreamt. What? Worst is beginning. How they change the venue when it's not what they like. Ask you do you like mushrooms because she once knew a gentleman who. Yet if I went the whole hog, say: I want to, something like that. Because I did. She too. Offend her. Then make it up. Pretend to want something awfully, then cry off for her sake. Flatters them. She must have been thinking of someone else all the time. What harm? Must since she came to the use of reason, he, he and he. First kiss does the trick. Something inside them goes pop. Mushy like, tell by their eye, on the sly. First thoughts are best. Remember that till their dying day. Molly, lieutenant Mulvey that kissed her under the Moorish wall beside the gardens. Fifteen she told me. But her breasts were developed. Fell asleep then. After Glencree dinner that was when we drove home the featherbed mountain. Gnashing her teeth in sleep. Lord mayor had his eye on her too. Val Dillon. Apoplectic.

There she is with them down there for the fireworks. My fireworks. Up like a rocket, down like a stick. And the children, twins they must be, waiting for something to happen. Want to be grownups. Dressing in mother's clothes. Time enough, understand all the ways of the world. And the dark one with the mop head and the nigger mouth. I knew she could whistle. Mouth made for that. Why that highclass whore in Jammet's wore her veil only to her nose. Would you mind, please, telling me the right time? I'll tell you the right time up a lane. Say prunes and prisms forty times every morning, cure for fat lips. Caressing the little boy too. Onlookers see most of the game. Of course they understand birds, animals, babies. In their line.

Didn't look back when she was going down the strand. Wouldn't give that satisfaction. Those girls, those girls, those lovely seaside girls. Fine eyes she had, clear. It's the white of the eye brings that out not so much the pupil. Did she know what I? Course. Like a cat sitting beyond a dog's jump. Woman.

Never meet one like that Wilkins in the high school drawing a picture of Venus with all his belongings on show. Call that innocence? Poor idiot! His wife has her work cut out for her. Sharp as needles they are. When I said to Molly the man at the corner of Cuffe street was goodlooking, thought she might like, twigged at once he had a false arm. Had too. Where they get that? Handed down from father to mother to daughter, I mean. Bred in the bone. Milly for example drying her handkerchief on the mirror to save the ironing. And when I sent her for Molly's Paisley shawl to Presscott's by the way that ad I must, carrying home the change in her stocking. Clever little minx! I never told her. Neat way she carries parcels too. Attract men, small thing like that. Holding up her hand, shaking it, to let the blood flow back when it was red. Who did you learn that from? Nobody. Something the nurse taught me. O, don't they know? Three years old she was in front of Molly's dressing-table just before we left Lombard street west. Me have a nice pace. Mullingar. Who knows? Ways of the world. Young student. Straight on her pins anyway not like the other. Still she was game. Lord, I am wet. Devil you are. Swell of her calf. Transparent stockings, stretched to breaking point. Not like that frump today. A. E. Rumpled stockings. Or the one in Grafton street. White. Wow! Beef to the heel.

A monkey puzzle rocket burst, spluttering in darting crackles. Zrads and zrads, zrads, zrads. And Cissy and Tommy ran out to see and Edy after with the pushcar and then Gerty beyond the curve of the rocks. Will she? Watch! Watch! See! Looked round. She smelt an onion. Darling, I saw your. I saw all.

Lord!

Did me good all the same. Off colour after Kiernan's, Dignam's. For this relief much thanks. In *Hamlet*, that is. Lord! It was all things combined. Excitement. When she leaned back felt an ache at the butt of my tongue. Your head it simply swirls. He's right. Might have made a worse fool of myself however. Instead of talking about nothing. Then I will tell you all. Still it was a kind of language between us. It couldn't be? No, Gerty they called her. Might be false name however like my and the address Dolphin's barn a blind.

Her maiden name was Jemima Brown

And she lived with her mother in Irishtown.

Place made me think of that I suppose. All tarred with the same brush. Wiping pens in their stockings. But the ball rolled down to her as if it understood. Every bullet has its billet. Course I never could throw anything straight at school. Crooked as a ram's horn. Sad however because it lasts only a few years till they settle down to potwalloping and fullers' earth for the baby when he does ah ah. No soft job. Saves them. Keeps them out of harm's way. Nature. Washing child, washing corpse. Dignam. Children's hands always round them. Cocoanut skulls, monkeys, not even closed at first, sour milk in their swaddles and tainted curds. Oughtn't to have given that child an empty teat to suck. Fill it up with wind. Mrs. Beaufoy, Purefoy. Must call to the hospital. Wonder is nurse Callan there still. And Mrs Breen and Mrs Dignam once like that too, marriageable. Worst of all the night Mrs Diggan told me in the city arms. Husband rolling in drunk, stink of pub off him like a polecat. Have that in your nose all night, whiff of stale boose. Bad policy however to fault the husband. Chickens come home to roose. They stick by one another like glue. Maybe the women's fault also. That's where Molly can knock spots off them. It is the blood of the south. Moorish. Also the form, the figure. Hands felt for the opulent. Just compare for instance those others. Wife locked up at home, skeleton in the cupboard. Allow me to introduce my. Then they trot you out some kind of a nondescript, wouldn't know what to call her. Always see a fellow's weak point in his wife. Still there's destiny in it, falling in love. Have their own secrets between them. Chaps that would go to the dogs if some woman didn't take them in hand. Then little chits of girls, height of a shilling in coppers, with little hubbies. As God made them He matched them. Sometimes children turn out well enough. Twice nought makes one. This wet is very unpleasant.

Ow!

Other hand a sixfooter with a wifey up to his watchpocket. Long and the short of it. Very strange about my watch. Wonder is there any magnetic influence between the person because that was about the time he. Yes, I suppose at once. Cat's away the mice will play. I remember looking in Pill lane. Also that now is magnetism. Back of everything magnetism. Earth for instance pulling this and being pulled. That causes movement. And time? Well that's the time the movement takes. Then if one thing stopped the whole ghesabo would stop bit by bit. Because it's all arranged. Magnetic needle tells you what's going on in the sun, the stars. Little piece of steel iron. When you hold out the fork. Come. Come. Tip. Woman and man that is. Fork and steel. Molly, he. Dress up and look and suggest and let you see and see more and defy you if you're a man to see that and legs, look look and. Tip. Have to let fly.

Wonder how is she feeling in that region. Shame all put on before third person. Molly, her underjaw stuck out, head back about the farmer in the ridingboots with the spurs. And when the painters were in Lombard street west. Smell that I did, like flowers. It was too. Violets. Came from the turpentine probably in the paint. Make their own use of everything. Same time doing it scraped her slipper on the floor so they wouldn't hear. But lots of them can't kick the beam, I think. Keep that thing up for hours. Kind of a general all round over me and half down my back.

Wait. Hm. Hm. Yes. That's her perfume. Why she waved her hand. I leave you this to think of me when I'm far away on the pillow. What is it? Heliotrope? No. Hyacinth? Hm. Roses, I think. She'd like scent of that kind. Sweet and cheap: soon sour. Why Molly likes opoponax. Suits her with a little jessamine mixed. Her high notes and her low notes. At the dance night she met him, dance of the hours. Heat brought it out. She was wearing her black and it had the perfume of the time before. Good conductor, is it? Or bad? Light too. Suppose there's some connection. For instance if you go into a cellar where it's dark. Mysterious thing too. Why did I smell it only now? Took its time in coming like herself, slow but sure. Suppose it's ever so many millions of tiny grains blown across. Yes, it is. Because those spice islands, Cinghalese this morning, smell them leagues off. Tell you what it is. It's like a fine fine veil or web they have all over the skin fine like what do you call it gossamer and they're always spinning it out of them, fine as anything, rainbow colours without knowing it. Clings to everything she takes off. Vamp of her stockings. Warm shoes. Stays. Drawers: little kick taking them off. Byby till next time. Also the cat likes to sniff in her shift on the bed. Know her smell in a thousand. Bathwater too. Reminds me of strawberries and cream. Wonder where it is really. There or the armpits or under the neck. Because you get it out of all holes and corners. Hyacinth perfume made of oil of ether or something. Muskrat. Bag under their tails. Dogs at each other behind. Good evening. Evening. How do you sniff? Hm. Hm. Very well, thank you. Animals go by that. Yes, now, look at it that way. We're the same. Some women for instance warn you off when they have their period. Come near. Then get a hogo you could hang your hat on. Like what? Potted herrings gone stale or. Boof! Please keep off the grass.

Perhaps they get a man smell off us. What though? Cigary gloves Long John had on his desk the other. Breath? What you eat and drink gives that. No. Mansmell, I mean. Must be connected with that because priests that are supposed to be are different. Women buzz round it like flies round treacle. O father, will you? Let me be the first to. That diffuses itself all through the body, permeates. Source of life. And it's extremely curious the smell. Celery sauce. Let me.

Mr. Bloom inserted his nose. Hm. Into the. Hm. Opening of his waistcoat. Almonds or. No. Lemons it is. And no, that's the soap.

O by the by that lotion. I knew there was something on my mind. Never went back and the soap not paid. Two and nine. Bad opinion of me he'll have. Call tomorrow. How much do I owe you? Three and nine? Two and nine, sir. Ah. Might stop him giving credit another time. Lose your customers that way. Pubs do. Fellows run up a bill on the slate and then slinking around the back streets into somewhere else.

Here's this nobleman passed before. Blown in from the bay. Just went as far as turn back. Always at home at dinnertime. Looks mangled out: had a good tuck in. Enjoying nature now. Grace after meals. After supper walk a mile. Sure he has a small bank balance somewhere, government sit. Walk after him now makes him awkward like those newsboys me today. That's the way to find out. Ask yourself who is he now. *The Man on the Beach,* prize tidbit story by MrLeopold Bloom. Payment at the rate of one guinea per column. And that fellow today at the graveside in the brown mackintosh. Corns on his kismet however. Healthy perhaps absorb all the. Whistle brings rain they say. Must be some somewhere. Salt in the Ormond damp. The body feels the atmosphere. Old Betty's joints are on the rack. Mother Shipton's prophecy that is about ships around they fly in the twinkling. No. Signs of rain it is. The royal reader. And distant hills seem coming nigh.

Howth. Bailey light. Two, four, six, eight, nine. See. People afraid of the dark. Also glowworms, cyclists: lighting up time. Jewels diamonds flash better. Light is a kind of reassuring. Not going to hurt you. Better now of course than long ago. Country roads. Run you through the small guts for nothing. Still two types there are you bob against. Scowl or smile. Not at all. Best time to spray plants too in the shade after the sun. Were those nightclouds there all the time? Land of the setting sun this. Homerule sun setting in the northeast. My native land, goodnight.

Dew falling. Bad for you, dear, to sit on that stone. Brings on white fluxions. Might get piles myself. Sticks too like a summer cold, sore on the mouth. Friction of the position. Like to be that rock she sat on. Also the library today: those girls graduates. Happy chairs under them. But it's the evening influence. They all feel that. Open like flowers, know their hours, sunflowers, Jerusalem artichokes in ballrooms, chandeliers, avenues under the lamps. Nightstock in Mat

Dillon's garden where I kissed her shoulder. June that was too I wooed. The year returns. And now? Sad about her lame of course but must be on your guard not to feel too much pity. They take advantage.

All quiet on Howth now. The distant hills seem. Where we. The rhododendrons. I am a fool perhaps. He gets the plums and I the leavings. All that old hill has seen. Names change: that's all. Lovers: yum yum.

Tired I feel now. Drained all the manhood out of me, little wretch. She kissed me. My youth. Never again. Only once it comes. Or hers. Take the train there tomorrow. No. Returning not the same. Like kids your second visit to a house. The new I want. Nothing new under the sun. Care of P. O. Dolphin's barn. Are you not happy in your? Naughty darling. At Dolphin's barn charades in Luke Doyle's house. Mat Dillon and his bevy of daughters: Tiny, Atty, Floey, Sara. Molly too. Eightyseven that was. Year before we. And the old major partial to his drop of spirits. Curious she an only child, I an only child. So it returns. Think you're escaping and run into yourself. Longest way round is the shortest way home. And just when he and she. Circus horse walking in a ring. Rip van Winkle we played. Rip: tear in Henny Doyle's overcoat. Van: bread van delivering. Winkle: cockles and periwinkles. Then I did Rip van Winkle coming back. She leaned on the sideboard watching. Moorish eyes. Twenty years asleep. All changed. Forgotten. The young are old. His gun rusty from the dew.

Ba. What is that flying about? Swallow? Bat probably. Thinks I'm a tree, so blind. Metempsychosis. They believed you could be changed into a tree from grief. Weeping willow. Ba. There he goes. Funny little beggar. Wonder where he lives. Belfry up there. Very likely. Hanging by the heels in the odour of sanctity. Bell scared him out, I suppose. Mass seems to be over. Yes, there's the light in the priest's house. Their frugal meal. Remember about the mistake in the valuation when I was in Thom's. Twentyeight it is. Two houses they have. Gabriel Conroy's brother is curate. Ba. again. Wonder why they come out at night like mice. They're a mixed breed. Birds are like hopping mice. What frightens them, light or noise? Better sit still. All instinct like the bird in drouth got water out of the end of a jar by throwing in pebbles. Like a little man in a cloak he is with tiny hands. Weeny bones. Almost see them shimmering, kind of a bluey white. Colours depend on the light you see. Instance, that cat this morning on the staircase. Colour of brown turf. Howth a while ago amethyst. Glass flashing. That's how that wise man what's his name with the burning glass. Then the heather goes on fire. It can't be tourists' matches. What? Perhaps the sticks dry rub together in the wind and light.

Ba. Who knows what they're always flying for. Insects? That bee last week got into the room playing with his shadow on the ceiling. Birds too never find out what they say. Like our small talk. And says she and says he. Nerve they have to fly over the ocean and back. Lots must be killed in storms, telegraph wires. Dreadful life sailors have too. Big brutes of steamers floundering along in the dark, lowing out like seacows. *Faugh a ballagh.* Out of that, bloody curse to you. Others in vessels, bit of a handkerchief sail, pitched about like snuff at a wake when the stormy winds do blow. Married too. Sometimes away for years at the ends of the earth somewhere. No ends really because it's round. Wife in every port they say. She has a good job if she minds it till Johnny comes marching home again. If ever he does. Smelling the tailend of ports. How can they like the sea? Yet they do. The anchor's weighed. Off he sails with a scapular or a medal on him for luck. Well? And the tephilim poor papa's father had on his door to touch. That brought us out of the land of Egypt and into the house of bondage. Something in all those superstitions because when you go out never know what dangers. Hanging on to a plank for grim life, lifebelt round round him, gulping salt water, and that's the last of his nibs till the sharps catch hold of him. Do fish ever get seasick?

Then you have a beautiful calm without a cloud, smooth sea, placid, crew and cargo in smithereens, Davy Jones' locker. Moon looking down. Not my fault, old cockalorum.

A lost long candle wandered up the sky from Mirus bazaar in aid of funds for Mercer's hospital and broke, drooping, and shed a cluster of violet but one white star. They floated, fell: they faded. And among the elms a hoisted lintstock lit the lamp at Leahy's terrace. By the screen of lighted windows, by equal gardens a shrill voice went crying, wailing: Evening Telegraph, extra edition. Result of the Gold Cup races: and from the door of Dignam's house a boy ran out and called. Twittering the bat flew here, flew there. Far out over the sands the coming surf crept, grey. Howth settled for slumber tired of long days, of yumyum rhododendrons (he was old) and felt gladly the night breeze lift, ruffle his many ferns. He lay but opened a red eye unsleeping, deep and slowly breathing, slumberous but awake. And far on Kish bank the anchored lightship twinkled, winked at Mr. Bloom.

Life those chaps out there must have, stuck in the same spot. Irish Lights board. Penance for their sins. Day we went out in the Erin's King, throwing them the sack of old papers. Bears in the zoo. Filthy trip. Drunkards out to shake up their livers. Puking overboard to feed the herrings. And the women, fear of God in their faces. Milly, no sign of her funk. Her blue scarf loose, laughing. Don't know what death is at that age. And then their stomachs clean. But being lost they fear. When we hid behind the tree at Crumlin. I didn't want to. Mamma! Mamma! Frightening them with masks too. Poor kids. Only troubles wild fire and nettlerash. Calomel purge I got her for that. After getting better asleep with Molly. Very same teeth she has. What do they love? Another themselves? But the morning she chased her with the umbrella. Perhaps so as not to hurt. I felt her pulse. Ticking. Little hand it was: now big. Dearest Papli. All that the hand says when you touch. Loved to count my waist coat buttons. Her first stays I remember. Made me laugh to see. Little paps to begin with. Left one is more sensitive, I think. Mine too. Nearer the heart. Her growing pains at night, calling, wakening me. Frightened she was when her nature came on her first. Poor child! Strange moment for the mother too. Brings back her girlhood. Gibraltar. Looking from Buena Vista. O'Hara's tower. The seabirds screaming. Old Barbary ape that gobbled all his family. Sundown, gunfire for the men to cross the lines. Looking out over the sea she told me. Evening like this, but clear, no clouds. I always thought I'd marry a lord or a gentleman with a private yacht. *Buenas noches, senorita. El nombre ama la muchaha hormosa.* Why me? Because you were so foreign from the others.

Better not stick here all night like an oyster. This weather makes you dull. Must be getting on for nine by the light. Go home. Too late for *Leah, Lily of Killarney. No. Might be still up*. Call to the hospital to see. Hope she's over. Long day I've had. Martha, the bath, funeral, house of keys, Museum with those goddesses, Dedalus' song. Then that brawler in Barney Kiernan's. Got my own back there. Drunken ranters. Ought to go home and laugh at themselves. Always want to be swilling in company. Afraid to be alone like a child of two. Suppose he hit me. Look at it. Other way round. Not so bad then. Perhaps not to hurt he meant. Three cheers for Israel. Three cheers for the sister-in-law he hawked about, three fangs in her mouth. Extremely nice cup of tea. Imagine that in the early morning Everyone to his taste as Morris said when he kissed the cow. But Dignam's put the boots on it. Houses of mourning so depressing because you never know. Anyhow she wants the money. Must call to the Scottish widow's as I promised. Strange name. Takes it for granted we're going to pop off first. That widow on Monday was it outside Cramer's that looked at me. Buried the poor husband but progressing favorably. Well? What do you expect her to do? Must wheedle her way along. Widower I hate to see. Looks so forlorn. Poor man O'Connor wife and five children poisoned by mussels here. The sewage. Hopeless. Some good motherly woman take him in tow, platter face and a large apron. See him sometimes walking about trying to find out who played the trick. U. p: up. Fate that is. He, not me. Also a shop often noticed. Curse seems to dog it. Dreamt last night? Wait. Something confused. She had red slippers on. Turkish. Wore the breeches. Suppose she does. Would I like her in pyjamas? Damned hard to answer. Nannetti's gone. Mailboat. Near Holyhead by now. Must hail that ad of Keyes's. Work Hynes and Crawford. Petticoats for Molly. She has something to put in them. What's that? Might be money.

Mr. Bloom stooped and turned over a piece of paper on the strand. He brought it near his eyes and peered. Letter? No. Can't read. Better go. Better. I'm tired to move. Page of an old copybook. Never know what you find. Bottle with story of a treasure in it thrown from a wreck. Parcels post. Children always want to throw things in the sea. Trust? Bread cast on the waters. What's this? Bit of stick.

O! Exhausted that female has me. Not so young now. Will she come here tomorrow? Will I?

Mr. Bloom with his stick gently vexed the thick sand at his foot. Write a message for her. Might remain. What?

I.

Some flatfoot tramp on it in the morning. Useless. Tide comes here a pool near her foot. O, those transparent! Besides they don't know. What is the meaning of that other world. I called you naughty boy because I do not like.

AM.A.

No room. Let it go.

Mr. Bloom effaced the letters with his slow boot. Hopeless thing sand. Nothing grows in it. All fades. No fear of big vessels coming up here. Except Guinness's barges. Round the Kish in eighty days. Done half by design.

He flung his wooden pen away. The stick fell in silted sand, stuck. Now if you were trying to do that for a week on end you couldn't. Chance. We'll never meet again. But it was lovely. Goodbye, dear. Made me feel so young.

Short snooze now if I had. And she can do the other. Did too. And Belfast. I won't go. Let him. Just close my eyes a moment. Won't sleep though. Bat again. No harm in him. Just a few.

O sweety all your little white I made me do we two naughty darling she him half past the bed him pike hoses frillies for Raoul de perfume your wife black hair heave under embon senoritayoung eyes Mulvey plump bubs me bread van Winkle red slippers she rusty sleep wander years dreams return tail end Agendath lovey showed me her next year in drawers return next in her next her next.

A bat flew. Here. There. Here. Far in the grey a bell chimed. Mr. Bloom with open mouth, his left boot sanded sideways, leaned, breathed. Just for a few.

Cuckoo.

Cuckoo.

Cuckoo.

The clock on the mantelpiece in the priests' house cooed where Canon O'Hanlon and Father Conroy and the reverend John Hughes S. J. were taking tea and sodabread and butter and fried mutton chops with catsup and talking about.

Cuckoo.

Cuckoo.

Cuckoo.

Because it was a bird that came out of its little house to tell the time that Gerty MacDowell noticed the time she was there because she was as quick as anything about a thing, was Gerty MacDowell, and she noticed at once that the foreign gentleman that was sitting on the rocks looking was.

Cuckoo.

Cuckoo.

Cuckoo.

(*to be continued*)

THE LITTLE REVIEW

VCL· VII. SEPTEMBER-DECEMBER No. 3

CONTENTS

DESHIL Holles Eamus, Deshil Holles Eamus, Deshil Holles Eamus. Send us, bright one, light one, Horhorn, quickening and wombfruit. Send us, bright one light one, Horhorn, quickening and wombfruit. Send us bright one light one, Horhorn, quickening and wombfruit.

Hoopsa, boyaboy, hoopsa! Hoopsa, boyaboy, hoopsa! Hoopsa, boyaboy, hoopsa!

Universally that person's acumen is esteemed very little perceptive concerning whatsoever matters are being held as most profitably by mortals with sapience endowed to be studied who is ignorant of that which the most in doctrine erudite and certainly by reason of that in them high mind's ornament deserving of veneration constantly maintain when by general consent they affirm that other circumstances being equal by no exterior splendour is the prosperity of a nation more efficaciously asserted than by the measure of how far forward may have progressed the tribute of its solicitude for that proliferent continuance which of evils the original if it be absent when fortunately present constitutes the certain sign of omnipollent nature's incorrupted benediction. For who is there who anything of some significance has apprehended but is conscious that that exterior splendour may be the surface of a downward tending lutulent reality or on the contrary anyone so is there inilluminated as not to perceive that as no nature's boon can contend against the county of increase so it behooves every most just citizen to become the exhortator and admonisher of his semblables and to tremble lest what had in the past been by the nation excellently commenced might be in the future not with similar excellence accomplished if an invercund habit shall have gradually traduced the honourable by ancestors transmitted customs to that thither of profundity that that one was audacious excessively who would have the hardihood to rise affirming that no more odious offence can for anyone be than to oblivious neglect to consign that evangel simultaneously command and promise which on all mortals with prophecy of abundance or with diminution's menace that exalted of reiteratedly procreating function ever irrevocably enjoined?

It is not why therefore we shall wonder if, as the best historians relate, among the Celts, who nothing that was not in its nature admirable admired the art of medicine shall have been highly honored. Not to speak of hostels, leperyards, sweating chambers, plaguegraves, their greatest doctors, the O'Shiels,

Overleaf: table of contents, *Little Review*, September–December 1920

the O'Hickeys, the O'Lees, have sedulously set down the divers methods by which the sick and the relapsed found again health whether the malady had been the trembling withering or loose boyconnell flux. Certainly in every public work which in it anything of gravity contains preparation should be with importance commensurate and therefore a plan was by them adopted (whether by having preconsidered or as the maturation of experience it is difficult in being said which the discrepant opinions of subsequent inquirers are not up to the present congrued to render manifest) whereby maternity was so far from accident possibility removed that whatever care the patient in that allhardest of woman hour chiefly required and not solely for the copiously opulent but also for her who not being sufficiently moneyed scarcely and often not even scarcely could subsist valiantly and for an inconsiderable emolument was provided.

To her nothing already then and thenceforward was anyway able to be molestful for this chiefly felt all citizens except with proliferent mothers prosperity at all not to can be, and as they had received eternity gods mortals generation to befit them her beholding, when the case was so having itself, parturient in vehicle thereward carrying desire immense among all one another was impelling on of her to be received into that domicile. O thing of prudent nation not merely in being seen but also even in being related worthy of being praised that they her by ancipation went seeing mother, that she by them suddenly to be about to be cherished had been begun she felt!

Before born babe bliss had. Within womb won he worship. Whatever in that one case done commodiously done was. A couch by midwives attended with wholesome food reposeful cleanest swaddles as though forthbringing were now done and by wise foresight set: but to this no less of what drugs there is need and surgical implements which are pertaining to her case not omitting aspect of all very distracting spectacles in various latitudes by our terrestrial orb offered together with images, divine and human, the cogitation of which by sejunct females is to tumescence conducive or eases issue in the high sunbright wellbuilt fair home of mothers when, ostensibly far gone and reproductitive, it is come by her thereto to lie in, her term up.

Some man that wayfaring was stood by housedoor at night's oncoming. Of Israel's folk was that man that on earth wandering far had fared. Stark ruth of man his errand that him lone led till that house.

Of that house A. Horne is lord. Seventy beds keeps he there teeming mothers are wont that they lie for to thole and bring forth bairns hale so God's angel to Mary quoth. Watchers they there walk, white sisters in ward sleepless.

Smarts they still sickness soothing: in twelve moon thrice an hundred. Truest bedthanes they twain are, for Horne holding wariest ward.

In ward wary the watcher hearing come that man mild-hearted eft rising with swire ywimpled to him her gate wide undid. Lo, levin leaping lightens in eyebling Ireland's westward welkin! Full she dread that God the Wreaker all mankind would fordo with water for his evil sins. Christ's rood made she on breastbone and him drew that he would rather infare under her thatch. That man her will wotting worthful went in Horne's house.

Loth to irk in Horne's hall hat holding the seeker stood. On her stow he ere was living with dear wife and lovesome daughter that then over land and seafloor nine years had long outwandered. Once her in townhithe meeting he to her bow had not doffed. Her to forgive now he craved with good ground of her allowed that that of him swiftseen face, hers, so young then had looked. Light swift her eyes kindled, bloom of blushes his word winning.

As her eyes then ongot his weeds swart therefor sorrow she feared. Glad after she was that ere adread was. Her he asked if O'Hare Doctor tidings sent from far coast and she with grameful sigh him answered that O'Hare Doctor in heaven was. Sad was the man that word to hear that him so heavied in bowels ruthful. All she there told him, ruing death for friend so young, algate sore unwilling God's rightwiseness to withsay. She said that he had a fair sweet death through God His goodness with masspriest to be shriven, holy housel and sick men's oil to his limbs. The man then right earnest asked the nun of which death the dead man was died and the nun answered him and said that he was died in Mona island through bellycrab three year agone come Yule and she prayed to God the Allruthful to have his dear soul in his undeathliness. He heard her sad words, in held hat sad staring. So stood they there both awhile in wanhope, sorrowing one with other.

Therefore, everyman, look to that last end that is thy death and the dust that gripeth on every man that is born of woman for as he came naked forth of his mother's womb so naked shall he wend him at the last for to go as he came.

The man that was come into the house then spoke to the nursingwoman and he asked her how it fared with the woman that lay there in childbed. The nursingwoman answered him and said that that woman was in throes now full three days and that it would be a hard birth unneth to bear but that now in a little it would be. She said that she had seen many births of women but never was none so hard as was that woman's birth. Then she set it forth all to him that time was had lived high that house. The man hearkened to her words for he felt with wonder women's woe in the travail that they have of motherhood and he wondered to look on her face that was a young face for any man to see but yet was she left after long years a handmaid. Nine twelve bloodflows chiding her childless.

And whiles they spake the door of the castle was opened and there nighed them a mickle noise as of many that sat there at meat. And there came against the place as they stood a young learning knight yclept Dixon. And the traveller Leopold was couth to him sithen it had happed that they had ado each with other in the house of misericord where this learning knight lay by cause the traveller Leopold came there to be healed for he was sore wounded in his breast by a spear wherewith a horrible and dreadful dragon was smitten him for which he did to make a salve of volatile salt and chrism as much as he might suffice. And he said now that he should go into that castle for to make merry with them that were there. And the traveller Leopold said that he should go otherwhither for he was a man of cautels and a subtle. Also the lady was of his avis and repreved the learning knight though she trowed well that the traveller had said thing that was false for his subtility. But the learning knight would not hear say nay nor do her mandement he have him in aught contrarious to his list and he said how it was a marvelous castle. And the traveller Leopold went into the castle for to rest him for a space being sore of limb after many marches environing in divers lands and sometime venery.

And in the castle was set a board that was of the birchwood of Finlandy and it was upheld by four dwarfmen of that country but they durst not move more for enchantment. And on this board were frightful swords and knives that are made in a great cavern by swinking demons out of white flames that they fix in the horns of buffalos and stags that there abound marvellously. And there were vessels that are wrought by magic out of seasand and the air by a warlock with his breath that he blares into them like to bubbles. And full fair cheer and rich was on the board that no wight could devise a fuller ne richer. And there was a vat of silver that was moved by craft to open in the which lay strange fishes withouten heads though misbelieving men nie that this be possible thing without they see it natheless they are so. And these fishes lie in an oily water brought there from Portugal land because of the fatness that therein is like to the juices of the olive press. And also it was a marvel to see in that castle how by magic they make a compost out of fecund wheat kidneys out of Chaldee that by aid of certain angy spirits that they do into it swells up wondrously like to a vast mountain. And they teach the serpents there to entwine themselves up on long sticks out of the ground and of the scales of these serpents they brew out a brewage like to mead.

And the learning knight let pour for the traveller a draught and halp thereto the while all they that were there drank every each. And the traveller Leopold did up his beaver for to pleasure him and took apertly somewhat in amity for he never drank no manner of mead and anon full privily he voided the more part in his neighbour glass and his neighbour nist not of his wile. And he sat down in that castle with them for to rest him there awhile Thanked be Almighty God.

This meanwhile this good sister stood by the door and begged them at the reverence of Jesu our alther liege Lord to leave their wassailing for there was above one quick with child a gentle dame, whose time hied fast. Sir Leopold heard on the upfloor cry on high and he wondered what cry that it was whether of child or woman and I marvel, said he, that it be not come or now. Meseems it dureth overlong. And he was ware and saw a franklin that hight Lenehan an that side the table that was older than any of the tother and for that they both were knights virtuous in the one emprise and eke by cause that he was elder he spoke to him full gently. But, said he, or it be long too she will bring forth by God His bounty and have joy for she hath waited marvellous long. And the franklin that had drunken said, Expecting each moment to be her next. Also he took the cup that stood tofore him for him needed never done asking nor desiring of him to drink and, Now drink, said he, fully delectably, and he quaffed as far as he might to their both's health for he was a passing good man of his lustiness. And Sir Leopold that was the goodliest guest that ever sat in scholar's hall and that was the meekest man and the kindest that ever laid husbandly hand under hen and that was the very knight of the world one that ever did minion service to lady gentle pledged him courtly in the cup. Woman's woe with wonder pondering.

Now let us speak of that fellowship that was there to the intent to be drunken an they might. There was a sort of scholars along either side the board, that is to wit, Dixon yclept junior of Saint Mary Merciable's with other his fellows Lynch and Madden., scholars of medicine, and the franklin that hight Lenehan and one from Alba Longa, one Crotthers, and young Stephen that had mien of a frere that was at head of the board and Costello that men clepen Punch Costello all long of a mastery of him erewhile gested (and of all them, reserved young Stephen, he was the most drunken that demanded still of more mead) and beside the meek Sir Leopold. But on young Malachi they waited for that he promised to have come and such as intended to no goodness said how he had broke his avow. And Sir Leopold sat with them for he bore fast friendship to Sir Simon and to this his son young Stephen and for that his langour becalmed him there after longest wanderings insomuch as they feasted him for that time in the honourablest manner. Ruth red him, love led on with will to wander, loth to leave.

For they were right witty scholars. And he heard their aresouns each gen other as touching birth and righteousness, young Madden maintaining that put such case it were heard the wife to die (for so it had fallen out a matter of some year agone with a woman of Eblana in Horne's house that now was trepassed out of this world and the self night next before her death all leeches and pothecaries had taken counsel of her case). And they said farther she should live because in the beginning they said the woman should bring forth in pain and wherefore they that were of this imagination affirmed how young Madden had said truth for he had conscience to let her die. And not few and of these was young Lynch were in doubt that the world was now right evil governed as it was never other howbeit the mean people believed it otherwise but the law nor his judges did provide no remedy. This was scant said but all cried with one acclaim the wife should live and the babe to die. And they waxed hot upon that head what with argument and what for their drinking but the franklin Lenehan was prompt to pour them ale so that at the least way mirth might not lack. Then young Madden showed all the whole affair and when he said how that she was dead and how for holy religion sake her goodman husband would not let her death whereby they were all wondrous grieved. To whom young Stephen had these words following, Murmur, sirs, is eke oft among lay folk. Both babe and parent now glorify their Maker, the one in limbo gloom, the other in purge fire. But what of those Godpossibled souls that we nightly impossibilise? For, sirs, he said, our lust is brief. We are means to those small creatures within us and nature has other ends than we. Then said Dixon junior to Punch Costello wist he what ends. But he had overmuch drunken and the best word he could have of him was that he would ever dishonest a woman whoso she were or wife or maid or leman if it so fortuned him to be delivered of his spleen of lustihead. Whereas Crotthers of Alba Longa sang young Malachi's praise of that beast the unicorn how once in the millennium he cometh by his horn the other all this while pricked forward with their jibes wherewith they did malice him, witnessing all and several by Saint Cuculus his engines that he was able to do any manner of thing that lay in man to do.

There at laughed they all right jocundly only young Stephen and sir Leopold which never durst laugh too open by reason of a strange humour which he would not betray and also for that he rued for her that bare whoso she might be or wheresoever. Then spoke young Stephen orgulous of mother Church that would cast him out of her bosom, of law of canons, of bigness wrought by wind of seeds of brightness or by potency of vampires mouth to mouth or, as Virgilius saith, by the influence of the occident or peradventure in her bath according to the opinions of Averroes and Moses Maimonides. He said also how at the end of the second month a human soul was infused and how in all our holy mother foldeth ever souls for God's greater glory whereas that earthly mother which was but a dam to bring forth beastly should die by canon for so saith he that holdeth the fisherman's seal, even that blessed Peter on which rock was holy church for all ages founded. All they bachelors then asked of sir Leopold would he in like case so jeopard her person as risk life to save life. A wariness of mind he would answer as fitted all and, laying hand to jaw, he said dissembling that as it was informed him and agreeing also with his experience of so seldom seen an accident it was good for that Mother Church belike at one blow had birth and death pence and in such sort deliverly he scaped their questions. That is truth, said Dixon, and, or I err, a pregnant word: Which hearing young Stephen was a marvellous glad man and he averred that he who stealeth from the poor lendeth to the Lord for he was of a wild manner when he was drunken and that he was now in that taking it appeared eftsoons.

But sir Leopold was passing grave maugre his word by cause he still had pity of the terror causing shrieking of shrill women in their labour and as he was minded of his good lady Marion that had borne him an only manchild which on his eleventh day on live had died and no man of art could save so dark is destiny. And she was wondrous stricken of heart for that evil hap and for his burial did him on a fair corselet of lamb's wool, the flower of the flock, lest he might perish utterly and lie akeled (for it was then about the midst of the winter) and now sir Leopold that had of his body no manchild for an heir looked upon him his friend's son and was shut up in sorrow for his forepassed happiness and as sad as he was that him failed a son of such gentle courage (for all accounted him of real parts) so grieved he also in no less measure for young Stephen for that he lived riotously with those wastrels and murdered his goods with whores.

About that present time young Stephen filled all cups that stood empty so as there remained but little if the prudenter had not shadowed their approach from him that still plied it very busily who, praying for the intentions of the sovereign pontiff, he gave them for a pledge the vicar of Christ which also as he said is vicar of Bray. Now drink we, quod he, of this mazer and quaff ye this mead which is not indeed parcel of my body but my soul's bodiment. Leave ye fraction of bread to them that live by bread alone. Be not afeard neither for any want for this will comfort more than the other will dismay. See ye here. And he showed them glistering coins of the tribute and goldsmiths' notes the worth of two pound nineteen shillings that he had he said for a song which he writ. They all admired to see the foresaid riches in such dearth of money as was herebefore. His words were then these as followeth: Know all men, he said, time's ruins build eternity's mansions. What means this? Desire's wind blasts the thorntree but after it becomes from a bramblebush to be a rose upon the rood of time. Mark me now. In woman's womb word is made flesh but in the spirit of the maker all flesh that passes becomes the word that shall not pass away. This is the postcreation. *Omnis caro ad te veniet.* No question but her name is puissant who aventried the dear course of our Agenbuyer, Healer and Herd, our mighty mother and mother most venerable and Bernardus saith aptly that she hath an *omnipitentiam deiparae supplicem,* that is to wit, an almightiness of petition because she is the second Eve and she won us, saith Augustine too, whereas that other, our grandam, which we are linked up with by successive anastomosis of navelcords sold us by all lock, stock and barrel for a penny pippin. But here is the matter now. Or she knew him, that second I say, and was but creature of her creature, *vergine madre figlia di tuo figlio* or she knew him not and then stands she in the one denial or ignorancy with Peter Piscator who lives in the house that Jack built and with Joseph the Joiner patron of the happy demise of all unhappy marriages *parceque M. Leo Taxil nous a dit que qui l'avait mise dans cette fichue position c'etait le sacre pigeon, ventre de Dieu! Entweder* transsubstantiality *oder* consubstantiality but in no case subsubstantiality. And all cried out upon it for a very scurvy word. A pregnancy without joy, he said, a birth without pangs, a body without belmish, a belly without bigness. Let the lewd with faith and fervour worship. With will will we withstand, withsay.

Hereupon Punch Costello dinged with his fist upon the board and would sing a bawdy catch *Staboo Stabella* about a wench that was put in pod of a jolly swashbuckler in Almany which he did now attack: *The first three months she was not well, Staboo,* when here nurse Quigley from the door angerly bid them hist ye should shame you nor was it meet as she remembered them being her mind was to have all orderly against lord Andrew came as she was jealous that no turmoil might shorten the honour of her guard. It was an ancient and a sad matron of a sedate look and christian walking, in habit dun beseming her megrins and wrinkled visage, nor did her hortative want of it effect for incontinently Punch Costello was of them all embraided and they reclaimed him with civil rudeness some and with menace of blandishments others whiles all chode with him, a murrain seize the dolt, what a devil he would be at, thou chuff, thou puny, thou got in the peasestraw, thou chitterling, thou dykedropt, thou abortion thou, to shut up his drunken drool out of that like a curse of God ape, the good sir Leopold that had for his cognisance the flower of quietmargerain gentle, advising also the time's occasion as most sacred and most worthy to be most sacred. In Horne's house rest should reign.

To be short this passage was scarce by when Master Dixon of Mary's in Eccles, goodly grinning, asked young Stephen what was the reason why he had not cided to take friar's vows and he answered him obedience in the womb, chastity in the tomb but involuntary poverty all his days. Master Lenehan at this made return that he had heard of those nefarious deeds and how, as he heard hereof counted, he had besmirched the lily virtue of a confiding female which was corruption of minors and they all intershowed it too, waxing merry and toasting to his fathership. But he said very entirely it was clean contrary to their suppose for he was the eternal son and ever virgin. Thereat mirth grew in them the more and they rehearsed to him his curious rite of wedlock for the disrobing and deflowering of spouses, she to be in guise of white and saffron, her groom in white and grain, with burning of nard and tapers, on a bridebed while clerks sung kyries and the anthem *Ut novetur sexus omnis corporis mysterium* till she was there unmaided. He gave them then a much admirable hymen minim by those delicate poets Master John Fletcher and Master Francis Beaumont that is in their *Maid's Tragedy* that was writ for a like twining of lovers: *To bed, to bed,* was the burden of it to be played with accompanable concent upon the virginals. Well met they were, said Master Dixon, but, harkee, better were they named Beau Mont and Lecher for, by my troth, of such a mingling much might come. Young Stephen said indeed to his best remembrance they had but the one doxy between them and she of the stews to make shift with in delights amorous for life ran very high in those days and the custom of the country approved with it. Greater love than this, he said, no man hath that a man lay down his wife for his friend. Go thou and do likewise. Thus, or words to that effect, saith Zarathustra, sometime regious professor of French letters to the university of Oxtail nor breathed there ever that man to whom mankind was more beholden. Bring a stranger within thy tower it will go hard but thou wilt have the secondbest bed. *Orate, fratres, pro memetipso.* And all the people shall say, Amen. Remember, Erin, thy generations and they days of old, how thou settedst little by me and by my word and broughtest in a stranger to my gates to commit fornication in my sight and to wax fat and kick like Jeshurum. Therefore hast thou sinned against the light and hast made me, thy lord to be the slave of servants. Return, return, Clan Milly: forget me not, O Milesian. Why hast thou done this abomination before me that thou didst spurn me for a merchant of jalap and didst deny me to the Roman and the Indian of dark speech with whom thy daughters did lie luxuriously? Look forth now, my people, upon the land of behest, even from Horeb and from Nebo and from Pisgah and from the Horns of Hatten unto a land flowing with milk and money. But thou hast suckled me with a bitter milk: my moon and my sun thou hast quenched for ever. And thou hast left me alone for ever in the dark ways of my bitterness: and with a kiss of ashes hast thou kissed my mouth. This tenebrosity of the interior, he proceeded to say hath not been illumined by the wit of the septuagint nor as much as mentioned for the Orient from on high. Which brake hell's gates visited a darkness that was foraneous. Assuefaction minorates atrocities and Hamlet his father showeth the prince no blister of combustion. The adiaphane in the moon of life is an Egypt's plague which in the nights of prenativity and postmortemity is their most proper *ubi* and *quomodo*. And as the ends and ultimates of all things accords in some mean and measure with their inceptions and originals, that same multiplicit concordance which leads forth growth from birth accomplishing by a retrogressive metamorphosis that minishing and ablation towards the final which is agreeable unto nature so is it with our subsolar being. The aged sisters draw us into life: we wail, batten, sport, slip, clasp, sunder, dwindle, die: over us dead they bend. First saved from water of old Nile, among bulrushes, a bed of fasciated wattles; at last the cavity of a mountain, an occulted sepulchre amid the conclamation of the hillcat and the ossifrage. And as no man knows the ubicity of his tumulus nor to what processes we shall thereby be ushered nor whether to Tophet or to Edenville in the like way is all hidden when we would backward see from what region of remoteness the whatness of our whoness hath fetched his whenceness.

(*to be continued*)

THE COMPOSITION HISTORY OF *ULYSSES*

The *Ulysses* that appeared in the *Little Review* between March 1918 and December 1920 was very much a work in progress. When the first installments were published, Joyce still didn't have a clear vision of the novel as a whole, and he later expanded and revised the episodes he had written for magazine publication, before Sylvia Beach's Shakespeare and Company published the novel as a book in 1922. *The Little Review "Ulysses"* thus offers insight into the making of one of the twentieth century's most important works of art, since it differs in surprising, often revealing ways from the text with which we have now grown familiar. This concise history of the book's composition provides an overview of how *Ulysses* first took shape and gradually developed over the course of two and half years before it was deemed obscene and its publication in the United States prohibited. It also looks briefly at some of the key differences between the magazine and book versions, exploring how Joyce set about expanding and developing his work in ways that made it more complex, more rife with allusion, and more deeply structured around its Homeric themes and symbolic motifs.

This section does not aim to be a complete genetic history of *Ulysses.* Such a project certainly exceeds the limits of a book like this and is itself the subject of ongoing scholarly debate and research that we hope this book will facilitate. Joyce's drafting and revision process was incredibly complex and almost always additive. Indeed, he left distinctive margins of increasing width in his notebooks precisely to allow himself room for expansion and revision. And because so much of the draft and proof material for the book survives, scholars have been able to trace with great care the ways in which individual words and passages grew as the book advanced from draft to typescript to page proof. To fully track these changes, one would have to work through the vast archival materials published in *The James Joyce Archive* and *"Ulysses": A Facsimile of the Manuscript* (cited hereafter as the Rosenbach Manuscript), then study closely the three-volume critical and synoptic version of the novel prepared by Hans Walter Gabler. That research would then have to be supplemented by further analysis of the manuscripts now available online at the National Library of Ireland, most of which were not available when Gabler completed his work. The genetic study of Joyce's masterpiece, in short, is an active site of scholarly investigation and discovery. Inevitably, then, the short summaries in this section flatten the dynamic revision process in order to focus more generally on what makes the *Little Review* version of Joyce's novel distinct from the much longer, more complex version that appeared in 1922. But this section also aims to provide a valuable new tool to assist our understanding of both *Ulysses* and the dazzling mind at work behind it.

Finally, it is important to keep in mind that *The Little Review "Ulysses"* stands outside the 1922 edition's direct line of transmission. Joyce worked from copies of the typescripts he sent to Ezra Pound and Margaret Anderson—not from the magazine text itself. What the magazine version offers us, therefore, is a clear sense of how Joyce first envisioned *Ulysses* and of how that book appeared to its first readers. And what we offer here, in the novel's composition history, is less a definitive statement on the evolution of *Ulysses* than a concise look at what we now know about the book's first publication. Therefore, it is also an invitation to further research on what amounts to a first-draft version of the twentieth century's most important and most influential work of fiction.

ORIGINS

Ulysses's beginning emerged from a series of endings—from incompletely realized ideas Joyce had for a story that might have been added to *Dubliners* and then from a scene in the Martello tower that was originally intended for the final chapter of *A Portrait of the Artist as a Young Man.* The first surviving notes we now have that were clearly designed for *Ulysses* appear in a notebook that dates to October 1917. Across the top of the pages, Joyce wrote nineteen topic headings that included names of characters (Simon, Leopold, and Stephen), what would become key topics (Irish, Jews, and Art), and a handful of references to the classical structures that would eventually give shape to the book (including Homer, Rhetoric, and Oxen). The notebook's final page includes a tantalizing list of "Words," ranging from the resonant "heaventree" to the unremarkable "faucet." Luca Crispi calls these "subject headings" for *Ulysses,* arguing that this is one of Joyce's first known attempts to organize notes gleaned from other sources. "It seems likely," Crispi speculates, "that Joyce compiled the entries in the notebook over a relatively short period of time and then began using some of them to write and revise drafts almost immediately," though it is clear that Joyce returned to the notebook at later stages of his composition process as well ("First Foray"). Other notes survive, too, the most important of which are those held by the British Library dating from approximately 1919–1921. These are organized around the Homeric titles for each of the episodes, indicating that by this point Joyce had a clearer sense of the book's shape and classical motifs.

Although the earliest notes date to 1917, we know that the origins of *Ulysses* can be traced to a much earlier period. The title emerged in 1906 when Joyce wrote to his brother Stanislaus that he planned to use it for an additional story in *Dubliners* about a Dublin Jew attending the funeral of a friend. (For more on this origin, see the section below on "Hades.") The story seems never to have gotten beyond the title, though Joyce clearly kept in mind that mythically resonant name and slightly unusual character. The book's opening in the Martello tower also dates from a rejected idea for an earlier work. We know that Joyce started thinking quite early about extending *A Portrait of the Artist as a Young Man* to include his stay in this unusual property, because there is a late fragment of that novel in which a character named Doherty tells Daedalus (as Joyce then spelled the name), "We must retire to the tower, you and I" (Scholes and Kain 108). Doherty is an early version of Mulligan (and Joyce took care to preserve the three syllables in the name in every version). So the pieces of *Ulysses* were likely in place before 1910, including a classical frame, the Martello tower opening, and the idea of a story about an Irish Jew. But we don't yet know exactly when these fragments and ideas began to fuse.

The earliest drafts of the novel now extant date from 1917 and include sections of both "Proteus" (the third episode) and "Sirens" (the eleventh), though Joyce also wrote to Pound in April of that year that a version (now lost) of the "Hamlet chapter" was complete (*LI* 101). These drafts reside in a single notebook now held by the National Library of Ireland. They are significant both because they provide the first glimpse of the book as it was coming into being and because the material for "Sirens" contains the first narrative reference to Leopold Bloom. A few other notebooks from this period have survived, including a second draft of "Proteus" and three notebook drafts of "Scylla and

Charybdis." Beyond this, the only other manuscript available for the first ten episodes is the Rosenbach Manuscript—a fair-copy version of the novel that was written out primarily for use by the people who typed the text for Joyce. A richer archive of drafts survives for much, though not all, of the rest of the book, and the *Little Review* text itself can be seen as a kind of draft version of the book. We detail its development in the rest of this section by looking closely at each episode as we now think it took shape for its sometimes stuttering serialization in the *Little Review,* and at some of the important changes that took place as Joyce revised and expanded the book for its 1922 publication by Shakespeare and Company.

EPISODE I: TELEMACHUS

Ulysses begins at 8:00 A.M. on June 16, 1904—a date now celebrated around the world as "Bloomsday." We begin in a Martello tower on the coast of Ireland, in Sandycove, a pleasant suburb of Dublin. These towers were forts built in the nineteenth century to defend the coastline against a possible invasion by France, but as they became obsolete, some were rented out as dwelling places. Joyce lived there for a few days in September 1904 with his friend and rival Oliver St. John Gogarty, a medical student and poet of some regard. He left when another resident in the tower, Samuel Trench, woke from a nightmare about panthers and fired a pistol wildly in the room. Crying "leave him to me," Gogarty allegedly grabbed the gun and fired as well, prompting Joyce to storm out angrily (Ellmann 175). He was then forced to make the long walk to Dublin, where he spent some time at the National Library and wandered about the city in search of a new place to stay.

The parallels between these events in Joyce's life and the story narrated in the episode's opening pages are important but inexact and follow closely the technique used in *A Portrait of the Artist as a Young Man.* This opening episode, in fact, can easily be read as a sequel to *Portrait*—especially when, in the pages of the *Little Review,* it appears immediately after an advertisement for that earlier novel that emphasizes Stephen's "extreme completeness." In *Portrait,* Joyce drew heavily on the autobiographical details of his own life, just as *Ulysses* does, but they underwent a process of revision and invention that makes it difficult for us to know where to draw the boundary between fiction and fact, between Joyce's own life and the epic career he crafted for the struggling artist Stephen Dedalus.

Joyce most likely began work on "Telemachus" in June 1915, when he wrote to his brother Stanislaus, "Die erste Episode meines neues Roman 'Ulysses' ist geschreiben" [The first episode of my new novel 'Ulysses' is written] (*SL* 209). Just over a year later, in October 1916, he wrote to Harriet Shaw Weaver, "I have almost finished the first part and have written out part of the middle and end" (*LII* 387). It took almost another year, however, before the first part of the book was ready for a planned simultaneous serialization in the *Egoist* and the *Little Review*. None of these early drafts mentioned in the letters has survived. In mid-November 1917, Joyce mailed the manuscript version of the first three episodes to his friend Claud Sykes, in Zurich, who typed it out on a borrowed machine. The handwritten, fair-copy version appears today as part of the Rosenbach Manuscript, which includes some specific instructions for the typist. For example, when Stephen drags his ashplant along the ground, "squealing at his heels . . . . Steeeeeeephen," Joyce noted on the manuscript that there were "12 e's here" (Groden, *UP* 206), though the *Little Review* printed only seven of them (*LRU* 20). The typed copy of the manuscript was sent to Ezra Pound in London, who forwarded it to Margaret Anderson in New York. (The episode in fact came to Pound in what he called "chunks," which he forwarded to New York as he got them.) In December 1917, Pound wrote to Anderson that Joyce had told him that the first section was at the typists, so she could plan to begin printing the novel in March of the following year. By February, Pound had sent the entire episode and urged Anderson to print the whole thing in one issue, which she did (*Pound/Little Review* 190).

After the initial publication of the episode, Joyce did not return to it until he began preparing the 1922 Shakespeare and Company edition of the book. Despite receiving five sets of page proofs and placards, he did not take the opportunity to add or revise very much, making this episode somewhat unusual. He did make sure that "Steeeeeeeeeeeephen" got its twelve *e*'s, however. And he added an Irish saying that comes to Stephen's mind as Haines smiles at him on his departure: "Horn of a bull, hoof of a horse, smile of a Saxon" (*U* 1.732). Three very hard objects, to the Irish mind, and Stephen is thinking of himself as very Irish in the presence of the English (or Saxon) Haines. One of the most important additions to this episode for the book publication, though, is the Middle English phrase about Stephen's conscience, "agenbite of inwit," which comes to Stephen's mind as he is talking with Haines and Mulligan about washing (*U* 1.481); it returns to haunt him several more times in the course of the novel, especially during the tenth episode, "Wandering Rocks."

EPISODE II: NESTOR

The second installment of *Ulysses* finds Stephen teaching a class in a boy's school in Dalkey, a mile from the Martello tower where we last saw him. When the class adjourns for hockey at ten, Stephen visits Mr. Deasy, the headmaster, in his study, where he receives his wages and some advice from the old man, as well as a letter that Deasy has written about preventing foot and mouth disease in cattle. Aware that the younger man knows several journalists, he hopes to get some help in having it published. As Joyce's biographer Richard Ellmann notes, the episode is loosely based on Joyce's own short-lived experience early in 1904 with teaching at a boy's school, just south of Dublin, which also had a headmaster who, like Mr. Deasy, was an Ulster Unionist who supported English rule in Ireland (*James Joyce* 152–53). To this extent, the episode continues Joyce's initial idea that *Ulysses* would be a sequel to *A Portrait of the Artist as a Young Man,* his own life providing the incidents for his fiction.

Unlike later episodes, which Joyce composed while concentrating solely on *Ulysses,* "Nestor" was conceived and written while he was still working on several other books, including *Portrait* (see Groden, *UP* 5–6). Joyce had completed an initial draft of "Nestor" by June 1915, though no manuscript or notebook evidence of this early work survives. At the time, he was living in Trieste, a city now in Italy, but then a thriving multicultural port in Austria-Hungary and one of the world's major commercial capitals. With the outbreak of World War I, Joyce—a British subject—found himself in enemy territory and had to move hastily with his family to Zurich, in neutral Switzerland. In November 1917, during a stay in Locarno, Switzerland, where he was recuperating from an eye operation, Joyce returned to the episode and completed it (along with the other two episodes of the "Telemachiad," as Joyce referred to the first section of the novel), in anticipation of the book's serialization in the *Little Review* and the *Egoist* in 1918. In mid-December 1917, Joyce sent a fair-copy manuscript of the episode to Sykes, in Zurich, to be typed. The earliest surviving version of the episode, this draft is part of the Rosenbach Manuscript. Late in 1917, Joyce mailed two typed copies to Pound in London. Pound mailed one copy to Margaret Anderson, in New York, on January 23, 1918, and Anderson published the episode in the April 1918 issue of the *Little Review* (*Pound/The Little Review* 177).

We know Pound was not thrilled by the second episode: in a letter to H. L. Mencken, he wrote, "Joyce's new novel has a corking 1st chap. (which will get us suppressed), not such a good second one" (*Pound/Joyce* 130). Perhaps from his lack of enthusiasm, or simply his conclusion that the episode posed no threat to the magazine, Pound does not seem to have edited the typescript before passing it off to Anderson. When Joyce returned to the episode in 1921, he introduced only a few changes on five different proofs and placards. Like "Telemachus," this episode was fixed relatively early, again contributing to the idea that these opening chapters were more a continuation of *Portrait* than a radical break with the themes and techniques of that earlier novel.

The most substantial changes made in 1921 were a series of additions that included several new phrases, a few new sentences, and one new full paragraph: "Glorious, pious and immortal memory. The lodge of Diamond in Armagh the splendid behung with corpses of papishes. Hoarse, masked and armed, the planters' covenant. The black north and true blue bible. Croppies lie down" (*U* 2.273–76). Like most of the other additions, this one, which offers a mosaic of fragments from Irish history, extends and deepens the parts of the narrative that chart Stephen's stream of consciousness. A few of Joyce's late additions to "Nestor" also extend the web of cross-references in the novel by anticipating actions in later episodes. In the quotation above, for example, the sentence "Croppies lie down" is a song refrain that points ahead to the "Sirens" episode, where "The Croppy Boy" is sung by Ben Dollard, as well as to "Hades," where the song and singer are first mentioned together. Joyce may have been making some effort in these additions to flesh out his schema: in response to Stephen's idea of history as a "nightmare," Joyce, in 1921, has him think, "What if that nightmare gave you a back kick?" (*U* 2.379). By posing this fanciful question, Joyce manages, with a single stroke, to link the art of the episode (history) to its technic (catechism) and symbol (horse), while also anticipating the many violent shocks of the nightmare sections of "Circe."

Joyce's additions thickened his language, making parts of the 1922 version of this episode harder to understand than the serialized text. This thickening is magnified by the compression of a number of compound words that, in the magazine, stand distinct: "blotting paper" becomes "blottingpaper" and "all important" gives way to "allimportant." But errors in the *Little Review* text in turn create moments of confusion that are later absent from the book. Besides some obvious mistakes by the printer ("breats," "sopybook," "tehir"), there are three errors, possibly introduced when the typescript was created, in which entire lines from the manuscript were skipped. In the first two omissions, a line from later in the episode was swapped for the missing line, producing a confusing echo in the text: for instance, "Mr. Deasy **laughed, with rich delight, putting back his savings**box" in Joyce's manuscript becomes, in the magazine, "Mr. Deasy **stared sternly for some moments over the mantel**box," which is then repeated, several lines later: "Mr. Deasy **stared sternly for some moments over the mantel**piece" (Rosenbach Manuscript, *LRU* 30, *LRU* 30, boldface added). In the last of these errors, a line from the manuscript is simply left out; "Yes, sir, Stephen said, turning hard and swallowing his breath" (*LRU* 35) in the *Little Review* should, in fact, read this way (with the omitted line marked in bold):

> —Yes, sir, Stephen said, turning **back at the gate.**
> **Mr Deasy halted, breathing** hard and swallowing his breath. (*U* 2.435–36)

Since none of these mistakes shows up in the 1922 print edition, later readers of *Ulysses* are spared having to wonder why Mr. Deasy spends so much time staring sternly in this episode, or what is going on inside Stephen's head that would make him swallow his breath at Deasy's approach.

EPISODE III: PROTEUS

The third installment of *Ulysses* continues to follow Stephen through the early part of the day and concludes both the first section of the book and the first section of the manuscript that Joyce drafted and sent to Pound. It is now eleven in the morning, and Stephen has taken a tram to a muddy beach called Sandymount Strand, just south of Dublin's city center. Self-consciously alone, he is planning to pass some free time before meeting Mulligan at a pub called the Ship. He decides to break this appointment, however, withdrawing instead into loneliness while his mind wanders in an often complex and disorienting pattern that makes this episode particularly challenging to read. As in the other early episodes of *Ulysses,* this is not strictly a stream-of-consciousness narrative but instead a sometimes perplexing mixture of third-person narration and Stephen's first-person interior monologue. It too is basically a continuation of both the story and the mode of writing first developed in *Portrait,* but now turned even more inward on itself. There is almost no direct dialogue, and every quotation or fragment of dialogue we hear has been filtered through Stephen's mind. As readers, we labor to follow the young man as he walks and thinks and eventually writes a poem, and we glimpse images made familiar in previous installments (like the fox burying his grandmother—*LRU* 27) alongside others (like the pale vampire—*LRU* 46) that seem redolent with meaning yet somehow incomplete.

It is appropriate that the Greek sea god of change, Proteus, should stand symbolically over this episode, since it underwent surprising revision from its initial drafting to its final publication while nevertheless maintaining its core substance. "Proteus" is, in fact, the episode for which we have the longest record of composition, and it was likely one of the first pieces of *Ulysses* drafted as part of a book distinct from *Portrait* (along with portions of what would become episodes IX, X, and XII). It took shape in the summer of 1917 in what is now called the "coverless" notebook held by the National Library of Ireland (NLI MS 36,639/7A), but it contains traces of even earlier work, including one of the "epiphanies" Joyce first recorded in 1904. The notebook, as Daniel Ferrer discovered, contains the same key elements of the text published in the *Little Review* but in a radically different order. The draft contains approximately fifteen fragments separated by asterisks, suggesting that these were building blocks for a larger narrative (as Ferrer suggests) or perhaps a deliberately fragmented narrative similar to the piece titled "Nocturne" by Ben Hecht that follows it in the *Little Review*. More recently, Luca Crispi has contended that this notebook is less experimental than this and more likely a repository for draft material.

Instead of opening with the baffling, even pretentious phrase "ineluctable modality of the visible" (which doesn't even appear in the notebook), Joyce's 1917 draft begins with the ten lines describing the Martello tower from later in the episode (*LRU* 37, 43). As Ferrer notes, although these chunks of text might be in a different order, the key narrative and thematic structures are in place, including the distinctive "blend of first-person monologue and third-person narration, with some transitional sentences that may or may not be free indirect speech" ("What Song," 55). This manuscript, however, proved remarkably protean, since Joyce transformed it rapidly from a series of fragments into a more familiar shape by the fall of 1917 (Buffalo Notebook V.A.3). Shortly thereafter, he produced a fair copy and sent it to Claud Sykes so that it could be typed. Following custom, copies of this episode were then sent to Ezra Pound, who forwarded one to Anderson and Heap at the *Little Review* in time for publication in the May issue.

By the time this installment appeared in the magazine, *Ulysses* itself had begun to take on a more definite shape. Although Joyce had initially considered adding a fourth episode to the Telemachiad (tentatively titled "Lacedemon"), the early structure of the book was now essentially fixed. As with the other episodes of the Telemachiad, Joyce introduced very few changes to the original text before it appeared in the 1922 Shakespeare and Company edition. Nevertheless, there is some evidence of Joyce's accretive method of drafting, described by A. Walton Litz and others, though most of these additions are relatively minor and cluster around the few paragraphs describing Stephen's memories of Paris. Several of these additions strengthen parallels to both Homeric and Irish myths. Kevin Egan, for example, now tells the young poet "You're your father's son. I know the voice," a scene of recognition that both evokes Menelaus's meeting with Telemachus and captures the book's larger thematic concerns with paternity and filial recognition (*U* 3.229). Similarly, Joyce adds a few lines of dialogue in French between Egan and a waitress, who fails initially to understand that Stephen too is Irish (*U* 3.220–21). This question of national identity emerges as well in the short addition of the phrase "steeds of Mananaan" to describe the waves on the beach (*U* 3.56–57). This passage makes explicit Stephen's symbolic evocation of the mythic Irish hero Cuchulain, who, after accidentally murdering his son, took out his grief and rage by battling the waves until he was exhausted. Like the allusion to the *shan van vocht* in "Telemachus," in which the old woman who delivers milk becomes a figure of both Athena and the wandering Irish queen, this addition emphasizes Joyce's deliberate melding of Irish and Greek myth. The final significant revision of the periodical version is the addition of the sentence "His arm: Cranly's arm" in the middle of the passage on Wilde (*U* 3.451). This reference to Stephen's close friend from *Portrait* evokes that earlier book while also making explicit the young man's homoerotic anxieties—a theme that weaves its way through the rest of *Ulysses.*

EPISODE IV: CALYPSO

The first three episodes read like a continuation of *A Portrait of the Artist as a Young Man,* but this one comes from a very different place. In many ways it marks the start of *Ulysses* as a distinct project, a new departure for Joyce as he began to reach beyond the semiautobiographical character of Stephen. As a way of marking this change, the book essentially begins a second time, taking us back to eight in the morning, the same moment the novel began in episode I. Bloom's story begins, as Stephen's did, at home, and it details the familiar rituals of the morning: fetching the mail, doing some shopping, making breakfast, feeding the cat. There is little to suggest that anything particularly epic awaits him, and the episode retains from the previous chapters the "initial style" (as Joyce termed it), which swerves so effectively between everyday details and the central character's fluid thoughts (*LI* 129).

We know very little about the evolution of this episode. The earliest extant drafts are two fragmentary typescripts (Buffalo V.B.3.a and b) prepared in Zurich first in February and then later in the spring before Joyce sent a copy to Pound for publication in the *Little Review.* Although a fair copy dated to February 1918 is part of the Rosenbach Manuscript, Michael Groden demonstrates that it lies outside the main line of transmission (*UP* 208). The surviving typescripts were then used to introduce the first of what would become a growing set of additions to the episode across six levels of proofs completed between June and September 1921. These changes are complex, and almost all of them expand the length and richness of the work.

When Pound received the typescript for "Calypso" in 1918, he objected to its frank and detailed portrayal of Bloom relieving himself in the outhouse: "The contrast between Blooms [insert: interior] poetry and his outward surroundings is excellent," he writes, "but it will come up without such a detailed treatment of the dropping feces" (*Pound/Joyce* 131). So before he sent the episode to New York, Pound censored the passages he found objectionable, cutting all of one paragraph and parts of two others in which Joyce graphically describes Bloom's defecation. The annoyed Joyce retained them all for the Shakespeare and Company edition in 1922 and even expanded these same paragraphs, adding more graphic descriptions of smell, size, and sensation while embroidering them with new details and allusions.

It is beyond our purposes here to analyze each of Joyce's changes, but these key paragraphs illustrate his methods. The underlined passages are those Pound cut for the *Little Review,* while those in bold were added during the revision process in 1921.

> Deep voice that fellow Dlugacz has. Agendath what is it? Now, my miss. Enthusiast.
>
> He kicked open the **crazy** door of the jakes. Better be careful not to get these trousers dirty for the funeral. He went in, bowing his head under the low lintel. Leaving the door ajar, amid the stench of mouldy

> limewash and stale cobwebs he undid his braces. Before sitting down he peered through a chink up at the nextdoor windows. **The king was in his countinghouse.** Nobody.
>
> Asquat on the cuckstool he folded out his paper, turning its pages over on his bared knees. Something new and easy. **No great hurry. Keep it a bit.** Our prize titbit: *Matcham's Masterstroke.* Written by Mr Philip Beaufoy, Playgoers' Club, London. Payment at the rate of one guinea a column has been made to the writer. Three and a half. Three pounds three. Three pounds, thirteen and six.
>
> **Quietly he read, restraining himself, the first column and, yielding but resisting, began the second. Midway, his last resistance yielding,** he allowed his bowels to ease themselves quietly as he read, reading **still** patiently **that slight constipation of yesterday quite gone. Hope it's not too big bring on piles again. No, just right. So. Ah! Costive. One tabloid of cascara sagrada.** Life might be so. It did not move or touch him but it was something quick and neat. **Print anything now. Silly season.** He read on, **seated calm above his own rising smell.** Neat certainly. Matcham often thinks of the masterstroke by which he won the laughing witch who now. **Begins and ends morally.** Hand in hand. Smart. He glanced back through what he had read and, **while feeling his water flow quietly, he** envied kindly Mr Beaufoy who had written it and received payment of three pounds, thirteen and six. (*LRU* 62; *U* 4.491–505)

There is also this short but important passage, restored at the end, just before Bloom looks at his trousers:

> He tore away half the prize story sharply and wiped himself with it. Then he girded up his trousers, braced and buttoned himself. He pulled back the **jerky** shaky door of the jakes and came forth from the gloom into the air. (*U* 4.537–40)

As these additions and restorations suggest, when Joyce turned away from Stephen to begin writing about Bloom, the text itself began to expand in a variety of ways. The author was not only battling against the unexpected censorship by Pound, but also struggling to create a new kind of character, one embedded in a new web of reference and allusion. The number of changes here shows *Ulysses* emerging from its serial origin and mutating rapidly into something even more ambitious and complex.

EPISODE V: LOTUS EATERS

This episode continues to follow Bloom, who has now left his home on Eccles Street for the day and is passing the time walking about Dublin before he attends Paddy Dignam's funeral at eleven. The only surviving early draft material for the episode is the fair-copy version prepared in early 1918 (not part of the Rosenbach Manuscript). None of the typescripts generated from this copy, which Joyce sent to Pound, has been found, though we can surmise that the episode was drafted in the spring of 1917. Pound received the text from Joyce in late March or April 1918 and mailed it on April 23 to Margaret Anderson (*Pound/The Little Review* 212). It was published as a single installment in the July 1918 issue of the *Little Review.*

There are some small differences between the manuscript and the serial version, suggesting that Pound again decided to strike material he thought might lead to legal trouble for the magazine. The word "venereal" (*U* 5.72) was cut, as were the phrases "a stump of black gutta-percha wagging limp between their haunches" (*U* 5.218), "Has her monthlies [later changed to 'roses'] probably" (*U* 5.285) and "Where the bugger is it?" (*U* 5.527). More strikingly, the episode's final nineteen words were also cut (see below), shaving off all reference to Bloom's pubic area (*U* 5.570–72).

When Joyce turned to "Lotus Eaters" in the book manuscript, he retained the words previously cut by the magazine editors, as he did with "Calypso," and began a process of considerable expansion across eight levels of proofs and placards. He added 1,850 words to the 4,500 published in the *Little Review*—a growth of 41 percent. As usual, Joyce's changes were almost all additions, the vast majority occurring within Bloom's interior monologue. Accordingly, the external events recounted by Joyce's omniscient narrator in the *Little Review* version remain largely unchanged in the 1922 book edition, while the ideas in Bloom's head expand in range and complexity.

This growth of Bloom's interior monologue helps draw out the episode's lotus theme. Because his mental landscape consumes more of the narrative in the book version, Bloom seems more self-absorbed there, his ideas responding as often to his preceding thoughts as to external stimuli. (For a good example of this change, compare the opening paragraph in the two versions.) Moreover, adding more of Bloom's thoughts to the episode's unchanging time frame has the effect of slowing time down, which amplifies the episode's lethargic air. But the greatest increase in the episode's sleepy mood comes from Joyce adding numerous references to flowers and narcotics. Among the new phrases not found in the magazine version are: "His life isn't such a bed of roses" (*U* 5.8); "Cigar has a cooling effect. Narcotic" (5.272); "Prefer an ounce of opium" (5.327); "Good idea the Latin. Stupefies them" (5.350); "Blind faith. . . . Lulls all pain. Wake this time next year" (5.367–68); "Drugs age you after mental excitement. Lethargy then. Why? Reaction. A lifetime in a night" (5.474–75); "Overdose of laudanum. Sleeping draughts" (5.481).

Joyce's revisions also make the episode more cohesive. When he added, in 1921, a hundred-word meditation on the nature of confession to Bloom's thoughts within All Hallows Church, he helps us to relate what Bloom seeks from his secret correspondence with Martha, in the first half of the episode, to what church parishioners seek from the confessional, in the second half. Likewise, Joyce's restorations and additions to the episode's final paragraph draw it together around his schema (restorations are again underlined, additions marked in bold):

> Enjoy a bath now: clean trough of water, cool enamel, the gentle tepid stream. **This is my body.**
>
> He foresaw his pale body reclined in it at full, naked, **in a womb of warmth,** oiled by scented melting soap, softly laved. He saw his trunk and limbs riprippled over and sustained, buoyed lightly upward, lemonyellow: **his navel, bud of flesh: and** saw the dark tangled curls of his bush floating, floating hair of the stream around **the limp father of thousands,** a languid floating flower. (*LRU* 76; *U* 5.565–72)

Elements of the episode's schema—its scene (bath), organ (genitals: "limp father of thousands") and symbol (Eucharist: "This is my body")—are irreligiously wedded here, while the episode's technic (narcissism) presides over it all. Bloom, like Narcissus bending before his reflection, envisions himself in the water while thinking, moments earlier, that he will pleasure himself in the bath ("Also I think I. Yes I. Do it in the bath. Curious longing. Water to water. Combine business with pleasure"—*U* 5.503–5). Joyce's restorations and revisions also enhance the lotus theme by stretching out the paragraph and slowing it down: the third iteration of what Bloom saw in his bath nearly triples the length of the last sentence, which now weakly trails off with a resumptive modifier ("floating, floating") and an alliterative appositive ("father . . . flower"). Inducing lethargy with these appendages, Joyce appropriately depicts Bloom's limp penis as the lotus flower itself.

EPISODE VI: HADES

The sixth episode of *Ulysses* brings Bloom into the realm of the dead, where he wrestles with the tragedies of his own life. "Hades" shares a number of intertextual links with the last several stories Joyce composed for *Dubliners,* especially "Grace" and "The Dead." Thematically, both stories deal with questions of death, memory, and redemption, the latter closing with its protagonist seemingly carried away into a Hades-like realm "where dwell the vast hosts of the dead" (*Dubliners* 223). And almost the entire cast of characters from "Grace"—Martin Cunningham, Tom Kernan, and Jack Power—appear at Paddy Dignam's funeral. (In a deftly comic move, Joyce even has Bloom ask a reporter to list as a mourner the name of another character from "Grace," M'Coy, even though he doesn't actually attend the funeral.) In the process of revising the episode after its *Little Review* appearance, Joyce further strengthened these connections to *Dubliners* by adding references to the Gordon Bennett Cup (an auto race featured in "After the Race") and Ivy Day (a day of remembrance for Parnell), both of which are key settings in his first book.

This close set of connections to *Dubliners,* along with the story's setting at a funeral, suggests that "Hades" might have been the nucleus for the whole of *Ulysses.* From 1906 to 1907, Joyce lived and worked in Rome, a city he found obsessed with its own decaying past, memorably comparing it to "a man who lives by exhibiting to travelers his grandmother's corpse" (*LII* 165). In September 1906, having just finished "Grace," he wrote to his brother Stanislaus that he was planning a new companion story entitled "Ulysses," based on the experiences of a real Dubliner named Alfred H. Hunter, who was suspected of being Jewish and whose wife was rumored to be cheating on him. In *James Joyce and the Beginnings of "Ulysses,"* Rodney Owen argues that the early plan for this story involved Hunter attending the funeral of Matthew Kane, himself the actual Dubliner on whom Martin Cunningham is based. The main character might then have gone to a pub and been taunted. It appears that Joyce never actually drafted this story, writing in 1907 that it "never got any forrader than the title" (*LII* 209). That title, however, did remain, and in 1920, as the book neared completion, he wrote to Carlo Linati of its genesis in Rome: "Imagine, fifteen years ago I started writing it as a story for *Dubliners!*" (*LI* 146).

Despite this long gestation, none of the early drafts for "Hades" has yet been found. It likely first took shape as an episode between 1912 and 1914, along with pieces of what would become "Proteus" and "Lotus Eaters." By June 1917,

Joyce had completed an initial draft, though it wasn't typed until May 18 of the following year. This typescript for the *Little Review* reached Pound at the end of July. A partial copy of this typescript has survived, which Joyce then used when he began revising the episode. A collateral fair copy dating to the spring of 1918 survives as part of the Rosenbach Manuscript. "Hades" appeared first in the September 1918 issue of the *Little Review* and was later split into two installments for publication in the July and September 1919 issues of the *Egoist* as part of the aborted attempt to serialize the book simultaneously in the United States and Great Britain.

When Joyce prepared the episode for its 1922 publication, he added approximately 2,500 words or nearly 30 percent of its original length. The surviving typescript contains many of these changes in Joyce's hand, and many more appear across six levels of the placards as well. The substantive themes, characters, and events of the magazine version remain essentially intact; most of the changes involve filling out details or suturing the episode into the larger symbolic and thematic structures of the book. For example, ten new instances of the word "heart"—the organ associated with "Hades" in the schema—are added, many of them emphasizing a connection to death. The description of Cunningham's wife that initially concludes "wear out a man's heart" (*LRU* 85) was expanded to include a larger meditation on the suicide of Bloom's father and fears about the undead: "They have no mercy on that here or infanticide. Refuse christian burial. They used to drive a stake of wood through his heart in the grave. As if it wasn't broken already" (*U* 6.345–48).

Other patterns are woven into the text as well. Joyce strengthens the connection between "Hades" and "Proteus," for example, by having Bloom's thoughts strangely evoke the things Stephen sees on the tidal flats, including "slime, mudchoked bottles, carrion dogs" (*U* 6.444). Similarly, just as the younger man sat thinking about the drowned body being eaten by the fish in Dublin Bay, in the expanded version Bloom thinks, "Drowning they say is the pleasantest. See your whole life in a flash" (*U* 6.988). The book's major themes also expand, including Dublin's inhospitable anti-Semitism, which Bloom now explicitly names "hate at first sight" (*U* 6.1012). These revisions reach out to entangle the larger fictional double of Dublin that Joyce created in his earlier books. In addition to new references to stories from *Dubliners,* Bloom briefly mentions Dante Riordan, the character who sets off a bruising fight over Parnell and religion in *A Portrait of the Artist as a Young Man.*

Finally, as in many of the other episodes, Joyce restored a number of explicit references to the body and more specifically to sexuality that would never have made it past the American censors. In the manuscript and 1922 versions, for example, Bloom remembers Molly growing aroused while "watching the two dogs at it by the wall" and a "sergeant ['warder' in the manuscript] grinning up," and he wonders whether this might have somehow contributed to Rudy's death (*U* 6.78–79). Throughout the episode, women are more generally connected not just to sex, but also to death in added references to their traditional role in washing and laying out corpses. As a result, the 1922 "Hades" is a considerably richer text, its possible role as the origin of *Ulysses* reinforced as Joyce integrated it into a much more complex narrative and symbolic structure.

EPISODE VII: AEOLUS

For any student of *Ulysses* as a work in progress, this is a crucial episode, since, as Michael Groden demonstrates so thoroughly in *"Ulysses" in Progress,* it is here that Joyce dramatically altered his compositional method during the process of revision. As a result, the differences between the versions published in 1918 and 1922 are significant and immediately obvious. For readers of the book version, this departure from the first six episodes is evident in the first line, set in capital letters without attribution, quotation, or context: "IN THE HEART OF THE HIBERNIAN METROPOLIS" (*U* 7.1–2). There follows a more familiar narrative voice in the initial style, though it no longer focuses on either Bloom or Stephen. Instead, we find a description of the busy tramlines that cross at Nelson's Pillar in the city's center. This makes those first bold lines seem something like newspaper headlines or photo captions, and though these oversized text blocks are generally descriptive in the episode's opening pages, they become increasingly satiric as it progresses. They also present a real challenge to readers, since they are attributed neither to a character nor to the narrative voice. David Hayman argues that they belong instead to an agent he calls "the arranger," which he describes as "something between a persona and a function, . . . an unstated but inescapable source of control" (*"Ulysses": The Mechanics of Meaning* 122–23). Put another way, style itself seems to become a character in this episode, intervening in what had been until now a naturalistic novel layered with streams of consciousness. In an episode named after the god of wind, readers find themselves blown abruptly off course and onto a new kind of adventure.

For readers of the *Little Review,* however, this change of course did not occur, since the headlines and the intrusion into the initial style that they mark did not appear in the magazine. These were later additions, and so we see in this version of "Aeolus" a *Ulysses* still stylistically consistent with the first six episodes. We begin, as we have begun before, within Bloom's mind as he observes "dullthudding" (misprinted as "dullhudding") barrels of porter, watches printing presses at work, and sets about negotiating over an advertisement in the one real piece of business he pursues over the course of the day (*LRU* 101). In the middle of the episode, an important pivot occurs as Bloom leaves the newspaper office just before Stephen enters, marking their second near miss of the day. At this point, the narrative returns to its pattern from the first three episodes, recording events and dipping frequently into Stephen's stream of consciousness. Rather than the radical departure announced by the headlines in the book, the magazine version of the episode continues a much more familiar pattern, though it now alternates even more quickly between the two central figures.

Joyce composed this episode in Zurich in 1918, finishing it in August and sending a typescript to Pound, who forwarded it to Margaret Anderson for the October issue of the *Little Review.* None of the early drafts predating the preparation of the fair-copy Rosenbach Manuscript has survived. A copy of the typescript has been preserved (Buffalo V.B.5), and it contains numerous corrections and additions that did not appear in the *Little Review.* These include the addition of several rhetorical devices (such as the chiasmus that restructures the first two sentences of the magazine version), but not the capitalized passages suggestive of headlines. These were composed in June or July 1921 and sent to the printer, who prepared six different placards and page proofs. Joyce added the subheads on the first placards, which were prepared in early August. The headlines then underwent multiple changes on subsequent proofs before they reached their final form in the 1922 edition (Groden, *UP* 105–8).

In newspapers, headlines are editorial intrusions that label and shape the material following them. In "Aeolus," the headlines imitate and exaggerate this practice to the point of parody, and they make us aware of an authorial presence that regards the characters and events through many different textual lenses. There are other sorts of changes as well. Take, for example, this small revision (with the added or corrected material in bold type):

> —He's pretty well on, **professor MacHugh** said in a low voice.
> —Seems to be, J. J. O'Molloy said, taking out a **cigarettecase in mur-**

muring meditation, but it is not always as it seems. Who has the most matches? (*LRU* 110; *U* 7.461–63)

Joyce's revision does not change the sense of this trivial bit of conversation (though it becomes clearer when the comma that had appeared between "professor" and "MacHugh" in the *Little Review* is made to follow "well on" instead), but it mentions a particular mode of oral discourse—"murmuring meditation"—using an expression that is also, of course, an instance of alliteration, and adds a verbal cliché—"not always as it seems"—in order to direct the reader's attention to language itself and the ways in which people speak and think it. Joyce seems to have considered all sorts of linguistic habits and tricks "rhetoric" for the purposes of revising this episode. The aims of *Ulysses* are visibly moving here beyond a novelistic interest in characters and events, and toward a distinctly modernist concern with the medium, as well as a particularly Joycean concern with the way people use and abuse language.

In revising this episode, Joyce expanded it from around 8,000 words to 10,000; his additions came in the form of the new pseudo-headlines and small changes like the one illustrated above. Many larger changes took place as well, such as this one (with revisions and additions in bold type), which developed in six stages:

HOW A GREAT DAILY ORGAN IS TURNED OUT

Mr Bloom halted behind the foreman's spare body, admiring **a** glossy crown.

Strange he never saw his real country. Ireland my country. Member for College green. He **boomed** that workaday worker tack for all it was worth. **It's the ads and side features sell a weekly, not the stale news in the official gazette. Queen Anne is dead. Published by authority in the year one thousand and. Demesne situate in the townland of Rosenallis, barony of Tinnahinch. To all whom it may concern schedule pursuant to statute showing return of number of mules and jennets exported from Ballina. Nature notes. Cartoons. Phil Blake's weekly Pat and Bull story. Uncle Toby's page for tiny tots. Country bumpkin's queries. Dear Mr Editor, what is a good cure for flatulence? I'd like that part. Learn a lot teaching others. The personal note. M. A. P. Mainly all pictures. Shapely bathers on golden strand. World's biggest balloon. Double marriage of sisters celebrated. Two**

bridegrooms laughing heartily at each other. Cuprani too, printer. More Irish than the Irish. (*LRU* 102; *U* 7.85–100)

The major change in this passage is the addition of the long section in which we follow Bloom's thoughts, both personal and professional. Numerous passages like this one enrich our sense of Bloom, who reveals here an acute sense of business and a sympathetic awareness of other human beings. The *Little Review* version is easier to follow, but the expanded version is richer and funnier, as when Bloom's interest in "flatulence" is noted.

EPISODE VIII: LESTRYGONIANS

After alternating between Stephen and Bloom, the narrative focus here returns to the older man, who increasingly becomes the book's central character. At just under 10,000 words, "Lestrygonians" was the longest episode of *Ulysses* yet to appear in the *Little Review,* and it was the first to be divided into two or more sections, published in the January and February–March 1919 issues. It is possible that Joyce had difficulty completing the episode in time to meet the magazine's publication schedule, since an unexplained two-month break in the serialization occurs between episode VII, published in October 1918, and episode VIII in January. We know from Joyce that he sent his typescripts of the episode to Pound on October 25 (*LI* 120), and that Pound sent the "eighth bundle of Joyce" to Anderson on November 4 (*Pound/The Little Review* 256). That was, of course, too late for it to appear in the November issue, though a notice at the end of that issue announced, misleadingly, that "James Joyce's 'Ulysses' will be continued in the next number" (*LR* 5.7: 64). No drafts of "Lestrygonians" have so far been found, and according to Groden, the fair-copy Rosenbach Manuscript was likely a collateral copy prepared from another working draft (*UP* 118). A copy of the typescript for the episode sent to Pound does exist (Buffalo V.B.6), but it includes hundreds of marginal additions and revisions, meaning this is a copy that Joyce retained and used to prepare the book version in 1921. Many more changes were then introduced across seven levels of proofs in preparation for the 1922 Shakespeare and Company edition.

Besides being the first episode to miss its serialization deadline, "Lestrygonians" —which details Bloom's hunger after 1 P.M. and revolves about the themes of food, eating, digestion, and excretion—was the first episode (of four) to run afoul of the law. According to Clive Driver, Pound had performed some preemptive censoring before sending the episode to Anderson, notably deleting the phrase "men's beery piss" from the typescript (Bibliographical preface, 20). But after the subscription copies were mailed, the January issue was nonetheless confiscated; the offending section, according to Driver, was Bloom's sexually charged memory of Molly on Howth (21). A postal official wrote to his superior that the "creature who writes this Ulysses stuff should be put under a glass jar for examination" (Vanderham 28). The seized copies were burned, and the post office notified Anderson that it would block any further mailing of the issue (Ellmann 502; Driver 21).

The episode's increased length may relate, in part, to Joyce's developing use of interior monologue—which we may test by comparing "Lestrygonians" to "Lotus Eaters," the previous episode that focused exclusively on Bloom. In episode V, the narrative closely follows Bloom's perspective, yet most of the paragraphs are triggered by external events correlated with his physical passage through Dublin. By contrast, in "Lestrygonians" the number of paragraphs that originate inside Bloom's head dramatically increases, and there are several passages (such as Bloom's recollection of Chamberlain's visit to Dublin) in which a long series of paragraphs follow Bloom's thinking without establishing any clear reference to the world immediately about him. During these stretches, the external world gives way to the shifting landscape of Bloom's mind, and readers discover that they can no longer rely on Joyce's paragraph breaks to chart the character's location or signal the narrative's move in or out of his swelling consciousness.

With this expansion of Bloom's subjectivity, episode VIII in the *Little Review* looks ahead to the additions Joyce would make to "Lotus Eaters" in 1921, which suggests that he may have already decided to expand Bloom's interior monologue in the fall of 1918. Even so, when Joyce revised episode VIII for book publication, he managed to increase it by 2,700 words—the vast majority of these additions made to Bloom's interior monologue. The book version of "Lestrygonians" is thus 28 percent longer than its *Little Review* counterpart, and an episode that was already dense with interior monologue became denser. One notable example: in the 1922 book edition, Joyce takes the three-word paragraph "Poor Mrs Purefoy!" from the magazine version and expands it, on both sides, by 220 more words, introducing Bloom's reflections on a new character, Mrs. Dandrade, and expanding his thoughts about Mrs. Purefoy and her family (*LRU* 132; *U* 8.358–67). While these additions further weaken our grasp on the present moment in episode VIII, they strengthen the network of intratextual correspondences in the book by linking "Lestrygonians" to "Oxen of the Sun" (in which Bloom visits Mrs. Purefoy at the birthing hospital) and "Circe" (in which Mrs. Dandrade has a walk-on role).

Finally, Joyce's additions to Bloom's interior monologue allow him to reinforce the episode's thematic concerns with cannibalism, digestion, and of course food: "Good Lord, that poor child's dress is in flitters. Underfed she looks too. **Potatoes and marge, marge and potatoes.** It's after they feel it. **Proof of the pudding.** Undermines the constitution" (*LRU* 125; *U* 8.41–43). As this passage suggests, Joyce had some fun with these additions, folding in conventional phrases and puns that involve food in surprising ways: "Lucky I had the presence of mind to dive into Manning's **or I was souped**" (*LRU* 133; *U* 8.425–26); "**Drop him like a hot potato**" (*U* 8.444–45); "Pyramids in sand. **Built on bread and onions**" (*LRU* 135; *U* 8.489–90); "**Sandwich? Ham and his descendants musterred and bred there**" (*U* 8.741–42).

EPISODE IX: SCYLLA AND CHARYBDIS

Unlike many of the earlier episodes, which follow characters on their convoluted paths through the city, the scene in "Scylla and Charybdis" remains largely fixed in a single place: the National Library of Ireland, where Stephen is locked in conversation with some of Dublin's leading intellectuals. Despite its static setting, a sense of restlessness pervades the chapter. Here, for the first time in the magazine, hints of a new kind of stylistic experiment emerge as the initial style of *Ulysses* is suddenly, visibly interrupted by a musical score, dramatic dialogue, and disorienting wordplay (*LRU* 166, *LRU* 176). Although these new elements anticipate later changes in the narrative, the episode also looks backward. Indeed, parts of "Scylla and Charybdis" echo in theme and content not just the opening three episodes of *Ulysses* but the later chapters of *A Portrait of the Artist as a Young Man* as well. Even the theory of *Hamlet* that Stephen proposes in the library looks back: to "Telemachus," where it was first evoked, but also to the Renaissance, to a foundational English writer, and to questions about paternity, inheritance, and the burdens imposed by the past. It is as if both Stephen and the book are frozen in time and space as the young man struggles to escape a history he has already described as a "nightmare." Batting around obscure scholarly references, he clings desperately to "the now, the here, through which all future plunges to the past" (*LRU* 155). This feeling of paralysis grows more intense when we learn, near the chapter's end, that Stephen claims not to believe the theory of *Hamlet* he elaborates. Joyce here seems finished not only with Stephen, but also with his initial plan for the novel as a blend of naturalism and stream of consciousness. It should thus come as no surprise that on the manuscript draft, finished on the last day of 1918, Joyce boldly wrote "End of First Part of *Ulysses.*"

Like the other episodes that focus closely on Stephen, this one has its roots in Joyce's earlier work on *Stephen Hero* and *Portrait.* This chapter, in particular, shares a clear affinity with the densely argued aesthetic theory Stephen unwinds in the latter book, right down to the evocation of his friend Cranly—Stephen's chief interlocutor in those earlier novels, who, though mentioned occasionally, does not otherwise appear in *Ulysses.* We know more about the history of "Scylla and Charybdis" than many of the other early episodes and can trace its development from a series of lectures in 1912, through a draft spread across three copybooks in 1918, a collateral fair copy, the typescript prepared for the *Little Review,* subsequent manuscript additions and revisions to the typescript, and finally to seven levels of page proofs.

In his letters, Joyce persistently referred to this as the "Shakespeare" or "Library" episode, and it was likely one of the earliest pieces of the book that he conceived. Like "Telemachus," it might have been planned as part of *Portrait,* especially since, as Luca Crispi has discovered, it draws on entries from the same "Alphabetical Notebook" (Cornell MS 25) that Joyce used when writing that earlier book ("First Foray"). In 1912 and 1913, Joyce delivered a series of twelve public lectures on *Hamlet* at the Università Popolare in Trieste, where he and his family were then living. Although the text of these evening talks has not survived, we have a notebook and several manuscript pages from 1912. These contain notes about Shakespeare's life as well as transcriptions from scholarly and critical sources, many of them keyed to individual passages in the play. (For a full transcription of these notebooks, see Quillian, "Shakespeare in Trieste.") Joyce then returned to Shakespeare and *Hamlet* sometime around 1916, when he began a notebook with the title "Shakespeare Dates" on the cover (Buffalo Notebook V.A.4). It contains a list of major events in the dramatist's life, arranged chronologically, each page dedicated to a particular year. By no means a draft, it nevertheless suggests that Joyce was beginning work in earnest on what would become "Scylla and Charybdis," and it is possible that he completed a draft around this time.

About a year later, in April 1917, Joyce wrote in response to Pound's inquiry about new material that only the "Hamlet chapter" was ready (*LI* 101). The first complete draft we now have dates to the summer of 1918 (NLI MSS 36,639/08/A–C), though an earlier, more fragmentary version was identified as part of an auction in 1948 but was subsequently lost (see Slocum and Cahoon, *Bibliography of James Joyce*). The next extant version is the Rosenbach Manuscript, which was completed in late 1918; across its final page Joyce wrote "New Year's Eve 1918" and "End of First Part of 'Ulysses.'" Two carbon typescripts, likely prepared from another fair copy, were sent to Pound at approximately the same time, and the episode appeared in the April and May 1919 issues of the *Little Review.* Crispi notes, however, that there are differences between the Rosenbach and the typescripts, which means that neither the magazine version nor the book version derives directly from this manuscript version ("First Foray").

As was his habit, Joyce made several additions to this initial published version when preparing for the 1922 Shakespeare and Company edition. Many of these took place on the carbons that had been prepared for the *Egoist* and the *Little Review.* Compared to the extensive emendations made to many of the other surrounding episodes, however, the changes were relatively slight, amounting to fewer than 1,000 words in a chapter of around 11,000 total. Thus there is significant continuity between the magazine and book versions. Most of Joyce's additions to the typescripts and placards appear to reinforce the book's major themes and to emphasize the monstrous dialectic between Aristotle and Plato. The early passage on the link between idealist philosophy and Catholic mysticism ("Formless spiritual. Father, Son and Holy Breath"—*LRU* 154), for example, assumes a much clearer shape with this addition: "Allfather, the heavenly man. Hiesos Kristos, magician of the beautiful, the Logos who suffers in us at every moment" (*U* 9.61–63). Additional passages on Aristotle's materialism are included, such as this one, which links an apocryphal story about the philosopher freeing his slaves to King Charles II's dying concern about his mistress:

> —Antiquity mentions that Stagyrite schoolurchin and bald heathen sage [Aristotle], Stephen said, who when dying in exile frees and endows his slaves, pays tribute to his elders, wills to be laid in earth near the bones of his dead wife and bids his friends be kind to an old mistress (don't forget Nell Gwynn Herpyllis) and let her live in his villa. (*U* 9.720–25)

This addition forms part of a larger constellation of revisions that draw out the book's overarching themes of marriage, fidelity, family, and inheritance. The

Blooms' unconventional marriage, for example, is evoked by the theory that Ann Hathaway made a cuckold of Shakespeare as well as by the addition of passages that imagine the poet caught "between conjugal love and its chaste delights and scortatory love and its foul pleasures" (*U* 9.631–32). Bloom's refusal to resort to anger or violence in response to Molly's affair is similarly emphasized in Joyce's revisions by several allusions to the opera *Carmen,* in which a jealous man murders his lover.

EPISODE X: WANDERING ROCKS

The changes to narrative form and structure anticipated by the musical score and microdrama in "Scylla and Charybdis" emerge forcefully in the tenth episode, which consists of nineteen sections that give us glimpses of Dubliners about town between three and four in the afternoon. Joyce's schema calls this episode "Wandering Rocks," and he wrote it with a map of Dublin and a watch to ensure its accurate organization of space and time (Budgen 122–23). For the first time, we learn with certainty the precise date of the book's events, as a typewriter hammers it onto the page for us to read: "—16 June 1904" (*LRU* 195). With Stephen and Bloom reduced in the episode to just two of the many characters whom Joyce tracks, we realize that the city of Dublin has itself become a major character in the narrative, its citizens, streets, businesses, and advertisements taking on lives of their own, which radiate well beyond the horizon of Homer's epic or the novelistic story of Bloom, Stephen, and Molly. To accommodate this shift, Joyce developed a new style, one that depends on juxtaposition rather than continuity, simultaneity rather than development. The streams of consciousness that once flowed so freely are replaced by jagged perceptual shards, roughly sutured together on the page in patterns that resemble painterly cubism or cinematic montage. Here the book insists, at least temporarily, on the initial narrowness of its own vision and on the novel's inability to capture the breadth of human experience when it remains tied to questions of psychology and development. Put another way, *Ulysses* pauses in episode X to remind its readers that Stephen and Bloom are but two of many travelers through Dublin on this day and that many other odysseys are unfolding around them: voyages and struggles that the book can fleetingly acknowledge even if it elects not to follow them.

This decisive shift in *Ulysses* is plainly evident in the *Little Review.* "For the first time," Michael Groden argues, "a voice distinct from that of the characters or of the narrator clearly announces himself through both the new monologue subjects and the interpolations" (*UP* 38–39). In the magazine version, there were no headlines in "Aeolus" to anticipate this departure. Neither the Gilbert nor the Linati schema had yet been created at this point, so there was no catalogue of technics that might have helped distinguish subtly between the different narrative styles of the first nine episodes. "Wandering Rocks" thus appears in the magazine as something fundamentally new.

As late as May 1918, Joyce likely did not intend to include "Wandering Rocks" in the novel, since he described to Harriet Shaw Weaver a plan for book publication that lists only seventeen episodes: "If the Little Review continues to publish [*Ulysses*] regularly he [the American publisher B. W. Huebsch] may publish as a cheap paperbound book the *Telemachia,* that is, the first three episodes—under the title *Ulysses* I. . . . The second part, the *Odyssey,* contains eleven episodes. The third part, *Nostos,* contains three episodes" (*LI* 113). Based on this letter, Groden concludes that "Wandering Rocks" was thus the last piece of *Ulysses* that Joyce conceived (*UP* 33). No drafts of the episode have so far been found, and the earliest version extant is a fair copy written during the first two months of 1919. This copy, now part of the Rosenbach Manuscript, was written in two different hands, since Joyce suffered an eye attack during the drafting, prompting him to dictate the final seventeen pages to Budgen. A typescript was prepared in February, two copies of which still survive. The first (Buffalo V.B.8.b) contains a series of small corrections that Joyce made after its initial preparation. The second (Buffalo V.B.8.a) contains the original corrections as well as numerous additions made in 1921. This latter document was used to create the 1922 edition, which passed through seven levels of proofs and placards.

In his revisions to the serialized version of this episode, Joyce added about twelve hundred words, mostly in very short sections, making no drastic changes in tone or structure. Groden describes "Wandering Rocks" as the first episode in Joyce's "middle stage" of composing *Ulysses:* Joyce here extends the processes of narration used in the early chapters but does not radically alter them, as he does in the "last stage" (*UP* 52). As it happens, the *Little Review* version of *Ulysses* ends as the late stage begins. But Joyce came back to the middle-stage episodes and inserted material in preparation for the later chapters, introducing, for example, the dancing professor Maginni in his revision of the first section of "Wandering Rocks," to anticipate his appearance later in the "Circe" episode. He also added this passage about Gerty McDowell to the lengthy final section describing the viceroy's cavalcade: "Passing by Roger Greene's office and Dollard's big red printinghouse Gerty MacDowell, carrying the Castesby's cork lino letters for her father who was laid up, knew by the style it was the lord and lady lieutenant but she couldn't see what her Excellency had on because the tram and Spring's big yellow furniture van had to stop in front of her on account of its being the lord lieutenant" (*U* 10.1205–11). The rhythm and syntax of the passage clearly echo Gerty's interior monologue from the later "Nausicaa" episode. She plays a key role there—a role that eventually led the editors of the *Little Review* into criminal court and concluded with an American ban on the publication of *Ulysses*.

EPISODE XI: SIRENS

Throughout the day, Leopold Bloom has dreaded the approach of four o'clock, when he knows his wife will meet Boylan and likely consummate their affair. In episode XI, that time finally arrives. But Joyce does something surprising to mark the event: he brings both Bloom and Boylan to the Ormond Hotel, along with a host of lesser characters who have previously appeared in the book, and then sets their words, thoughts, and movements to music. In an impromptu concert in the bar, Simon Dedalus and Ben Dollard perform songs, and Joyce himself translates his writing into musical form: he uses musical devices in his prose, structures the episode's narrative around the formal features of a fugue, and prefaces it all with an overture that introduces readers to excerpts from the ensuing text.

In a letter to Harriet Shaw Weaver about "Sirens," Joyce says that he wrote the episode in five months, presumably between February and June 1919 (*LI* 128). But with the subsequent emergence of two early partial drafts of "Sirens" (NLI MS 36, 639/07/B and 36,639/09), we now know that Joyce began the episode as early as January 1918, and possibly earlier; therefore, it appears to be "one of the earliest episodes of *Ulysses* Joyce wrote" (Crispi, "First Foray"). In his account of these new manuscript materials, Michael Groden notes that Joyce first wrote "Sirens" straight and only later imposed his stylistic and musical innovations upon it ("National Library," 41); as Daniel Ferrer describes it, Joyce's "fugal idea is not consubstantial with the episode but a second thought" that was imposed at a later stage of composition ("What Song," 62). In the earliest draft, Bloom is wholly absent from the first half of the episode, which suggests that Joyce may have intended to present the scene in the bar first and then focus on Bloom separately, using for "Sirens" the structure that he eventually adopted for "Nausicaa" (58, 60). By the time Joyce wrote the second draft, in 1919, he had not only folded Bloom into the first half of the episode but also incorporated its characteristic musical structure. Ferrer surmises that the fugue's contrapuntal structure offered Joyce a way to integrate the episode and represent Bloom (and a multitude of other voices) in both halves (62).

Neither draft includes the episode's overture, but the second one confirms Joyce's musical intentions for "Sirens": on the inside front cover, Joyce jotted (in Italian) a list of eight musical terms that bears out the eight-part fugal structure he mentioned to Weaver (Groden, "National Library," 43-44; Brown, "Mystery of the Fuga"). As Susan Brown has persuasively argued, Joyce likely copied these terms from the entry for "Fugue" written by Ralph Vaughan Williams for the 1906 edition of *Grove's Dictionary of Music and Musicians.* One can still debate whether and how Joyce structured "Sirens" around eight different sections (which are not, by any means, the typical structure of a fugue), but we do know now that Joyce was thinking of these terms when he imposed his musical superstructure on the episode.

Neither Pound nor Weaver, the first two readers of "Sirens," much liked it, which depressed Joyce, since he feared that he had lost the confidence of his two strongest supporters. Weaver felt the episode was not up to his usual high standard, and Pound—writing to Joyce shortly after receiving the typescript—found the opening pages perplexing, objected that the episode was too long, feared that readers would be alienated, complained about the novel's constantly shifting styles, and reiterated his dismay at Joyce's preoccupation with excretion: "You have once again gone 'down where the asparagus grows' and gone down as far as the lector most bloody benevolens can be expected to respire" (*Pound/Joyce* 160, 157–59). Pound did not make any edits before forwarding the text to Anderson, but he did encourage Joyce to take the time (even if it meant missing his serialization deadline) to clarify the opening pages with "a few sign posts" and to prevent Bloom's explosive fart from appearing as "the climax of the chapter," by either suppressing it or moving it to the start of the next episode (157–59).

Joyce did not follow Pound's advice for revising "Sirens," but when he returned to it in 1921 he added just under 700 words—a relatively minor revision by his standards. Most of these additions expand Bloom's interior monologue, though about a third occur within the omniscient narration. A number of Joyce's edits accentuate the episode's musical theme: the phrase "they all three" from the *Little Review* version becomes "all trio" in the book, and "her hair uncombed" becomes "her wavyavyeavyheavyeavyevyevyhair un comb:'d" (*U* 11.808–9), which Stuart Gilbert identifies as an instance of *trillando* (*Joyce's Ulysses* 254). Joyce also adds such allusions to music as "paying the piper," "still harping on his daughter," "play on her heartstrings," and "a blade of grass, shell of her hands, then blow" (*U* 11.615–16, 644, 714, 1237). There is also more aural wordplay: "lovesoft word" becomes "lovesoft oftloved word," and Boylan's first name and eye color appear now fused in "Blazure's skyblue bow and eyes" (*U* 11.680, 394). Bloom's name is also subjected to more variations: "Bloom went by" becomes "Bloowho went by," and "Bloom's dark eye" becomes "Bloowhose dark eye," the declarative sentence in both instances mutating into a noun and relative clause (*U* 11.86, 149). This verbal pun both pokes fun at Bloom's sadness (boo-hoo) and sets up other sound associations that Joyce exploits: "Bloom sighed on the silent bluehued flowers" and "Blmstup. O'er ryehigh blue," which is a further variation on the song title "When the Bloom Is on the Rye" (*U* 11.457–58, 1126). Despite these later changes, Joyce's primary structural and technical innovations in "Sirens" were essentially fixed when the episode appeared in the August and September 1919 issues of the *Little Review.*

EPISODE XII: CYCLOPS

Something unsettling happens in the twelfth episode of *Ulysses:* an entirely new voice takes command of the story, one that belongs neither to the central characters nor to the increasingly active narrative voice that orchestrated "Sirens" and "Wandering Rocks." Instead, we listen to a new, unnamed narrator: a barfly who relates with considerable panache the story of an encounter between Bloom and an Irish nationalist referred to only as "the citizen," which took place earlier in the day at Barney Kiernan's pub. Adding to the disorientation, this retrospective tale is itself interleaved with another, often jarring voice that fractures the story with a series of passages Joyce's schema for the chapter calls "gigantism." These interruptions, which critics call interpolations, take a variety of forms, ranging from the detailed legal language of a contract to comically inflated lists. These sections have no direct bearing on the story itself, and the characters remain unaware of their existence, despite the fact that their words or actions often trigger them.

With "Cyclops," then, the book reaches a state of narrative fragmentation

—one previously glimpsed only in "Wandering Rocks"—that transforms the meaning and trajectory of *Ulysses* as a whole. The mutating style again becomes an active character, vying with Bloom, Stephen, and Molly for the reader's attention. The "gigantism" of the twelfth chapter soon after gives way to the magazine-inflected voice of Gerty MacDowell in "Nausicaa," to the anthology of prose styles that ranges across "Oxen of the Sun," and, in the 1922 book edition, to the dramatic form of "Circe," in which once again fantastic events occur without the characters noticing. Joyce, in short, moves definitively away from the traditional shape and constraints of the novel into entirely new territory. This shift in *Ulysses* mirrored the *Little Review*'s growing interest in avant-garde experiments, which drew the attention of American censors, leading to the partial suppression of "Cyclops" and growing financial difficulties for Anderson and Heap's magazine.

Several note sheets for "Cyclops" as well as two complete copybooks with lengthy drafts (Buffalo Notebooks V.A.8 and V.A.6; NLI MS 36,639/10) have survived, as has the fair-copy Rosenbach Manuscript, the typescript prepared for the *Little Review,* and several page proofs prepared for the 1922 Shakespeare and Company edition. We thus have an unusually large record of Joyce's work on this episode, beginning with his earliest notes. In "*Ulysses" in Progress,* Groden analyzes these materials, noting that Joyce began by first drafting several of the interpolated parody sections in June 1919 (*UP* 116–18). There is little narrative in these first manuscripts, and the names of individual characters rarely appear. Instead, much of the writing focuses on passages like the one that describes Barney Kiernan's pub in mock-heroic style and begins "In Inisfail the fair there lies a land, the land of holy Michan" (*LRU* 256). The small pieces of narrative that Joyce does initially supply are inconsistent, and though in the final version the parodies don't seem to intrude on the events of the story itself, in the draft this boundary is much more indistinct. As Groden notes, even the lines of dialogue prove mutable. In one of the drafts (Buffalo Notebook V.A.6), for example, Stephen is among those gathered in the pub, and he utters an anti-Semitic remark (later attributed to J. J. O'Molloy) in response to John Wyse Noland's question "why can't a jew love his country like the next fellow?" (*LRU* 291). Joyce eventually decided to remove Stephen from the episode entirely, delaying his meeting with Bloom to "Oxen of the Sun" and mitigating any antagonism between them. Stephen's anti-Semitism, furthermore, is deferred, making the song he later sings about a Jew cutting off a child's head all the more shocking when it appears in "Ithaca."

The instability of these early drafts and their emphasis on stylistic experiment at the expense of narrative continuity make it clear that Joyce had reached a turning point. In these copybooks, Groden argues, Joyce "stopped writing one kind of book, basically concerned with Stephen and Bloom, and began to write another, in which a succession of parody styles, and eventually a group of schematic correspondences, began to take over" (*UP* 126). In fact, "Cyclops" becomes a launching point for the rest of *Ulysses,* since the parodies are models for the more daunting array of technics that will follow. Having decided on this turn, Joyce began to work quickly, completing his drafts in September. A typescript was then prepared, to which Joyce made a few minor additions before sending it to Pound for publication in the *Little Review.* It appeared in four installments from November 1919 to March 1920.

Joyce's new conception of *Ulysses,* which Karen Lawrence calls "an odyssey of style," profoundly shaped the revisions he made to "Cyclops" for the 1922 book publication. He expanded the parody sections considerably, making the episode one of the most heavily revised of all the book's chapters. Working from the typescript (a copy of which was sent to the *Little Review*), Joyce introduced well over 150 changes, almost all of them additive. As the French printer in Dijon prepared page proofs and sent them to Paris, new additions and revisions appeared. In the end, Joyce made changes to eight of the nine proof sheets he received, each time expanding the text and requiring the episode's pages to be continually reset.

This expensive and labor-intensive process constituted a "gigantism" of its own and became an essential part of the book's larger composition process. The list of heroes attending the citizen (*LRU* 258), for example, grows from twelve to eighty and becomes comically absurd. The list of exclusively Irish names such as Cuchulin and Brian of Kincara that appears in the *Little Review* was expanded to include Shakespeare, Gutenberg, Benjamin Franklin, and "The Man that Broke the Bank at Monte Carlo" (*U* 12.185–86). Other kinds of lists and catalogues were expanded too, in a manner that points forward to the encyclopedic entries in "Ithaca." These include the roll of Irish industries that the citizen enumerates (*U* 12.1241–56), the punning register of wedding guests (e.g., "Miss Gladys Beech"—*U* 12.1267–98), and the collection of saints attending the citizen's invocation of Saint Patrick (*U* 12.1679–1712). Entirely new sections were added as well. The account of the hanging, for example, was almost doubled in length, becoming the longest interpolation in the episode (*U* 12.525–678); and Joyce added the description of "the muchtreasured and intricately embroidered ancient Irish facecloth" that appears after the citizen spits disdainfully in response to Bloom calling himself Irish (*U* 12.1438–64).

These changes made the version of "Cyclops" that appeared in 1922 substantially different from the one that first appeared in the *Little Review,* as well as 28 percent longer, which is striking, since the episode was already, by far, the longest that had appeared in the magazine. Indeed, the installments of "Cyclops" in the *Little Review* are like drafts themselves, allowing us to see vividly the development of a distinctive literary "gigantism" that dramatically changed the shape of *Ulysses* as a whole.

EPISODE XIII: NAUSICAA

When "Nausicaa" begins, we shift once more to an entirely new narrator, this time slipping into the thoughts of a young Irish girl named Gerty MacDowell as she looks at Bloom, first with curiosity and then with desire, as he masturbates on the beach. Just after the moment of climax, marked overtly in the text by the explosion of fireworks, the scene shifts away from Gerty and back into Bloom's mind. He then watches the woman limp away and wanders the beach in a dissolute state of mind, much as Stephen did in "Proteus." For a moment, his mind turns to the events in the pub some three hours before, and he questions his actions before reminding himself to "look at it. Other way round" (*LRU* 330). Such doubled vision, which is essential to the episode's split perspective, offers a powerful counterpoint to the narrowness of "Cyclops."

The language in Gerty's section is by turns sentimental and erotic, further emphasizing the abrupt transition from the mix of satire and violence at the end of "Cyclops." This frank exploration of sexuality brought the magazine's editors to trial for obscenity, generating an enormous amount of publicity for the publication of the novel in book form while ensuring that it would be banned in the United States. The obscenity in question required some careful reading to detect, though it seemed evident both to the lawyer who first complained of it to the authorities and to the three-judge panel that eventually ruled on it in court.

"Nausicaa" marks a significant point of transition for Bloom as the long day of June 16 passes into night and this modern Odysseus prepares to return home and confront the fact of his wife's adultery. Having connived earlier in the day at his wife's affair and committing now his own act of infidelity with another woman, Bloom is justifiably uncertain about his identity in this episode, which ends with one of the most famous cruxes in the book: Bloom takes a stick and writes "I. AM. A." in the sand, leaving the declaration unfinished before he "effaced the letter with his slow boot" (*LRU* 331). The remaining episodes put Bloom's identity and perhaps even his sanity to the test—though readers of the *Little Review* did not have a chance to see how the book itself attempted to end Bloom's enigmatic sentence.

Joyce conceived the plan for "Nausicaa" in Zurich, began drafting it in Paris in 1919, and finished it in February 1920. He sent the typed copy to Pound in London, who forwarded it to Margaret Anderson for publication. A relatively long episode, it was spread over three issues of the magazine, starting in April. The process Joyce followed in revising this episode for publication in the book version was similar to that used for many of the others. He took a copy of the typescript used for the *Little Review* version and made corrections and additions in the margins. This was then sent to the printer in Dijon, who produced five proofs set from this corrected typescript. Joyce then made further revisions to each set of proofs he received. In this process of revision, the word count went from around 14,250 to 16,600. Most of the revisions ran from a word or two to a few lines, leaving the basic structure unchanged but considerably enriched—especially the sections presented through the mental processes of Gerty MacDowell and Bloom. Here is a sample of Joyce's revisions to Gerty's daydreaming about cooking for her future husband and other aspects of their married life (revisions in boldface and deletions in square brackets):

> Her griddlecakes **done to a goldenbrown hue** and queen Ann's pudding **of delightful creaminess** had won golden opinions from all because she had a lucky hand also for lighting a fire, dredge in the fine **self-raising** flour and always stir in the same direction, then cream the milk and sugar and whisk well the white of eggs **though she didn't like the eating part when there were any people that made her shy and often she wondered why you couldn't eat something poetical like violets or roses** and they would have a [nice drawingroom] **beautifully appointed drawingroom** with pictures and **engravings and the photograph of grandpapa Giltrap's lovely dog Garryowen that almost talked it was so human and** chintz covers for the chairs and that silver toastrack in Clery's summer **jumble** sales like they have in rich houses. (*LRU* 306; *U* 13.225–35)

This revision shows the pains Joyce took to enrich our sense of Gerty's world—a slightly incoherent world, at once comic and pathetic, its gentility shaped by popular magazines. He also manages to sneak in a reference to the dreadful dog Garryowen, which we met in the "Cyclops" episode but here is thoroughly sentimentalized and even humanized in Gerty's thoughts.

Joyce also enriched our sense of Bloom in his section of the episode. There are many interesting additions, but this brief one is typical. Bloom is musing about the Catholic church service just heard from the nearby chapel (additions in boldface): "Mass seems to be over. **Could hear them all at it. Pray for us. And pray for us. And pray for us. Good idea the repetition. Same thing with ads. Buy from us. And buy from us.** Yes, there's the light in the priest's house. Their frugal meal" (*LRU* 328; *U* 13.1122–25). This is quintessential Bloom, with the advertising man recognizing the similarity between what he does and what the priests do.

Pound and Anderson were both keenly aware of the legal risks involved in publishing this episode in the *Little Review.* As they had done in other episodes, the editors cut some passages from the typescript that Joyce sent. Here is the passage that appeared in the typescript (cuts in square brackets): "O sweety all your little white [up] I [sawdirty girl] made me do [love sticky] we two naughty darling she him half past the bed [met] him pike hoses frillies for Raoul" (*James Joyce Archive* 13.266). These small cuts clearly seek to remove the allusions to Bloom's masturbation, but they did little to preserve Joyce's work from the American censors. (For a full account of the ensuing obscenity trial, see *LRU* 422–24.)

EPISODE XIV: OXEN OF THE SUN

In this episode, Joyce finally brings Stephen and Bloom together, at ten, in a maternity hospital on Holles Street, where Mina Purefoy is suffering through a prolonged labor. Though they meet there by accident, Joyce has staged the episode so that Bloom and Stephen undergo a symbolic rebirth, in the "womb" of the hospital, as father and son. By the end of the episode, Mrs. Purefoy has given birth to her ninth child, Bloom has acquired feelings of paternal responsibility for Stephen, and Joyce has brought English prose up to the twentieth century. But these are developments that the first readers of *Ulysses* did not get to witness, since the serialization of Joyce's novel in the *Little Review* abruptly ends after the first installment of episode XIV, only a quarter of the way into that text and four episodes shy of the novel's conclusion.

Joyce composed "Oxen of the Sun" while living in Trieste in 1920, between early February and late May; he claimed that the intricately wrought episode took him 1,000 hours to draft (*Pound/Joyce* 164; *LI* 141) in a stressful environment: "I live in a flat with eleven other people and have had great difficulty in securing time and peace enough to write" (*Pound/Joyce* 168). In a letter to Harriet Shaw Weaver, Joyce again described the difficulty that "Oxen" caused him: "I am working now on the *Oxen of the Sun* that most difficult episode in an odyssey, I think, both to interpret and to execute" (*LI* 137). Despite these forbidding accounts of composing this formidable episode, Groden notes that Joyce wrote "Oxen" "without major complications," perhaps because he had by this time mastered the middle-stage style of parodic narration that began in "Wandering Rocks" (*UP* 52).

Two drafts of "Oxen" have survived, the first dating from early February 1920 (Buffalo Notebook V.A.11–12; NLI MS 36,639/11/A–B) and the second traced by Luca Crispi to March and April (Buffalo Notebook V.A.13–18; NLI MS 36,639/11/C–F). The Rosenbach Manuscript preserves a fair copy prepared for typing in May 1920, and a copy of the complete typescript sent to the *Little Review* also survives (Buffalo V.B.12.a). Richard Ellmann recounts how Joyce, while drafting "Oxen," "kept before him a diagram showing the ontogeny of the foetus during nine months," along with a copy of Saintsbury's *A History of English Prose Rhythm* (*James Joyce* 475). James Atherton has shown that William Peacock's anthology *English Prose from Mandeville to Ruskin* was another important resource for Joyce. In tracking down the sources Joyce used to create "Oxen," scholars have been assisted by a series of twenty note sheets on which Joyce copied out snippets of text from his reading that he later incorporated into the episode. Now housed in the British Museum, these sheets contain about 3,000 notes: "Approximately 2,000 entries contain examples of period diction, and the remainder relate to embryology, the history of the English language or detail from previous episodes" (Davison, "Joyce's Incorporation"). Armed with Joyce's notes, as well as a knowledge of the books in his library in Trieste, scholars have established that Joyce used many more sources than had previously been imagined: by 1967, Robert Janusko had identified 400 different sources; by 1983, 800; and by 2002, Gregory Downing had raised the number to over 1,000 (Davison).

Despite his troubles in composing the episode, Joyce made only minor revisions as he worked through five proofs in the fall of 1921 (Groden, *UP* 52). He expanded by just 160 words the portion of the text that appeared in the *Little Review,* including the following additions to Stephen's thoughts on contraception (additions in boldface): "But, **gramercy,** what of those Godpossible souls that we nightly impossibilise, **which is the sin against the Holy Ghost, Very God, Lord and Giver of Life**?" (*U* 14.225–27). Joyce also introduced the following dense sentence between Stephen's reference to Fletcher and Beaumont, and Dixon's joke about their names: "**An exquisite dulcet epithalame of most mollificative suadency for juveniles amatory whom the odoriferous flambeaus of the paranymphs have escorted to the quadrupedal proscenium of connubial communion**" (*U* 14.352–55). Joyce's revisions include the addition of individual words that heighten his writing's archaic style, such as "have joy **of her childing** for she hath waited" (*U* 14.176–77) and "That is truth, **pardy,** said Dixon" (*U* 14.259). He also replaced some words with others: "Yule" becomes "**Childermas,**" a couple instances of "the traveller" become "**childe Leopold,**" and "they reclaimed **the churl**" instead of "him" (*U* 14.103, 160, 325). Perhaps to avoid an anachronistic cliché, Joyce translates "lock, stock and barrel" into "**seed, breed and generation**" (*U* 14.301).

Not all the strange-looking words that appear in the *Little Review*'s "Oxen," however, are of Joyce's devising. The magazine's chronic difficulty with printer's errors is significantly aggravated in this episode, where so much of the language already appears to be misspelled. Thus, the phrase "county of increase" in the magazine should actually read "bounty of increase"; "by ancipation"—anticipation; "lightens in eyebling"—eyeblink; "certain angy spirits"—angry; and "a body without belmish"—blemish.

Despite the finding by the Court of Special Sessions that *Ulysses* was an obscene book, Joyce continued to draft the novel through the summer of 1921. Indeed, as the charges brought against Anderson and Heap were being argued in New York, he worked first in Trieste and then in Paris on "Circe"—an episode set in a brothel and laden with sexually explicit imagery. By the autumn of 1921, he had completed a full draft of the novel, including the equally explicit "Penelope" episode, which turns its attention away from the inconclusive encounter between Stephen and Bloom in order to recast the day's events through the memories and fantasies of Molly. The last four episodes were not written with the expectation of serial publication, and thus their evolution is somewhat different from the others'. As Joyce completed his work in 1921, he turned to the extraordinary Sylvia Beach, who patiently saw *Ulysses* through its massive revisions and then published it under the imprint of Shakespeare and Company in 1922.

THE MAGAZINE CONTEXT FOR *THE LITTLE REVIEW "ULYSSES"*

In "The Composition History of *Ulysses*" above, we examine how Joyce composed each episode of *Ulysses* and note some key differences between the text that appeared in the *Little Review* and the first book edition of the novel published in 1922. In this section, we situate *The Little Review "Ulysses"* within the printed context of the magazine itself. We aim to give some account of what besides *Ulysses* appears in each issue and to relate each installment of the novel to its neighboring texts. This should foreground for readers how *Ulysses,* far from being a timeless classic sprung wholly out of its creator's head, belongs to and emerges from a time and place that Joyce shared with other writers—writers who were responding in various ways to a common social and artistic environment and building collaboratively, in magazines like the *Little Review,* a new kind of art that we today call modernism.

JOYCE'S MAGAZINE NETWORK

Before we examine the magazine installments of *Ulysses* one by one, we need to take a step back and provide a broader view of the place that Joyce and his novel occupy in the *Little Review,* drawing in part from data that have been made available about the journal by the Modernist Journals Project (MJP).[1] The *Little Review* serialized the first thirteen episodes of *Ulysses* (along with the start of episode 14) in twenty-three issues over the better part of three years, from March 1918 through December 1920. The novel appeared in every issue of the magazine from this period except four—August 1918 (a special number devoted to Henry James), November 1918, December 1918, and October 1919. Each of the first seven episodes was published in a single installment, and the next six, which were on average twice as long as the previous seven, were broken into multiple installments: episodes 8–11 each appeared in two issues, episode 12 in four issues, and episode 13 in three. Episode 14 was slated for multiple installments as well, but only the first quarter of it appeared, in the September–December 1920 issue, before the novel's serialization was prematurely brought to a halt.

There are a couple of ways to measure the size of *Ulysses*'s footprint in the *Little Review* during its serialization. One way is to count the number of titles (or items) that the magazine published in the twenty-three issues in which *Ulysses* appeared. The MJP's catalogue records for the journal indicate that 624 titled items (excluding advertisements) appeared in these issues, including 202 poems, 197 articles, 90 pieces of fiction, 67 letters, 63 images, and 5 dramatic works. Viewed this way, the 23 installments of *Ulysses* make up less than 4 percent of the titles but more than 25 percent of the pieces of fiction in these issues.

The novel's footprint in the magazine looks much bigger if we instead examine the MJP's transcripts for the *Little Review* and count the number of words in Joyce's text. The twenty-three installments of *Ulysses* amount to 122,285 words, while everything in these issues (including advertising and peripherals, not just titled items) comes to 527,536 words. By this measure, *Ulysses* makes up over 23 percent of all words in the magazine, or nearly a quarter of the *Little Review* during its serialization. What follows is a chart of how this breaks down, issue by issue:

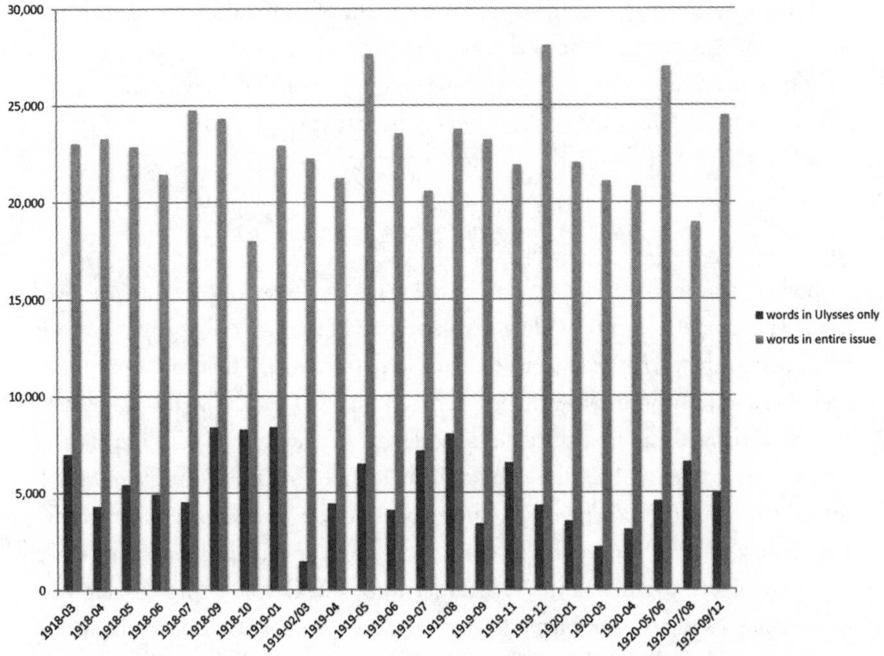

Comparison between *Ulysses* episodes and the *Little Review* issues in which they appeared (number of words)

By the same measure, *Ulysses* makes up nearly 42 percent of all fiction published in the magazine (292,337 words) during the period of its serialization.

We can also measure Joyce himself against the other contributors to the magazine during this time. Once we reconcile obvious name variants among the authors and artists in these twenty-three issues, we come up with 180 unique contributors. Over 62 percent of them (112 of 180) had only one contribution each, and fewer than 17 percent (30 of 180) had more than five contributions. Measured by the number of items published, Joyce, with one contribution in each of the twenty-three issues, ranks as the sixth most prolific contributor, following Ezra Pound (with forty-three items), John Rodker (thirty-seven items), the two editors of *The Little Review*—Jane Heap (thirty-three) and Margaret Anderson (twenty-eight)—and Else von Freytag-Loringhoven (twenty-five). Among contributors of fiction, Joyce ranks first, followed by Dorothy Richardson (whose novel *Interim* was serialized in ten of the *Ulysses* issues), Sherwood Anderson and Ben Hecht (each with eight fiction contributions), and Djuna Barnes (with six).

Another way to measure Joyce's standing in the magazine is to look at the company he keeps in each issue's table of contents, which is reproduced in this book before each installment of the novel. This approach foregrounds who Joyce's neighbors are in the community of the *Little Review*'s significant contributors, and it gives a sense of how readers would have seen the material assembled in each issue. Though 180 persons contributed to these twenty-three issues, fewer than a hundred show up on the magazine's contents pages, where Joyce's name appears on average among twelve other contributors' names and just ten other unique contributors.[2] After Joyce, Pound shows up most frequently on these contents pages, with contributions to thirteen of these issues; he is followed by Rodker (eleven), Richardson and S. Anderson (ten each), Hecht and William Carlos Williams (nine issues), and Maxwell Bodenheim and M. Anderson (eight each).

We can also measure Joyce's neighbors on these contents pages by contingency—whose name rubs up against Joyce's and whose work directly precedes or follows *Ulysses* in the magazine itself. By this standard also, Pound proves to be Joyce's closest neighbor, appearing four times immediately before Joyce and twice after him in the pages of the magazine. Richardson, S. Anderson, and Heap are Joyce's next-closest neighbors, butting against him three times each.

By these different measures, we get a sense of the network of authors in the *Little Review* in which Joyce was a member by virtue of having his work published alongside theirs. But if we examine the magazine over time, we can discern two groups of contributors appearing in its pages. Anderson and Heap edited the *Little Review* throughout *Ulysses*'s serialization, but Ezra Pound served as its foreign editor, based in London, only for the first year—during which time he brought to the magazine not only Joyce's novel but also the works of a number of other writers, including his own. Pound's influence over *Ulysses* continued throughout its serialization—Joyce sent each episode to Pound when it was ready—but his influence over the magazine and its content dropped off sharply after he resigned his post in the spring of 1919.

As a result, Pound had a commanding influence in eight of nine issues containing *Ulysses* during the first year of its serialization (the exception being an American number that Heap edited herself in June 1918), while the remaining fifteen issues were assembled by Anderson and Heap without Pound's assistance. The difference in community is evident: Pound's issues have significantly fewer authors and titles—about 60 percent fewer of each—even though these issues are only slightly shorter than the ones that followed his departure.[3] Not only did Pound devote more space to fewer authors than did Anderson and Heap, but the authors in his circle are also strikingly more international. As Anderson promised readers when Pound first came on board, his addition as foreign editor meant "that a great deal of the most creative work of modern London and Paris will be published in these pages" (*LR* 3.10: 25), and that indeed is what happened: twice as many European as American contributors appear in the Pound issues, while just the reverse—twice as many Americans as Europeans—were published in the issues that followed in his wake.[4] Likewise, in Pound's issues, non-Americans are the lead authors in seven of the eight issues, while in the post-Pound issues Americans take the lead spot nearly half the time (in seven of fifteen issues).

So which authors belong to these two circles? The smaller circle of European authors in the Pound issues includes the "men of 1914," as Pound's protégés were later called, authors such as Wyndham Lewis and the London-based T. S. Eliot, but other non-Americans also figure prominently: Rodker, Ford Madox Hueffer, May Sinclair, and W. B. Yeats all appear among the top eight contributors after Pound himself (whose work appeared in seven of his eight issues). In the fifteen issues Pound didn't edit, the top ten most frequent contributors besides Joyce are Richardson (with ten contributions), M. Anderson, S. Anderson, and Williams (eight contributions each), Rodker and Bodenheim (seven each), Barnes, Freytag-Loringhoven, Emanuel Carnevali, and Pound (six each).

As the composition of these two lists suggests, more women showed up in the magazine following Pound's departure. When we count how many women appear on the contents pages of all twenty-three issues, we discover twice as many female authors in the issues that Anderson and Heap edited without Pound's help. Only after Pound left the magazine did the editors begin serializing Richardson (in June 1919) and also promoting such female talents as Barnes and Freytag-Loringhoven. In three of Pound's issues, Yeats appears as the lead author; in two post-Pound issues Barnes heads off the contents page, and in a third her picture provides the magazine's frontispiece. Though Pound's issues involve fewer contributors, three of the eight nonetheless include no women at all and two others include only one woman each. By contrast, issues edited by Anderson and Heap include on average contributions by three or more women; three issues published five women, and two more published six. Likewise, in Pound's eight issues, a female author (May Sinclair) has a lead article only once, while in the remaining fifteen issues female authors head the contents page nearly half the time, featuring Barnes, Richardson, Jessie Dismorr, Freytag-Loringhoven, and Mary Butts.

One of the interesting implications of these figures is that while *Ulysses* was developing in the pages of the magazine and moving away from its initial realistic style to become more experimental in later episodes, the magazine in which it appeared was changing as well, featuring more women and more American writers, along with even more aggressively avant-garde art. In what follows, we discuss many of the authors whose work collides with Joyce's writing in the pages of the magazine, underscoring the richness of the periodical culture in which *Ulysses* first reached its readers.

EPISODE I: TELEMACHUS

Little Review *4.11: March 1918*

Ulysses began running in the March 1918 issue of the *Little Review.* The magazine had already been hauled into court for publishing obscenity, and the issue of the previous October had been suppressed, because of Wyndham Lewis's story "Cantelman's Spring-Mate." Ezra Pound, who had become foreign editor in May 1917, got around to addressing this matter in the March issue, in a piece titled "The Classics 'Escape,'" mainly by quoting what he called "the amazing, grotesque, and unthinkable, ambiguous law of our country":

I have been unable to speak promptly regarding the suppression of the October number; I am a long way from the New York Post Office.

However, as I, whom the law appears to concern, was ignorant of it, it is possible that others with only a mild interest in literature may be equally ignorant; I therefore quote the law:

Section 211 of the United States Criminal Code provides:

"Every obscene, lewd, or lascivious, and every filthy, book pamphlet, picture, paper, letter, writing, print, or other publication of an indecent character and every article or thing designed, adapted or intended for preventing conception or producing abortion, or for any indecent or immoral use; and every article, instrument, substance, drug, medicine, or thing which is advertised or described in a manner calculated to lead another to use or apply it for preventing conception or producing abortion, or for any indecet [sic] or immoral purpose; and every written or printed card, letter, circular, book, pamphlet, advertisement, or notice of any kind giving information directly or indirectly, where, or how, or from whom, or by what means any of the hereinbefore-mentioned matters, articles, or things may be obtained or made, or where or by whom any act or operation of any kind for the procuring or producing of abortion will be done or performed, or how or by what means conception may be prevented or abortion produced, whether sealed or unsealed; and every letter, packet, or package, or other mail matter containing any filthy, vile or indecent thing, device, or substance; any every paper, writing, advertisement, or representation that any article, instrument, substance, drug, medicine, or thing may, or can be, used or applied for preventing conception or producing abortion, or for any indecent or immoral purpose; and every description calculated to induce or incite a person to so use or apply any such article, instrument, substance, drug, medicine, or thing, is hereby declared to be non-mailable matter and shall not be conveyed in the mails or delivered from any post-office or by any letter carrier. Whoever shall knowingly deposit, or cause to be deposited for mailing or delivery, anything declared by this section to be non-mailable, or shall knowingly take, or cause the same to be taken, from the mails for the purpose of circulating or disposing thereof, or of aiding in the circulation or disposition thereof, shall be fined not more than five thousand dollars, or imprisoned not more than five years, or both".

> That, gentle reader, is the law, the amazing, grotesque, and unthinkable, ambiguous law of our country. (*LR* 4.11: 32–33)

Pound's quarrel with America, which was long and bitter, stemming from disappointed hopes, is embodied in that string of adjectives he uses to describe the same law that, nearly three years later, would be wielded against *Ulysses.* Thus, from its very first appearance in the *Little Review,* Joyce's novel was presented alongside the obscenity law that eventually ended its serialization in the magazine. It was a law that, as Pound complains, submitted all literature in America to "the taste of one individual," the postmaster general, who is "selected without any examination of his literary qualifications" (*LR* 4.11: 34). It was also a law that exempted only the classics, as Judge Augustus Hand admitted in his November 1917 ruling against the magazine, because the classics were sanctioned by "age and fame" and were read by so few people—an opinion that Pound called the most "damning indictment of American civilization" ever written.

Despite the legal challenges of his day, Pound's efforts to bring modern art and literature to America were untiring, and every writer in the March 1918 issue knew him. Wyndham Lewis, who has an "Imaginary Letter" in the issue, worked with Pound on Lewis's short-lived avant-garde magazine *Blast.* Ford Madox Hueffer (later Ford), Pound's occasional tennis partner, had published Pound's poetry in his magazine, the *English Review.* In this issue of the *Little Review* he published the second installment of his book *Women and Men.* Jessie Dismorr, who has a prose poem in this issue, was a visual artist whose work had appeared in *Blast.* And Arthur Symons, who has a story in this issue, was a poet and critic well known in the 1890s; his book *The Symbolist Movement in Literature,* first published in 1899, was an important influence on Yeats and other modern poets. He was one of Pound's first friends after he came to London in 1908.

Pound himself is everywhere in this issue. Besides his article on the obscenity law, he contributed a review of the 1917 *Others* anthology, surveys of three authors he considered underappreciated, and a glowing appraisal of Wyndham Lewis's novel *Tarr,* which Pound had arranged to have serialized in the *Egoist* after Joyce's *A Portrait of the Artist as a Young Man* had appeared there. But the issue begins with "Telemachus," the first episode of *Ulysses,* which appears immediately after an advertisement from Joyce's New York publisher, B. W. Huebsch, promoting *Portrait, Dubliners,* and Joyce's forthcoming play, *Exiles.* By situating *Ulysses* in the wider context of Joyce's other works, the advertising blurbs on the left-hand page offer the only assistance that readers get in this issue for understanding the novel that begins on the right, linking Stephen Dedalus back to *Portrait* and to the "quintessential and unfailing reality" —H. G. Wells's comment about Joyce's previous book—that Joyce breathes into him there.

EPISODE II: NESTOR

Little Review *4.12: April 1918*

"Nestor," the second installment of *Ulysses,* appears as the fifth of eight items in the April 1918 issue of the *Little Review,* where it is surrounded by pieces that are unabashedly avant-garde in identity and technique. Preceding the episode are May Sinclair's essay on Dorothy Richardson's groundbreaking novel series *Pilgrimage,* an experimental short story by B. Windeler, and Jules Romains's bizarre "Reflexions" about group consciousness (with commentary by Ezra Pound). Following it are Ben Hecht's poetic urban musings in "Fragments," as well as the latest installments in series by Wyndham Lewis and Pound ("Imaginary Letters") and Ford Madox Hueffer ("Women and Men").

Of these texts, Sinclair's lead essay holds the greatest significance for Joyce's fiction. Whereas *Ulysses* today is probably the English-language novel most commonly cited as illustrating stream of consciousness, Sinclair's review, famous in its own right, is responsible for introducing that term—coined by William James and until 1918 used only in psychology—into a literary context. Sinclair uses it to describe Richardson's experimental fiction, but she explicitly relates this narrative technique to what Joyce does in *A Portrait of the Artist as a Young Man,* and much of what she says in her essay resonates with *Ulysses.* She describes how Richardson breaks with nineteenth-century realism by doing away with its conventional plot trappings ("there is no drama, no situation, no set scene"), suspends "the wise, all-knowing author" (her narrator "must not interfere; she must not analyse or comment or explain"), and collapses the clear distinction "between what is objective and what is subjective" (*LR* 4.12: 5–6, 5, 5, 9). Richardson does all these things, according to Sinclair, so she may plunge into the perspective of her main character, Miriam Henderson, and present "the firsthand, intimate and intense reality" of what is happening in her mind, in "the fragmentary way in which people appear to most of us" (9, 5).

We can easily imagine how readers of the *Little Review,* baffled by the second installment of *Ulysses,* might have turned to Sinclair's essay for help. On the first page of "Nestor," Sinclair's piece can explain why Joyce's opening lines are disorienting (because his narrator withholds any explanation of who is talking, when, where, and why), why there are no quotation marks around the spoken dialogue (to elide the difference between the objective and subjective), and why the narrative suddenly reverts to obscure broken phrases (to indicate that we have plunged into the stream of Stephen's consciousness). Sinclair's essay might also explain to readers why most of the commentary we do get about the classroom and students in this episode comes from Stephen's mind, and why that commentary is itself so fragmented (since he is not addressing us, and mixing what he observes with reflections on his past along with other personal associations and imaginings). Richardson today is linked in our minds with Joyce as a fellow modernist novelist, but Sinclair's essay relates the two, perhaps for the first time, in the *Little Review*—and the magazine further cemented that relationship when it serialized the fifth novel of *Pilgrimage,* which ran alongside its serialization of *Ulysses* for an entire year, between June 1919 and May 1920.

Another aspect of the magazine that resonates with the subject matter in "Nestor" is the criticism it directs at the literary establishment. When Sinclair introduces Richardson, she cites the *Little Review*'s motto—about making no compromise with the public taste—as consonant with Richardson's own stance toward her audience, and she claims that the critic who seeks to understand Richardson's work must "throw off the philosophic cant" of the nineteenth century and not be "content to think in clichés" (*LR* 4.12: 3, 4). Ezra Pound, who secured Sinclair's review and the other texts that appear in the issue, is even more vocal in his enthusiasm for putting the past behind him. In a "squib" (or a small explosive device) titled "The Criterion" that appears immediately after Sinclair's piece, he writes this:

> "Art", said the chimpanzee, "which *I* have to *study* before *I* can understand it, is fatally lacking somewhere." "Upon this principal", said the chimpanzee, "we must reject Mr. Browning's *Sordello.*" (11)

This is a preemptive strike against readers who dismiss the literature in the magazine because they find it challenging. In Pound's estimation, such readers are simply apes.

In his notes on Romains's difficult piece about the French avant-garde movement called Unanimism, which directly precedes *Ulysses* in the magazine,

Pound takes further aim at the older generation that still presides over cultural affairs in America, "certain fusty old crocks [who] have pretended to look after American 'culture'" (*LR* 4.12: 26): "These suave old gentlemen, and these vulgar middle-aged automatons have given us a long example of intellectual cowardice; all their lives they have striven to prevent the impact of any real value, of any equation of life, from reaching the minds of their readers" (27). The old gentlemen back in America whom Pound castigates here in fact resemble Mr. Deasy, the headmaster at the school where Stephen teaches in "Nestor." And if we read Deasy through the lens of Pound's aggressive contempt for fusty old crocks, we can easily mount a damning critique of him. We might, for example, note Deasy's unfounded certainty about himself and his opinions; his inability to listen; his provincial suspicion of foreign people and cosmopolitan ideas; his larding up his letter with empty verbiage and clichés; and his general lack of self-awareness: "I don't mince words, do I?" he asks Stephen, even as the latter, while reading Deasy's letter, has yet to reach its main point, for all its hot air (*LRU* 32).

It is tempting to promote Stephen at Deasy's expense, especially since the younger man's notions of history (a "nightmare") and god (a "shout in the street") are both offered as alternatives to what Deasy thinks (*LRU* 33, 34). Yet contrary to Pound's example, Stephen displays considerable restraint while standing before the old man in charge: he remains respectful, only mildly dismissive, and not at all incendiary. By contrast, Deasy, in thinking the young teacher a Fenian, mistakes him for someone more like Ezra Pound. Stephen's stance displays, in short, a more measured view of the literary establishment than we would associate with Pound. And that should interest us, since Pound surely saw the serialization of *Ulysses* in the *Little Review* as a bomb for blowing up the old house of literature.

EPISODE III: PROTEUS

Little Review *5.1: May 1918*

In the March and April 1918 issues of the *Little Review,* the first two installments of *Ulysses* appeared without direct introduction or commentary, though readers had been prepared for the serialized work by an advertisement on the back cover of the February number. They were assured by an anonymous critic (almost certainly Ezra Pound) that Joyce's new novel was "rather better than

Flaubert" and that the magazine was "about to publish a prose masterpiece" (*LR* 4.10: np). When Margaret Anderson and Jane Heap published the third installment of the novel, "Proteus," they broke the magazine's silence about the book. The letters in the "Reader Critic" section all endorse the magazine's willingness to publish *Ulysses:* as Alice Groff writes, "the *Little Review* has been a delightful youth, gifted, daring, insolent, swash-buckling, with flashes of divine discernment and discrimination," but "with the March number it comes to its majority" (*LR* 5.1: 64). Daphne Carr similarly writes to thank the magazine "for sticking out in these beastly times," and Israel Solon calls the April number "the best single number I have yet come across" (64, 62). In two of these three letters, *Ulysses* is mentioned for the first time and treated as emblematic of the magazine itself; Solon expertly links its stream of consciousness to other items that had recently appeared, including May Sinclair's essay on Dorothy Richardson. He writes that Joyce has "plunged deep into himself" and that he "adventures slowly and painfully with a huge stone deliberately tied to his middle, that he might sink readily and stay under long and be all but unable to retreat" (63). These letters, the first published critical commentary on *Ulysses,* emphasize key themes that preoccupied the book's critics for the next decades, including its potential to offend, its obsession with interiority, its ruthless honesty, and a difficulty so daunting that, as Solon writes, "none but the most disciplined, the most persistent and sympathetic are able to break through" (63).

Ulysses, however, is not the only thing that appears in this number, and similar concerns with honesty, difficulty, offensiveness, fragmentation, and subjectivity emerge elsewhere as well. Hueffer's lengthy serialized piece "Women and Men" is striking because it reflects on the burgeoning periodical culture of the early twentieth century and the consequent fragmentation of the reading public. In some ways a counterpart to Pound's series about magazines called "Studies in Contemporary Mentality," which was serialized in the *New Age* in 1917 (and republished in Scholes and Wulfman), the article examines different kinds of newspapers and magazines, concluding that it is no longer possible to identify a single public, since "it is almost impossible to say even who will not read any given paper" (*LR* 5.1: 58). Although *Ulysses* is now largely shrouded in its own mystique of highbrow difficulty, when it appeared in the *Little Review* it too engaged many similar concerns about the fragmentation of audiences. It is unlikely, for example, that any single reader of the magazine text would have been able to grasp the full range of references and allusions in "Proteus," which primarily occur as Stephen cycles through memories of his past, since their compass includes local Dublin politics, European literature, Yeats's poetry, Catholic heretics, Irish myth, and the Vulgate Bible. Like the magazines that Hueffer describes, this episode of *Ulysses* is distinctly marked by the diversity of readers and publics it can accommodate.

As the letters in the "Reader Critic" section suggest, what remains most striking about "Proteus" is the distinctive "initial style," as Joyce called it, of *Ulysses* as a whole (*LI* 129)—the narrative form he employs through the first eleven episodes (albeit with increasingly significant changes) that mixes stream of consciousness with third-person narration and allows a generally unobtrusive narrator to fade frequently in and out of a character's mind. The *Little Review* subtly highlights this effect by juxtaposing "Proteus" with Hecht's "Nocturne," which runs immediately after it. It too records the jumbled thoughts and impressions of a self-consciously artistic first-person narrator as he makes his way through a city. "I walk on and on," Hecht writes, "and the adjectives form themselves into remarkable thoughts that sometimes startle me and cause me to forget to listen to the castenets of my heels upon the lonely pavement" (*LR* 5.1: 45). This passage is strikingly similar to Stephen's own wandering on the beach as he listens to the "crush, crack, crick, crick" of his steps, wondering about language, poetry, and art (*LRU* 37).

Thus "Proteus," along with several of the other early installments of *Ulysses*, appears in the *Little Review* as part of the magazine's larger experiment not just with the new forms of art we now associate with modernism, but also with the particular set of techniques then being developed for representing the scattered patterns of sensation, association, and thought that Sinclair had described the previous month as a "stream of consciousness." Joyce was unaware of the connections between his work and the larger concerns of the magazine, but "Proteus" nevertheless appears as part of a complicated aesthetic debate about art, realism, and representation that Pound, Anderson, and Heap deftly orchestrated in their selection and juxtaposition of material in the magazine's pages.

EPISODE IV: CALYPSO

Little Review *5.2: June 1918*

"Calypso" seemed somewhat out of place when it appeared in the June 1918 *Little Review.* This issue, identified as "An American Number" on the magazine's green cover, offers "a review of work being done in America by writers who are called artists" (*LR* 5.2: 62), and it features poems by Wallace Stevens, William Carlos Williams, Amy Lowell, Carl Sandburg, and Mark Turbyfill; an essay on love by Williams; and short fiction by Ben Hecht, Sherwood Anderson, and Djuna Barnes. Episode IV of *Ulysses,* which introduces us to the book's protagonist, Leopold Bloom, and is laden with intimate details of Dublin life, appears toward the end of the magazine, and Joyce's byline on the contents page sits forlornly at the bottom of a long list of American names, as though highlighting its lack of belonging. Perhaps anticipating that readers might wonder at the magazine's departure from the more cosmopolitan issues previously edited by Pound, Jane Heap explains, in the notes at the back, that she was "responsible for this issue" and that "it was made with no compromise to Margaret Anderson and Ezra Pound," but also that it is neither "a revolt against our 'foreign all-star cast'" nor "a 'return to our former ways'" (62). Indeed, the editors' "interest and intent the past year [in the *Little Review*] has been to span the Atlantic, to end America's intellectual isolation" (55). When viewed in this light, an occasional American issue seems exactly what Anderson and Heap wanted for the journal during their serialization of Joyce's novel.

Heap underscores her commitment to *Ulysses* in the "Reader Critic" section of the magazine. For the first time, the editors include letters that object to Joyce's novel, a possible sign of their growing confidence in its power and importance. In responding to these readers, Heap rises to Joyce's defense, stirring an often raucous debate that helped cement the magazine's place at the center of the avant-garde. When one reader complains about the novel's "obs[cen]e commonplaces," Heap counters that "it is impossible for Joyce to be obscene," explaining, "He is too concentrated on his work. He is too religious about life" (56). And an item the editors titled "What Joyce Is Up Against" contains this letter from "S. S. B., Chicago":

> Really now: Joyce! what does he think he is doing? What do you think he is doing? I swear I've read his "Ulysses" and haven't found out yet what it's about, who is who or where. Each month he's worse than the last. I consider myself fairly intelligent. I have read more than most. There are some few things I expect of a writer. One of them is coherence. Joyce will have to change his style if he wants to get on. Very few have the time or patience to struggle with his impressionistic stuff—to get nothing out of it even then. (54)

In her response, Heap expresses the policy of the magazine and its opposition to that of Harriet Monroe's *Poetry,* which bore on its back cover Walt Whitman's claim that "to have great poets there must be great audiences too." In her usual ironic mode, Heap writes this:

> You consider yourself an intelligent, "well-read" person. Did it ever occur to you to read anything on the nature of writers? If it should you might help to remove from the mind of the reading public—Whitman's great audience—some of the superstition of its importance to the writer; some of its superstition of being able to put any compulsion upon an artist. All compulsion exists within the artist. It would take too long to discuss this fully here. The only concern of the artist is to try in one short lifetime to meet these inner compulsions. He has no concern with audiences and their demands.—*jh.* (54)

Heap's defense of Joyce's art as having "no concern with audiences and their demands" additionally aligns the *Little Review* with the *Egoist,* which still hoped to run its own serialization of *Ulysses* in London. A full-page advertisement for the *Egoist* on the inside front cover of this issue makes plain the shared aims of these two small magazines:

> This journal is not a chatty literary review: its mission is not to divert and amuse: it is not written for tired and depressed people. Its aim is rather to secure a fit audience, and to render available to that audience contemporary literary work bearing the stamp of originality and permanance: to present in the making those contemporary literary efforts which ultimately will constitute 20th century literature.
>
> The philosophical articles which *The Egoist* publishes, by presenting the subject-matter of metaphysics in a form which admits of logical treatment, are promising a new era for philosophy. The power of its fictional work is investing that commonest but laxest of literary forms—the novel (as written in English)—with a new destiny and a new meaning. In poetry, its pages are open to experiments which are transforming the whole conception of poetic form, while among its writers appear leaders in pioneering methods radically affecting the allied arts.

Versions of this ad appeared in a number of issues. Both magazines were voices of the modernist avant-garde, challenging readers and viewers on either side of the Atlantic to measure up to the new modes of writing and visual art. And that was the context in which Joyce's work appeared in both journals, *A Portrait of the Artist as a Young Man* having appeared in the *Egoist* in 1914–1915. Eventually, only four episodes of *Ulysses* appeared in *The Egoist* in 1919, that magazine's plans for serialization frustrated by objections from printers and publishers about its wide-ranging obscenity.

EPISODE V: LOTUS EATERS

Little Review *5.3: July 1918*

"Lotus Eaters" appears in the July 1918 issue of the *Little Review,* over which Ezra Pound clearly presided. Featuring works by the French authors Jules Laforgue, Arthur Rimbaud, and the Goncourt brothers, as well as an article about T. P. Jyotishi's Bengali poem "Saptam Edoyarder Svargabohan," the July issue includes contributions by Pound (writing as himself, as "E. P.," and as "Thayer Exton"), Ben Hecht, Iris Barry, Sherwood Anderson, Iseult Gonne (whose mother, Maud Gonne, appeared in revisions Joyce made to "Lotus Eaters" in 1921), Ford Maddox Hueffer, and a dozen letters by readers.

One resonance between these surrounding texts and *Ulysses* is the concept of the "average" person, which shows up in the title of Hueffer's "Average People" but is also central to the Goncourts' preface to their 1865 novel *Germinie Lacerteux,* which Pound reprinted in the magazine and describes as "the whole case for realism" (*LR* 5.3: 56). Hueffer explores the problem of identifying the average person by offering two contrasting portraits: his "average man" is a wealthy Londoner idling away his life, and his "average woman" is a peasant woman consumed by manual labor. Leopold Bloom, of course, is neither; but as the unlikely everyman hero of *Ulysses,* he raises, especially when compared with Odysseus, similar questions about the way social norms in literature involve class and status. (Hueffer's average man, we might note, falls victim, in his daily routine, to the lethargy and aimlessness that tempt Bloom throughout episode V.)

In their defense of novelistic realism, the Goncourt brothers make the case for recasting serious literature around lowly subjects like Hueffer's "average woman":

> Vivant au dix-neuvième siècle, dans un temps de suffrage universel, de démocratie, de libêralisme, nous nous sommes demandé si ce qu'on appelle "les basses classes" n'avait pas droit au roman; si ce monde sous

> un monde, le peuple, devait rester sous le coup de l'interdit littéraire et des dédains d'auteurs qui ont fait jusqu'ici le silence sur l'âme et le coeur qu'il peut avoir. (*LR* 5.3: 57)
> [Living in the nineteenth century, in a time of universal suffrage, of democracy, of liberalism, we wondered if the so-called "lower classes" were not entitled to the novel; if this world beneath a world, the common people, should remain under the shadow of forbidden literature and disdained by authors who have thus far been silent about what heart and soul they may have.]

Pound specifically intended this preface to justify the realism in *Ulysses,* telling Margaret Anderson that "it is the answer to all that may be said against Joyce" (*Pound/The Little Review* 226), though in the magazine he remains silent about this motive. More complexly for the magazine's American readers, Pound published the Goncourts' defense of the ordinary untranslated, leaving its justification of Joyce's naturalism to be deciphered only by those readers able to read the original French.

It is not just naturalism, however—and the idea that a novel may be "true" to life by coming out of the street ("vient de la rue," *LR* 5.3: 56)—that aligns *Ulysses* with French literature in this issue. With "Our Tetrarchal Precieuse"—Pound's prolix free translation of Jules Laforgue's retelling of "Salome"—and the six prose poems from Rimbaud's *Illuminations* translated by Helen Rootham (who is best known today as Edith Sitwell's governess and companion), the July issue brought French Symbolist literature, with its associated air of decadence, into English. And it is possible to see Joyce's "Lotus Eaters" doing much the same: its atmosphere of somnolence, drugged languor, self-indulgence, and unnatural pleasures all recall French decadence. When we read the episode against the dense hothouse aestheticism of Salome's palace and the aimlessness of Rimbaud's vagabonds, we sense behind Joyce's lotus flowers (and Bloom's flâneur) the influence of Baudelaire's *Flowers of Evil* as well as Verlaine's poem "Langueur," whose speaker—an empire in decline—is so heart-sick with indolence and ennui that he has lost all will for adventure.

Readers of the *Little Review* clearly noticed this air of decadence, in both *Ulysses* and the magazine itself. For some, the news was good: Rex Hunter, who was impressed by the magazine's decision to print "almost an entire number in French" (in February 1918), describes Hecht's "Lust" in the June issue as being "delightfully decadent, with a sort of Huysmans quality," and commends the drawings of Szukalski by claiming that his soul, like Beardsley's, "wanders darkly in a mysterious rose garden full of monstrous roses" (*LR* 5.3: 62). More readers, however, were deeply disturbed: Frank Stuhlman claimed that "decadence commenced" at the *Little Review* in 1916 and that "Ezra Pound, Joyce and Co." ought to be fired (64). Louis Puteklis similarly accused Pound of leading the magazine into "decadent blunderings": "rotten stuff . . . so ugly that one can not read it" (63). *Ulysses*'s appearance in the magazine contributed to these charges of decadence and decline. Stuhlman accused Joyce of "throwing chunks of filth into the midst of incoherent maunderings" (64), and R. McM. (in the June issue) complained that the *Little Review* promoted "cerise abnormal art" and that Joyce rated poorly even when compared with "anaemic, palely diseased" writers such as Wilde, Baudelaire, and Swinburne (*LR* 5.2: 55, 56).

In response to this critique, Hart Crane, in the final letter of the July issue, "Joyce and Ethics," offers an impassioned defense of Joyce's art and morality. At the time, Crane was only nineteen years old, but he was already an insider at the *Little Review*, having sold advertising for the magazine and published a short poem, "In Shadow," in the December 1917 issue. Crane defends Joyce against the charge of decadence, first by dissociating him from Wilde and Swinburne (who, in his estimation, both lack Joyce's intelligence) and then by asking that readers "let Baudelaire and Joyce stand together" (*LR* 5.3: 65). Their common "penetration into life," he contends, makes people discover "their entrails," which some resentful readers confuse with decadence—whereas "sterility," Crane proclaims, "is the only 'decadence' I recognize."

EPISODE VI: HADES

Little Review *5.5: September 1918*

When the September 1918 issue of the *Little Review* appeared, the four-year agony of World War I was reaching its bloody end. American troops had entered Europe in force, and in August the Germans began a final retreat from the stalemated trenches in which millions had died. When read in this immediate historical context, the extended meditation on death, memory, and grief in Joyce's "Hades" takes on a powerful new valence. For almost exactly four years, Europeans (and more recently, Americans) had passed steadily into graveyards to bury their dead, making passages like this seem urgent: "How many. All these here once walked round Dublin. Besides how could you remember everybody?" (*LRU* 98). Set in 1904, *Ulysses* is nowhere explicitly about the war, but its effects pervade the text and radiate out through the rest of the magazine in a collection of shared themes, images, and motifs that all cohere around death and the afterlife.

Ben Hecht's story "Decay," for example, might itself have been titled "Hades," given its deliberate invocation of hell in a powerful description of a slum ravaged by poverty: "Here in this street the half dead begin to give forth an odor. The rows of sagging little houses are like the teeth in an old man's mouth. From them arise the exhalations of stagnant wood, of putrescent stairways, of bodies from which the sweats of lust have never been washed, of ulcerous shadows and soft, bubbling alleys. The stench is like a grime that leadens the air" (*LR* 5.5: 39). The narrative describes the life of a brutalized woman whose husband essentially rapes her as their child lies dying in the next room. These visions of death and suffering are picked up in the four poems by T. S. Eliot that appear in this issue. "Sweeney among the Nightingales," for example, describes a darkly urban scene in which a man is surrounded by prostitutes. Evoking the same epic parallels that structure *Ulysses,* it concludes by comparing these women to those who "sang within the bloody wood / When Agamemnon cried aloud" (11). Unlike Joyce's everyday Odysseus, who escapes his encounter with death, the Greek king that Eliot focuses on here returned from war only to be murdered by his wife. Similar themes appear in the rest of Eliot's poems in this issue, including "Whispers of Immortality," which opens with allusions to authors who meditated on corpses and who, like John Webster, "saw the skull beneath the skin." Even Sherwood Anderson's short story "Senility," though seemingly about a mad old man in a railway station, nevertheless evokes the war, which not only ravaged bodies but also destroyed the minds of many shell-shocked veterans.

Although traces of the war pervade the issue, it appears explicitly only twice: once in a brief notice in the "Books" column about the death in action of the poet Isaac Rosenberg (*LR* 5.5: 50) and, more prominently, in W. B. Yeats's "In Memory of Robert Gregory." This elegiac poem about the combat death of Yeats's wealthy patron's son opens and thus frames the entire issue, so Bloom's meditation on those he has lost connects powerfully with Yeats's attempt to "name the friends that cannot sup with us" (1). Unlike Bloom's escape from the gates of death at the end of "Hades," however, Yeats seems unable or unwilling to complete the work of mourning, and the poem ends not with a strong sense of resolution but with a self-confessed failure as the poet loses "all my heart for speech" (4). Indeed, this uncertainty upset Gregory's family, prompting Yeats to write a second elegy, "An Irish Airman Foresees His Death," and in November the *Little Review* reprinted a short article in which the poet unambiguously praises the dead man as an artist, hero, and genius.

The unsettling difficulties of "In Memory" exemplify the strain of literary modernism that Ezra Pound sought to champion in the *Little Review.* Suspicious of old forms and easy sentiment, this new mode of experiment depended instead on irony, difficulty, and the jarring juxtaposition of images; it was also not timid about standing up to criticism. Perhaps with such literary ideals in mind, Pound launched a scathing critique of American poetry in this issue by publishing Edgar Jepson's essay "The Western School." Jepson's piece was originally commissioned by Harriet Monroe, the editor of *Poetry* magazine. In an acid note introducing the essay, Pound writes that it had been "rejected for its lack of flattery, its lack of kow-tow to certain local celebrities" (*LR* 5.5: 5). He then gets in another jab at the *Little Review*'s rival, warning that there is "no intolerance like that of a 'great public.'" The essay touched off furious responses from *Poetry* as well as American newspapers, and the *Little Review*'s "Reader Critic" column sustained this often bruising debate for months.

The vision of modernism that emerges from the September 1918 issue is largely familiar to us, the list of contributors in the table of contents reading almost like names in an anthology. Joyce's *Ulysses* thus seems comfortably ensconced among other resonant names such as Eliot, Pound, Yeats, and Anderson. The "Reader Critic" column reminds us, however, that for most readers *Ulysses* remained a confusing, uncertain, even chaotic text. Without the benefit of the schemas or a sense of the book's deeper epic structure, Marsden Hartley struggled to make sense of its welter of detail. Himself a talented painter, Hartley tries to map Joyce's innovations onto the revolutionary changes that were remaking visual art. After calling *Ulysses* a kind of "cross-hatching which has not the distinction of Rembrandt," he goes on to argue that the text's apparent fascination with detail and its weak, even nonexistent plot make it akin to pointillism (*LR* 5.5: 60). "Is Joyce," he asks, "a Seurat [or] a Signac in wordy dots?" (61). Hartley, like the editors and readers of the *Little Review,* clearly sensed that Joyce's novel was something different, but he was still waiting to see whether the book might possess the "artistry [that] comes in fullness" (62).

EPISODE VII: AEOLUS

Little Review *5.6: October 1918*

The October 1918 issue of the *Little Review* begins with seven poems by Yeats and a critical essay by Pound. This is fitting, since it was Yeats who first introduced Pound to Joyce's work, which in turn led to the publication of *A Portrait of the Artist as a Young Man* and *Ulysses* in journals in which Pound had some influence. In his critical essay, Pound discusses Jean de Bosschère's study of the symbolist poet Max Elskamp. De Bosschère, a Belgian artist and critic, had taken refuge in London during the war, where he met Pound and other poets. Some of his poems, in French, appear in this issue, along with images of his visual art.

French literature is the concern of two other pieces by Pound that frame Joyce's "Aeolus" in this issue; in both, Pound invokes his study of modern French poets that appeared in the *Little Review* in February 1918, a month before the start of *Ulysses*'s serialization. Referred to subsequently as the *Little Review*'s French number, this issue sampled the work of over a dozen recent French poets, whom Pound unapologetically published untranslated, announcing up front that "the time when the intellectual affairs of America could be conducted on a monolingual basis is over" (*LR* 4.10: 3). After a mildly critical review of the French number appeared in the April issue of *Poetry,* the *Little Review* countered in October with a "Note upon Fashions in Criticism," which painstakingly enumerates the reviewer's many small inaccuracies. Signed by J. H. Le Monier, the piece, which immediately precedes "Aeolus" in the magazine, is almost certainly by Pound himself, writing in French and posing as a French literary authority. The other piece by Pound that immediately follows *Ulysses* in the October issue describes a less defensive response to his French number, this time by a real person. In "Albert Mockel and 'La Wallonie,'" Pound reprints a letter that Mockel—the symbolist poet who edited the Belgian review *La Wallonie* from 1886 to 1892—sent Pound in response to his French number; in it, he says he feels a kinship ("une sorte de cousinage") between the *Little Review* and the journal he edited thirty years earlier, even describing *La Wallonie* as "notre *Little Review* à nous" (*LR* 5.6: 52, 51). In the remainder of the piece, Pound introduces readers to the "permanent value" of Mockel's "small magazine" by reprinting a dozen of the poems it published, including works by Mallarmé (63). Pound thus rounded out the October issue with another anthology of untranslated French poems, which figures as a sort of bookend to the February number. In fact, when he later republished his study of *La Wallonie* in his collection *Instigations* (1920), Pound simply added it, along with his piece on De Bosschère, to the end of his "Study of French Poets" as a natural extension of that work.

The deep interest in French literature that Pound displays in the October issue (and elsewhere) is something he shares with Joyce. As seen in "Lotus Eaters" (episode V), Joyce also had a special relationship, as a native English speaker, to French literature and culture; he admired Flaubert's realism, and he credited the symbolist author Édouard Dujardin with inspiring his own use of interior monologue, which he had noticed in Dujardin's novel *Les Lauriers sont coupés* ("The laurels are cut down"), translated by Joyce's friend Stuart Gilbert as *We'll to the Woods No More.* But the two French texts by Pound that frame *Ulysses* in this issue have an additional, specific resonance with "Aeolus," since they show Pound looking to French literature for the artistic fellowship, appreciation, and shared sense of purpose that he had difficulty finding for his work back home—and that speaks to the outsider status of Joyce's two protagonists in *Ulysses,* excluded from the mainstream of social and cultural life of Dublin, which is very much on display in episode VII.

In "Aeolus," we find Bloom and Stephen in the same Dublin newspaper offices, and though they don't actually meet, they are nonetheless connected by their common sense of exclusion: Bloom is repeatedly locked out of the camaraderie of the newspaper men and made to scramble to get his ad placed, and Stephen shows himself, with the parable of the plums he relates, to be out of step with the rhetorical inflation around him at the press. Like Pound, Stephen has cosmopolitan literary ambitions that put him at odds with the popular journalism of the day. His search for his true literary paternity will eventually lead him to the foreign-looking Bloom, who figures as his father in Homer's Greek tale; in much the same way, Pound seems to find in the older Mockel a symbolic foster parent for his own literary ambitions, which remained unfulfilled in America. Indeed, as Pound wistfully imagines it, the magazine office of *La Wallonie*—located in Liège, "in the heart of French Belgium"—was in its day a site of exemplary literary value and fellowship: "Permanent literature, and the seeds of permanent literature, had gone through proof-sheets in their office. There is perhaps no greater pleasure in life, and there certainly can have been no greater enthusiasm than to have been young and to have been part of such a group of writers working in fellowship at the beginning of such a course, of such a series of courses as were implicated in *La Wallonie*" (*LR* 5.6: 63). This vision of literary and professional camaraderie eludes both Stephen and Bloom in the newspaper offices in "Aeolus," and it was likewise one that Pound had trouble achieving at the *Little Review,* where his tenure as a foreign editor was coming to an end. Nonetheless, by reprinting the poems from *La Wallonie* in this issue, Pound positioned himself as Mockel's literary heir, incorporating his forebear's symbolist work into his own avant-garde little magazine.

EPISODE VIII: LESTRYGONIANS

Little Review *5.9 and 5.10/11: January and February–March 1919*

There was a two-month break in the *Little Review*'s serialization of *Ulysses* after "Aeolus" appeared in October 1918. Though the war ended during this period, the delay seems to have stemmed merely from the difficulty that Joyce had completing "Lestrygonians" in time to meet the journal's monthly serialization schedule. Episode VIII runs about 1,500 words longer than the previous longest episode, and its increased length probably led the editors to break it into two installments.

The two issues in which "Lestrygonians" appeared, spanning the first three months of 1919, also happen to be the last in which Pound played a significant role as an editor at the magazine. Notable texts published in the January 1919 issue include Yeats's one-act verse drama *The Dreaming of the Bones;* the first installment of May Sinclair's autobiographical novel *Mary Olivier: A Life*—a female *Portrait of the Artist* whose first section, recording the author's impressions from infancy, was serialized in the magazine's next three issues; a four-person discussion of Joyce's drama, *Exiles;* and the second half of Israel Solon's "The Boulevard," a sort of Yiddish Cinderella story set in Chicago. The February–March issue, dedicated to Remy de Gourmont, features five pieces on the work of the French Symbolist, who died in 1915. The issue also contains Pound's retrospective piece "The Death of Vorticism" (which he claims to be wildly exaggerated), illustrated with woodblock images by the *Blast* contributor Edward Wadsworth, and a letter by Edgar Jepson that represented the latest installment of his ongoing controversy with Harriet Monroe about the merits of American poetry. Whereas Pound, in his final issue as editor, aptly situated Joyce's novel amid other European artists and art movements he championed, the January issue helps place "Lestrygonians"—and *Ulysses* generally—in the context of Joyce's work as a playwright.

In particular, the January issue allows readers to relate *Ulysses* to the innovative work of the Irish theater. Yeats modeled his play *The Dreaming of the Bones* on a Japanese Noh play that Pound and Ernest Fenollosa had translated into English. Despite its publication here, *Dreaming* was not performed until Dublin's Abbey Theatre staged it in 1931. Set during the 1916 Easter Rising, the play is about a young republican who, while hiding in the country hills, encounters the wandering ghosts of Dermot and Dervogilla, two lovers from Ireland's distant past who are doing penance for an affair that had disastrous consequences for the country. After Dermot stole Dervogilla away from her husband, he recruited Normans to invade Ireland, which eventually led to the English occupation of the country. Having thus "sold their country into slavery" (*LR* 5.9: 11), the couple will remain cursed until someone in Ireland forgives them—which, the play suggests, will not happen any time soon, since the young rebel withholds his forgiveness. Like *Ulysses,* Yeats's play aligns Dublin and contemporary Ireland with ancient history. And like both *Ulysses* and *Exiles,* it makes spousal infidelity a central concern.

Joyce wrote *Exiles* in 1914, but it wasn't published in England and America until May 1918, which occasioned its discussion in the *Little Review.* At the time, the play had yet to be produced; Joyce had offered it twice to the Abbey Theatre, but Yeats turned it down both times, presumably because it was too sensational for its audience (Ellmann 401). Yeats likely worried about the play's libertine views toward adultery and free love; but the discussion of *Exiles* in the *Little Review,* while acknowledging its affront to conventional morality, sees the play as controversial in other areas. All four discussants find subconscious desires at work in Joyce's drama. John Rodker describes a battle between will and instinct among its characters, and Samuel Tannenbaum offers a psychoanalytic reading that draws out the "repressed but most urgent impulses" of the author himself (*LR* 5.9: 23). The unconscious impulse that Tannenbaum and Israel Solon both regard as the play's central theme is homosexuality—a sexual attraction between the two male friends, Richard and Robert, which secretly motivates the love triangle they form with Bertha, Richard's wife. Jane Heap (writing as *jh*) also acknowledges Robert's homosexual love for Richard, but takes this interpretation a step further by tracing the source of sexual conflict in the play to the way in which both Robert and Bertha desire to be Richard.

This discussion of *Exiles,* which immediately precedes *Ulysses* in the January 1919 issue, invites readers to notice likenesses between the two works. They might have wondered, for instance, whether "Exiles" provides a better name for Joyce's novel than "Ulysses," since the play's title easily describes both Bloom and Stephen—the wandering Jew who is out of place in Catholic Dublin, and the alienated artist who, like Richard Rowan, has recently returned to Ireland from Europe. More significantly, the love triangle at the heart of *Exiles,* hinging on whether the hero's wife will give herself to a male friend, may have helped some readers discern its more obscure counterpart in *Ulysses* and thus make sense of Bloom's recurring anxiety in "Lestrygonians" about Molly and Boylan. It is difficult to say whether the magazine's original readers took Bloom to be homosexual, but even this idea, suggested by the *Exiles* discussion, might have helped them reflect on the underlying cause of his troubled and apparently abstinent relationship with Molly. And those readers who could secure a copy of Joyce's play might have further recognized Bloom's behavior in the surprising passivity Richard displays toward his wife's affair. Robert's defense of multiple partners for women, Richard's insistence on Bertha's freedom to be faithful or not, and Richard's secret longing to be betrayed by her and Robert may all shed light on Bloom's unexplained unwillingness to prevent Molly's adultery.

Though we can see today how the January number illuminates *Ulysses,* we know that some of the magazine's original readers were unable to fashion such insights themselves—for the simple reason that their issue never arrived in the mail. After Anderson sent a batch of magazines to subscribers, "Lestrygonians" was deemed obscene by U.S. postal authorities, who barred Anderson from mailing additional copies of the January issue. Episode VIII thus became the first of four episodes of *Ulysses* to run afoul of the law (*Pound/The Little Review* 261).

EPISODE IX: SCYLLA AND CHARYBDIS

Little Review *5.12 and 6.1: April and May 1919*

After the seizure of the January 1919 issue, Anderson became wary of the increasing attentions of the postal authorities. Without consulting Joyce, she cut several passages from the second part of "Scylla and Charybdis," which appeared in the May 1919 issue, signaling these omissions in the text with an extended ellipsis and a note:

> * The Post Office authorities objected to certain passages in the January installment of "Ulysses," which prevents our mailing any more copies of that issue. To avoid a similar interference this month I have ruined Mr. Joyce's story by cutting certain passages in which he mentions natural facts known to everyone. —M. C. A. (*LRU* 170)

The passages Anderson removed were explicit but relatively innocuous, the most significant describing the mysterious W. H. of Shakespeare's sonnets performing "the holy office an ostler does for the stallion" (*U* 9.664). In the book's larger scheme, this passage evokes Bloom, who, by passively accepting Molly's affair with Blazes, performs the role of an "ostler" or stable hand. These small cuts, however, proved insufficient, and the post office impounded the May issue of the magazine as well. "This is the second time I have had the pleasure of being burned while on earth," Joyce ruefully wrote, comparing himself to a martyred saint (*LI* 137).

Amid these ominous signs, the magazine underwent a number of significant changes. Pound had been growing restless with the editors and increasingly suspicious of their commitment to his cause. He wrote to Joyce in December 1918, urging him to speed up his work, out of concern that "these women in New York may go bust" (*Pound/Joyce* 147). The real trouble, however, was that the stipend John Quinn had given Pound to solicit and publish work in the *Little Review* had been spent. As a consequence, Pound began to withdraw from the magazine, the last issue in which he had a significant hand appearing in March 1919. Two months later, Anderson launched the sixth volume with a new masthead, which appeared in the middle of the magazine, and Pound's name was noticeably absent. John Rodker and Jules Romains were now listed as "Foreign Editors," and a newly created "Advisory Board" appeared, listing Jane Heap ("jh") as its sole member. This same issue contains a short commentary by Pound titled "Avis," the Latin term for "bird," which invokes his flight from the magazine. In it he expresses his frustration with American writers who "in utter and abject intellectual cowardice seek to avoid international standards" (*LR* 6.1: 70). Pound closes by affirming the kind of cosmopolitan aesthetic he had long advocated in the magazine, then declares himself unwilling to repeat himself yet again on this point. Despite breaking his editorial connection with the paper, he nevertheless continued to serve as a conduit for Joyce, sending Anderson the typescripts for installments of *Ulysses* as they were finished. He also published some additional essays and poems in its pages—including Ernest Fenollosa's "The Chinese Written Character as a Medium for Poetry," edited by Pound and serialized in the last four months of 1919—though by 1920 he looked back on his involvement with Anderson and Heap with distaste. Even as they faced prison for publishing *Ulysses,* he wrote to Joyce that "the editrices have merely messed and muddled, NEVER to their own loss" (*Pound/Joyce* 184). In 1921, Pound's name did appear once more on the *Little Review* masthead, but only after the magazine had been reorganized as a quarterly and begun its decline.

When Pound left in 1919, the magazine took on a different look. The covers, which had been printed on heavy stock in vibrant solid colors, appeared instead on decorative paper with elaborate designs evocative of wallpaper. The first issue of the new volume was also considerably longer than previous ones, running to eighty-four pages, compared with the sixty-eight in the April number. The familiar, even iconic "Reader Critic" section, which used to appear at the end, was now in the middle—a space traditionally reserved in magazines for editorial comment—and was retitled "Discussion." Most of these changes, however, proved short-lived: three months later, the old covers returned, as did the "Reader Critic" column soon thereafter. Nevertheless, the changes in May 1919 suggest that with Pound's departure, Anderson and Heap sought to take the magazine in a new direction.

Most strikingly, this issue features a number of items by and about women, including Djuna Barnes's elliptical story "The Valet," which explores the strange erotic relationships surrounding a dying man. Both the April and May 1919 issues contain serial installments of May Sinclair's semiautobiographical novel *Mary Olivier: A Life.* A year before, Sinclair had offered her now-famous meditation on the use of stream of consciousness in books by Dorothy Richardson and Joyce. Now her own work featured similar narrative experiments in a novel that reads as a kind of feminist response to the early episodes of *A Portrait of the Artist as a Young Man.* This same issue also features three radically avant-garde poems by the eccentric Else von Freytag-Loringhoven, extended commentary in the "Discussion" section on a play by Susan Glaspell, and book reviews by Babette Deutsch.

There is also a notable shift in emphasis toward American writers, framed by the serialized publication of William Carlos Williams's "Prologue" to what will become *Kora in Hell.* In "Prologue I," he strikes out against both the idea that he should be an American writer and Pound's belief that poets should measure up to international standards. In this, he articulates a project for himself that might well describe Joyce's aims in *Ulysses:* "There is nothing sacred about literature, it is damned from one end to the other. There is nothing in literature but change and change is mockery. I'll write whatever I damn please, whenever I damn please and as I damn please and it'll be good if the authentic spirit of change is on it" (*LR* 5.12: 8). This radical embrace of artistic autonomy remained a driving force in the *Little Review* even after Pound's departure, and it shaped the new episodes of *Ulysses* that appeared in the coming months—episodes that eventually landed the magazine and its editors in court.

EPISODE X: WANDERING ROCKS

Little Review *6.2 and 6.3: June and July 1919*

"Wandering Rocks" appeared in the June and July 1919 issues of the *Little Review,* divided by the editors into two installments, just like the two episodes that preceded it in 1919. In addition, the June and July issues include the first two installments of Dorothy Richardson's novel *Interim.* As the fifth work in Richardson's long sequence of autobiographical novels collectively called *Pilgrimage, Interim* was serialized in eleven consecutive issues of the *Little Review,* concluding in May–June 1920. Since the last installment of *Ulysses* appeared only two issues later, Richardson's *Pilgrimage* was a sustained presence in the magazine for the remainder of *Ulysses*'s serialization, appearing with Joyce's novel in ten issues and back-to-back with it in three. Word for word, Richardson's novel overlaps with nearly 40 percent of *Ulysses* published in the magazine, while the two novels together constitute over two-thirds (68 percent) of all fiction and over two-fifths (41 percent) of all words printed in the ten issues in which they both appear. By their size alone, the novels exert a strong gravitational pull on each other as well as on everything else published with them in the magazine.

As one segment of a modernist saga written by a woman, *Interim* provides a significant counterpoint to Joyce's novel and helps draw out the gender differentiation within modernism that was increasingly felt in the journal after Pound's departure. Significantly, it was Margaret Anderson, not Pound, who had reached out to Richardson earlier in 1919, after reading reviews of *The Tunnel,* the fourth novel in *Pilgrimage,* in order to secure permission to serialize *Interim* in the *Little Review* (Fromm 117–18). Anderson may have wanted to publish something by Richardson ever since May Sinclair's article "The

Novels of Dorothy Richardson" appeared in the magazine's April 1918 issue. But the announcements on the inside front cover page of the June 1919 issue indicate that its appearance in the magazine also coincided with the disappearance of Pound:

> Beginning—*Interim,* a new novel by Dorothy Richardson, the fifth in a series called "Pilgrimage". *Pointed Roofs, Backwater, Honeycomb* were published in America by Mr. Knopf, who is also bringing out the fourth volume, *The Tunnel.*
>
> . . .
>
> Ezra Pound has abdicated and gone to Persia. John Rodker is now the London Editor of the Little Review. (*LR* 6.2: np)

Rodker may have replaced Pound as London editor, but the space in the magazine that Pound had aggressively secured for his authors became occupied by Richardson's novel and by an increasing number of contributions from the likes of Djuna Barnes, Mary Butts, and Else von Freytag-Loringhoven. By identifying *Interim* as the fifth novel in "a series called 'Pilgrimage'" and then naming all four preceding novels, the announcement characterizes Richardson's work as an epic that can stand up to *Ulysses.* Whereas Joyce uses parallels to Homer's *Odyssey* to magnify the lives of his modern characters, Richardson turns the ordinary experiences and inner life of Miriam Henderson, her central character, into the subject of an epic spiritual journey extending over many novels.

In *Pointed Roofs* (1915), Miriam's pilgrimage begins in 1893 when at age seventeen she leaves her parents' suburban home in southwest London and travels to Germany, where she teaches English for five months at a girls' boarding school in Hanover; in *Backwater* (1916), the second novel, she returns to England to teach for three terms at the Wordsworth House in drab North London; and in *Honeycomb* (1917), she becomes a governess in a wealthy household in the upscale Newlands region outside of London. In *The Tunnel* (1919), Miriam works as an assistant in a dental office on Wimpole Street in London; living in the attic of Mrs. Bailey's lodging house in Bloomsbury, she mixes with an intellectual crowd, befriends some "new women," attends lectures and the theater, earns a raise at work, and learns to ride a bicycle. *Interim* continues to chart Miriam's London experience, from Christmas Eve 1896 to August 1897. During those eight months, she tutors her landlady's girl in French, attends piano concerts, walks about London both day and night, visits restaurants, welcomes her sister Eve to London, reads Ibsen's *Brand,*

and buys a bicycle. The novel records her involvement with other boarders at Mrs. Bailey's, including an eligible Canadian doctor, von Heber, who expresses romantic interest in her.

Of course, the everyday events recorded in these novels are noteworthy primarily for the access they afford us, through Richardson's innovative use of interior monologue, into the developing thoughts and reflections of Miriam, who figures as a fictional counterpart of Richardson herself. In this way, the early novels of *Pilgrimage* resonate with Joyce's *A Portrait of the Artist as a Young Man,* since both texts use experimental means to recover the authors' pasts and retrace the paths they took in coming into their own as writers. Miriam resonates with Stephen Dedalus in *Ulysses* as well. Though raised in middle-class families and well educated, both characters have been cast out into the world by a bankrupt father, which forces them to turn to teaching in order to scrape by. Both characters also struggle emotionally with the recent deaths of their mothers—in Miriam's case, by suicide, at the end of the third novel. When *Interim* opens, Miriam is twenty-one years old—about the same age as Stephen in *Ulysses*—and both characters, having come of age, have moved to their native metropolises to find their way.

There is one more surprising connection between Miriam and Stephen in these two novels: their authors bring both characters into the orbit of a Jewish man who may significantly change their lives. Among the boarders that Miriam meets at Mrs. Bailey's is Bernard Mendizabal—a raffish, clever foreigner who is fluent in multiple languages and whom Miriam is drawn to as an expression of the cosmopolitan spirit. One night as she steps out for a walk, Mendizabal accompanies her, leading her eventually to Ruscinos', a continental café where he feels at home in London (*LR* 6.6: 52–53). Though Miriam's nighttime excursions with Mendizabal to the café are innocent enough, a scandal ensues when word of them gets back to the boardinghouse. Dr. von Heber breaks off relations with Miriam, declaring her to be lost before he abruptly leaves the country. Miriam subsequently learns that von Heber's rejection of her was clinched by Mendizabal's fatuous boast that he had her tied around his finger (*LR* 6.10: 24); apparently, the idea of Miriam's succumbing to a foreigner and a Jew marked her as hopelessly contaminated in von Heber's eyes. Both *Interim* and *Ulysses,* then, involve a Jewish figure who draws out characters' racial prejudice but also looks after the novel's young hero. In Miriam's case, she is arguably better off for having met Mendizabal, who unwittingly saved her from an unfulfilling middle-class life as a doctor's wife in Canada.

Miriam's free movement about London, which winds up affecting her social reputation, is also a point of resonance, in the June and July issues, between *Interim* and "Wandering Rocks." In this episode, Joyce continues to depart from the initial style of *Ulysses* to chart the movement of multiple characters, including Stephen and Bloom, as they make their way about Dublin between 3 and 4 P.M. Joyce's fragmented narrative, which captures the chop and change of bustling city life, contrasts sharply with the narrative technique of *Interim,* which immerses us in extended stretches of Miriam's singular consciousness—a contrast that is felt most sharply when she, like Joyce's characters in "Wandering Rocks," walks about town. Miriam tends to project her thoughts and feelings onto her London environment, as when she walked along Oxford Street after reading Ibsen and "wandered on and on forgetful in an expansion of everything that passed into her mind out and out towards a centre in Norway" (*LR* 6.6: 44). But the city can also be confrontational, challenging her composure, as it does in chapter 1 when she walks alone about North London on Christmas Day:

> She wandered along the little roads turning and turning until she came to a broad open thoroughfare lined with high grey houses standing back behind colourless railed-in gardens. Trams jingled up and down the centre of the road bearing the names of unfamiliar parts of London. People were standing about on the terminal islands and getting in and out of the trams. She had come too far. Here was the wilderness, the undissembling soul of north London, its harsh unvarying all-embracing oblivion. . . . . Innumerable impressions gathered on walks with the school-girls or in lonely wanderings; the unveiled motives and feelings of people she had passed in the streets, the expression of noses and shoulders, the indefinable uniformity, of bearing and purpose and vision, crowded in on her, oppressing and darkening the crisp light air. She fought against them, rallying to the sense of the day. (6.2: 20)

We find Miriam here especially vulnerable in an unsympathetic locale, attempting to hold off the mostly unpleasant memories it awakens in her as she struggles to pull herself out of dejection.

Miriam's relationship to city space in *Interim*—her exploration of different regions of London, drawing out different parts of herself—has no counterpart in "Wandering Rocks"; in Dublin, respectable women do not freely wander the streets in search of experience. Though women appear in the episode, the great majority of characters milling about the city are male, and the handful of women encountered are, for the most part, located safely inside—like the blond girl who works in Thornton's shop; or Miss Kennedy and Miss Douce, who look out the bar window in the Ormond Hotel; or Lady Dudley, who rides in a carriage in the viceroy's cavalcade; or even Molly, whose "plump bare generous arm" is thrust out a window to throw a coin down to a beggar (*LRU* 192). The character in "Wandering Rocks" that perhaps comes closest to Miriam's female flâneur is Stephen's younger sister Dilly, who roams Dublin in search of material and spiritual sustenance. But we do not get into Dilly's head as we do Miriam's, and neither do we find in *Ulysses* a female character who approaches Miriam's sustained free wandering, in either thought or step, until we encounter Gerty MacDowell, whose erotic activity with Bloom on a public beach in episode XIII led the U.S. courts to ban *Ulysses.*

EPISODE XI: SIRENS

Little Review *6.4 and 6.5: August and September 1919*

During the summer of 1919, the *Little Review* published, for the first time, works by Emanuel Carnevali (in June), Malcolm Cowley and Yvor Winters (in July), Mary Butts (in August), and Aldous Huxley (in September). Meanwhile, the side-by-side serialization of *Ulysses* and *Pilgrimage* continued uninterrupted, encouraging its audience to read them together. By September, the first critical responses to Richardson's novel appear, by William Carlos Williams and John Rodker, who both relate Richardson's writing to Joyce's. In "Four Foreigners," Williams commends the prose of the two novelists for capturing the living present—"Their form lives!"; "They plunge naked into the flaming cauldron of today"—which he finds missing from the recent war poetry of D. H. Lawrence and Richard Aldington (*LR* 6.5: 38). Surprisingly, Williams claims that Joyce and Richardson are truer to the experience of war than these two poets because they do not try to capture its reality directly in their work: "Insofar as their form goes the war exists in it, carries its own meaning. It is a different war, it is not like other wars, it is modern, it exists" (38).

Rodker's article "Dorothy Richardson" likewise relates the two authors, though only as part of his larger complaint that the method of Richardson's *Pilgrimage,* by its fifth iteration in *Interim,* has become tiresome, leaving readers with a welter of material details that fail to amount to much. "Her method has been compared to that of Joyce," Rodker writes. "This is mere footling since anyone with a sufficiently sympathetic and cultured brain can follow Joyce and be moved by him; but Miss Richardson's associations are as free as a choppy sea and with the same effect. Miss Richardson is too intellectually subtle" (*LR* 6.5: 41). Regardless of how one rates either author, there is some merit to Rodker's observation that their methodologies have parted ways. Each installment of *Interim* in the magazine continues to unfold, in close focus, Miriam Henderson's web of mind and life, whereas each corresponding installment of *Ulysses* draws further away from *Ulysses*'s initial style, pursuing instead one stylistic experiment after another in successive episodes. There is little in previous chapters of either *Pilgrimage* or *Ulysses* to prepare readers for what appears in "Sirens," the last of four *Ulysses* episodes to be published in two installments.

There are other texts in the August and September 1919 issues of the *Little Review,* however, that resonate strikingly with Joyce's new experimental writing in "Sirens" and point to the magazine's reinvention after Pound's departure. In this episode, which features singing in the saloon of the Ormond Hotel, Joyce transforms his own writing into song, opening the chapter with an overture and then invoking a fugue to braid together the voices of his characters. At first glance, the episode's opening section, with its series of short incoherent lines, appears more like poetry than prose—and the prose poems by Jessie Dismorr that begin the August issue seem to be its proper literary kin. Even stronger resonance can be discerned in the lead item from the September issue, Else von Freytag-Loringhoven's "Iron Cast Lover." Whereas Joyce uses the fugue, a musical form drawn from the Renaissance, to create a distinctively modern text in "Sirens," in "Iron Cast Lover" Freytag-Loringhoven has composed a love song that draws on the conventions of love poetry—the poet complains of unreciprocated love, uses archaic language throughout, and employs such traditional devices as inventorying the lover's cherished features—only to turn them on their head, resulting in the "half-inarticulate frenzy" of a sensualist (according to Maxwell Bodenheim) who "claw[s] aside the veils and rush[es] forth howling, vomiting, and leaping nakedly" (*LR* 6.7: 64).

In its concern with music, "Sirens" reverberates with still other texts in the August and September issues. In episode XI, Joyce turns an Irish barroom with amateur singers and a piano into a concert hall, but the many references to music and singing in the magazine's other pieces remind us that a vibrant musical culture, including both amateur and professional performers, was not limited to Dublin at the time. Significantly, each installment of *Interim* in these two issues finds Miriam Henderson attending a piano recital in London. And the *Little Review*'s editor, Margaret Anderson, was herself a committed amateur pianist who brought her love for the instrument into the magazine. From the very first issues, in 1914, Anderson contributed concert reviews, appreciations of operatic singing by Mary Garden and of piano performances by Ignacy Paderewski and Harold Bauer, as well as discussions of the future of modern piano playing. Anderson's love of music is also on display in the piano ads for Mason & Hamlin ("The Stradivarius of Pianos") that appear on the inside cover pages of the August and September issues. An oddity among the magazine's other advertisements, these ads stem from a deal that Anderson struck early on with the piano company: so long as she ran the ads for free in the magazine, she got free use of a Mason & Hamlin piano at her home (Anderson 67). The *Little Review* underwent striking changes over the years, but the advertisements for Mason & Hamlin were one of its few constants. They are a reminder of Anderson's lasting commitment to the piano and music, which was perhaps rivaled only by her dedication to publishing *Ulysses*.

EPISODE XII: CYCLOPS

Little Review *6.7–6.10: November 1919–March 1920*

"Cyclops," which continues Joyce's increasingly extravagant experiments with narrative technique, appeared in the *Little Review* across four issues and five months, from November 1919 to March 1920. The installments vary in length, ranging from sixteen pages in the first issue to just six in the last one. Anderson and Heap divided this episode for publication in a way that emphasizes its parodic interpolations, since all three of the last installments begin with or just before one of the sections Joyce called examples of "gigantism," passages in which the narrative is disrupted by inflated disquisitions on often unrelated topics. The January issue, for example, opens with this sentence: "The fashionable international world attended en masse this afternoon at the wedding of the chevalier Jean Wyse de Nolan, grand high chief ranger of the Irish National Foresters, with Miss Fir Conifer of Pine Valley," whose maids of honor, we then learn, are her sisters, "Miss Larch Conifer and Miss Spruce Conifer" (*LRU* 284). The narrative thread from the previous section of "Cyclops"—promised by the persistent "to be continued" tag that concludes each installment—thus becomes particularly difficult for the magazine's readers to follow as the epic saga of Stephen and Bloom becomes lost amid amusing but bewildering puns on the names of trees.

The disruptive elements of "Cyclops," however, were consistent with the *Little Review*'s larger turn in these issues toward avant-garde experiment at the limits of meaning. Indeed, next to the work of Else von Freytag-Loringhoven, whose poems appear in two of the same issues (and are the subject of discussion in all four), Joyce's writing seems constrained. A flamboyant Greenwich Village personality whom Heap called "the first American dada" (*LR* 8.2: 46), Freytag-Loringhoven made her life and body a work of art by stealing flagrantly from people, assembling elaborate costumes made from trash, and starring in a film by Man Ray and Marcel Duchamp titled *The Baroness Shaves Her Pubic Hair.* Her writing was provocative and erotic, even as it attacked the very idea of meaning. The March 1920 issue, for example, features a tone poem titled "Narin—Tzarissamanili (He is dead!)" that uses nonsense words to emphasize the pure sonic capacity of verse. It begins "Ildrich mitzdonja—astatootch / Ninj—iffe kniek— / Ninj—iffe kniek!" and concludes with a tension between silence and energy: "Sh— Sh— / Vrmm" (*LR* 6.10: 11–12). The emphasis here on the material quality of sound resonates clearly with Joyce's turn away from narrative in "Cyclops" and toward his own playful experiments with language.

These same energies pervaded the pages of the *Little Review* in this period as the magazine became increasingly militant in its embrace of experimentation and its affirmation of the imagination's supremacy. The issue that begins with Joyce's arboreal puns concludes with a poem in the "Reader Critic" section by the cartoonist Weare Holbrook, written in response to an anonymous editor's lament, "*If this be modern, give us Wordsworth!*" Promising the editor some kitschy natural artifacts and offering to do yard work for him, the poet writes, "I give you Wordsworth—lots of him! / I hope you choke" (*LR* 6.9: 63).

Similar kinds of attacks on conventional poetry appeared throughout the magazine, often taking place in the expanding "Discussion" section at the center of each issue. In these pages, which typically occupied a quarter of the contents, Anderson and Heap published letters, short essays, and commentary that engaged in a wide-ranging debate about the nature of art. After a lengthy letter from Evelyn Scott, for instance, that tries to force Heap's thinking into a kind of logical consistency, there appears only this response: "I feel that I have been permitted a glimpse of the gentle mystic soul of an adding-machine" (*LR* 6.10: 47). In the December issue, Heap offers a short piece titled "Sincerity," which takes direct aim at the magazine's critics and borrows from Oscar Wilde to mount a defense of the creative mind's power to shock, rankle, and offend: "When primitive man abandoned sincerity civilization began. . . . And still one has to stand champing at the bit while some good citizen gushes over the sincerity of this or that public man or assures us that our magazine would be 'all right' if the artists contributing to it were only sincere and not trying to be so extreme. Who could face the situation of a sincere world: the boredom, the sights and sounds, the danger!" (*LR* 6.8: 32). These consciously provocative defenses of an aesthetic clearly shaped by the anarchic energies of Dada resonate throughout the magazine. In the March issue, for example, Anderson prints a letter from a subscriber ("The Good Old Days") that echoes questions about the magazine's editorial turn raised by similar correspondents in earlier issues: "Your *Little Review* bewilders me. All the things I like best you disparage and all your enthusiasms I think . . . should be preserved as samples of the madness of the present age" (*LR* 6.10: 60). Anderson responds, "I really don't know what to say to all these denunciations—these neurotic excesses that we are so generally accused of." Less acerbic than Heap, she nevertheless offers a strong defense of the experiments conducted by Joyce and others, concluding that "art is a challenge to life" (61, 62).

The risks that Anderson and Heap took extended well beyond the injection of Dadaist aesthetics, however, since the magazine was entering a period of legal and financial crisis. *Ulysses* again caught the attention of the postal censors when the third installment of "Cyclops," in the January 1920 issue, was seized and burned, despite the editors' efforts to forestall such action. Heap believed the seizure resulted from Joyce's poor treatment of Queen Victoria and King Edward, though no formal cause was listed. Anderson herself had hoped to prevent such difficulties in the November issue by striking some twenty lines from *Ulysses* "to avoid the censor's possible suppression" (*LR* 6.7: 49). This passage includes Alf Bergan's graphic discussion of the erections produced by hanging and the interpolated passage in which Bloom delivers a lecture on the effect in the guise of "Herr Professor Luitpold Blumenduft" (*U* 12.456–78). Anderson was not cautious enough, however, and the seizure of the January issue led to the cancellation of the February number and thus a gap in the dating sequence of the magazine.

These legal difficulties also put in jeopardy a renewed push by Anderson to secure more advertising from book publishers. The results of these efforts are visible in the December 1919 issue, which contains ads from eight publishing houses, including Huebsch (Joyce's American publisher) and Doran (which published best-selling authors like Gilbert Cannan). In this same issue, Anderson pens an open letter, "To the Book Publishers of America," in which she describes her attempts to canvas New York publishers for advertisements, telling them that the *Little Review* gave a start to many of their own successful writers and that the magazine was owed some financial support. As she notes in the letter, however, "some objected so strongly to our policy and to Mr. James Joyce that nothing would induce them to appear" (*LR* 6.8: 65). She then closes with a request to the publishers: "I ask whether you can give your support, at least once a year, to the one magazine in America in which the man of letters may obtain a hearing among his peers, ungarbled in editorial rooms to suit the public taste" (67).

Judging by the number of new advertisers in the December issue, this campaign seemed promising. Following the seizure of the January number, however, only one significant ad, from Houghton Mifflin, appears in the March issue, which closes with another open letter from Anderson, this one titled "Some of the Causes for the Omission of the February Number" (*LR* 6.10: 64). She describes the censorship by the U. S. postal service as well as a number of other difficulties both personal and financial, including the loss of the apartment where the magazine had been based and cases of influenza contracted by the editors. This page-long letter concludes with the news that the magazine had lost its "temperamental printer" and was facing growing costs for labor and raw materials in the aftermath of the war. Within a few months, the situation would grow even more precarious as Anderson and Heap began printing "Nausicaa," the episode that led to a legal ban on the American publication of *Ulysses*.

EPISODE XIII: NAUSICAA

Little Review *6.11, 7.1, and 7.2: April–August 1920*

"Nausicaa," which brings Bloom within sight of Gerty MacDowell and her friends on Sandymount Strand at 8 P.M., ran in three issues of the *Little Review*, the April, May–June, and July–August numbers of 1920—with the final installment, in which Bloom masturbates on the beach, bringing the wrath of the censors down upon the magazine. In the April issue, we find artwork and poems in French by Jean de Bosschère, stories by Djuna Barnes and Emanuel

Carnevali, an eight-part lyric poem by Malcolm Cowley, and the latest installments of Richardson's *Interim* and Sherwood Anderson's *A New Testament.* Also included is a book review by Ezra Pound of *Economic Democracy*—a work by Major C. H. Douglas, which had been serialized in 1919 in the *New Age,* to which Pound was a regular contributor. Pound's interest in the economic theories of Douglas led him through a field of political and economic thought that finally ended in his disgust with democratic capitalism and his support for the Fascism of Mussolini in Italy.

Readers of the *Little Review* who had waded through "Cyclops" might have uttered a sigh of relief when they began "Nausicaa," which greets them with a sentimental and unsophisticated prose style that comes partly out of the popular commercial magazines for women, like *The Princess Novelettes,* that Gerty read. The *Little Review* had little in common with such magazines, but we may nonetheless observe that the downward shift in register that Joyce uses so effectively in this episode is at work in another piece in the April issue—Charles Henry's review of the Fourth Annual Exhibition of the Society of Independent Artists. The exhibition, which took place on the roof of the Waldorf-Astoria hotel in New York, brought together the latest work of American avant-garde artists that the *Little Review* was interested in, including Stuart Davis and Charles Ellis, who both would have drawings published in the July–August issue later that summer. Instead of rising to the task of seriously critiquing the artwork on the roof, however, the reviewer sets his sights at street level and compares the art and artists seen at the exhibition to advertisements, buildings, bridges and businesses seen about Manhattan, framing it all with references to bull—specifically, the "Bull Durham" tobacco bull then advertised in Times Square. Written in a breezy, conversational style, the piece is less art review than gossip column—a who's who about town—of the kind more commonly found in the popular press.

In the May–June issue, the second installment of "Nausicaa" is immediately preceded by the conclusion of Richardson's *Interim,* which produces the interesting juxtaposition of Gerty MacDowell and Miriam Henderson, two very different female characters, both closely observed by their authors. The issue begins with a tribute to W. H. Hudson, the British naturalist and author of *Green Mansions* and *The Purple Land,* with essays by Ford Madox Hueffer, Ezra Pound, and John Rodker. The issue includes stories by Sherwood Anderson and William Carlos Williams, and images of sculptures by Chana

Orloff, with a discussion of her work by Muriel Ciolkowska. The *Ulysses* installment was immediately followed by this exchange in "The Reader Critic":

> Can you tell me when James Joyce's "Ulysses" will appear in book form? Do you think the public will ever be ready for such a book? I read him each month with eagerness, but I must confess that I am defeated in my intelligence. Now tell the truth,—do you yourselves know where the story is at the present moment, how much time has elapsed,—just where are we? Have you any clue as to when the story will end?
>
> ["Ulysses" will probably appear in book form in America if there is a publisher for it who will have sense enough to avoid the public. Joyce has perfected a technique that has enabled him to avoid almost all but those rabid for literature. We haven't any advance chapters in hand, but it would seem that we are drawing towards the Circe episode and the close of the story. The question of time seems simple and unobscured. The story is laid in perhaps the talk centre of the universe, but time is not affected; the time of the present chapter is about five thirty or six in the evening of the same day on which the story started,—I think Tuesday. Mr. Bloom has had a long day since he cooked his breakfast of kidney, but he has lost no time.—*jh.*] (*LR* 7.1: 72)

Actually, as we know, the time of day was a bit later, but Heap has it essentially right. It is indeed the evening of the same day. "Circe," however, was by no means the close of the story, and the *Ulysses* that appeared in 1922 turned to Molly in ways that the readers and editors of the magazine could not have expected.

"Nausicaa" concluded in the July–August 1920 issue, which opens with a photograph of Joyce, looking very stern and serious—hardly the image one might expect of a man whose writing, published in the back pages of the issue, would be declared obscene by the U.S. postal service. In fact, Joyce's alleged appetite for obscenity is debated in all three issues in which "Nausicaa" appears. In the April issue, one reader, "F. E. R.," writes to criticize postal authorities for confiscating the January issue, arguing that they "should recognize that only a few read" Joyce and that those few are not "the kind to have their whole moral natures overthrown by frankness about natural functions" ("Obscenity," *LR* 6.11: 61). In the next issue, another reader, Helen Bishop Dennis from Boston, who identifies herself as one of the "prudes" who don't like

Joyce, offers a contrary view of Joyce's handling of natural functions, which she compares to the behavior of the insane: "There is a certain form of mental unbalance—about the lowest form—that takes delight in concentration on the 'natural functions. . . All attendants in insane asylums are familiar with it. Does James Joyce belong to those so affected? Do 'the few who read him' belong? If not, and Joyce and his readers are to be considered fairly sane, would he—and they—be willing to perform their 'natural functions' in public? If not, why take out a desire for dabbling in filth, in writing in public?" ("The Modest Woman," *LR* 7.1: 73–74). Even if we disagree with the thrust of these questions, we ought to marvel at the letter's timing, since both Joyce and Bloom show a great willingness, in the next issue, to perform some "natural functions" very much in public view.

One writer who clearly disagreed with Helen Dennis was Else von Freytag-Loringhoven, who in the following issue turns the tables on her, asserting that Dennis is in fact unhealthily immodest in strutting about in public "with your cotton-tuft in ear," and that instead of asking Joyce to suppress his writing about natural functions, she—along with all Americans—needs to stop making a public display of her uneasiness: "why have you to show it to the world at large? afflicted people should stay at home—with family" ("'The Modest Woman,'" *LR* 7.2: 39, 38). Though she admits that she has not read *Ulysses* and that Joyce's obscenities are the only thing by him that she could enjoy "with abandon" (40), Freytag-Loringhoven somehow comes up with a perfect defense of the charged matter in "Nausicaa," with its marriage of the sacred and profane, which follows her piece in the issue: "To show hidden beauty of things—there are no limitations! Only artist can do that—that is his holy office. Stronger—braver he is—more he will explore into depths" (39).

EPISODE XIV: OXEN OF THE SUN

Little Review *7.3: September–December 1920*

The first installment of "Oxen of the Sun"—and the last installment of *Ulysses*—appeared in the September–December 1920 issue of the *Little Review,* which was billed as a double number on the cover and likely came out in late November. Only in October did Joyce learn from Pound that the July–August issue of the magazine had been confiscated in New York and the editors were being tried on obscenity charges (*Pound/Joyce* 184; *LI* 149). Having heard nothing from Margaret Anderson, Jane Heap, or John Rodker about these troubles, Joyce tried to find out how much (if any) of "Oxen" had appeared in print and whether the *Little Review* was still being published (*LIII* 27–28). By mid-December, it was clear that Joyce had not seen a copy of the latest issue, since he mistakenly believed that it contained the entire episode (*LIII* 33).

In the opening pages of the September–December issue, the editors break the news to readers about why the magazine was delayed: "The hazards and exigencies of running an Art magazine without capital have forced us to bring out combined issues for the past months. Publication has been further complicated by our arrest on October fourth: Sumner vs. Joyce. Trial, December thirteenth" (*LR* 7.3: 2). During the trial, which took place in February 1921, Anderson and Heap reluctantly agreed to follow the advice of their lawyer, John Quinn, that they remain silent and not speak in defense of Joyce's work (Anderson 219–20). But there is no such self-censoring in the pages of this issue, with each editor sounding off with her own lead item.

In "Art and the Law," Heap expresses her indignation that a work of art like *Ulysses* should be subject to legal review, and she sees the obscenity charges against Joyce's novel as an indictment of American culture, "insensitive and unambitious to the need and appreciation of Art" (*LR* 7.3: 7). Heap also argues that Joyce's "Nausicaa," with its "record of the simplest, most unpreventable, most unfocused sex thoughts possible" (6), does not have the power to corrupt readers, and she refutes the chivalrous premise that the law especially needs to protect young girls against *Ulysses*, noting the irony that she and Anderson were being prosecuted for corrupting the thoughts of a young girl—by exposing her in part to the thoughts of another young girl, Gerty MacDowell.

In "An Obvious Statement (for the millionth time)," Anderson offers her defense of Joyce by shifting the argument to what she believes the court should be discussing: "the relation of the artist—the great writer—to the public" (*LR* 7.3: 8). Anderson thinks that an artist like Joyce is not responsible to the public, though the public is certainly responsible to him; and she says there is no point in trying to limit his expression, since the true artist is immune to all such efforts. Like Heap, Anderson expresses her frustration with an American public that, in its misguided egalitarianism, fails to recognize the artist's cultural superiority and believes it can judge a work of art without any special expertise. Skirting elitism, Anderson concludes: "Of the little freedoms that can be attained or respected, . . . let us respect those of the superior people rather than of the inferior people. It is far more important that a great artist's freedom to write as he pleases be respected than that Mr. Sumner's freedom to suppress what he does not know to be a work of Art be respected" (11). This is not an argument likely to succeed in court, but it is a defiant reaffirmation of the magazine's bold motto (adopted from Pound, and still being printed on its cover in 1920) to make "no compromise with the public taste."

Although the serialization of *Ulysses* abruptly ended with this installment, there are three coincidences—or encounters—in the September–December issue that provide a sense of closure to the novel. The first takes place within "Oxen of the Sun." Only the first quarter of the episode appears in the magazine, but that happens to be enough to include what has been repeatedly pushed back in the novel, the much-deferred meeting between Stephen and Bloom: "Sir Leopold sat with them [the scholars drinking at the birthing hospital] for he bore fast friendship to Sir Simon and to this his son young Stephen and for that his langour becalmed him there after longest wanderings" (*LRU* 339). For readers wondering whether the two major characters of *Ulysses* would ever come together, Bloom's meeting Stephen here, and his decision to look after him, provides some sense of completion, even if their encounter is obscured by archaic prose and comes after a wait of nearly three years and 120,000 words.

The second encounter occurs within the layout of the magazine. Immediately preceding *Ulysses* in this issue is a short prose piece by Carlo Linati, "Bergamasque," which lovingly recalls a day the author spent in Bergamo, Italy, with a friend. Linati, an Italian writer and translator, dedicated this piece to Ezra Pound, but he was a friend of Joyce as well, and translated *Exiles* and parts of *Ulysses* into Italian. To help Linati better understand the novel, Joyce famously sent him in 1920 an outline, now known as the "Linati schema," that spelled out the Homeric parallels and other organizational structures in each episode. Thus, Joyce made his exit from the *Little Review* after being introduced by a friend and colleague who would play an important role in the proliferation of scholarship on the novel.

The third encounter draws together two of the greatest modernist writers in English. In the "Reader Critic" section at the very end of the September–December issue, a piece titled "The World Moves (from the *London Times*)" discusses Joyce's writing. No author is listed, but readers today will recognize the text as part of Virginia Woolf's essay "Modern Novels" (later reworked and retitled "Modern Fiction"), which appeared as the lead article in the *Times Literary Supplement* on April 10, 1919. In describing how Joyce's work comes "closer to life" than that of his predecessors, Woolf famously writes: "Let us record the atoms as they fall upon the mind in the order in which they fall, let us trace the pattern, however disconnected and incoherent in appearance, which each sight or incident scores upon the consciousness. Let us not take it for granted that life exists more in what is commonly thought big than in what is commonly thought small" (*LR* 7.3: 93–94). Clearly, Woolf's review, with its reference to *Ulysses* "now appearing in the Little Review" (94), was reprinted as a plug for the magazine. But it was also confirmation, from the world beyond America, of the views that Anderson and Heap expressed about Joyce earlier in the issue, in the small oasis of their embattled publication. Woolf expresses misgivings about Joyce's indecency; but far from branding him a purveyor of obscenity, she claims that "Mr. Joyce is spiritual." By abandoning in *Ulysses* the limiting conventions inherited from the past, Joyce manages not only to express "much of life [that] is excluded and ignored" but also to capture "life itself."

Thus Joyce appears censored and suppressed in America at the start of the September–December issue, but by the end we see him moving the world forward, at the forefront of a new generation of writers.

THE END OF *THE LITTLE REVIEW "ULYSSES"*

The serialization of *Ulysses* in the *Little Review* reached its end when Margaret Anderson mailed out unsolicited copies of the July–August 1920 issue, which contained the final installment of "Nausicaa." One of these gratis copies reached the home of a New York lawyer, where it was read by his daughter. Her father sent a letter of complaint to the district attorney, urging him to read passages on pages 43, 45, 50, and 51 and asking whether "such indecencies don't come within the provisions of the Postal Laws" (Vanderham 37). The matter was then directed to John Sumner, the head of a group called the New York Society for the Prevention of Vice, a nongovernmental agency that nevertheless possessed powers of censorship and investigation. Sumner found the issue clearly offensive. He purchased several additional copies at the Washington Square Bookshop, intending to have its owner tried for selling obscene materials. Anderson and Heap intervened, however, and had themselves substituted as defendants with the intention of using the case to further publicize *Ulysses* and their own magazine. At a preliminary hearing on October 21, the list of objectionable passages grew to include at least fourteen of the sixteen pages printed in the issue. Anderson and Heap were both held over for trial on bail of $25 each.

The legal issues at stake in the case were relatively straightforward, since obscenity in U.S. law at the time was governed by a test called the *Hicklin* rule. It defined obscenity as "the tendency of the matter charged . . . to deprave and corrupt those whose minds are open to such immoral influences" (*Regina v. Hicklin* 1868). It furthermore held that this test had to be applied to individual passages and not to the work as a whole; thus, if even a single passage or phrase, taken entirely out its context, was judged obscene, then the entire work could be suppressed. By this standard, "Nausicaa" was plainly in violation of the law. John Quinn nevertheless agreed to take the case, despite telling Anderson and Heap that "it would serve them damnably right if [the magazine] was permanently excluded from the mails" (Vanderham 42). Quinn, however, had a serious investment in the book and its publication, having funded Pound's work at the magazine and purchased Joyce's manuscript for *Ulysses* (what is now called the Rosenbach Manuscript). His own efforts, therefore, were bent not just toward defending Anderson and Heap, but also toward protecting *Ulysses* as well as Joyce's copyrights in it.

Quinn initially sought to delay the trial as long as possible, in the hopes, Paul Vanderham argues in *James Joyce and Censorship,* that "Joyce could finish *Ulysses* and have it published in a single volume before the conviction could be handed down" (46–47). Quinn, in fact, had urged both Joyce and Pound to forgo magazine publication, precisely to avoid this kind of legal entanglement. *Ulysses,* he wrote, "is a very unique work of art, but it is not a work of art to [be] published in a magazine. . . . There are things in *Ulysses* that would be alright in a book, but which it was stupid to think could be got away with in a monthly magazine" (55). In this case, his advice proved sound. Despite Quinn's plans to draw out the case, the trial was scheduled promptly before a three-judge panel in the Court of Special Sessions and conducted over two days—February 14 and 21, 1921. Although the court permitted some testimony on the book's literary merit, such evidence wasn't important, given the strict standards of the *Hicklin* rule. Quinn tried the only real line of argument available, contending that the portion of the episode at stake was too difficult to understand and thus could not corrupt an innocent mind. The district attorney, however, read out in court portions of the passage where Bloom masturbates. The court reached its now infamous decision: Anderson and Heap were found guilty and fined $50 each. The court also barred the editors from printing any additional portions of *Ulysses* in their magazine (53).

This decision brought to an end *The Little Review "Ulysses,"* despite the fact that one additional section of episode XIV had appeared in the September–December 1920 issue. In the first issue to appear after the trial's conclusion, Margaret Anderson shared her thoughts about the whole ordeal in "'Ulysses' in Court." In this essay she offers her own arguments for the importance of Joyce's book, laments the state of American law, takes issue with Quinn's legal strategies, and notes that some of her friends thought her "both insane and obscene . . . for publishing Mr. Joyce" (*LR* 7.4: 25). She combatively describes the disappointing outcome, leveraging it as best she can for the magazine's avant-garde image: "This decision establishes us as criminals and we are led to an adjoining building where another bewildered official takes our fingerprints!!!"

Anderson's article is followed by a small inset box that announces the effective end of *Ulysses* in the magazine: "Owing to editorial mediation as to what passages must be deleted from the next instalment of 'Ulysses' Episode XIV will not be continued until next month." Anderson had perhaps not yet recognized the force of the injunction against the magazine, but its consequences were clear to Quinn and Joyce. Having been judged obscene, *Ulysses* could not be printed or sold in the United States unless deep and substantial changes were made. Joyce refused to censor himself, and B. W. Huebsch wrote to Quinn in April 1921 that he could not publish the book. In frustration, Joyce turned to a woman who owned a small bookstore in Paris called Shakespeare & Company. Her name was Sylvia Beach, and their partnership created a way for Joyce not only to publish what he had written, but also to explore new kinds of radical experiments with form and content that could never have appeared in the pages of the *Little Review.*

Thus began the saga of a new and very different *Ulysses*—one American readers would not legally see for over a decade. In 1933, Judge John Woolsey essentially overturned the outcome of *People of the State of New York against Margaret C. Anderson and Jane Heap,* allowing Bloom, Stephen, and Molly safe passage into world literature.

Notes

1. Readers can find the MJP's data files for the *Little Review* online at http://sourceforge.net/p/mjplab/home/Home/.
2. To arrive at this lower figure, we counted just once those authors with multiple contributions to an issue and also reconciled obvious name variations for an author—for example, "E.P." was identified as Ezra Pound.

3. In the Pound issues, there are on average six fewer titles and six fewer names listed on the table of contents. And while the issues edited by Pound have on average 10 percent fewer pages than the non-Pound issues, they contain about the same number of words—22,695 versus 23,065, which is a difference of only 1.6 percent.
4. In Pound's issues, we identified the thirty-two unique contributors listed on the contents pages as 28 percent American, 56 percent European (37.5 percent British, 19 percent non-British European), and 16 percent indeterminate, while in the non-Pound issues the corresponding figures for their eighty-one unique contributors are 53 percent American, 28 percent European (16 percent British, 12 percent non-British European), and 19 percent indeterminate.

ESSAYS, LETTERS, AND COMMENTS ON *ULYSSES* IN THE *LITTLE REVIEW* (1918–1921)

Those who encountered *Ulysses* in the pages of the *Little Review* knew they were reading something unique, even extraordinary—a new kind of novel that was difficult, allusive, beautiful, and bewildering all at once. It was easy to get swamped by the details of Dublin life or become lost in a network of references that extended from classical Greece through Irish myth to contemporary European literature. And then there was the book's style—or rather, its succession of styles, which began with what May Sinclair called (in an essay printed below) the stream of consciousness before mutating into a diverse array of antic parodies and innovative experiments. The twelve items reproduced in this section offer a sampling of the many responses to *Ulysses* that Anderson and Heap published in their magazine—some positive, some negative, and others simply baffled. They include the editors' often caustic responses to letters critical of the book, as well as explanations of the difficulties they endured in getting their magazine past vigilant postal inspectors. This section concludes with the editors' accounts of the court case that brought their serialization of *Ulysses* to an end and their final, eloquent defense of free expression. These documents remind us just how new *Ulysses* truly was even as they give some sense of what it might have been like to watch a literary revolution unfold.

1. From LR *4.12 (April 1918): 3–11*

THE NOVELS OF DOROTHY RICHARDSON

May Sinclair

Pointed Roofs.
Backwater.
Honeycomb.

(*Duckworth and company, London*).

I HAVE been asked to write — for this magazine which makes no compromise with the public taste — a criticism of the novels of Dorothy Richardson. The editors of the *Little Review* are committed to Dorothy Richardson by their declared intentions; for her works make no sort of compromise with the public taste. If they are not announced with the same proud challenge it is because the pride of the editors of the *Little Review* is no mate for the pride of Miss Richardson which ignores the very existence of the public and its taste.

I do not know whether this article is or is not going to be a criticism, for so soon as I begin to think what I shall say I find myself criticising criticism, wondering what is the matter with it and what, if anything, can be done to make it better, to make it alive. Only a live criticism can deal appropriately with a live art. And it seems to me that the first step towards life is to throw off the philosophic cant of the XIXth Century. I don't mean that there is no philosophy of Art, or that if there has been there is to be no more of it; I mean that it is absurd to go on talking about realism and idealism, or objective and subjective art, as if the philosophies were sticking where they stood in the eighties.

In those days the distinction between idealism and realism, between subjective and objective was important and precise. And so long as the ideas they stand for had importance and precision those words were lamps to the feet and lanterns to the path of the critic. Even after they had begun to lose precision and importance they still served him as useful labels for the bewildering phenomena of the arts.

But now they are beginning to give trouble; they obscure the issues. Mr. J. B. Beresford in his admirable introduction to *Pointed Roofs* confesses to having felt this trouble. When he read it in manuscript he decided that it "was realism, was objective." When he read it in typescript he thought: "this . . is the most subjective thing I have ever read." It is evident that, when first faced with the startling "newness" of Miss Richardson's method and her form, the issues did seem a bit obscure to Mr. Beresford. It was as if up to one illuminating moment he had been obliged to think of methods and forms as definitely objective or definitely subjective. His illuminating moment came with the third reading when *Pointed Roofs* was a printed book. The book itself gave him the clue to his own trouble, which is my trouble, the first hint that criticism up till now has been content to think in clichés, missing the new trend of the philosophies of the XXth Century. All that we know of reality at first hand is given to us through contacts in which those interesting distinctions are lost. Reality is thick and deep, too thick and too deep and at the same time too fluid to be cut with any convenient carving knife. The novelist who would be close to reality must confine himself to this knowledge at first hand. He must, as Mr. Beresford says, simply "plunge in". Mr. Beresford also says that Miss Richardson is the first novelist who has plunged in. She has plunged so neatly and quietly that even admirers of her performance might remain unaware of what it is precisely that she has done. She has disappeared while they are still waiting for the splash. So that Mr. Beresford's introduction was needed.

When first I read *Pointed Roofs* and *Backwater* and *Honeycomb* I too thought, like Mr. Beresford, that Miss Richardson has been the first to plunge. But it seems to me rather that she has followed, independently, perhaps unconsciously, a growing tendency to plunge. As far back as the eighties the de Goncourts plunged completely, finally, in *Soeur Philomène, Germinie Lacerteux* and *Les Frères Zemganno*. Marguerite Audoux plunged in the best passages of *Marie Claire*. The best of every good novelist's best work is a more or less sustained immersion. The more modern the novelist the longer his capacity to stay under. Miss Richardson has not plunged deeper than Mr. James Joyce in his *Portrait of the Artist as a Young Man*.

By imposing very strict limitations on herself she has brought her art, her method, to a high pitch of perfection, so that her form seems to be newer than it perhaps is. She herself is unaware of the perfection of her method. She would probably deny that she has written with any deliberate method at all. She would say: "I only know there are certain things I mustn't do if I was to do what I wanted." Obviously, she must not interfere; she must not analyse or comment or explain. Rather less obviously, she must not tell a story, or handle a situation or set a scene; she must avoid drama as she avoids narration. And there are some things she must not be. She must not be the wise, all-knowing author. She must be Miriam Henderson. She must not know or divine anything that Miriam does not know or divine; she must not see anything that Miriam does not see. She has taken Miriam's nature upon her. She is not concerned, in the way that other novelists are concerned, with character. Of the persons who move through Miriam's world you know nothing but what Miriam knows. If Miriam is mistaken, well, she and not Miss Richardson is mistaken. Miriam is an acute observer, but she is very far from seeing the whole of these people. They are presented to us in the same vivid but fragmentary way in which they appeared to Miriam, the fragmentary way in which people appear to most of us. Miss Richardson has only imposed on herself the conditions that life imposes on all of us. And if you are going to quarrel with those conditions you will not find her novels satisfactory. But your satisfaction is not her concern.

And I find it impossible to reduce to intelligible terms this satisfaction that I feel. To me these three novels show an art and method and form carried to punctilious perfection. Yet I have heard other novelists say that they have no art and no method and no form, and that it is this formlessness that annoys them. They say that they have no beginning and no middle and no end, and that to have form a novel must have an end and a beginning and a middle. We have come to words that in more primitive times would have been blows on this subject. There is a certain plausibility in what they say, but it depends on what constitutes a beginning and a middle and an end. In this series there is no drama, no situation, no set scene. Nothing happens. It is just life going on and on. It is Miriam Henderson's stream of consciousness going on and on. And in neither is there any grossly discernible beginning or middle or end.

In identifying herself with this life which is Miriam's stream of consciousness Miss Richardson produces her effect of being the first, of getting closer to reality than any of our novelists who are trying so desperately to get close. No attitude or gesture of her own is allowed to come between her and her effect. Whatever her sources and her raw material, she is concerned and we ought to be concerned solely with the finished result, the work of art. It is to Miriam's almost painfully acute senses that we owe what in any other novelist would be called the "portratis" of Miriam's mother, of her sister Harriet, of the Corries and Joey Banks in *Honeycomb*, of the Miss Pernes and Julia Doyle, and the north London schoolgirls in *Backwater*, of Fräulein Pfaff and Mademoiselle, of the Martins and Emma Bergmann and Ulrica and "the Australian" in *Pointed Roofs*. The mere "word painting" is masterly.

" . . . Miriam noticed only the hoarse, hacking laugh of the Australian. Her eyes flew up the table and fixed her as she sat laughing, her chair drawn back, her knees crossed — tea was drawing to an end. The detail of her terrifyingly stylish ruddy-brown frieze dress with its Norfolk jacket bodice and its shiny leather belt was hardly distinguishable from the dark background made by the folding doors. But the dreadful outline of her shoulders was visible, the squarish oval of her face shone out — the wide forehead from which the wiry black hair was combed to a high puff, the red eyes, black now, the long, straight nose, the wide, laughing mouth with the enormous teeth."

And so on all round the school tea-table. It looks easy enough to "do" until you try it. There are thirteen figures round that table and each is drawn with the first few strokes and so well that you see them all and never afterwards can you mistake or confuse them.

You look at the outer world through Miriam's senses and it is as if you had never seen it so vividly before. Miriam in *Backwater* is on the top of a bus, driving from North London to Piccadilly:

"On the left a tall grey church was coming towards them, spindling up into the sky. It sailed by, showing Miriam a circle of little stone pillars built into its spire. Plumy trees streamed by, standing large and separate on moss-green grass railed from the roadway. Bright, white-faced houses with pillared porches shone through from behind them and blazed white above them against the blue sky. Wide side streets opened, showing high balconied houses. The side streets were feathered with trees and ended mistily.

"Away ahead were edges of clean, bright masonry in profile, soft, tufted heads of trees, bright green in the clear light. At the end of the vista the air was like pure saffron-tinted mother-of-pearl."

Or this "interior" from *Honeycomb*: . . . "the table like an island under the dome of the low-hanging rose-shaded lamp, the table-centre thickly embroidered with beetles' wings, the little dishes stuck about, sweets, curiously crusted brown almonds, sheeny grey-green olives; the misty beaded glass of the finger bowls — Venetian glass from that shop in Regent Street — the four various wine glasses at each right hand, one on a high thin stem, curved and fluted like a shallow tulip, filled with hock; and floating in the warmth amongst all these things the strange, exciting dry sweet fragrance coming from the mass of mimosa, a forest of little powdery blossoms, little stiff grey — the arms of railway signals at junctions — Japanese looking leaves — standing as if it were growing, in a shallow bowl under the rose-shaded lamp."

It is as if no other writers had ever used their senses so purely and with so intense a joy in their use.

This intensity is the effect of an extreme concentration on the thing seen or felt. Miss Richardson disdains every stroke that does not tell. Her novels are novels of an extraordinary compression and of an extenuation more extraordinary still. The moments of Miriam's consciousness pass one by one, or overlapping, moments tense with vibration, moments drawn out fine, almost to snapping point. On one page Miss Richardson seems to be accounting for every minute of Miriam's time. On another she passes over events that might be considered decisive with the merest slur of reference. She is not concerned with the strict order of events in time. Chapter Three of *Pointed Roofs* opens with an air of extreme decision and importance: "Miriam was practising on the piano in the larger of the two English bedrooms," as if something hung on her practising. But no, nothing hangs on it, and if you want to know on what day she is practising you have to read on and back again. It doesn't matter. It is Miriam's consciousness that is going backwards and forwards in time. The time it goes in is unimportant. On the hundredth page out of three hundred and twelve pages Mirian has been exactly two weeks in Hanover. Nothing has happened but the infinitely little affairs of the school, the practising, the "Vorspielen", the English lesson, the "raccommodage", the hair-washing. At the end of the book Fräulein Pfaff is on the station platform, gently propelling Miriam "up three steps into a compartment marked Damen-Coupé. It smelt of biscuits and wine." Miriam has been no more than six months in Hanover. We are not told, and Miriam is not told, but we know as Miriam knows that she is going because Pastor Lahmann has shown an interest in Miriam very disturbing to Fräulein Pfaff's interest in him. We are not invited to explore the tortuous mind of the pious, sentimental, secretly hysterical Fräulein; but we know, as Miriam knows, that before she can bring herself to part with her English governess she must persuade herself that it is Miriam and not Mademoiselle who is dismissed because she is an unwholesome influence.

In this small world where nothing happens "that dreadful talk with Gertrude", and Fräulein's quarrel with the servant Anna, the sound of her laugh and her scream, "Ja, Sie Können Ihre paar Groschen haben! Ihre paar Groschen!", and Miriam's vision of Mademoiselle's unwholesomeness, stand out as significant and terrifying. They *are* terrifying; they are significant; through them we know Gertrude, we know Fräulein Pfaff, we know Mademoiselle as Miriam knows them, under their disguises.

At the end of the third volume, *Honeycomb*, there is, apparently, a break with the design. Something does happen. Something tragic and terrible. We are not told what it is; we know as Miriam knows, only by inference. Miriam is sleeping in her mother's room.

"Five o'clock. Three more hours before the day began. The other bed was still. "It's going to be a magnificent day", she murmured, pretending to stretch and yawn again. A sigh reached her. The stillness went on and she lay for an hour tense and listening. Someone else must know . . . At the end of the hour a descending darkness took her suddenly. She woke from it to the sound of violent language, furniture being roughly moved, a swift, angry splashing of water

. . . something breaking out, breaking through the confinements of this little furniture-filled room . . . the best gentlest thing she knew openly despairing at last."

Here Miss Richardson "gets" you as she gets you all the time — she never misses once — by her devout adhesion to her method, by the sheer depth of her plunge. For this and this alone is the way things happen. What we used to call the "objective" method is a method of after-thought, of spectacular reflection. What has happened has happened in Miriam's bedroom, if you like; but only by reflection. The firsthand, intimate and intense reality of the happening is in Miriam's mind, and by presenting it thus and not otherwise Miss Richardson seizes reality alive. The intense rapidity of the seizure defies you to distinguish between what is objective and what is subjective either in the reality presented or the art that presents.

Nothing happens. In Miriam Henderson's life there is, apparently, nothing to justify living. Everything she ever wanted was either withheld or taken from her. She is reduced to the barest minimum on which it is possible to support the life of the senses and the emotions at all. And yet Miriam is happy. Her inexhaustible passion for life is fed. Nothing happens, and yet everything that really matters is happening; you are held breathless with the anticipation of its happening. What really matters is a state of mind, the interest or the ecstasy with which we close with life. It can't be explained. To quote Mr. Beresford again: "explanation in this connection would seem to imply knowledge that only the mystics can faintly realise". But Miss Richardson's is a mysticism apart. It is compatible with, it even encourages such dialogue as this:

" 'Tea' " smiled Eve serenely.

" 'All right, I'm coming, damn you, aren't I ?'

" 'Oh, Mimmy!'

" 'Well, damn *me*, then. Somebody in the house must swear. I say, Eve!'

" 'What?'

" 'Nothing, only I *say*.'

" 'Um.' "

It is not wholly destroyed when Miriam eats bread and butter thus: "When she began at the hard thick edge there always seemed to be tender places on her gums, her three hollow teeth were uneasy and she had to get through worrying thoughts about them — they would get worse as the years went by, and the little places in the front would grow big and painful and disfiguring. After the first few mouthfuls of solid bread a sort of padding seemed to take place and she could go on forgetful."

This kind of thing annoys Kensington. I do not say that it really matters but that it is compatible with what really matters. Because of such passages it is a pity that Miss Richardson could not use the original title of her series: "Pilgrimage," for it shows what she is really after. Each book marks a stage in Miriam's pilgrimage. We get the first hint of where she is going to in the opening of the tenth chapter of *Pointed Roofs*: "Into all the gatherings at Waldstrasse the outside world came like a presence. It removed the sense of pressure, of being confronted and challenged. Everything that was said seemed to be incidental to it, like remarks dropped in a low tone between individuals at a great conference." In *Backwater* the author's intention becomes still clearer. In *Honeycomb* it is transparently clear:

"Her room was a great square of happy light . . . happy, happy. She gathered up all the sadness she had ever known and flung it from her. All the dark things of the past flashed with a strange beauty as she flung them out. The light had been there all the time; but she had known it only at moments. Now she knew what she wanted. Bright mornings, beautiful bright rooms, a wilderness of beauty all round her all the time — at any cost."

And yet not that:

"Something that was not touched, that sang far away down inside the gloom, that cared nothing for the creditors and could get away down and down into the twilight far away from the everlasting accusations of humanity . . . . Deeper down was something cool and fresh — endless — an endless garden. In happiness it came up and made everything in the world into a garden. Sorrow blotted it out; but it was always there, waiting and looking on. It had looked on in Germany and had loved the music and the words and the happiness of the German girls, and at Banbury Park, giving her no peace until she got away.

"And now it had come to the surface and was with her all the time."

There are two essays of Rémy de Gourmont in *Promenades Littéraires*, one on "l'Originalité de Maeterlinck," one on "La Leçon de Saint-Antoine." Certain passages might have been written concerning the art of Dorothy Richardson: —

"Si la vie en soi est un bienfait, iet il faut l'accepter comme telle on la nier, le fait même de vivre le contient tout entier, et les grands mouvements de la sensibilité, loin de l'enrichir, l' appauvrissent au contraire, en concentrant sur quelques partis de nous-mêmes, envahies au hasard par la destinée l' effort d' attention qui serait plus uniformenent reparti sur l' ensemble de notre conscience vitale. De ce point de vue une vie ou il semblerait ne rien se passer que d' élémentaire et quotidien serait mieux remplie qu'une autre vie riche en apparence d' incidents et d' aventures" . . . . "Il y a peut-être un sentiment nouveau a créer, celui de l' amour de la vie pour la vie elle-même, abstraction faite des grandes joies qu'elle ne donne pas à tous, et qu' elle ne donne peut-être à personne . . . Notre paradis, c' est la journèe qui passe ,la minute qui s' envole, le moment qui n'est déjà plus. Telle est la leçon de Saint. Antoine."

2. From "The Reader Critic," LR *5.2 (June 1918): 54*

WHAT JOYCE IS UP AGAINST

S. S. B., Chicago:

Really now: Joyce! what does he think he is doing? What do you think he is doing? I swear I've read his "Ulysses" and haven't found out yet what it's about, who is who or where. Each month he's worse than the last. I consider myself fairly intelligent. I have read more than most. There are some few things I expect of a writer. One of them is coherence. Joyce will have to change his style if he wants to get on. Very few have the time or patience to struggle with his impressionistic stuff—to get nothing out of it even then.

[You consider yourself an intelligent, "well-read" person. Did it ever occur to you to read anything on the nature of writers? If it should you might help to remove from the mind of the reading public—Whitman's great audience—some of the superstition of its importance to the writer; some of its superstition of being able to put any compulsion upon an artist. All compulsion exists within the artist. It would take too long to discuss this fully here. The only concern of the artist is to try in one short lifetime to meet these inner compulsions. He has no concern with audiences and their demands. *—jh.*]

3. From "The Reader Critic," LR *5.2 (June 1918): 55–57*

JAMES JOYCE

R. McM., Los Angeles :

You are a firm believer in cerise abnormal art, I take it. Has art then no elasticity, no tolerance, no humor, If Joyce is an artist put him beside Turgeniev, Chekhov, Goethe . . . Even in decadency—anaemic, palely diseased,—how do you stack up beside even poor Oscar Wilde, Beaudelaire, possibly Swinburne? They had intellect added to their art ears. I'd like to hear convincing justification of Joyce other than mere statement that "his work is art". I should be reluctant to say "this is art" of anything until time has proved its staying power. The human mind and perception is so finite and insular, why be so sure you and your group, small, select, and exotically interesting, are absolutely correct? We have with us in the world other than Joyce, Lewis, etc. Rolland *(Jean Christophe),* Barbusse *(Under Fire* —much overrated, by the way), Nexo and many who have virility, intellect, philosophy and art,—not sexually perverted. The prostitute who paints an already beautiful body may have added unnatural charm, but why call it art? Justify some of Joyce's obsence commonplaces taken from life neither for power nor beauty nor for any reason but to arrest attention, cheap Bowery vileness.

[Yes, I am a believer in "cerise abnormal art." Why all this effort to bring shame upon cerise ? Colour is a vital necessity in the organization of the universe, as vital and necessary as form. The artist has recognized and used both as means of expression.

They are difficult words—normal and abnormal; they may be used with many turns. I believe in abnormal art because Art is abnormal : at least up to the present it hasn't been a normal occupation of normal men. All activities that are not art activities might as easily seem sub-normal to the artist. Where do we get?

If only some of your reluctance to call a thing art might stay with you in discussing artists, how becoming . . . If you were reluctant to call Wilde, Beaudelaire and Swinburne so many "cerise" adjectives . . . .

You seem to want some justification of our position in classifying work as Art before time has proved its staying powers. We do not belong to that part of humanity whose life in its first half is directed by its parents and grandparents, and in its second half by its children and grandchildren. If an engineer builds a bridge across a river a group of other skilled engineers would probably be able to tell whether it were a bridge or merely a decoration in the air, without leaving the matter to time and chance. Crudely, it is something like this with Art. Time has made some asinine mistakes: in the galleries of Europe, time, represented by town councils, has collected some wierd specimens—on a more or less "tag-you're-it" basis.

It is impossible for Joyce to be obscene. He is too concentrated on his work. He is too religious about life. You perhaps think yourself pure-minded: everything should then be pure to you. If you are not you can not put what you are not upon Joyce. The other day a young woman said to me: "Tell me about this 'to the pure all is pure'. I suspect them both". *I* suspect all who find either purity or obscenity in Art.

How could anyone begin to discuss Joyce except with a person who has an intense grip on modern thought? The earth slimes with a slightly-informed protoplasm called humanity: informed with a few instincts. Some few have become aware of cerebral irradiations. Fewer attain active cerebration. The artist has always known that outside or beyond or beneath or before both these lie irradiations, psychic or x or n-th, and has tried to describe and record them. Joyce has perfected a technique which eliminates description. He conceives and records.—*Jh.*

4. From "The Reader Critic," LR *5.3 (July 1918): 65*

JOYCE AND ETHICS

Hart Crane, Cleveland, Ohio :

The Los Angeles critic who commented on Joyce in the last issue was adequately answered, I realize,—but the temptation to emphasize such illiteracy, indiscrimination, and poverty still pulls a little too strongly for resistance.

I noticed that Wilde, Baudelaire and Swinburne are "stacked up" beside Joyce as rivals in "decadence" and "intellect". I am not yet aware that Swinburne ever possessed much beyond his "art ears", although these were long enough, and adequate to all his beautiful, though often meaningless mouthings. His instability in criticism and every form of literature that did not depend almost exclusively on sound for effect, and his irrelevant metaphors are notorious. And as to Wilde,—after his bundle of paradoxes has been sorted and conned,—very little evidence of intellect remains. "Decadence" is something much talked about, and sufficiently misconstrued to arouse interest in the works of any fool. Any change in form, viewpoint or mannerism can be so abused by the offending party. Sterility is the only "decadence" I recognize. An abortion in art takes the same place as it does in society,—it deserves no recognition whatever,—it is simply outside. A piece of work is art, or it isn't: there is no neutral judgment.

However,—let Baudelaire and Joyce stand together, as much as any such thing in literary comparison will allow. The principal eccentricity evinced by both is a penetration into life common to only the greatest. If people resent a thrust which discovers some of their entrails to themselvs, I can see no reason for resorting to indiscriminate comparisons, naming colours of the rainbow, or advertising the fact that they have recently been forced to recognize a few of their personal qualities. Those who are capable of being only mildly "shocked" very naturally term the cost a penny, but were they capable of paying a few pounds for the same thinking, experience and realization by and in themselves, they could reserve their pennies for work minor to Joyce's.

The most nauseating complaint against his work is that of immorality and obscenity. The character of Stephen Dedalus is all too good for this world. It takes a little experience,— a few reactions on his part to understand it, and could this have been accomplished in a detached hermitage, high above the mud, he would no doubt have preferred that residence. *A Portrait of the Artist as a Young Man,* aside from Dante, is spiritually the most inspiring book I have ever read. It is Bunyan raised to art, and then raised to the ninth power.

5. From "The Reader Critic," LR *5.5 (September 1918): 59–62*

DIVAGATIONS

Marsden Hartley, Taos, New Mexico :

I suppose I must count myself lover of stylistic radiance. It is not enough for me to have sun; I want the distribution of the prismatic facet, the irridescence wrapped around the sphere. There must be the web for the dew to hang on, there must be a free sky for an avid moon. This cannot, I think, be achieved without a rigid adherence to the significance of essential values.

Between the mania of a Flaubert for exatitude, and the monosyllabic detail of a James Joyce there is, as one may observe, a wide divergence. I want for myself most of all the poetry of a scene, and poetry is just as much a well placed "good morning" as it is a wandering ode. I think it is well for the writer of real purposes to escape the less interesting faculty for journalistic rendition, as it is well for the over-paid reporter to elaborate on the fact not present. The successful reporter is not one who tells the truth in conjunction with fact, he is that one who can weave a labyrinth of romantic insinuation around an improbability.

For the novelist, journalistic voluminousness is possibly a valuable adjunct to the swelling out of facility as well as of the page. Poetry has the greater value to one who would write well. It would teach him brevity, compactness. A narrative of a page's length in Frost is as significant a rendetion of its theme as is a chapter of Balzac. It is more important that the artist know exactly to the hair his own limitations as well as his excellences. Verhaeren's page or two on his own Belgique is as telling as an entire play of Shakespeare on England, excepting of course that Verhaeren is what his Belgique was, and Shakespeare is the world.

Essences are volumes of another degree merely. The atmosphere of a story should be just as solid as the action. We should know the teacup on the kitchen table of a labourer's family, just as we should know the cataclysm in his soul. It seems to me the novel should be just as mathematical as the good poem, or the excellent bit of prose. It may be the novel is harder both in terms of difficulty as well as consistency, that is to say when psychological inevitability is concerned. Not a term involved which does not swing directly between the moment and its creator. Outside of the fine stylists you get so much of slipping over the surface of the scene. Jane Austen, Thomas Hardy, and Henry James are certainly various, but you get the sense of consequence in them. The Joyce species of entertainment is a restive feathering of the acid upon a not too expansive plate. You are fed with a fascination of little touches. It is Messionierism in words. Cross-hatching which has not the distinction of Rembrandt. There is a humoristic tracery in Joyce which will amuse any ardent lover of the touch. I wonder if we do not hear the strumming of the mosquitoe's wing a little excessively in Joyce. Is the space around things large enough? Does he care for entirety as much as the whimsie en passant? Is it not a too close relationship of tense values. I have only "Ulysses-Episode IV" to begin my premise. I know one who makes an exquisite drawing solely by means of the point of the pen. He is a large amiable person, who finds a hair from an elephant's tail around his wrist an engaging preoccupancy. I find it charming in suggestion also, for there is the whole jungle in that small brown strand tickling his wrist. I find the little thing circling around a portion of a very big smiling fellow a pleasant bit of fun. But these dots made by the point of the pen are placed, as far as I can tell, with scientific accuracy under the force of an expensive and spacious magnifying glass, and after two years of labour to a finality in dots, what is there is but the passing of an afternoon cloud beyond a spreading oak, the which comes forth as an accompaniment to a dull poem on the page of a correct magazine. Dot for dot is more what I am thinking, is the case of Joyce; Dürer used dots also, and a host of very vivid lines, and his plates were mostly small. What about the plate of Joyce. Is there the expanse in it, is there encompassed, or does Joyce spread the masses esewhere in his theme. We had Seurat with his very intelligent pointillism, a fine artist, and the only distinguished one in that field of discovery, as superior to Signac and Cross as

Cross is superior to Signac. Is Joyce a Seurat of a Signac in wordy dots? I have, I confess, a proud admiration for the flawless line of Ingres, and the dignity of Mass in Courbet, the superb orchestration in the arrangements of Delacroix. I like to excess, the swinging into untouched ethers of Francis Thompson, who has I think given more of the floridness of frigidity than any other poet of modernity. The sanitillance that trickles out of Henry James at his best, and the incomparable fluidity and lucent earthiness of his brother William James, cover my moments with delight. But I wonder if novelists outside the revolutionary academic crew care much for stylistic radiance. I wonder if being too near the diamond does not shatter its dust. Does the ruby glow with an eye fastened on its skin, or the emerald send up seabottoms of delicious fancy with a hot finger on its face. There are so many sprightly indications in Joyce, almost too much of vividness, which in the presence of so much uncoloured production, might seem unjust.

These are skimmings of reflection of an August afternoon, where the desert shines like a sheet of scorched metal.

Language is after a something wonderful in itself, and as for the perfect word it all but sinks in space for its rarity.

Is not the average line of the acknowledged story-telled a dullard, as to its propensities for initiation? Is not plot the demon of the dream? Should there not be a kind of poetry of line in the unfolding of experience, as well as the giant of edges? A good drawing is that one which holds the form consistently between its outlines. Artistry comes in fullness. Seurat was successful. Perhaps Joyce is, also. Joyce amuses. Seurat satisfies.

6. From LR *6.10 (March 1920): 64*

SOME OF THE CAUSES FOR THE OMISSION OF THE FEBRUARY NUMBER :

THE extreme leisure of on the part of the Obscene Department of the U. S. P. O. in deciding the fate of the January *Little Review.*

The house in which we have had our office for the past three years has been sold. We are forced to find new quarters.

The entire staff of the *Little Review* (both of us) is just recovering from the influenza.

And—we have lost our temperamental printer. The following letter may throw some light on printing conditions in New York City:

> Dear Miss Anderson:
>
> Tomorrow will be a week that I received copy with money in advance as agreed, and was not able to start and will not be able before next week. It is no use Miss Anderson to be so nervous. You want always first-class work and I cannot make. Do you not know that we had war? Workingman is now king. If you would pay me three thousand dollars I will not make good work. This is other times. I wrote you about this many times and will not repeat any more, but wish to say if you pay all in advance and two, three hundred per cent more as now, you must not expect good work or on time. I want no responsibility.

The vast improvement in our financial condition can be gauged from the above.

7. From "The Reader Critic," LR *6.11 (April 1920): 61*

"OBSCENITY"

F. E. R.:

And what caused the suppression of the January issue? The Joyce, I suppose. I have been through the whole number very carefully and the "Ulysses" is the only offender I can find. But why cavil about Joyce at this late day?—it would seem to me that after all these months he could be accepted, obscenity and all, for surely the post-office authorities should recognize that only a few read him, and those few not just the kind to have their whole moral natures overthrown by frankness about natural functions.

8. From "The Reader Critic," LR *7.1 (May–June 1920): 72*

"ULYSSES"

Dear Little Reviewers:

Can you tell me when James Joyce's "Ulysses" will appear in book form? Do you think the public will ever be ready for such a book? I read him each month with eagerness, but I must confess that I am defeated in my intelligence. Now tell the truth,—do you yourselves know where the story is at the present moment, how much time has elapsed,—just where are we? Have you any clue as to when the story will end?

["Ulysses" will probably appear in book form in America if there is a publisher for it who will have sense enough to avoid the public. Joyce has perfected a technique that has enabled him to avoid almost all but those rabid for literature. We haven't any advance chapters in hand, but it would seem that we are drawing towards the Circe episode and the close of the story. The question of time seems simple and unobscured. The story is laid in perhaps the talk centre of the universe, but time is not affected; the time of the present chapter is about five thirty or six in the evening of the same day on which the story started,—I think Tuesday. Mr. Bloom has had a long day since he cooked his breakfast of kidney, but he has lost no time.—*jh.*]

9. From "The Reader Critic," LR *7.1 (May–June 1920): 73–74*

THE MODEST WOMAN

Helen Bishop Dennis, Boston:

I notice that the first letter under the Reader Critic in your April issue suggests that "after all these months James Joyce might be accepted, obscenity and all, for . . . . only a few read him, and those few not just the kind to have their whole moral natures overthrown by frankness about natural functions."

The mistake you people make is in thinking that we "prudes" who don't like Joyce are concerned with morals. *Morality* has nothing to do with it. Does morality have anything to do with the average person's desire for privacy concerning the "natural functions"? Not at all; it is delicacy, lack of vulgarity. I do no think we need to apologize for this delicacy and lack of vulgarity, even to your superior beings.

There is a certain form of mental unbalance—about the lowest form—that takes delight in concentration on the "natural functions. . . All attendants in insane asylums are familiar with it. Does James Joyce belong to those so affected? Do "the few who read him" belong? If not, and Joyce and his readers are to be considered fairly sane, would he—and they—be willing to perform their "natural functions" in public? If not, why take out a desire for dabbling in filth, in writing in public?

The only cure for the nausea he causes is the thought that "only a few read him." I think the *Little Review* has become a disgustingly artificial and affected publication. You started out to be sincere, unconventional, to refuse to pander to commercialism, etc.: a wonderfully courageous and admirable ambition. But you are a great disappointment to those of us who hoped great things for you. You are like a crowd of precocious, "smarty cat," over-wise children, showing off. I know of no one who has anything for you now but pity, mingled with contempt and disappointment—and this from people who were once your friends and admirers.

[Yes, I think you must be right. I once knew a woman so modest that she didn't wear underwear: she couldn't stand its being seen in the wash.]

10. From LR *7.3 (September–December 1920): 5–7*

ART AND THE LAW

by jh

THE heavy farce and sad futility of trying a creative work in a court of law appalls me. Was there ever a judge qualified to judge even the simplest psychic outburst? How then a work of Art? Has any man not a nincompoop ever been heard by a jury of his peers?

In a physical world laws have been made to preserve physical order. Laws cannot reach, nor have power over, any other realm. Art is and always has been the supreme Order. Because of this it is the only activity of man that has an eternal quality. Works of Art are the only permanent sign that man has existed. What legal genius to bring Law against Order!

The society for which Mr. Sumner is agent, I am told, was founded to protect the public from corruption. When asked *what public?* its defenders spring to the rock on which America was founded: the cream-puff of sentimentality, and answer chivalrously "Our young girls." So the mind of the young girl rules this country? In it rests the safety, progress and lustre of a nation. One might have guessed it. . . . but—why is she given such representatives? I recall a photograph of the United States Senators, a galaxy of noble manhood that could only have been assembled from far-flung country stores where it had spat and gossiped and stolen prunes.

The present case is rather ironical. We are being prosecuted for printing the thoughts in a young girl's mind. Her thoughts and actions and the meditations which they produced in the mind of the sensitive Mr. Bloom. If the young girl corrupts, can she also be corrupted? Mr. Joyce's young girl is an innocent, simple, childish girl who tends children . . . she hasn't had the advantage of the dances, cabarets, motor trips open to the young girls of this more pure and free country.

If there is anything I really fear it is the mind of the young girl.

I do not understand Obscenity; I have never studied it nor had it, but I know that it must be a terrible and peculiar menace to the United States. I know that there is an expensive department maintained in Washington with a chief and fifty assistants to prevent its spread—and in and for New York we have the Sumner vigilanti.

To a mind somewhat used to life Mr. Joyce's chapter seems to be a record of the simplest, most unpreventable, most unfocused sex thoughts possible in a rightly-constructed, unashamed human being. Mr. Joyce is not teaching early Egyptian perversions nor inventing new ones. Girls lean back everywhere, showing lace and silk stockings; wear low cut sleeveless gowns, breathless bathing suits; men think thoughts and have emotions about these things everywhere—seldom as delicately and imaginatively as Mr. Bloom—and no one is corrupted. Can merely reading about the thoughts he thinks corrupt a man when his thoughts do not? All power to the artist, but this is not his function.

It was the poet, the artist, who discovered love, created the lover, made sex everything that it is beyond a function. It is the Mr. Sumners who have made it an obscenity. It is a little too obvious to discuss the inevitable result of damming up a force as unholy and terrific as the reproductive force with nothing more powerful than silence, black looks, and censure.

"Our young girls" grow up conscious of being possessed, as by a devil, with some urge which they are told is shameful, dangerous and obscene. They try to be "pure" with no other incantations than a few "obstetric mutterings."

Mr. Sumner seems a decent enough chap . . . serious and colourless and worn as if he had spent his life resenting the emotions. A 100 per cent. American who believes that denial, resentment and silence about all things pertaining to sex produce uprightness.

Only in a nation ignorant of the power of Art . . . insensitive and unambitious to the need and appreciation of Art . . . could such habit of mind obtain. Art is the only thing that produces life, extends life—I am speaking beyond physically or mentally. A people without the experience of the Art influence can bring forth nothing but a humanity that bears the stamp of a loveless race. Facsimile women and stereotyped men—a humanity without distinction or design, indicating no more the creative touch than if they were assembled parts.

A beautiful Russian woman said to me recently, "How dangerous and horrible to fall in love with an American man! One could never tell which one it was—they are all the same."

There are still those people who are not outraged by the mention of natural facts who will ask "what is the necessity to discuss them?" But that is not a question to ask about a work of Art. The only question relevant at all to "Ulysses" is—Is it a work of Art? The men best capable of judging have pronounced it a work of the first rank. Anyone with a brain would hesitate to question the necessity in an artist to create, or his ability to choose the right subject matter. Anyone who has read "Exiles," "The Portrait," and "Ulysses" from the beginning, could not rush in with talk of obscenity. No man has been more crucified on his sensibilities than James Joyce.

11. From LR *7.3 (September–December 1920): 8–12*

AN OBVIOUS STATEMENT (FOR THE MILLIONTH TIME)

by Margaret Anderson

MR. SUMNER is a representative intelligence (I will say later what value I put upon the "representative"),—a serious, sincere man, very much interested in proving his conviction that James Joyce is filthy to read and contaminating to those who read him.

My first point is that Mr. Sumner is operating in realms in which it can be proved that he cannot function intelligently, legitimately, or with any relation to the question which *should* be up for discussion in the court.

That question is the relation of the artist—the great writer—to the public.

> *First, the artist has no responsibility to the public whatever; but the public should be conscious of its responsibility to him, being mysteriously and eternally in his debt.*
>
> *Second, the position of the great artist is impregnable.* You can no more destroy him than you can create him. You can no more limit his expression, patronizingly suggest that his genius present itself in channels personally pleasing to you, than you can eat the stars.

I should begin my (quite unnecessary!) defense of James Joyce with this statement: I know practically everything that will be said in court, both by the prosecution and the defense. I disagree with practically everything that will be said by both.

I do not admit that the issue is debatable.

I state clearly that the (quite unnecessary!) defense of beauty is the only issue involved.

James Joyce has never writen anything, and will never be able to write anything, that is not beautiful. *So that we come to the question of beauty in the Art sense,*—that is, to the science of aesthetics, the touchstone which establishes whether any given piece of writing, painting, music, sculpture, is a work of Art or merely an effort in that direction by a man who, however he may wish or work, has not been born an artist.

You will say this brings us to an impasse; that we now arrive at that point where two autocracies of opinion can be established—one which says "This is Art" and the other which says "It is not." And you will tell me that one is quite as likely to be right as the other,—and that therefore every man is thrown back upon his personal taste as a criterion, etc.

I answer: *Autocracy? It is entirely a matter of autocracy of opinion. And the autocracy that matters, that can prove itself, as against that which cannot, is the only thing we are concerned with in this discussion.* It is the only thing to be considered in any Art discussion, but the last that ever *is* considered. Why is this? Because it never occurs to the Mr. Sumners of the world that Art is a highly specialized activity to which they must bring something beyond mere knowledge. *They are content to approach even without knowledge.* If Mr. Sumner were asked to judge pearls, for instance, he wouldn't dream of expressing an opinion unless he really knew how a good pearl must feel to the touch, how it must weigh, what color it must be. If he were asked to buy a string of corals for a connoisseur he wouldn't undertake the commission unless he knew that Japanese corals are more "beautiful" than Italian corals, and that he couldn't buy an acceptable string for less than $3,000. In short, unless he were a connoisseur he wouldn't be doing these things.

In Art (and this is the crux of the whole business) *one must judge with a touchstone beyond even the capacity of the connoisseur.* It is not the taste, the judgment of connoisseurs that has established what are the great works of Art in the world. *It is the perception of the great artists themselves,—the judgment of the masters.*

In begininng to talk of this kind of perception, of *who are the masters,* it is necessary to begin with the fundamentals of aesthetics. *In aesthetics it can be established;*

> *First, that to a work of Art you must bring aesthetic judgment, not moral, personal, nor even technical judgment.* It is not the *human feelings* that produce this kind of judgment. *It is a capacity for art emotion, as distinguished from human emotion, that produces it.*
>
> *Second, that only certain kinds of people are capable of art emotion (aesthetic emotion). They are the artist himself and the critic whose capacity for appreciation proves itself by an equal capacity to create.*

In an old race of people, like the Hindoos, where the artist is protected from the assault of the philistine by as definite a caste system as exists in all other phases of Hindu life, the kind of thing that will happen to us in a United States court could not take place. That civilization is founded on the autocratic recognition of certain values,—the artist as the highest manifestation of life; the critic who recognizes him; the philosopher who explains him. An autocracy—the recognition of the valuable as against the less valuable,—is the only sound basis for life. Anything else is shameful. Anything else means that the exceptional people must suffer with the average people,—from the average people. This is the ethics of the western world. Nearly everyone believes this to be inevitable,—even desirable. Mr. Sumner believes it. He has quoted to me a remark of Victor Hugo's to the effect that personal freedom extends just to that point where it does not interfere with the personal freedom of another. I have said to him "Mr. Sumner, that is an inepetitude. There is no *thinking* in that kind of remark." I don't know just where Victor Hugo makes this banal and curiously unthoughtful statement. Perhaps he makes it only in connection with physical freedom,—in which case it is not entirely senseless. But when a good mind begins to reflect on the subject of the more subtle freedoms, what does it say? *First of all, that there is no such thing as freedom. There is only interdependence. And of the little freedoms that can be attained or respected, in this great maize of the interdependence of all life, let us respect those of the superior people rather than of the inferior people. It is far more important that a great artist's freedom to write as he pleases be respected than that Mr. Sumner's freedom to suppress what he does not know to be a work of Art be respectd.*

Why is there no such autocracy in this country?—why is there no caste feeling which makes a man humble before what he does not understand—before what he does not know that he does not know—rather than confident that he has some special capacity to deal with it? It is because in America every human being, no matter what his training, his business, his qualifications, *makes some mysterious identification of himself with the artist.* He says "I love the better things of life, I go to concerts and art galleries, I couldn't live without these things"—and that is supposed to endow him with some creative participation. I can't tell you how many people have said to me: "I don't know anything about Art, I couldn't write a poem or compose a piece of music to save my life, but I know what I like, I have a very good critical sense, and I *feel* the way the artist does." They mean that they eat Art, live on it,—go to hear good music in order to drown in the emotions it gives them. In America, where the emotional life has been allowed so few direct outlets, this is what happens everywhere. But if this is the way the majority of humanity acts, it is not the way the artist acts. And the thing that will puzzle me to the end of time is this: You can tell a man who knows a great deal about insurance, for instance, that he doesn't know enough mechanical engineering to build a bridge, and he doesn't feel insulted. But if you tell a plumber, or an engineer, a business man, a lawyer, a scholar, a club woman, a debutante, that they are not artists, not creators in this special sense, they take it as the deepest insult. Of course, I suppose this shouldn't exasperate me. I should take it all as the deepest tribute a man can pay to that mysterious phenomenon, the artist, with whom he thus identifies his own highest instincts. Well, I wouldn't be exasperated; I could look upon it all as a rather charming foolishness, if it weren't for the prosecution of that human being whom all mankind in its best moments is trying to impersonate.

This at least begins the argument. Next month I shall report all the blatant ineptitudes of the court proceedings and answer them simply, obviously, and patiently,—unless I shall have succumbed in the meantime to the general sense of devastating futility which is really the only good sense one can hope to preserve in these contentions.

[...]

12. *From* LR *7.4 (January–March 1921): 22–25*

"ULYSSES" IN COURT

by Margaret Anderson

THE trial of the *Little Review* for printing a masterpiece is now over—lost, of course, but if any one thought there was a chance of our winning . . . in the United States of America. . . .

It is the only farce I ever participated in with any pleasure. I am not convivial, and I am usually bored or outraged by the state of farce to which unfarcical matters must descend. This time I had resolved to watch the proceedings with the charming idea of extracting some interest out of the fact that things proceed as one knows they wlil proceed. There is no possible interest in this fact, but perhaps one can be enlivened by speculating as to whether they will swerve the fraction of an inch from their predestined stupidity.

No, this cannot engage my interest: I have already lived through the stupidity. So how shall I face an hour in a court room, before three judges who do not know the difference between James Joyce and obscene postal cards, without having hysterics, or without trying to convince them that the words "literature" and "obscenity" can not be used in conjunction any more than the words "science" and "immorality" can. With what shall I fill my mind during this hour of redundant human drama? Ah—I shall make an effort to keep entirely silent, and since I have never under attack achieved this simple feat, perhaps my mind can become intrigued with the accomplishment of it.

It is a good idea. There are certain civilized people who proceed entirely upon the principle that to protect one's self from attack is the only course of action open to a decent and developed human being. My brain accepts this philosophy, but I never act upon it—-any more than Ezra Pound does. I am one of those who feels some obscure need to have all people think with some intelligence upon some subjects. . . .

But I am determined, during this unnecessary hour in court, to adopt the philosophy of self-preservation. I will protect my sensibilities and my brain cells by being unhearing and untalkative.

The court opens. Every one stands up as the three judges enter. Why must I stand up as a tribute to three men who wouldn't understand my simplest remark? (But this is reasoning, and I am determined to be vacuous.)

Our attorney, Mr. John Quinn, begins pertinently by telling who James Joyce is, what books he has written, and what are his distinguished claims as a man of letters. The three judges quite courteously but with a bewildered impatience inform him that they can't see what bearing those facts have on the subject—they "don't care who James Joyce is or whether he has written the finest books in the world"; their only function is to decide whether certain passages of "Ulysses" (incidentally the only passages they can understand) violate the statute.— (Is this a commentary on "Ulysses" or on the minds of the judges?) But I must not dream of asking such a question. My function is silence. Still, there is that rather fundamental matter of *who is the author?* Since *Art is the person—!* But this is a simplicity of logic—they would think I had gone mad.

Mr. Quinn calls literary "experts" to the stand to testify that "Ulysses" in their opinion would not corrupt our readers. The opinions of experts is regarded as quite unnecessary, since they know only about literature but not about law: "Ulysses" has suddenly become a matter of law rather than of literature—I grow confused again; but I am informed that the judges are being especially tolerant to admit witnesses at all—that such is not the custom in the special sessions court. . . .

Mr. John Cowper Powys testifies that "Ulysses" is too obscure and philosophical a work to be in any sense corrupting. (I wonder, as Mr. Powys takes the stand, whether his look and talk convey to the court that his mind is in the habit of functioning in regions where theirs could not penetrate: and I imagine the judges saying: "This man obviously knows much more about the matter than we do—the case is dismissed." Of course I have no historical basis for expecting such a thing. I believe it has never happened. . . .

Mr. Philip Moeller is the next witness to testify for the *Little Review,* and in attempting to answer the judges' questions with intelligence he asks if he may use technical terminology. Permission being given he explains quite simply that the objectionable chapter is an unveiling of the subconscious mind, in the Freudian manner, and that he saw no possibility of these revelations being aphrodiasic in their influence. The court gasps, and one of the judges calls out, "Here, here, you might as well talk Russian. Speak plain English if you want us to understand what you're saying." Then they ask Mr. Moeller what he thinks would be the effect of the objectionable chapter on the mind of the average reader. Mr. Moeller answers: "I think it would mystify him." "Yes, but what would be the effect?" (I seem to be drifting into unconsciousness) *Question*—What is the effect of that which mystifies? *Answer*—Mystification. But no one looks either dazed or humourous, so I decide that they regard the proceedings as perfectly sensible.)

Other witnesses (among them the publishers of the *Dial,* who valiantly appeared at both hearings) are waived on the consideration of their testimony being the same as already given. Mr. Quinn then talks for thirty minutes on the merits of James Joyce's work in terms the court can understand: "Might be called futurist literature"; "neither written for nor read by school girls"; "disgusting in portions, perhaps, but no more so than Swift, Rabelais, Shakespeare, the Bible"; "inciting to anger or repulsion but not to lascivious acts"; and as a final bit of suave psychology (nauseating and diabolical), aimed at that dim stirring of human intelligence which for an instant lights up the features of the three judges—"I myself do not understand 'Ulysses'—I think Joyce has carried his method too far in this experiment" . . .

"Yes," groans the most bewildered of the three, "it sounds to me like the ravings of a disordered mind—I can't see why any one would want to publish it."

("Let me tell you why"—I almost leap from my chair. "Since I am the publisher it may be apropos for me to tell you why I have wanted to publish it more than anything else that has ever been offered to me. Let me tell you *why* I regard it as the prose masterpiece of my generation. Let me tell you what it's about and why it was written and for whom it was written and why you don't understand it and why it is just as well that you don't and why you have no right to pit the dulness of your brains against the fineness of mine" . .)

(I suddenly feel as though I had been run over by a subway train. My distinguished co-publisher is pounding me violently in the ribs: "Don't try to talk; don't put yourself into their hands"—with that look of being untouched by the surrounding stupidities which sends me into paroxysms. I smile vacuously at the court.)

Mr. Quinn establishes, apparently to the entire satisfaction of the judges, that the offending passages of "Ulysses" will revolt but not contaminate. But their sanction of this point seems to leave them vaguely unsatisfied and they state, with a hesitation that is rather charming, that they feel impelled to impose the minimum fine of $100 and thus to encourage the Society for the Prevention of Vice.

This decision establishes us as criminals and we are led to an adjoining building where another bewildered official takes our fingerprints! ! !*

> Owing to editorial mediation as to what passages must be deleted from the next instalment of "Ulysses" Episode XIV will not be continued until next month.
>
> M. C. A.

*In this welter of crime and lechery, both Mr. Sumner and the judges deserve our thanks for one thing: our appearance seemed to leave them without any doubts as to our personal purity. Some of my "friends" have considered me both insane and obscene, I believe, for publishing Mr. Joyce.

BIBLIOGRAPHY

Anderson, Margaret C. *My Thirty Years' War: An Autobiography.* 1930. New York: Horizon, 1969.

Atherton, James S. "The Peacock in the Oxen." *A Wake Newslitter* 7 (October 1970): 77–78.

Brown, Susan. "The Mystery of the Fuga per Canonem Solved." *Genetic Joyce Studies* 7 (Spring 2007). www.geneticjoycestudies.org.

Budgen, Frank. *James Joyce and the Making of "Ulysses."* 1934. Bloomington: Indiana University Press, 1960.

Crispi, Luca. "A First Foray into the National Library of Ireland's Joyce Manuscripts: Bloomsday 2011." *Genetic Joyce Studies* 11 (Spring 2011). www.geneticjoycestudies .org.

Davison, Sarah. "Joyce's Incorporation of Literary Sources in 'Oxen of the Sun.'" *Genetic Joyce Studies* 9 (Spring 2009). www.geneticjoycestudies.org.

Driver, Clive. Bibliographical preface to *"Ulysses": A Facsimile of the Manuscript,* 1:13–38. Philadelphia: Octagon, 1975.

Eliot, T. S. "'Ulysses,' Order and Myth." 1923. *Selected Prose of T. S. Eliot,* 175–78. London: Faber and Faber, 1975.

Ellmann, Richard. *James Joyce.* New and rev. ed. Oxford: Oxford University Press, 1982.

Ferrer, Daniel. "What Song the Sirens Sang . . . Is No Longer Beyond All Conjecture: A Preliminary Description of the New 'Proteus' and 'Sirens' Manuscripts." *James Joyce Quarterly* 39, no. 1 (Fall 2001): 53–68.

Fromm, Gloria G. *Dorothy Richardson: A Biography.* Athens: University of Georgia Press, 1994.

Gifford, Don. *Ulysses Annotated.* Berkeley: University of California Press, 1988.

Gilbert, Stuart. *James Joyce's "Ulysses."* 1930. New York: Vintage, 1955.

Groden, Michael. "The National Library of Ireland's New Joyce Manuscripts: A Statement and Document Descriptions." *James Joyce Quarterly* 39, no. 1 (Fall 2001): 29–52.

———. *"Ulysses" in Progress.* Princeton: Princeton University Press, 1977. Abbreviated *UP* in the text.

Hayman, David. *"Ulysses": The Mechanics of Meaning.* Rev. ed. Madison: University of Wisconsin Press, 1982.

Janusko, Robert. *The Sources and Structures of James Joyce's "Oxen."* Ann Arbor, Mich.: UMI Research Press, 1983.

Joyce, James. Buffalo Joyce Collection, c. 1903–1940. University of Buffalo. Reproduced in *The James Joyce Archive.* Referred to in the text by catalogue titles and page numbers.

———. Cornell Joyce Collection, c. 1893–1941. Cornell University. Reproduced in *The James Joyce Archive.* Referred to in the text by manuscript number.

———. *Dubliners.* New York: Viking, 1967.

———. *The James Joyce Archive.* Edited by Michael Groden et al. New York: Garland, 1977–1979.

———. The Joyce Papers 2002, c. 1903–1928. National Library of Ireland. http://catalogue.nli.ie/Record/vtls000194606. Abbreviated "NLI MS" in the text and using the NLI's catalogue titles.

———. *Letters of James Joyce.* 3 vols. Edited by Richard Ellmann and Stuart Gilbert. New York: Viking, 1957–1966. Abbreviated *LI, LII,* and *LIII* in the text, and cited by volume and page number.

———. *Selected Letters of James Joyce.* Edited by Richard Ellmann. New York: Viking, 1975. Abbreviated *SL* in the text.

———. *"Ulysses": A Critical and Synoptic Edition.* 3 vols. Edited by Hans Walter Gabler, Wolfhard Steppe, and Claus Melchior. New York: Garland, 1984. Abbreviated *U* in the text and cited by episode and line number. A one-volume edition of this version—containing the text of the novel but no critical apparatus—was published by Vintage in 1986.

———. *"Ulysses": A Facsimile of the Manuscript.* 3 vols. Philadelphia: Octagon, 1975. Referred to as the "Rosenbach Manuscript" in the text.

Kiberd, Declan. *"Ulysses" and Us: The Art of Everyday Life in Joyce's Masterpiece.* New York: Norton, 2009.

Lawrence, Karen. *The Odyssey of Style in "Ulysses."* Princeton, N.J.: Princeton University Press, 1981.

Little Review. Edited by Margaret Anderson and Jane Heap. 1914–1922. http://modjourn.org/render.php?view=mjp_object&id=LittleReviewCollection. Abbreviated *LR* in the text, and cited by volume, issue, and page number.

Litz, A. Walton. *The Art of James Joyce: Method and Design in "Ulysses" and "Finnegans Wake."* London: Oxford University Press, 1961.

Morrisson, Mark. *The Public Face of Modernism.* Madison: University of Wisconsin Press, 2001.

Owen, Rodney. *James Joyce and the Beginnings of "Ulysses."* Ann Arbor, Mich.: UMI Research Press, 1983.

Pound, Ezra. *Instigations.* New York: Boni and Liveright, 1920.

——. *Pound/Joyce: The Letters of Ezra Pound to James Joyce.* Edited by Forrest Read. New York: New Directions, 1967.

Quillian, William H. "Shakespeare in Trieste: Joyce's 1912 *Hamlet* Lectures." *James Joyce Quarterly* 12, nos. 1/2 (Fall 1974/Winter 1975): 7–63.

Rosenbach Manuscript. See Joyce, *"Ulysses": A Facsimile of the Manuscript.*

Scholes, Robert, and Richard M. Kain, eds. *The Workshop of Daedalus: James Joyce and the Raw Materials for "A Portrait of the Artist as a Young Man."* Evanston, Ill.: Northwestern University Press, 1965.

Scholes, Robert, and Clifford Wulfman. *Modernism in the Magazines.* New Haven, Conn.: Yale University Press, 2010.

Scott, Thomas L., and Melvin J. Friedman. *Pound/The Little Review.* New York: New Directions, 1988.

Slocum, John J., and Herbert Cahoon. *A Bibliography of James Joyce, 1882–1941.* New Haven, Conn.: Yale University Press, 1953.

Thomson, George H. *A Reader's Guide to Dorothy Richardson's "Pilgrimage."* Greensboro, N.C.: ELT Press, 1996.

Vanderham, Paul. *James Joyce and Censorship: The Trials of "Ulysses."* New York: New York University Press, 1998.

Vaughan Williams, Ralph. "Fugue." *Grove's Dictionary of Music and Musicians,* 2:114–21. London: Macmillan, 1906.